I0822488

PRAISE FOR THE ARTEMIS LUPINE SERIES

"I would recommend this book to anyone who enjoys a howling good werewolf tale." ~*Written Word Review*

"Weaving a mysterious tale that's filled with werewolves, vampires and fae, Banks has written a great foundation within the Young Adult genre." ~*A Life Bound by Books*

"A truly spectacular read for any young adult paranormal romance fan!" ~*Fantasy Book Chick*

"How can you not love Catherine Banks' Artemis Lupine series? The answer is you can't! It's fascinating and too hard to put down. I have no idea how she does it, and honestly it doesn't matter. Her unique writing, the way she wraps her readers up in all the intense situations and outcomes is mind blowing and at the end of the day I don't need to know how she makes that happen. I just need to know that she won't stop any time soon." ~*The Bookshelf Sophisticate*

ARTEMIS LUPINE

THE COMPLETE SERIES

USA TODAY BESTSELLING AUTHOR

CATHERINE BANKS

TURBO KITTEN

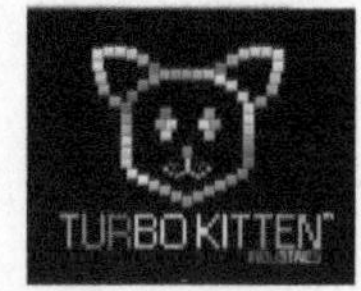

Artemis Lupine, The Complete Series by Catherine Banks.

Cover design by Covers by Juan.

Logo by Avery Banks.

Published by Turbo Kitten Industries.

www.CatherineBanks.com

Turbo Kitten Industries

PO Box 5012, Galt, CA 95632

Special thanks to the following people who backed my Kickstarter and helped et these gorgeous books out into the world.

Amanda Jenkins
Anij Fallows
Arlene Medder
Brandy Robinson
Ceciley Snook
D. T. Brook
Davide B.
Deissy Hermunslie
Emily Suzanne Davis
Emjrabbitwolf
Fawn of the Woods
Francesco Tehrani
Gary Phillips
Helen Jensen
Jamie Forster
Jeff Lewis
ennifer & Jamie Wallace
Jennifer Laslie
Jon Tarbox
Ken Anderson
Kylie Corley
Louise Kendall
Matthea W. Ross
MelX
Michelle Fritz
Michelle Johnson
Michelle R. McFarlin
R.J. Blain
Ran Frimark
Russell Nohelty
Russell Ventimeglia
Stormie Harlan
Synergica
Taka Angevine
Tara Harrington
Zack Newcomb
Amanda Haynes
Erin Hayes
Amber
Emma
The Creative Fund
Rebecca Laffar-Smith

CONTENTS

SONG OF THE MOON

KISS OF A STAR

HEALED BY THE FIRE

BATTLES OF THE NIGHT

THE COMPLETE SERIES

USA TODAY BESTSELLING AUTHOR

CATHERINE BANKS

SONG OF THE MOON

ARTEMIS LUPINE SERIES, BOOK ONE

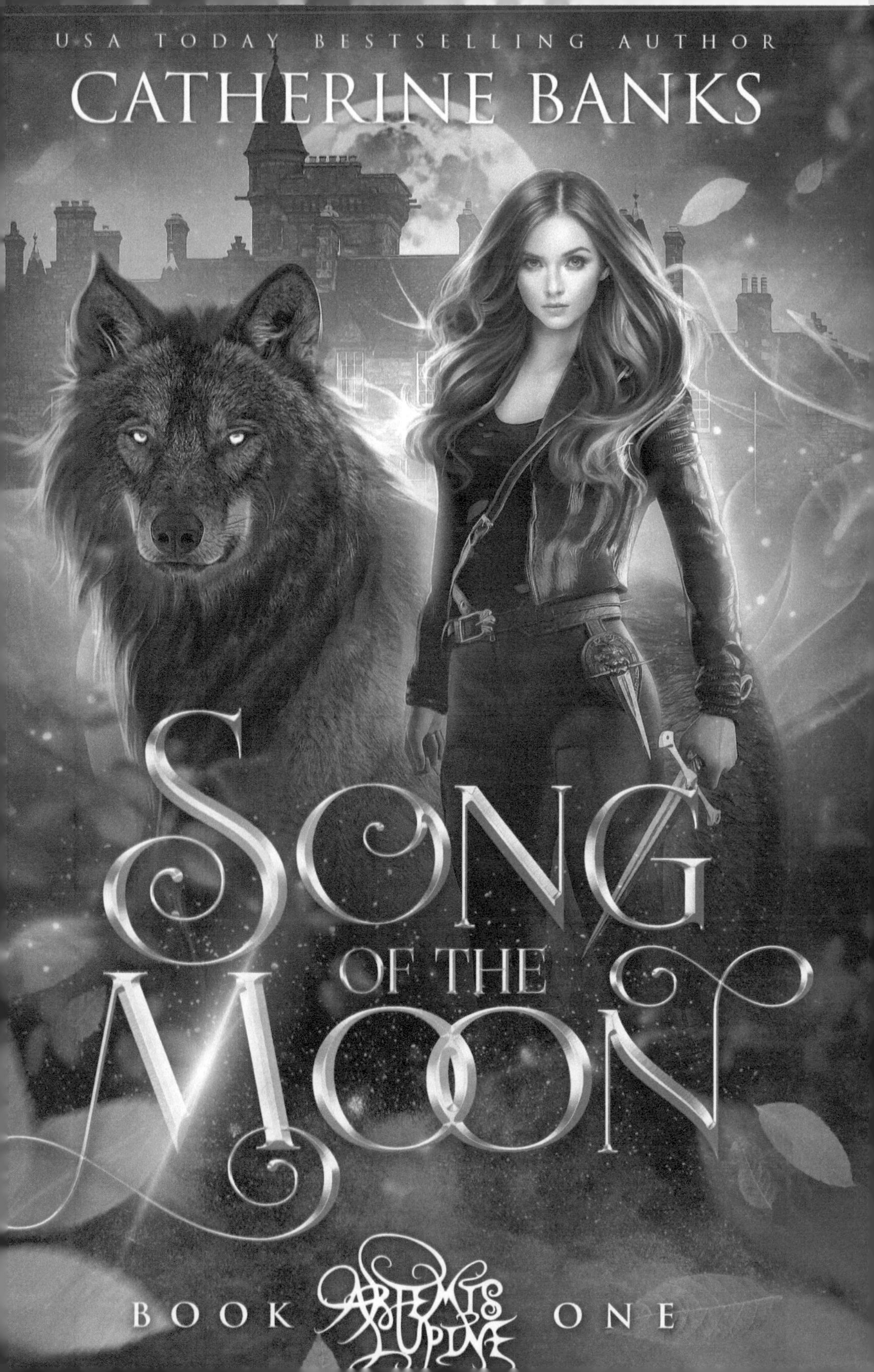

USA TODAY BESTSELLING AUTHOR

CATHERINE BANKS

SONG OF THE MOON

BOOK ONE

ARTEMIS LUPINE

Song of the Moon by Catherine Banks.

Cover design by Covers by Juan.

Logo by Avery Banks.

Published by Turbo Kitten Industries.

www.CatherineBanks.com

Turbo Kitten Industries

PO Box 5012, Galt, CA 95632

Acknowledgments

Avery, my best friend and soulmate, thank you for being you and allowing me to be myself. Without you, these books would not have been written or published. You are more than I could have ever wished for in a partner. You are my ever constant moon, bringing light to my life in even my darkest times. I love you.

Ms. Challis(Donovan), thank you for encouraging me in high school and assisting me with the originally released books. Teachers like you are indispensable.

CHAPTER ONE

It was our third day away from home. Darren, my father, decided that we needed a vacation away from the drama of our small-town life. I didn't know what drama he was talking about, but it *was* nice to get away. Darren sang along quietly to the song on the radio as we drove towards our third destination: South Lake Tahoe.

The first day, well, technically night, had been Las Vegas with its bright lights and non-stop gambling. I wasn't actually twenty-one, but somehow Darren got fake ID's that allowed both Bret and me to gamble and drink. Vegas had been fun, but the men were very abrasive, throwing offers at me like I was a street walker. Darren had, of course, protected me, but Bret was the one to make them back off. Bret was my best friend of thirteen years and the star quarterback of our high school football team. He just accepted a full ride scholarship to Notre Dame for the upcoming semester. It was the main reason he had come with us, so that we could have one last trip together before he left California for Indiana.

Our second day was spent in Reno, which was a smaller version of Vegas minus the brightly lit streets. We went to a rodeo, much to Darren's dismay, and then gambled more of Darren's savings away.

That was yesterday though. Tonight, we would get to enjoy Tahoe. Bret silently stared out the back passenger window of Darren's nimbus grey metallic, VTEC Honda Ridgeline. The townspeople made fun of Darren for buying an import truck, but I loved it. What's more reliable than a Honda? I drove a small blue Honda Del Sol. Bret hates my car, often telling me, "It's a death trap waiting to happen." I ignore his domestic car-loving mentality and enjoy driving the small car with my targa top off every summer.

Just as I felt my eyes starting to droop, Darren cleared his throat. "Welcome to South Lake Tahoe."

I turned to the left and stared out at the perfect blue water. The mountains which lined the lake still held on to a thin layer of snow, making the scene twice as lovely. "Wow! It's beautiful."

Bret sat up straight and asked, "Do we get to go swimming?"

Darren laughed. "Of course! I would never bring you to Tahoe and not let you enjoy the lake. That's like taking you to San Diego and making you stay away from the beach."

I started bouncing up and down on the seat. "I can't wait to jump into that lake!"

"You won't be jumping in. You'll be flying in," Bret said as he laughed.

I scoffed. "Like you could catch me!" I knew he could catch me easily, but it was fun to roughhouse with him. We spent a lot of time wrestling and goofing around. He easily outmuscled me, but that's to be expected since I'm a small girl and he's a football player. It just makes me feel better to play tough sometimes.

Darren laughed quietly. "Now, children, remember we are supposed to be acting like adults."

Bret shrugged. "You said we only had to act in our early twenties, and I guarantee any guy in his early twenties would try to throw Artemis in the lake."

I rolled my eyes. *Boys are so weird.*

Darren sighed. "I don't think you two will ever grow up."

Bret and I shrugged in unison and then laughed together.

Darren finally stopped in front of a large hotel. "This is my favorite hotel, so no screwing things up. You can use an underground tunnel to go from this hotel to the one across the street."

"Awesome!" I said

"That means there are twice as many restaurants for us to eat at," Bret said with a smile on his face.

Darren and I groaned at Bret.

"You always think about food," I complained.

"Come on! It's been like four hours since lunch. I know you're hungry, too," Bret said.

I started to deny his statement, but my stomach growled loudly, giving me away. I sighed. "Guess I can't deny it now." I looked down at my stomach and whispered, "Traitor."

Darren shook his head smiling. "Come on. Let's get checked in and put our bags away and then we'll get some food."

Darren pulled into the valet parking line and handed the valet the truck keys. I stepped out of the truck, jogged to the back, and opened the compartment in the bed to get out my duffel bag of clothes. I hated those girls who packed five bags of crap for only being gone three days, so I made sure to pack as light as possible.

I started to sling my bag over my shoulder when Bret took it from me. He slung it over his shoulder with his. I smiled at him as I followed them into the hotel.

Darren checked us in, getting our room keys before guiding us towards the elevators. No one was waiting, so we got the elevator to ourselves. I breathed slowly, trying to fight my paranoia. I kept imagining the elevator reaching the highest floor then plummeting back to the first level, killing us. Bret hugged my shoulders and rubbed my arm to calm me. Darren rolled his eyes at me and pushed the button for the tenth floor.

I groaned. "*Tenth* floor?"

Darren shrugged. "At least it's not the top floor. There are fourteen."

I snarled. "Four more isn't that big of a difference."

Darren smiled sideways. "It is when you are falling to the ground. Four less floors may be the difference between death and being permanently paralyzed."

I started breathing faster and turned my face into Bret's side. Bret shook his head. "Darren, was that necessary?"

Darren scoffed. "She's such a baby about heights. One day she'll have to get over her fears."

I shook my head. "It's not the heights, Dad. It's the elevator. I would more than gladly take the stairs up. I just hate the thought of plummeting to my death in this tin can."

Bret rolled his eyes. "But you drive the Del Sol and feel safe. Isn't that kind of backwards?"

I shook my head. "Nope. *Nikkou* is very safe." *Nikkou* was the Japanese word for "sunshine" and my little car always makes me think of the sun.

Darren rolled his eyes as the elevator door opened.

I ran out from under Bret's arm and sat on the tile of the tenth floor. "Oh, thank God. We made it."

Bret picked me up under the arms and set me on my feet. "Come on scared-y cat. Let's go."

Bret and I followed Darren as he wound the way down the hallways towards our rooms. Darren stopped next to two doors. "That one is your room and this one is mine." He handed Bret a keycard and then walked into his room without another word to us.

Bret turned to our door and opened it with the keycard. I walked in before he could and looked around. It was a large room with two queen sized beds and a gorgeous view of the mountains. I walked into the bathroom and giggled happily. A large jetted tub sat to the side waiting for me to get in. I turned on the bath and then walked out to the bedroom.

Bret flipped through the channels on the television and then groaned. "All that is on is some breaking news story."

I shrugged. "I have a few minutes before my tub is full. Let's watch it."

Darren burst in through the side door that connected our rooms and took the remote from Bret, turning off the television. "No TV! I told you that before we left!" His voice was raised, he was breathing heavily, and his face was flushed.

"Why are you so angry?" I asked.

Bret shrugged. "It's alright. Whatever you want, Darren. I was just curious what the breaking news story was."

Darren shook his head. "You aren't allowed to watch TV. I told you we were getting you both away from the drama and watching TV won't do that. Now dammit, enjoy yourselves without the TV!"

I stared at my dad as he tried to play off his anger and become playful. I wasn't buying it.

"I'm taking a bath." I grabbed my bag and walked into the bathroom. I could hear Darren and Bret talking quietly, but I focused on relaxing. I set my bag down in the area with mirrors, grabbed a towel and set it next to the tub as I turned on the jets, and climbed in. I loved hot baths and any free time I had was spent in the tub. I let my body relax with the gentle humming of the jets. In a matter of minutes, my mind began to wander, and my subconscious took over.

My breath steamed out in front of me as I ran through the thick forest. The other five people around me panted and sucked in air as we fled from our pursuers. The three wolves hunting us yipped in delight, and fear made me trip on a tree root. I dodged around the trees as fast as I could. I knew I only had to run faster than the last three people. I knew I couldn't run my fastest or I would increase my chances of hitting one of the trees and ending up in the claws of those pursuing us. The sounds of the others grew faint as I darted around more trees. Sweat plastered my shirt against my chest. I heard movement beside me, but dodged too late. A large animal slammed into my side, sending me flying sideways. I wrapped my arms around my head to protect it as I slammed into a tree and slid to the ground.

The animal stood over me, snarling and snapping its teeth, but made no move to hurt me. I moved one arm to my stomach and one to my throat to try to protect my most vital parts. I opened my eyes and gasped. A wolf the size of a horse stood over me, snarling. I had never seen such a beautiful animal before. The wolf's jet black fur reflected the moonlight as its muscles flexed. The wolf sat, staring at me with its deep amber eyes. It seemed strange to me for so much hate to be emanating from such a beautiful creature. I reached out and stroked the soft furred neck, and the wolf quieted. I slowed my breathing as I stroked the wolf. I looked down the wolf's body and saw the male sheath and smiled. "Hello, boy. Why don't you change and let me see how beautiful you are in human form?"

The wolf snarled, and I pulled back my hands. The words seemed to come out even though I wasn't sure of their meaning. "I only meant that you are so beautiful in wolf form that I have no doubt that you are gorgeous in your other form as well." The wolf stepped back and stood up on its hind legs. I scooted backwards to get farther away from him and watched in amazement as the wolf's body rippled like water and became human. The man before me smiled and walked forward. I couldn't help but stare at his naked perfection, although I kept my gaze above his belly button so as not to offend him. "What's your name?" I asked.

The man smiled and held his hand out to me. He spoke with a voice like honey and said, "Ares."

The dream ended as quickly as it had started. I sat up and stared at the wall in front of me. I slowed my breathing as I focused on reality, and then sighed heavily. It was the same dream I had been having for the past week. I wished it wouldn't end in the same spot every time. I wanted to know what happened next.

Bret knocked on the bathroom door. "Are you alright, Artemis?"

I inhaled one more long breath then called back, "Yes, I'm fine. Just fell asleep in the tub." I climbed out of the now lukewarm water and dried off quickly.

Bret sighed. “Well, hurry. I’m starving.”

My stomach growled in agreement, and I groaned. “Alright. Sorry.” I threw on a pair of jeans and a low-cut t-shirt then ran my brush through my shoulder length black hair before throwing it up into a ponytail. I pulled open the door and ran into Bret’s chest.

He stumbled backwards and smiled at me. “Shit, you caught me off guard.”

I smiled back. “Don’t lie. You know I’m just stronger than you.”

Bret rolled his eyes. “Yes, you, a five foot two, hundred and ten-pound girl, are stronger than me, a six-foot, hundred and eighty-pound guy. Not likely.”

I shrugged. “It’s okay that you don’t want to admit it. I know the truth.”

Bret sighed and motioned towards the door. “Let’s go eat.” I hurried out into the hall to find Darren, who stood against the opposite wall waiting for us. He acknowledged us with a smile and then started walking down the hall towards the elevators. I tried to listen to the guys’ conversation, but all I could think about was the wolf-man of my dream.

Darren interrupted my thoughts by pushing me into the elevator. I frowned at him, but ignored his taunting. *Could the man be real?* I shook my head. *Of course not. There aren’t men who can turn into wolves or vice versa. That’s all just fantasy. Wait... wouldn’t he be a werewolf then?*

Darren cleared his throat making me look up at him. “Are you alright?” he asked.

I nodded. “Sorry. I fell asleep in the tub and I’m still trying to wake up.” Wrapping my arms around myself, I kept taking slow, deep breaths to calm my fear of being in the elevator.

Darren rolled his eyes. “I was thinking we would go to a steak house.”

I licked my lips. “Steak sounds great!”

Darren frowned at me, and Bret laughed. “I swear if we took

red meat away from you, you would end up eating one of us just to get your fill."

I wrinkled my nose in disgust. "I don't think you would taste very good."

Darren rubbed his temples. "Let's not discuss eating each other." He walked out of the elevator as soon as it opened and led us through the now crowded hotel. A line of at least thirty people formed at the steak restaurant, but Darren strolled up to the front and the hostess nodded as he spoke to her. She darted into the restaurant. Bret and I walked up to Darren who stood, looking smug. The hostess came back and waved us in with a smile. Darren followed her and sat down at the largest booth. Two waiters came up and handed us menus and took our drink orders without even asking for ID.

I turned to Darren. "Why are they treating you like royalty?"

"The owner is a longtime friend of mine," he said.

A short, very muscular man with a three-inch-tall, bright green Mohawk walked over to our table. His very nice, very expensive looking suit fit every curve of his body.

Darren smiled wider, but it seemed to almost look like a grimace. "Koda! I didn't think you would be here. I thought you were still in Germany."

Koda smiled wide, flashing perfectly white teeth. I stared at his face and guessed him at about twenty-five, but that made no sense to me since Darren was close to forty. "We came back from Germany a few weeks ago. I'm sure you know why."

Darren smiled slipped down into a frown. "Yes, yes I do." Darren's sudden mood change made me stare at Koda longer. He was very handsome and looked strong. Darren shook his head and smiled again. "Where are my manners? Koda, I'd like you to meet my daughter, Artemis, and her friend Bret."

Koda turned his attention to me, and his brows lifted. His bright blue eyes pierced through me as he stared into mine. He slowly reached his hand out towards me, and I took it, shaking hands like Darren had taught me. His skin was extremely warm, and I felt a small tingle rush up my arm and to my head. Koda smiled and shook my hand back with an equally firm, yet gentle shake. "It is a pleasure to meet you, Artemis. I have heard so much about you."

I frowned. "Unfortunately, I cannot say the same. But it is nice to finally meet one of Dad's friends."

Koda dropped my hand abruptly, making the tingling disappear, and turned to Darren. "She hasn't heard about me?"

Darren swallowed hard and he couldn't meet Koda's gaze. "I have not told her of my past life."

Koda's lip twitched in a snarl. "That is very interesting indeed." Koda turned to me, smiling again. "If you want some time away from your father and friend please feel free to find me. I am always around this restaurant and, if not, my staff can reach me at any time, day or night." He took my hand again and kissed the back of it. "And I would be more than happy to show you around."

Bret stiffened beside me, and I smiled nicely at Koda. "Thank you, Mister…"

Koda shook his head then winked at me. "Call me Koda."

I smiled wider. "Thank you, Koda, but we are only here for one night and I'm sure the guys have a lot planned."

Bret relaxed back against his seat, and Darren let out the breath he had been holding.

Koda shrugged. "As you wish, but the offer is open any day."

Koda smiled at me then stepped closer to Darren and whispered into his ear. Darren's face fell, and he nodded once, very short and quick, as if he were afraid to make any other movement. Koda walked away without glancing back. The waiters came by and took our orders. Darren smiled again and shook his head. "It has been too long since I've seen him. So, how does gambling for a few hours, then a trip to the hottest dance club in town sound?"

Bret smiled. "Awesome!"

I groaned. "A dance club? Why don't you just stab me in the eye with this fork?"

Bret and Darren talked in about the night to come, but I couldn't listen to them. I stared in the direction Koda had disappeared and wished I could find a way to speak to him further. I remembered the strange tingling and wondered what had caused it. My ruminations ended as our food came and I ate my medium rare steak quickly. I ate the fries and salad as fast as my steak. Then downed my beer. I looked at Darren and Bret. "I need to use the restroom. I'll be right back." I started to get up then realized I had no clue where the bathroom was.

Darren noticed my problem. "Straight back and to the left."

I walked in the direction he had told me and felt butterflies as I realized it was the same way Koda had gone. I turned right down a dark hallway and ran into Koda's wide back. I hadn't seen him in the darkness. He spun around, and his surprised expression turned into a warm smile. "Hello, Artemis. Get tired of your friend so soon?"

I laughed. "Hi, Koda. Sorry. I was just going to the bathroom and wasn't paying attention."

Koda shrugged. "No harm done."

He stepped to the side to allow me to pass him, but I stayed still. "Koda, what did my dad mean about not telling me about his past?"

Koda's eyes squinted in anger. "I'm sorry, Artemis, but it's not my place to discuss your father's past with you. Your father will have to tell you."

I sighed. "Alright."

I continued past Koda and into the restroom. I went pee then washed my hands and walked out of the bathroom. Koda stood in the same spot as before, talking quietly on his cell phone. I hurried to the table where Darren and Bret had already finished their food. "Time to gamble?" I asked.

Bret nodded. "Let's go!"

Darren rolled his eyes. "So eager to waste my money?"

"It was your idea." I lifted a brow at him.

Darren laughed. "True, very true."

We started to walk out of the restaurant when I felt someone's hand on me. A quick rush of heat raced up my arm, making me gasp. I spun around and stared at Koda. He dropped my arm and the heat stopped. "My apologies, Artemis, I didn't mean to frighten you."

I smiled. "It's alright. No harm done."

His smile widened at my reminder of his comment. He held out a small piece of white paper. "Take this. If you ever need anything feel free to call me."

I slowly took the paper and nodded. "Th-thanks."

He winked at me. "No problem."

I couldn't help but stare at his backside as he walked away. Darren cleared his throat, and I hid the piece of paper in my hand and turned to him.

Darren asked, "What was that about?"

I shrugged. "He was just saying bye."

Darren stared at me for a second then shrugged. "He's a nice guy." We started walking out of the restaurant again, and I put the piece of paper in my pants pocket. There were so many questions about Darren that I wanted answers to. Maybe I would call Koda and see if he could answer them. Darren stopped in the middle of the gambling area and turned to us. He pulled out his wallet and made three piles of bills. He handed one pile to me and one pile to Bret before pocketing the third pile for himself. "Now make this last at least two hours."

"I'm sure I can do that, but Bret will probably spend it in ten minutes," I said with a laugh.

Bret rolled his eyes. "You only spend it slowly because you play slots."

I shrugged. "I think slots are fun."

Darren laughed. "Play nice, kids. I'll meet you back here in two hours." He started towards the blackjack tables.

I turned to Bret and smiled. "See you in two hours."

He rolled his eyes again. "Have fun with the slots."

"I will," I said. I strolled towards the slot machines when the hairs on the back of my neck stood on end. Was someone staring at me? I rubbed the back of my neck and looked around, but couldn't see anyone. I shrugged it off and walked faster towards the five cent slot machines. I felt a warm tingling sensation spread over me and turned to my right.

Koda stood a few feet away, talking to someone whose back was towards me. Koda's eyes widened when he saw me, and he whispered something to the man he was with. I smiled at Koda and waved, starting to walk away when the man turned around. I gasped and stopped moving. The man with Koda smiled politely at me, but I stood dumbfounded. He was the man from my dreams, the werewolf man.

Koda walked quickly to my side and whispered, "Breathe!"

I inhaled a big breath and then stopped breathing again as the man walked towards me. I started to ask his name when Darren, appearing seemingly out of thin air, grabbed my arm and yanked me behind him. The man snarled softly at Darren, and I gasped at his wolf-like growl. I shook my head, clearing my thoughts. *I'm just projecting what I want to hear.*

The man seemed angry and stood in a loose fighting stance, like he was preparing for an attack. "What are you doing?" His voice was tinted with anger as he glared at Darren.

"Leave my daughter alone," Darren said with menace in his voice as he pushed me farther behind him and away from the man.

The man smiled. "I haven't done anything and you know I would never hurt our kind, especially not one as beautiful as her."

My cheeks instantly flushed. What did he mean by that, though?

Darren's lips twitched up in a snarl. "Are you here for what I think you are here for?"

The man frowned. "Darius sent us here to continue our mission, yes."

Darren sighed then walked backwards and grabbed my arm. "Come on, Artemis. We're leaving."

I shook my head and stared at the gorgeous man in front of us. "I don't want to leave." I could feel the man's dangerous potential and yet I could tell he was good. How did I know this? I had no idea.

Darren looked from me to the man and then back again. He shook his head and dragged me away by the arm. "We are leaving."

I grabbed at my stomach so that I wouldn't reach out towards the man from my dreams like I wanted to. The man blew a kiss at me, and I felt my blush intensify. I forced myself to turn away from him and followed Darren. Darren grabbed Bret, and we hurried to our rooms. We walked in silence until we reached our rooms, and then Darren turned to us suddenly. "I can't explain this, Artemis, but you two need to trust me. We have to leave, now."

I nodded and hurried into the hotel room to pack my bag. Bret grumbled about being on a streak as he packed his bag, too. I turned to walk out of the room and stopped dead. Koda stood at the end of the hallway by the elevators staring at me. I dropped my bag and hurried to him.

He frowned. "I wanted to make sure that you did as your father says and leave. Do not come back."

"Who was that man? I-I've had dreams about him," I said while wringing the bottom of my shirt.

Koda's eyes widened, his jaw dropped, and then he shook his head. "Just leave. If you want to call me later you can, but do not try to call me for at least two days."

I started to ask him why, but the elevator opened and Koda hurried inside, staring at the back of the elevator. The elevator doors closed a few moments before Darren spoke from his room. "Where's your bag?"

I turned around and smiled. "Sorry, I was trying to catch the elevator and dropped it by the door." I rushed back down the hallway and grabbed my bag as Bret followed me out, shutting the door and handing Darren the keycard. Darren watched me curiously, but didn't say anything. We took the elevator down and Darren paid the front desk clerk. I walked quickly towards the doors which led to the valet area, but I felt someone looking at me again and turned around, raising my gaze to the second story of the lobby. The man from my dreams stood on the upper level staring at me. He started to move towards the escalators, but Koda and another man grabbed him and held him back. I hurried out the door and inhaled the cool, refreshing night air. Darren walked out just as the valet brought the truck up.

I threw my bag to Bret and climbed into the truck, slamming my door and putting on my seatbelt. Darren climbed into the truck and started it, sighing as the motor started up. I looked back in the hotel and saw the man and Koda inside the lobby. Koda was holding onto the man's arm and talking sternly to him. The man was yelling at Koda, but he stopped mid-rant and turned to look at me. I stared into his beautiful blue eyes and wanted nothing more than to have him hold me.

Darren yelled, "Artemis!"

I stopped moving and realized that I had unbuckled my seatbelt and was opening my door. I slammed the door and put my belt back on and faced forward. Darren put the truck in gear and raced away from the hotel, leaving Koda and the mystery man behind. We drove in silence for an hour, and then Darren pulled into a small diner. We got out, and I numbly followed them into the diner. Darren ordered a burger for me and shoved a soda under my chin.

I drank as I thought about the mystery man. Who was he? Why did I feel so strange when I was near him? The news chiming on the television brought my attention back. I stared at the news reporter as his sad face told me that it wasn't going to be a happy report. "We know you all have heard of the devastation that is sweeping the Orient. It started in Japan and spread through China at an alarming rate…"

Darren yelled, "Can we change the channel?"

Our waitress came over, smiling politely. "I'm sorry, Sir, but there are more people here that want to watch it than those who don't."

Darren sighed loudly and stood up, dragging me with him. The news reporter continued. "We just learned that Russia has been…"

Darren shoved me out of the diner so hard and fast that I fell on my face on the concrete outside. Bret rushed to my side and picked me up in his arms. Bret growled. "What the hell is wrong with you, Darren?"

Darren shook his head. "Get in the truck!"

Bret set me down in the truck and got in the backseat. I stared at Darren, eyes wide. "What's happening? Why won't you let us watch the news? What's going on?!" I screamed at him, knowing he was up to something.

"Just do what I say." He started the truck and took off out of the parking lot, spraying gravel from his tires as we raced to the highway again.

My anger rose at Darren and my body began to heat up. I turned to yell at him then felt my body starting to twitch. I grunted in frustration as I had a seizure.

Bret screamed, "Darren!"

Darren pulled over and Bret held me down against the seat so I wouldn't thrash around and hit my head. Darren grabbed a cold water bottle, unscrewed the lid and splashed it on my face. I closed my eyes and focused on the cold feeling, willing myself to calm down. My body slowed its convulsions and then stopped altogether.

Bret sighed. "I wish I knew what the hell caused those."

Darren just stared at me with anger and worry filling his eyes as I regained control.

I whispered, "You can let go, Bret. I'm fine now."

Bret sat back in his seat and Darren started driving again. We listened to the radio in silence the rest of the way to town.

We hurried home, and I climbed straight into bed. Bret followed me in and closed the door behind him. He set our bags down and sat on the bed next to me.

"I'm sorry we had to leave so early," I said to Bret.

Bret shrugged as he settled himself next to me. "It's not your fault, Artemis."

I rolled over and laid my head on his chest. We had been sleeping like this for so long that I barely thought about it. I focused on the beat of his heart and closed my eyes. Bret softly rubbed my back, and I fell asleep.

The rain poured like a giant waterfall down my face as I scanned the forest. I swiped at my face, but nothing helped. I put my hands over my eyes and screamed in frustration. I tensed as a wolf howled nearby, answering my scream. I walked backwards into the cave, pressing my back against the wall. My heart hammered against my chest, threatening to break through as I wiped the water from my eyes, and stared at the black opening of the cave. Lightning flashed, allowing me to see outside, and my entire body stilled. A large black wolf stood in the cavern's mouth, smelling the ground. The wolf turned its head towards me and sniffed three times quickly. I tried to slow my breathing, but my adrenaline was pumping too quickly to allow it. The wolf walked into the cave and whimpered. I shook my head and closed my eyes. The sound of bones snapping and popping echoed in the cave. I hugged myself tighter, fear consuming my rational thought. A familiar male voice whispered, "It's alright. I won't hurt you. I'm Ares."

I sat up in bed and focused on slowing my breathing down. I looked around the room and realized I was in my bedroom, not a forest, and Bret was sleeping soundly beside me. I crawled over the top of him and walked into the bathroom. After I flipped on the light, I stared at the blank wall where a normal household would have a mirror. I opened the wooden medicine cabinet and took out my nighttime contacts. I forgot to put them in, in my hurry to get to sleep. I took out the ones already in and threw them in the garbage. I let my eyes rest for a minute without any contacts in, and then put eye drops in to refresh my eyes. A sigh escaped me as I slowly put in the nighttime contacts.

It took me a while to be able to put contacts in since we didn't have a mirror, but I learned to do a lot of things without mirrors. So much so, that I never even look at one when away from home. Bret thought it was weird that I didn't have a mirror, but to me it was just how I was raised, like the kids who didn't have televisions. I closed the medicine cabinet and walked out into the living room. The TV was turned to the news, but Darren wasn't there. Gunfire in the distance let me know he was out target shooting or coyote hunting. I sat down and turned the news up so I could hear it.

CHAPTER TWO

The news reporter frowned, and he spoke in a sad, monotone voice. "Just two hours ago, devastation wrought the town of South Lake Tahoe."

I gasped.

"So far, no survivors have been found within a ten-mile radius." I blinked at the television channel, shaking, not wanting to believe the report.

Bret walked out of the bedroom rubbing his eyes. "What are you doing?"

I shushed him and pointed at the television. "Everyone is dead in Tahoe."

He stared at me, his brows furrowed. "What?"

I patted the seat beside me and said, "Watch."

He sat down next to me and stared at the television.

The reporter continued, "At full dark, something began to kill people. We do not know what it was, but the bodies were found exactly like those in Japan and Russia. Their throats torn out and—"

Darren ran into the house and turned off the television. Bret jumped up. "What the hell are you doing?"

Darren pointed his finger at us. "I said no television!"

"Now you are being stupid, Dad. Something is happening, and we need to know. Why aren't you letting us watch the news?"

Darren shook his head. "I can't tell you. Just trust me that you do not want to watch the news."

I snarled at him. "I do want to watch the news. I want to know what is going on."

"It's not safe, especially not after tonight. Now go to bed," Darren said in his no back talk allowed tone. He was mad at me, but I hadn't done anything that bad. I knew I wasn't supposed to talk back to him, but he had never been this angry before. I wanted to argue more and find out what had happened in Tahoe, but Darren was not someone I liked to see mad.

I groaned at him and stomped to my room. I thought at times like this it was perfectly normal to act bratty. Bret followed me in and laid back down and stayed silent.

Something is going on and I am going to find out what. Whether Darren likes it or not, I need to know what is going on.

Bret hummed softly and rubbed my back lulling me to sleep before I wanted to.

The sun shining in my room woke me up. I stretched and yawned, feeling refreshed. I looked beside me and realized Bret was gone. I smelled bacon cooking which let me know that Bret and Darren were in the kitchen. I hurried to the bathroom and changed my contacts to the daytime prescription. Apparently, my eyes were so bad that I needed two different sets of prescriptions. I rushed to the kitchen and found Bret sitting at the kitchen table. I sat down next to him and started sipping the hot chocolate that was on the table for me. Darren finished the bacon and set it on a plate in the middle of the table. I started to reach for a piece and he smacked my hand. "You wait for the rest of us."

I groaned. "But it smells *so* good!"

He smiled and started making scrambled eggs. I bounced my

leg as I waited impatiently for my food. Darren scraped the eggs into a bowl then placed it on the table. Before I could move, he smacked my shoulder. "Wait!"

I groaned and started bouncing both my legs at the same time. Darren opened the fridge and tossed Bret the butter tray and then the bottle of syrup. Darren then opened the freezer, which was on the bottom of the fridge, unlike most refrigerators, and took out frozen waffles.

I started bouncing on my chair. "Come on. Hurry!"

Darren rolled his eyes at me as he put ten frozen waffles in the microwave. I watched anxiously as the microwave table spun in small, slow circles. I felt my mouth watering as the eggs and bacon sat waiting on the table. The microwave dinged and I jumped up. Darren growled at me, and I sat back down, sipping my hot chocolate. Bret laughed at me as I waited until Darren gave us each a waffle before he smiled. "Go on."

I grabbed four pieces of bacon from the plate and spooned two large portions of eggs next to the bacon. Bret held the butter tray and spread the butter on his waffles slowly. I groaned and started bouncing my legs again. He handed me the butter with an exaggerated slowness. I yanked it from his hand and slapped butter on my waffle then took the syrup and poured it all over my plate dousing the waffle, eggs and bacon. Then I set the syrup bottle down and looked up to find Darren and Bret staring at me. I giggled nervously, and then started eating. I shoveled the food in my mouth as fast as I could chew. The delicious food elicited a groan of happiness from me, and I ate without any more noises until my plate was empty. Once finished, I sat back and sighed in contentment, resting my hands on my full stomach.

Darren rolled his eyes at me and continued to slowly eat his food. I picked up my hot chocolate and sipped it like a dessert. I tried to think of a way to broach the subject with Darren when Bret did it for me. "Darren, what the fuck is going on?"

Darren blinked at Bret. "Well Bret, I think that is the first time I have heard you cuss."

Bret frowned. "It won't be the last time if you don't answer my question."

Darren sighed. "There is a lot of bad stuff going on in the world, and I am trying to keep you two out of it so that you can enjoy your last week together."

I stared at Darren, and for some reason, knew he was lying. It was like a punch in the gut. I started to say something, but Bret interrupted me. "Well, if it might interfere with our safety, I think you should tell us."

Darren said, "You're fine for now. I promise that I will tell you, if it gets to that point. Now go enjoy the day."

I stood and walked past Darren and out the back door. Bret followed me, and together we walked out to the open fields that lay behind my house. This is the one place of countryside I still had. On TV, they always showed the industrialized parts of the world. None of that interested me. Just give me open fields or forests and I'm happy. I was about to head towards the forest when Darren called to us, "Don't go to the forest. I saw a group of wolf tracks in that area this morning. I'm not sure if they are passing through or not, but just don't go that way."

I nodded and walked the opposite direction, farther into the open fields. Bret followed me, staying silent, but close. Our cattle mooed in the distance and my horses neighed. I started running through the open fields just enjoying the feel of the early morning sun and wind on my face. Bret ran beside me. I smiled at him and increased my speed. He easily caught up with me, and we ran for a few more minutes. When I felt I'd run enough, I collapsed to the ground and closed my eyes.

Bret laid down next to me and asked, "What do you think is really going on with Darren? Why would he want to keep this all hidden from us?"

I shrugged. "How should I know?"

Bret stroked the side of my face with his hand. "If anything does come, I'll protect you."

I rolled my eyes. "Shut up Bret. Nothing is going to come."

A high pitched voice yelled from the road near the field. "Bret! Bret, what are you doing?!"

I groaned and opened my eyes. "Skankzilla is calling you."

Bret rolled his eyes at me. "Yeah, I hear her." He sat up more so that she could see him and waved. "Hey guys."

Guys? I sat up and the two guys and two girls that had been smiling and waving at Bret from a lifted Chevy Blazer frowned at me. I smiled at them knowing they hated that Bret spent so much time with me.

"Oh, you're busy I see," said the girl whom I call "Skankzilla". I could hear the discontent in her voice.

I smiled wider "Actually, we're just hanging out. Shouldn't you be getting back to your corner? Wouldn't want some other skank to take it."

She flipped her blonde hair behind her back and turned away from me.

Bret sighed. "She was just kidding! What are you guys up to?"

J.D., one of Bret's best friends spoke up. "We're going to the lake. You two wanna come?"

Skankzilla sighed and asked, "Why did you invite her?"

I stood and put my hand on my hip and flipped my hair behind my shoulder in an imitation of her. "Because if you don't invite me, Bret won't come, Skankzilla. And we all know how bad you want Bret's balls in your mouth."

The skank frowned at me. "That's just disgusting, Artemis."

I shrugged. "You're the one who does it." I wasn't usually so abrasive, but she rubbed me the wrong way.

J.D. and the other three people in the truck laughed loudly at Skankzilla. She screamed in frustration and turned away from me. Bret sighed and whispered, "Do you always have to get her all riled up?"

"It wouldn't be any fun if I didn't. Besides, what did I say that wasn't true?" I walked towards the truck and smiled up at the two boys in it. "Hey J.D. Hey Billy. One of you strong boys wanna give me a boost?"

They both started to reach towards me, but Bret grabbed me. "I got her guys."

J.D. rolled his eyes. "Yeah, Bret. You've always got her."

In reality all of the kids just put up with me because Bret was my friend. If they had their choice, I would be the biggest loner ever. Billy smiled kindly at me and moved over so I could sit in the front beside him. Bret started to sit beside me and I shook my head. "Go sit in the back with Skankzilla. I'm sure she needs some consoling after my insults."

Bret rolled his eyes at me, but did what I asked. J.D.'s girlfriend, Jessica, smiled at me. "Hey. Chicky." Chicky was Bret's nickname for me, not sure where he got it from, but it stuck.

I smiled back at her knowing she was just being polite. "Hey, Jess."

Billy started the truck and drove off towards the lake. I put my seat belt on and watched the landscape go by as we drove. Billy turned country music on the radio and everyone started singing along except me. I ignored the rowdy teens and watched the fields. Billy asked, "So, how was your trip?"

I shrugged. "It was alright. We gambled and drank and had fun. And Bret tried to get in a fight in Las Vegas."

J.D. asked, "What happened?"

I turned to Bret and nodded. "You can tell them."

"When we were in Vegas, these older guys were trying to proposition Artemis." Bret said without hesitation.

Billy kept looking at me out of the corner of his eye. All of them did this, like they couldn't let me out of their sight. Like they were *scared* of me. I didn't understand it, because I had never done anything to any of them, but I was used to it by now. Bret continued telling them all about our adventures. The lake started to become visible and I got excited. I loved the water and couldn't wait to get in it.

Billy parked the truck, and I hopped out before anyone else and ran down to the new dock the townspeople had built. I threw off my shirt and pants and ran straight off the dock and into the lake without making the dock squeak. As I went under the surface I swam farther out, pushing against the water and loving the feel of it on my skin. I could hear the rest of them jumping into the water and surfaced when I knew I was far enough away that none of them could jump on me.

I turned around and gasped as Billy splashed me in the face. I splashed him back and we started a girls versus boys splashing war. Of course, the boys always won, but I liked to think that we let them win. Boys had very sensitive egos. Billy splashed me again, and I launched myself at him, pushing him under the water. He pulled me down with him and I went willingly, glad that, for once, one of them was treating me like a friend. I started to swim up when Billy pulled me against him and kissed me under the water. I froze in shock as he went up for air. I sat under the water not comprehending what had happened when Bret pulled me up. I gasped and stared at Billy.

Bret yelled, "What the hell did you do to her?!"

I shook my head and put my hands on Bret's chest. "No, Bret. It's okay. He didn't do anything. I was just seeing how long I could hold my breath." *And wondering why Billy had kissed me and why it had felt so strange.*

Bret frowned at me and then shrugged. "Sorry, Billy."

Billy smiled. "No prob. We know you are protective of her. Just like a big brother."

Bret flinched at the words, and I ignored him. I dove under the water as far down as I could go. I swam right to Billy's legs and pulled him under. His arms flailed as he tried to stay up, but I tugged harder, surfaced before he did, and swam a few feet away. Billy came up, sputtering, and smiled at me. Bret glared at me, and

I shrugged at him trying to look innocent. The girls started fighting with individual boys and, as I suspected, Skankzilla went to Bret. I floated on my back, enjoying the sun on my face. I heard the water moving and turned my head to see Billy floating next to me. He spoke softly, "Hey."

"Hey Billy. Nice day, huh?"

He nodded and then turned serious. "I'm sorry Bret's leaving."

I shrugged. "Yeah, but it's great for him."

He nodded. "Yeah, but bad for you."

I stopped floating and treaded water so I could look at him better. "What do you mean?"

He dropped down too and smiled. "Artemis, we know how you feel about him."

I shook my head. "No, you don't."

He rolled his eyes. "So, you're trying to tell me that you don't like him?"

I frowned. "Of course I like him, but not like J.D. and Jess like each other. You said it right. He's like my big brother."

Billy flinched. "Don't tell that to Bret. You'll kill him."

I shrugged. "I've never told him any different."

He frowned. "So, you've never done anything with him?"

I laughed. "No! I've never done anything with anyone." I suddenly felt embarrassed and turned away.

"It's okay, Artemis. I know it's hard for you here since everyone treats you bad," Billy said softly.

I shrugged. "I'm used to it."

Billy moved closer to me and said, "When Bret leaves, you can spend time with me, if you want to."

I turned around and stared at him. "You're not afraid of me?"

He smiled. "A little, but I'm tougher than Bret and he can handle you so, I figure I shouldn't be too scared."

Skankzilla screamed and pointed behind me. "Oh my God, do you guys see those bears?"

I turned and looked in the direction she was pointing and gasped. "Those aren't bears, they're huge wolves!"

Two gray wolves and one beautiful black wolf were standing on the sandy edge of the lake drinking. They looked up when they heard her, and I felt drawn to them.

I started swimming towards them and they turned to stare at me. The black wolf in the middle took a step forward and the other two snarled at him. He stopped moving and they all started to turn away. I called to them, "Wait! Don't leave!"

Billy grabbed me. "What are you doing, Artemis?"

I shook free of him and swam faster towards them. "Please! Wait!" I recognized the middle one and knew where I had seen him before. He was the wolf in my dream last night. He was Ares, the mystery man in my dreams and the man at the casino. The wolves ignored my pleas, running into the fields before disappearing into the forest. I sighed and Bret grabbed me in his arms.

I growled, "Put me down."

"What were you thinking?" He shouted at me.

"You wouldn't understand." I pushed off of him and swam towards the shore. The girls were already dressed and headed towards the truck. I put my clothes back on and my shoes and started walking.

Billy caught up to me. "Where are you going? Come on, I'll give you a ride home."

I shook my head. "No thanks. I'll talk to you later, Billy."

He stared at me as I started running down the road. I heard Bret grunt and stopped running. I yelled, "You go with them! I need time alone!"

Bret started to shake his head as he tried to put his pants on, and I ran down the road as fast as I could. Dirt kicked up behind me as I sprinted towards home. I felt stupid for even believing that wolf had been Ares.

A werewolf? How stupid am I? I have a wild imagination.

I stopped suddenly and stared in surprise at my house.

How did I get here so fast?

I shrugged and walked up the steps of the front porch.

Darren opened the door before I could reach for it and narrowed his eyes at me. "Where's Bret?"

"With his friends. I left early to come home."

He shrugged. "Okay. Now what are you doing?"

"Taking a shower and then eating lunch. Is that okay with you?" I glared at him, my hands forming fists at my sides.

He raised his hands in surrender. "Yeah, yeah, kid."

I hurried into the bathroom and undressed.

What the hell is wrong with me? I keep having wolfman dreams then I think I see the man that is from my dreams. Koda said I couldn't call him for two days. Why not? Oh shit. Is he still alive?

I started to get nervous and wanted to call him, but breathed slowly, letting my body relax again.

I can wait until I'm done. If he is dead... I swallowed hard... *rushing won't do anything.*

I would have rather taken a bath, but I needed a shower after swimming in the lake. I climbed into the hot stream of water and washed my body and hair absent-mindedly.

Why had I felt so strongly that the wolf was Ares? It was stupid to even consider that my dreams were real, right? But how was he in my dreams? Why was he in my dreams?

"Artemis, are you alright?" Bret called through the door.

I sighed. "Yes, Bret. I'm fine. I thought I told you to hang out with your friends?"

He sighed heavily, and the door creaked from him leaning against it. "I know what you are doing."

I stared at the wall waiting for his answer.

"You think by pushing me away it will make it easier on you when I leave."

I sighed. "Yeah, well, what am I supposed to do?" I turned off the shower and wrapped the towel around myself. I opened the door and looked up at Bret who stood, frowning at me. I walked past him and into my room to get dressed. Bret shut the door behind me waiting in the hallway as I got dressed as slow as possible.

When I walked back outside Bret was still scowling at me. I put my hands on my hips. "What?"

He frowned. "Looked like you and Billy were pretty friendly at the lake."

"He was just trying to be nice since you are leaving and everything. He offered for me to hang out with him, so that I wouldn't be lonely."

Bret rolled his eyes. "Right, so you wouldn't be *lonely*. What a dirtbag!"

I frowned at him. "Why are you upset? Most of the time, your friends won't even talk to me so, shouldn't you be happy that he is being nice to me?"

Bret scoffed. "I'm sure he'll be real nice once I'm gone."

I stared at Bret and realized what was going on. "You're jealous."

Bret's face twisted from shock to sadness. "No, I'm not. Why would I be jealous of Billy?"

"Because you think that when you leave I am going to hook up with Billy and then when you come back, it won't be the same between us."

Bret played with a string at the end of his shirt. "That's not it. I just ... I just don't want him to hurt you."

I smiled. "You mean emotionally, right?"

He smiled back. "Well, not physically. I think you could take Billy if you wanted to."

I rolled my eyes. "I could take you if I wanted to." I pushed his chest, and he fell backwards onto the floor.

He swept my legs out from under me, making me fall on my back beside him. He rolled over and before he could do anything else, I punched his chest and arm. His face lit up with a giant smile as we wrestled in the hallway. We both admitted defeat when we were breathing heavily and sweating. Bret stood and then held out his hand to help me up.

I folded my legs under me and stayed sitting as I looked up at him. "Tell me the truth, Bret."

Bret's face turned serious, making him look older and a little handsome. "I don't want to leave. I want to stay here with you." I started to protest but he squatted down, grabbed my arms and shook his head. "I'll play for one of the colleges close to here. We can live in my parent's house and—"

I shook my head. "Bret, Notre Dame is an amazing opportunity. I'll make new friends."

"I don't want to be away from you Artemis. I lov—"

I pushed him away and ran from the house. *I am not doing this right now.* I could hear Bret calling after me, but I didn't want to deal with him and his stupid attempts at making me into something more than his friend. I just didn't see him that way. Bret was catching up to me, and I knew I couldn't outrun him, so I stopped. He stopped a few feet behind me, trying to catch his breath. I focused on my own breathing and realized that I wasn't even winded, but I normally never got winded. Bret said it wasn't human for me to be able to run so fast or long without getting winded, but I just told him he was just mad that I was in better shape than him.

I started to turn around to look at Bret when I heard a soft growl from beside me. I turned my head slowly and saw one of the wolves from the lake standing in the forest. The black wolf. Bret grabbed my arm before I realized I was moving towards the wolf. The wolf snarled loudly, and I knew he was snarling at Bret. Darren appeared beside me and yelled, "Get in the house!"

I jumped away, since I hadn't even heard him run up to us.

I started to protest leaving, but Bret picked me up and started running. I tried to fight Bret, but he was a lot stronger than me. I twisted in his arms so I could see the wolf as he watched us leave. Darren raised his gun and aimed at the wolf.

I screamed, "No!" and pushed myself from Bret's arms. He stumbled as I made him lose his balance, and I ran to Darren.

He had his finger on the trigger, gun aimed at the wolf.

I ran as fast as I could into Darren, making his gun go off high in the air, and he fell to the ground. I jumped up and looked to the forest hoping the wolf was fine and smiled when I saw him standing proudly in the clearing. The other two wolves from the lake came to him, and together they ran off into the forest. I turned on Darren. "What the hell are you doing? That wolf didn't do anything."

Darren snarled. "That wolf is dangerous! He needs to be killed."

I shook my head. "You were the one who taught me that predators are not always dangerous and shouldn't be shot just because they *might* harm your animals. He was just sitting there."

"He growled at you!" Darren yelled at me, his face blushing with his anger.

"He growled at Bret, not me, and he was just standing there," I said as I glared at Darren. "I can't believe you were going to shoot him. You are not the man I thought you were." I started to get angry and felt my body temperature rising. My hands started shaking, and I sighed as the first of the convulsions brought me to my knees. I fell to the ground on my back and started to twitch hard.

Darren yelled, "You bastard!" in the direction the wolves had gone then stared into my eyes. "Artemis, breathe honey. Slow your breathing and calm yourself. You can work through this. Focus on happy thoughts."

I clenched my teeth and closed my eyes. I tried to slow my breathing and pictured how beautiful the wolves had looked at the lake and Ares' smiling face from my dreams. My body slowed, cooled down and then stopped twitching. Bret started to pick me up, but I pushed him away, standing on my own. I brushed my backside off and ran towards the house. We had no clue why I had the seizures and Darren refused to take me to the doctors. I threw clothes, contacts and my toothbrush in my backpack and ran back out of the house. Bret was following me and I stopped running to wait for him. He caught up to me frowning. "Where are you going?"

I snarled. "Away from my father."

"Are you coming to my house?" he asked smiling.

"I hadn't really thought about it actually," I said quietly.

He smiled wider. "You know you are always welcome to stay with me."

I stared at his smiling face and felt sadness overwhelm me, knowing that in a week I would no longer have him. I would be alone, just like the first week of kindergarten. I started to tell him I couldn't when Billy drove down the street. I waved at him and he stopped the truck, waving back at me. I smiled at Bret. "I think I'll go hang out with Billy for a while."

Bret's smile fell and a quick anger replaced his happiness. "Fine. Do whatever you want." His anger faded and he rubbed the back of his neck in his nervous gesture. "If you want to stay the night at my house, I'll leave the door open for you. I think I'll go hang out with the guys for a while if you won't be with me."

I could see the hope in his eyes that I would go with him, but I smiled reassuringly. "I'll meet you at your house for dinner, 'kay?"

He nodded and attempted a smile. "Alright. I'll see you at six."

I stood on tiptoe and kissed his cheek. "Bye, Bret."

He smiled at me with a little gleam of hope in his eyes. "Bye, Artemis."

I ran to Billy's truck and hopped up into the open door. I threw my bag in the back before turning to him. "Hey, Billy. You know you have perfect timing?"

He laughed. "Well, that's a first." He looked at my bag. "You going somewhere?"

"Just running away from home for a little while. Not like my dad won't know where to find me, but I need some space." Billy's face fell, likely because he realized I meant Bret's house. "So, Billy, you want to go somewhere? Bret's hanging out with the guys for a while and I'm not supposed to be back at his place for dinner 'til six."

Billy smiled. "We could go to the mall."

I nodded. "Great. I need to do some shopping."

Billy smiled wide. "Cool." He started the truck back up and drove away down the road towards the highway. I buckled my seatbelt and sat back against the seat. Billy talked about his 'after high school' plans and I tried to pay attention, but all I could think about were the wolves. I had never seen wolves come so close to humans before, especially twice in one day. Billy must have noticed my wandering mind because he turned on the radio and didn't talk the rest of the way to the mall. We parked on the top level of the garage and walked towards the mall.

I smiled reassuringly at Billy and asked, "Do they have cell phones in here?"

Billy shrugged. "I don't remember. I have one you could borrow, though."

"Thanks. I just need to make a call tomorrow."

"No problem." He opened the door for me and I walked in and inhaled the smell of sugar and sweetness. Billy laughed. "It's the cinnamon bun place. It's like two feet from the department store. If you want, we can get something there?"

I licked my lips, realizing that I hadn't eaten after my shower. "Actually, I think I need to get food, like more than a cinnamon bun."

Billy rubbed his stomach and said, "I'm always hungry."

"What is it with boys and always being hungry?" I asked.

He shrugged and then flexed his arms, showing off his muscular biceps. "It's from all of the working out and growing big."

I huffed a laugh. "That must be it. Working out your big egos."

He rolled his eyes. "Come on, there is this great Chinese food place in here I love."

I shook my head. "No way. I need meat!"

He laughed and put his hand on the center of his chest. "A woman after my own heart." We walked through the department store to the exit, which led to the rest of the mall. I dodged people as I hurried to the food court, which was about fifty feet away. I turned and looked at all of the places surrounding me, trying to figure out where to go. Billy started pointing out places. "There's the fast food burger place or the place that makes giant burritos that are like *ten* pounds. You can get an all meat burrito I bet."

I licked my lips at the thought of spicy shredded beef in a burrito. "Burrito place it is." He led the way to the restaurant which thankfully had no line. I ordered the largest burrito of spicy shredded beef, rice, sour cream, refried beans and cheese they could make. Billy ordered his burrito then got us chips and salsa with our drinks as well. We sat down at an empty table and started in on our chips and salsa. I moaned happily. "I forgot how much I love chips and salsa."

"My mom always keeps chips and salsa around at the house. We could watch a movie afterwards and chow down on some more chips and salsa there if you want?" Billy offered with a tentative smile.

I shrugged then talked around a chip in my mouth. "Maybe, it depends on how I feel after shopping. I generally get tired from dealing with the Barbie girls here."

Billy frowned. "What Barbie girls?"

I looked around us and saw at least ten blonde haired, big-chested, scantily clad girls and laughed. "Look around us Billy. It's like an 'I wanna be Barbie' convention at this mall."

He looked around us and smiled. "I guess I see what you mean."

I scoffed. "As if their looks weren't bad enough, these girls all act dumb and talk in high-pitched voices." I changed my voice to as high pitched as I could get. "Like *oh my God,* Billy! Did you see her hair? It is like *totally* last summer."

He laughed at my mocking and shook his head, rubbing a tear

from the corner of his eye. "So, why is it that you have been the outcast in our group when you are so much fun to hang out with?"

I shrugged and tried to hide the pain from my face. "I think because Bret forced me on everyone so they didn't get a chance to decide if they liked me or not. Then you have Skankzilla who wants Bret so bad that she will do anything she can to try to get rid of me."

Billy looked nervous as he dipped a chip in the salsa. "Yeah, she definitely hates that Bret is with you."

I felt my face wrinkle in disgust. "I told you that I'm not *with* Bret! We are just friends. I told you that at the lake."

He shrugged. "You don't have to lie to me Artemis. I see the way you are together."

I shook my head. "You obviously don't. Bret is my friend and that's all. Ugh. I hate it when people assume we are together."

He smiled and asked, "So, you guys aren't a couple?"

I shook my head. "No. He is just so damn protective of me that he makes everyone think that."

Billy smiled wider. "Oh. Well, I'm glad I know now."

I finished eating my burrito and finally felt full.

Billy finished his burrito with a sigh. "Man, that was good."

I nodded. "Yep. Definitely hit the spot. So, are you ready to shop?"

He smiled. "Always!"

"Are you one of those guys who is a secret shopaholic?" I asked after laughing at his enthusiasm.

He put his head down in a bashful manner. "Maybe."

I laughed. "Great. I think I'm coming here for a relaxing time and you're going to be going to all of the sales."

His eyes got big and darted around the mall. "There's a sale?! Where?"

I rolled my eyes. "Come on, tough football player. Let's shop!" I stood and he followed me, throwing away our tray on the way.

I started to walk past the teen clothing store with a giant SALE sign and Billy cleared his throat. "Uh, I wasn't kidding about being a shopaholic."

I laughed and followed him into the store. He rushed right to the discounted racks and started pulling out t-shirts with the clothing store's logo on them. I had to admit that Billy had decent taste in clothes.

He cleared his throat, and I looked up from the floor that I had at some point started looking at. He smiled. "What size are you?"

I frowned. "Why?"

He sighed. "Just play along."

I sighed back at him. "Medium."

He nodded then turned back to the discounted racks. I walked over to one of the display stands and sat on it. It was definitely going to be a long day of shopping. Billy walked across the store with a pile of clothes over his shoulder to another rack which had sunglasses. He put on a pair of the old style aviators, and I couldn't help but laugh. He turned to me and frowned. "You don't like them?"

I shook my head. "No." I walked over to the sunglass rack and found a nice pair of sunglasses and put them on him. He looked in the mirror and smiled. I nodded. "I like those."

He reached over to the girls' side and handed me a pair with diamonds on the frame. "Put them on."

I frowned and put the sunglasses on. I had never really been a big fan of sunglasses so I didn't own any. I tilted my head to the side as if I was modeling them.

"I like those. They look good on you."

I blushed. "You think so? You don't think they make me look—"

He moved closer to me and whispered, "Hot? Yes, definitely." I turned to face him and he kissed me on the lips, sending an unpleasant shock down my spine. He pulled away from me, smiling, and took the glasses off my face. "I'm buying you these."

"I have my own money, Billy."

He shook his head. "Nope, I picked the store, so I'm buying."

He walked over to another rack and started looking at belts.

I sighed too softly for him to hear. "I'm going next door to get my shopping out of the way while you're finishing up."

"Okay. I'll meet you in there. I think I'm almost done."

I laughed as he scowled at a pair of jeans, trying to decide if they were worth it with the ten percent off or not. I hurried to the store right next door and walked in. It was my favorite place: a jewelry store. I didn't wear jewelry, but I loved looking at everything. I walked down to the men's jewelry spot and looked at the necklaces. They were all chains and reminded me of rappers on TV. I rolled my eyes and then found the necklace I had been looking at since I found out Bret was leaving. I smiled at the clerk who stood silently waiting for me to ask for help and pointed at the necklace. "I'd like that one please."

She smiled. "That's a nice one." She took it out and put it in a box. I watched the silver chain with the football on it sparkle and hoped Bret liked it. It would be my last present to him before he left. I paid for it and walked outside, almost running into Billy.

He smiled and looked down at the bag. "Gift for Bret?"

I sighed. "My going away present for him. Something so he'll remember me."

Billy rolled his eyes. "Like anyone could forget you."

I smiled at him and started walking towards the exit. He walked quietly beside me and opened the door for me. I looked down at his hands and gasped. "How much did you spend?"

He shrugged. "A couple hundred dollars. Not much."

I gaped at the ten bags he held. "Oh my God. I don't think I've spent that much in five years of clothes shopping."

He rolled his eyes. "Are you sure you're a girl?"

"Are you sure you're not gay?" I asked.

He frowned. "Would I have kissed you if I was gay?"

I fought the frown that wanted to form and forced a playful look. "You did just question if I was a girl."

He rolled his eyes at me and started walking to his truck. I walked beside him and smiled at how easy it was to be around him. I felt, for once, normal. We were almost to his truck when we heard screeching tires. I turned my head and saw Skankzilla driving J.D.'s truck and swerving out of control. Billy jumped in front of me to protect me from the careening truck. I tensed, waiting for impact, but nothing happened. I opened my eyes slowly and saw the truck had stopped just inches from Billy. He exhaled and turned around to face the truck. "You almost killed us!"

Skankzilla shrugged. "I wasn't aiming for *you,* Billy."

Bret frowned from the passenger seat and shook his head. "I can't believe you just said that. Are you alright, Artemis?"

I patted my arms and legs and nodded. "Yeah. Billy saved me by blocking Skankzilla's path."

Bret's forehead creased further in anger.

Billy stepped in my view of him and looked me over. "You sure you're alright?"

I laughed. "Billy, I'm fine. If anyone would have been hurt, it would have been you for jumping in the way. You could have died."

He smiled. "Well, I couldn't just let you get hurt. I had to protect you." He kissed my cheek and I felt the blush spread across them. He turned around and yelled, "Don't ever let her drive again!"

Bret glared at Billy as he walked to the truck. Bret hopped down and walked towards me. "You having fun with Billy?"

I shrugged. "Actually, yes. We ate then we shopped…" Billy whistled and I turned just as he tossed the sunglasses he bought me at my chest. I caught them easily and put them on, smiling at Bret. "You like them?"

He nodded and smiled. "Yes. They look good on you."

Billy called, "That's because I picked them out."

Bret snarled. "So, you and Billy dating now?"

I frowned and pushed the sunglasses on top of my head. "Bret, I have to make friends, right? You'll be gone in a week. And we just talked about this."

He scoffed and then glared at me. "Friends? *Right,* more like bed buddies."

I shoved Bret in the chest as hard as I could, making him stumble a few steps backwards. "Don't ever say something like that about me again. You know I'm not like that. I can't believe you said that. Here. Take this." I tossed the bag with his necklace in it at him and walked away. Bret started walking towards me and I turned around and yelled, "Screw you! I've been your friend for over ten years and never *ever* done anything with you. How dare you assume that I'm with him for a few hours and I'm screwing him. If that's what you think of me then you should just leave for Indiana now."

Bret called, "I'm sorry, Artemis. Wait. Please."

I hurried to Billy's truck where he stood with the door open. I pulled my sunglasses down, so he wouldn't see me crying, and hopped up into the truck. He shut my door and got in the driver's side, starting the truck quickly and pulling out of the parking lot. We wove our way down the parking garage while I cried as silently as I could. Billy put his hand on top of mine and rubbed small circles on it, trying to be soothing. His touch began making me nauseous so I patted his hand to let him know it was alright and turned to face the passenger door. I let the tears fall, then shook my head.

I am not going to let him ruin my day.

I turned to Billy. "Sorry about that, Billy."

He rolled his eyes. "Bret is a jerk to you and you apologize to me? That's a little backwards, Artemis. I can't believe he said that to you."

I shrugged. "He's just upset. I'm sure he feels like a jerk especially after seeing the necklace." I thought about it and realized that I didn't want to see Bret. "Is it okay if I come over and eat chips and salsa and watch movies?"

Billy smiled wide. "Yeah. My parents are still out of town so we'll have the place to ourselves."

I smiled. "Cool. So, what are we watching?"

He shrugged. "I have like a thousand movies so I'll let you pick."

The trip passed quickly, and we stopped in front of his house. I climbed out of his truck and grabbed a couple of his bags. He opened the door and waited for me to go in.

I called over my shoulder, "Where do you want the bags?"

He whispered, "Here is fine."

I jumped since I hadn't realized how close he was.

He laughed. "Sorry. I whispered so I *wouldn't* scare you."

I smiled. "It's alright." I set the bags down in the entryway and walked to his kitchen. I had been to Billy's house a few times to watch movies with everyone. I took out a soda for each of us and Billy took out the salsa and got the chips down. We walked to his living room and I gasped. A new gigantic TV sat, taking up his entire living room wall.

"Holy crap," I exclaimed. "How big is that?"

He shrugged. "It's a seventy-three inch. We're going to get the eighty-inch next month."

I turned to my right and gasped again. The wall was an array of shelves of movies. "What order are they in?"

"Release year."

I walked to the wall of movies and started going through the titles. I finally decided on one of my favorite movies. "Here."

He looked at the movie then up to me again. "This one?" he asked. "Are you sure?"

I nodded smiling. "It's one of my favorites. You don't like it?"

He laughed. "No, I love it! It's just that I thought you would pick a comedy or something…"

I finished, "Something girly?" He nodded and I laughed. "Nope, I like action movies."

"Alright, *300* it is." He walked to the stand which held the movie player and what seemed like every game console ever made and put the movie in. I sat down on the couch and opened my soda and ate a chip with salsa on it. He turned the lights off and sat down beside me as the previews started to play. I relaxed into the couch and felt the stress press down on my shoulders. Billy sat back against the couch beside me and clicked the menu button to start the movie. I smiled excitedly as the movie started to play. I could practically say each line along with the movie, but I kept quiet so Billy could enjoy the movie as well. Halfway through the movie a message blinked at the bottom of the screen. Billy sighed. "Breaking news alert again."

I turned to him and asked with a shaky voice, "Can you turn to it?"

He shrugged. "Sure. I'm surprised you want to after how much has already gone on."

I frowned harder. "I haven't heard anything. Darren has been keeping me and Bret away from the television so we haven't heard about what's going on at all."

Billy's mouth fell open. "So, you don't know what's happening?" I shook my head. "Then you need to watch this." He hit pause on the movie and changed inputs to go to the news.

The reporter was the same monotone reporter we had seen at the diner. His face seemed more solemn than before. "Another attack and another country completely decimated..."

I turned to Billy. "What is he talking about?" He shushed me and pointed at the television. Pictures started flashing on the TV of a city with buildings on fire and hundreds of dead bodies everywhere. I gasped. "What's happening?"

The reporter came back on screen. "The entire country of Mongolia is completely devoid of human life." The bodies in every town have all been left in the same state of mutilation: their throats ripped out and their blood drained. Some even seem animal ravaged, but we believe that may be from scavengers who smell the decaying corpses. We haven't been able to find a single shred of evidence as to the cause. Scientists are baffled, saying that they do not believe this is some type of disease, but no answers have been found as to what or *who* has been causing this. Video surveillance is unable to pick up anything either. So far the following places have been hit... Japan, Russia, North and South Korea, Nevada and now Mongolia."

I gasped. "Oh my God! Why wouldn't Darren let us know about this? It's kind of important."

Billy shrugged. "I don't know."

The shock slowly set in. "We were just in Tahoe. What if we had been there...?" I remembered Darren making us leave so quickly from Tahoe and then it had been massacred. *Could Darren be in on it?* I shook my head, dismissing that thought. Then I stood. "I have to go."

Billy followed me to the door. "Okay, but will you come back?"

"Not tonight. Thank you for a great afternoon." I put on my best smile and put a hand on the doorknob.

He held up one finger. "Hold on. I got you something." He walked over to his bags and rummaged through them. I twitched nervously as he came back with a small white box. He handed it to me. "Here, I thought you would like this."

I opened the little white lid and gasped. A silver chain with a silver wolf hanging from it glittered in the white box. I stared at the small wolf and whispered, "It's beautiful."

He kissed me lightly on the lips. "You can come by anytime you want."

I smiled at him and kissed his cheek. "Thanks. I love the necklace, and I'll hold you to that offer." I ran from the house to his truck and grabbed my backpack. It still didn't feel right when Billy kissed me. *Was it just me, since I hadn't been kissed before?* I ran down the road, past the feed store and the side street that led to Bret's house, leaving behind the town's cozy ambiance as I left the town's border.

Darren sat on the front porch, cleaning one of his shotguns.

I frowned at him as I walked up the steps. "You shoot one of the wolves?" I asked nervously.

He shook his head and sighed. "I wasn't going to kill the wolf, Artemis. I was just going to scare it a little." He looked at the necklace box and sunglasses on my head and smiled. "Bret, get you those?"

I shook my head. "No, Billy did. Bret and I aren't speaking right now."

He frowned. "Not speaking? When have you ever not been speaking? What happened?"

I groaned. "I don't want to talk about it. I *do* want to talk about what's been going on that you've been hiding from us. Why didn't you tell us that people are dying or being killed? That's kind of important, Dad! Especially when it happens at a place right after we leave."

He flinched. "I know. I was just trying to keep you kids happy and not worrying about what was going on."

I shook my head. "You knew about the attack in Tahoe. How?"

"I can't tell you that," he said sternly.

I groaned. "You are always keeping secrets from me, you have ever since I was born. Why?"

He shook his head. "I can't tell you. I'm sorry. If I tell you, it will put you in danger and I want you to be safe and happy."

I sighed then turned around when I heard someone running down the street. Bret was running up our road with his necklace shining in the sun. I groaned. "Great. Just freaking great."

Bret looked down at my necklace box and frowned, but turned to Darren. "What the hell, Darren? Why didn't you tell us what was going on?"

"I've heard this, so I'm going inside to pack better." I walked away, leaving the boys to talk and went to my room. I pulled out more pairs of underwear and a couple of pajama tops and bottoms and shoved them into my backpack.

I heard Bret come in my room, but ignored him and zipped up my bag. He whispered, "So, how was your day?"

I shrugged. "It was great until my best friend called me a slut and I found out my dad has been hiding things from me."

Bret sighed. "I'm sorry, Artemis. I didn't mean what I said."

I raised my hand stopping him and looked up into his eyes. Tears had started to well up in mine. "Don't apologize for something you meant."

He wrapped his arms around me. "I didn't mean it."

I shrugged and pulled out of his embrace. "Whatever. I'll be at Billy's if you need me." I started to walk out of the room and Bret grabbed me by the arms and kissed my lips hard. I felt the strength he had in his hands and knew I couldn't fight him off even though his kiss sent my stomach rolling.

He pulled back from the kiss and whispered, "Please don't go over there. I'm better than him. Stay with me. Please."

I stared up at his face and knew that if I didn't go with him that it would crush him. Yet the disgust I felt each time I was kissed by him or Billy was too much to deal with. "I'm sorry Bret. I need some time alone."

Bret frowned. "You can't go out alone with the wolves constantly showing up."

I snarled at him. "I can do whatever I want. Besides, I'm sure you need time to go see Skankzilla." I pulled away from him and walked out of the house. If it had been any other girl than Skankzilla I wouldn't have cared since I didn't like him in that way. Why her? Why my nemesis?

Darren called after me, "Where you going?"

I yelled, "Away from you!"

"She's trying to go somewhere alone," Bret said in a sharp tone.

Darren frowned at me. "You going to the stable?"

I nodded.

Darren quickly put his gun back together and handed it to me. "Take this then. Just in case you need it."

I slung my bag over my shoulders and took the gun and the box of shells sitting next to Darren. "Thanks."

I walked away from Bret, who was frowning in frustration at Darren for not stopping me, and through our field. The stable sat in the center of our property and was basically an empty building for the horses and cows to use to get out of the sun, rain or snow. The trees swayed slightly in the breeze and birds and insects chirped and clicked and built an endless stream of music as I walked. I raised my arms to the wind and reveled in the feel of it against my skin. The outdoors had always drawn me more than buildings. The forest felt like a friend waiting for me to walk with. And I could feel the moon's presence like a buzzing in my veins, though I couldn't see her. I jogged through the pastures, past grazing cattle, until I finally came to the stable. The building was dark brown instead of red, and I could see a few horses dozing inside under the shade. I approached slowly, making kissing noises so I wouldn't frighten them. The horses bobbed their heads and waited patiently for me to come to them. I stroked the three horses' heads and crooned and cooed to them. Two feral cats stared at me from their perches on the beams. Cats had never liked me or Darren, so the only cats that we got were the feral ones who ate mice in the stable. In the back, east corner was a ladder that led up to the small loft.

I climbed up and shook out the bedroll to make sure there weren't any creepy crawlies hiding within the folds. The horses nickered and snorted and talked to each other, relaxing my nerves. I set the gun against the wall and opened the necklace box. The wolf charm sparkled in the sunlight that was streaming through the windows. I picked the charm up in my hand and screamed in pain as it burned my fingertips. I dropped the charm and stared at the red blisters now present on my fingertips. The silver had burned me? I held my palm out flat and laid it against the charm and screamed again as the charm burned me.

"What the hell?" I cradled my hand against my chest and squinted against the tears trying to squeeze out.

Something isn't right.

I needed to get cream for the burn or it would get infected. "So much for my alone time," I muttered as I used the bedroll to put the necklace back in its box and close the lid. I grabbed the gun again and grimaced at the pain from holding the gun against my burn. I climbed down from the loft and ran through the pastures towards Bret's house.

I hadn't forgiven him, but I needed to take care of my burns and I didn't want to see Darren or Billy.

How could I explain that the necklace burned me?

Bret's house came into view and I saw him sitting on his back porch talking on the phone. As soon as he saw me, he hung up and ran out to meet me. "Hey."

I frowned and looked down at the ground. "I haven't forgiven you, but I hurt my hand and need to treat it before it gets infected. So, even though I'm still mad at you can I please stay the night?"

Bret held his hand out for the gun. I gave it to him and gritted my teeth as I released the cold metal from my burnt hand. I followed him into the house and into the bathroom. He tried to help me with it, but I told him to leave. I sat down on the toilet and stared at the wolf-shaped burn on my palm. I squeezed burn ointment on it and wrapped gauze around my hand. I smeared some ointment on my fingertips and walked out to the living room where Bret was watching a movie.

I kept quiet the rest of the night so that I wouldn't start any more trouble between us. I leaned against Bret as I started to get tired. He put his arm around me and rubbed my arm as he watched the movie. I rested against his familiar body basking in his familiar cologne. I used to hate cologne, but Bret's had just become his smell. I shivered and Bret walked to the closet and got a large afghan out. He laid down against the back of the couch and I laid down in front of him as he wrapped us up together. He put his arm out and I laid my head on it in the perfect curve of his elbow. This had become such a common occurrence that I could be practically incoherent and still do this. Although doing it now felt wrong somehow. I shook my head and ignored that thought.

I was almost asleep when I heard two gun shots. Bret jumped up, and we ran to the window to see what was going on. Billy stood a few feet in front of Bret's house facing away from us and aiming his gun into a clump of trees. I stared into the trees and saw the reflection of amber eyes.

Wolves.

I ran to the door, flinging it open and ran outside. The wolves had started to walk towards Billy, snarling. I ran in front of Billy and put my arms out, "No. You three leave."

The wolves stopped and stared at me. I instantly recognized the three wolves as the ones that had been around the area today. They looked extremely large, but were always too far away for me to be able to tell. The middle one was obviously the alpha and took a step forward so I mimicked him by taking a step towards him. Billy started to grab me, but I waved him away.

Bret whispered loudly, "What are you doing?"

"Trying to show the wolf that he is not dominant to me. I am alpha here, not him," I answered quietly.

Bret groaned. "Great, you're going to make the wolf attack you."

I shook my head at him then squared my legs and stared straight in the wolf's eyes. He stared back at me, unwilling to be seen as submissive. One of the other two wolves nudged the alpha in his side. The alpha's hackles rose and he snarled. I stayed perfectly still and for once wished I had a tail so I could show that I wasn't scared of him. The other wolf nudged the alpha and the strangest thing happened…the alpha sighed. The alpha snapped his teeth at me and then ran off into the trees with his two pack members.

I turned to Billy and saw the white of his face. "What's wrong?

They weren't really going to hurt you, Billy." I reached out to him and he backed away.

"Don't touch me, Artemis," he said quickly as he backed up.

I stared at him in shock. "Why are you acting like you are afraid of me? All I did was use some of my nerdy research to show the head wolf that I wasn't afraid of him. I did it to save your life. It's not like I *talked* to the damn wolf."

Bret stood beside me and stared at Billy. "Dude, what is your problem?"

Billy shook his head. "You can't expect me to believe that you just used common wolf knowledge to show you were tougher. You *had* to have been communicating with him."

I rolled my eyes. "Right, communicate with a wolf. Have you lost your mind?"

He shook his head. "I'm sorry, Artemis, but I can't see you anymore." I frowned at him and was about to say something when he tossed me a large box. "Here, now you don't need mine."

I stared at the box and read the label. "Pay as you go cell phone. Uh, thanks."

He nodded and ran down the street away from us. Bret folded his arms across his chest. "No wonder the wolf was going to eat him. Billy's a puss."

I huffed a laugh and walked back inside the house, opening the cell phone box as I went. I put the phone together and plugged it in so that I could use it to call Koda tomorrow. Hopefully he would answer. Bret turned on the news channel, and we laid back down on the couch under the afghan. I sighed in contentment against his arm as my body warmed back up.

The monotone news reporter came on the channel looking as somber as ever. "What I am about to show you is very disturbing. If you have small children or sensitive individuals, you should have them leave the room." I looked back at Bret, and he shrugged, staring at the TV.

"A cell phone caught footage of an attack in London. We aren't sure how the video got to the internet, but sources believe the boy had set his phone to automatically send when he was done recording. Please, brace yourselves for what you are about to see." A new grainy video came on the screen showing a dark London night where two men were surrounded by people as they prepared to fight. Just as one of the men arched back to throw his punch two of the people in the circle around them started screaming and were thrown across the road and into a building. Their bodies made disgustingly, loud, wet thuds as they hit the brick wall. Everyone started looking around, unable to see what was going on. Four more people in the circle disappeared screaming only to land a few blocks away on the cement, no longer breathing.

White mist appeared around one of the fighters, and he screamed in pain before flying through the air. The second fighter and the boy with the phone started to run, but three more patches of mist appeared in front of them. They started to back up and then the mist sped forward wrapping around them and their screams stopped with a loud crack and a strange hissing sound. I turned to Bret and saw he had the same shocked and scared expression on his face. The news reporter came back on. "As you can see, it appears that the strange mist is causing these deaths, but we aren't sure how the mist is capable of doing the physical damage we have seen done to the bodies. Some have had their throats torn out, some have had their necks broken and others have been found completely drained of blood. We will continue to keep you updated as we learn of new developments."

Bret turned off the television, and I shuddered against him. He wrapped his arms around me, and I wrapped the blanket tighter around us. I closed my eyes, willing them to forget the horrified expressions frozen on the victims' faces as they were thrown through the air. *What could cause this? What is the mist?* I shivered at the thought of what this could mean for us and closed my eyes. Bret stood and carried me to his bedroom. He gently laid me down and climbed in bed with me. I got into our sleeping position with my head on his chest and sighed as our bodies heated up the sheets around us and the heavy comforter made me feel even more secure. Bret hummed a soft song as I fell into a deep sleep.

The *branches stung as they hit my face. I ran as fast as I could, trying to keep up with Darren. He dashed and dodged and jumped over and around trees and bushes. I started to fall behind him and yelled for him to wait, but he ignored me. I could hear the wolves getting closer and I knew I didn't want to die. I increased my speed, but the wolves continued to gain ground. Darren was just ahead of me in a clearing and a small spark of hope seeped through me. I ducked under a low tree branch and stopped running. Darren's body twitched and convulsed then fur sprung out from under his skin. The wet splitting sound made me cringe in disgust, but what stood in Darren's place replaced my disgust with awe. A medium-sized brown wolf stood over Darren's shredded human skin. I stared at this wolf and gasped as its eyes turned to me. "Dad?" The wolf nodded and then bound away as the wolves following us pounced on top of me.*

I screamed and sat upright. I looked around and realized I was safe in Bret's bed. He opened one eye and looked at me sleepily. "Dream?" he asked with a yawn. I nodded. He pulled me back down and hugged me against him. "'S alright. I'm here."

I relaxed against him and tried to shake off the bad feeling. I wasn't sure I *was* alright. *It was just a dream. Darren can't become a wolf. That's crazy.* I repeated it a few times, making myself firmly believe what I said and closed my eyes.

"Artemis. Artemis honey, wake up," Bret whispered in my ear.

I groaned. "Five more minutes."

He laughed softly. "Breakfast is ready."

I inhaled and smelled bacon and eggs. I licked my lips and sat up. "Well, let's go." I jumped out of the bed and jogged to the kitchen. I stopped in the entryway and gasped. "You cleaned?"

He walked past me and smiling. "I knew it bothered you, so I cleaned."

I looked around the immaculate kitchen and smiled. "It's great Bret. I can't believe you did such a good job. I'm impressed."

He bowed at the waist and draped a hand towel across his arm. "A table, milady?" I curtsied and walked to the small dining table, where he pulled out a chair for me and I sat down in it. He laid the hand towel across my lap and pushed my seat in.

I inhaled the smell of the delicious looking food and licked my lips. He sat across from me, and I started shoveling food onto my plate and groaned in happiness when I saw the homemade waffles. I drowned all of my food in syrup and butter and started eating. I ate slowly, enjoying the food and chewing thoroughly. Darren sighed behind me and I growled. I turned around, and he smiled at me. "Guess her eating your food slow means she likes it more than mine."

Bret shrugged and I glared at him mouthing, "Traitor."

He rolled his eyes at me then smiled at Darren. "Come sit down. We just started eating."

Darren sat down next to Bret and looked at my plate. "I can see that."

I rolled my eyes at him and kept eating. Darren quietly spooned food on his plate while I started to eat my food faster.

Bret cleared his throat. "The wolves were back again."

Darren stopped moving and stared at me. "What happened?"

I ignored him and kept eating.

Bret sighed again. "They were being aggressive to Billy and he shot at them, but he apparently missed. Artemis ran out and yelled at them to leave and the head one the?" Bret turned to me. "The alphy?"

I sighed and set my fork down. "The alpha. The alpha male took a step forward and tried to show dominance to me and I did it right back to him. He was contemplating what to do when his two pack mates nudged him and I swear to God he sighed."

Darren frowned. "Sighed?

I nodded. "Yes, he sighed and then he snapped his teeth at me and they left."

Darren groaned and put his head in his hands. "Oh, no. He snapped his teeth at you?"

I nodded, and he groaned again.

"Shit! I knew this would happen one day, but why now? Dammit!"

I stared at him, frowning. "What are you going on about?"

He looked up slowly at me and sighed. "Nothing."

"Why are you being so secretive all of a sudden?" I asked, pounding a fist on the table. Darren ignored me, eating more of his food. Apparently, this was a battle I couldn't win right now. "Fine, be that way. I'll be leaving after I finish eating." Bret started to eat, faster and I waved my hand at him. "I'm going alone."

He sighed. "You shouldn't go alone with the wolves out."

Darren scoffed. "She'll be fine. They won't hurt her." We both stared at Darren and he shrugged. "She showed him she was dominant. If he wanted to hurt her, he would have done it then."

"He's right, Bret. Wolves aren't smart enough to plan a later attack."

Darren scoffed again and rolled his eyes. He saw us looking at him and resumed eating.

I shoveled the rest of my food into my mouth and walked to the plugged-in cell phone. I waved at Bret and Darren. "I have a cell phone if you need to reach me. I'll be back for lunch." I handed Darren the piece of paper I had written the phone number on.

Darren frowned at my bandaged hand. "What happened to your hand?"

I pulled my hand away and cradled it against my chest. "Nothing."

I ran out of the house carrying the phone in my pocket. I ran through the town ignoring the younger boys' calls and the stares of Billy and his group of friends. I knew by now he had told them what a freak I was for being able to communicate with the wolves. Boys were so dumb sometimes. I knew I would definitely have no friends when Bret left and that actually made me sad. I sighed and increased my speed, pushing my limits to get to the lake as fast as possible. When I finally got to the lake, I was thankful to find no one there. It was too early in the morning for anyone to want to try to swim. I sat down on the dock at the very end so I could dangle my legs in the water. I took out the cell phone and the piece of paper with Koda's number on it and took a deep cleansing breath. I quickly punched in the numbers and hit send.

The phone rang four times before someone answered. "Hello?"

I stopped breathing for a second then exhaled. "Koda?"

Koda sighed. "Artemis."

I nodded then realized he couldn't see me. "Yeah, how'd you know?"

He laughed. "Only four people have this number and two are with me and the other is a man so it kind of narrowed it down. What's up? Are you alright?"

I sighed. "No, I need to ask you some questions."

He was silent on the other end for a full minute before finally talking again. "Ask and I'll see if I can answer or not."

"Why am I dreaming about your friend?" I asked quickly before I lost my courage.

"What are you talking about?" he asked softly.

"I've been having these weird dreams and the man that was with you has been in them. I have had them for the past week and a half."

He whispered, "Exactly how many days?"

I thought back to when I had the first one and answered, "Ten days."

He groaned. "Shit. How do you know it was my friend and not just you dreaming about someone who looks like him?"

I asked, "Is his name Ares?"

Koda went silent again. I couldn't even hear him breathing. His voice boomed back making me pull the receiver away from my ear. "What happened in the dreams? Tell me every little detail!"

"Calm down," I said into the phone.

He growled. "I don't have time to be calm. Now answer my questions."

I quickly explained my dreams to him.

He groaned softly. "Hold on one minute."

"Alright," I said with a sigh. He talked quietly away from the phone, but I couldn't understand what he was saying. I heard a man with a thick British accent talking back to him, but still couldn't understand what they were saying. I kicked my feet around in the water as I grew impatient.

Koda came back on. "Alright. I can't really say anything to you except that they are just dreams."

"Why are you being so secretive with me?"

"It's your father's fault. If he had told you about us, there wouldn't be a problem. Shit, you would probably be with us right now."

I felt my breath whoosh out of my lungs and tried to think about what he had just said.

Koda grunted. "Shit. That was too much information."

I inhaled and asked, "Is your friend's name Ares?"

Koda groaned. "Yes, that's all I'm going to say though."

I nodded. "Fine. Well I did have another dream last night as well."

Koda sighed in exasperation. "Tell me." I explained the dream about my father and he sighed again. "You've been in contact with wild wolves."

It wasn't a question, but I answered anyways. "Well, sort of. There was a group of three wolves at the lake and I swore one of them looked just like the wolf in my dreams that turned into Ares and I just felt compelled to go to him. Well, his other two pack mates pushed him away. Then, another time the same group of wolves were being aggressive, and I showed the alpha a sign that I was dominant and he was debating what to do when his pack mates nudged him and I swear I heard him sigh. Then they left."

Koda scoffed. "He sighed. You know it's not very smart to show an alpha dominance when you aren't."

"What should I have done? Let him eat Bret's friend?" I said defensively.

He laughed. "It might have been funny."

"The asshole would have deserved it. He thought I was *communicating* with the wolves. How stupid is that?"

"Look, Artemis. I can't really tell you much and I'm sorry for that. I do have a feeling that we will be seeing you soon though."

"I have two more questions."

He groaned. "What?"

"Do you know what the white mist is and if it is going to come here?" I asked.

He exhaled. "You have to keep this completely secret. Even from your friend, okay?"

"Okay."

He whispered quickly, "I do know what the mist is and I promise it will not come for your town and you will be perfectly safe. Consider the wolves and your dreams a good omen."

I sighed as the heavy weight was lifted from my shoulders. "Okay. One more thing. Why does silver burn my skin?"

Koda spoke in another language fast and loud. I assumed he was cussing, but couldn't be sure. "I can't say anything. Just don't touch silver. Did any of it get in your blood?"

"No, just burned my palm."

"Good. Don't worry, Artemis. Soon you will be experiencing a lot of different things. I'll see you soon."

I yelled, "How soon?"

"A few weeks probably. We'll find out for sure next week."

"What happens next week?" I asked.

He laughed. "Can't tell you. Bye, Artemis."

"Wait! Why did you know that we had to leave Tahoe and how did you get out okay?"

"Bye, Artemis," he said again.

"Bye, Koda." I pressed the end button and stared at the phone in my hand. Why was everyone so secretive? I hated secrets and surprises. I remembered that Koda had said they would be coming soon and felt butterflies flip around in my stomach at the thought of seeing Ares again. "Just what I need, a crush on some older guy who won't be interested in me." I walked slowly back home and didn't care how late it was when I got there. It would only take me ten minutes at the most to get home anyway. *Stupid small town.*

I heard someone following me and stopped and turned around. Billy stood smiling behind me. "What is it, Billy?"

"I'm sorry I overreacted before," he said softly.

I scoffed. "Right. Calling me the wolf whisperer was just a small overreaction."

"I just said I was sorry." He started to move closer to me, and I held my hand up.

"I thought you said we couldn't see each other anymore, Billy? Why the change?"

He smiled. "I changed my mind. I don't want to be away from you."

I remembered what Bret had said about him being a horndog and asked, "Is it me or my body you don't want to be away from?"

He stopped moving and the smile left his lips. "What's that supposed to mean? I haven't tried anything with you."

I shrugged. "From what I've heard you think mostly with your smaller head and you're just being nice today so you can pressure me tomorrow."

Billy snarled. "That bastard will say anything to keep you to himself. I swear I am going to kick his stupid ass!" He started walking quickly down the road to Bret's house. I knew I should stop him, but this was actually a fight I wanted to see. We arrived at Bret's house quickly and Billy yelled from the yard, "Come out, come out wherever you are! You pussy-ass liar!"

I stared in shock at the angry Billy who was somehow more attractive now.

Bret walked out of the house with no shirt on, smiling. "Hey bro, what's up?"

Billy shook his head. "Don't call me bro! You tell Artemis the truth right now, or I'm going to whip your ass!"

Bret shrugged smiling smugly. "I did tell her the truth! I'm better than you."

Billy looked at me. "You didn't tell me that part."

I shrugged. "It didn't seem important at the time."

Billy turned around and glared at Bret again. "Tell her the truth!"

Bret smiled. "You aren't better than me. That's the truth."

Billy charged up the steps and slammed into Bret, knocking him down on the ground. Billy was one of the strongest football players on the team. I had seen him bench pressing and couldn't even add up all the weights that were on the bar. Billy started punching Bret in the face. Bret shoved Billy backwards and jumped up. Darren walked calmly out of the house and past the fighting boys to stand next to me. "What's going on?"

"Not much. Bret said Billy was a horndog and that he is better than him and now they are fighting," I said.

Darren smiled. "So, they're fighting over you?"

I frowned and then thought about it. "Shit! Now you tell me." I ran over to the boys and threw myself between them. Bret threw a punch that barely missed my face. "Hey!" I yelled as I ducked down. Bret at least had the decency to blush. "Look, I didn't really think this through. Now stop fighting."

Billy shook his head. "Not until he tells you the truth."

"Fine. Artemis, he isn't a horndog. He's a freaking spineless virgin!"

I stared at Bret in disbelief. "Why is that a bad thing? I'm a virgin."

Bret's face fell. "No, it's different for girls."

"You're one, too." I said quietly, nervous of his answer.

Bret sighed. "No, I'm not."

Billy smiled smugly. "He's been telling you that so he had a better chance of screwing you."

Bret punched at Billy and I kicked Bret in the shin. "We are done, Bret!" I ran into the house and grabbed my bag. I walked out of the house furious and shaking with anger. "I should let my dad kick your ass!"

Darren smiled and waved bye to me. I walked away with Billy walking beside me, silently. We got halfway through town and I stopped walking, turning to look at Billy. "Why didn't you tell me about Bret?"

"What was I supposed to say? 'Hey, Artemis, Bret's really just trying to get in your pants, but he is lying to you to do it'?"

I smiled. "Yeah that would have worked."

He scoffed. "Right, and then I wouldn't have him as a friend anymore because I broke the guy code."

I rolled my eyes. "The guy code. Stupid!" I realized I had no clue who Bret had slept with or anything. "Billy, who has Bret slept with?"

He cringed. "You sure you want me to answer that?"

I gasped. "Skanzilla! That's why she is always hanging on him and hates me so bad. Because he's been screwing her! That bastard!" I felt my body heating up more and groaned as I fell to the ground and started convulsing.

Billy held me down and whispered, "Breathe, Artemis. Come on, stop the seizure."

I gritted my teeth and focused on calming myself down. The twitching finally stopped, and I exhaled. The doctors always thought I was lying when I told them that I could stop the seizures, but obviously, they were wrong.

I looked up at Billy and asked, "How'd you know?"

He smiled. "Bret told us in case he wasn't there and you needed help."

I smiled back at him. "Thanks. You can let me up now."

He kissed my lips softly. "I don't want to let you up."

I suddenly felt pinned and my body started to heat up again. I thrashed against him, but he held me down. I screamed in anger and fear of being trapped and pushed against him lifting him up off the ground.

Trapped!

I fought with my mind to make it realize that I wasn't trapped, but nothing worked.

Darren appeared over the top of me and saw the fear in my eyes. "Billy get off of her!"

Billy stepped away and Darren backed up, too.

I sat up slowly and slowed my breathing down so I wouldn't hyperventilate. Billy shook his head. "What happened?"

Darren rubbed the back of his neck, a mirror of Bret's nervous habit. "She got scared and well…it's hard to explain."

"Sorry." I said, embarrassed.

"Are you okay now?" Billy asked. I nodded, and he smiled. "Good. Now let's go." I let him grab my hand and pull me up to a standing position. Once I had my balance I kissed his cheek. He smiled wider. "What was that for?"

I smiled back. "For being understanding about my…uh…stuff."

He shrugged. "You're too much of a catch to let a few minor things bother me."

I started walking away with Billy when Darren cleared his throat. I turned around to glare at him. "What?"

"When will you be home?"

I shrugged. "Why do you care?"

He frowned and spoke in his 'don't talk back' tone, "Artemis."

I sighed. "Tonight. You and I have things to talk about anyway."

He cringed. "What stuff?"

I smiled. "Things Koda and I were discussing."

He growled. "What did he tell you? And when did you talk to him?"

I shrugged and turned away, dragging Billy along with me. "Interesting things. Bye Darren."

Billy walked with me as I skipped like an elementary school girl. "What was that about?"

I smiled and started walking instead of skipping. "Apparently, my dad has been withholding information about my past so I have to make him sweat a little." Darren and I had never been close. He provided for me and I never starved or anything like that, but he had never been emotionally open to me. I'd never felt loved by him. I'd always blamed it on my mother's disappearance, but maybe it was more than that. I needed to get out of the town and away from Darren as soon as I could.

We arrived at Billy's house to find J.D. and Jess sitting on the porch. Billy smiled at them. "What's up guys?"

Jess and J.D. stared at us for a second before smiling. Jess held up a bottle of whiskey. "We come bearing gifts."

Billy licked his lips then looked at me. "You don't have to drink if you don't want to."

I shrugged. "I've never tried it before."

Jess laughed. "Oh, girl, you are in for a great time!"

We walked into the house and sat down around the kitchen table. J.D. grabbed four red plastic cups and poured some of the alcohol into each glass. I sniffed the cup and gagged. It was horrible smelling, like rubbing alcohol.

Billy laughed. "Don't smell it! Just down it."

I stared at the brown liquid. "Down it?"

J.D. tipped his cup up and gulped down the drink in one swallow. "Woo!" He yelled.

Jess smiled. "Like that." She held up her cup towards me. "Ready?"

I lifted mine up and hit the side against hers. "I guess." I looked at the liquid one more time then tipped the cup up and swallowed. The liquid burned my throat and I exhaled and set the cup down. "Whoa."

Billy poured another round and raised his cup. "Cheers!"

We all hit cups then downed the alcohol. My stomach felt warm for a moment as the liquid settled then the warmth disappeared. J.D. frowned. "You sure you haven't drunk before?"

Jess giggled beside me. "I'm a lightweight no matter how much I drink!"

Billy snorted. "You're just a lush!"

Jess rolled her eyes. "You're a boozer!"

I could see the difference in Jess already, but I didn't feel any different. J.D. poured another round and we touched cups then downed yet another drink. Billy took out a deck of cards and taught me a drinking game which consisted of taking as many shots as corresponded to the card you pulled. Jess and J.D.'s eyes became glazed over, and they started acting drunk. Billy was slurring his words and smiling a lot. I frowned as I realized I didn't feel any different. I went to the bathroom for the fifth time, and as I walked out of the restroom ran into Billy. He wrapped his arms around me, and I felt instantly disgusted as his alcohol breath stole my fresh oxygen. He tried to kiss me, and I pushed him away, heading for the door.

Billy frowned and followed me. "What's wrong? Aren't you having any fun?"

J.D. scoffed. "No 'cus we're drunk and she's not. Artemis has been holding out on us."

I rolled my eyes and smiled at Billy. "I have to see my dad, remember?"

"Are you coming back tonight?" He asked.

I shook my head. "No, but you can come over in the morning, and I'll make you breakfast."

He pulled me against him in a hug. "That sounds great."

I pulled away from him and grabbed my backpack. "Bye."

He let me go and waved as I walked down his porch steps. Once I was in the night completely, I stopped and inhaled. I had always loved the night time. It was like more sights and sounds and smells came alive in the dark. I stared up at the half moon and smiled. The full moon would be here soon. I could feel her song flowing through my body like a second pulse. The full moon always made me feel safer and more powerful. As if that made any sense. I jogged across town towards my house and inhaled loudly trying to separate the different smells. I reached the house much faster than I had wanted to and looked up at the moon one last time before walking up the porch. Darren sat in one of the chairs staring at me. I smiled. "Hey, Dad."

"What did he tell you?" He asked with a big frown on his face.

"Nothing really. He said that if I had known about our past that I would probably be with them right now. Then he said that they would be coming to visit in a few weeks, and we would know for sure in the next week."

Darren frowned. "Why would they visit? They have no reason to come here." He groaned. "Unless it's to discuss a punishment for me not telling you. Dammit."

I shrugged. "I'm not worried about it. He said that mist won't be harming our town so I'm not scared anymore."

Darren smiled. "The mist would never come near our town with me here. Bastards."

I frowned. "You say that like the mist are people. What the hell is it?"

He shook his head. "If you knew, they would *definitely* come for us."

Darren's evasiveness proved that he was hiding something big. I needed to find a way to get out of the town and soon. Someway, somehow, I would leave. He was trying to keep me here, hidden, and I wasn't sure why.

I took out a frozen bean burrito and popped it in the microwave. I heard Darren come in and ignored him as he sat down on the couch and turned on the TV. The microwave dinged, scaring me. I took out the burrito which had split open and hurried to my room. I sighed and ate my burrito slowly. A quiet chiming made me stop eating. I looked down at my pants and remembered I had the cell phone still. I took it out and stared at the number. "Koda." I smiled then frowned wondering why he was calling. I flipped open the phone and answered, "Hello?"

The person on the other end was silent for a second and then sighed heavily. His voice made me shiver in delight. "I thought you were a figment of my imagination at the hotel, but everything is the same."

My hands shook, and my heart beat pick up as I recognized the voice. "Who is this?"

He laughed softly. "Do you really need to ask?"

"No. I…I'm just confused."

"I know you are, and it's your father's fault. You would be able to understand the connection an alpha male has with a new female if he had told you."

"Alpha male? You mean like wolves? What are you talking about?" I asked. He wasn't making sense.

He scoffed. "That's what I mean. You have no idea! I can't talk long because Koda will have a cow if he finds out that I am talking to you since it breaks all the rules, but I had to hear your voice. I had to know that you weren't just a girl in my dreams that I made real at the hotel."

I gasped. "You've been dreaming of me?"

He laughed quietly. "Yes, every night for the past ten days. I can't explain what's going on between us because I'm not completely sure. Has Koda told you that we are coming to get you?"

"Get me? Where are you taking me?" I asked, suddenly nervous, though I wasn't sure if it was a good or bad nervousness.

"We are taking you with us to where you belong. You do not

belong in that town with those...*people*. I'm not sure how long before we get there, but I will come for you. I have to go."

I felt my heartbeat becoming frantic. "Wait! Don't go. Please."

"Don't worry. I will speak with you again, and I will see you soon as well. Sweet dreams, little wolf lover."

"Bye, Ares," I said quietly. I'd wanted to say more, but it didn't seem right. I turned the phone off and tossed the leftover burrito and plate in the trash can. Paper plates are very convenient sometimes. I took my pants and bra off and climbed into bed under the covers. I played his voice over in my head and smiled knowing he was coming for me.

CHAPTER
THREE

The rest of the week went by quickly with Billy coming for breakfast every morning in place of Bret and us spending the entire day together. He was extremely understanding and fun and luckily hadn't tried to kiss me again. Darren grumbled a lot, but didn't say anything to us. The news stories continued on the television with no new leads. Darren watched the news and told me that he would let us know if anything new came up. I didn't worry because I knew Ares was coming for me. I never told Darren, because it seemed like he didn't like Ares. I had gone without worrying almost a full week until Friday night, when Bret ran into our house. It was just before eight o'clock and the sun was starting to set, casting purple and red hues across the sky. I could feel night coming like a chill creeping up my arms to my neck. Bret spoke quickly to Darren and Billy, and then turned and ran from the house.

Darren sighed and faced me, "Apparently, there is new information we need to hear. Everyone is gathering at the pub." We walked quickly from the house towards the pub.

The town's streets and buildings sat deserted with an unnatural silence. The only light and noise was coming from the pub. Children were placed in a separate room, left to play, so that they wouldn't watch what was happening. I stood in front with Darren as the news reporter began talking. Billy had walked to the back with the other teens.

The reporter, a man with a deep voice and salt-and-pepper hair, sat in front of a stone wall, wearing jeans and a t-shirt. He whispered and looked around warily, "The scene here in Washington is chaos and devastation. Some are calling it the end of the world. Revelations and doomsday. I don't know what to call it, except gruesome. It started three hours ago at full dark. People started falling down, their throats cut or ripped out by something with claws. Some found in dark alleys with their blood completely drained from their bodies and two small puncture wounds on their necks. No one has been able to catch a glimpse of the attackers as they move faster than the wind and just as quietly."

The cameraman crept forward showing the hundreds of bodies littering the streets of Washington. Blood ran down the drains like rain. Cars were turned upside down and some were even on fire. The street lamps cast a halo around a group of three teenagers' bodies lying on top of each other.

The reporter cleared his throat making the cameraman turn back to him. "It appears to be the same situation as what is happening all over the world, but we appear to be the only survivors in town. We don't know if the attackers are moving on, or have stopped. I wish we could be more help, but..." The reporter suddenly flew through the air, screaming as he sailed into the side of a building, smacking it with a solid thud.

The cameraman panned around frantically, trying to see what had done it, but nothing was visible. We all watched as he stared down a dark alley, his breathing speeding up. He swallowed hard and whispered, "Fuck." The mist sped forward and wrapped around him, but the camera fell and the screen went black as we heard his screaming begin.

Darren turned off the television and turned to everyone with sad eyes. "We have to start our plan."

Glen, the oldest in town, nodded. "Darren's right. Something killed those people and it's getting closer."

Darren spoke before any of the others could. "Tomorrow morning, meet at my place at five. Bring your guns. If we all know how to use a gun, we might stand a chance against them. Or at least go down swinging."

I headed to the rest of the teenagers who sat in the back of the room, whispering quietly. "Hey guys." The three girls and four boys looked up at me. I sighed. "Come on. It's not that bad. We are in such a small town that I doubt these things would come after us, whatever they are."

Trixie, Skankzilla's youngest sister, shook her head. "No. Did you see what happened? Whatever it is will find us. It was like fog. How can fog hurt you?!"

Bret sighed and stood. "Artemis is right. We just have to get ready and prepare for any possibility. Nothing is invincible."

Skankzilla rolled her eyes. "Of course, you agree with her. When haven't you agreed with her?"

I ignored her comment because it didn't matter anymore. I would leave soon and this would all be over with. The children came in from the other room and were reunited with their families. The quiet whispers of each family showed how scared each was. Everyone began to disperse to their homes, to get ready for bed. Billy led me from the pub out to the dark evening. I pulled away from him and inhaled the sweet smell of night and basked in the moon's glow. I closed my eyes and stopped walking. I love the night.

Billy laughed. "I swear, if I didn't know better, I'd say you were a vampire or something."

"Yes, let me suck your blood." I said in a mock accent.

Skankzilla smiled. "I bet he has something you could suck."

I turned to her and let my anger loose. "Shut up you dirty

whore! I've had enough of you!" I started to move towards her, and then smiled. "You know what…it's not worth it. I'll be out of here in a week anyway."

Billy frowned. "A week? Where are you going?"

I was about to answer him when Darren came up. "Tomorrow we are waking up early to start preparing, so we need to go home."

"What are we preparing for?" I asked.

Darren sighed. "Come on, girl, let's get home."

Billy kissed my cheek then waved. "Later, Chicky."

I smiled at him. "Later, B."

Bret growled behind us. "Great, she already found someone else."

I ignored his comment and started walking towards home. Darren smiled and spoke to the teens, "Five a.m. we are doing shooting practice. I expect you all to be there with your gun of choice."

Bret saluted Darren. "Yes, sir."

Darren shook his head and walked after me. He smiled at me as I walked beside him towards the house. The streets were still eerily empty, but a soft glow fell from each house's porch light. We walked in silence, as we always did at night, enjoying the smells and noises only available in the dark. I looked up at the moon and smiled. Only a few more days until the full moon. Darren had said the reason I was named Artemis, Goddess of the Moon, was because I had been born on a full moon, and every milestone I ever reached was on a full moon. I think he just wanted to make me feel special.

We arrived home, and I hurried to bed. The image of the three dead teenagers was still in my head. I sighed and prayed Koda was right and the town would be okay, even after I was gone.

"Artemis, get up." Darren said.

I opened my eyes and looked at the dark sky. "Dad, it's still night time. I just went to sleep."

He laughed. "Come on lazy. You just have to shoot once, to

show that you can handle your gun, and then you can come back to bed."

I sighed and got up, changing into my jeans and putting a bra on under my shirt. I hurried through my morning routine and walked out to the kitchen, where Billy, Bret and Darren were eating breakfast. I smiled at Billy's excited face. Billy patted the chair beside him, but I shook my head and took my normal chair across from Darren. I ate the eggs, bacon and toast which were already on my plate. Bret had added strawberry jelly to my toast as usual, which made me feel sad that we weren't really friends anymore. The milk was a little warm, but still delicious. Darren and Bret placed their plates in the sink and started towards the door. I sighed and followed their leads. Billy followed behind me. I pulled on my boots and grabbed the hunting rifle Darren had given me last year for Christmas. Bret held his hunting rifle down by his leg. We had been taught since we could walk that you never point a gun at something you aren't willing to kill. Billy followed us with two revolvers. I looked at Darren's empty hands and asked, "Where's your gun, Pop?"

"I'm teaching, not shooting. I'll practice later tonight." Darren answered.

Bret shook his head. "I don't understand how you and Artemis can see those targets at night."

Darren and I shrugged then walked out the door with Billy and Bret following closely behind. The entire town sat on our front lawn, waiting to start the lesson. The children had already started playing in the tree house and swinging in the tire swing my father built for me and Bret. Bret smiled at the children and nudged me with his arm. "That used to be us."

I nodded and felt a twinge of sadness at the thought that I wouldn't see Bret again for a long time, if ever. "Yeah, used to be." I walked away from him, with Billy following me, around the back of the house to the shooting range Darren had set up. Darren believed that everyone needed to know how to use a gun in case of emergency. Now, with the threat of some unseen monster, it was even more important.

I stood at the mark for the first target and chambered a shell. I sighted down the barrel at the beer bottle that had been set up and exhaled. I pulled the trigger and smiled as the bottle shattered. I heard Trixie say, "Wow" from behind me. I lowered my gun and walked to the back porch, setting my gun in the safe and locking it with the key. Bret walked to the next mark and aimed his gun. He pulled the trigger shattering another bottle just like I had.

Skankzilla clapped her hands and cheered, "Yay, Bret!"

I fought the urge to take my gun back out and end her miserable existence.

Bret pointed his gun at the ground, ignoring Skankzilla, as he walked towards me. He motioned at the gun safe and smiled.

I unlocked it and waited while he put his gun inside.

Billy waved at me. "I'm going to go listen to your dad."

I nodded and walked into the house, Bret following closely behind. Darren rolled his eyes at us and began instructing the rest of the town who did a lot less shooting than Bret and me. I sat down on the couch and turned on the television, flipping through the channels in search of cartoons. Bret sat down behind me, stretching his long arms along the back of the couch. I groaned as every channel was a news alert. The light in my head clicked on, and I stopped on one of the channels. Bret leaned forward beside me, his mouth dropping open.

The reporter spoke softly, standing in the middle of Oregon, surrounded by dead bodies. "The scene here is a duplicate of every other city. No one saw it coming and whatever has done this has vanished with the morning light. Every human found is dead. Hundreds are missing. The only clues as to what monster has done this are the claw marks we found on one body left beside a dumpster in an alley. Police from surrounding states have come to investigate this tragedy. Thousands are dead, leaving us to wonder what or whom is doing this. We found one surveillance tape, but please be warned, this tape contains graphic scenes not suitable for some audiences."

The view changed to a grainy surveillance camera. A man stood pressed against a brick wall as a large, dark shape moved towards him. It looked like mist, but moved unlike any mist I had ever seen. The mist covered the man, who screamed in terror. A sharp crack resonated through the alleyway, and the man stopped moving. The shadow disappeared. The reporter from our local news came back on, "This is replayed footage from New York. We have been told that there are indeed no survivors living in New York City, or any of the surrounding cities. The President has issued a warning to all states, saying, 'We need to prepare for the worst. There is no way to tell where it will strike next.' The reports are conflicting, but with the mist and claw marks, we do know that something is killing and *kidnapping* people. Yes, you heard right, not all of the bodies are accounted for. We can only assume that with no signs of any of their personal belongings that they've been taken."

Bret stood up and ran outside. He yelled for Darren who came running into the house. I changed the channel to another station that showed the same scene all over again.

Darren sat down beside me, shaking his head. "Shit."

I felt my body begin to shake with fear, and Bret pulled me up, wrapping his arms around me. He whispered, "It's going to be alright, Artemis. I'll be here for you."

Darren stood and walked outside, telling the rest of the town what had happened. I pushed Bret away. "It won't matter, because neither of us will be here. I'm leaving in a few days, and so are you."

He frowned. "I love you, Artemis. Why can't you see that?"

I felt the tears in my eyes and turned away, walking to my room. I laid down on my bed, facing the wall, and closed my eyes. Bret climbed on the bed behind me, and pulled me against him. I shook my head and tried to pull away from him, but he held me tight. I whispered, "I can't Bret."

Bret nodded against the back of mine. "I know that you feel betrayed, but I love you. I always have."

I sighed. "You're my friend, Bret. That's it. I can't date my friend. It never works out. Especially when that friend has been trying to screw me."

Bret shrugged and hugged me tighter. "What doesn't work about this?"

I pushed against him. "Just leave."

He sighed and stood up. "Fine, but just know that I'll wait for you. I love you."

I waited until he shut the door, and closed my eyes. I focused on relaxing my body and fell into a deep sleep.

Billy softly shook me awake. I opened my eyes to the dark and rolled over so I could see him. He whispered, "Your dad is outside shooting right now, but you need food."

My stomach growled with vigor anyone could hear.

Billy snickered. "It's been doing that for fifteen minutes so I figured I should wake you up."

I looked out the window and saw the dark sky. "What time is it? How long have I been asleep?"

Billy stood up. "It's eight o'clock and you've been asleep for a long time. I'm sure you will be awake all night now."

Why had I slept so long? I didn't usually sleep so long.

I stretched my arms and legs then sat up throwing my legs over the edge of the bed. Billy extended his hand to me, and I took it to stand. He pulled me against him and kissed my lips. I stood frozen as he pulled away and smiled at me. He laughed. "What's wrong?"

I pulled away from him. "I can't, Billy. I'm leaving soon."

He smiled. "So, that means I can't get a few last kisses in?"

Bret walked into the room and glared at Billy's arms around me. He pushed Billy off of me and kissed my lips hard. I pushed against his chest, but couldn't do anything. He pulled back and asked, "Who's do you like more?"

I groaned. "Why? Why are you doing this?"

Bret reached for me, but I dodged his hand, running towards the door. Bret grabbed me around the waist and pulled me back, hugging me against him. "Just admit that you liked mine more. Just admit that you want me to do it again without him here."

Billy yelled, "Let her go, Bret!"

I shook my head and fought against Bret, but he was much stronger than me. I suddenly felt trapped, and fought as hard as I could against him. I kicked at him and tried to elbow him, but he juggled me around so that I couldn't make contact. I pushed at his arms and they started to give.

He exclaimed, "What the hell?"

I pushed his arms off of me and ran away into the kitchen. I turned back towards them and panted and fought to control my emotions. I was no longer trapped and felt better, but I had a strange urge to fight Bret.

Bret walked into the kitchen staring at me in shock. "What is going on with you, Artemis?"

Billy smiled. "Obviously, she doesn't want you touching her."

I shook my head and held out my hands. "Don't come near me, either of you. I don't...I felt trapped."

Darren walked into the house and stared from Bret to Billy to me and back. "What's wrong?"

"I was holding her, and she started attacking me and got some burst of strength. She pushed my arms away and says she felt trapped," Bret said.

Darren frowned and stared at me, but talked to the boys. "Bret and Billy, I think you both should leave."

Bret frowned. "Why? She's fine now. I think I just scared her."

Billy scoffed. "No, he kissed her, and she didn't want him to."

Darren set his gun down on the table and walked towards me.

I took a step back and hit the wall. I shook my head as the urge to run tried to take over. I whispered, "Stop."

Darren stopped moving and whispered, "You want to run, don't you?"

I nodded and stared at him. "How'd you know that?"

He sighed. "I can't explain right now." He turned to the boys. "Look, you know I've never had a problem with you being here before, but we have family matters to discuss."

Bret nodded. "I understand."

Billy nodded, too.

Bret walked towards me and stopped a few feet away, raising my instinct to flee two notches higher. Bret asked, "Can I get a hug or are you going to go all crazy again?" He finished the last part trying to hide the hurt in his face.

I shook my head. "Both of you, please, just leave. I'm sorry."

Bret smiled. "Night, Chicky. Night, Darren."

Billy waved, with an obvious look of concern on his face. "Bye, Chicky."

Darren watched them leave. I plopped down into one of the kitchen chairs and put my face on the table. "Dad, what's happening to me?"

Darren rubbed his face with his hand. "I can't tell you everything yet, but you are coming into adulthood. It's a transition period for our family that few others here have to go through. It's because of your interactions with Ares and Koda. You are going to have to stay indoors for the next week and I'm going to have to forbid anyone from coming over here until your transition is finished."

I gasped, "But Bret is leaving in a few days!"

He sighed. "I'm sorry."

I stared at him in disbelief. "What are we?" I asked, fear creeping up my spine.

He smiled. "We're human, but with a little extra spice in our blood. I told you I can't explain it yet. You'll understand in a few days."

I asked, "Are we like the things that have been killing all of those people? The mist?"

Darren shook his head, his hands fisting on the table as he scowled. "NO! We are nothing like those things. I promise, in a week or so, you'll know everything." He sighed heavily. "Whether you like it or not."

I stood, wanting to ignore the jumbled new information in my head, grabbed some food, and walked to the television. I turned on the TV. "Dad, there's another video."

He walked over and sat on the couch beside me. The news reporter showed video of a city being wiped out by the mysterious monsters. No new information was available, and the same signs had been shown. Claw marks, two puncture wounds, blood completely drained and broken necks. I wondered what these things were, but knew Darren wouldn't tell me.

"Can they be killed?" I asked Darren.

He smiled a purely evil smile. "Yes, but not very easily."

"Why won't you just tell me what they are?"

"I fear that speaking their name will bring them to us. They have spies everywhere and can be almost anywhere. I would rather they left our town alone, but I fear they will be here much sooner than I wanted." He picked his gun up off the table and walked towards the door. "I'm going shooting, but stay here. If either of the boys come back, don't let them in."

I shrugged. "Whatever you say, Dad."

He smiled. "That's my girl. I'll be back in a few hours. Do some chores or something to keep yourself occupied."

"Alright." I stood and headed towards the kitchen. I turned on the water, and started doing the dishes. Something was going to change my life.

But what? What are these things, and how does what I am relate to it?

I kept myself busy for the next two hours cleaning the kitchen and scrubbing the floors, but I grew bored. I hated staying inside the house. I went to my room and cleaned everything. I started a load of laundry. I walked into Darren's room, but was careful not to touch any of his books or research. He was always researching something, but I never knew what, because he kept his door closed and told me I couldn't go in his room.

However, curiosity overrode the warnings in my brain, and I picked up a stack of papers and read the title. "*Lycanthropy and Its Effects on Humans, by Darren Smith.*" I gasped.

Dad had written this? What the hell is lycanthropy?

I sat down and started to turn the first page when I heard the front door open and close. I set the papers back down and hurried out of his room, closing the door quietly. I ran into the bathroom across the hallway and turned the water on, splashing my face. I grabbed the towel and walked out of the bathroom, drying off my face.

Darren frowned. "The cows are missing, but your horses are fine."

I nodded. "Thanks."

He smiled. "Yep. Hey, you want to play a board game?"

I stared at him. "We haven't played a board game together since I was ten."

He nodded again. "I think it's time we played one then."

I shrugged and walked towards the closet that held all of our games. Darren had always kept an abundance of board and card games around in case of bad weather. I pulled down Risk and set it on the table. He locked his gun up in the safe and walked back, smiling. I pulled out the board and set it up. We played for a few hours, but I started to grow sleepy again. I yawned and stretched my arms. "Why am I so sleepy?"

He smiled. "It's all part of the transition. Don't worry. When the full moon gets here, you'll be as good as new." He tried to smile, but it didn't reach the corners of his mouth or his eyes.

I nodded and walked to the bathroom to change my contacts. I hurried to my bedroom and fell asleep faster than ever before, dreaming of wolves running together in a pack, playing and hunting.

I stretched my arms as I woke up with the sunrise. I sat up and looked around my room. Everything was where it should've been, but something felt wrong. I walked to the bathroom, changing my contacts, and then toward the living room. I stopped moving when I saw the television. Darren sat, watching the news report of another attack. This one was in Nevada again. Darren sighed as he heard me walk up. "You better sit down for this kid. Someone got a glimpse of the beasts."

I sat down quickly and pulled my legs up, wrapping my arms around them. A cell phone video popped up on the screen. Two men were fighting in front of a bar with people forming a circle around them. Suddenly a black shape jumped on top of the fighters, clawing and biting them. The men screamed and all of the people started to run away. Mist moved towards two people that had started to run away and stopped them.

I stared at the black figure, as the phone focused on it. The men who had been fighting were no longer moving, and blood gathered in a massive pool around their bodies. The black figure tore a chunk of meat from one of the men's sides and tilted its head back swallowing. The video panned out and you could see the rest of the massive black figure.

I shook my head as I realized what it was. "A wolf? No way. Wolves don't get that big."

Well except for the three that have been around here.

Darren said nothing as the video continued playing. The wolf dropped its head and looked at the person recording it. I stared in awe at the wolf with its black fur and perfect amber eyes. I gasped, "Ares!"

Darren turned to me and frowned. "What?"

I shrugged. "Nothing."

I stared back at the wolf as it stalked towards the person

recording him. The wolf walked with such pride, such power. I shivered as it stared directly into the camera and howled loud and long. I gasped for breath, and my body started to convulse. Darren growled. "Fuck. That piece of shit."

I fell off the couch and continued to convulse, unable to get air. My bones began aching and felt like they were trying to separate. I closed my eyes and could see a white wolf with a blue mane and purple eyes. I stared into the wolf's eyes and realized it was me. *Impossible, I don't have purple eyes.* The wolf-me nodded, tilted her head back, and howled loudly, shaking my entire body. I felt Darren's hands on my body seconds before cold water covered me. I gasped for air and stood up, staring at Darren's infuriated face. I shivered and stared at up him. "How did we get to the creek at the edge of our property?"

He smiled. "I had to stop you. It's not time yet."

I growled, and the sound vibrated my chest, sounding like a wolf. I pictured the wolf with purple eyes and felt my body warming up. Darren grabbed me and snarled in my face. "You aren't allowed to change yet."

My body cooled and the vision of the wolf disappeared. I collapsed into his arms and asked, "What's happening to me?"

Darren stroked my hair and whispered, "It's alright. Just sleep. You'll understand when you wake up."

I nodded and relaxed, as he picked me up and carried me to the house, and to my room. I started to get up to change my contacts, but he just rolled me over, so I could take them out. He whispered, "You won't be needing those."

I curled up under the covers, not having the energy to ask any more questions, and fell asleep. I dreamt of Ares and pictured his gorgeous face. I could see him in front of me running through the forest. I ran after him as fast as I could, but my human legs wouldn't keep up with him. He turned to me and howled, summoning me. I tried to reach him, but he was too far away. Another howl broke through my dream, waking me up. I sat up on my bed with sweat running down my face. The windows were dark, so it was still night. I inhaled and smelled wolves.

I ran from my room to Darren's, but he wasn't there. I ran to the gun safe and unlocked it, taking out a gun and loading it. I grabbed a handful of shells and put them in my jeans pockets. I walked quickly to the back door and stopped moving.

Darren stood on the porch with his hands to his sides with no weapons. On the ground twenty feet away from him stood three giant wolves. I instantly recognized the middle wolf.

"Ares," I whispered quietly. I pushed open the door and walked out, setting the gun on the porch and taking the shells out of my pockets. I started to walk past Darren to Ares, but Darren grabbed me, pulling me against him.

Ares snarled at us, but I felt no fear.

Darren snarled back sounding just like Ares. "She's my pup. You can't take her like this. She hasn't changed yet."

I felt anxious at Darren's words and wanted to go to Ares. I pulled away from Darren, but he grabbed me, holding me tighter.

Ares walked forward and sat on his haunches, tilting his head to the side.

Darren shook his head. "No, Ares. She can't be yours. I don't care if she is the one who answered your call. She's not ready. She doesn't even know yet."

I looked up at Darren and smiled. "They said that was your fault."

He frowned. "You've talked to them?"

I shrugged. "I've had dreams about Ares and he's had them about me. I had to talk to them."

Darren sighed and looked at Ares. "If you want to see her reaction, then go ahead."

Ares stood up and shook his body. I held my breath as his body rippled like water and turned human just like in my dreams.

Darren ran into the house and returned quickly with a pair of pants which he tossed to Ares.

Ares put the pants on then smiled at me. His blue eyes sparkled like crystals. He took a step towards me, and I looked at Darren. "We're werewolves, aren't we?

Ares frowned. "Why haven't you told her? The full moon is tomorrow."

Darren sighed. "I didn't want to scare her. She has no idea what she is. She thinks she is human."

Ares snarled. "You would rather her be scared shitless when she changes for the first time? That is the worst way to find out."

Darren snarled. "She is my pup to do with as I please."

Ares shook his head. "I am alpha to you and she is my *passt genau*. I am taking her. I will teach her the ways of our kind."

Darren pushed me behind him and squatted down in an attack stance. "You will not touch her. She will not become like you."

Ares snarled. "And what am I?"

Darren spit. "A monster."

The two wolves behind Ares growled and took a step forward. Ares held up his hand and they stopped moving. Ares sighed. "I understand you don't agree with what is being done. Neither do I, but I am following my alpha's orders. If I could, I would stop it."

Darren sighed. "What do you want with her, Ares?"

He smiled at me as I looked around Darren. "She is mine. She answered my call."

"What call?" I asked.

Ares took a step towards the porch and Darren growled. Ares sighed. "I'll stay here, but not because you are dominant to me. Keep pushing it, and I'll remind you who is dominant."

Darren sighed and walked to one of the chairs on the porch a few feet away from me.

Ares cleared his throat. "I sent out a call through the video that only my true match could answer. You answered me. I was still in Nevada when I heard you."

I shook my head. "I don't understand. What are we? I mean, are you really a werewolf?"

Ares smiled. "I'm a lycanthrope, also known as a werewolf."

I gasped and turned to Darren. "Your papers in your room. They were talking about lycanthropy."

Darren sighed. "Yes, because I am a lycanthrope as well, and you, being my child, have had the disease passed on to you."

I stared at Ares and asked because I had to be certain, "I'm a werewolf? How is that possible? I thought werewolves were myths?"

Ares snarled. "There are many myths that are true, but the humans forced us into hiding a few centuries ago. We have just been waiting for the right time to come out and take over."

I stared at him and shook my head. "You are killing all of these innocent humans because of what other humans did centuries ago? How can you do that? They had nothing to do with it."

Ares frowned. "You think these would be any different? You think that if I were to show myself to the humans of this century that they would not hunt us down? You are very naïve, and it is your father's fault for not teaching you our history."

Darren sighed. "I just wanted her to have a normal life. I had no idea when you would be returning. I had hoped that she could live out her life until she was an adult without changing, but when she saw the news, she started showing the signs. And then you had to call her and speed up her process. I had to force her change back once."

Ares bowed his head. "My apologies for that. But I had to know if she was my match or not."

I took a step down the porch towards Ares. He smiled at me, but Darren growled making me stop moving. Ares ran up the porch in a blur of tan skin, grabbed Darren by the throat, held him up with one hand, and choked him. "I warned you already. I am the alpha here, not you. Do not hinder her again."

I ran to them and pleaded, "Please don't kill him."

Ares dropped Darren back into the chair and smiled. "I would not kill him. He is your father and just needed a small reminder."

I stared at his handsome face and couldn't help but look over his muscular body. His light tan skin was the color of caramel and his perfect blue eyes were like a June sky. I reached out toward him, and almost touched him, when I heard the wolves behind us snarl. I turned around and saw Bret standing on the side of the house with his rifle aimed at the wolves.

Ares snarled and the two wolves moved towards Bret.

I screamed, "No!" and ran as fast as I could to Bret, standing in front of him.

He lowered the gun. "Artemis, what the hell are you doing? Don't you see the wolves? They are the same as the ones that have been killing people."

I looked back at the wolves, still moving forward and Ares close behind me. I turned to Ares. "Tell them to stop moving. He won't shoot them. Please."

Ares sighed and held his hand up. The two wolves stopped moving, sitting on their haunches, narrowing their eyes at Bret.

I reached for Bret's gun, but he backed up. I shook my head. "Bret, give me the gun or they will kill you."

Bret reached towards my face and asked, "Why are your eyes purple?"

I heard Darren speaking to Ares. "I made her wear contacts because they changed when she hit puberty."

I ignored Darren, and turned to Bret. "Look Bret, there is a lot of shit I can't explain right now, but if you don't give me the gun, they are going to kill you."

Bret stared at Ares and the two wolves and shook his head. "They are going to kill me anyway. I can see it in his eyes."

I turned to Ares and snarled. "You won't touch him."

Ares snarled back at me. "You are not dominant enough to make such demands."

I shook my head. "I don't care about dominance. If you try to hurt him, I will die protecting him."

Ares shook his head. "Do not threaten me, pup."

Clearly this was not the way to end this. I needed to think wolf-like. "Please, Ares. I am asking you as a submissive. I am pleading with you as the one who answered your call."

Ares smiled. "Only if you promise to leave with me."

I looked up at Bret's shocked face and turned back to Ares. "Only if you and all of your people leave this town unharmed." *Good thing he doesn't know that I was already planning on leaving with him.*

Ares sighed and rubbed his temples. "I should have known you would be smart. Very well, if you leave with me, we will leave this town unharmed including this boy."

I reached down and grabbed Bret's gun out of his hand before he could react. I ran over to the gun case, and locked it inside before Bret could reach me.

He spun me around and shook me. "What have they done to you? Have they brainwashed you?"

I felt the tears falling down my face and shook my head. "I'm sorry, Bret. I had no idea about any of this. I have to go, though."

Bret stormed towards Ares and glared at the shorter man. "Who the fuck is he that you would leave me for him?"

Ares smiled up at Bret. "She's my one and only, destined since she was born to be mine."

Bret spit on the ground beside Ares. "That's a bunch of shit. We've been together since we could walk. She is mine, not yours."

Ares smiled wider, but it made the hair on the back of my neck stand up. "Would you put it to a test?"

Darren stood and walked quickly to Ares. He dropped to his knees and begged, "Please don't do this to him. He does not know anything about us. Please, Ares."

Bret stared at Darren in shock. "Why are you groveling to him? He's just another man."

Ares laughed. "Just another man! How funny."

I grabbed Bret's hand and pulled him to me. "Just leave, Bret.

You have to move on. I'm sorry, but I won't be here. It's for the good of the town."

Bret shook his head. "You're not making any sense. Why would your leaving benefit the town?"

Ares smiled and motioned at the two wolves. "Because your town is just another one to be destroyed. She has bargained for your lives; can't you see that?"

"I won't let you leave with him," Bret said in a harsh tone.

I should have been pissed about him forcing that kiss on me. About him holding me when I didn't want him to, but knowing I was leaving, I smiled and hugged him. "I have always known you were my best friend, but this is bigger than us. I have to protect everyone, including you," I whispered and then pulled away and backed towards Ares.

Bret shook his head. "No, don't leave me. I am the one who is supposed to protect you, remember?"

I smiled. "We always knew it would end with me protecting you, Bret. You just never wanted to admit it."

Ares extended his hand to me, smiling, "Come, little Moon Goddess. Let me take you away and show you your true nature."

I smiled back at him and took his hand. The instant our skin touched an electric shock went through our bodies. I collapsed forward, falling into his arms.

He picked me up and held me against his bare chest. "I'll treat you like a queen."

I looked one last time at Bret's distraught face, and then relaxed as Ares began running as he held me. I heard the two wolves following closely behind us. I expected his running to be bouncy, but it was smooth. It was like we were standing still, with the air whizzing past us. They ran for a few hours, taking us into a thick forest. When they finally stopped, Ares set me down on the ground. I wrapped my arms around myself and sighed. Tears escaped from my eyes before I could stop them. Ares sat down beside me and wiped the tears away with his thumb while he rested his palm against my cheek. I leaned into his hand, enjoying the warmth. He whispered, "You will be happy again soon. I promise."

I nodded and turned away from him. The two wolves stared at me with curious expressions on their faces. I turned to Ares and asked, "Why are they looking at me like that?"

He smiled. "They want to know how it's possible that you do not know what you are. And why you have not changed."

I shrugged my shoulders, "I don't know. My father never changed in front of me, so until you changed, I had no idea."

One of the wolves shook its head, I heard popping and snapping. It sounded like bones breaking. I cringed as I watched his head reform into a human head. His green Mohawk was a dead giveaway.

I smiled. "Koda!"

He smiled at me as I stared at his human head on the giant wolf body. "Hey, Artemis."

I smiled. "I should have known you would be here. Why aren't you changing back all of the way?"

Ares rolled his eyes. "He is trying to save you from embarrassment. If he changes completely, he will be naked and we have no clothes with us for him to change into."

I blushed. "Oh."

The other wolf shook his head and changed it to human. He looked exactly like Koda, but had a blue Mohawk and spoke with a British accent. I recognized him as the other man from the hotel. "She's blushing. That is very cute, Love."

I turned away from them and walked a few steps away.

Ares snarled. "Nice job, Matt."

"What? You can't tell me that it's not cute that she blushes like a human," Matt said.

I turned around and snarled at them. "I am a human!" I clamped my hands over my mouth and turned away again.

Holy shit. What is happening to me?

Ares whispered, "It's okay that you are scared."

I shook my head. "I'm not scared. I just want to know what's happening." Okay, I was scared, but I didn't want to admit it.

Ares spoke softly to me. "You are going to change for the first time when the full moon rises tomorrow night. Your body is going through your transition phase and during that phase you can be a little bit temperamental."

"*Great*! So, it's like getting your period all over again."

Ares smiled. "Sort of. How old are you, Artemis?"

I looked at his face and gauged him at about twenty-three. "Seventeen. Well, I'll be eighteen tomorrow."

Ares smile fell slightly at the corners. "You're turning eighteen?"

I nodded. "Yep. I'm hoping to make it a couple more years, too."

Koda and Matt laughed, but Ares just regained his full smile. "It would be a truly amazing feat for you to hold off your change on your eighteenth birthday, but I do not think it will be possible. You're getting a double whammy of full moon and eighteenth birthday."

I shrugged. "Can't hurt to try."

Matt laughed again. "I like her. She has a much older soul than her human years."

Ares nodded. "It has to do with the fact that she is my match."

I sighed. "I don't understand this whole match thing. I mean, I don't even remember answering your call or whatever. I started having convulsions after I saw you on TV and my dad stopped them by throwing me in the creek. I went to sleep, and when I woke up, I could smell wolves. When I went outside, you were there."

"You must have answered before your dad threw you in the creek."

The memory of my wolf self howling played in my mind and my eyes widened. I asked, "So, what happens now?"

Ares stood and held out his hand for me. I stood without his hand, brushing off my pants. Ares smiled and walked towards

Koda and Matt. "Now, we continue moving towards our destination. Once there, we will take you to a special place to wait for your first change."

I shook my head. "I won't change tomorrow night."

Ares smiled. "We'll see about that, but we must hurry."

I looked at Matt and Koda in their wolf bodies and human heads, and at Ares, and scowled. "Why is this happening to me? Why couldn't I just have a normal life?"

Ares frowned. "Your father said you were an outsider anyway."

I laughed. "An outsider to everyone but Bret and Billy."

Ares snarled. "You have to forget about them. You will never see them again."

I frowned at him. "What? Why? You promised not to kill them." I felt my anger boiling up and my skin started to turn hot. I took a step towards him and growled. A deep wolf growl came from my throat, but I didn't cringe.

Ares growled back. "Do not try to fight me, Artemis. You are completely human until you change, and I don't want to hurt you."

“Then answer my questions." I snarled at him.

Ares snarled back at me, taking a step closer.

I fought my body and stayed still, not stepping back from him even though I could feel the pressure building against me.

"I will only let your aggressive gestures last so long. I understand that you are not used to the werewolf way, but I am your dominant, and you must treat me as such. Your friends will be alive and fine, but you will not be allowed to visit them or anyone else. After you have your first change, your food instincts are a little off."

I stopped snarling and stared at him. "You mean that I might end up trying to eat them?"

Ares nodded. "Exactly.”

I frowned. “Aren’t humans the top of the food chain?”

“Humans were never the top of the food chain,” Ares answered with a scoff.

“What is?”

“We are,” Ares answered.

I decided to leave the food chain topic alone, and walked towards Koda and Matt. "How old are you three?"

Koda frowned. "You don't want to know."

"Try me."

Matt laughed. "Just wait until you know everything about us before we tell you our age."

I sighed. "Fine, be secretive. See if I care. Now let's go. I'm starving."

Koda smiled. "Me, too."

I looked at him and realized he was trying to make a joke. I laughed and turned to Ares. "So, I guess you'll be carrying me again?"

Ares shrugged. "Would you rather ride one of them?"

I looked at Matt and Koda and asked, "Would one of you let me?"

Koda stepped forward and nodded. "Of course, hop on." He coughed, and I cringed as his face snapped and popped and extended into its wolf form.

I shivered. "At least you look natural again, but that's disgusting to hear."

"Wait until it's your body doing it," said Matt.

Ares snarled, and Matt quickly changed his head back to wolf. I reached out towards Koda and stopped mid-way. I looked back at Ares. "Are they still them?"

He tilted his head to the side in a very canine-like manner. "You mean are they still thinking like themselves or are they thinking like a dog?"

I nodded. "Yeah. If I pet him, is he going to try to bite me?"

Ares shrugged. "Depends on what kind of mood he is in."

I looked into Koda's eyes and said, "Don't bite me." I reached forward and stroked his fur with my hand. "It's so thick."

Koda laid down so I could get on to him easier. I climbed up and grabbed a fistful of his fur, enjoying the feel of it in my hands. He stood up slowly and started walking. I tucked my legs up slightly to get a better hold, since he was too large to ride like a horse. Koda crouched down and then sprang forward in a full run. I held on tightly, leaning forward so the wind and branches wouldn't hit me. We ran much faster than before and came out of the forest in a few minutes to a flat grass field. Koda slowed, and Ares walked to stand beside us. He looked around, then nodded. Matt walked forward into the open field and looked around carefully. He got to the middle of the field and howled loudly. I watched as five wolves ran from the trees on the other side of the field, and walked up to Matt. They smelled each other's faces and then sat down on their haunches. Matt turned back to us and nodded. Koda and Ares walked together towards the group. I lay down flat on Koda's back trying to hide as much as possible in his fur.

We reached the group and Koda sat down, making it harder for me to hang on, but I gripped his fur tighter not wanting to fall. Ares, still in his human form, said, "Greetings, fellow wolves. We come to seek shelter in your town."

Another man who had changed forms answered, "Greetings, Prince Ares. Of course, you may stay with us. You need not even ask our permission."

"Thank you, Gregory, but I wanted to be polite and not insist you let me stay with you." Ares said in a lighthearted tone.

My grip slipped through Koda's fur, and I hit the ground making an "oomph" sound as I landed. The other man growled. "What do you have with you?"

I peeked around Koda and Ares smiled at me. "It's alright, Artemis. Come here."

I walked slowly toward Ares, eyeing the other wolves cautiously. "Are you sure they aren't going to hurt me?"

Ares smiled and held out his hand. "You are one of us, and you are mine. They will not harm you." I took his hand and hurried the rest of the way to his side. He said, "Gregory, I would like you to meet Artemis, my *passt genau.*"

Gregory, the only naked man, shook his head in disbelief. "Your match? I did not think it was possible for a wolf to find a match."

Ares smiled and kissed the back of my hands sending chills up my spine. "Neither did I, but we had been dreaming of each other. I sent out a call and she answered from a state away. Her father did not tell her about our kind and kept her away. She has yet to change though."

Gregory blinked at me. "How old?"

"Seventeen, eighteen tomorrow."

Gregory shook his head. "Amazing. It must have something to do with her not being around our kind."

Ares nodded, staring at my face. "That's what I assumed. Her father has even refused to change in front of her. She had no idea that werewolves even existed until a few hours ago, when I came to her."

I couldn't help but look at Gregory's body. He was muscled like Ares and naked. I started to look lower, but Ares tapped my face making me look at him. He whispered, "I assure you that there is nothing special for you to look at on him."

I blushed and turned away from both of them. "You can't get mad at me. I hadn't seen a naked man before you changed at my house."

Ares snorted. "Don't lie. I could tell that you have slept with that boy."

"Define slept with. I have been asleep in the same bed with him, if that is what you mean, but I have never even kissed him, more than a kiss on the cheek."

Ares sighed. "Now is not the time to discuss this. We must hurry to your place. The full moon comes tomorrow, and she will need her rest."

I nodded. "Especially if I'm going to stop the change."

Gregory shook his head. "You can't stop it."

I glared at him, no longer unable to meet his eyes. "Do not tell me what I can or cannot do."

Ares laughed. "See Gregory. She is perfect."

Gregory smiled. "She is something, great Prince. Hurry and follow me then."

He changed back to a wolf, his body popping and snapping as it changed. I cringed at the sound and moved towards Ares, but he was changing, too. I ran to Koda and hopped up on his back as he started to stand up. I clung to him as he ran with the others.

CHAPTER FOUR

We ran for a few hours through the trees before coming to a large clearing filled with little log cabin houses and a bigger concrete warehouse building. Adults and children of various races walked around smiling, talking and laughing as our pack of wolves ran by them. I gaped, not believing that this sight wasn't scaring them.

How can this be normal? Are all of these people werewolves?

I shuddered at the thought of so many werewolves being in one place.

Aren't werewolves supposed to be angry and bloodthirsty?

Our group stopped in front of the largest house, and the men changed from wolves to human. I kept my face burrowed in Koda's fur as they walked inside so that I wouldn't have to look at their naked bodies. Koda turned his head to me and nudged my arm. I looked up, and he snorted. I slid from his back and walked forward until I was on the steps of the house. I could hear Koda's body popping and snapping and cringed with each sound.

He made a stretching noise and said from very close behind

me, "Come on. Everyone went to get clothes so that they wouldn't embarrass you anymore."

I felt the heat on my cheeks and was glad that I didn't have to look at him. I walked into the house quickly before any more naked men showed up. When I was inside the doorway, I stopped. The house had a very warm feeling. The entryway had rows of pictures of people and wolves and a chandelier made of deer antlers hanging over the doorway. The living room sat off to the left, the bedrooms to the right, and the kitchen was straight ahead. I frowned at the set-up and then shrugged.

Not my house to decide how to set it up.

I loved how normal everything looked and hoped that my life wouldn't have to change too much.

Ares walked out of one of the bedrooms in a pair of blue jeans and nothing else, and I stared at him as he walked towards me. His flawless caramel skin begged for me to lick, it and his piercing blue eyes would be perfect staring down at me while he...

I broke the thought off and turned away as a burning blush roared up my cheeks. I felt Ares behind me and desperately wanted to turn around and touch him, but I stayed still, digging my fingers into my arms to hold myself together.

You don't even know this guy and you're already thinking about doing things you have never done with any other man before. I swallowed hard. *Man. He was definitely a man.*

"Artemis," Ares whispered behind me. If his voice was a physical element, it would be velvet.

I swallowed hard. "Yes?"

He moved closer to me so that a large thought would make us touch. "Are you alright?"

I nodded quickly then sighed. "I...I..."

Ares wrapped his arms around my waist, and I moaned at the feel of his burning skin against mine. He placed his lips next to my ear and asked, "Would you like me to give you some space?"

I tried to say yes, but my mouth said, "No." I spun around in his arms and stared at his gorgeous face. His rugged physical features reminded me of the men who often camped in the nearby mountains. If he had wanted to, he could have been a model. I felt the muscles of his arms against me and his chest muscles as he wrapped his arms around me. My eyes rolled in the back of my head. He laughed quietly and set me down in a chair walking across the room. I stared after him and fought my body to stay in the chair. He smiled, and I smiled back at him.

Matt whistled from the doorway and spoke in his thick British accent, "Wow, she really is all bonkers fer ya. I can't believe you have *a passt genau.*"

Ares smiled and nodded. "She's perfect. Well, except that she hasn't changed yet."

I frowned. "I'm not going to change."

Ares shrugged and smiled. "Whatever you say."

I smelled steak and licked my lips. "Are we going to eat soon? I'm starving." Ares started walking towards me and wicked thoughts about parts of him I wouldn't mind nibbling on instantly sprang to mind. I shook my head trying to clear it and asked, "Did you put some type of spell or something on me?"

He whispered from behind me. "No. It's just how we are together."

I groaned. "Great. Just great."

Matt and Koda walked into the room and sat down on the love seat. They were both wearing only pants like Ares and it took all of my willpower to look away from their bodies and stare at my hands as I sat down on the farthest seat of the couch. I pressed myself into the corner, trying to hide and disappear even though I knew it was impossible. I continued staring at my hands, even when someone sat down next to me on the couch.

Matt whispered, "What's wrong, Love?"

I looked up slowly making sure to avoid staring at his body and going straight for his face. "I don't really want to answer that truthfully."

Matt smiled. "Is it because of how we're dressed?" I looked back down at my hands as another blush spread over my cheeks. Matt laughed. "It's alright. We won't get mad if we catch you looking at us."

"It's not that, well it sort of is, but that's not completely it." I said quietly.

Someone else sat down on the couch beside Matt. Koda asked, "You can't tell me you haven't seen your guy friends with their shirts off before."

I felt my blush deepen and shook my head. "I didn't really have any friends besides Bret and I never paid attention to the guys anyway." *And I guarantee none of them had bodies like yours.*

Matt snarled. "Was Bret the one trying to shoot us?"

I sighed and looked up at him. "Yes. You can't hate him for that, though. I've never seen wolves your size until we watched the videos on TV and then to see two of them at my house." My throat constricted as I thought about never seeing Bret again. After taking a deep breath I continued. "Bret has always vowed to protect me, and he was just worried for my safety. He didn't shoot you, right?"

Matt shrugged. "I didn't say I hated him. I just don't like humans in general."

I grimaced. "You don't like me?"

Matt smiled sweetly. "Love, you aren't human. Your father made you believe you are, but you are a werewolf." He stared at my eyes and shook his head. "And something else, because I have never met anyone with purple eyes before."

I frowned. "What are you talking about? I don't have purple eyes."

Koda and Matt stared at me in shock.

I shook my head. "I don't know what you are talking about."

Koda called, "Ares." Ares walked over and stood in front of me. I stayed staring at Koda. Koda said, "Ares, you need to take her to the bathroom."

I looked up at Ares' face, waiting for his reaction. Ares frowned. "Why? Are you not feeling well?"

Koda shook his head. "Ares, she doesn't know what her eyes look like."

Ares looked down at me, eyebrow raised. "What color are your eyes Artemis?"

I shrugged. "Brown. At least that's what Bret always told me. Darren never had a mirror in the house and I never really thought about it. Whenever I walked by a mirror I just never looked into it."

Ares picked up my hand then turned it over, staring at the burn from the wolf necklace. "What happened?" he asked softly.

I sighed. "Billy gave me a necklace with a wolf pendant and the wolf burned my hand."

Ares asked, "Silver?" I nodded and he whispered, "Don't touch silver." He pulled me to the bathroom down the hall. We passed Gregory, who watched us with curiosity. Ares pushed the bathroom door open and pushed me in front of the mirror. I stared at him, not sure what he wanted.

Ares sighed. "Look in the mirror."

I turned my head and looked at the mirror and gasped. I put my hand up to my face and rubbed my cheek. I knew I looked like my mother because Darren had told me, but I hadn't realized how much I looked like her. I looked deep into my dark purple eyes. I turned to Ares and asked, "This isn't some illusion, is it? Is this really what I look like?"

"Yes, Artemis. That is what you look like. Didn't you own a mirror?" I shook my head and ran my fingers through my thick black hair. I felt the tears running down my face before I saw them in the mirror. I turned away from the mirror and sat down on the floor holding my face in my hands. Ares sat down next to me and wrapped his arms around me. "It's alright, Artemis. Everything will be alright."

I stopped crying and rubbed my eyes with my arms. "I'm sorry.

It's just that I haven't seen my face before, and I didn't realize how much I look like my mother. I thought this whole time that I was just ugly and that's why everyone treated me like an outsider." I stopped talking because I felt like I was being arrogant to say that I thought I was beautiful.

Ares tilted my head up with his finger under my chin and smiled. "You're very beautiful, Artemis. I'm sure the reason they treated you like an outsider has nothing to do with your looks. I'll explain it to you later, but we need to eat."

I nodded and stood. I turned to him and asked, "Do you know of anyone else who has purple eyes? And why is it that I feel like I have known you my entire life, when I have only known you a few hours?"

He smiled and ran a fingertip along my jaw line. "I keep telling you that you were destined to be with me. I'm not making it up. And yes, I have met someone with purple eyes, but it has been a very long time since then."

I asked, "Does everyone have someone to answer their call?"

He shook his head. "No. The one that did, had to wait a long time to find the person who answered."

I asked, "How long did you wait?"

He shook his head. "Not yet. Wait until we explain everything about our culture to you."

I sighed. "Fine. But can you explain it soon?"

Ares laughed. "Of course." He walked from the bathroom back to the living room where everyone was sitting. I followed him and sat down in my spot in the corner of the couch.

Gregory brought out three plates piled with burgers and set it down on the coffee table. Gregory smiled. "Dig in!"

Matt and Koda jumped from the couch and grabbed two burgers each. Ares stood up and grabbed two also then all three sat down on the floor and began eating. I stared at the normal setting of guy friends eating burgers in a living room and wondered if all things about werewolves were the same. *Well except for the body changing part.* Ares looked up from his burger and frowned at me. "You need to eat."

I sighed and stood up grabbing one burger and sat back down pressing myself harder into the corner of the couch. I took a small bite from the burger and groaned in pleasure. "This is the best burger I have ever tasted!" I ate the burger quickly then grabbed another from the table, scarfing it down, too. Gregory handed everyone cups of soda then sat back down. I swallowed mine quickly, sighing in happiness when I was done. I felt a burp coming and fought to hold it down, but Koda burped loudly below me so I let mine out. I burped loud and long and laughed when I was finally done. "Excuse me."

All of the men stared at me in shock then started laughing loudly. Matt said, "Koda, she beat your burp like you were still a pup."

Koda smiled. "Looks like we may have a good burping contest with her around."

I blushed and looked down at my hands.

Koda groaned. "You embarrass, too easily. I know you don't know us, but we really aren't bad, and we aren't trying to embarrass you. Just treat us like we're your friends.

I stayed looking at my hands, no longer embarrassed, but now sad.

I wonder what theory Ares has about why I didn't have any friends.

Koda sighed. "What did I say wrong?"

I looked up at him and smiled. "Nothing, Koda. I just didn't have any friends besides Bret, so I don't really know how to act around a group of people."

Koda frowned. "But your friend was the all-star football player. You would go everywhere with him."

I furrowed my brow. "How did you know that?"

Koda smiled. "I can recognize the type."

"Sure, I went with him everywhere, but he was the only one that wanted me there, and no matter how hard I tried to fit in, it never worked." I laughed bitterly. "I'm sure they are ecstatic that I'm gone."

Ares shook his head. "They might be, but Bret won't be."

I smiled. "I wish I could see their faces when they make a comment, and he tears their heads off. Well, for the next day or two, until he leaves." I sighed. "He was always sticking up for me." I looked at Ares. "It wouldn't be possible for me to go back and explain everything to him, would it?"

Ares smiled. "Maybe someday, but not soon. You are in for a long couple of weeks of dealing with the transformation and the new things that come with it.

I nodded. "Sure. Will you explain everything now?"

Ares nodded then looked at Gregory. Gregory asked, "What do you know about werewolves?"

I shrugged. "Only what I've seen in movies."

All of them groaned. Gregory shook his head. "I don't understand why your father was so stupid not to tell you about what you are. Alright, I'll explain from the beginning. There are three ways to become a werewolf. One is to be bitten, which injects the Lycanthropy disease. The second is to be cursed by a witch, which sort of implants the disease in your body. The third is genetic, where you receive the disease from either the sperm or egg."

I stared at him as he continued his editorial. "You were born which means that either one or both of your parents were werewolves. We obviously know your father was one, but aren't sure about your mother what with your purple eyes and all." Ares cleared his throat, and Gregory continued. "Werewolves are special from humans not only in the fact that we can change shape, but also that we move fast and heal much faster than humans. We don't live forever, but if we find someone who will tie themselves to us, then we will live an endless number of years. Basically, if one of you dies, the other dies, too. Luckily, it's difficult to kill us. It's really the only drawback."

I felt my jaw drop open and looked around at the men around me. "You...you're all old, aren't you?"

They all frowned at me as I looked at all of their handsome faces and sculpted bodies. I looked at Ares last and asked in a voice barely louder than a whisper, "How old are you?"

Ares smiled. "I honestly don't know how old I am. I tried once to go back and figure it out, but I always lose count around the time of the Battle of Actium in Greece. I was old by human standards then, though."

I felt my jaw drop open. "Why are you interested in a seventeen-year-old then? Isn't that kind of like being a pedophile?"

Ares frowned deep, his forehead furrowing together and anger stretching his eyes tight. "I am not a pedophile! The rules are different when you live for hundreds of years. I am technically only in my mid-twenties. And besides, you are the one who answered my call. No matter what your age, you would be the only one for me. If you had been an infant, I would still have taken you and cared for you until you were old enough to truly love me like we are meant to."

I felt my face fall. "Love?"

What the hell is he talking about?

Ares sighed. "You don't get it. You and I are destined to be together for eternity. We are the only couple that does not have to be bound to live forever. You and I will live an endless number of years and if one of us dies the other will not."

I stared at the ground. "I did not mean to upset you, but fifty was old to me. How can you not expect me to be upset that you are over two *thousand* years old?"

Koda cringed. "Don't tell her my age. I may be younger than Ares, but not by her standards."

"You might as well tell me. If I am really going to live for eternity, I will find out later," I said.

"Later. Keep going, Gregory," Koda said.

Gregory smiled. "When someone is bitten, they change at the

next full moon, the same as with being cursed by a witch. But when you are born, you don't change until you hit puberty."

I stared at him and shook my head. "That's wrong. I hit puberty at thirteen."

All of the men turned and stared at me. Ares asked, "Thirteen? Have you ever stopped your transformation before?"

I thought about it and shrugged. "I don't know. I didn't know I was a werewolf until you came, remember?"

Ares snarled. "I'm really starting to dislike your father more and more. Have you ever had an instance where you thought you were having a seizure or heart attack or something?"

I thought back through my childhood and then remembered everything. I felt my eyes widen and said, "Shit. You've got to be kidding me."

They all stared at me, waiting for me to answer.

I groaned. "When I was ten, yeah ten, I had what appeared to be a seizure at school. My dad refused to take me to the doctors though, which pissed off the town. Then I kept having them. Not every day or anything, but once every few months. The last three years I've had them about every month, sometimes three times a month. Like once when I was thirteen, when I hit puberty, I started getting the shakes really bad. Darren kept me home from school and I fought my body to stop the shaking. Then when I was fifteen, I had another seizure episode at school in the middle of the cafeteria, but obviously it wasn't a seizure. One time I was at the lake with Bret and this girl slapped me in the face. I punched her back, but then fell on my hands and knees and started seizing."

Gregory's eyes were wide as I continued.

"Yesterday I started seizing, but Darren threw me in the creek, which stopped it."

"Holy shit," Koda said.

Matt nodded. "Love, you are amazing."

I looked at Ares who was smiling happily at me. "What does

this mean, Ares? That I have been fighting my transformation since I was ten?"

Ares nodded. "I believe so. I don't know why you started before you hit puberty or why you were able to stop them for so long. No one has ever stopped their first transformation before. And it is very unheard of to stop any of them."

I asked, "Can you stop them?"

He nodded. "I can, but not all of the time."

I shivered. "Oh, God. Why didn't Darren tell me this before? I felt like I was handicapped or something with the seizures."

Ares snarled. "I think you may get your wish to visit your town. I need to speak with your father."

"You aren't going to hurt him, are you?" I asked nervously.

Ares smiled. "Not if you don't want me to."

I shook my head. "I don't. So, when we go back, do I get to speak with Bret?"

Ares snarled. "With supervision."

I snarled back. "I don't need supervision."

Ares shook his head. "I won't let you see him alone."

I stood up, glaring at him. "You cannot tell me what to do. I may be stuck with you the rest of my life, but I don't have to bow to you just because you have some stupid title among the werewolves."

Ares stood and growled at me. I flinched, but didn't take a step back. I felt something pushing at me and looked around, but there was nothing. I felt a thick substance, like mud, spread around me seeping upwards until it covered me and I couldn't breathe. I fell to the floor gasping for breath as Ares stood over me.

Was he pushing his power over me? I looked up at his eyes and if I had had any breath would have gasped.

His eyes were completely black, like the pupil had expanded to cover everything. He snarled. "I am dominant to you and although you do not understand our ways, you will not try to belittle me."

I began to see grey spots as my body tried to black out with the lack of oxygen. I shook my head and rolled over on to my stomach. I felt a flame flare inside my core and focused on it. It flared higher and higher until it filled my entire body up. I looked up at Ares and smiled as I realized I had my own magic. Ares stared down at me, eyes widening, as I pushed with my hands and the internal flame at the invisible mud covering me. The internal flame extended past my hands and pushed the mud back enough for me to breathe. I gasped for breath and pushed harder with my power. Ares shook his head, and I watched in amazement as his eyes cleared back to normal. The invisible flame from me snapped back inside and only a small flicker like a candle flame stayed in my reach. I collapsed against the ground and closed my eyes in exhaustion.

No one spoke or moved for ten minutes. Ares finally cleared his throat and spoke. "Well, that was interesting."

"Did she just use magic against you?" Koda asked.

Ares laughed. "Yep. Darren has been holding out on us. I thought he had been bitten, but apparently, he comes from a line that was cursed, or he was cursed. That bastard. Now I really have to speak with him."

I sat up slowly and looked up at Ares. "What just happened?"

Ares smiled. "When you are cursed by a witch, or come from a line which is cursed by a witch, you gain magical powers. Apparently when I used my powers on you it let yours emerge."

I shook my head and laughed. "Werewolves, witches and now magical powers? You've got to be kidding me."

Ares frowned. "You've seen us change and you felt what just happened. You can't honestly think I am making this up?"

I sighed. "No. It's just a lot to take in. Are there any more mythological creatures I don't know about?" Everyone nodded, smiling. I groaned. "Great. So, when do I get to know which ones are real?"

Ares shrugged. "When we come across one."

I sighed. "Okay, fine. Look, I'm tired. Can I go to sleep?"

Ares smiled. "Of course. I'll show you to your room."

Ares extended his hand to me, and I took it, following him past the bathroom and into one of the four doors down the hallway. He held the door open for me, so I could walk in. The room was small, just big enough for a bed and a dresser, but it was inviting. I sat down on the bed and smiled at the feel of the soft mattress. Ares closed the door behind him and turned to me. I felt my heart speed up as I realized that we were alone in the room together. He smiled at me and shook his head. "Don't get nervous; I just want to talk."

I slowed my breathing down and crossed my legs on the bed. Ares leaned against the door and frowned. "You really have to watch how you act. I know I told you that I was going to give you slack about treating me as Prince, but I am dominant to you. If you had been any other werewolf, I would have punished you severely for what you did."

I sighed. "I'm sorry, but I have to speak with Bret, alone."

Ares shook his head. "It is out of the question, Artemis. I can't allow you to be alone with that human. If he hurt you, I would never forgive myself."

I frowned. "Bret would never hurt me."

Ares sighed. "You may think that, but when humans find out what we are, they turn into different people. It makes me wonder who the real shifters are," he said almost to himself.

"Bret would never hurt me. He has always been my protector. It would be kind of hypocritical to protect me from everything then hurt me himself."

Ares frowned. "You'd be surprised."

"Can't we at least try to compromise?"

Ares smiled. "Alright. What do you propose?"

"Well, since you won't let me meet with him alone, can I choose who goes with me?" I asked.

"Who did you have in mind?"

I shrugged. "Koda or Matt?"

He nodded. "Koda."

I smiled victoriously. "And he stands in the back of the room while I talk to Bret."

Ares shook his head. "No. We may be fast, but I won't take the chance on him hurting you before Koda can get there."

"Fine, after I tell Bret what I am, and Koda sees his reaction, he will stay in the back."

"Only if Bret's reaction is decent."

I nodded. "Fine."

Ares nodded. "Fine."

I raised my pointer finger. "One last thing."

Ares groaned. "What?"

I stopped smiling, keeping a serious face. "Koda won't repeat what is said to you or anyone else. Everything that is said stays in that room."

Ares snarled. "What is it that you will say that you don't want me to hear?"

I looked at the ground. "Just agree."

Ares sighed and rubbed his face. "Fine."

I smiled at Ares and wondered if things would work out.

Could I be happy with him? They seemed okay so far, but it takes a while to find out how people really are. Can I really believe that there are other mythological creatures running around?

Ares sat down on the bed beside me and smiled. "I promise that I will work my hardest to make you happy. I know that this must be hard for you."

I rolled my eyes. "No, learning that I'm not human and that I was destined to be with a man I don't know and having to deal with the fact that I'm going to have to stop my transformations all the time because I'm a werewolf isn't hard at all."

"If your father had done the right thing and told you about us, this wouldn't be that difficult for you. He and I are going to have a long talk when we go visit them."

"Fine, but if you kill him, I won't forgive you." I said with as much anger as I could muster.

Ares smiled. "I won't kill him. Promise." I smiled back at him and tensed as he leaned towards me. He lifted his hand, and reached towards my face, causing my heart to speed up even faster. His hand was an inch away from my face when someone knocked on the door twice. I stood up quickly, moving to the window which looked out at the village. I felt the blush on my cheeks and shook my head so that my hair fell around my face. Ares sighed. "Come in."

The door opened and Koda said, "Ares, the King is here."

Ares groaned. "What is he doing here?"

Koda laughed. "Not sure, but he is requesting to speak with you."

I continued facing the window, not wanting to go anywhere or talk to anyone. Ares stood up from the bed and walked to stand behind me. "I know you are tired, but I would like you to meet the King."

I sighed and asked without turning around, "Will you keep your agreements about our visit?"

Ares laughed softly. "Yes."

I turned around slowly and nodded. "Alright."

Ares smiled and kissed my cheek. "Thank you."

The blush erupted on my face before I could even blink. Ares walked out the door leaving me alone with Koda. He smiled and shook his head.

I held up my hand at him. "Don't even say anything."

He held his hands up in surrender. "I wasn't."

I growled and walked past him out of the bedroom. When I got down the hallway, Koda started laughing in the bedroom. I blushed darker and walked faster towards the living room. Matt stood by the entrance and smiled at me. "Ready, Love?"

I shrugged. "What's one more werewolf?"

He frowned. "What's that supposed to mean?"

I shook my head. "Nothing. Forget about it." I squared my

shoulders, and walked past Matt, to stand beside Ares, but stopped halfway when I saw the man he was talking to.

To say he is a large man is a lie. *He's ginormous.* At least six and a half feet tall, he towered over Ares' five-foot-seven frame easily. His body looked like a professional wrestler and I was just waiting for him to yell, "I'll crush you!". I had never been intimidated by anyone before, but he definitely intimidated me. His dark hair hung to his shoulders, and his beard hung to his belly. I instantly thought of a biker and wondered if he had been living here this whole time as one. Ares turned to me, smiling reassuringly, and reached his hand out to me. I thought about rejecting his hand, but knew I would feel safer if he held mine.

How childish is that?

I walked quickly to Ares, taking his hand and pressed myself against his side.

Ares cleared his throat. "Darius, this is Artemis, my mate."

Darius smiled, but it didn't make him any less menacing. "Your mate? I thought you said you were waiting for the one who would answer your call?"

Ares nodded, looking down at me with gentleness in his eyes. "I did."

Darius stared at me for a second then his eyes bulged in surprise. "This child answered your call?"

I glared at him. "I'm not a child."

Ares nudged my arm to quiet me. "Forgive her, Darius. Her father decided that he was not going to tell her about us until she changed for the first time, so she knew nothing of us until I came to get her."

Darius stared at me in wonder. "She answered your call without having her first change?"

Ares nodded. "We have learned that she has actually been fighting her changes since she was ten years old."

Darius shook his head. "Impossible. No one can fight their first change."

Ares shrugged. "Apparently, she can. She has done it numerous times already. Tomorrow will be the ultimate test though."

I rolled my eyes. "I keep telling you that I will not change tomorrow. Why won't you believe me?"

Darius snarled. "Because it's impossible."

I shrugged. "We'll see. I'm still going to try."

Darius laughed. "She does seem to be a perfect match for you Ares."

Ares nodded, smiling at me. "She seems so, so far."

I tensed beside them, unsure of what they meant, but Ares rubbed his thumb across my knuckles, calming me.

Darius sighed. "Well, I am just on my way through. We are going to the meeting place."

Ares nodded. "I have one stop to make after tomorrow night, and then I will be through. We should probably be there in three or four days, depending on how things go tomorrow night."

Darius nodded and appraised me. "Does she have magic?" Ares nodded. Darius snarled. "Why do you have purple eyes, pup?"

I shrugged. "I have no idea. I didn't even know I had purple eyes until a few minutes ago."

Ares smiled. "She has, literally, been kept in the dark."

Darius frowned and seemed like he wanted to say something else to me, but shook his head. "Well, I better get going."

Ares nodded and bowed to Darius. I looked behind me and found Matt and Koda bowing, too. I curtsied and looked at the ground as Darius walked past us and out the door. Ares stood up and so did I. He turned to me smiling. I dropped his hand and moved away from him. "What?"

He laughed. "You really are amazing."

I shook my head. "I don't know what you mean."

He smiled and moved towards me making me stare at his naked upper body. "I know you don't understand. You will soon though."

I turned towards the windows as I felt the sun coming up and sighed. "The sun is here."

Koda stared at me. "You can feel when the sun comes up?"

I nodded. "Since I can remember. I have always loved the moon and it's like an alarm in my head goes off when the switch between moon and sun is about to happen."

Ares stared at me in shock for a moment and then whispered, "Oh, Goddess, she might be her."

I turned and looked at him. "Who?"

Koda shook his head. "She can't be her."

Matt nodded. "She has the right powers and abilities."

Koda shook his head. "But she is obviously not full werewolf."

Ares shook his head. "The prophecy says she'll be a mixed blood."

I walked slowly away from them, towards the bedroom. Ares called, "Where are you going?"

I turned around. "You probably aren't going to explain it anyway and I'm tired. I need to sleep."

Ares smiled. "Of course." He walked towards me, making my heart speed up again. He smiled wider and when he was close enough whispered, "I hope your heart speeding up isn't because you are frightened of me."

I shook my head. "No, not frightened in the regular sense."

He smiled and bent down towards me. I tried to move away, but my body wouldn't let me. He bent over my lips with just a breath between us and whispered, "I know you are fighting your feelings, and I understand, but if you would just let go it would be truly amazing." I went to answer him, but he stopped me by kissing me on the lips. I stayed tense as his lips pressed softly, but warmly against mine. My body wanted to wrap my arms around him and kiss him back, but my brain refused to admit that I could have any feelings for this man I had just met hours before. He pulled away and laughed, "You are a fighter. I admire that. Now go on to sleep. We will be in the rooms beside you if you need anything."

I turned quickly away from him without another glance and walked as fast as I could without jogging to my room. I slammed the door shut and threw myself onto the bed. My lips burned where he had kissed me as I buried my face in my pillow. I shook my head back and forth.

I can't have feelings for this old half man, half wolf. I just met him hours ago. Shit.

I groaned and rolled on to my side, closing my eyes.

Things will work out. I can control myself long enough to find an escape plan.

I pulled the covers over my head and hummed the song my father had always sung to me as I drifted to sleep.

"Artemis. Artemis, wake up." Koda said softly.

I opened my eyes and looked up at Koda's smiling face. "Hi, Koda."

He laughed softly. "Hello. It's time to get up."

I looked out the window and saw that there was no light coming through. "Is it night-time already?"

He nodded. "You slept through the day. The only reason I am waking you now is because your stomach has been growling loud enough that we heard it in the other room. Ares thought it would be best if you ate before you fought your change as well."

I nodded and stood, stretching my arms over my head. I squealed as I finished my stretch and smiled. Koda laughed. "I see you're calmer today."

I shrugged and smiled. "I figured that being nervous all the time and thinking about things I can't change is stupid. I am just going to relax and learn to enjoy how my new life is." *Until I can think of a plan to escape from you.*

Koda frowned. "What was that?"

I stared at him in confusion. "What do you mean?"

He sighed. "You flinched as you finished saying that. That usually means that you are lying or thinking something bad."

I felt my eyes widen and turned away from him.

Shit. Why the hell is he so perceptive?

"I'm sorry, it's just that I can't believe I am saying this and feeling so comfortable with you all when I don't even know you."

"I know how you feel, Artemis. I helped a wolf that wasn't told about being a werewolf until one month before his first change. He was scared and it was in the eighteen hundreds when the werewolf and witch hunts began. At least for you, things are a lot better and will be getting much, much better soon."

I turned to him and asked, "What do you mean, 'soon'?"

He smiled. "The preternaturals or mythological creatures as you like to call them, are taking the world back from the humans."

I gaped at him as I remembered the London and Las Vegas scenes. "You're killing all of the humans?"

He shook his head and waved his hands at me. "No. No. No. Okay, we kill some, but we capture most of them."

I snarled. "So, you can eat them later?"

Matt walked into the bedroom laughing. "Now that's original. Of course not, Love. We are taking them as slaves. It's the only way for them to live as humans. Either you are a slave or you become one of us."

I growled and felt my power rising inside me. "That is ridiculous. Who are you to decide how they live?"

Matt snarled at me. "They decided to kill us centuries ago. To avoid that fate, we were forced to hide in sewers and nearly starve."

I clenched my teeth and shook my head, my power radiating off of me in waves and slapping against Koda and Matt. Every time a wave would hit them, they would take a step back. "It was not these people, but the people who lived during that time. It would be like the African-Americans forcing Caucasians into slavery because of what happened hundreds of years ago. That's ridiculous, because we live peacefully together, no matter what color the other is. How do you know it wouldn't be the same for you?"

Koda laughed. "Are you serious? Do you honestly think the

humans would live peacefully with a werewolf? They would be too worried that we would hurt them."

I growled loudly and moved towards the bedroom door. Matt blocked me, making me snarl and growl louder. "Move!" I felt my body starting to shake and stopped growling. I stayed perfectly still and breathed slower, taking big, deep breaths. Matt and Koda stared at me, eyes wide, as I kept my body calm and collected. I sighed and looked up at Matt. "I said move."

Matt moved to the side, and I hurried past him into the kitchen. I opened the fridge and found lunchmeat and took it out, swallowing the pieces of turkey and ham whole.

Koda and Matt watched me from the doorway as I finished the two packs of lunchmeat. I opened the freezer and pulled out a block of ground beef. I put it in the sink and turned the water on scalding hot to defrost it as quickly as possible.

After watching me for a few more seconds, Matt walked away from the kitchen and out of the house.

I ignored Koda, as I waited anxiously for the meat to defrost. I poked at the meat and smiled as it started to give way. I heard the front door open, but ignored it, continuing to poke at the block of beef. I started dancing from side to side as I grew antsy for the meat to defrost. I snarled and flipped the meat over to allow the water to defrost the other side. I felt someone standing next to me but ignored him.

Nothing matters but food right now.

Blood started to run down the sink and I pulled the meat out holding it in my hands. I licked my lips hungrily and looked around for a plate. Ares, who was standing beside me, handed me a plate. I took the plate quickly and placed the meat on it. I sat on the ground, and started eating the ground beef. I groaned in happiness as I swallowed the beef and blood. Someone's hand reached towards my plate and I snarled and pulled the plate away. The hand disappeared, and I went back to scarfing down the food. When I had finished the ground beef, I stood up and put the plate in the sink. I went back to the fridge and took out the milk. I turned for a glass, but Ares was already handing one to me. I took it and poured a glass of milk, then swallowed it quickly. I put the milk back and put the glass in the sink, before sighing in contentment. I looked around at the three men staring at me, and felt self-conscious. I wiped at my mouth and ran to the bathroom to see if I had food or blood on me. I stared at my face a moment longer than necessary, unused to using a mirror.

My face was clean, so I walked back out into the living room where they had moved and begun to whisper together. I sat down on the couch and stared at my hands, as they finished talking.

Ares cleared his throat making me look up at him. "How are you feeling?"

I shrugged. "Fine. Why?"

"You don't know what just happened do you?"

I shrugged. "I started to get shaky and I calmed myself down, but then I was really hungry so I ate."

He laughed and turned to Koda and Matt. "You see? She has no idea what just happened."

"You want to explain to me what happened?" I said angrily.

"You just stopped your transformation again. This time you stopped it so fast that the only need you had was food. Usually you are extremely tired when you stop it too, but you stopped it so fast and so early that you aren't tired."

I stared at him in surprise as I comprehended what he said. I smiled at him and laughed. "So, I stopped the transformation again?"

He nodded.

I smiled wider. "I told you I could."

Koda snorted. "Just because you said so doesn't mean you can. If I hadn't seen it with my own eyes, I would have told them they were crazy."

"Oh. Well, can we go see Darren and Bret now?"

Ares shrugged. "I guess it is safe, since you didn't change."

I blinked at him. "You thought I was going to lose control and try to eat Bret, didn't you? Is that the main reason you wanted Koda with me?"

Ares nodded. "You would never forgive yourself if you hurt him."

I nodded, solemnly. "You're right. So, does this mean I can meet with him alone?"

He sighed and rubbed his temples. "You are so pushy, but since it's your birthday, I'll let you."

I smiled at him and walked towards the door. "Come on. Let's go. You can decide when we get there." I walked out the door and stopped in my tracks. Bret stood a few feet away from the door frozen in shock. I shook my head and whispered, "Bret? What are you doing here?"

His surprise turned into a wide-toothed grin as he picked me up spun me around. "Oh, thank God, you're alright. Come on let's get you home." I shook my head as he set me down and started to pull me down the porch. I grabbed his arm and pulled him back. He stared at me in shock. "Come on, Artemis."

I shook my head. "Bret, you need to leave, now. It's not safe for you here. How the heck did you even find me? You need to leave."

"Why? Because of all of the big wolves around? I can handle myself. I need to take you out of here. I just followed the direction you left. It was almost like I knew which way you would go. Now, let's go," he said fiercely.

Ares, Matt, and Koda walked on to the porch and glared at Bret with his hand on my arm, and mine on his.

I placed my body in front of Bret's. "Just listen to me for a second, okay?"

Ares, Matt and Koda nodded in unison.

"He thinks you are going to hurt me, and he came to save me. You can't hurt him for that."

Ares shook his head. "No, but he can't go free."

I shook my head. "He doesn't know anything. He hasn't figured it out."

Bret pushed me to the side and asked, "Figured out what? Why do I feel like I am missing some big secret?"

I smiled and turned to Ares. "See? He doesn't know. Just let me take him home. You want to talk to my dad anyway, right?"

Matt snarled. "You plan on telling him anyway. Then he will know how to get here. We can't let him go."

I snarled back at him and put myself in front of Bret again. "You are not going to hurt him."

Koda smiled. "We never said we were going to hurt him."

I snapped my teeth at Koda. "You aren't going to kill him either."

Ares waved his hands in the air. "Calm down, Artemis. We aren't going to kill him. But he can't go free. He is going to have to stay with us."

I looked from Ares to Koda to Matt and back to Ares. "Why do *I* feel like I'm missing something now?"

Ares sighed. "If I tell you, you are going to freak out."

I shook my head and took a step back pushing Bret back with me. "Then it's definitely no."

Bret asked, "What is going on, Artemis?"

I snapped. "I'm trying to save your life, Bret. Just shut up and let me handle this."

He scowled, but didn't say anything. Ares and Matt took a step towards me while Koda took one to the side.

I snarled and crouched down. "Please stop. I don't want to fight you."

Ares glared at me. "You are willing to fight us over him?"

I nodded. "He has done nothing wrong and you are trying to do something horrible to him."

Ares smiled. "You don't even know what it is."

I snarled. "No. You told me that he would be unharmed."

Ares nodded. "Yes, but that was when he was at your town. Now he knows the way here and will tell the others."

Bret shrugged. "Why would I tell anyone about this place? Just let me take Artemis back and we'll forget about it."

Ares shook his head. "She can never go back."

I felt a tear fall down my face and shook my head. "Shut up. All of you, just shut up!"

I heard someone behind us and spun around to see Koda coming towards us. I growled loudly and jumped in front of Bret as Koda ran towards him. Koda smashed into me, sending me flying through the air. I felt my body hit the wall and shook my head to clear my daze. I jumped up and saw Matt and Ares holding Bret. I snarled loudly and snapped my teeth at them as I moved towards them. I felt my body begin to shake and sighed. I breathed slowly and stopped the shaking. I looked up at Bret's face and stopped moving. He stared at me with a mixture of horror and fear on his face.

Bret asked, "What's wrong with you?"

I shook my head. "Nothing Bret."

He shook his head at me. "You aren't human, are you?"

I looked at Ares and snarled. "Let him go. Please."

Ares dropped Bret's arm and moved towards me. "Artemis. I didn't want this to happen."

I shook my head and moved away from him. "Bret, you need to leave."

Bret shook his head. "Whatever you are, I...I can deal with it. Come home with me."

I laughed bitterly and shook my head. "It's never been my home, Bret. I can't go back there again. You're right, I'm not human. That's why I never fit in."

Bret asked, "If you aren't human, then what are you?"

I looked up at Ares' worried face and sighed. "I'm a werewolf."

Bret laughed loudly and said, "Yeah, right. So, really though. What's going on with you?"

I looked Bret in the eyes. "I'm a werewolf, Bret. So are the three men around you."

Bret looked at three men holding him who were all shorter, but more muscled. He shook his head in disbelief. "No way."

"Bret. You remember Ares was there at my house, right?"

Bret nodded.

I went on, "So were Koda and Matt, just not in human form."

I watched as Bret comprehended what I said. "The wolves? The giant wolves?" His face grew more worried as he looked at the men holding him.

I nodded. "Yes. And I'm one of them, but I haven't changed shape yet."

Bret shook his head. "Then how do you know that you are one of them?"

I looked at Ares who nodded. I groaned. "Because my dad is one."

Bret's face fell, and he stopped talking. He stared at me for a full minute before shaking his head. I walked towards him, but he backed up as much as Matt and Koda would allow.

I stopped walking and looked at the ground. "I would never hurt you." I looked back up at him and smiled.

Bret shook his head. "You can't be a werewolf I can't be in lov..." He stopped talking and looked up at me. I let the pain and shock show on my face. "I won't believe you are a werewolf until you change."

I groaned. "I'm not going to change. I refuse."

Bret smiled. "Then it's alright. We can go on with our lives like normal."

I groaned again. "Don't you see, Bret? I'm not normal. I don't belong with you and your friends. I belong here with other wolves. Eventually, I'll change and I know that. I won't be able to hold it off forever. When that happens, I don't want to be near you. I could kill you."

"I don't believe you. If you don't love me or don't want to be with me, then just tell me. Don't make up these crazy lies." Bret's eyes were pinched, like he was in pain.

Ares laughed. "Damn, you are persistent. Would you rather I changed and showed you?"

I snarled at Ares. "Don't even think about it."

Ares snarled back. "Do not threaten me. I have the power to force you to change if I want."

I snapped my teeth at him. "Let Bret go, and you and I can finish this."

Ares shook his head. "I already told you that we can't let him go. He knows too much."

I shook my head. "No way. You are going to make him a slave or something and I won't let you."

Ares growled. "You wouldn't be able to stop me, even if that was what I was going to do."

Koda cleared his throat, "Prince." Ares looked at Koda and stopped snarling. Koda smiled. "Perhaps I should just get this over with so we don't have to stand here and talk all day?"

Ares nodded, smiling. "Okay." I took a step forward as I saw Koda open his mouth. I watched in amazement as fangs extended. I finally knew what they were going to do and ran forward. I dodged around Ares as he tried to grab me and lunged at Koda. Koda grabbed Bret around his arms and bit into his shoulder. Bret yelled in pain as Koda bit down harder, drawing blood.

I screamed, "No!" and charged into Koda knocking him backwards and away from Bret. Koda landed with a large thud as I rode his body down to the ground. I pushed off of him, running back to Bret. Matt was kneeling beside him and I charged forward smashing into him and sending him flying backwards into the side of the house.

Ares snarled at me from the other side of Bret. "Stop, Artemis. It's too late now. He's already infected."

I shook my head and ran back, picking Bret up in my arms and running as fast as I could. I had to fight to keep a hold on Bret because he was too tall to be carried easily. I could hear someone following me, but I didn't care. My only concern was getting Bret to safety. I ran faster and weaved in and out of the trees, trying not to hit one. I saw a clearing and ran for it. I set Bret on the ground and ripped open his shirt. I stared at the wound which was still bleeding. I placed my lips over the wound and sucked as hard as I could. Bret screamed in pain as I sucked his blood and another bitter tasting substance into my mouth. I sucked until my mouth was full then turned and spit. I clamped my mouth over the bite again and sucked. Bret screamed with every suck and thrashed his legs.

Ares sighed beside me. "It's no use, Artemis. Even if you suck up what is there, some has already gone into his bloodstream. Look at his eyes."

I pulled back from the bite and spit what was in my mouth. I looked at Bret's eyes and gasped. They were wolf amber and glowing. I shook my head and let the tears fall. "No! No, I can stop it."

Ares reached towards me.

I snarled at him. "Get away!" I clamped my mouth over Bret's bite and sucked as hard as I could, making Bret scream in pain. No more bitter taste came and I stopped sucking. I spit what was in my mouth out and stared at Bret.

He breathed slowly staring at me with amber eyes.

I cried harder and hugged him. "I'm so sorry, Bret. I'm so sorry. I could have tried harder. Now you are going to be like me and never be able to go back to our town. Never finish football."

Bret laughed. "It's alright, Artemis. I don't care about that as long as I have you."

Ares growled. "She is not yours."

I pushed off of Bret and shoved Ares in the chest. "I am not yours, either, you asshole! You think after you take my friends humanity away, that I am going to stay with you?"

Ares frowned. "I did not bite him."

I snarled. "But you let Koda. You could have told him not to, and that makes you just as liable. It was your plan all along to have him changed, wasn't it? That was what you didn't want to say to me. You bastard."

Ares sighed. "I'm not going to fight with you anymore tonight. He is changing already and there is nothing you can do about it."

Bret stood up behind me and grabbed my arm hard. I looked up at his black eyes and said, "Bret, just calm down. You can fight the change."

Bret snarled. "I'm hungry."

I smiled. "Well, let's go get you some food."

Bret shook his head then inhaled above my head. "I have food here."

I felt my mouth drop open as I realized he was talking about me. Ares moved forward so that he was standing beside me and Bret. "She is not food." Ares said in a strained voice

Bret turned to Ares and snarled. "She smells like food."

The tension in the air was growing thicker. Ares shook his head. "You do not know what food smells like. Come with me and I will show you real food."

Bret snarled and pulled me against him. "You just want her to yourself. No!"

Matt and Koda jogged into the clearing and came to stand behind Ares. Koda whispered, "What's going on?"

I cried softly and whispered, "Bret wants to eat me."

Matt and Koda looked from me to Bret to Ares and back to me. When they settled back to me their faces held more of a softer look. Matt said. "Love, I'm sorry. This has never happened before."

Koda nodded. "Never. Maybe it's because you haven't changed yet."

Matt nodded. "That's it. You need to show him who is dominant to convince him that you aren't food."

"So, I have to fight him?" They all nodded. I looked up at Bret, who was staring intently at Ares in a battle of wills. I groaned. "Shit." I yanked my arm from Bret's arm and ran away from him as fast as I could. I heard rustling and yelling, but kept running. When I was far enough away that they couldn't see me clearly, I jumped up the nearest tree and climbed up. They came running and pushing each other, searching for me.

Why are Ares, Koda and Matt pushing each other?

I didn't have time to decide because Bret passed under me. I jumped down from the tree on to his back, forcing him to the ground. I drove my knee into his spine as he fell making him scream in pain. He rolled over and I jumped up straddling him. I bent to press my knee into his throat when someone slammed into me and grabbed me.

I grunted from the impact and said, "Stop."

The person stopped and I looked up to see Matt's excited amber eyes. I shook my head. "Matt, what the hell are you doing?"

He inhaled loudly then sighed. "Sorry. You got us all excited when you ran away like that. Our wolf sides kicked in."

I groaned and pulled away from him, going back for Bret who was standing up, now.

He smiled and licked his lips.

I shook my finger at him. "I am not food. I am your alpha."

He snarled. "You are not dominant to me."

Ares appeared behind him. "I am." He grabbed Bret around the neck and proceeded to choke him until he passed out. He laid Bret on the ground and wiped his hands off against each other to symbolize he was done.

I snarled. "I was supposed to dominate him. Now he is still going to think I'm food when he wakes up."

Ares shrugged. "He won't wake up for a few days anyway. We'll worry about it then."

Koda ran to us. "You really have to learn not to run like that. I got all excited and almost pounced on you."

"You were nowhere near me. None of you knew where I was," I said with a suppressed laugh.

Ares looked up at the tree branches above us. "Yeah, how did you get up that tree so fast?"

I shrugged. "My life depended on it."

The three men laughed loudly at my joke and the tension disappeared.

Koda reached down and picked Bret up under his arms. "We better get back and put him in the hibernation room."

Ares nodded. "We'll leave him here while we go talk to Darren."

"I'll stay here with Bret," I said.

Ares shook his head. "He tried to eat you. I'm not leaving you here. You have to come with us."

I groaned. "Why are you always so pushy? Can't you just suggest that I go with you and then let me decide?"

Ares thought in silence for a minute before speaking. "Then I suggest you come so you don't get eaten."

I nodded. "Sounds like a good idea."

Ares laughed. "You agreed with me for once."

"Trust me, it won't happen again. Besides, as soon as I can, I'll be leaving." The words left my mouth before I could stop myself.

Ares and Matt blinked at me. Ares asked, "What do you mean by that?"

"Nothing. Forget I said it."

Ares grabbed me by the arms and stared into my eyes. "I am sorry that we turned your friend. You have to forgive me."

I laughed bitterly. "I told you that I wasn't going to stay with you."

Ares face fell, pulling at my heart. "How can you say such a thing? Do you not feel for me?"

I stared at his handsome face and desperately wanted to kiss him, to heal the pain I had caused. I shook my head. "I refuse to admit anything."

The pain in his eyes made me flinch, but I held my ground. Ares asked, "Do you want to leave? To go back to your father and the little town you came from when Bret won't be there?"

I groaned and looked at the ground. "I can't believe you allowed this to happen."

Ares whispered, "If I had known how you would react, I would not have let it happen. I figured you would be happy that your friend is now like you, and will live almost as long as you."

I shook my head. "But he is in love with me. The day before you came, he was trying to make me his girlfriend. Don't you get it? You have just prolonged his life, to watch me be with you."

Ares smiled. "So, you admit that you have feelings for me?"

I shook my head. "I didn't say that. What I am saying is that I do not love him in that way. And that you would not even let us try, because you believe I am destined to be with you." I rolled my eyes at the thought of destiny.

Ares frowned. "Why do you roll your eyes?"

"Destiny is not something I believe in. I believe that we make our own destiny, not that it is pre-set for us."

Ares shrugged. "Either way, you still answered my call, which means that you are essentially mine. You can call it whatever you want, but you and I are meant to be together. I am sorry that your friend will have a tough time dealing with that, but it is the truth. It is why your father could not stop me from taking you. He could feel the connection between you and me when you came out the door."

I frowned. "What if I do not love you? What if I never love you?"

Ares smiled. "Just give it time, and do not strangle your feelings. You will see."

I looked at the ground. "It's really irritating that I can't be mad at you for very long."

Ares nodded. "I'm sure I will find out how that is soon enough."

I looked up at his face and asked, "Will you let Bret stay with us, or will you send him away?"

Ares shrugged. "I'll leave that up to you and him to decide. If he thinks he can handle staying and seeing us together, then he is welcome to join us, but if he wishes to stay with the wolves in this village, then I will let him."

I nodded and started walking back toward the village. I called over my shoulder, "We better get him to your hibernation thingy."

Koda and Matt picked Bret up and carried him behind me. Ares walked beside me, smiling. I tried my best to ignore him, but couldn't help glancing at him occasionally. He never looked at me, but every time I glanced at him, his smile seemed to get bigger. It took us longer to get back because I was walking, but I didn't care. When we made it to the clearing, I stopped moving and, tilting my face up to the full moon, closed my eyes.

Koda and Matt continued past me with Bret, leaving me and Ares alone.

I put my arms out to the side and inhaled as deep as I could. I loved the smell of the forest and the night. I opened my eyes and bathed in the warmth of the moon, pulling my arms back down to my sides. I turned to Ares and smiled.

He had his face upturned to the moon and his eyes closed, breathing deeply. He opened his eyes and smiled at me. "You enjoy the moon, too, I see."

I nodded. "The moon makes me feel at peace."

Ares smiled. "Me, too. Of course, I should have assumed someone with the name of the Goddess of the Moon would like the moon."

I laughed. "Yeah, but I guess my connection to the moon is more because of my werewolf side."

Ares shrugged his shoulders. "We are the Children of the Moon. Our power to change comes from the moon. I have always liked the moon's glow. It's much better for your skin to moonbathe than sunbathe."

I laughed and took a step closer to him, feeling a strange pull. I thought about fighting it, but remembered him asking me to not strangle my feelings. He lifted a brow at me, his body tense, but he did not move. I took another step, closing the distance so that only one foot of space separated us. I looked up at his uncertain face and smiled. He smiled back at me, but stayed perfectly still, his breathing speeding up slightly. I slowly reached a shaky hand out to him and placed it on his chest. His muscle flexed then relaxed as I stroked down his chest and across his chiseled abdominals. His skin was so hot against my hand that I had to keep moving it, or it was too much. I ran my hand back up his stomach and across his chest and up the side of his neck to rest on his face. I stared a little longer at his sky blue eyes and realized that there was a slight slant to the corners.

I wonder if he is part Asian.

I started to stand on tiptoe to reach his lips when I heard something moving through the trees. I quickly dropped my hand and turned around towards the sound.

Ares stepped around me so that he was standing beside me.

A small grey wolf cub covered in blood walked from behind a tree to stare at us.

Ares squatted down and opened his arms as if inviting the wolf for a hug.

I watched in amazement as the wolf's body snapped, popped, and twisted to form a small boy. The boy ran to Ares and collapsed into his arms.

Ares cradled the boy and whispered to him. "What happened?"

The boy shivered against Ares and whispered, "The humans figured it out. They…they killed my pack."

Ares asked, "Are you hurt?"

The boy shook his head. "It was my pack's blood. I hid under the bodies so the humans wouldn't kill me."

Ares stood with the boy still in his arms and walked towards Gregory's home. Gregory opened the door before we got there and took the boy from Ares' arms.

The boy turned to Ares. "Prince, wait."

Ares stayed still and waited for the boy to speak.

The boy cleared his throat. "One of them there is a wolf. He is helping them find us. They have guns and knives with silver. Stay downwind of him."

Ares nodded. "Do you know his name?"

The boy snarled, "Darren."

I gasped and shook my head. "It must be someone else."

Ares asked, "What did he look like?"

The boy sighed. "I didn't get a good look, but he had her hair."

The boy pointed to me then gasped. "Is she with them? Is she going to kill us?"

I shook my head. "No, I'm not with them and won't hurt you."

Ares smiled at the boy. "It's alright, she's my *passt genau*."

The boy nodded. "Okay."

Gregory took him inside and shut the door.

Koda and Matt walked up the porch steps to stand beside us.

I looked at Ares. "What's pause...gee...now?"

Ares laughed at my poor attempt to speak the words he had just done. "It's *passt genau,* German for what you are to me."

"What does it mean, Ares?" I asked again.

He smiled. "Perfect match."

I fought to frown, but my mouth formed a smile. I shook my head and asked, "What are we going to do about the humans and that werewolf?"

Ares frowned. *"You* aren't going to do anything. You are still very human. Until you change you aren't doing any fighting."

I groaned. "Ares, I have to go. What if it's my dad?"

Ares sighed and rubbed his temples.

Koda said, "I think she should stay here. You will be too worried about her to focus on the fight."

Matt nodded. "I agree with Koda."

I sighed. "Fine. You go off and battle the humans and leave me here alone to worry. I'll just find things to break while you're gone. And fight my change."

Ares smiled. "You would worry for us?"

I nodded then hissed, "Damn you!"

Ares laughed and grabbed me, pulling me against him. "Koda is right, I would worry too much about you if you went. You worrying for us will be a lot less of a problem. Please stay here. If it is your father, I will try my hardest to simply restrain him and bring him here. But if it comes down to it, and I must, I will kill him."

I nodded and relaxed into the warmth of his body, leaning my head against his chest. "I understand. Be careful."

He pushed me back and kissed my lips softly. I kissed him back and then quickly pulled away, running into the house and shutting the door. My lips burned even hotter than before as I leaned against the front door. Gregory and the boy sat in the middle of the living room. The boy had been given clothes much too big for him, but he sat playing a card game with Gregory, smiling.

How can he be smiling after his pack was killed? I would be devastated.

Gregory saw me and smiled. "You want to play?"

I shrugged my shoulders. "I guess I should. They are leaving me behind."

Gregory shrugged. "Ares would be too focused on your safety to worry about his. It's better this way."

I groaned and sat down beside them. I turned to the boy and said, "Hi, I'm Artemis."

He smiled at me. "Jason."

I smiled back at him as Gregory passed out cards. I watched as he dealt us each thirteen cards and asked, "What are we playing?"

Gregory smiled. "Thirteen."

I sighed. "I don't know how to play."

Gregory laughed. "It's alright. We'll teach you."

I listened intently as Gregory explained the game to me. The game was like war, where you had to put a card down which was higher in either number or suit and the first one out of cards won. I arranged my cards from lowest, three, to the highest, two then started playing. Gregory put down the three of clubs, the lowest card in the game. I put down a three of hearts which was higher in suit so it beat his card. Jason put down a king, making Gregory and I groan. Gregory put down an ace then I put down a two. Jason and Gregory groaned.

Jason said, "Pass."

Gregory nodded. "Pass."

I smiled and laid down a six card straight. Both groaned again and said, "Pass" in unison. I put down a pair of fives and Jason laid down a pair of eights. Gregory passed and I put down a pair of tens.

Jason sighed. "Pass." Gregory nodded and waved his hand for me to go. I put down my final card, an ace and raised my hands in the air. "I'm out."

Jason groaned. "I thought you said that you haven't played this?"

I smiled. "I hadn't played this before. It's a very fun game though. Can we play again?"

Gregory smiled. "Sure."

Jason turned and looked at me frowning. "Why are you nervous?"

I looked down at him and frowned. "Why do you think that I am nervous?"

His eyes went wide. "Aren't you a werewolf?"

I nodded. "Yes, but what does that have to do with why you think I am nervous?"

Gregory smiled. "Jason, she hasn't had her first change yet."

Jason's eyes went even wider. "What! How is that possible?"

I smiled and shrugged. "I didn't know I was a werewolf until yesterday and apparently, I have been fighting the change since I was around your age."

Jason gasped, "No way. Asena's children were the only ones who were supposed to be able to do that."

I frowned. "Who's Asena?"

Jason and Gregory stared at me in shock. Gregory asked, "You don't know who Asena is?"

"I told you that I didn't know I was a werewolf until yesterday. Your speech last night was the first I have heard about us."

Gregory sighed. "I thought they were joking and just wanted me to talk. Alright. I'll have to tell you our story then."

I smiled. "Okay." I adjusted myself so that I was a little more comfortable before he began.

Gregory cleared his throat. "All of us that are born werewolves are descendants of the Mother of all werewolves, Asena. She, herself, was not a werewolf, but...I'm getting ahead of myself. A village was raided by soldiers, killing everyone but one infant, who the general took pity on and only gave the infant cuts on his arms and legs. Asena, a great she-wolf with grey fur and sky-blue mane saved the boy and nursed him back to health. The boy eventually impregnated her and she gave birth to ten boys. Those ten boys were half man, half wolf. The very first werewolves. They ruled over the Empire, but many of the boys became bored of their home and left to explore the world. They went to Iceland, Germany, Scotland, England and many other places. The men would mate with women in those countries, thus passing on their half wolf traits to their offspring. That's how we came about. There are some who came from Greece who claim that they are descendants of Lycaon who tried to trick Zeus into eating human flesh and then was turned into a wolf by Zeus, but I don't believe that. They are just descendants of Asena like us."

I stared in disbelief of the story he had just said, but strangely it made sense. "Why are you killing all the humans now?"

Gregory frowned. "During the medieval times in Europe, there was a rash of wolf killings. Instead of realizing the reason there were so many more wolf kills was that the wolf population had gotten out of control, they started the search for werewolves. Unfortunately for some of us, we really did exist and lived in Europe at that time. I don't know how the notion of werewolves got into their heads, but they started looking. Soon after that they started searching for witches as well. I had many witch friends who died. It was horrible. We all went into hiding then. Some of us managed to come to America and start over here, but others went into the sewers with the vamp...with the others."

I shook my head. "What were you going to say?"

He shook his head back at me. "I can't tell you that part yet. I'm sure soon, but not yet. Anyway, the others decided it had been long enough and we planned our take over. I give it three months before the world is completely taken over by us preternaturals."

I shook my head. "What's a preternatural?"

He sighed. "I'm telling you too much already. Preternatural means exceeding what is natural or regular. All races that possess gifts, as you humans call them, are called preternaturals. Basically, anyone that has characteristics that surpass natural human abilities is a preternatural."

I nodded. "Like witches."

Gregory smiled. "Yes, like witches. Now let's play some more thirteen."

I smiled and nodded. "Alright. How long do you think it will be before Ares is back?"

Gregory smiled. "I'm not sure, but you don't have to worry about Ares. He is the toughest of us. Did he tell you that's how he became prince?"

I shook my head. "We haven't really talked much." I felt a blush starting and shook my head.

Gregory sighed. "Well, I will let Ares tell you about the ways to become powerful." He picked up the cards on the floor and started shuffling them. I turned and saw that Jason was staring at me curiously.

"What is it Jason?" I asked.

He looked down. "Nothing."

I laughed. "You can ask me whatever you want. I promise I won't get mad."

Jason looked up and smiled. "I was just trying to remember where I saw purple eyes before."

Gregory frowned. "Enough Jason."

Jason sighed. "Alright."

I frowned at Gregory. "What? Why can't he tell me where he has seen purple eyes before? It might help me find my mom."

Gregory shook his head. "Sorry. We can't tell you that. When Ares wants to, he will."

"Whatever. Let's play." I said to change the subject.

We played for a few more hours, but the sunlight started to peek through the curtains, and I couldn't stay awake anymore. Jason fell asleep on the floor, snoring softly. I stood up and started to walk back to my room when I felt Ares. I threw the front door open and ran out on to the front porch. I looked around, but couldn't see him anywhere. I inhaled and could smell him. *How the hell do I know it's him? Is this one of those weird things about being tied to him? I know he is here. Where is he?* I continued to scan the yard and turned as Gregory came out.

"What is it Artemis?" He asked me, looking around too.

"Ares is here, I can feel him and smell him, but I can't see him."

Gregory inhaled then nodded. "You're right. He must be close for me to be able to smell him, too. Come on, let's go look for him." I followed Gregory down the porch steps, still frantically searching for Ares. Gregory led us towards a large white warehouse and stopped me at the black metal door, "You can't come in here. I'll be right back."

I inhaled deeply and jumped up and down. "He's in there. Hurry."

Gregory stared at me strangely, but walked in the large warehouse, shutting the door tightly behind him. I paced back and forth in front of the door as I waited. People passed me with odd expressions on their faces, but I ignored them pacing back and forth and back and forth. Ten minutes passed, and I started to get worried as I reached for the door handle, the door swung open nearly hitting me in the face. Koda looked around and finally saw me standing next to him. He frowned. "What are you doing here?"

I sighed. "I can feel Ares and smell him. What's wrong? Is he hurt?"

Koda laughed and grabbed my shoulders stopping me from jumping around. "He's fine Artemis. Calm down. I'll go get him for you."

"Why can't I come in? Gregory went to get him for me ten minutes ago."

Koda sighed. "Just stay here, and I'll get him."

I snarled and crossed my arms over my chest. "Fine, but you better hurry."

Koda shut the door behind him as he went back inside.

I picked up my pacing route as I waited yet again for Ares to come out. I walked a few feet away from the door then spun around as I heard it open.

Ares stared at me then smiled and walked quickly towards me.

I walked as fast as I could without running to him wrapping my arms around his neck as he wrapped his around my waist. "Are you okay?" I asked frantically.

Ares nodded, inhaling my hair. "I am now."

I sighed in happiness and pulled back to kiss him on the lips softly. He kissed me back, pressing harder. I pulled away and asked, "What's going on? Why didn't you come see me?"

He frowned. "I was talking to our prisoner."

I gasped, "Is it my dad? Was it him that was taking the humans to find the wolves?"

Ares pulled away from me and nodded. "Yes, but your dad is not the prisoner I have. Darren got away before we could catch him."

I sighed. "Does that mean you are going to go after him?"

Ares shook his head. "I ran into Darius again and he said he will take care of it." I started to say something, but he held up his hand. "He promised not to kill him until you and I speak with Darren."

"Thanks." I realized that I still had my arms wrapped around his neck and pulled away from him blushing.

Ares laughed. "I wondered how long it would take you to pull away from me. I don't understand why you won't just enjoy it?"

"Because I shouldn't have such strong feelings for you so soon. It's not normal."

Ares smiled. "We aren't normal anyway. And by the way, Bret is doing well. We should be able to let him out tomorrow, to spend time with you."

I smiled. "That's great. Thank you." I sighed and looked back up at Ares. "Is it true that you are one of the strongest of the werewolves?"

Ares frowned. "Has Gregory been telling you stories?"

"He explained about Asena and Lycaon, but said it was your choice to tell me about how you became prince and how that works."

Ares smiled and extended his hand to me, waiting for me to take it. "I'll explain everything back in the house."

I took his hand reluctantly, but once our skin touched, I felt much better. We walked in silence back to Gregory's house and into my bedroom, so Jason could sleep. I sat cross-legged on my bed, with my back against the headboard, as Ares closed the bedroom door.

He sat down cross-legged facing me and smiled. "Alright, here it is. I come from a family of kings and queens who ruled humans in Europe. Of course, my ancestors are from Asena and that is where my slanted eyes are from." He noticed my shocked face and whispered, "Yes, I saw you looking at them." He shifted on the bed before continuing. "Anyway, I technically was a prince in Europe, but in the order of werewolves to be king or queen is by fighting. I fought my way up to Prince one hundred years ago, and have stayed there because no one has tried to fight me for that place. Darius just became king a few years ago, after defeating our old king. His wife, who happens to be my mother, got her place because her husband, the old king, made a decree that a king could choose his own queen or have the queen he wanted kill the old one or keep the current queen. Unfortunately for my mother Darius chose to keep her." Ares snarled as he finished his explanation.

I gaped at him, "Darius killed your step-dad and is sleeping with your mom?"

Ares snarled. "No one said they were doing anything like that. Although, sometimes the ruling pair do end up becoming a breeding pair. That is not the case with my mother and Darius."

I shrugged and couldn't help smiling a little. "Whatever helps you sleep at night."

Ares sighed. "Anyway, I killed Darius' son to become prince and I think that was his motivation to become king."

I asked, "Are you going to fight him to be king?"

Ares laughed bitterly. "Someday, but not anytime soon."

I stopped talking and stared at his thoughtful face. "Have you ever done modeling?"

Ares smiled and nodded. "I actually did. When I lived in London, I did some modeling for money. Why would you ask that?"

I blushed. "Don't make me say it."

Ares crawled forward on his hands and knees until his face was just in front of mine. "I love that you blush for me."

I looked up slowly, and my breath caught in my throat.

He is too handsome.

I reached out and stroked the side of his face with my hand. His muscles were hard as he clenched his jaw. I smiled. "Why are you clenching your jaw?"

He slowly relaxed his jaw and whispered, "I am trying to hold myself back."

I shook my head. "From what? I don't understand." I ran both my hands down the sides of his face and felt him clench his jaw again. I leaned forward and kissed the right side of his jaw softly. "Stop clenching your jaw."

He relaxed his jaw then leaned forward kissing me on the lips. His lips were burning hot and all I wanted was to kiss him back. I wrapped my arms around his neck and kissed him back, letting him feel how much I wanted him. He grabbed my legs and uncrossed them pulling me down the bed so that I was lying under him. Our lips melted together as we kissed. I felt his joy and it was suddenly my own.

Why had I been so reluctant to give into him?

I heard the door open, but did not stop. Ares tried to pull away, but I held him in place, kissing him harder and flicking my tongue across his lips. He groaned and pulled away from me, jumping off the bed.

I smiled at him then turned to the door.

Bret stared at me with wide eyes and I watched as the hurt sank into his eyes.

I sat up quickly and shook my head. "Bret, I…I didn't know you were there."

Bret shook his head, looking at the ground. "I should have knocked. I'm sorry."

He turned away to leave, and I jumped off the bed running to him. "Please don't...I'm sorry. I don't know what got into me."

Ares sighed. "I'll leave you two to talk." He started to walk past me, but I saw the sadness in his eyes.

"Ares, what's wrong?" I asked.

Ares shook his head smiling. "I know you are young and inexperienced, so I won't hold tonight against you."

I groaned. "What did I do?"

Bret sighed. "You are trying to please both of us and can't, Artemis. You tell me that you don't know what came over you, that you weren't in your right mind, but that means that you are telling Ares that what happened wasn't what you wanted. Either way you are hurting one of us. Just tell us the truth, don't try to please us."

I groaned and turned away from both of them. "I don't know what to say. Did I enjoy kissing Ares? Yes, but I didn't want it to happen in front of you, Bret."

Ares cleared his throat. "I know that you want to talk, but I can't let you two be alone while he is still adjusting to his instincts."

Bret growled. "I would never hurt her."

I scoffed. "No, not hurt me, just eat me."

Bret's eyes widened and then turned to Ares. "Did I try to eat her?"

Ares shook his head. "No, but you were saying that she smelled like food and that you *were* going to eat her. You didn't hurt her or touch her, though."

Bret grimaced. "And that's because you protected her, right?"

Ares nodded. "Yes, but you were not in your right mind."

Bret sighed. "I don't want to talk to her in front of you."

I turned to Ares. "Can we use the same deal that I had set up with you before?"

Ares groaned. "I don't know why you are trying to be secretive with me, but I'll agree to it. Koda!"

Koda appeared in the doorway without making a sound. "Yes?"

Ares smiled. "These two need to talk, but they can't be alone so you are going to stay here and make sure he doesn't try to eat her again." I cleared my throat and Ares sighed. "And whatever they say you can't tell me."

Koda frowned. "Are you sure about that last one?"

Ares looked at me and smiled. "For her, I'd do almost anything." He walked towards me then looked at Bret and sighed. "Good night, Artemis."

I kissed his cheek quickly. "Good night, Ares." He smiled and walked out of the room towards his bedroom.

Koda sat in the chair which was beside the bed.

Bret walked towards me slowly with his hands out, but when he was close enough to touch me, he dropped his hands. "I'm sorry I tried to eat you."

I laughed. "It's alright, Bret. I know it wasn't really you. I'm sorry I got you into all of this and you ended up becoming one of us."

Bret shrugged. "There are a lot of upsides to being a werewolf, especially since they are taking over the world now."

I groaned. "Don't remind me."

Bret laughed. "I know. I'm torn about how to deal with it as well. At least our town is okay."

I nodded. "Yeah." I looked up at his face and realized that I no longer thought of him as very attractive.

I guess when you have to compare him to the God of War, he isn't really that handsome. Still attractive, but no contest. Okay, Ares isn't the mythical God of War, but he is very handsome.

I groaned. "I'm sorry about everything, Bret. I didn't want any of this to happen. The plan was that I would leave, and the town would go on like normal while I started my new life with Ares. You would stay home and fall in love with one of the local girls and live happily ever after."

Bret shook his head, smiling. "I already fell in love with one of the local girls."

"Bret, I can't be with you. Whether I like it or not, Ares and I do have a connection. I can't explain it, but I crave...I...ugh! I don't want to talk to you about this, but I want you to know."

Bret sighed. "I can see how you two look at each other. I know you have feelings for him."

I shook my head. "It's deeper than that. We are connected so much that when he feels sad, I feel sad. It's why I could feel him yesterday. He was worried and I started getting worried. I thought he was in trouble and had to find him." The truth to that statement shocked me. Until then, I hadn't even been aware of that fact.

Bret frowned at me. "That's not possible to be like that."

Koda scoffed. We turned to look at him and he shrugged. "Sorry, but you two do not know about the connections our kind can have. If Artemis's father had taught her, she would have felt similar to that with Darren. She could have been connected to him like Ares, but obviously not the physical attraction part."

I shivered in disgust. "Thanks for that visual."

Koda rolled his eyes. "Don't you understand? If you form a connection with another werewolf you feel what they feel. Now, of course, you and Ares' connection is a lot different because your ties are like when you bind yourself to someone, but without the death factor. What I'm saying is that although Ares and Artemis's connection is very unique, you can have a much smaller version with any werewolf you wanted."

I nodded. "I understand."

Bret shrugged. "Whatever you say. The point is that I love you Artemis and that won't change. I know you are with Ares and can't be with me, but I want to be close to you. I want to stay with your group."

I asked, "Even if that means having to see me *with* Ares?"

Bret sighed. "Yes. I will have to deal with it."

I smiled and hugged him tightly. "Thank you for staying with me."

Bret hugged me back and kissed the top of my head. "Anytime."

Koda stood up. "Alright, time to go."

Bret kissed my cheek quickly then walked out the bedroom door. Koda smiled. "Good night, Artemis."

I smiled back at him. "Night, Koda." I waited until Koda closed the door to throw myself on my bed burying my face in my pillows.

Why me? Why do I have to deal with two men? What happens if I start to develop feelings for Bret? Oh God!

I shook my head and started thinking about Darren. I tried to focus on my thoughts, but sleep overtook me.

CHAPTER FIVE

I woke up slowly, although I wasn't sure what had woken me up. I tried to roll over, but something held me down around my waist. I started to panic and looked down to see an arm lying over my stomach. *An arm?* I rolled over and bumped noses with Ares. I jumped out of the bed and snarled. "What are you doing?"

Ares woke up and smiled at me. "Good morning. Did you sleep well?"

"Ares what are you doing in bed with me?"

He whispered, "I heard you crying and you sounded scared, so I came in here to check on you. You wouldn't stop shaking, and I was worried that you were going to shift for the first time so I laid down next to you to take the transformation from you. When I laid down you stopped shaking and crying and went quiet. I was too worried about you changing, though, so I stayed with you."

I stared at him in disbelief. "How do I know you're telling the truth?"

He smiled. "If I wanted to sleep with you, I wouldn't sneak in here. You know that I have been behaving myself and letting you decide what happens between us."

I sighed. "I know that. I'm sorry. You just caught me off-guard. And how can you take my transformation?"

"Only those with enough power can take someone's transformation. It's one of the ways I became prince. I took my opponent's transformation from him and changed myself when he couldn't to kill him. We are a lot easier to kill in human form."

I gaped at him. "You killed to get to your spot?"

He nodded. "I had to. I have to take the throne away from Darius and free my mother. I already told you that."

I sighed and nodded. "I know."

He patted the bed. "Come back to bed, it's still too early."

I shook my head. "No. Get out."

He groaned. "You were fine just a minute ago."

I snarled. "I was asleep and didn't know you were there."

He smiled. "You said my name."

I gasped. "No, I didn't. You're lying."

He held up three fingers in a boy scout salute. "I swear on my mother's grave that you did."

I blushed. "Great." I turned away from him and heard the bed move as he stood up.

He wrapped his arms around my waist and placed his face next to mine. "It was very sweet to hear you say my name in your sleep."

I blushed deeper and tried to pull away from him, but he just spun me around to face him. He kissed my lips softly and crept backwards towards the bed. "I promise I will do nothing but cuddle with you while we sleep."

I blushed a shade darker. "Alright, but if you try anything, you have to leave."

Ares smiled widely and nodded. "Promise." He lay down and scooted back so there was plenty of room for me to get on. I climbed into the bed, facing away from him. He spooned his body to mine and sighed in contentment. "It's no different than you sleeping in the same bed with Bret."

I closed my eyes and relaxed against him as our bodies warmed up the covers again. "It is very different than sleeping with Bret," I whispered.

He kissed the back of my head then wrapped his arm back around my waist, pulling me tighter against him. I tensed for a second, but then relaxed. I felt safe again and fell into a deep sleep.

Ares shook my arm. "Artemis, get up."

I groaned and sat up. "What? I'm up."

He pulled me back off the bed holding me in his arms. "Someone is here."

I opened my eyes and stared at a dark shadow in one corner of the bedroom. "What is that? Why is that shadow so strange looking?"

Ares snarled. "Why are you here? And why sneak in?"

I watched in amazement as a man stepped out of the shadow making it disappear. I gasped. "Holy shit. How did he do that?"

The man bowed at the waist and smiled at me revealing fangs. "My apologies for sneaking in, Ares. I wanted to see your *passt genau* while she was not hiding her feelings for you."

I snarled. "Word travels fast I take it."

Ares sighed. "Victor, this is Artemis. Artemis, this is Victor. I almost killed you before I smelled you, you know?"

Victor laughed and it made me shiver, thinking of sexual things.

Ares snarled. "Knock off the voice powers."

Victor bowed at the waist again. "My apologies. Your *pass*...Artemis has an aura I seem drawn to test."

Ares sighed, setting me down on my feet beside him. "I know what you mean."

I stared at the two of them and asked, "Why are we suddenly friendly with the weird guy with fangs who appeared out of a shadow?"

Victor blinked then asked, "She does not know about us yet?"

Ares shook his head. "I have much to tell you, old friend."

I gasped. "Friend? This freak...no offense...is your friend?"

Ares snarled. "Be nice, Artemis. He is not a freak, just a jerk. And yes, he is my friend."

"Great. Well, I need breakfast," I said. I had no idea why I was able to accept this all so quickly, but not really having an option seemed a likely reason.

Ares nodded, "I'm hungry, too."

Victor smiled flashing his fangs again. "I could eat."

Ares snarled. "You be nice, too, Victor. She knows nothing of you, so stop."

Victor sighed. "Very well, but I really could use something to eat."

I walked from the bedroom with them following me. Koda, Matt and Gregory stood at the end of the hallway ready to attack. I smiled. "Sorry boys, but it's a friend of Ares apparently."

Koda and Matt smiled at Victor as he walked out. Victor shook their hands. "Hey, Matt and Koda. How are my favorite twins doing?"

I stopped walking and turned back. "Twins? You guys never told me that."

Matt shrugged. "You were a little preoccupied with Ares to notice, Love."

I stared at Matt's face and his blue Mohawk then turned to Koda and gasped. "Holy shit! You guys are identical twins minus the different colored Mohawks!"

Koda smiled shaking his green Mohawk. "I was the first one to do the Mohawk, but he had to copy me."

Matt rolled his eyes. "I didn't even know you had one. I was in London while you were in Germany with Ares. There's no way for me to have known."

I shook my head at the siblings and walked to the kitchen where Gregory had started taking out food. I saw a bag filled with red liquid and asked, "What is that?"

Gregory smiled. "Food for Victor."

I frowned. "What the hell is it?"

Gregory shook his head smiling. "I'm not spilling the beans on this one."

Ares and Victor walked in whispering, but when they saw me, they stopped.

I scoffed. "Real subtle, I have no idea you were talking about me just now."

Ares smiled and walked towards me. "What else should we talk about?"

I shrugged and stood on tiptoe to kiss his cheek. "Whatever you want, *great* Prince."

Ares laughed. "You're a smart ass? Great."

"I *was* raised by a man," I reminded him with a smile.

Victor frowned and asked, "How long have you been together?"

Ares kissed my cheek then went and grabbed food from Gregory. "Two days."

Victor's eyes opened in surprise. "Then she really is your *passt genau.*"

Ares took a bite out of the piece of raw steak he was holding and nodded. "I wouldn't lie about that. She answered my call from a state away."

Victor turned to me, and for the first time I noticed his eyes, solid black like the pupil had taken over. Victor asked, "Is it true that you haven't changed yet?"

I nodded and licked my lips. "Can I ask you something?"

He nodded.

I cleared my throat, "Why are your eyes black?"

He laughed, making me moan in pleasure.

Ares growled loudly and rushed to stand between me and Victor. "Knock it off! You are my friend, but don't push me too far."

Victor bowed at the neck. "I apologize to you both."

I grabbed Ares' arm and pulled him back to me. "I'm sorry to cause drama between you two."

Victor smiled. "It's not your fault. And I'll let Ares explain my eyes later."

I groaned. "Why is it that everyone makes Ares tell me things? I'm not going to freak out and run away if one of you tells me."

Ares frowned. "What else are you waiting for me to tell you?"

I pointed to the bag of red liquid. "What that is?"

Ares' eyes widen, and he turned to stare at Gregory. "You didn't tell her?"

He shook his head. "Nope, I thought you should be the one to explain about Victor. She obviously has no clue."

I snarled. "I'm not stupid."

Gregory shook his head. "I didn't say that. I just meant that you have no idea what Victor is."

Victor frowned. "Why doesn't she know what I am?"

Ares answered before I could. "Her idiot father decided he wasn't going to tell her about being a werewolf until she changed for the first time. Problem is that she has been fighting her change since elementary school and he stopped her change when she answered my call. She was never taught about us or you or any of the others."

My eyes widened and I asked Ares, "Others? What do you mean others? Oh, wait like the witches?"

Victor shook his head with a sneer. "What a fool. We don't have very much time to teach her, though."

Ares sighed. "I know. I was hoping you would help."

Victor smiled. "I would be honored to."

I walked to Gregory and asked, "Do you have any real food?"

Gregory frowned. "You really should eat one of these steaks. Especially if you are going to continue to fight your change."

I sighed and nodded. "All right, fine. But can you at least warm it up?"

Gregory smiled and nodded. "Sure."

I walked back over to Ares and put my hand on the inside of his arm. I suddenly felt scared and pressed my body to his arm. He stopped talking to Victor and looked down at me. "What's wrong?"

I shrugged. "I'm not sure, I just suddenly got really scared."

Ares sniffed the air then picked me up in his arms holding me tight against him. "Someone is here. Victor, did you bring anyone with you?"

Victor shook his head sniffing the air. "No, but I know who it is." Victor walked quickly towards the front door, throwing it open. I stared at the tall man standing on the porch looking in. He looked like Victor's twin, but without the black eyes. Victor hissed. "What are you doing here?"

The man frowned. "Is that any way to treat your father and your king?"

I stiffened in Ares' arms and wrapped my arms around his neck so that I was pressed tighter to him. Ares rubbed my leg with the hands that were holding them and whispered, "It's alright, you don't have to be scared of him while I'm here."

I nodded and pressed my forehead to his cheek, inhaling his smell and calming my nerves.

Victor's father walked into the house and bowed at the waist to Ares and me. "Greetings Ares, Prince of the Werewolves."

Ares set me down beside him and bowed at the waist to him. "Greetings Maurice, King of the Vampires. To what do we owe the pleasure of your visit?"

I gasped as he said the word, "vampires" and moved a step closer to him so that I was touching my entire left side to his entire right side. *How come I didn't guess that? Fangs equals vampire. Duh.* Maurice stared at me in confusion then looked up at Ares. "Did I do something wrong?"

Ares laughed and shook his head. "No, King Maurice..."

Maurice shook his head. "Just Maurice, Ares."

Ares smiled. "Of course. No, Maurice. She is, well...I would like to speak with you and Victor about this in private if you wouldn't mind."

Maurice stared at me second before inhaling. "She's a werewolf, but that other smell and those eyes. I know them, but can't think of where. Let's go talk before I figure it out and give something away you did not want her to know."

Ares started to walk to the living room with Maurice and Victor and I grabbed his arm, pulling him back to me. I whispered, "Don't leave me alone."

He sensed the worry in my voice and smiled. "It's alright, Koda and Matt will protect you." He looked up at Koda and Matt and smiled, "Right?" Koda and Matt nodded in unison with serious faces on. Ares snarled. "And you both know that if anything happens to her that I *will* have to punish you."

Koda smiled. "I would have it no other way."

Matt snarled. "Death may be a good punishment for that much of a failure."

I frowned at them. "Why are you so willing to be punished if something happens to me? It makes no sense. You don't even know me."

Ares sighed and shook his head. "I have to go. Keep her safe." I watched with growing nervousness as Ares walked from the kitchen to the living room. Once he was out of my sight, I started to shift from foot-to-foot.

Matt sighed. "Artemis, it's okay. Victor and Ares have been friends since they were born and Maurice will not do anything to any of them because of that."

I sighed and walked towards Koda. Koda stood perfectly still as I leaned my head against his chest. I exhaled a shaky breath and said, "I know you don't know me and I don't have any right to ask, but could you just hold me for a second? I would ask Bret, but he is not allowed to be alone with me, and I don't fully trust him."

Koda exhaled the breath he was holding and said, "I'm sorry about Bret. And I will do whatever you ask me to do."

I wrapped my arms around his waist as he wrapped his arms around my shoulders. I whispered, "I'm sorry for causing so much drama here. I really am not a drama queen, by any means."

Matt snorted. "You apologize too much, Artemis. We know you

aren't a drama queen, and the drama that has been happening is not your fault."

I turned to him and could see the jealousy in his eyes. I pulled away from Koda and walked towards him. "Why are you jealous? I did not pick Koda over you, I just assumed Ares would feel less threatened if he found Koda hugging me then you."

Matt rolled his eyes. "I think Ares would be mad to find any of us hugging you, but if you are in need of consoling he would get over it. And I am jealous, but I'm trying to get over it."

I stood one foot from him and looked up at his handsome face. "I swear I did not pick Koda because I favor him."

Matt smiled. "Love, it's alright. I am just jealous when it comes to my brothers."

I frowned. "Brothers? Who is your other brother?"

Matt frowned and looked over my head at Koda. "Shit."

Koda sighed. "Yes, shit is right."

I sighed. "Just let Ares tell me. I'm used to it by now."

Matt smiled and placed his hand against my face. "Thanks, Love."

I frowned at him. "Why do you call me Love?"

He shrugged. "I call most girls Darlin or something like that, but you are definitely Love. Mine or not, that is who you are."

I blushed and looked down at my hands.

Matt laughed and whispered, "I love that you blush."

I pulled away from him and walked towards my bedroom. I heard them following me and sighed. "Can we go outside?"

They both answered, "No," in unison.

I groaned. "Fine, then can we sit at the dining table and play a game?" I turned around and looked up at their matching faces.

Koda shrugged. "Sure."

I smiled and walked back to the table and sat down at the head. Koda and Matt sat across from each other, staring at me. I smiled. "We're going to play one hundred questions."

Matt groaned. "You tricked us."

I smiled and nodded. "Sort of. So, I'll go first. Why am I so attached to Ares already?"

Koda smiled. "You are his *passt genau,* his perfect match. Only the strongest of our kind get one. You are born with a sort of mental and physical connection to him. Almost like you were literally *made* for him."

I asked, "How many before have had a match?"

Matt tapped his chin in thought for a moment. "Just one set that I know of, the Mother and Father."

"Who are they?" I asked.

Matt sighed and put his hand against his forehead. "I can't believe your father never told you any of this. The Mother is Asena..."

I interrupted him. "Oh, yeah, the she-wolf that saved the baby then ended up mating with him to create werewolves."

Matt nodded. "Yes, and the boy she saved is who we refer to as the Father."

I nodded. "I understand that part, but how do you know that they were born for each other? What if it was just a coincidence?"

Matt shook his head. "It was not a coincidence. The boy sent out a call like the one Ares did and Asena answered."

I shook my head. "But he was human, not a werewolf."

Matt shrugged. "I don't make the stories; I just tell them. That's what happened according to Asena."

I shrugged. "If you say so. Okay, your turn."

Matt and Koda looked at each other for a moment then Matt asked, "Have you ever slept with Bret?"

I felt my eyes widen and shook my head. "No, never. I'm a virgin."

Koda smiled. "Have you ever kissed Bret?"

I shrugged. "Not like a boyfriend type of kiss, but a friend kiss. He did kiss me the night Ares called to me, but I didn't kiss him back."

Koda and Matt exchanged a look then Matt asked, "Have you ever done anything with Bret or any other boy?"

I shook my head. "I haven't even touched another boy besides Bret, well, and Billy, but I didn't do anything then either."

Koda asked, "Why not?"

I stared at him for a second then sighed. "I've always been the outcast in my town. Bret was the only one who would be my friend, let alone touch me. And Billy was only talking to me and stuff towards the end. I think he was just trying to...well you know."

Matt frowned, "Your dad never explained why to you?"

I frowned and asked, "He knew why?"

Matt and Koda nodded in unison.

Koda said, "It's because you're a werewolf. Humans can sense that we are predators and fear us. Bret must have just ignored the feeling because of your physical appearance."

I felt the first tear fall down my face and asked, "What's life like when you are raised with others of our kind?"

Matt shrugged. "Like the humans except that we are much closer, like a family. I firmly believe that your childhood would have been a lot easier if you had been around your own kind."

I felt the tears falling and asked, "How close is the nearest group?"

Koda whispered, "This one and it's about one hundred miles."

I stood up and started to walk towards my bedroom when Ares walked into the dining room. He frowned and walked quickly to me, wrapping his arms around me. "What's wrong?"

I shook my head. "It's nothing, Ares."

He growled. "What did you two say to her?"

Koda said. "She asked us about why she was an outcast with the humans and what it would have been like to grow up around us."

Ares sighed. "Sorry, Koda."

Koda laughed. "Don't worry about it, Ares."

Ares pushed me back and said, "I'm sorry about your father. If I could change time for you I would."

I nodded and wiped at the tears on my face. "I know Ares. It's alright."

He snarled. "It's not alright. I'm going to find your father."

I shook my head. "You can't leave me again. Please!" I grabbed both of his arms and gripped as hard as I could.

Ares stared in shock at my face, and Matt cleared his throat, making me release my hold a little.

Matt said, "She is starting to show the symptoms, Ares."

Ares looked over my head at Matt. "Describe."

Matt said, "She started to panic when she watched you walk away from her and grew increasingly nervous when you were out of her sight. She had to have Koda hold her to stop her panic."

Ares looked down at me and asked, "Is that true?"

I felt the blush on my cheeks, looked down, and lied, "No."

"You have no reason to be embarrassed. It's part of what we are. It means that you are finally letting go and soon you and I will be fully connected."

I shrugged, still looking down. "So, I was a little nervous."

Matt gave a short bark of a laugh. "You were about to run after him."

"Shut up, Matt."

Ares shook his head, smiling. "It's really alright, Artemis. I promise I won't leave you unless I have to."

I felt my heart pick up and shook my head. "That's not a good enough promise." I growled. "I don't like this feeling."

Ares nodded. "I understand, Artemis. I feel the same way."

I stared at him and said, "You don't act like it."

He smiled. "I hide it. Wouldn't you think I was a little odd if I got all nervous when I walked away from you?"

I nodded. "Yeah, I guess you're right."

He hugged me against him. "We'll get through this first part and get on to the easier parts soon. I came in here to get you, though. Will you come with me to speak with Victor and Maurice?"

I shrugged. "As long as I can touch you while I'm near them."

Ares nodded. "Deal. I'm not sure why you are scared of them though. Your werewolf side should make you feel safe around them."

I shrugged. "Maybe it's my other side."

Ares frowned. "Yes, probably. I hope Maurice and I are wrong about what you might be."

I frowned. "What is that?"

Ares shook his head. "I can't tell you right now. Come on." I let him lead me by the hand to the living room where Maurice and Victor sat in chairs facing the couch. Ares sat down on the couch pulling me down with him. I scooted as close as I could without being in his lap.

Victor smiled. "I promise we won't hurt you or Ares."

I nodded and licked my lips nervously. "Okay."

Maurice smiled, making his face look less frightening. "How old are you?"

"Eighteen."

He frowned. "How old were you when you stopped your first transformation?"

I shrugged. "I think ten."

His eyes widened a little bit, almost unnoticeable if you weren't watching for it. "Have you ever changed?"

I shook my head. "No, I almost did when Ares called to me or whatever, but my dad threw me in the creek and stopped it."

Victor asked, "Do you remember hearing Ares' call?"

"When he howled on TV? If that was his call, then, yeah."

Victor asked, "Do you remember answering?"

I shook my head. "No, I was watching the TV and thinking how gorgeous he was in wolf form and that it was strange that I wasn't afraid of him at all when I saw him killing people, then I started convulsing. Then my dad threw me in the creek and put me to bed.

When I woke up, I felt something was wrong, no, I thought wrong, but it was more like I felt drawn outside and there was Ares and Koda and Matt."

Maurice asked, "Why don't you want to change?"

"I don't want to answer that in front of Ares." I said softly.

Ares groaned. "You might as well, because I'm going to be asking you anyway."

I groaned and scooted a little way away from Ares, not looking at him. "I don't want to change yet. If there is a chance that I could be human..."

Maurice interrupted me. "No. I'm sorry, child, but even if you don't change, you are still half werewolf and half..."

Ares cleared his throat stopping Maurice from finishing. I growled and glared at Ares. "Why won't you let him tell me?"

Ares smiled. "It is too dangerous for you to know."

I snarled at him. "Just tell me."

He snarled back. "No, and watch yourself. I will not allow you to challenge my authority."

I sighed and pushed down my anger, staring down at my hands. "Sorry, Ares. It's hard to control my anger sometimes."

He sighed. "I understand. If you would change it would be a lot easier."

I groaned. "I get it, alright? I need to change. Just give me some time."

Ares tilted my head up and smiled at me. "I'll give you however much time you need."

I smiled back at him and then looked at Victor and Maurice who were watching us intently. I pulled away from Ares and blushed. "Sorry. I forgot you two were here."

Maurice spoke softly, "She is delightful, Ares, but you must teach her how to act properly."

Ares nodded. "I'm sorry, Maurice. I didn't know you were coming otherwise I would have."

Victor laughed. "I think you should leave her be. It's nice to have someone not treating you differently."

Ares smiled. "She's good at it."

I stared at the three of them. "I think I missed something?" They all nodded, and I shrugged. "Whatever."

Maurice asked, "Do you remember your mother?"

I shook my head. "No, she left when I was five years old."

Maurice's eyes widened considerably from shock. "When you were five? Exactly?"

I nodded. "I remember it because it was the day before my birthday."

Victor asked, "Did your father ever tell you about her?"

I shook my head. "At first, he said she was going on a trip, but the more years that passed he just said that he didn't want to talk about it. I have seen a picture of her, but that's it. I stopped asking Darren about her when I turned ten."

Victor asked, "When you started having the seizures?"

I nodded. "Yeah, but I guess that was really me trying to change."

Maurice nodded. "Yes, it was."

I sighed and said, "My mother left because of me, and I know that. I don't know why, but someday I will."

Maurice smiled. "I'm sure you will. Now, what did your father tell you about yourself? How did he explain your purple eyes?"

"I didn't know I had purple eyes until Ares came to get me. I always had contacts in and we didn't have a mirror in the house. He always made me change out my contacts in the bathroom, too. It's why Bret didn't know either."

Victor asked, shock evident in his tone, "You didn't have a mirror?"

I shook my head. Ares explained, "She didn't even know what she looked like until she came here and I made her look in the mirror."

Maurice rubbed his chin. "I'm beginning to understand Ares'

desire to find your father. To not tell your daughter about her heritage or to let her meet others of her own kind is monstrous."

I looked at Maurice. "Can I ask you a question?"

"Of course."

I whispered, "What are you?"

Maurice smiled and looked at Ares. "May I?"

Ares nodded. "Yes. I was going to have Victor tell her later anyway."

Maurice smiled and said, "Do not be frightened child, I will not harm you, alright?"

I nodded and moved closer to Ares. He held my hand and smiled. I watched as Maurice looked down at the ground and inhaled. I could feel a strange pressure, like the tide pulling at my legs, moving towards him. He looked up at me, and I gasped, jumping over the back of the couch behind Ares.

Maurice's eyes were solid black like Victor's and he smiled revealing long fangs where his small canines used to be. He said, "I told you not to be frightened."

I nodded and swallowed. "I know, but I couldn't help it."

Maurice smiled flashing his fangs again. "I will not hurt you; I have already eaten today."

I felt my heart speed up and asked, "Please tell me what you are."

He looked down and I felt that tide push past me, leaving his body. He looked back up and his face and teeth were back to normal. "I'm a vampire."

"Like Dracula?" I asked curiously.

Maurice groaned and rolled his eyes. "Honestly, Vlad was always looking for attention. That bastard."

I stared at him in shock. "Dracula was real?"

He nodded. "Of course he is."

I asked, "The fog that was killing people that was vampires, wasn't it?"

He nodded again. "Yes. We were trying to hide our existence."

"Why are vampires and werewolves working together? I thought they hated each other?"

Ares laughed and said, "That's a story we made up so the humans would not hunt us both at the same time."

I frowned. "What do you mean?"

Victor smiled. "Vampires and werewolves have been allies since we found out about each other. The original vampires could not go out in the sunlight so the werewolves became our daytime bodyguards. It was mutually beneficial because they would protect us during the day and then the vampires would work at night and pay for everything for the werewolves. When the witch hunts of the seventeenth century and werewolf hunts of the eighteenth century happened, we decided it was time to go into hiding and wait for our chance to take over the world."

I nodded. "I understand about waiting to take over, but I had no idea about you guys being allies."

Victor laughed. "Neither do the humans. It really is a great plan. So far, the humans just think that the wolves are so fast that when a human walks in the fog, they just run over and kill them."

"I remember seeing the video. It was creepy to see the fog move." I stared at Victor for a second until all of the pieces clicked into place. "You can change into fog! You can shapeshift!"

Victor and Maurice smiled. Maurice said, "She is very smart."

Ares nodded. "Yes. Smart like a werewolf."

"Is that how he formed out of the shadow?" I asked curiously,

Ares nodded again. "Yes. They can shift to shadow, mist, wolves, fog, bat, rats and some others I don't remember."

My eyes widened at the extensive list. How would you even be able to tell the difference between a vampire in animal form and a regular animal? They could have been around me all of my life and I never knew it. "Good thing you are on our side."

All three men laughed, causing me to blush and looked down at my hands. Maurice asked, "Do you know what a vampire is?"

I shook my head. "Only what I've seen in movies."

Maurice said, "We are no more than a cursed soul. Like the werewolves are cursed with lycanthropy."

I looked up at him in shock. "So, you aren't a living dead monster?"

Maurice frowned, wrinkles appearing on his forehead. "Definitely not. I can't believe humans even believe that kind of thing."

Victor sighed. "It's not like they came up with it on their own. One of us told them that."

"Okay, so you just have a curse which gave you fangs and the ability to shapeshift and you have to eat blood to survive?"

Victor and Maurice nodded.

I shrugged. "Okay. So, is that all? Can I go eat?"

Ares raised one of his eyebrows. "You aren't scared, nervous or going to ask questions?"

I shook my head. "I can't be prejudiced. I mean it's not like they chose it."

Ares smiled. "Well, that's refreshing to hear."

My stomach growled loudly. "Can I please get some food?"

Ares nodded. "Sure."

I stood and quickly walked to the kitchen.

Koda stood by the fridge holding a piece of steak.

I took it from him and threw it in the microwave turning it on for forty seconds. I watched as the steak rotated inside the microwave.

Koda cleared his throat behind me making me turn to him. "Are you alright?" he asked.

I shrugged. "Yeah, why wouldn't I be?"

He frowned and started to reach a hand out towards my face. "You're pale."

I focused on my body and noticed that I was shaking. I held up my hands and felt my eyes widen as I saw them shaking uncontrollably.

Koda grabbed my hands and stared into my eyes. "What's wrong, Artemis?"

"It's that feeling again. Like the one I had when Maurice was at the door. I'm just suddenly *terrified*."

Koda picked me up in his arms and ran into the living room.

Ares snarled when he saw me in Koda's arms, but stopped when he saw my face. He asked, "What's wrong?"

Koda said, "She's scared. Her hands are shaking really bad, and she said it's the same feeling she got when Maurice was at the door."

Ares turned to Maurice. "Did you bring someone with you?"

Maurice stood and shook his head. "No." He inhaled and then spit. "That's not a vampire. It's an—"

Before he could finish his sentence, the wall to the living room smashed into pieces.

Koda turned his back to the wall and crouched down to protect me from the flying pieces.

I heard the popping and snapping of bones telling me that someone was changing into a wolf and tried to look, but Koda was suddenly running through the house.

I held on to his neck as hard as I could as he ran with me.

He turned his shoulder towards the bedroom wall and smashed through it.

I gasped as the sun shone in my eyes. We started running through town, in a blur of colors.

Koda kicked open the door to the concrete warehouse, never missing a beat. "Bret!" He yelled.

Bret appeared in front of us out of nowhere and stared at my face. "What happened?"

I tried to frown, but suddenly couldn't move. I gasped for air and stared at Bret's worried face.

Koda looked down and growled, "Shit!" He set me down on the floor on my back and ripped open my shirt.

I tried to protest, but couldn't do anything.

Bret held down my arms, although unnecessarily, and whispered, "This is going to hurt."

I tried to look down at what was happening, but my entire body was numb.

Koda inhaled then I felt something rip out of my chest.

I screamed in pain and then couldn't breathe again. I gasped for air and started to flail, but a short man with glasses squatted down beside me and spoke in a soothing tone. I stopped flailing and sat still as I felt him poking below my chest.

He pushed down on one spot, and I cringed, but still couldn't get any air. A sharp snap startled me, then I inhaled and air rushed down my throat and filled up my lungs.

I breathed in deep and held the air in for a second as my throat burned from the oxygen it finally received.

Bret stroked the side of my face as I relearned how to breathe.

Koda's face appeared above mine. He asked, "Are you doing alright?"

I whispered, "Better now. What happened?"

His face was guarded as he tried to hide his true emotions from me. "A piece of wood pierced your lung."

I blinked at him. "How am I breathing then?"

He smiled. "You aren't human, Artemis. We heal a lot faster than humans."

"Well, I guess it's a good thing I'm not human then. Ares would be really mad at you."

Koda groaned. "Don't remind me. He's already going to be pissed that I let you get hurt at all."

I sat up and saw the children huddled in the back corner with two large wolves standing in front of them. I looked up at Koda. "What's going on?"

His lips twitched as he snarled. "Ogres are attacking the village. That's why you got scared, because you could smell them. Stupid creatures. Come on, we have to get you out of the village."

Large explosions and screams sounded outside of the warehouse. I stared at the children and shook my head. "Not if the children are staying here."

Koda groaned and bent down so that our cheeks were touching as he whispered in my ear, "They are not as important as you. We can make more children, but we cannot replace you."

I gasped and pulled away from him. "That's horrible! I won't leave."

Koda snarled and reached down to grab me, but Bret pulled me backwards and crouched down in front of me in an attack stance. Koda shook his head. "Back off, Bret. I'm not going to hurt her. I just want to take her to safety."

"She doesn't want to leave," Bret said with clenched fists.

Koda growled, his eyes turning solid black. "Do you want her to die, Bret?"

Bret slowly stood up and sighed. "No."

Koda nodded. "Neither do I. Now come on and help me protect her while we leave the village." The sounds of fighting continued outside as they talked.

Bret turned towards me, and I jumped up and backwards out of his reach. "No. I'm staying here. Someone has to protect these children."

Koda motioned at the wolves and children. "There are two guards in front of them already."

I shook my head fiercely. "What if that's not enough? If I leave and then find out later that these kids were killed, I won't ever be able to forgive myself."

Koda smiled, his eyes back to his natural blue. "You said you wouldn't forgive Ares for turning Bret, but you seem to be getting along just fine."

I snarled. "Only because Bret is okay with being a werewolf."

Bret laughed. "Okay? I'm ecstatic! These new abilities are amazing."

"Anyway, it's not fair to compare that to the current situation. It's almost impossible for me to harbor hard feelings for Ares. It's so frustrating."

Koda nodded and I realized that he and Bret had moved closer to me while I was ranting.

I started to jump backwards, but Koda grabbed my arm and held me against him. I struggled as hard as I could, but he held on to me.

He picked me up in his arms and looked back over his shoulder. "You coming, Bret?"

"No, I'm going to stay here to help guard the kids," Bret answered.

I leaned over the top of Koda's shoulder to look at Bret. He smiled at me and I shook my head. "Bret, you don't have to. You can come with us." A loud explosion made me jump in Koda's arms.

He shook his head. "Koda can protect you. I'll help the kids."

"Thanks, Bret."

He nodded and pushed Koda. "No problem, Chicky. I'll see you soon."

My throat was dry and it was becoming difficult to get words out. "Alright."

Koda whispered, "Now tuck into as small a ball as possible against me and hold on."

I wrapped my arms around his neck and did as he asked.

He wrapped his arms around me and ran out of the warehouse through the door Bret held open.

I gasped at what I saw as we came out. All of the houses were on fire and bodies littered the ground. Most were thankfully ogres, but there were some werewolves.

Koda pushed my face down and started running as fast as he could. The air whipped around us as we were going much faster than humanly possible. The sound of fighting and screams slowly died away until the only sound I heard was the beating of Koda's heart. His heartbeat did not speed up as he ran, but stayed a constant steady thrum. I felt my eyes beginning to close and shook my head, but it wasn't enough. Slowly, sleep won and I slept without dreaming.

CHAPTER SIX

I opened my eyes slowly and found myself lying on top of Koda in a parallel line with him, with my head on his chest and the rest of our body parts lining up. I lifted my head up slowly and looked around. We were lying in the middle of a forest in the dark of night. The forest was too dense to be able to see any stars as I looked up.

Koda whispered, "The ground is really hard and this was the only way I could think to keep you comfortable."

I smiled at him. "Thanks, but you really didn't have to do that. It's not fair that you are uncomfortable."

He shrugged. "I'm fine. I'm used to sleeping on the hard ground. Although it would have been better in wolf form, but I didn't want to scare you."

I laughed at the image. "That would have been interesting. Would you like me to get off you now?"

He smiled at me seductively. "Only if you want. I'm pretty happy." I smiled back at him, unsure what he meant until I felt him flexing under my lower body.

I hopped up off of him and turned away as the blush spread over my entire face.

Koda laughed. "Wow. I didn't expect that reaction out of you. Hasn't that ever happened with Bret before?"

I groaned and stayed facing away from him. "Yes, it has, but you aren't Bret. You're Koda, and I barely know you."

Koda sighed. "Well you better get to know me fast because we are going to be spending the rest of our lives together."

I turned around and stared at him. "What do you mean by that? Did something happen to Ares?"

He smiled. "Calm down. Nothing happened to him. I just mean that I am Ares' pack and guard and I'm guessing yours, too, and that I will be alive hopefully as long as you, which is going to be hundreds of years."

I stared into his blue eyes and whispered, "Are you only protecting me because you are afraid of Ares' discipline?"

He stared back into my eyes and whispered, "No. I'm protecting you because I can see what you will become· and I have spent time with you and I couldn't bear the thought of you being hurt or...or dying. I fear it would tear me apart as much as it would Ares."

He sat up, pulled me down so that I was now sitting in his lap with my legs around his sides, and stroked the side of my face softly. "I promise to protect you from whatever tries to cause you harm, whether it be another person or even Ares."

I nodded, unable to speak.

He leaned forward and kissed my lips. I felt a spark flare up in the core of my body, but ignored it, suddenly overwhelmed with a strange sensation.

I kissed Koda back, forcing his mouth open with my teeth.

He groaned in pleasure and wrapped his arms around me, pressing us together as he deepened the kiss. He leaned forward, making me lie backwards on to the ground and pressed himself against me.

I moaned and bit his lip playfully. I pulled back from him and lay on the ground catching my breath.

He smiled back for a second and then turned his head to the side. He started to stand up, but was suddenly flying through the air with a wolf on his back.

I started to go after them, but Matt grabbed my arm. "Love, you better just wait here."

I shook my head as I realized Ares had tackled Koda. "No, Ares might hurt him and it wasn't his fault. Someone is messing with our emotions; I can feel it." I pulled away from him and ran through the forest after them. I yelled, "Ares! Please stop. It's not his fault. Someone is messing with our emotions."

I ran toward the sound of snarling and found Ares growling over Koda who was lying in human form on his back with his hands to his sides. I ran up and reached toward Ares, but he turned to me and snapped his teeth. I stopped walking and stared at him. "Would you really hurt me, Ares?"

Ares' wolf face softened, and he walked backwards off of Koda.

I whispered, "Someone is manipulating our emotions Ares. I can feel it."

He changed back to human and stood perfect and naked in front of me.

I licked my lips and fought to keep my eyes above his chest.

He snarled. "Why were you kissing him?"

"I just told you that someone is manipulating our emotions and I'm not lying. I swear Ares that I would not have kissed him under my own volition."

"Thanks. I guess I'm just chopped liver," Koda said playfully.

Ares growled. "Don't push me, Koda!"

I laid my hand on Ares' arm and whispered, "I'm sorry I kissed him. I promise it won't happen again."

Ares turned to me and for the first time I saw the pain in his eyes. "Don't promise something you can't keep."

I shook my head and wrapped my arms around his upper body. "I promise, Ares. I am sorry that I lost control."

He sighed and hugged me back. "It's alright. I know you're telling the truth. Matt, go find who has been manipulating them."

Matt ran off into the woods without a word.

Koda stood up and walked toward Ares. He dropped to his knees and said, "Please forgive me, Prince Ares. I did not know what I was doing and I swear it will not happen again. I will work to gain more control over myself."

Ares spoke in a stern voice, "You are forgiven. Stand."

Koda stood and smiled. "Thank you."

Ares looked down at me and smiled. "And of course, I wouldn't hurt you. I was just upset at finding you eating each other's mouths."

I cringed. "I already apologized, and you don't have to rub it in."

"I'm sorry. Are you alright?"

"Of course, I am. I mean, we had a little issue, but—"

Ares interrupted me. "What issue?"

Koda groaned. "You couldn't have waited, Artemis? I mean shit, I just got his forgiveness and now you are throwing me under the bus again."

"Sorry," I said sympathetically.

Ares spoke through gritted teeth, "Someone better tell me what happened."

Koda dropped to the ground on his hands and knees in front of Ares and said, "I failed you my Prince. When the ogre smashed through the wall, I was not fast enough to turn away. A piece of wood pierced her lung, collapsing it."

Ares looked down at my body just below my bra and traced the scar with his fingertip, making me shiver.

I was suddenly very aware of the fact that I didn't have a shirt on.

"It's alright Koda. You got her out of the village as quick as you could and that was the best thing to do."

I gasped. "Oh, my God. Bret and the children—are they okay?"

Ares nodded. "Bret was actually very helpful in protecting the children. They are all calling him their protector. I don't think he is going to be leaving with us."

I smiled, but felt a twinge of sadness at the news. "That's great." I turned away from Ares and started walking through the trees.

He grabbed my arm and stopped me. "I'm sorry he won't be coming with us."

I shrugged. "'S alright. It's better for him this way."

Koda stood beside us. "When did you get that tattoo?"

Ares glared at Koda. "How have you seen it when I haven't yet? Is that something else you did before I came?"

I could see the anger building in Ares and sighed. "You just didn't pay attention to where it was or you would have seen it already, too."

Ares' frown evened out and a twinkle of intrigue returned to his eyes. "Can I see it?"

I shrugged and turned my back to him. He traced his fingertip across the snarling wolf head in the center of my lower back. Ares asked, "When did you get this?"

"Two years ago."

"Did your father see it?"

I shook my head emphatically. "No, he would have killed me for getting a tattoo."

Ares smiled. "It's actually very nice."

I blushed. "Thanks."

Koda shook his head. "I can't believe your father never said anything to you even though you had such a fascination with wolves."

I shrugged. "My fascination with wolves was normal compared to other girls' fascinations with horses or whatever other animal."

"I think we should find some clothes before we leave," Ares said quietly. I realized I was staring at Ares' lower body and blushed, looking away from him. He hugged me tightly, "I love that you blush. I hope you always do it."

"I don't."

Matt ran back through the trees and frowned. "I couldn't find anyone."

I sighed. "Great. Well, let's get back. I'm still hungry."

"Sorry about that. Those damn ogres attacked without warning. Lucky that you got scared in time for me to change," Ares said.

I remembered the vampires and asked, "Are Victor and Maurice alright?"

Ares nodded. "Maurice managed to get to cover before the sun got him. Both were a big help in defeating the ogres actually. From now on, all werewolf posts are going to be assigned two vampires. We're going to be taking a vampire along with our group as well."

I frowned. "Why?"

Ares answered instantly, "For better protection of you. Plus, he wants to observe our relationship anyway."

I groaned. "Great. Now I'm an experiment? Why don't you just hand me over to the humans?"

Ares snarled. "I would never do that. Those monsters would torture you worse than you could imagine."

I stared at him and wondered if he had been tortured by humans. I almost asked, but knew it would probably just make him angrier. "So, what's the vampire's name that is joining us?"

"Victor."

My throat felt dry again. "Great. Well let's go."

I started walking, and Ares cleared his throat. "You're going the wrong way." I giggled and followed behind him, staring at his muscled back and butt as he walked. I felt proud of myself that I had managed not to stare at his crotch while we were talking. I could hear Koda and Matt whispering behind me, but couldn't understand what they were saying. I tried to ignore them, but curiosity got the better of me.

I turned around, stopping in front of them. "What? What are you two whispering about?"

Koda and Matt stopped walking and stared at me for a full minute. Matt finally sighed. "Love, we would appreciate it if you wouldn't make us tell you."

I growled. "Why? Because Ares is here and would get mad?"

I felt Ares beside me, but didn't look over at him. Matt groaned. "Alright. We wanted to know why it is that you say you have never been with a man before, but you are so comfortable walking around in your bra and with Ares being naked if that's true?"

I stared at them for a minute as I added up what they had said. *Why am I so comfortable being in my bra around them? And why am I not blushing with Ares walking naked in front of me?* I shook my head. "I...I don't know why I'm comfortable. I mean Ares being naked might be because of our weird connection thingy, but I've never even worn a two-piece bathing suit in front of anyone before. I...I should be embarrassed, but strangely, I'm not."

Ares smiled. "You're probably just adjusting to being around us. Also, wereanimals generally like to wear as little clothing as possible. You know, the whole shapeshifting thing? We lose a lot of clothes the first year because we end up shifting while dressed and human clothes don't fit very well on large wolves."

Koda rolled his eyes. "Tell me about it. I've shredded more jeans than I can count."

I wrapped my arms around my stomach. "Well whatever it is, now you boys have your answer." A blush rushed up my cheeks, and I groaned. "And now I'm properly embarrassed. Can we go?"

Matt smiled. "We didn't *want* to embarrass you; we were just wondering if you might have been lying to us."

I shook my head. "I'm only eighteen for crying out loud."

Koda laughed. "Shit, eighteen was the beginning of my man-whore days."

Ares groaned. "Don't remind me. You weren't very discreet

about it either. I still haven't forgiven you for screwing that girl in my room while I was sleeping in there."

"Ew," I said wrinkling up my nose. "This is why I tried to hide from everyone. Girls are catty and cynical and guys are gross and only think about one thing."

Matt said, "Food."

Ares said, "Hunting."

Koda said, "Fighting."

My mouth gaped open at them for a moment. "Seriously? Sex! All men think about is sex. And obviously Koda is a prime example," I said, pointing towards him.

Koda rolled his eyes. "Don't ask about Ares then."

I looked sideways at Ares and wondered how many women he had slept with.

He is really old. Probably best not to ask.

I shook my head. "Let's go guys. I'm hungry."

Ares smiled. "If you would change, we could take you on a real hunt."

I shook my head. "I'm not going to change."

Ares groaned. "You'll have to change eventually Artemis. Just because you don't change doesn't mean you aren't a werewolf."

"Whatever. I'm not changing yet."

Ares snarled. "You know; I could force you to change."

I snarled. "Don't even try it."

Matt stepped between us. "Calm down. Everyone, calm down. Let's get home and find some food."

Ares stopped snarling and shook his head. "Whoever is messing with us is very powerful. I'll need to speak to Victor right away."

I squatted down in an attack stance as Ares took a step towards me.

He sighed. "Artemis, I promise I am not going to try to change you right now. I just wanted to carry you so that we could get back to the village faster."

I shook my head. "Let Matt carry me if you are telling the truth."

Ares snarled. "Would you rather Matt or Koda carry you than me touch you? If I hadn't come when I had, would I have found you and Koda doing other things?"

I stopped snarling and stared at him, seeing the hurt in his eyes. I straightened and shook my head with my hands on top of my head. "I'm sorry. This isn't like me. You're right, we need to get back soon because this person is screwing with me really bad."

Ares picked me up in his arms and ran without another word. He ran through the thick forest, dodging trees and jumping over fallen logs like it was a flat surface. I enjoyed the feel of his hot naked flesh against my arm and face.

I rubbed my face in the crook of his neck as he ran.

He shivered and slowed down.

I kissed the point where his neck and shoulder met and kissed my way up his neck to his ear. He moaned and grabbed my face with the hand that had been holding my legs. I dropped to the ground and he snarled at me making me lie flat on the ground, waiting for my punishment.

He growled into my ear. "Do not tease me. I understand it is hard to control these emotions, especially since you have not had them before. My control is waning though, and I do not want to try to finish what you are starting if that is not what you want. So, stop teasing me and sit still until we get back."

I glanced down his body and saw what he meant about his waning control. I swallowed hard and looked back up at him. "I'm sorry." I leaned up and licked his cheek, short and quick. I gasped and lay back down, shocked by what I had just done.

Ares smiled. "Don't worry, that's a submissive apology that wolves do to each other. It's natural that you would do that to me in this situation." He licked my cheek back and said, "You're forgiven." He stood up and turned to Matt. "You need to carry her. I fear that my control has been extremely diminished."

Matt laughed. "I can *see* that." Matt walked over and held out his hand to me. "Come on, Love. I'll carry you the rest of the way."

I took his hand and let him help me stand. He picked me up in his arms and ran faster than any of them had carried me before. The wind whipping my hair and face excited me, and I suddenly had the urge to run. I tore his arms away and fell to the ground on my feet. I started running as fast as I could, blowing past Ares and Koda. I yelled in joy and felt a burst of energy and began running even faster.

I could hear Ares, Koda and Matt behind me, but I didn't care about anything except running. It was the freest feeling I had ever experienced. I dodged around the trees, which I could see surprisingly well for how fast I was going. It was more like I could sense them. The night air spilled around me, and I could suddenly smell everything. The birds and small animals in the trees, the three men/wolves behind me and the larger animals a few miles away. I had no idea how I knew everything, but I did.

We ran into the clearing of the village and I gaped. Houses were burned to the ground and the warehouse had a gigantic hole in the side of it big enough to fit a whale in. I ran to what was left of Gregory's house. The living room was now nothing more than a covered patio and the kitchen was completely gone. I screamed, "No!" And ran to where the kitchen used to be. I found the fridge on its back a few feet away and pulled it open. Meat and various other groceries lie on the back of the fridge defrosting. I reached in and grabbed as much meat as possible and pulled it out. I looked around for the microwave and found it under what used to be the kitchen sink. I looked at Matt. "Can you grab that?"

Matt picked up the microwave and followed me into the house. I walked to the bathroom and pointed at the plug. "Plug it in there please." He did as I asked and opened the door to the microwave. I pushed the meat inside and shut the door and turned on the microwave to heat up the meat. I waited anxiously shifting from one foot to another as the meat twirled inside the microwave. The "ding" of the microwave made me jump, and I hurried to grab the meat out, shoving an entire steak in my mouth and chewing. I moaned in pleasure and talked around my full mouth of food, "This is so good."

Ares walked into the bathroom and stared at the pile of meat in my arms. "Hungry?"

I snarled as much as was possible with a full mouth. "Don't make fun of me."

His lip twitched slightly as he tried to hide a smile. "Sorry. Can I have a piece?"

I grumbled, but handed him one of the smaller steaks. Matt laughed. "At least she is generous."

I snarled and swallowed the piece of meat that was in my mouth. "You shut up." I plopped down on the closed lid of the toilet and ate my meat quickly. Matt and Ares walked away sharing the piece of meat I had given them.

Victor walked in and smiled at me. "Hey." I frowned and continued to eat my meat without saying anything. He laughed. "I can see that you are eating, but I just wanted to formally introduce myself now that I am going to be joining your little faction."

I nodded and pushed the food in my mouth to the side. "Nice to meet you. I'm usually not this rude, but I'm really hungry."

Victor nodded. "I understand completely. It must take a lot out of you to stop your changes."

I shrugged. "Don't know. Just always do it."

Ares came back in. "You need to rest."

I nodded and kissed Ares' cheek as I walked to my bedroom and laid down on the bed, rolling on my side to face away from the door. I heard the door open and someone come in and assumed it was Ares. I ignored him, closing my eyes. I started to fall asleep when someone grabbed my arms and forced me on my back with my arms stretched and held above my head on the bed. My eyes snapped open. Gregory stood over me with a knife in his hand. I swallowed hard. "What's going on?"

Gregory snarled, "I'm doing what should have been done the night you were born, but your father was too much of a coward to do it."

I stared at the knife in his hand and asked, "Are you going to kill me?"

He smiled. "Yes, and I'll love every second of it. If that boy hadn't been here before, you would already be dead."

I looked backwards and saw a man I had never seen before holding my arms. "You both know that Ares will kill you when he finds out, right?"

Gregory laughed quietly. "He won't know who did it because we are going to take your body out in the woods and make it look like suicide."

I rolled my eyes. "I would never kill myself. He won't believe it."

Gregory smiled. "Oh, I think he will." He raised the knife and started to plunge downwards towards my chest. I rolled to the side of the bed tearing my arms out of the other man's hold. Gregory snarled, "Grab her!"

I ran around the bed and towards the door, but Gregory grabbed me. I screamed, "ARES!!!!" as Gregory threw me back on to the bed and picked up the knife he had dropped. I kicked as hard as I could at Gregory, but he moved out of the way. The other man grabbed on to my arms again, and I screamed as loud as I could.

The wall beside me burst into pieces as Bret ran through it. He grabbed the other man and threw him out of the room and against the house across the street. Ares ran through the bedroom door and tackled Gregory, pulling the knife from his hand and stabbing it into Gregory's stomach. I jumped off the bed and ran to Matt who had come into the room behind Ares. He held me against him, his muscles strained as he fought to control himself. Ares grabbed Gregory's throat and squeezed then pulled backwards ripping his throat out. Blood sprayed over Ares and the bedroom. Ares tossed the piece of Gregory's throat outside the bedroom and into the street then grabbed Gregory's head and twisted and pulled, ripping his head off his body. Ares threw Gregory's body and head out of the bedroom and into the street next to his piece of throat.

Ares turned to me, and his eyes were amber wolf eyes. I felt no fear though he was covered in blood and I had just watched him rip Gregory's head off. I pulled away from Matt and walked towards Ares. Ares took a step back from me and shook his head speaking in a voice which was more of a growl than natural. "If you touch me you'll change. I have no control over my power right now."

I shook my head and continued to walk towards him. "I won't change." I reached out and touched his face and felt my body twitch hard once. I groaned and fought to control myself.

I stared into Ares' eyes and felt lust, admiration, and...love. My body cooled and released its tension. Ares eyes cleared as I felt power flow into my body.

He stared in awe at my face and whispered, "I knew you were perfect, but this is remarkable. Even I do not have this power."

I stood on tiptoe and kissed his lips softly.

He kissed me back and whispered, "I will protect you at all costs."

I smiled. "I know you will."

Bret growled. "I saved you, too! Why does he get all of the attention?" He squatted down, and I saw his body beginning to change.

I walked to him, and he snarled at me.

Ares started to come towards us, but I held up my hand walking towards Bret. "You are not my alpha, Bret. You cannot snarl or growl or try to show dominance that you do not have. If you try to attack me, I will hurt you. Friend or not, I am your alpha."

Bret snapped his teeth at me and started to change. I reached into him with my power and felt the power of the moon and wolf in him. I pulled those powers into me absorbing them.

Bret fell to the ground completely human and asleep.

Matt whistled. "Wow. I've never seen anyone but Ares do that."

I smiled then felt exhausted. I put my hand out for the bed, but missed and started to fall.

Ares caught me and picked me up in his arms. He whispered, "You have to learn to pace yourself. Using too much magic too quickly will drain you."

I shrugged. "I'm a newb, what can I say?"

He tilted his head to the side in confusion, reminding me of a canine once again. "A newb? What is that?"

"It means I'm a newbie. Some of Bret's nerdy friends used to say it when talking about video games." I said quietly.

Ares shook his head. "The humans have used a lot of different slang over the years. Most of it I think is ridiculous. Like groovy. What is groovy? Stupid, that's what it is."

I giggled and asked, "Where am I going to sleep now?"

He winked. "How about my room?"

I blushed, and Ares smiled. "I was just teasing. We'll put you in Koda's room and make him sleep on the couch."

Koda groaned. "Why me?"

Ares snarled. "You kissed her, remember?"

Koda rolled his eyes. "Fine, if that's my punishment, then alright."

Ares shook his head. "That's only the beginning of your punishment. You still have lots of punishing left."

I sighed. "It wasn't his fault, Ares."

Ares shook his head again. "Spells like that can't put thoughts in people's heads. They can only intensify what they are thinking."

I looked at Koda and blushed. I turned my face into Ares' neck and said, "Okay, take me to his room."

Ares walked quickly to Koda's room and laid me down on the bed. "I know this must be hard, but I assure you that I will do all that I can to make you happy." He bent down and kissed my cheek then hurried out, shutting the door behind him.

I groaned and rolled on to my side closing my eyes.

Great, I am falling in love with him at a ridiculously rapid pace. Of course, my life would be complicated like this.

CHAPTER SEVEN

Two knocks on the bedroom door woke me from my peaceful sleep. I groaned and stood up from the bed, walking clumsily towards the door. I reached for the light, but couldn't find the switch.

The person knocked again, louder this time.

"Hold on, I'm trying." I groaned. I finally opened the door, no longer trying to find the light. The light from the hallway blinded me for a second, and I had to wait for my eyes to adjust. I blinked three times then finally saw who was there. "Bret? What's wrong?"

Bret walked into the bedroom, flipping on the light switch and closing the door.

I glared at the light switch, angry at not being able to find it.

Bret turned to me and demanded, "Why did you humiliate me yesterday?"

I stared at his face as I tried to remember what he was talking about. It was odd to see his face, the one I had seen for years and thought handsome and now I thought was only average. I smiled.

I guess when you are dating the God of War that it's hard to compare anyone else to that.

Bret snarled. "Why are you smiling?"

I sighed. "Look, Bret. In the world of werewolves, you have to have a pecking order. Sure you can be friends and lovers, but you have to keep the order and you tried to break it. I didn't mean to humiliate you, but you challenged me in front of others. I had to remind you who your alpha is."

Bret growled. "You aren't alpha; you are just screwing the alpha."

I growled back at him shoving my finger in his chest. "You don't know anything! I'm not screwing anyone and I *am* your alpha. Do you need a reminder?"

Bret snarled. "Try it and see who the real alpha is."

I felt my body temperature rising with my anger and felt my body starting to twitch. I looked at Bret's body and saw him beginning to change as well. I groaned, "Fuck it!" I let my body take over and transform. I could feel the bones popping and sliding around to change my shape. My skin split apart, making a disgustingly wet sound as it ripped into pieces and then started falling below me. I closed my eyes and inhaled, holding my breath as I finished the transformation. I slowly re-opened my eyes and looked out with much clearer, much sharper eyes with a muzzle between them that surprisingly didn't interfere with my view. I picked each foot up and wagged my tail and then pulled my lips up in a smile.

I shook my body and turned to look at Bret. He was bigger than me in height, width, and weight, but I knew I could still defeat him. It was too cramped in the bedroom to move around easily though. He snarled at me, and I snarled back. I sighed in happiness, finally finding a body that felt right.

This body was like home for me.

I no longer cared to school Bret, I just wanted to run. I ran through the bedroom door, breaking it into pieces and continued down the hallway.

Bret barked and growled as he ran after me, but I didn't care.

As I turned from the hallway towards what used to be the

living room, I saw Ares, Koda, and Matt in the kitchen. When they saw me, their mouths dropped open in shock. Ares ran towards me, but I couldn't wait for him because Bret was right behind me.

I ran through the giant opening and towards the closest stand of trees. The early morning air was crisp and clean as I breathed through my new mouth and nose. I ran faster into the trees, dodging and weaving through them. I could feel the energy in the trees and plants and asked their permission to frolic among them. The trees seemed to anticipate my moves, leaning out of the way to give me more room to run faster and enjoy my newfound freedom. I could hear the others running after me, and it made me smile. For once I was in charge. I ran through the forest and inhaled the smells for what seemed like the first time.

I could feel Ares gaining on me and turned to watch him. His black fur glistened in the dawn light as his muscles bunched and stretched to run and catch up to me. He was truly magnificent, and I knew he was alpha. He was much larger than Bret and huge compared to me. His majestic head tilted to the side as he caught my eye.

I lolled my tongue out in a playful show.

His voice whispered through my head. *Why are you a wolf?*

I snapped my tongue back inside my mouth and stopped running, staring at him. *How can I hear you in my head?*

He snorted. *All wolves can communicate through mind-to-mind telepathy. Some, like me, Koda, and Matt can do it while in human form.*

I sighed. *Bret was challenging me again, and I decided to let myself…*

Bret slammed into my side, sending me head over heels.

My head missed a nearby tree by only a few inches. I wasn't sure if the trees had moved or not, but I thanked them anyway. I jumped up and snarled, but Ares already had Bret on his back on the ground.

What is your problem, Bret? She didn't do anything to you.

Bret snarled. *She humiliated me yesterday.* He turned his head to look at me. *And I'm right about the alpha thing.*

I snarled and launched myself so that I pushed Ares off of Bret and took his place above Bret, snarling with my teeth by his throat. *Do you want to die Bret? I will kill you if you don't stop trying to fight me. I am alpha as much as Ares.*

Bret snorted. *Ares is alpha, but you are just his bitch. The only reason no one will challenge you is because of him.*

I shook my head. *I am alpha with or without Ares. I don't want to kill you Bret, but you are leaving me little choice.*

Ares, Koda, and Matt surrounded us.

Matt growled softly. *Don't kill him. Let the loser go back to the village and live there with them. He is only pissed because you chose Ares over him. And he doesn't believe you aren't screwing Ares because what other reason would you chose Ares over him? Right Bret?*

Bret snarled, and I bit down into his throat. He yelped loudly as blood began to leak down his coat. *You better knock it off Bret. I don't care what you think, because I know I am alpha. With or without Ares, I am your alpha.*

I released my hold on his neck and stepped backwards to join Koda, Matt, and Ares.

Bret rolled up to his feet and shook his head. *You are definitely not the same girl I fell in love with.*

I snarled. *Because you fell in love with a lie my father had set up. This is the real me, and if you don't like it then too bad. I'm already taken anyway.*

Bret coughed. *Yeah, good luck being his slut. Although you seem pretty good at it so far.*

Ares charged forward, knocking Bret to his side. *Enough! You cannot talk to her that way. She is not a slut, and she is your alpha. Now go back to the village before I kill you.*

Bret stood and ran back to the village without another word.

I walked forward and turned around so I could look at the three wolves with me. I giggled internally at the thought that they were wolves now and not men. I could see Koda, Matt, and Ares having some type of dialogue among them, but had no idea what about. I snarled, making them all look at me. *It's not nice to talk about me when I can't hear you and am standing right here.*

Matt tilted his head to the side. *You should be able to tap into our conversation if you want to.*

I shook my head. *Nope, I can't. So, what are you talking about?*

They looked at each other and Ares finally turned to me. *We were discussing how beautiful you are in wolf form and how much like the Mother you look. You are exactly as she is drawn and described, except for the purple eyes.*

I frowned. *I still have purple eyes? I thought your eyes were supposed to change to wolf eyes?*

Koda nodded. *They're supposed to, but it may have something to do with you being half.*

I nodded and looked around the forest. I wished the moon was out, but it was my own fault for not changing sooner. We walked back to the house in silence, or at least, I was in silence. I waited while the others changed and walked into the house. I was about to start to change when Ares walked back out wearing a pair of pants. He smiled at me. "You alright?"

I nodded, feeling my ears flop as I did. I sat on my haunches and pictured my human self. My bones popped, and I shrank in size until I could feel the cold wood porch beneath my butt. I curled into a ball, trying to hide my body as Ares handed me a large blanket. "It's all I could find quickly."

I wrapped my self up in it and stood. "Thanks."

Ares smiled. "You need to put some clothes on though, because we're leaving."

I frowned. "Where are we going?"

He shook his head. "It's a secret."

I sighed. "Like everything else in my life."

Ares took a step towards me, and my heart beat instantly picked up speed. I swallowed, and he smiled. He reached out slowly and stroked my cheeks softly. "I'm very lucky to have gotten you as a match."

I opened my mouth to say something, but Ares stopped me with a kiss. My legs felt like jelly and Ares wrapped his arms around my waist to keep me from falling. I pulled back from his kiss and whispered, "It's not fair that you make me feel this way and I have no effect on you."

Ares laughed and shook his head. "You have a great deal of an effect on me. I'm just better at hiding my emotions."

Koda cleared his throat, making us turn towards him. "Ares, we should get back soon."

Ares sighed and nodded. "Right." He pulled away from me, and it felt like a scab being pulled off.

I bolted inside to Koda's bedroom where a pile of clothes lay on the bed. I changed faster than I ever had before and walked out to the porch where Ares, Koda, Matt, and Victor were talking. I leaned against the porch railing and stared out at the abused town knowing it was my fault.

Matt walked to stand next to me and smiled. "How are ya doin', Love?"

I shook my head. "So much fighting and death and damage all because of me? It doesn't make sense. I'm not special."

The other men stopped talking, and I turned around to face them.

Ares shook his head. "You are special. You and I are special together. There are going to be people trying to get you and use you for themselves, but you must never think it's your fault."

Two black SUVs pulled up in front of the house and Koda smiled. "Time to go."

I walked towards the SUVs, ignoring Ares and Victor as best as I could. They were both whispering too quietly for me to hear their conversation, but obviously they were talking about me. I climbed into the first SUV and crawled into the center seat, looking out the side window.

Ares sat down beside me and placed his hand palm side up on my knee. I stared at it for a moment then sighed, giving into my desire, and placed my hand in his. My heart picked up tempo, and I felt content. I closed my eyes, and Ares sighed happily beside me. "Thank you."

I rested my head against his shoulder. "It's getting much harder to fight. Plus, it's not like I don't *like* holding your hand."

Ares laughed and kissed the top of my head. "I like holding your hand, too. You should sleep now. It'll be a while before we reach our destination." I closed my eyes and enjoyed the feel of his hand holding mine, but sleep wouldn't come.

I shifted on the seat, and Ares released my hand so he could pull me down into his lap. I started to protest, but knew I would be more comfortable. I laid my head in his lap, and he draped his left arm across my stomach and began stroking my hair with his right hand. I rubbed my cheek against his pant leg and sighed happily. For once, it felt right to do this. With Bret, it had always felt wrong somehow.

Could it have been because I was meant to be with Ares?

Time dragged on, but Ares never stopped rubbing my hair. The vehicle finally stopped, and I sat up stretching my arms above my head. Ares frowned. "You didn't sleep?"

I shook my head. "No, but it was relaxing."

He smiled at me, and it was so gorgeous that my heart skipped a beat. Koda cleared his throat pulling me out of my trance. "I'm hungry."

Ares sighed. "You're always hungry."

I looked out the window and gasped, "My town!"

Ares smiled. "We need to rest for a day and I thought you might like to get some of your other things from your house."

I climbed out of the SUV and looked around the deserted streets. The only lights were coming from the pub and I could hear everyone talking loudly from inside. I turned to Ares and hugged him. "Thank you."

He kissed my cheek softly. "I'll have to remember to do things like this more often."

I looked at his naked chest and frowned. "Maybe you should find a shirt first?"

Ares frowned. "Are you embarrassed by my body?"

I laughed. "Definitely not! I just don't want to have to beat all of the girls off of you when we go inside."

He smiled. "Aw, you're jealous."

I snarled. "Don't patronize me."

Koda tossed Ares a shirt from inside the car and Ares quickly put it on.

I started towards the pub before Ares could tease me anymore. I turned around before opening the door to make sure that Matt, Koda, and Ares were fully clothed then walked into the pub. Everyone ignored me as they watched the news of another attack. I walked to an open booth and waved at the waitress, Darcy.

She smiled at me and nodded. I waited until all of the guys sat down then sat on the edge seat beside Ares. He smiled at me and continued whispering to the others.

The news story ended and Tyler, Skankzilla's dad, turned off the television.

Darcy hurried over and smiled at me. "Hey Darlin'! I was worried about you and your dad when you both disappeared."

I smiled. "Oh, we just went camping. You know how Darren loves camping."

She laughed. "So, what do ya'll want?" I rolled my eyes and Darcy laughed. "The usual?"

I nodded. Ares nudged me and I sighed. "Darcy this is Ares, my boyfriend."

Darcy looked him over with lust in her eyes. "You do know how to pick them. Well, what do the rest of you want?"

I looked around the pub as the others ordered and caught Skankzilla glaring at me and storming towards me. I tensed, and my lip pulled up in a snarl. I quickly pulled my lip back down and smiled at her. She put her hands on her hips and glared at me. "Where's Bret?"

I batted my eyelashes. "Why would I know that, Skankzilla?"

She growled at me, and it sounded so pathetic that I almost laughed. "Listen, you hooker trash. I've taken your crap because of Bret, but if you've done anything to him—"

I stood up an inch away from her face. "You'll do what?"

She stuttered and took a step back. "I…I…" Ares cleared his throat, and Skankzilla looked around me to him. Her breath caught in her throat when she saw him. "Oh, hi."

He smiled. "Bret moved. He said to tell you he's sorry he didn't say goodbye."

She stepped around me and flipped her hair over her shoulder. "Oh, well I'm Trish."

Ares winked. "I'm Ares, Artemis' boyfriend."

Skankzilla's eyes widened and she gaped in disbelief. "You're dating *her*?" Ares nodded and she asked, "What did she have to do to date you?"

I reached back to punch her when Billy grabbed my arm. "Calm down, Artemis. She's not worth it. You know she's just mad that Bret left without saying bye to her."

Ares glared at Billy's hand on me, but stayed perfectly still in his seat.

I pulled my arm away from Billy's hand gently. "You're right, Billy."

Skankzilla turned to talk to Koda, but he waved his hand dismissively at her. "Beat it, child."

Billy looked at the four men sitting at the table with me and frowned. "Who're they?"

I smiled. "Billy, this is Ares, Koda, Matt, and Victor."

Billy nodded at them. "So, are you staying, or you on your way out?"

Ares was still glaring at Billy, and I remembered that Billy had tried to shoot them while they were wolves.

I shook my head. "Just stopping at my house for some things and staying the night. We'll be leaving tomorrow morning."

Billy smiled at me. "So, you'll be here tonight? You could come over—"

Ares shook his head. "She's taken, boy."

I glared at Ares. "Ares, I can handle this."

He folded his arms across his chest and continued to glare at Billy.

Billy frowned. "What's he talking about?"

I sighed. "Ares is my…I'm dating Ares."

Billy looked Ares up and down. "How long?"

I frowned. "What?"

Billy looked at me. "How long have you been with him?"

"Not long."

Billy shook his head. "Artemis he's…" He pulled my arm gently turning me away from the table.

I heard Ares growl softly, but it was too low for Billy to hear.

"Artemis, I don't like this guy."

I smiled and patted his back. "Good thing it's not up to you then. It was nice seeing you, Billy, but my food's here."

I turned to sit down, and Billy grabbed my arm hard, pulling me back toward him. "What's does he have that I don't?"

I stared down at his painful grip on my arm and opened my mouth when Ares spoke slowly beside me. "Manners for one. Release your hold on her before I lose my temper."

Billy smiled smugly. "And why should I worry if you lose your temper, huh, freak?"

Ares smiled, and the promise of pain was plain on his face. "Try me."

Billy started to tighten his grip, and I punched him in the face with my other hand. He let me go and stumbled backwards, falling against the bar.

Ares pulled me back against him.

I glared at Billy. "You were always so jealous. I thought it was just of Bret, but you're just too insecure."

Billy glared at me. "You've always just been Bret's pet freak."

Ares moved across the aisle faster than I could see and picked Billy up by his throat with one hand. "I would prefer it if you refrained from insulting my girlfriend. As you can see, I lose my control when that happens."

Ares dropped Billy to the ground, and Billy gasped for breath.

J.D. started to move towards us, but Jess grabbed his arm and shook her head.

I smiled at Jess and she smiled back. She pointed at Ares then put two thumbs up nodding her head smiling.

I smiled back at her and pulled on Ares' arm. "Come on, let's eat before it gets cold. He's just a loser like Bret."

Ares looked at my arm where a small red mark still sat from Billy gripping me. He kissed it softly. "Do you see what I've told you? I'm fast, but not fast enough at times."

I kissed his cheek. "It's alright."

He sat down, and the judgmental eyes of the others in the pub glared at me.

I sat down and we ate in silence. The noise started up again in the pub, but I could hear every painful comment from everyone talking about me. I finished my burger and chocolate shake and walked out of the pub.

Jess walked out behind me and smiled. "Hey."

I smiled at her. "Hey. Sorry about that."

She shrugged. "Why are you apologizing to me? That's the most excitement we've had in a long time! And your boyfriend is sexy. Man. I couldn't believe how he held Billy up with one hand," she said in awe.

I giggled nervously. "Yeah, he gets really angry when people hurt me."

She sighed. "I'm sorry about how we treated you before, Artemis. You don't have to leave, you know?"

I shrugged. "No worries."

Ares walked out of the pub and wrapped his arms around my

waist. The feel of him holding me released all of the tension in my body. Ares asked, "So, have you told her your good news?"

I frowned. "Um…no."

Ares started pouting. "Well, that's one way to hurt my feelings."

Jess gasped, "Are you pregnant?"

I yelled, "Hell no!"

Ares frowned. "What she meant to say is that we're engaged."

Jess looked at my hands. "I don't see a ring."

Ares sighed. "I told you to let me get you a ring."

"No, you—"

He pinched my stomach and smiled. "She was very worried about Darren finding out. But we're eloping."

Jess frowned. "Eloping? I thought you said you haven't been with him for very long?"

Ares laughed. "We've known each other a while, but we've only been officially dating a little bit. We're family friends."

Jess smiled. "Oh. That's cool. Well, I hope you have fun. Maybe we'll see each other again soon?"

I shrugged. "Maybe."

I walked away from her, and Ares followed me silently. Koda, Matt, and Victor caught up with us when we were at the feed store. I stopped and turned around to glare at Ares. "What the hell was that?"

He frowned. "What?"

I yelled in frustration, "Eloping! What is it with you and making sure everyone knows I'm yours? Can't you just let me deal with them? I mean, it's bad enough that I'm stuck with you…" I gasped. "Ares, I…I didn't mean that."

He shook his head. "Yes, you did. I'm sorry. That boy just set me off."

"We better get to the house. I've got a lot of hunting to do," I said, happy for the subject change.

Koda asked, "Hunting?"

I smiled. "Come on." Ares walked back with Matt and Koda, talking quietly to them.

Victor walked beside me and whispered, "You shouldn't be so hard on him. He's trying."

I scoffed. "So am I, Victor. This isn't easy."

Victor nodded. "Think how hard it is for him."

I frowned. "What do you mean?"

He sighed and rubbed his temples. "Ares is the second fiercest warrior of all of the werewolves in the *world*. He doesn't bow to anyone except the King and now he's got you to deal with. You're pigheaded, strong-willed, and he's been bending over backwards to try to make this easy on you when it's tearing him up inside."

I stopped and stared at Victor. "How?"

Victor sighed again. "Being tied or having a match requires almost constant touching in the first few months and most often requires you to seal the bond. You're young and inexperienced, so Ares isn't pushing you, but you keep pushing him away and refusing to touch him, and we all know you would refuse to seal the bond. It's eating at his control. If we aren't careful, he could snap."

I frowned. "So, I'm causing him pain?"

Victor nodded. "More pain than you could imagine."

Ares frowned when he saw us standing still. I whispered, "What do we have to do to seal it?"

Victor smiled. "I'm sure you can figure that out."

I groaned. "No! No way, Victor."

He shrugged. "Would it be so bad?"

I watched Ares walking gracefully towards us and felt my lower body tighten. Ares stopped walking and stared at me in shock. I groaned and covered my eyes with my hands. "No, anything, but that. Not yet. Can't we just cut each other's palms and press them together or something?"

Victor laughed quietly. "This is why he is giving you space, but just think about the pain you're causing him. I'm not telling you to do it tonight, but it will need to be done soon. The sooner you seal your bond, the safer you both will be."

Ares frowned. "What are you two talking about?"

Victor smiled. "Nothing."

I shook my head and jogged towards my house. Headlights raced down the street towards me. I stopped jogging and the truck skid to a stop in front of me spraying gravel. Ares pulled me backwards and I sighed. "He wasn't going to hit me."

Billy climbed out of the truck with Jake and Jeff.

Ares shook his head. "We need to go."

I saw the seriousness on his face and wondered what was wrong. I looked at Jake and Jeff and noticed they were holding bats. I asked, "What are the bats for, boys?"

Jeff smiled. "In case things get out of hand."

I smiled. "Do I really scare you that much, Jeff?"

He frowned. "What?"

Jake, one of Bret's other good friends, laughed and tossed his bat into the truck bed.

I smiled. "Thanks, Jake."

Jake winked at me. "You ever need a change of men, call me."

I rolled my eyes. "You know you couldn't handle me."

He sighed. "Too true."

Ares frowned. "Is there something I don't know about?"

I shrugged. "Just that I'm too scary for the boys here to deal with."

Ares snorted and stroked my cheek. "Scary? Not hardly. Sexy? Definitely."

Billy asked, "Artemis what's happened to you? This isn't like you. Why are you with these scumbags?"

I frowned. "Nothing's happened to me. And they aren't scumbags."

Billy rolled his eyes. "They are obviously much older than us, and I'm sure Ares is really after your *heart*."

Ares snarled, and I put my hand on his chest, stopping him from moving forward.

Jeff smiled. "Silenced by the bitch? Wow, that's a new low."

I pointed at Jeff. "You! You sleazy jerk. You have no room to call me names. I've seen the girls you go out with and the diseases you give them. And I didn't silence him. He is just letting me fight my own battle. And whatever Ares is after is none of your—"

Jeff smiled. "So, you've already given him what he wants. Interesting."

I snarled and leapt towards him. He swung at me with the bat, and as I put my hands up to block it Ares moved forward, grabbing the bat from Jeff's hands. Jeff's eyes bulged as Ares took the bat from him and tossed it into the truck. Ares pushed his finger into Jeff's chest, making him step backwards. "Just because she has better taste then to date you does not mean she's given up anything. Not that it's your business, but she hasn't. If you ever try to lay a finger on her again, I'll kill you."

Billy pointed at Ares. "And he's better than me how?"

I swung around and punched Billy in the face, knocking him to the ground. "I'll be leaving tomorrow, and you'll never see me again. So, just shut up." I turned to Jeff. "And do something useful with your life. Football is useless."

Victor frowned. "I like football."

I sighed. "Not now, Victor."

We walked the rest of the way to my house, and I stared up at the porch steps. This had been my strange, but cold home. The house used to be a place of fun, but now it only brought me sadness. I walked into the house and straight to the cupboard under the sink. I pulled out Darren's hidden bottle of whiskey and took three giant gulps before Ares jerked it away from me. The burning of the liquor distracted me as I wiped my mouth. "What?"

Ares snarled. "What are you doing?"

I shrugged. "It's not like I can get drunk easily."

Koda laughed. "No. Wait, how do you know that?"

I smiled. "I drank with Billy and Jess and J.D. one night, but nothing happened. They were smashed, but I wasn't."

Ares snarled. "Did he do anything?"

I rolled my eyes. "No."

Victor opened the fridge, and I watched in astonishment as he flipped a switch and a hidden compartment slid forward. Victor grabbed two bags of blood and closed the compartment again. Victor smiled at me. "It's customary for werewolves to keep blood on hand in case a vampire comes to visit."

I turned to Ares and asked, "So, now what?"

He smiled. "We rest here tonight."

The desire to touch him started intensifying, and I remembered Victor's words that it hurt Ares more. I walked forward slowly and leaned my head against his shoulder. The pain receded, and Ares sighed. I walked into the living room and sat down. "So, when you told Jess we were engaged, you weren't just being possessive were you?"

Ares shook his head. "How many times do I have to tell you this? You and I are the perfect couple."

"I'm an eighteen-year-old girl tied to a man I barely know who likes to kill people." I said irritably.

Ares frowned. "I don't *like* to kill people. It's just necessary."

Koda snorted. "Unless it's a Sidhe, then you like it."

Ares snarled at him and I asked, "What's a Sidhe?"

Ares sighed. "Another preternatural I do not want to discuss with you until necessary."

I frowned. "Why not?"

He spoke in clipped words. "Because I refuse to. I refuse to acknowledge their existence. Now, moving on, when we get to Victor's place there are going to be other werewolves there. Don't look the alphas or betas in the eyes, and you have to act submissive to them. The females are very aggressive towards each other, so for now, try not to make any eye contact with other females. You're especially going to be a target."

I frowned. "Why me?"

Koda smiled. "Because Ares was the hottest bachelor when we left. They've been drooling for him to come back and now you've taken him. So, they'll try to kill you so that he'll want them more."

I felt my jaw drop open and looked at Ares. He was gorgeous, but worth killing someone over? I tried to imagine him with another woman and a large growl ripped through my chest. My wolf stretched in my body, and I pleaded for her to go to sleep. Ares stared at me and I giggled in embarrassment. "Sorry, just testing a theory." I sighed. *Dammit I can't be willing to even think about killing someone over a man. It's so...true. Dammit. I barely know him and the thought of him with another woman makes me want to rip her head off!*

Ares smiled. "You have any questions?"

I nodded. "Do you have alpha females?"

Ares nodded. "We have ranks like the vampires. King, queen, prince, etcetera. To get to a place of high rank for werewolves, we have to defeat the current person in that rank in a battle. Vampires are all about bloodlines and crap, but our method is that the strongest and most powerful are the rulers. Survival of the fittest at its best."

I asked, "Are werewolves like vampires, where they get stronger or more powerful the older they are?"

Victor looked at me curiously. "I never told you that."

I smiled. "You can learn a lot from movies."

Ares nodded. "To a certain extent. Darren is very old, but not very powerful. It depends on your aura and abilities."

"But as a new werewolf, I'll be pretty much helpless against older ones?" I concluded.

Ares smiled. "That's why you have me. No one will be able to defeat me to get to you."

"If I am ever going to gain the respect of anyone in the pack, I have to fight my own battles!" I said, my hands forming fists. Ares frowned at me, and I could tell he wanted to order me not to get into battles ever. I rubbed my eyes. "I think we've talked enough tonight. I have a lot to think about and I'm tired." I started walking down the hallway to my room when I felt him behind me. "What, Ares?"

He laughed softly. "How'd you know it was me?"

I shrugged and turned to face him. "I can smell you. Plus, you have a weird feeling about you, like I want to bow to you." I groaned realizing I had said the last part out loud. "I didn't mean that."

Ares smiled. "It's normal for all wolves. As beta, I have a lot of authority, and it gives me a powerful aura."

I frowned, remembering Darren had discussed auras with me when I was younger. "Do you have an aggressive aura?"

Ares' brow furrowed. "What do you mean?"

I shrugged. "Darren said that people with aggressive auras are more likely to go on a rampage."

Ares shrugged back at me. "You can't see your own aura so you'd have to ask someone else."

"Well, I can't see anyone's aura." I said. Ares smiled at me and put his hand against my face. I instantly started to lean into his hand and jerked back. "I don't like that I'm like this."

Ares smiled. "What? That all you can think about is me touching you? I told you that you're my *passt genau*. We are destined to be together, forever."

I frowned. "What if I don't want to be with you forever?"

His smile slipped away into a look so filled with rejection, that I instantly regretted my words. He asked softly, "Am I not pleasing you? Is there something you would like me to change?"

I looked at his sculpted body and his handsome face and knew nothing needed to be changed. The girls I knew would do almost anything to be with a man like him. And here I was trying to throw it away before I even gave him a chance. I spoke softly. "It's not that Ares. I'm just really overwhelmed by my feelings for you and the fact that I don't know you. Maybe you could tone down on reminding me that I'm stuck…I mean that I'm supposed to be with you forever. I've never even had a boyfriend, and to be told I'm destined to be with you seems like a sentence, not a blessing."

Ares nodded and smiled a little. "I'll try. Just know that I'll do anything for you. No matter the cost."

I smiled. My hands ached to touch him and I gave in, letting my body rush forward and hug him quickly. I pulled away before I kissed him and darted into my bedroom and on to my bed. I listened to all of the new sounds I could hear with my heightened senses and smiled as the sound of the creek at the other end of our property gurgled. I drifted in and out of consciousness, but couldn't get the feeling that someone was going to attack me out of my head. I decided I needed sleep and even if I looked like a child, I would ask one of them to sleep in the room with me. I opened my door and screamed.

Victor, Koda, and Matt ran down the hallway then sighed in relief when they saw Ares sitting on the floor outside my door.

Ares frowned. "I'm sorry. I didn't mean to frighten you. I just didn't want to be too far away."

I finally regained my composure. "It's okay—you just startled me." He looked at me as if waiting for me to continue, and I looked at the ground. "Could you sleep in here tonight? I'm just—"

Ares jumped up and smiled. "Of course, I would prefer it actually, but I didn't want you to get the wrong idea."

I smiled at him and nodded. Victor winked at me, making me blush. I walked to my bed and heard him close the door quietly. I quickly took my shoes off and climbed into bed, closing my eyes. Ares climbed in behind me, and I tensed. *Not exactly what I had meant about sleeping in here.* He put his arm around my stomach, but kept space between our bodies. As much as I wanted to object, it was comforting to have him with me. I pulled the blanket around me tighter then realized I was sweating.

Ares whispered, "Having two werewolves in a bed at once usually makes blankets obsolete." I nodded and kicked the blankets off. We settled in, once again, and my brain shut off. The sound of arguing woke me. I opened my eyes and was instantly lost in Ares' sky blue eyes. He smiled at me. "Good morning."

I swallowed the lump in my throat at the realization that I had just technically slept with a *man*. Okay, okay. I know it's not the same thing, but he was in my bed because I asked him to sleep with me. "Morning. Who's fighting?"

"They're discussing politics. Nothing important." He rubbed my back slowly. "Did you sleep well?" He rolled on to his back, and I scooted over laying my head on his warm, bare chest. I inhaled his now familiar smell and nodded. "Very well."

He asked, "Are you feeling better?"

I sighed. "I'm realizing that being a werewolf isn't as scary as I first thought. I'm still worried I could go on a killing spree…"

Ares stroked my back with long, even movements. "I won't let you do that."

I smiled and looked up at his face.

I had expected him to be smiling, but he was serious. He stared into my eyes with a desire I had never seen before and then I felt it.

I reached up slowly, fearful of his reaction and ran my hand down his face.

A small smile played at the corners of his lips, and I couldn't hold myself back.

I moved up on the bed and kissed him on the lips.

The instant our lips connected fire shot through me and I moaned.

Ares' responding moan let me know that he was feeling the same thing. He kissed me back with a need of his own and wrapped his arms around me.

I ran my hands over his chest as we kissed and felt my lower body tighten. I gasped and tried to pull away, but Ares had repositioned us so that he was lying on top of me. I ran my hands through his thick black hair and kissed him harder, grabbing a chunk of his hair in my hands and pulling him to me.

He moaned again and thrust his tongue into my mouth. He kissed my lips once more and then moved down my jaw to my neck. My breathing sped up, and he smiled at me. The smile was perfect. Admiration, desire and happiness all in one. He kissed my lips one more time, before he jumped off me.

I frowned. "Where are you going?"

He smiled at me from the bedroom door. "I want you for your heart, not your body, but if I stay any longer with you kissing me like that, I don't know if I can hold myself back." He walked out of the room and my face erupted into a blush. I grumbled to myself as I changed clothes and went through my morning routine.

I walked out into the living room and stared at the pile of dishes in the sink. I opened the fridge and growled. "What happened to all of the food?"

Koda laughed. "You have three male werewolves in your house and you wonder where your food went? It's in our stomachs!"

I glared at him. "And you didn't think to leave some for me?" Koda's smile faded, and I sighed. "I'm sorry, I'm just hungry." I tapped my foot then sighed. "Well I guess we'll just have to go to the pub."

Ares asked, "Do you have money for the pub?"

I laughed. "You don't know Darren very well do you? I told you I had to go hunting." I walked to the bottom middle kitchen cabinet and pulled all of the canned food out onto the floor. A piece of tape held down a tiny white string, and I pulled on it, opening the small compartment Darren built into the cabinets. He always hated banks and being a couple hundred years old explained it better. I reached into the compartment and pulled out the long slender bag hidden inside. I shut the compartment and put the canned food away then tossed the bag to Ares. I walked quickly into Darren's room and tried to move the bed, but it was too heavy. I turned to see Koda in the doorway, smiling at me. "Can you move this?"

He shrugged and walked over to the bed. He put his foot

against the base and with a slight movement sent the bed flying across the room and into the wall. Ares ran in the room and sighed. "Koda."

Koda smiled. "Sorry. Couldn't help myself."

I rolled my eyes at him and walked to where the center of the bed used to be and sat down. I traced my fingertip along the edge of the two boards and smiled when I felt the air coming up on the edge of one. I pressed against the very end of the board and it popped up. The boards were only three inches wide so I had to turn my hand sideways to get it in. When my hand was in down to my wrist I had an evil idea. I hid my smile and then screamed as if in pain and acting like I was trying to pull my arm out. Koda rushed over to me and started trying to pull my arm out. He looked at my face, and I smiled. "Sorry, couldn't help myself."

Koda sighed. "Shit."

Ares laughed. "Looks like she'll be a handful for you too, Koda.

Koda groaned. "Damn, a prankster and a smart aleck like me. Wonderful."

I finished reaching under the floorboards and pulled the bag up. Darren must have added more while it was in the hole because it wouldn't come out. I stared at the small space and didn't want to ask for Koda's help again. As a werewolf, shouldn't I be able to break it apart? I made a fist and punched the board next to the open one and smiled as it broke apart. I punched the board on the other side of the hole and it broke open, too. Koda watched me with a small smile on his face. I cleared the piece of the board and grabbed the bag. I gasped when I realized how heavy it was. What used to be a three-inch by three-inch bag was now a ten-inch by ten-inch bag. I smiled and tossed it to Ares. "I think we have enough for a while."

He opened the two bags and smiled. "Darren didn't like banks, did he?"

I shook my head. "Not one bit."

Koda frowned. "What's in the bags?" Ares tossed him one and Koda's eyes lit up. "Damn, that's a lot of money."

I stood up then frowned at my hands. A couple of pieces of the boards were sticking out of my hand and it was bleeding. Ares rushed over to me and tossed the other bag of money to Koda. He picked my hand up gently and sighed. "This is why you don't punch wood."

"Thanks for telling me now." I said through gritted teeth. He started to pull a piece of wood out of my hand, and I groaned. "Ow. Ow. Ow."

He sighed. "You're going to have to let me pull these out."

I gritted my teeth. "Fine, but do it fast."

Koda laughed. "That's what he's best at."

I turned to him and wanted to ask what he meant, but Ares snarled. "Shush. Let's get this over with so she can eat." He smiled at me and then kissed my lips softly. Fire exploded on my lips, and I stared into his blue eyes. *Maybe being tied down to him wouldn't be so bad. I mean, man is he gorgeous.* He kissed my cheek and then dropped my hand. "That wasn't so bad now, was it?"

I frowned and looked down at my hand. All of the pieces of wood were out and the wounds were already healing. "Wow."

Koda snorted. "She's easily impressed."

I shook my head. "I've never really been injured so I never knew we could heal so fast."

"There are downsides to that." Koda said.

"Like what?" I asked curiously.

He smiled. "Healing too fast and having to cut out the pieces of wood."

I cringed. "Ow."

Koda nodded. "Definitely."

Ares asked, "Are we ready to go eat?"

I looked at him wearing Darren's jeans and t-shirt and smiled, "Almost. I need to pack some stuff." I took the money bags from Koda and walked to my bedroom, finding one of my backpacks. I shoved clothes and hygiene products into it, slung it on my back and then the men talking quietly out on the porch. I started to walk down the steps when Ares cleared his throat. I stopped and turned around. "Yes?"

He sighed. "Don't laugh, but can I hold your hand?"

I stared at him in shock for a second, then looked at Victor's face. He tilted his head to the side and I smiled at Ares. "Sure." I held my hand out towards him and he gave me his perfect smile again.

He interlaced our fingers, and we walked through town toward the pub. It felt good to be holding his hand. No, it felt perfect. He picked our hands up and kissed the back of my hand quickly. "Thank you."

I rubbed my face against his shoulder and sighed in contentment. "No problem."

The pub was slow, as usual, so we got a seat right away. I looked around for Darcy, but a new waitress I had never seen before walked over to our table. The instant Ares saw her, his entire body tensed. She smiled and spoke with a thick southern drawl. "How y'all doin'? What type of drinks can I start ya' off with?"

I smiled. "You're new here. I'm Artemis."

She laughed. "Oh, I know who you are, honey. I'm Sally."

I frowned. "You know who I am?"

She nodded and tilted her head towards the bartender. "He talks a lot about you and yer dad."

I smiled. "Oh. Well I'll have a soda." The men stared in frozen shock at her. I frowned. "What do you guys want?"

Ares shook his head. "It's time to leave."

I frowned. "Why?" I looked more closely at the waitress and didn't see anything out of the ordinary except that she was very attractive. I shrugged. "Guess we aren't eating here."

As I started to get out of the booth, she frowned. "Why her? Why not me?"

I stared at her, and Ares sighed. "Sally, she's my *passt genau*."

Sally's eyes widened, and she shook her head. "I don't believe you. You're just with her because she's younger. I'm not that old." She lowered her voice. "I'm only a hundred. You know that's young and you know I'm better."

Ares shook his head. "Sally, it wouldn't have worked between us even if I didn't find Artemis."

Sally snarled. "Let me kill her and prove I'm better."

Ares anger exploded from his body and his authority as beta beat against me like a wave of fire. He pushed me gently out of the booth and Koda grabbed me, wrapping his arms around my body. The instant Koda touched me, Ares' anger and authority stopped pressing against me. Ares spoke slowly, "Sally. She is my *passt genau*. You know the rules about that. If you kill her, it's an automatic death sentence. What would you gain?"

She smiled. "It's not a death sentence if she agrees to the fight."

Ares arms flexed, and she fell to her knees. "You will not speak of fighting or killing Artemis again. If you do, I will let the King judge you for attempted assassination."

She whimpered. "I just want to be yours."

Ares temper faded, and the pressure released as he squatted down and looked into her eyes, "You can find many others that would willingly be with you. I'm sorry, but I'm taken." Ares stood, and reached out for me. Koda released his hold on me and I walked quickly to Ares. He led me past the weeping waitress and outside.

We were almost to the SUVs when she burst out of the pub. "No! No I won't let her win. She's only a pup and not fit to be your mate."

I stared at the furious woman and could see the bloodlust in her eyes. Ares started to let go of my hand and I grabbed his bicep. "Please. Please don't kill her."

Ares frowned. "She wants to kill you."

I shook my head. "Being shunned for another woman younger

than you, is defeat enough. Let's just leave. Order her as beta to go to the nearest wolf town and stay there."

He frowned at me. "You want to spare her life, even though she's admitted that she wants to kill you?"

I nodded. "It's not worth it. Please Ares."

He sighed and rubbed his temples. "Alright Artemis." He kissed my cheek and walked towards Sally who was glaring at me with utter hatred. I turned to face Matt, and he put his arm around my shoulders. Ares picked my hand up and whispered, "It's done."

Sally stood and give Ares one last pain-filled look, and me, a look of contempt before running into the forest.

"Thank you." I stood on tiptoe and kissed his cheek. We started walking again and I couldn't get the look of pain she had had out of my brain. I stopped Ares. "How many women have you been with?"

He frowned. "What?"

I sighed. "How many, Ares? How many women am I going to have to deal with like Sally?"

He sighed. "I'm not sure."

I swallowed the lump in my throat and fought the tears away. *How can you not know for sure?* "More than fifty?" He nodded. I asked, "more than a hundred?"

He groaned. "I'm not sure."

Tears started to leak out, and I wiped them quickly. "At least I know." I walked away from him as quickly as I could towards the SUVs. My stomach growled loudly, and I scolded it, "We'll eat soon enough, just wait."

Ares spoke from beside me. "I didn't know I was going to have a match until you were born."

"I'm sure that stopped you." I frowned, crossing my arms over my chest.

He grabbed my arms and turned me towards him. I looked to my right to avoid making eye contact with him. He whispered, "Artemis. Artemis look at me." I turned my face and looked at him with the best frown I could muster. "I've been alive a long time and only when you were born, did I know that you might be my match. It wasn't even a positive thing then, either. Once I felt you, I couldn't be with another woman again."

I frowned. "What do you mean—felt me?"

He smiled. "The instant you were born my heart no longer looked at women. It was like they stopped being female and were just another wolf. I didn't know what was happening, until I talked with Darius."

I looked at Koda. "Is he telling the truth?"

Koda nodded. "He wouldn't even go to strip clubs with me."

Matt sighed. "We left Germany for America so he could get away from the females he had been with."

I frowned. "So, they think you've deserted them for eighteen years, but are hoping that you will come back, and then they can start up with you again?"

"I'm afraid so. If I had been positive about you, I would have told them the reason, but at the time, it was easier to just leave. Women can be very aggressive when they think you're choosing another over them."

I shrugged. "I guess I understand." I walked to one of the SUV's and climbed into the middle seat. I kept looking out the side window, not wanting to talk to Ares anymore. I knew it wasn't his fault, but it didn't hurt any less to know that he had been with so many women. We drove in silence through the smaller towns until we reached a drive-thru window.

Ares asked, "What do you want?"

I sighed. "Don't laugh. Five cheeseburgers, extra ketchup and a large chocolate shake."

Ares smiled. "Why would I laugh?"

Victor ordered food for everyone and Ares handed him money from my bag. Koda poked my arm from the back seat. I turned around, and he smiled. "How are you doing?"

I looked from Ares to him and shrugged. "Fine."

Koda sighed. “Come on. We’re pack now.”

I frowned. “Pack?”

Ares nodded. “Koda, Matt and I are a pack. And now that you are my mate you are part of our pack.”

I furrowed my brow. “You only have one female in your pack and that’s only because it’s me?”

Ares shrugged. “Matt and Koda haven’t found mates yet.”

Matt snorted. “Not looking either.”

I frowned. “Isn’t it like a natural instinct to find a mate?”

Matt shrugged. “You can fight your natural instincts. I don’t feel like being with a crazy female just because my *instinct* says I should.”

Victor tossed back the bags of food and handed Ares the drinks. I grabbed my burgers and shake and dug in, no longer wanting to engage in conversation. Victor continued driving, and after I was done eating, my eyelids started to droop. Ares put his arm around my shoulders and pulled me against him, pushing my head against his shoulder, “You need to rest.”

I shook my head. “All I do is sleep or eat.”

He kissed my forehead. “Your body is adjusting. It needs time to rest and recuperate.”

I looked down at the wolf burn on my hand. “How come this hasn’t gone away?”

Ares rubbed the small burn on my palm. Then he picked it up and kissed it, making the spot tingle. “Silver permanently scars us.”

I groaned. “Great.” I closed my eyes as I leaned against Ares. He hugged my shoulders and rubbed his chin against my forehead.

We drove with the radio on for a few hours and then Victor groaned, “Traffic.”

I looked up and saw the line winding into the airport. “Where are we going?”

Victor turned around and smiled. “France.”

I gasped and turned to Ares. “France! Do we get to visit the Eiffel Tower?”

Ares laughed. "Sure." My wolf seemed to wake inside me and stretched. I gasped, and Ares inhaled loudly. "She wants to hunt."

I blinked at him. "How'd you know?"

He smiled. "I could feel her and smell her."

I frowned. "But I can't even tell what she wants. She just woke up and stretched."

Matt laughed. "They never wake up unless they want something."

I lifted a brow. "Is she another personality?"

He shook his head. "No, she is you with some different instincts. She's a more primitive version of you. Of course you still think, but sometimes her instincts will take over. Which is why you need a strong alpha nearby to help you."

I smiled. "Which is why it's good to have you?"

He kissed my cheek. "Yes."

Victor finally pulled up to the front of the airport, and we all climbed out. Koda took my bag from me and we walked toward the counter. Ares held my hand and, even in the crowd of people I felt completely safe. The woman at the counter asked for our IDs. Victor handed her IDs and then waved his fingers. Her face went slack then she smiled and handed him our tickets. Ares pulled me towards the gate and when we were far enough away whispered, "Vampire powers come in handy with humans quite often."

Victor handed me my ID and plane ticket. I stared at my ID. "Artemis Lupine? Lupine isn't my last name." I said.

Ares smiled. "Lupine is my last name."

"Oh." I said in shock. He was already making changes that married couples make. I couldn't say my name with his last name though. It didn't seem right yet.

I looked at the plane tickets and my hands started to sweat. Ares frowned. "What's wrong?"

I licked my lips nervously. "I...I've never been on a plane and well..."

Koda laughed loudly. "She's scared!"

I growled at him, and my wolf snarled inside me. Koda's eyes flicked with golden specks, and he growled back. Ares grabbed both of our arms and his power hit me like a tidal wave of hot water. "Enough."

I kept my gaze even with Koda's, ignoring Ares as best as I could. Ares snapped his teeth at me and my wolf disappeared, leaving me weak. I started to fall forward and Ares put his arm around my waist, holding me up. I whimpered, "I…"

Ares shook his head, a golden tint to his eyes. "Be quiet."

Ares handed our tickets to the stewardess who smiled at me. "First flight?" I nodded, and she waved. "Have fun."

Ares led me inside the airplane and to our seats. I pulled away from him and stared out the window. Ares sighed. "Artemis, I wasn't trying to upset you."

I sighed. "I know. My wolf doesn't like the idea that Koda is dominant to me."

Ares rested his hand on mine and whispered, "All wereanimals hate enclosed metal places. It's natural for us to hate what amounts to a flying cage."

I looked up at his sincere face and asked, "Does it bother you?"

Ares nodded. "Very much, but when you're as old as me, you learn to hide the things that bother you. When enemies learn what bothers you, they use it against you."

The plane began moving down the runway and I gripped Ares' hand tightly. He rubbed his thumb across my hand and whispered, "I won't let anything happen to you."

I closed my eyes as the plane increased speed and began tilting upwards and lifting off the ground. "Would we survive a plane crash?" I asked quietly.

Ares laughed softly. "Well, it depends, but most likely." The plane leveled out and a high pitched ding made me open my eyes to look at the sign allowing us to move around the airplane. Ares picked my hand up to his lips and kissed the back of it softly. "You alright?"

I looked at the blood trickling down his hand and gasped. "Ares, I'm…I'm sorry." I tried to let go of his hand, but he held on to me.

"Calm down, Artemis. Look." He repositioned my hand in his so that he was still holding mine, but I could see the wounds I had made from my fingernails. The half circles that were filled with blood slowly stopped bleeding and then the skin closed completely with no sign of the cuts except the blood staining his hand.

Victor leaned over the back of our seats and handed Ares a handkerchief. "Would you mind? I'm hungry and I don't think you want another incident like Bosnia."

Ares rolled his eyes. "You should have eaten before we left, and Bosnia wasn't my fault. Koda bit me."

Koda sat down in an empty seat across from us. "I was only ten and you were being rude."

Victor scoffed. "It took me three *days* to heal from that crash, and my father spent five thousand dollars on outside help to finally convince the humans that it had been a lightning strike."

Ares rolled his eyes. "That's pocket change to your father and besides it would have been fine if you had eaten *before* we got on the plane with two hundred humans."

I looked at Victor as the pieces of what they were talking about fit into place. "You ate two *hundred* humans?"

Victor shushed me and whispered, "No, I tried to eat Ares and he changed and the humans freaked and I *killed* the two hundred humans."

I looked at Ares. "You killed them?"

Ares shook his head. "No, I was fighting with Koda because he was trying to eat the humans. Victor killed them."

Koda shrugged. "I'd only changed twice and humans smell *very* good when you're a pup."

I wrinkled my nose in disgust. "If you say so."

"You don't think they smell good?" asked Koda.

"They smell like humans, not food." I said seriously.

Ares smiled at me. "Really?"

I blushed and looked down. "Something else that makes me not normal?"

Victor was tapping his chin with his finger loudly. "It must be because she was raised around them and that boy was so close to her when she was fighting the changes so many times. She must have just associated their smell with friends. You know the wolves' friend, foe or food mentality."

Koda scoffed in the seat across from us. "Food can be foe or friend also."

I looked up at him in shock. "You'd eat a friend?"

Ares shook his head smiling. "Not a friend as in another wolf, but like a friendly dog."

I stared at Ares then saw the smile Victor had to the side of me. "That's really not funny."

Victor and Ares laughed loudly and the overweight woman in front of us turned her head and shushed us. I stuck my tongue out at her and she turned back around whispering loudly to the balding man beside her about "disrespectful youth".

Ares reached across me, and my heart sped up instantly at the nearness of his body to mine. His smile widened as he pushed up the window cover so we could see outside the plane. I closed my eyes as he and Victor looked out the window. Ares whispered, "Artemis, just look. It's very beautiful."

I shook my head and squinted my eyes closed harder. "No thanks. I'll pass."

Victor sighed. "And here I thought the Great Ares would get an adventurous mate, but it looks like he got a wimp."

I nodded with my eyes still closed. "Yep, sorry Victor, not falling for the bait."

The plane bounced around as we hit a patch of turbulence, and I gripped the arms of the seat and squealed in fear. The arms began moaning in protest of my grip, and Ares pried my left hand off the arm between us and laced his fingers with mine. "Artemis, do you think I'm a liar?"

I turned my head towards him and opened one eye. "What?" The plane jolted again, and I closed my eyes, squeezing tightly on his hand and the right chair arm.

He whispered, "I told you that I wouldn't let anything happen to you and yet you're destroying the plane in your fear of falling out of the sky. Do you think I'm lying when I tell you that I'll protect you?"

The pain and sincerity in his voice made me open my eyes and loosen my grip. I looked at him and it caused my stomach to knot up at the sight of his pain. "I don't think you're a liar, but you couldn't possibly protect me from everything."

Ares frowned. "So, you do think I'm a liar? I'll just have to prove it to you." He leaned towards me and cupped my face with his hands. His skin was warm and his breath was hot as he kissed me on the lips. Fire exploded in my body, and I wrapped my arms around his neck. He pulled away from the kiss and whispered, "Nothing matters to me now except you. This plane could fall on my mother's house and my only worry would be your safety. Trust me to protect you."

I nodded and licked his cheek. "I'm sorry."

He smiled. "You licked me again?"

I shrugged. "I am a wolf."

He whispered, "Will you accept your place in my pack now?"

I frowned. "What do you mean?"

Matt whispered from behind me, "He means will ya' accept him as yer' mate and me and Koda as yer' packmates?"

I turned my head so I could see Matt through the crack in the seats. "What happens?"

Matt smiled. "We go on a hunt and you finally sleep with us."

My eyes widened, and Matt shook his head. "Love, your mind is filled with dirty thoughts. I only meant that we sleep in the same bed with you, not *sleep* with you."

Ares growled. "No, not the latter."

Koda sighed. "Ares has never been good about sharing."

Ares sighed. "We hadn't eaten in four days and I killed it! Besides I apologized the next day."

I smiled and asked, "What happened?"

Koda leaned around Ares and talked just loud enough for me to hear, but not for the humans on the plane. "We were running through Germany and hadn't been able to find a house or food for a few days. Well as you can imagine we were ravenous. Ares here sees a lone stag and takes off after it, killing it in like three seconds. I walked over to eat my share, and he attacks me!"

I gasped, "No!"

Matt stood up and leaned over the tops of our seats. "So, while Ares is chasing Koda around, I run over and started eating off the stag. As you can imagine that wasn't alright with Ares. So, he leaves Koda and charges after me!"

Koda laughed and shook his head. "We had to keep drawing him away and then sneaking in to eat like that for two hours before we got our fill and then we both ran off and let Ares eat."

Ares sat back in his seat and frowned. "I apologized afterwards. Besides I'm supposed to eat first and you both know it."

Matt asked, "When are we going to test the new dominance layout?"

"It depends on how she feels. I don't want to push her too soon." Ares said softly.

"You're talking about me like I'm not here." I pouted.

Ares smiled and rested his hand on my knee and closed his eyes. "Sorry, baby."

I smacked his hand off my knee and snarled, "Don't call me baby!"

Ares opened one eye and looked at me with a completely calm, neutral face. "What would you like me to call you?"

I frowned. "I don't know, but not baby or darling or…well I can't think of anything you could call me."

Ares closed his eye again and replaced his hand on my knee. "I'll think of something."

Matt smiled. "Glad I took Love already."

Ares scoffed. "Yeah, thanks."

I relaxed back into my seat and noticed the window still open from the corner of my eye. I closed my eyes and reached over, searching along the wall for the window cover. I finally found it and pulled the cover down and then opened my eyes again, only to find Ares, Koda and Matt watching me. I blushed and looked down at my hands in my lap. Koda sighed. "You think she'll ever stop blushing?"

Ares rubbed his thumb across my kneecap. "I hope not."

More blood rushed to my face and Victor whispered from behind Ares, "I can smell her from here. Knock it off."

Ares laughed softly and pulled his hand off my leg. "My apologies, Victor. We should all rest. It's going to be a *long* night once we arrive."

The absence of his hand was like a bee sting. I pushed up the middle arm, scooted closer to Ares and leaned my head against his shoulder. I closed my eyes and reveled in the happy electric current thrumming through my body. Ares kissed the top of my head and then laid his head on top of mine.

CHAPTER EIGHT

I pulled myself out of a dreamless sleep as I heard the stewardess talking quietly to Ares in another language. Instantly my anger began to well up. I opened my eyes and found myself inches from her breasts. I sat up quickly and was about to snarl when Ares grabbed my hand, and the anger disappeared. I stared at his hand as though it were a bear trap and asked, "How'd you do that?"

The stewardess handed me a pillow and then walked away. Ares whispered, "I wasn't doing anything with the stewardess, and I very politely explained that we were getting married. I had no idea she would start discussing it with me and then she insisted on getting a pillow for you even though we're about to land."

The pillow fell off my lap as I moved back into my own seat and faced the closed window. "I didn't say anything."

Ares whispered, "You didn't have to. I could feel your anger like a growing forest fire."

I looked at him and asked again, "How'd you do that?"

He smiled. "I took your anger from you. It's a handy trick you learn when you become an alpha." The stewardess stood in the front of the plane and picked up the intercom. She began speaking in fluent French, and I felt my anger rising again. She was pretty and thin, model thin. Ares sighed. "I would never cheat on you."

My anger rose at the thought of Ares with another woman and my body temperature began rising. Matt growled softly behind me, and Ares growled back. Koda whined softly and I took a giant breath then let it out slowly. The anger vanished, and my body cooled down. Matt snorted and Koda sighed. Ares thumped my arm softly. "Cool down."

I smiled and looked at his golden eyes. "I am. You seem to be upset still though."

Ares shook his head and the gold faded. "To feel your strong emotions is hard on me. Our connection is still new and not finished yet. The connection between our emotions is designed this way to keep you safe, but you're a little more volatile than most your age."

His words stung as I deciphered between the lines and got the unspoken word of "immature." The seatbelt light chimed over our heads giving me a chance to look away from Ares and put my belt on. The plane began to descend, and I gripped the armrests tightly. Ares held out his hand, but I ignored him by closing my eyes and leaning back against the seat as the plane landed on the runway. I kept my eyes closed until the attendant got back on the intercom and I could hear people beginning to stand up. I unbuckled my seatbelt and stood facing the front of the plane.

Koda walked up from the back, carrying my backpack. I held out my hand, and he shook his head, smiling. "I'll carry it."

I wanted to argue, but Ares was watching and we were next to walk out of the plane. "Thanks." The desire to touch Ares was growing stronger, but I refused to give in. There was no reason I had to touch him *all* the time. Victor led the way out of the airport and to a waiting limousine. I smiled at him. "I've never gotten to ride in a limo before."

He smiled at me. "Well then, get in."

I ducked into the limo and climbed over on the seat to look out the large side windows. The others climbed in behind me and the driver started the limo. I moved from one side of the limo to the other as we drove through France. The Eiffel Tower loomed over us as we drove by it and I asked, "Do we get to go see it?"

Ares frowned. "If we have time."

I was about to pout when Koda said. "Matt and I will take you tomorrow while Ares is in meetings."

Ares shook his head and folded his arms across his chest. "Absolutely not. She's not to be away from me while we're here."

Matt glared at Ares. "You think we wouldn't be able to protect her?"

Ares growled. "I think there are too many leeches, no offense Victor, in this city."

Victor frowned. "Why would any vampire want to bother Artemis? There are only a few people who have seen her and those are either in America or my father."

Ares shook his head. "I'm alpha of this pack and I say that I don't want her out of my sight."

"Ares, you're being overprotective. No one would want to take Artemis or hurt her. Gregory was just psycho and an exception and Darren was supposed to have killed her years…uh oh." Koda stopped talking, looked down at the ground and rubbed the back of his neck.

My eyes bulged out of my skull as I looked at each of the four men who were quickly averting their gazes from me. "What do you mean Darren was supposed to have killed me?"

Ares looked up. "You're a mixed blood, Artemis. Mixed bloods aren't supposed to be made let alone allowed to live. Your father was ordered by the king at the time you were born to kill you. As we can see he never did."

The words sunk in slowly until the painful truth hit. "He'd been planning it for after Bret left."

All of the men looked at me in shock. Ares asked, "What do you mean?"

Tears began running down my cheeks and I hugged my knees to my chest. "I heard Darren talking on the phone a few times about his plans. He would tell the person that it was going to be harder to do than he originally thought and to just give him until after Bret left. He always told me that I didn't need to worry about trying to find friends after Bret left, and I thought he meant that I'd find others, not that I'd be dead."

Ares growled and rushed across the limo, picking me up and holding me in his lap. "He won't hurt you now. I won't let him."

I buried my face in his chest and inhaled his scent, which was fast becoming familiar and comforting. In a matter of minutes, the sorrow at my revelation disappeared, and I was relaxed again. Deciding to ignore the news about my father, I whispered, "Can I go see the Eiffel Tower tomorrow?"

Ares sighed. "Dammit."

I lifted my face and licked his cheek. "Please."

Ares groaned. "Alright! But you have to stay with Koda and Matt at all times, even bathroom trips."

I kissed his lips quickly and jumped across the limo to look out the window. "I can't wait!"

Matt turned on the seat beside me and started pointing out places we would visit as the limo drove on. The city faded into countryside, and I sat down in my seat sighing loudly after thirty minutes. "When are we going to be there? I'm hungry."

Victor smiled showing his fangs. "Care to make a bet on who's hungrier?"

Ares growled. "Don't test me Victor."

My legs began to go numb from sitting so long and I slid to the floor, kicking my feet. "Dang it, my legs are falling asleep."

Victor smiled. "We're almost there. I'd say five more minutes, tops."

I folded my legs into my body and asked, "What's it like?"

Victor shrugged. "You'll see."

Ares held his hand out towards me, and I took it, giving into the longing I'd been trying to ignore for the last hour. He pulled me up on to the seat beside him, and I laid my legs across his lap. He started massaging my calves, and I moaned in pleasure. "Wow, you're really good at that."

"I'm very good at a lot of things." Ares winked at me, and I blushed, closed my eyes and enjoyed the massage.

Koda asked, "Do we have to dress up tomorrow?"

I opened my eyes to see the interaction. Ares nodded. "Of course. I don't want to go before them dressed in Darren's clothes."

Koda sighed. "I know. I just hate wearing a jacket all the time."

Victor shrugged. "You could wear dress casual instead."

Matt shook his head. "If we dress at all we will dress formal. It's how Ares likes it."

Ares shrugged. "If I'm going to try to look good I might as well look great."

"When don't you look great?" I gasped as the words slipped out of my mouth. I yanked my legs away from Ares and curled up into a ball trying to hide my blush.

Ares picked me up in my ball position and set me on his lap. "Thank you."

I mumbled, "You're welcome," from inside my ball.

Ares rested his head against my shoulder and whispered into my ear, "You always look great, too."

Part of me wanted to climb out of Ares' lap, but a larger part of me enjoyed his arms around me. I gave into the larger part and relaxed out of my ball to wrap my arms around his shoulders and rest my face in the crook of his neck. The temptation to bite him gnawed at me so I nipped his throat lightly. He growled, "No."

I whined and nipped his neck again letting the wolf instincts take a little bit of reign over my human ones. Ares growled at me again and bit my shoulder hard enough to make me gasp, but not hard enough to really hurt. I nipped his chest and jumped out of his arms to crouch on the floor of the limousine. Ares was crouched on top of the seat smiling at me and I swore I could see an image of a tail wagging behind him. Koda yipped excitedly behind me and jumped towards me. I rolled away from him, and Matt jumped on top of me. I nipped his arm and rolled away from him running into Ares who bit my bottom. I snarled and jumped around, biting his shoulder and then jumping on top of the seat beside Victor. Victor shook his head and sighed. "Wolves. You're all so silly."

I looked down at the crouched position I was in and plopped down on my butt sitting like a human and blushing at the things I had just done. Ares was staring at me with golden eyes. "You don't want to play anymore?"

I shook my head and blushed. "No."

Koda whined. "Play."

Matt nodded vigorously.

Victor sighed. "Point a sharp object at them and they'll rip your head off without a second thought, but offer to play tag and they become children pouncing around like fairies." Ares growled and Victor smiled "You know what I meant."

A large rod iron gate with swirls and flowers decorating it came into view and Victor sighed. "Finally."

Ares, Matt and Koda shook their heads and sat down on the seats normally. Koda and Matt folded their arms across their chests angrily, and Ares stared out the window ignoring me. They were mad at me. The gate opened, and we drove past rows and rows of grapes. "The vampire capitol of the world is in a vineyard?" I asked.

Victor shook his head. "It's a winery."

I rolled my eyes. "You know what I meant."

Victor smiled. "There are hundreds of miles of tunnels below us and we earn money from the winery to sustain a comfortable way of life. The humans get great tasting wine, and we get a place of solitude. It's a win-win situation for everyone."

I frowned. "Except for the people you eat."

Victor shrugged. "Eat a few, release a thousand. It's still a good deal."

The mansion we pulled up in front of was easily three times the size of any celebrity's in the United States I had ever seen on TV. Two muscular men stood beside two giant wooden doors. I looked closely at their bodies and turned to Ares. "The vampires use werewolf guards?"

Ares smiled. "I'm surprised you could tell they are wolves from here."

"Low amounts of body fat and high amounts of muscle suggest steroids or inhuman metabolisms. I figured the vampires would feel safer with werewolves than steroid using humans."

Victor laughed, making me shiver in delight. "You are very perceptive."

Ares frowned. "You need to eat, Victor."

Victor cleared his throat. "Sorry about the voice thing. As Ares said I need to eat or…well let's not discuss that." The driver opened the door for us and Victor climbed out first, smiling at the driver with a flash of his fangs, and walked up the steps towards the werewolf guards at the entrance. Koda and Matt climbed out next, waiting a few feet away from the limousine.

Ares smiled at me. "It'll be alright. No one will harm you, especially not with me beside you." I nodded, but licked my lips nervously. Ares asked, "Would you let me hold your hand? It'll make me feel better."

He climbed out of the car before I could answer, and I sighed in relief. *All I want is for him to hold my hand.* I climbed out of the car and reached for his hand. He squeezed my hand reassuringly and we started up the steps. The two guards at the door placed their fists over their hearts and bowed at the waist to us. Ares mimicked their gesture and smiled. "Greetings, brothers."

The guards smiled and spoke in unison, "Greetings, Prince."

Ares pointed at me. "My *passt genau* is with me during this visit.

If she needs anything, you come to her aid. Her needs are the most important out of anyone's here."

The guards sniffed the air, and Ares face went neutral as he waited. I stared at the two guards who were at least six and a half feet tall and built like walls. My feet started to move towards them and Ares nodded, simultaneously letting my hand go. I walked slowly up to the guards and inhaled the smell of forest, fur and also getting their individual smells mingled in as well. They inhaled deeply and smiled wide. They both spoke in unison again, officially creeping me out, "Greetings, sister."

I smiled. "Greetings, brothers."

Ares took my hand and pulled me away from the guards and into the mansion. The mansion was dimly lit and there were only a few servants running around in uniforms. Ares whispered, "The vampires are all downstairs since it is still daylight. When the sun sets, they will all come up here to mingle."

I asked, "Do I have to dress up tomorrow, too?"

Ares nodded and kissed my cheek. "Don't worry. One of the seamstresses will have something to fit you."

I wanted to protest, but a beautiful woman walked up to us speaking in rapid French. Ares nodded and then spoke back to her in French. She looked down at me and frowned, slowly letting her eyes travel up my body from my feet. She looked back at Ares and spoke again, pointing rapidly at me then back to herself and then at Ares. Ares sighed and shook his head. "Sophe..." His words were French again so I couldn't keep up, but at least I knew her name.

Koda ran his hand down my right arm and my body relaxed a little. He smiled at me. "It's alright. He's just explaining who you are."

I frowned and looked at the beautiful French woman. "She's one of the women he's slept with, isn't she?"

Ares turned to me and frowned. "Artemis..."

I pulled my hand out of his and smiled. "It's alright. Talk to her, and I'll talk to Koda."

Ares looked like he wanted to object, but Sophe was speaking angrily to his back trying to get his attention. Koda opened his arms, and I stepped forward into his body. Matt walked up behind me and hugged me from behind, wrapping his arms around Koda in the process. I asked, "Aren't you going to make a comment about him hugging you?" I asked Koda.

Koda shook his head. "We're pack and the touch of our pack mates is soothing. Like Ares' touch to you, but not the sexual part. Matt is my brother."

Matt kissed the top of my head then stepped back. "Don't be so upset, Love. He's simply trying to calm 'er down. Angry female werewolves are not fun to deal with."

I pulled away from Koda and stared at the animated conversation that was going on between Ares and Sophe. "She loves him."

Koda nodded. "She does, but she also knows that he never loved her."

"I can't handle this." I started to walk away, but Koda and Matt walked beside me. Ares watched me out of the corner of his eyes, but was trying to pay attention to the yelling French woman in front of him.

Luckily, she kept his attention while we started on our way. Koda gave me a tour of the main floor of the mansion, which consisted of a dining room, a living room, a kitchen bigger than my house, a game room with poker tables, pool tables and two giant televisions, and six bedrooms. We were about to walk out to the back patio and to the pool that Matt said was just beyond, when Ares caught up to us. He whispered, "I'm sorry, Artemis." He held out his hand, and I accepted it. He hugged me against him. "Are you alright?"

I shook my head. "No, but there's not much that can be done."

He tilted my chin up and kissed my lips. "Would an hour-long back massage make up for it?"

I smiled. "It'll help." Ares smiled at me, and I couldn't stay mad at him. I groaned. "It's not fair that I can't stay mad at you."

Ares kissed me again. "Not fair at all."

Matt cleared his throat. "Could we continue now?"

Ares bowed at the waist. "Of course, my liege. Forgive my rude interruption."

Matt rolled his eyes. "Jerk."

Ares smiled. "Baby."

Matt opened the patio door for me and continued the tour of the acre patio with dining tables and candelabras, and then onto the two-acre wide pool. Ares and Koda debated over whether it should technically be considered a pond or lake, since it was so large, but Matt argued that the fact that they used a pool pump and chlorine made it a pool. I tried to engage in their debate, but there was a strange weight resting on my chest and back. I tried to figure out what it was when the words popped into my head on their own: powerful darkness. The presence became heavier as the sun moved down towards the horizon. Ares rubbed my arm and kissed my cheek, as we walked back towards the mansion.

Koda led the way down the hallways as if he owned the place and into a large bedroom. The bedroom had one giant bed, which could sleep at least five people comfortably. A desk and chair as well as a couch sat against the walls on the room. One door led to the bathroom with Jacuzzi tub and open shower. The second door led to a walk-in closet bigger than my bedroom had been. Ares stopped at the entrance to the bedroom and spoke quickly to a maid in French. The maid left and then Ares came to stand beside me at the large bed. "We had these specifically made for those wishing to sleep in packs."

I jumped up on to the bed and sank into the cushions, sighing in pleasure. I started to push the mound of pillows off the bed, but decided it might be rude. I buried myself under the pillows instead. The bed moved and I smelled Ares before he pulled the two pillows that were covering my face off. "Does this mean you like it?"

I nodded and took the pillows back, recovering my face with

them. The men were talking about something serious and boring, so I decided to take a shower. I climbed off the bed and rearranged the pillows as close to the original shape as I could remember, and then walked toward the bathroom. Ares asked from close behind me, "Are you taking a shower?" I nodded then froze when I felt him behind me.

"Ares, please."

Ares shrugged and picked me up in his arms walking towards the bathroom.

I gasped, "No! Ares, that's not what I meant!"

He set me down and frowned. "Why are you scared?"

My heart was beating faster than it ever had before. "Ares, you can't come in there with me."

He sighed. "Oh, I see. I was raised better. I'm sorry."

I hurried into the bathroom and showered quickly. I wrapped myself in a towel and peeked my head out the door. "Can one of you bring my bag?"

Koda started towards the door with the bag, but Ares took it from him and handed it to me. Koda stuck his tongue out at Ares behind his back, making me giggle. Ares turned around, but Koda sucked his tongue back in and winked at me. I quickly changed into my bathing suit and turned on the giant tub and its jets. I walked back to the bathroom door and opened it before hopping into the large tub. A few moments later Ares stuck his head inside then smiled. "You know that is a tub, right?"

I shrugged. "It looks and feels like a spa to me. Plus, it's big enough to fit me and at least three other people." He walked in and sat on the edge of the tub trailing his hand in the bubbling water. I swallowed the nervousness I was feeling and asked, "Would you like to join me?"

He smiled at me and then disappeared from the bathroom. I heard low quick whispers and then he was back in the bathroom wearing a pair of swimming shorts. I stared at his muscular body and couldn't help the reaction of my lower body. I sat up straighter as he climbed into the spa. He frowned. "Isn't this a little hot for you?"

I shook my head. "No, but if it's too hot for you I can turn it down." I reached behind me to the complicated controls and hit the down arrow to decrease the temperature. Sometimes modern technology is a godsend.

He smiled at me. "You look great in that bikini."

I blushed and looked down at the water. "Thanks." I started swirling the water with my hands and felt the water move as he shifted across the tub.

He sat down beside me and whispered, "I know this is all new to you, and I'll try to be as well behaved as I can."

I turned to him and saw the desire in his eyes. I suddenly reached up and kissed him on the lips. He kissed me back and heat exploded between us. He wound his hand through my thick hair and gripped the back of my neck pulling me against him. I wrapped my arms around his shoulders and ran my hand through his hair. His hair was as thick as mine. Our kiss grew until he pulled back to gasp for air. I smiled at him and ran my hand across his sculpted chest. He flexed his chest, but it didn't appear to be on purpose, simply a reaction to my touch. I leaned forward and kissed his lips again, and he stayed perfectly still. He slowly released his grip on my hair and slid his hand away from my neck to rest beside him in the water. I could see the need in his face and could tell just how much he was holding back by the stiff posture and the white of his knuckles as he made a fist. I hadn't ever been with a boy or man before and didn't know what to do or not do. I kissed his cheek then his lips and climbed off of him to sit beside him. He exhaled, and I realized that he had been holding his breath. I stared at the water and wondered what he thought of me and my moments of hormonal insanity.

He stayed very still for a few minutes then turned to me. His eyes blazed with power and he asked deadpan, "Why did you stop?"

I smiled at him. "You were holding your breath and I didn't want you to die."

He smiled. "With you touching me I would fight death to the end.

I frowned at him. "You can't die."

His smile faded, and he wrapped his arms around me holding me against him. "I won't die as long as I have you."

I sniffed and realized I was crying. "You're all I have."

Someone cleared their throat and Ares and I turned around slowly, with Ares keeping his arm around my shoulder the entire turn. I wiped my face with the back of my hand, but that only spread the water from my hand on to my face. Koda and Matt stood in the doorway smiling. Koda spoke with a soft voice that had an Irish lilt to it. "You have more than Ares. You have us, too. We're pack now and if Ares leaves or dies we will still be with you."

I stared at him, realizing that he was opening himself up to me. I waved at him to come closer and Matt and Koda jumped into the tub still wearing their jeans and t-shirts. Water splashed over the sides of the tub and onto the floor. I moved forward and hugged them both at the same time. They inhaled and I did too, taking time to memorize the smell of my pack. They both smelled like the forest and underneath lingered a scent of crisp clean grass. Koda and Matt hugged me for a while then let go and pushed me back towards Ares. Ares put his arm around my waist and squeezed me against him. "See Artemis, you aren't alone anymore and you won't ever be again."

I started to cry again, and they all held me in the center of them in a group hug. My wolf swirled inside me and reached out with some invisible force to touch each of their wolves. I could see all of their wolves staring at me and I wasn't afraid. *These wolves won't hurt me. These wolves are my pack and they will do everything to protect me and keep me happy.* I realized it was my wolf's thinking and frowned at her, but she was too happy to pay attention to my feelings. We sat in our huddle for a few minutes longer as my tears faded and then everyone got out. I dried off then sighed at my now wet bag on the floor. I started to pull everything out when something cold fell into my hand then began burning. It felt like acid burning my skin, but it was solid, not liquid. I dropped to my knees and screamed in pain trying to pull my hand out.

Ares, Koda, and Matt surrounded me and started growling. Ares reached towards the bag, but jerked his hand back at the last second. "Victor!" Ares yelled.

Victor appeared over me and hissed, flashing his fangs. The others moved back some ways to give him room. Victor reached down and pulled the bag off exposing my hand and what was attached to it. I stared at the silver photo frame with a picture of a tall slender woman with purple eyes and wondered how it had gotten into my bag. Victor started to pull the frame from my hand, but it was burned into the skin and hurt like hell. Ares growled and Victor frowned. He spoke in soothing tones to the wolves surrounding me, "I have to get it out of her hand before this enters her blood and kills her."

Ares nodded, but was still snarling at Victor. Koda had dropped down and was cradling my head in his lap. Apparently, I had fainted at some point. Matt held my other hand as Victor yanked the frame from my hand. I screamed and blacked out.

CHAPTER NINE

I woke up surrounded by heat and tried to kick the blankets off, but kicked empty air. I was fully clothed when I had previously been in a bikini. I turned my head and realized I was surrounded by Koda on my right, Ares on my left and Matt at my feet. I started to sit up when searing pain made me whimper and stare at my bandaged hand. All three men sat up at once and stared at me. They were all wearing blue jeans and no shirts, making me look from one muscled chest to another. Ares stroked my face and frowned. "You're sweating."

I nodded. "It's too hot."

He gave a single quick nod and Matt and Koda climbed off of the bed, letting a cool wave of air hit me. I inhaled and then coughed, nearly gagging. "What is that smell?"

Ares stroked my cheek. "Your burnt flesh."

I groaned as I remembered the picture frame. "I didn't even pack that. I'm guessing it was silver and that's why it burned me?"

Ares nodded. "Silver is our weakness. I'd like to know how it got into your bag."

I frowned. "I don't know, but I think it was a picture of my mom. Can I see it?"

Ares shook his head. "Victor had to destroy it."

"What?!" I gasped. "He couldn't have just taken the picture out and then destroyed the frame?"

Victor spoke from behind me, "I did not have time. Your pack's instinct to protect you was on overload. They might have attacked me if I took too long."

I whimpered. "I didn't even get a good look at her. I only remember fragmented memories. Enough to know that I look like her."

Victor sat one hip on the edge of the bed beside me. He was wearing a pair of black slacks and a dark blue button up shirt that looked like silk. He smiled. "I am sorry that I did not think about what you would have liked. I just wanted to get it away so I didn't have to fight your pack."

I nodded and turned my gauze wrapped hand around. "Thank you."

Ares asked, "Why would Darren have had a silver frame anyway? He wouldn't have been able to hold it either."

I smiled. "It was my mom's frame."

"How do you know that?" asked Ares.

"Dad said he only had one thing of hers and never let me see it, so I'm guessing the picture frame was it," I responded quietly.

Ares whispered, "I'm sorry we didn't keep the picture for you."

I shrugged. "It's alright." I felt something tingling on my hand under the gauze and squeaked like a scared mouse. "What the hell?" I started unwrapping my hand and Ares and Victor tried to stop me. Once I had it unwrapped, I stared in shock at the mutilated skin that used to be my hand. The tingling increased and the burned skin shed off on to the floor as a new layer of skin replaced the old. "What happened?" I gasped.

Ares smiled. "Interesting."

Victor said, "It must be because of her other—" Ares growled, stopping him from speaking further. Victor bowed his head and continued, "It must be from her mother. Perhaps silver is not a permanent problem for our little goddess."

I frowned at Ares. "Why won't you let me know what my mother is and what I am?"

He smiled. "I will soon, but for now it's best if you don't know."

I didn't believe him, but decided not to press the matter. I ran a finger over my newly healed skin and smiled. "Wow."

Koda walked over. "The seamstress is here with the clothes for Artemis to choose from."

I looked around Koda to see a girl, no older than twenty, standing beside a rolling clothes rack filled with dresses. I looked at Ares and groaned. "A dress? You're making me wear a dress?"

"Don't you want to look nice for the King and Queen of the Vampires?" Ares asked.

I folded my arms across my chest. "The King has already met me. I've never even worn a dress before."

Ares kissed my cheek. "Then this will be a good learning experience for you. Besides, don't you want to look nice for me?"

There was no winning this argument, so I sighed and walked towards the girl. She looked from my toes to my head and then back again, frowning nonstop. "She is the one I am supposed to dress?" Her thick accent caught me off guard and it took me a moment to decipher what she had said.

Ares bowed at the waist to the girl. "Hello, Lucy. It's always an honor to see you."

Lucy folded her arms over her chest. "Flattery will not win you any points with me, Ares. I'm not a magician you know." She looked at me in disgust again. "Am I to bring our beautician in as well? She looks to need it."

I opened my mouth to call her one of the rude names I could think of, but Ares spoke before I could say anything. "Lucy, it would be wise to remember your place as well as what mine is. She is my *passt genau*; treat her with respect. Your insults of her are direct challenges to me."

Lucy's bottom lip quivered, but then she shook her head and straightened her back before turning back to me. "I apologize for my insults. I'm old and 'ow you say? Cranky, yes, 'zats the word."

I looked at her face and frowned. "Old? You don't look old."

Lucy smiled. "That is one of the benefits of being a dhampir." She saw my puzzled face and frowned at Ares. "You bring 'er to the vampire's 'ome without training as to what we are?"

I waved my hand at her. "I know what a dhampir is, half-vampire and half-human. I've just never seen one before. And I thought you were supposed to be enemies with vampires?"

Ares said, "I have much to teach her, Lucy. I only found her a few days ago."

Lucy turned back to me. "Dhampirs and vampires are enemies, but my father is very powerful and 'as enough pull to keep me alive and 'appy as long as I don't kill any of the vampires."

"I understand," I told her.

She sighed heavily. "Let's get started. We 'ave only an 'our to prepare you."

She walked to the dress rack and tapped her chin thoughtfully. Ares walked towards her, and she hissed. "Go get ready. I do not want you breathing down my neck while I prepare 'er. I will do my best to make 'er perfect for you." Her French accent seemed to grow stronger whenever she spoke to Ares.

Ares sighed. "Fine. Koda will stay in the room with you, Artemis."

Lucy blinked at Ares. "You do not trust me?"

Ares smiled. "I don't trust anyone to be alone with her." Ares walked over and kissed my lips quickly before hurrying to the bathroom. My skin began itching, and I began breathing faster.

Koda walked over to me and touched my shoulder. The smell of forest and wolf slowed my breathing, but the desire to run after Ares was still very strong. Lucy smiled. "Interesting." She turned back to the dresses and picked out a purple one and held it up to my face. "It matches your eyes, but I am not sure if it will work. Put it on."

I pulled off my jeans and t-shirt, trying hard to ignore the fact that Koda was right behind me, and pulled the dress on over my head. The bust was a little tight, but manageable and the material was soft against my skin. I spun in a slow circle for Koda and Lucy. Lucy tapped her chin and turned to Koda. "What do you think, Wolf?"

Koda smiled. "It's perfect."

Lucy frowned. "Hmm…per'aps I will like it more once the makeup and 'air is done. I'll fetch the beautician."

She pushed her cart out of the room leaving me alone with Koda. The bathroom door cracked open and Ares asked, "Did you find a dress?"

Koda answered, "Yes and it's very nice."

Ares asked, "Did Lucy leave?"

"Yes," I answered.

Matt walked out of the bathroom with a towel tied around his waist. I found myself staring at his abdominal muscles and remembering what it felt like to touch Ares in the tub. Ares growled softly. "Artemis, what are you thinking about?"

I swallowed. "Uh, nothing."

Matt laughed. "It's alright, Love. And that dress looks amazing on you."

Ares groaned. "I want to see it."

I yelled, "NO! You can't see me until you're ready. Plus, I'm not *ready* yet."

Ares sighed. "Fine, but stop thinking whatever it is that you were thinking."

I blushed and looked towards the bedroom door. Two soft knocks brought Koda's attention to the door as well. He opened it to reveal a tall, thin French woman in a business suit and four inch heels. She winked at Koda. "'Ello 'andsome."

Koda smiled. "Hey there, Madeleine. You're looking scrumptious as ever."

Madeleine walked to me and frowned, crossing her arms over her small breasts. "Let's get started. I 'ave much work to do."

I growled softly. "Why are the French so rude?"

She shrugged. "We're French, it's in our blood to 'ate Americans." She grabbed my forearm and led me to the desk, carrying a large suitcase that I was sure held torture devices in every imaginable shape. I sat down in the chair, and she opened the suitcase to reveal the devices which were much worse than I had imagined. Ares walked out of the bathroom and Madeleine spread her arms out to hide me. "What are you doing? Get out of 'ere!" She yelled.

I looked through her arms to see Ares averting his eyes. "I'm not even looking at her, Madeleine. Artemis, I'm going out for a little bit. Matt will stay here with you."

My stomach cramped, and my pulse started beating in double time. "When will you be back? Where are you going?" I asked nervously.

Madeleine sighed happily. "Aw, it's so nice to see true love."

Ares ignored Madeleine. "I'm just going out for a little bit. I'll only be gone thirty minutes and Koda is coming with me."

"Hurry, please."

Ares sighed happily. "Of course." Koda blew me a kiss and followed Ares out of the room.

Matt sat down on the desk and was, thankfully, wearing a pair of shorts and a t-shirt. Matt placed his hand on mine on the desk and smiled. "He'll be back before you're even ready."

I picked his hand up and inhaled the back of it. I could still smell wolf fur and his smell, but the soap he had used took away the forest. "I don't like feeling like this. I understand he's my match and we're pack, but I *really* don't know him. My wolf is getting harder to ignore, too."

Madeleine watched me curiously. "How long 'ave you known you're a wolf?"

Matt answered for me as I continued to inhale the smell of his skin. "Only a few days. As long as she's known Ares."

Madeleine's eyes widened. "She must be at least sixteen. 'Ow 'as she not known?"

Matt sighed and rubbed my hair softly. "Her father chose to not tell her and kept her away from our kind."

Madeleine looked at me with pity in her eyes. "That must 'ave been very difficult. Come, let me make you gorgeous for your mate."

I growled. "Don't call him that."

Matt shook his head at Madeleine. "Don't ask."

Madeleine sighed. "Wolves are always full of drama." Matt held my hand as she worked on my face. My nervousness increased as the minutes ticked by without Ares near me. Madeleine brought in another woman who brushed and fixed my hair into a half up and half down style, with everything lightly curled. Ares came in just as they made the final touches to my makeup and hair. The two women and Matt covered me as Ares walked by to the closet. I thanked Madeleine and the other woman and then walked to the bathroom to use the restroom. Madeleine had refused to let me go while she was working.

I started to come out of the bathroom, but Koda blocked my exit. "Ares is finishing getting ready. It's your turn to wait."

I looked over Koda's tailored suit that fit all of his muscles nicely. His Mohawk was gelled up and the gel made the green dye seem even brighter. "You look nice," I said honestly.

He spun in a slow circle. "Thank you." He smiled at me. "You look great, too, very beautiful."

I blushed and then asked, "How much longer is he going to take? I'm hungry." A chill swept over my body as the sun set and the powerful presence I had felt the previous afternoon caused fear to close my throat. I wrapped my arms around myself and shivered.

Ares spoke from outside the bathroom. "What's wrong Artemis? Why are you so frightened?"

"It's a strange…I know I'm going to sound stupid when I say this, but there is this powerful darkness I've been feeling since we came here. It got really strong just now, when the sun set."

Koda smiled. "It's alright dahlin' it's just the vampire King."

Ares spoke from farther away in the room. "I'm almost done—just finishing my hair."

I turned and looked at the mirror in the bathroom and stared at the woman looking back at me. I still couldn't believe it was really me. I raised my hand up to my face and pushed on my cheeks. Koda smiled at me, but stayed quiet as I stared at the purple eyes my mother had given me. Ares spoke from near Koda, "Are you ready?"

I scoffed. "I've *been* ready." I turned around and instantly felt self-conscious. *What if he thinks I look horrible? What if he decides I'm not good enough for him to be with? He's got so many attractive women vying to be with him and I'm just…*

Ares interrupted my thoughts by stepping into the bathroom and staring at me with wide eyes. He looked perfect. His suit looked like it had been stitched to him and his black hair gleamed with the gel in it and looked spiked, but still natural somehow. His blue eyes sparkled and I wanted him to want me, to approve of me.

He smiled and walked forward slowly. "Artemis, you look…"

I blushed and looked down at my hands. "Don't…"

Ares wrapped his arms around me and kissed me on the lips, hard, squeezing me against his muscular body. He smelled like wolf, Ares and cinnamon. He pulled back from me and whispered, "Perfect. Beautiful. Delicious."

The worry fluttered away, and I smiled. "You look great, Ares."

He shook his head. "Nothing can compare to your beauty." I blushed even hotter and he smiled. "I got you something." I stared at him in shock as he pulled out a white box. He opened the lid to reveal a beautiful diamond heart necklace. Ares took the necklace out and whispered, "So that you will know that my heart is yours alone."

I shook my head as I stared at the shining diamonds on the necklace. "That's too expensive. I couldn't…"

Ares raised his hand, and I stopped talking. He walked to stand behind me and put the necklace on. "Nothing is too expensive for you. Besides, I have quite a bit of money saved up, and I can spend it however I like."

I touched the heart lying on my upper chest and smiled at Ares. "Thank you. It's beautiful."

He kissed the side of my neck, sending chills down my spine. "You're welcome. Are you ready to meet the vampires?"

I curtsied to Ares and spoke with a deep voice trying to sound seductive, "Is my lord ready?"

Ares bowed at the neck and smiled. "Always for you, m'lady." He extended his bent elbow to me and I put my hand on the inside of his arm. He asked, "How do you know what to say?"

I shrugged. "I watched a lot of renaissance movies."

He kissed the back of my hand. "You're the most beautiful Princess in the lands."

I frowned. "Wait. In order to be Princess wouldn't I have to fight the others?"

Ares shook his head. "As my mate, you become my equal in power."

I frowned harder. "So, since you're Prince then I am Princess? What if someone else wants my position?"

Ares sighed. "That's something we'll discuss much later. For now, let's focus on the task at hand."

I curtsied again. "Of course, my lord."

"You really are perfect," he said as he squeezed my hand and led the way out of the bedroom. Koda walked in front of us while Matt walked behind us silently. There were a lot of people walking down the hallways and all stopped to stare or moved aside to let us pass, while others whispered. Koda led us downstairs and into a well-lit underground portion of the mansion. Koda maneuvered around the confusing hallways, going in what seemed to be circles. Ares squeezed my hand reassuringly, as we stopped in front of two large ornate doors.

Victor walked up to us with two identical looking male vampires. "You all ready?"

Ares nodded. "As ready as I ever am to walk into a room filled with vampires."

Victor winked. "We've already eaten for the night."

I asked, "What are they celebrating tonight anyway?"

Victor smiled. "They are celebrating the return of the Prince of the Vampires and the continued alliance with the werewolves."

I nodded. "That's right. You're a Prince, too."

Ares scoffed. "It's more impressive when you have to get it for being the strongest, but Victor is one of the most powerful vampires."

Victor sighed. "Yes, you are truly a powerful wolf, Prince Ares."

I shook my head smiling. "This is all so strange."

Koda rolled his eyes. "Tell me about it."

Two werewolf guards opened the doors and we walked inside behind Victor. The room was, by far, the largest room I had ever seen. Twelve long tables with bench seating filled up most of the room. Crystal chandeliers hung from the ceilings and gave a soft reflective light from the hundreds of candles that hung on the walls and sat on the tables in elegant holders. In the center of the room sat a thick wooden table with three thrones in the center. The vampire King looked like Victor's twin, but unlike Victor, he was wearing a puffy pirate shirt that was open to the middle of his hairy chest. His pants were black and looked like a replica of pirate's pants too. A beautiful woman, wearing a blood red dress, sat beside him on his right side. Victor walked down the center aisle, which was adorned with a dark red rug, and bowed to the king and queen. The twin vampires dropped to one knee beside Victor.

The king held up his hand and the room silenced. He stood up and smiled. "Welcome Prince Victor of the Vampires. It has been too long since you have returned to your home."

Victor stood up straight then bowed his head at the neck. "Greetings, King Maurice and Queen Isabella. I am glad to return home."

Maurice, still smiling, said, "Stand, faithful guards of the prince, Jean Pierre and Francois." As he said each of their names they stood up as though they were puppets and the king, the puppeteer.

Victor spoke just loud enough for everyone to hear, "May I introduce our allies, Prince Ares of the Werewolves, his mate Artemis and his two guards, Koda and Matthew."

Ares began walking forward, and I stayed beside him as we walked. He moved his arm to the side so he could bow and I curtsied as low as I could, staring at the ground. Maurice spoke with a voice that caressed around my body like a warm hand. "Greetings Prince Ares and his wolves." Ares stood up and I stood with him, all the while keeping my hand on his arm. Maurice continued, "I see that you are still convinced that she is your mate."

Ares spoke loudly. "She is my *ivraie vivace*. My perfect match."

The room was filled with gasps and then whispers of shock. Maurice raised his hand and the room silenced. Maurice stared down at me and for a moment I returned his gaze. I felt his power and quickly averted my eyes to his chin. He spoke in a soothing voice, "I had not thought it was true. Could you tell us how you found her?"

Ares spoke loud enough for everyone to hear, with a voice of power, and yet it was soft at the same time. "I felt her presence when she was born and all other women paled before me. None held my interest any longer and I craved no woman's caress. I searched for a long time, all over the world, until I had my first dream of her and her of me. By chance, we met and the dreams continued. I sent out my call shortly after meeting her and she answered in half transformation, and then subdued her wolf."

The crowd began whispering loudly again. Isabella raised her hand and the crowd silenced, but more slowly than they had for Maurice. She smiled and asked, "Are you to tell me that for the past eighteen years, you, the Prince of Wolves, have restrained from the temptations of a woman's bosom?"

Ares smiled. "I have."

She continued as if he had not spoken, "You, the most powerful bachelor, have not so much as craved a woman's touch or the sweet words of a female for eighteen years?"

Ares turned his head to me and smiled. "Not until I found her."

Maurice walked down from the throne he was sitting on, to stand in front of me. My wolf's fear spiked through me, making my heart beat faster. I forced myself not to step back and instead squeezed Ares' hand. Maurice smiled. "You have no need to fear me child. I will not harm you."

I said nothing and stared at his chin. I wasn't sure if the movies were right, about the vampires being about to take control of you with a look in their eyes or not. It wasn't a chance I was willing to take. Maurice inhaled. "Obviously she is not full-blood as we discussed previously, but she also does not smell of *you* Ares."

Ares nodded. "She is young and I am giving her time to adjust. And I would still ask your courtesy in not divulging her bloodlines."

Maurice nodded. "Wise of you in these times. She looks like someone..." He gasped, "You are the daughter of Darren?"

I nodded and spoke softly, "I am." The room filled with loud murmurs, and Maurice raised his hand to silence them.

He spoke again and his voice filled me with warmth and brought a smile to my face. "What is your father's view on this?"

Ares spoke with obvious hatred. "Her father is an outlaw, whose punishment, when found, will be severe."

Maurice smiled. "I see. How do you feel about this, Artemis?"

I frowned because it didn't sound like a question the King of the Vampires should ask. "It's a lot to deal with at first, but I love my pack and am pleased to be the Prince's match."

Maurice frowned. "You are not sure though."

I frowned in response. "As I said, it is a lot to deal with and I have only known this all for a few days."

Queen Isabella asked, "You did not know what you are?"

I shook my head. "Until Ares found me, I thought I was human."

The room was filled with shocked responses and she asked, "How could you have not known what you are? Your kind changes before eighteen."

Ares shook his head. "Not all of us, great Queen. A few have been known to fight the change until their eighteenth birthday, but they had at least changed one part and knew. The Princess did not change any part and her father made her believe she was having human seizures."

Isabella gasped. "She was around 'umans while fighting the change?"

Her change in accent was disturbing, but I answered her. "I went to school with humans and some would even hold me, while I fought the changes."

Isabella raised her hand to stop the others from speaking before she got a chance. "You fought off your change while in the presence of 'umans?" I nodded. She asked, "'ow many times?"

I tried to calculate, but math was not my best subject. "About six times a month since I was ten years old."

The crowd erupted in conversation so loud that I couldn't hear myself think and yet I couldn't make out what any of them were saying. The cartoon where all the kids hear is "Wa Wa" suddenly made sense. Maurice raised his hand to quiet the crowd. He spoke in a voice that no longer caressed me, but scared me. "You fought your change, surrounded by humans, with them touching you and then did not attack them?"

I nodded. "I never felt the urge to attack them. Usually I would be angry when I started the seizure...I mean attempt to change. I would calm myself down and it would stop. Then I would eat red meat and be fine."

Maurice turned to Koda and Matt. "Have you two witnessed this?"

Matt and Koda both nodded. Koda responded, "Her wolf was not present during the times she tried to change around the humans. Her father made sure to keep her away from other wolves and even hid his wolf from her."

Maurice asked, "Is her wolf present now?"

Ares nodded. "Yes. Her wolf exposed herself to Artemis on the day I sent my call."

Maurice stared at me with an expression that made me want to run. The look of need was not like Ares' passion-filled gaze, but instead a look of needing power. The look bore into me until I sensed his hostility and realized he would kill me if he could. I stepped back towards Koda and Matt and they pressed their chests to my back. Victor saw my face and our stance and turned towards his father. "Perhaps we could end the discussion for today and allow our guests to sit for the meal?"

Maurice's face changed back to his politician's smile and he nodded. "Of course. Please take a seat."

Ares walked with me pressed against his side, so close that I stepped on his shoes a few times before we were at the table. They sat us beside the king and queen's table and faced us towards the center of the room. Koda and Matt didn't sit beside us, but stood behind to keep guard. Once we were seated, Ares leaned over and whispered, "What happened to make you so nervous?"

I flipped my hair to the other side of my face and pretended to be merely leaning my head on Ares' shoulder. I whispered as quietly as I could, "The look he gave me was not friendly. I know you probably think I'm full of crap, but I could feel his need and then his hostility."

Ares kissed the top of my head. "I don't think you're full of crap, but let's not discuss this until later, when there aren't so many ears to hear." I kissed his cheek and sat up straight. Victor was now sitting beside his father and speaking very quietly to him. Was Victor a bad guy? Servants brought out bottles of wine and then plates of meat. The servants looked scared more than pleasant. I sniffed one as he passed by and realized he was human. I turned to Ares and he shook his head. I ate my food in silence until the king and queen stood. Everyone in the room including Ares stood with them, so I did too.

Maurice smiled at everyone. "Thank you for coming, my friends, but I must bid you *adieu,* the sun is rising soon and I need my beauty sleep." He took Isabella's hand and together they walked out of the room through the door we had come through. After they had disappeared through the doorway, Victor and Ares led me hurriedly back to our bedroom.

I jumped on to the bed and sighed. Ares laid down beside me on his side facing me and smiled. "That was fun, right?"

I scoffed. "About as fun as cleaning poop out of fifty horse stalls in the middle of a hot day in summer."

He ran his hand up and down my arm slowly with just his fingertips touching me. "I'm sorry you had to deal with that, but being my mate means that you will be forced to do that many more times with many different races. Can you handle it?"

I smiled. "I don't know. What's in it for me?" He leaned over and gave me a very chaste kiss. I frowned. "Definitely not worth it."

He smiled. "Really? Then how about this?" He rolled on top of me and kissed my lips with the need I had seen in his eyes from the tub. I kissed him back and power exploded inside me and ran into him. He grunted, but didn't stop our kiss as warmth built between us. He rolled us over so that I was lying on top of him and ran his hands down my back and over my rump. He squeezed lightly and the power in me slammed into him, making him grunt in pain and grip me harder. I moaned, and he deepened the kiss. The kiss grew, and I felt increasingly woozy. He slid his hands father down until they were at the bottom of my dress and pushed it up so he could put his hands on my bare butt. Thongs are good for not showing lines in your dress, but they do expose many things when your dress isn't on. He snarled and bit my lower lip. I gasped and kissed him with my own bites and nibbles of his lower lip. We were so busy with each other that we didn't pay attention to anything else. Cold water splashed over us and made me gasp. I spun around in a crouching attack position and snarled at the water throwers. Koda and Matt stood, smiling together, holding two empty buckets. Ares stood up beside me and frowned. "What was that for?"

Koda said, "You told us not to let you get too carried away with her until she was ready."

I snarled at him. "I wasn't pushing him away, was I?"

Matt shook his head. "No, but you aren't ready either."

I took a step towards them, growling, and felt my wolf ready to come out. Koda squatted down and growled back at me. I snapped my teeth at him. "You aren't alpha!" I yelled.

Koda snarled at me. "Neither are you, but I am beta."

I shook my head. "No, I am."

Matt squatted down and growled at both of us. "Knock it off, you two."

I snapped my teeth at him and saw his wolf's anger. He dropped his left hand in a crouching stance mimicking both Koda and me and snarled. Ares stared at us, frowning. I felt my wolf wake up and smiled. I pulled my dress off over my head and took my shoes off. Ares sighed, "Artemis." I unhooked my bra and pulled my underwear down while keeping eye contact with the two others and then let her come. My body stretched, and my bones cracked as she rose from my body in four quick steps. When I was finished changing, I felt the soreness that would be present when I returned to human shape, but I didn't care. Matt and Koda stood before me in their wolf forms and I suddenly realized how much smaller I was. They were both at least one and a half times my size, whereas Ares was twice my size. Koda took a step towards me, and I ran forward slamming into him. He skidded backwards, but did not fall. I bit into his side, pulling a piece of flesh off, and jumped away as Matt ran at me. They turned to face me, and I realized they were fighting together.

Ares snarled from behind them and dropped his clothes. I stared at his naked perfection and waited anxiously for him to be wolf, too. He changed in one fluid motion like in my dreams and walked forward to snarl at me. I stared at him in shock as he stood between Koda and Matt. I took a step back from him and then shook my head. I snarled and snapped my teeth against the three who were against me. The door opened, but I didn't want to risk looking away so I stayed, staring at the other three. Koda turned towards the door and I saw my opening. I threw myself forward and bit into his neck, but he shook me off. I jumped back and tried to hit him with my paw, but Ares blocked me, snarling. I backed away from him and sat on my haunches. Why was he attacking me? Ares took a step towards me, and Francois and Jean Pierre appeared in front of me. Their faces looked terrifying as they hissed, flashing their fangs with their fingers elongated into claws. Ares narrowed his eyes at them as they protected me from my own pack.

One of the twins, I couldn't distinguish between them, spoke with a deep voice, "Why are you attacking your mate?"

Ares barked and the vampire shook his head.

"Dominance battles are between them, you know this. How dare you interfere?" the vampire scolded Ares.

Ares moved forward and I did, too. The vampire twins and werewolf twins began fighting each other and I stared at Ares in shock. He snapped his teeth at me and snarled. I knew he was alpha, but he had no reason to be interfering in my dominance with the others as the vampire had said. I decided to do the only thing I could, submit. I dropped to my side and rolled on my back, exposing my neck and stomach to Ares. He continued to snarl and growl as he walked forward and stood over my body. His teeth were inches from my neck and he opened his jaw, when Victor ran in and flung Ares aside.

Victor stood between Ares and me and then raised his hands. "Silence." The wolves stopped growling and stared at him. Victor said, "You are under a spell. Please listen. Change back."

Ares changed back quickly and frowned. "What is going on?"

Victor smiled. "You owe me now, friend. You were about to take her life."

I changed back and stared, wide-eyed, at Ares. Ares shook his head. "I wouldn't have killed her."

Victor shrugged. "Perhaps not, but I did not wish to take that chance."

I stood and ran to the bathroom, shutting the door behind me and locking it. I shivered with the cold tile touching my feet and turned to the tub. I turned it on and heard Ares knock. "Artemis, please let me in." I stared at the water as it filled up the giant tub. "This door isn't very hard to break down. I'll do it if you don't let me in."

I sighed and walked over to the door, unlocking it, and then ran and hopped into the halfway-filled tub. I turned on the jets and stared at the bubbling water. My sore body began to relax, and I asked, "Were you going to kill me?"

Ares sighed and knelt beside the tub to look at me. I kept my gaze on the water waiting for his reply. "Of course not. I wouldn't kill you no matter what spell I was under."

I asked, "Why did you interfere? I have to prove my dominance in order to have a place in the pack."

Ares shook his head. "No, you get your place in the pack from your mate."

I looked up at him and frowned. "So, I could be the weakest wolf in the pack and become the alpha's mate and be alpha female?"

Ares nodded. "Yes."

I scoffed. "That's ridiculous."

Ares shrugged. "Sort of. Most alphas only choose strong mates anyway. We wouldn't choose the weakest, because she may not give us strong offspring."

I gaped at him. "Offspring?"

He looked down, obviously embarrassed. "Some do have offspring."

I rolled the idea over in my head of having children and scoffed. "No, thank you."

He looked up at me and frowned. "You don't want kids?"

I laughed. "Werewolves having kids? That's crazy. What if you go all insane one day and kill one?"

He smiled. "You wouldn't kill your offspring."

I frowned. "No, but someone else might."

His smile faded, and he nodded. "Rival alphas have been known to kill other's offspring, but not very often, and definitely not mine."

I shook my head. "I don't want to talk about it."

He reached towards me. I moved away and he sighed. "I told you I wasn't going to kill you."

I blushed. "I'm naked."

He looked down at the water, then at himself and frowned. "So, am I."

I looked at his face and saw the need there again. I shook my head. "I'm not ready for that. Not yet."

He sighed. "I understand. I'll leave you to your bath." He walked slowly from the room, and I couldn't help but stare at his muscular glutes. He looked back and winked. Then he walked out of the bathroom and shut the door. I exhaled a breath I hadn't realized I had been holding and groaned. I couldn't be this caught up in him already? How can he have such an effect on me? I groaned again and dunked my head under the water. Had I imagined Maurice's reaction to me? I pictured his face and shook my head. No, I was right. I climbed out of the tub and pulled on clothes out of my bag. I frowned at a wet pair of jeans lying on the floor and reluctantly pulled them on, then pulled on a blue t-shirt over my head. Wet jeans suck to walk in.

I walked slowly out of the bathroom and sat down between Jean Pierre and Francois and whispered, "Thank you."

They both nodded.

The one on the right patted my shoulder in response, but they were both staring at Victor, who was speaking to Ares. Koda and Matt stood in front of the bed, staring at me.

I frowned at them then stood. "What?"

They both looked down then back up at the same time. Twins are freaky. Koda said, "I'm sorry." I stared at him in shock, not believing what I just heard. He smiled. "I'm sorry for trying to fight you."

Matt nodded. "And I'm sorry for ganging up on you."

I frowned. "Yeah that was odd. I didn't even want to fight you, but you had to jump in."

Matt smiled. "Koda is my twin and we always fight together, so it was really mere instinct."

I continued to frown as my emotions built. "So, it was instinct for you two and Ares to try to fight your newest pack member? Nice. Now I know whose side you're on and that I need to watch my own ass." I crossed my arms over my chest and looked at the ground.

Koda groaned and moved to sit in front of me, but one of the vampire twins hissed at him making him stop. "Leave her alone, wolf. She needs time to adjust."

Koda snarled. "I agree, Francois, but she also has to know that we aren't her enemies and that we are sorry."

Francois, the one on the right, shook his head. "Later. Leave her be." He put his arm around my shoulders, and I leaned against him, resting my head on his chest. It was odd to be so comfortable around him so quickly and yet still had the urge to run, and the hair on the nape of my neck stood. It became easier to ignore the urge to run around vampires though.

Koda growled and took a step towards us, but Ares shook his head. "Leave it alone."

Koda groaned and stormed off to the bathroom, slamming the door shut behind him.

Ares approached me and for the first time, I felt nothing for him. He squatted down in front of me and sighed. "Artemis. Please forgive us. I would not have hurt you and the others didn't mean it personally."

I stared at him and sniffed the air and listened to his heartbeat. Dammit, he was telling the truth. "You can't expect me to be fine with it, when you may have hurt me if Victor hadn't come."

Ares smiled. "I understand how you feel and do not expect you to be over it immediately, but quickly would be best. We have to decide our next move." He looked at Francois then sighed. "And also, it would probably be best if you did not appear so friendly with vampires. It's not natural for our kind to be so cozy with theirs."

I smiled. "I am not *cozy*, but I just feel comfortable with Francois and Jean Pierre."

Francois nodded. "I would never harm the little goddess."

I groaned and stood up. "I need to go for a walk." Jean Pierre and Francois stood and smiled at me. I sighed. "Dammit, can't we go somewhere where I won't need babysitters?"

Ares smiled. "You will always have guards Artemis. You are too valuable not to be protected."

I whispered, "Valuable to whom?"

Ares frowned and grabbed my arm and pulled me against him. Fire burned where his hand touched against my skin as he stared into my eyes. "You are valuable to me and your pack. Don't you understand yet?"

I sighed. "I did not mean it that way. I simply meant that it seems that I am *valuable* to more people than I should be and that my value to them is probably not what you would approve of."

Ares fury settled and the fire vanished. "Who are you talking about?"

I shook my head. "You said I shouldn't speak of it until there weren't 'ears to hear'."

Ares face lifted. "Can you be so perceptive to have seen an expression on his face that I did not?"

"It was more than that. I could see his need and its nothing like the look of need you have towards me." I blushed as I finished saying it and looked down.

Ares kissed my cheek softly. "My needs can wait, but we must speak with Victor regarding this new problem." He turned around with his hand on my arm, but I stayed still. Ares sighed and turned back to face me. "You have to describe what you saw to Victor."

I frowned. "Fine, but after this I'm taking a walk with whichever person I choose as my guard."

Ares smiled. "As you wish."

I felt my face relax from its frown and spread to a look of shock. "You know the movie Princess Bride?"

Ares smiled. "Of course. Who doesn't?"

Koda called from behind the bathroom door, "Rodents of unusual size? I don't think they exist."

I smiled. "Koda."

Koda peeked out from the bathroom. "You rang?"

I inhaled and spoke quickly so I wouldn't lose my nerve, "I forgive you and Matt for ganging up on me since I am a new pack member, but if it happens again don't expect me to be so willing to forgive you."

Koda smiled and ran from the bathroom to me. He picked me up in a big bear hug, squeezing the air from my lungs and kissing my cheek repeatedly. He set me down then grinned. "You'll do great here."

I scoffed and Ares frowned down at me. "So, you'll forgive them, but not me?"

I shrugged. "I expect more of the alpha, as anyone would." His frown deepened, and I couldn't stand to see that look on his face. I hugged him and kissed his cheek. "I forgive you."

He shook his head. "No, you're right. I should've had more control than that. I would've never stopped a dominance fight before, and I don't know why I stopped yours. And turning on you was extremely unacceptable. Such an indiscretion would have resulted in a punishment that would have lasted many days."

I kissed his lips softly and whispered, "We all make mistakes. I'm sure I'll make a ton in the first years with you. Besides wolf pups are always getting scolded in the wild, so it's only natural for us to make mistakes."

He finally smiled and kissed my lips back. "You're a fascinating person, Artemis. I'm more than lucky to have you as my match."

I pulled away from him so he wouldn't see my blush and walked over to Victor who was sitting at a desk on the far wall by the fireplace. I sat down in front of the fireplace and looked up at him. He smiled at me, set his pencil down and spoke with a voice filled with a fluid French accent, "'ow may I 'elp you *mon papillon?*'

I frowned. "What does that mean?"

"It's my new pet name for you."

"Okay, well I need to talk to you about something that happened in the ceremony, and it's something no one else can hear."

His eyes widened, and, speaking without the French accent, he said, "Francois and Jean Pierre, go and make certain that there are no ears to hear nearby."

Francois and Jean Pierre hurried out of the room together.

Victor repositioned his chair so that he was facing me and smiled. "How are you feeling?"

I shrugged. "Overwhelmed, but I'm just trying to deal with it one part at a time."

He nodded thoughtfully. "So, you are over the shock of being told you are a werewolf?"

I sighed. "I can't change what I am and there is no sense in dwelling on something that I cannot change. I am still upset that I am something else besides werewolf and do not know though."

"Ares only keeps from you what will harm you. He cares very much for your safety."

I blushed and looked down. "I know."

Victor leaned forward and whispered, "And how are you feeling about your alpha?"

I sighed and whispered back, "Honestly, it's really weird. I understand him being my alpha and that I am his match, but it seems wrong to feel so strongly for him. And the whole mate thing is just too much to think about so I try not to."

Victor tapped his chin thoughtfully. "So, you feel strongly for him and believe you should not because you have only known him a few days?" I nodded and Victor smiled. "That is easily fixed. No one will judge you for your feelings towards him because legend tells that a matched pair is instantly in love. Besides, who would argue that being in love is a bad thing?"

"My father."

Victor hissed. "Your father is a stupid man. Forget him. He *would* put such vile concepts into your head. Sweet *papillon,* your feelings are just that, your feelings. Do not let others decide how you should feel. If you hate Ares, then hate him and tell him. But if you love Ares, then love him and tell him. Love is a wonderful thing, little *déesse*. Do not waste it."

I sighed. "Are you going to tell me what the last thing you called me means?"

"Déesse means Goddess. If I wanted to be more accurate, I would call you *déesse lunaire*."

I smiled. "Moon Goddess, right?"

He nodded.

"Most languages have a few words that sound similar. I figured *lunaire* was like lunar."

Victor grinned. "Perhaps I will teach you some French."

Ares scoffed from behind us. "No, thank you."

I jumped at his voice, not realizing he was standing there. I stared at Victor's chest and asked, "How long have you been standing there?"

Ares replied, "When you asked what the last thing he called you meant. Why? Were you talking about me?"

I looked up at him with my smart ass remark on the tip of my tongue and froze. His face was openly fearful and sad. "We were talking about you, but nothing you need to worry about. Actually, Victor was helping me."

Ares looked at Victor suspiciously. "Are you trying to stake a claim?"

Victor put a hand to his chest with his mouth open in an "O" shape trying to look innocent. "*Moi*?! Of course not!"

Ares snarled. "Because if you are, then I'll be forced to fight you."

Victor laughed softly. "You have been away too long *mon ami.* I would never think of trying to do such a thing. She is yours as you are hers, and I would not dream of interfering."

Ares sighed, obviously relieved, and smiled. "Thank you. I do not want to imagine how difficult it would be to kill you."

Victor rolled his eyes. "It would be impossible because you wouldn't be able to do it."

I waved my hands at them. "Enough. Let's not discuss something that won't happen."

Ares stood a little ways from us to make a triangle of our group. Jean Pierre and Francois walked in and bowed. "All is clear," they said in unison.

Victor glanced their way. "Good, now you and the wolf twins go monitor, so new ears do not wander close." Francois and Jean Pierre bowed again and left the room. Koda and Matt bowed to

Victor then to Ares and walked out. Victor turned to me and smiled. "Now, begin from the beginning."

I inhaled and described to him the way the king had looked when every bit of new information hit him and the final look that I swore was hostility. Victor nodded as I spoke and then sighed when I finished. I whispered, "If I'm wrong, then I'm wrong, but that's how I felt and what I saw."

Victor shook his head. "You are not wrong per se, but if this is true, then it is a bad thing indeed."

Ares groaned. "So, you think she's right?"

Victor's lips drew thin. "He has been searching for a way to increase his power. I think we should heed this as a warning to keep Artemis guarded at all times."

Ares frowned, his anger building. "Do you think he will try something?"

Victor rubbed his temples. "I don't know. I don't think he would risk a full-out assault for her because the wolves are still important to us. But he hasn't been king for so many years because he's stupid. He's a smart man. He might try something discreetly."

Ares reached his hand out towards me. I swallowed quickly, knowing that as soon as I touched him his power would wash over me. I slowly reached out and took his hand and then frowned. Nothing happened. He smiled at me. "I can control my powers when I think about it."

I smiled and looked at the ground. "I'm sorry."

He tilted my chin up and looked into my eyes with such a serious face that I couldn't turn away. "I will protect you. You know that, right?" I nodded and his anger began to build again. "No one will take you from me."

I whispered, "Damn, and here I thought I was going to get an out."

A small smirk tilted up one corner of his mouth. "Even if you ran of your own free will, I would find you. You're mine."

I put a hand on each side of his neck just below his chin and pulled him down to me. "And you are mine." I stood on tiptoe and kissed his lips hard. He responded by putting one hand on the back of my head and one around my waist to pull me against him. Our kiss deepened until I heard Victor clear his throat. I had forgotten he was even there. I blushed and pulled away. "Sorry, Victor."

Victor laughed. "Do not apologize. You did nothing wrong. I will be heading to my room now. Jean Pierre and Francois will come to you in the morning, Ares." He stood up beside me.

Ares frowned. "We need to discuss our plan…"

Victor waved his hand, interrupting Ares. "Later. I am tired and need rest. Tomorrow, let your guards take Artemis out to enjoy the town, and we will discuss business then." Victor bent down and kissed my cheek softly. "Good night, *mon papillon.* May your dreams be as sweet as you are." He left the room in the floating gait vampires had.

Koda and Matt came back in, smiling at us. I asked, "I take it that I don't get to take a walk tonight?"

Ares shook his head and kissed my lips softly. "Not tonight, sweetheart." He dropped my hand slowly and walked to the bathroom. The click of the lock echoed in the still room.

Koda scoffed, breaking the silence. "What pissed him off?"

At the bed, I bent down to get inside my bag. "Someone wants me and he is afraid that they might attack you to get me." I grabbed my favorite pair of pajama pants that were covered in pictures of a wolf, snarling, with the line, "Bark Off" under his feet. I reached farther in and grabbed the night shirt that matched it. I started to undress to put them on when I remembered Koda and Matt. I sighed. *I'll have to get used to indecent exposure eventually.* I stripped my jeans and t-shirt off and put the pajamas on. When I turned around, Koda and Matt were staring at me in shock. I frowned. "What?"

Matt smiled. "You changed in front of us?"

I shrugged. "What's the big deal?"

Ares walked out of the bathroom and frowned at us. "What's going on?"

Koda pointed at me. "She changed in front of us."

Ares frowned. "You changed clothes in front of them?"

I shrugged. "I'll be naked a lot in front of them if I keep changing to my wolf form and besides I had a bra and underwear on and was facing away from them."

I folded the dress I'd worn earlier and set it on the bedside table to return to Madeleine. Ares spoke quietly to Koda and Matt so I hopped up on the bed and pulled one of the pillows down and snuggled in. I felt the bed move, but remained facing the bedroom door. Koda stood in front of me and waved his hands in a shooing motion. "Move over, bed hog."

I frowned. "What?"

He sighed. "We're a pack and a pack sleeps together. We did it last night. Now move over."

I smiled. "So, this must have looked really awkward when it was just the three of you?"

Ares lifted a brow. "Yes, there were many questions floating around."

I backed up on the bed until I touched someone's body and repositioned my head on my pillow. Koda took his shirt off and climbed onto the bed facing away from me. I felt someone at my feet and sat up to see Matt along the bottom of the bed. I frowned. "Why does Matt always have to sleep down there?"

Koda turned his head and body so he could see me. "It's a pecking order thing."

I shook my head. "Come on. At least trade every night."

Koda frowned. "You don't want me to sleep beside you?" Ares growled softly and Koda shook his head. "You know what I meant, Ares."

"It has nothing to do with who it is, it's just not fair that he has to sleep at our feet all the time. Tonight, you can sleep here Koda, but tomorrow Matt gets to sleep up here."

Ares asked, "Are you going to try to make me sleep at the foot of the bed too?"

I shrugged. "Why shouldn't you? We're all a pack, right? And that means that your pack mates wouldn't try to make a move on me anyway. Right? So, then you should be a gracious alpha and sleep at the foot of the bed every third night."

Ares frowned, and Matt laughed. "Oh, I love this'n."

I smiled at him and rolled over to face Ares for a second. "Am I overstepping boundaries?"

Ares kissed my lips softly. "Definitely, but for you, I will concede this issue. We will rotate sleeping patterns, except for you. You must stay at the center of us."

I frowned. "Because you're worried about someone trying to get me?"

Koda leaned over us. "It's a lot harder to take someone from the center of the pile than the outside."

I sighed. "Fine." I kissed Ares' lips one more time and rolled over onto my back. Ares and Koda spooned themselves to me and Matt wrapped himself around us all. The heat started to become too much, but I quickly fell asleep to the sound of my pack's breathing.

CHAPTER TEN

As Victor had instructed, Ares left early the next morning to strategize with him and the twin vampires, while Koda and Matt took me out to explore Paris. We took a limo from the mansion to the heart of the town nearest the Eiffel Tower. It was a three-hour drive from the winery, so we walked everywhere once in town. The shops were cute, and I bought a few souvenir shirts with the money I had taken from Darren. We also ate at a lovely outside diner. Koda ordered snails just so we could look at them. As we walked from the diner towards the Eiffel Tower, I felt someone watching us and looked around, but there were too many people looking at us for me to be certain. My purple eyes didn't help our tourist looks, but Matt spoke fluent French so we were left alone and didn't have to ask for directions. I moved closer to Koda when I still felt the threatening presence nearby. Koda looked down at me with the smile he had had on all day, but quickly vanished into a frown when he saw my face. "What's wrong?"

I whispered, "Someone's watching us."

Koda looked around and smiled. "There are many people watching us."

I shook my head. "No, it's…it's like I can taste their aggression, their threat."

Matt sniffed the air and sighed. "There are too many bloodsuckers living in this city for me to be certain, but I can sense a little of the aggression she is speaking of."

Koda rubbed the back of his neck. "Maybe we should go back."

I groaned. "Dammit. And we're so close." I looked longingly up at the Eiffel Tower and sighed. "Alright, let's go back."

We turned around and started down the road towards the other town we had started from. Matt pulled out a cell phone and spoke quickly in French. He whispered, "The driver is still at the town waiting for us."

I nodded and tried to breathe slower. We turned down another road, which was nearly deserted, and walked faster. We were almost to the end when three people stepped into the alley, blocking our path. Koda pushed me behind him and Matt pressed himself against my back. Koda asked, "What do you want?" I peeked around Koda's arm so I could see what was happening.

The three men continued to walk towards us and I watched their feet, but they didn't float like the vampires. The man in the center spoke in a deep voice, "You know what we want. Just hand her over and no one dies."

Koda growled. "You're pack! You can't betray us!"

The man shrugged. "The leeches pay higher, and besides, after we kill you, no one will know what happened."

Koda took a step forward, and I grabbed his hand. He spun around and glared at me. "Koda, please don't. I don't want you to die."

Koda snarled. "If I let them take you I might as well die! You are my pack and what they will do to you will make you wish you were dead."

The man laughed deeply. "Oh, we'll be extra nice to the little pup. Won't we, men?"

The other men smiled wickedly. I swallowed hard and stepped back into Matt's arms. Koda stepped forward and exhaled. The two men, who hadn't spoken, ran forward and attacked Koda. Koda dodged and countered their attacks faster than I could keep track of. Grunts and cracking sounds made me cringe and hope Koda was alright. I watched in amazement as Koda grabbed the smallest man and threw him at the man who had spoken originally. The impact was as loud as a car crash, as their bodies slammed to the ground. Koda grabbed the last man's throat and squeezed tight.

I started to move forward to stop him, but Matt put his arm around my chest and whispered, "This is the only way. Either we kill them now, or Ares will order us to kill them later. They have admitted to trying to kidnap you, the Prince's mate. It is unacceptable."

I watched in horror as Koda dug his fingers in and ripped out the front of the man's throat, exposing bone. The man fell to the ground convulsing, and the other men stared, eyes wide. Koda reached into his pocket and pulled out a long black bag. He opened the bag to expose a silver stake inside. Making sure not to touch it himself, he drove the stake into the convulsing man's body then yanked it back out. The body stopped twitching, and his veins turned black. The two men who had been watching started to get up, but Matt let me go and ran over to them. He grabbed them by their throats and mimicked the attack Koda had done, reaching into his own pocket to take out a similar black bag. The three dead men with their throats ripped out, holes in their chests and black veins, lay in the alley. Koda and Matt took out black handkerchiefs and wiped the blood off their stakes. When done, they carefully closed the bags and put them back in their pockets.

Koda walked back towards me and reached his hand out. I

flinched away from him, and he smiled. "It's alright. They're dead now."

I whispered, "You killed them. Why?"

Koda squatted down and stared into my face. "Artemis, they were going to kidnap you. Do you know what they would have done between the time they took you and the time they got you to whoever wanted you?"

I shook my head. "You didn't have to kill them. Don't you have werewolf prison or something?"

Koda shook his head. "We kill men who are this dangerous to our packs or they will just come out of prison even angrier than before. If I hadn't killed them, they would have come back for you. They wouldn't have stopped until they had you, or they were dead. I couldn't let them have you." He extended his hand to me again.

I frowned, but took his hand and let him lead me past the dead men. We were almost to the street when three more men stepped in our way, making us stop. I turned around and gasped. "Koda, there's more behind us." Koda turned to the three other men walking behind us. Matt came to stand beside me so that I was in the between him and Koda. I sniffed the air and frowned. "More wolves."

The men held long hammers with silver heads as they walked towards us. I grabbed Koda's arm and whispered, "I don't want you to die for me."

Koda shook his head. "I won't let them take you, Artemis."

I pleaded, "No! Please, Koda."

Matt grabbed me around the waist and pulled me back against him as the six men circled around us. Koda frowned. "State your intent."

The six men looked at each other for a few seconds until one of them finally stepped forward. He was tall and muscular and scary. A scar over his right eye made him look even tougher. "We are here for the girl."

Koda shook his head. "Not going to happen."

The man smiled. "We are here for the girl and your lives don't matter. We will kill you and take her."

Koda leapt forward and attacked the man. They punched and kicked, and I soon realized that Koda knew some type of martial arts. The other man, however, knew some as well. As Koda and the leader fought, the other five men moved forward. Matt started to attack them, but there were too many, and after a minute, three of them held Matt down. Koda punched the leader as hard as he could, knocking him back into Matt, but the leader had recovered and with one of the other men, they grabbed Koda and tackled him to the ground. The last man took his hammer and held it up as if ready to kill them with it. I ran forward and held my hands up in front of them. "Wait!"

The man put his hammer down and the leader asked, "What are you doing? Someone grab her."

I turned to the leader and spoke in a voice barely audible to human ears, "If I go willingly, will you let them live?"

Koda thrashed on the ground. "No! Artemis! No!"

The leader frowned at me but nodded. "We will knock them out so they can't follow us, but we won't kill them."

Koda got one guy off of him, but the leader pinned him down with a knee to his face. I cringed. "Please! Please don't hurt them. I'll go with you, but you have to promise that you will only knock them out and not kill them or hurt them severely."

The leader turned to the other men and nodded. They all stood up, holding Koda and Matt who were trying to fight. Tears slipped down my face and I whispered, "Tell Ares that I'm sorry, but I can't let you die."

Matt shook his head. "No! Artemis, you don't understand. You don't know what they'll do to you!"

I wiped at the tears on my face. "You'll be alive and that's all that matters."

Koda snarled, and his body started to twitch. "If you do anything to her, I will find you all and kill you!"

The leader grinned. "We won't harm a single hair on her head. Knock him out before he changes!"

The man that was left took out a small black object and walked up behind Koda. He swung the object and hit Koda in the lower back of the head knocking him out instantly. Koda's body slumped forward and they lowered him to the ground. Matt trashed and snapped his teeth. "No! Artemis!"

I smiled. "You'll be alright Matt. It's a small price to pay to keep you alive."

Matt began twitching, and the man hit him with the black object making Matt's body go limp. They set him on the ground next to Koda and turned towards me. With all of their eyes on me, I suddenly realized that it may have been smarter to run, but it was too late. The leader grabbed my arm and led me from the alley towards a large black van with tinted windows. "Why do bad guys always drive vans to kidnap people?" I asked myself.

I looked back once at Koda and Matt and let the sobs come. They would live and that's all that mattered. The leader opened the doors to the van, and I climbed inside. After everyone was in, they drove off in silence. I stared out the window, watching the scenery go by, and hoped I might remember how to get back. The leader who was sitting next to me, frowned. "Why did you come willingly? Did you believe they didn't have a chance against us?"

My heart ached in my chest. "I don't know if they could have taken you or not, but I don't want their deaths on my hands. I'm not important enough to die for."

The leader huffed and took out a black handkerchief. He held out the handkerchief to me. "Put it on."

I folded it and wrapped it around my eyes and tied it so that I couldn't see anything but darkness. I leaned back against the seat and closed my eyes, hoping that whatever was in store for me wouldn't be as bad as I imagined. We drove for hours in silence and then finally stopped. I heard the doors opening and closing and then the blindfold came off. The leader stood in front of me. "Come on. Bathroom break."

I followed him out of the car and made sure not to make eye contact with any of the other men. They were all wolves and all dominant, which seemed wrong. We were at a gas station. I followed the leader to the side of the building and walked into the bathroom. I shut the door and sighed. *What had I done? What are they going to do to me?* I went to the bathroom then washed my hands in the sink. I stared at my reflection—at the stranger in the mirror and sighed. *Would Ares think I betrayed him? Would he even try to find me?* I pictured his furious face when Koda and Matt came back without me. *Would he kill Koda and Matt?* I clenched my jaw. *No, he wouldn't kill them because they had tried. Would he kill me if he found me?* Tears brimmed in my eyes, and I quickly wiped them away. I inhaled deeply and walked out of the bathroom.

The leader asked, "Better?"

I nodded and followed him back to the van.

He climbed in beside me and frowned. "What are you feeling?"

I frowned back at him. "What?"

He shook his head. "I can't understand your feelings. They're mixed."

I glared at him. "Why do *you* care?"

He sighed. "I know you must think the worst of us, but I swear that I will not harm you. We are just taking you to the leader."

I frowned. "Who is the leader and why does he want me?"

He shrugged. "We aren't told those things. We just get our money, a person, and instructions."

I sighed. "Great." *Could the vampire king be the one kidnapping me? These guys wouldn't have been told that though.* "What's your name?" I asked the leader.

He smiled. "Jesse."

"And you're a wolf?"

His lips thinned. "Bitten wolf."

I frowned. "A who?"

He narrowed his eyes at me. "You don't know the difference?"

I rubbed my temples. "I only found out that I was a werewolf a few days ago. I'm not really up on the details."

He gasped at me. "How old are you?"

I sighed. *Why did I have to go through this all the time?* "I'm eighteen and didn't change until after…yes, *after* my eighteenth birthday. I'm pretty sure I changed part way when Ares called me, but we aren't sure."

Two men up front gasped and spun around. "Ares!" they exclaimed in unison.

I frowned at them. "How did you know to get me and not know whose I am?"

Jesse blinked at me. "What do you mean whose you are?"

"You really should find out more information before you go on a mission. I'm Artemis Lupine, daughter of Darren, *passt genau* of Ares." The van jerked to a stop and everyone stared at me in shock. I frowned. "Didn't you figure out I was Ares', when his two pack mates were with me?"

Jesse groaned. "Dammit, no wonder he got the better of me at first. Koda's a freaking martial arts nut. Shit."

The man in the front passenger seat asked, "What are we going to do Jesse? We can't separate a match."

Jesse snarled. "It's done. We can't just go hand her back to Ares and hope he doesn't kill us. You know him, he'll kill us before he asks questions. He didn't get the nickname, 'God of War', for being a sweetheart."

I asked, "Is he really that ruthless?"

Jesse smiled. "You do not understand the ways of the wolf yet. He is ruthless because he must be. If he wasn't, he wouldn't be Prince, and if all of us weren't we wouldn't be alive." I sighed and Jesse frowned, "We'll need to find a place for the night and figure this all out."

I turned to him, hopeful. "If you take me back, I'll make sure Ares doesn't kill you."

All of the men laughed. Jesse shook his head. "No. He won't allow us to live after this.

"Then take me back close by, and I'll walk. I'll say I snuck out and they won't have to know it was you. I don't even know you guys so I won't be able to tell them who you are." I pleaded.

Jesse shook his head. "Koda saw us and Ares will smell us on you and his brothers."

The man in the driver's seat said, "It's probably a really good thing that we didn't kill them. If Ares had found them dead, he would have started the hunt immediately. Now he won't know until Koda and Matt make it back after waking up."

Jesse's brow furrowed. "Let's find a hotel."

The driver started driving again and then pulled into a motel a few minutes later. Two of the men went to the clerk and paid for a hotel for the night. We drove to our room and everyone piled out and into the room. Jesse held the door open for me and gave me a friendly smile. *Aren't kidnappers supposed to be mean and violent?* My stomach grumbled and everyone looked at me.

Jesse said, "Mark, go buy some food."

The driver of the van walked out of the room quickly and shut the door behind him. I turned to Jesse and asked, "What are you going to do?"

He shook his head. "I'm not sure yet. For now, you just go sleep on that bed." He pointed at one of the two twin beds. *I'm not tired yet, and how could I sleep when my life was being discussed?* I walked to the bed anyway and lay down on it. I could hear them whispering together, but they were too quiet for me to hear. A few minutes later, Mark came back with five bags of fast food and drinks. He handed me a drink and two cheeseburgers before going to the other men and separating the food between them. I ate my food and stared at the men holding me captive. They were all scary looking and yet the fear that was painted on their faces made them seem less intimidating. I wondered if Ares was really so bad that they should fear him this much. They were still talking an hour later, so I curled up on the bed and went to sleep. If I was going to try to get away tomorrow, I needed my sleep now. I closed my eyes and tried to get comfortable, but without my pack sleeping around me I was freezing.

I awoke to find two hands on me. A small whimper escaped my lips before I could stop it and a man laughed softly. "I ain't gonna hurt ya. I just wanted to ask if ya was cold?" I nodded, not looking at the man. He said, "I'll get a blanket from the car. These hotels are nastay." I heard the door to the room open and close, and then a car door and then the room again. I frowned. *Had my hearing really improved that much?* He shook out the blankets and then laid it on me. "There ya go. If ya need anything else, just ask."

I turned to look at him and asked, "Why are you being nice to me?"

He frowned wrinkling his forehead and asked, "Why wouldn't we be nice to ya?"

I sat up. "You kidnapped me. Koda and Matt seemed to think I was in more danger of you all than anything else."

He smiled showing two identical dimples. "We're hired help, but we aren't scum. We were told to bring you to the leader alive and that was all. Why would we hurt ya?"

I frowned. "So, you aren't going to torture me?"

He laughed loudly and shook his head. "Naw. We aren't. Darn kids watch too much television." He walked over to the other bed and lay down.

I curled up in the blanket and closed my eyes. *Maybe I could survive this.* I had just started to fall asleep hearing the soft sounds of snorting when the bed moved. I opened my eyes, but stayed still. The bed groaned softly as someone climbed on to it next to me. I started to sit up, but a large hand covered my mouth and the man whispered in my ear, "Now you be real quiet, girl, or I'll kill you." I frowned. Hadn't the other man just said they weren't going to kill me? He ran his hand down my face and neck and towards my chest. I slapped his hand, and he grabbed my wrists in one hand, keeping the other hand on my mouth. "It'll be easier on us both if you don't resist."

He kissed my neck and then licked my upper chest. He moved my knees apart and pressed himself against my jeans. I whimpered, realizing what he was doing. He rubbed himself against the front of me and I lost control. I reached my leg up and kicked him in the side. Sometimes being flexible is a great thing. He grunted, but didn't release his grip. He slammed his lower body against mine and I started crying. I realized now that this was what Koda and Matt had been worried about. I felt my body starting to shake and welcomed my wolf. She glared at this man trying to take advantage of me and fury radiated from her as she took over my body. My mouth changed to teeth as he started to kiss down my chest again. I bit into his hand, drawing blood and making him scream. I kicked him backwards and finished my change without any pain. I rolled over and snarled at him.

He held his hand up and growled. "You, dumb bitch! I'll kill you for that!" The lights for the room turned on, temporarily blinding me, and the five other men stared at us in shock. I jumped forward and bit into my attacker's crotch, tearing through his jeans and into his flesh. He screamed and tried to hit me, but I jumped back before he could land his punch. The other men rushed forward and grabbed him.

Jesse glared at him. "What the hell do you think you're doing?"

The man whimpered. "She bit me."

I snapped my teeth at him. Jesse's eyes went wide. I jumped up on to the bed and sat down. Jesse asked, "Artemis?"

I rolled my eyes and barked at him. The other men were staring at me with open mouths.

Jesse blinked several times. "Am I the only one seeing this?"

Mark shook his head. "She looks like Asena."

Jesse smiled. "I knew I wasn't the only one seeing it."

Someone banged on the door, making everyone jump. I glared at the man who had tried to rape me and smiled as he fell to the ground from pain and blood loss. This was one man I wouldn't mind killing. I sniffed the air and snarled. Vampires. Two figures in black cloaks floated into the room and stopped in front of the bed. One of them spoke, and I almost barked in joy. "Is this the girl?"

Jesse nodded. "That's Artemis."

The man lifted his hood back just enough for me to see his face and wink at me. Francois! He put his hood back down. "Why is she in wolf form?"

Jesse looked nervous and started stuttering. "Www…well you see…"

Francois held up his hand. "Enough. I see the wounded man on the floor. You are lucky that we are in a generous mood today." Francois took out a pair of jeans and a t-shirt and tossed them on the bed. "Change, girl, so that we may take you."

I changed back to human form and pretended to be upset, putting on my clothes and glaring at the man on the floor. I asked, "Could I take him as a souvenir? I'm sure your leader will be hungry so early at night."

Francois nodded. "You were told not to harm her and so he will be the price." Jesse started to move forward, but Francois held up his hand. "It is done." The other vampire, who I guessed was Jean Pierre, picked up the man and carried him outside. I followed them out to their silver car and climbed into the passenger seat. The second vampire stuffed the injured man into the trunk and then climbed into the backseat.

Once all the doors were closed, Francois pulled his hood back and the other man did, too. I stared at the other man for a second then asked, "Who is he?"

Francois smiled. "An accomplice. Now you stay quiet, and we can all stay pleasant."

I frowned. "What do you mean? Aren't you taking me to Ares? How did you find me so quickly?"

Francois drove down the road without another word. I

watched where we were going, but had no idea where we were. After a few miles, I asked, "Francois, why aren't you talking to me?"

He shook his head. "I am sorry for this Artemis, but I must obey my maker."

My mind clicked and it felt like liquid was in my brain. "You aren't here to save me, are you?"

The other vampire laughed. "Save you? We are here to take you the rest of the way."

I glared at Francois. "Why? Why are you doing this?"

"I told you that I must obey my leader. She is my maker, and I can't rebel against her. I'm sorry." He said softly through gritted teeth.

I frowned. "But you're a born vampire, you went out in the sun just now. How can you have a maker?"

He smiled. "You're perceptive. I was on death's bed, and she offered me her blood, but in doing so, I became as enthralled to her as any made vampire."

I stared at the window letting my mind numb itself. "Am I going to die?"

"No. She wants you alive." We drove the rest of the way in silence, and I found myself becoming more and more upset. I clenched my teeth to keep from flying off the handle and pressed my cheek to the cold glass. We stopped in front of a small cottage in the middle of nowhere and the two vampires got out. I climbed out with them and followed them to the house. It was fully dark now, and I could feel the presence of a powerful dark force. I swallowed, as I stepped inside the cottage and came face-to-face with Isabella.

She was still as beautiful as I remembered and still as scary. She smiled. "Welcome Artemis. I have been waiting for you." She waved her hand at the table, which was covered in food, like a buffet.

Though I started to drool, I shook my head. "No. What do you want Isabella?"

She laughed, making me shiver in delight. "Straight to the point. I like that." She walked to a small living room and sat in an overstuffed chair. I sat on the chair opposite her and frowned. She smiled wider. "As soon as I heard that Ares had a match, I knew it must be you. Your father disappeared so long ago, that it was apparent that he failed in his duty and kept you alive. I guess it worked out for the best, because now you are here."

I glared at her. "Why do you want me? I'm not special."

She frowned, somehow making herself even more attractive. "But you are special and that's why I went through so much trouble to get you away from that horrid Ares. He wouldn't use your abilities like he is supposed to."

She was confusing me. "Abilities? You mean changing to a wolf?"

Isabella gasped. "You do not know? You are not simply a wolf, but also Sidhe."

I frowned. "What's that?"

She smiled. "The humans call them fairies, I believe."

I stared at her. "Fairies? Like, wings and magical powers, fairies?"

She tilted her head. "Yes. Your mother is a very powerful Sidhe warrior. I knew when I saw your eyes who you were, and I knew I had to have you."

I frowned. "Why would you want me? You're a woman."

She laughed again, making me think of nefarious things. Vampires' voice powers are no joke in real life. "I do not want you for children, silly girl, but for your powers. You are going to help me take over this pathetic planet and push the wolves back to their proper place —as servants."

I folded my arms over my chest. "Does Maurice know what you are doing?"

She waved her hand dismissively at me. "Do not worry about

the king. Francois, here, will be working with you on your powers. As soon as you have gained them, we will move to the next step."

The second vampire brought in the man who had attacked me and threw him down on the ground between Isabella and me. I snarled at him and she smiled. "You seem displeased with this man."

I nodded. "He tried to rape me."

She hissed. "I gave them specific instructions not to harm you." She stood up and picked the man up off of the floor. She easily held him with one hand, and stared into his eyes. "Did you harm her?"

The man whimpered. "Please, beautiful queen, do not kill me."

She frowned. "Your lack of denial is an omission." She stood him up and smiled. I felt her power pulsating against him and groaned. She ran her fingertip along the man's cheek. "You disobeyed me, wolf." The man smiled happily, as though she called him her favorite pet name. She kissed his cheek then leaned his head back. Horror gripped me as her fangs extended, and she plunged them into his neck. He stayed still as she drank from him. I put my hand over my mouth to keep from vomiting and forced myself to watch. The man's eyes grew dimmer and dimmer until, with one last suck, the light disappeared from his eyes. I gasped as she let his body ago and it crumpled, lifeless, to the floor. "Clean that up, please Francois." She turned back to me and smiled, showing her bloody fangs. "Consider that retribution for the stress and pain he caused you. Now I must leave, but you must work hard and focus on your powers." She started to walk away, and I cleared my throat.

She turned around and frowned at me. I asked, "What if I refuse to help?"

She laughed, making me think of nefarious things. "That is not an option. You will help me or you die. It's as simple as that, *mon cheri. Adieu.*"

I watched her retreating back and felt hopeless. *How could I have powers besides my werewolf ones? Could I really be a fairy?* I looked over my back and frowned. No wings. The second vampire took the dead man's body out of the house. Francois smiled at me. "You should eat, Artemis."

I glared at him, but walked over to the table, no longer able to resist my hunger. I ate the food quickly, then folded my arms on the table. "What if I don't have powers?"

Francois frowned. "Then you will die. For now, let's think positive thoughts."

I scoffed. "Positive? Like I might escape and get to watch Victor tear you into pieces?"

Francois sighed. "I know you do not understand about my kind, but we have no choice but to do as our maker tells us. I am sorry, but we must begin your training." He sat across the table from me and frowned. "Put your palms face up and focus on them. You should be able to put energy in your palms and make fire."

"Fire… in my hands?" I asked doubtfully.

He lifted a brow. "You should be able to make fireballs."

I smiled and then frowned. *Why didn't I get to learn the cool stuff when I was with Ares?* I stared at my palms and pictured a flame. I clenched my eyes tight and wished for warmth or fire to my hands. I sat still for a few minutes, but nothing happened. I exhaled and looked at Francois. "Nothing's happening."

He shrugged. "Perhaps fire is not your element." I was beginning to hate hearing French accents. He tapped his chin thoughtfully. "Try picturing the ocean and see if you can make a water ball."

I raised an eyebrow. "A water ball? How is that useful?"

He sighed. "Just do it!"

I frowned at him, but focused on my hands. Then minutes later, I groaned.

He frowned in thought. "Hmm…maybe too much has happened today. Perhaps you should go to bed and try again tomorrow."

I sighed. "Great." I walked up the stairs and then stopped at the top. "Uh, where's my bedroom?"

He smiled. "Second door on the left." I started up again when he called to me. "And Artemis, don't even think about trying to escape. Andre and I have excellent hearing and are very light sleepers."

"Whatever. Stupid bloodsuckers." I mumbled the last as I walked into the bedroom that served as my prison. I plopped down on the bed and stared at the wood ceiling. Would Ares find me? Would he even be looking? I heard the front door open and shut, but ignored it. I rolled onto my side and closed my eyes, finally getting a peaceful night's rest. I awoke the next morning to the front door opening and closing again. I sat up and stretched my arms over my head. What now? Go downstairs and try to gain powers I don't have? Perfect. Maybe death would be better. I walked down the stairs and sat in the head chair of the dining table. "I'm hungry."

Andre frowned at me, but went into the kitchen. Francois sat down at the table, wearing a new set of clothes. He smiled. "How are you feeling this morning?"

"Like a captive who's hungry," I grumbled. Andre walked back into the room carrying a large tray of pancakes and bacon. I smiled. "Andre, if you weren't one of my prison guards, I would kiss you."

He set the tray on the table, flashed his fangs at me and walked away. I ate the food until I couldn't eat anymore and relaxed against the chair. Francois smiled. "Ready to begin your lessons again?"

I sighed. "Wouldn't it be better if someone with experience helped me? You know, someone who was also Sidhe?"

He frowned. "The Sidhe are not exactly friendly with the vampires. Besides, you can do it without their help. Just focus."

Although I didn't think I had the powers they were talking about, I was curious to try. Darren should have taught me about this, or Ares. Why did the bad guys have to be the ones to teach me?

I put my palms face up on the table. I focused on them and thought of fire, but after an hour with nothing happening, I grew tired. "I can't do it. Maybe I don't have magic."

"Well, it is lunch time, so maybe you just need food."

I groaned and stood, stretching my body. Andre walked in carrying a tray of food for me and two wine bottles for them. Although by now I knew it wasn't wine in the glasses. I ate my food in silence and stared at my prison guards. "How long will she keep me alive, if I don't have magic?"

Andre shrugged. "Your fey magic isn't all that she wants."

I frowned. "What did you call my magic?"

Andre looked at me as though I'd just asked what a foot was. "Fey is another term for the Sidhe or fairies. I can't believe Darren never told you about all of this. It is somewhat important."

"You knew my father?" I asked.

Andre sighed. "I fought with him in a battle once. He was a good fighter, but a bastard."

I scoffed. "Tell me about it."

Andre studied my face. I squirmed in my chair at his inquisitive stare. "Did you live with the humans like they say?" he asked.

I let out a slow breath. "I did. I went to school with them and played with them. I thought I was one of them."

Andre asked, "What are they like?"

I shrugged. "Most of the other students didn't like me. Ares said it was because they instinctively knew I was a predator. But there were a couple who accepted me for me and were great." I sighed remembering Bret.

I finished eating and leaned back in my chair. I snapped my fingers and imagined a flame like a lighter. Nothing happened though and no matter how good my imagination was, I just didn't feel magic in me. My wolf stirred inside me, making me gasp. Francois frowned. "None of that."

I shook my head. "I can't control her yet."

Francois frowned. "I forgot you have only changed recently. Your wolf needs an alpha to control her."

I frowned. "What? Why do you need Ares to control me? He hasn't yet." My wolf stirred harder in me, and I felt her trying to change me.

Francois hissed. "Stop it!"

I screamed in pain as a few of my bones separated, trying to remake my shape. I yelled, "I'm trying! But I can't stop her!" More bones and muscles separated and expanded. I fell to the floor screaming in pain. The change hadn't been this painful before. Andre jumped over the table and grabbed me, throwing me on the ground and pinning me. I snapped my teeth at him and shook my head. "You aren't helping Andre! My wolf doesn't like you."

He got off of me, and my body finished the transformation. I lay still on the ground panting and hurting. The pain started to subside, and I rolled over. Francois and Andre's faces were now that of the vampires I had nightmares of. Their fangs extended and their fingers turned into daggers. I growled at them softly, but stayed back. I suddenly knew how I could tell Ares I was captured. I ran to the front door and burst through it. I knew Andre and Francois were right behind me, but I had to do it. I stopped outside the door and raised my snout to the sky and howled as loud as I could. Andre reached for me and I jumped to the side, continuing my long howl. Dogs in the neighborhood near us began howling with me, and soon our songs filled the night air.

Within seconds I lost my breath, and Francois tackled me. I didn't fight and instead submitted to him. He frowned down at me, and then the faintest howl drifted on the wind to my ears. Ares had heard me and he was answering my call. He was coming for me. The thought made me happy and sad at the same time and if I had been in human form I would have cried. Francois dragged me by my scruff back into the house and hissed at me. I laid on the ground averting my eyes and staring at his shoes. He had on running shoes that were covered in mud.

Francois hissed again. "Change back."

I tried to change, but my wolf wouldn't let me. She liked being in control and didn't want to go back. I whimpered and Andre sighed. "Dammit. She doesn't have control over the wolf to change. You should have warned us that she was so new!"

Francois sighed. "The mistress did not care about her being new. Neither of us foresaw this as a possible reaction."

I watched them bicker and relaxed on the ground. Ares had heard my call and answered. He was coming for me. I just had to wait for him. Andre grabbed me by my scruff while I was lying down and threw me across the room. My instincts kicked in, and I pushed off the wall with my feet and landed on the ground. Andre's fangs were extended past his bottom lip and he screamed at me. It was a scream so full of rage and fury, that I flinched. He started towards me, but Francois stood in his path. "Our mistress ordered us not to kill her."

Andre hissed. "I won't kill her, but I'm going to make her wish she was dead."

I remembered Koda telling me that they would do that and I growled softly. Apparently, rape hadn't been the only thing they'd been worried about. I started moving around the table so it was between us, and Andre followed me. Francois let Andre go, and then began to come at me from the other side. It seemed that he liked Andre's reasoning and the thought of causing me pain wasn't a bad one. His fangs extended and he hissed at me. I snapped my teeth at them both and prayed Ares would come sooner rather than later. Andre jumped across the table at me. I had a second to decide my course of action and the wolf took over. I dove under the table and out the other side, while Andre tried to reach underneath.

I ran for the stairs and up into my bedroom. I focused on my human form and my body transformed faster than I had ever been able to before and with no pain. I ran forward and shut the bedroom door and locked it. I knew it was silly to think the small wooden door could keep the vampires out, but it was all I could think to do. I heard them move up the stairs and smelled them closing in on me, but the door didn't open. I curled up on the bed and waited for what they would do to me, because there was nothing else I could do. A few minutes passed and nothing happened. I listened harder and heard fighting downstairs. Had Francois come to his senses and begun to fight Andre? I strained to listen, but all I could hear was the thudding sound of fists hitting each other. I started to walk towards the door and decided it was better to stay here, until I knew who the winner was.

Five more minutes passed and then I heard footsteps up the stairs. I frowned because they were heavier than the vampires had been originally. Could they only float when using magic? I waited tensely as someone stopped in front of my door and inhaled. I suddenly wished I was in my wolf form, but she was too scared to move. There were soft whispers, then a knock on the door. I frowned. Why would they knock on the door?

A familiar male voice asked, "Artemis? Are you in there?"

I jumped off the bed and ran for the door, throwing it open. "Victor!" I ran into his arms and hugged him. "Oh, Victor, you're here."

Victor patted my back, then pushed me away.

I felt something hot and wet on my face and put my hand up to feel blood. I looked at Victor and gasped. "Are you hurt?"

He smiled, showing a little fang. "It's not my blood."

I looked around. "Where is Ares?"

He smiled at me. "He is not as fast as me, but he should be here in a moment. He wanted me to come ahead and to ensure your safety."

Jean Pierre stood just behind him, his face downcast. I reached my hand out to him and he took it, pulling me against him in a hug. "I am sorry for the pain my brother caused you, *mon ami.*"

I shook my head. "It is not your fault. You came to save me."

He pulled back, tears running down his face. "I had feared the dark mistress had taken control of him, but I had not dreamed he would do something so despicable."

"He did not hurt me. He was probably the only reason Andre did not hurt me." I frowned then. "Are they…"

Victor's lips thinned. "They are dead."

I exhaled in relief and began to shiver, thinking of what Andre had wanted to do. I heard someone come in the house and pressed myself against Victor, praying it wasn't Isabella.

Soft bone popping sounds traveled up the stairway and then loud footsteps followed.

I inhaled and smiled wide. I ran from Victor's arms towards the man I loved. I frowned at the realization and then quickly smiled again.

Ares held his arms out to me, a look of relief on his face as I jumped up on him. He held me against his body, and I kissed his lips. I felt his tension and remembered what I had done. I pushed away from him and knelt on the ground in front of him, with my head turned to the side offering my neck. I whispered, "Please forgive me. I did not go with them to betray you."

Ares squatted and lifted my chin up. "There is nothing to forgive. What you did was stupid, but I did not think you betrayed me."

Hot tears slipped down my face and I asked, "You aren't angry with me?"

He frowned. "I am angry with you." I let a few tears fall down my face, and he sighed. "But I am happier that you are alive and that my brothers are alive, as well."

I gasped. "Are they okay?'

Koda and Matt walked up the stairs, naked and smiling. I only glanced at their lower bodies because the nakedness was still so new to me, then ran to them. I hugged them at the same time and kissed each of their cheeks. Matt kissed my cheek back and Koda licked the tears from the side of my face he could reach. "Don't cry, Darling."

I pulled back. "I'm sorry, Koda. I know I am supposed to listen to you, but they wanted to kill you. They didn't even know who you were. I couldn't let you die for me. Please forgive me."

Matt put his hand on my cheek softly. "How could we not forgive you when you saved us? We are in your debt it seems now."

Koda snorted. "Don't tell her that."

I kissed Koda's cheek and whispered, "Now you'll never hear the end of it."

Koda sighed. "At least I'll hear it. We were so scared that you were…" Tears ran down his face and he dropped to his knees. "Forgive us for failing you."

Matt dropped to his knees beside Koda. "Forgive us our Prince and Princess."

Ares walked to stand beside me and asked, "Shall we forgive them my Princess?"

I extended my hands to Koda and Matt. "There is nothing to forgive. You fought, and there were simply too many."

Matt shook his head. "We could have taken them."

I sighed. "No more. I do not forgive you for there is nothing to forgive. You did your best at the time and that is all we can ask of you."

Matt stood up and kissed the back of my hand before smiling. Koda looked up at Ares. "What of you, my alpha? Am I to be punished for this unforgivable offense?"

Ares picked my hand up and placed it against his cheek. "We have our pack mate back, unharmed. I think if she can forgive, then for this instance, so can I."

Koda stared wide-eyed at Ares then stood up and kissed my cheek. "As Matt said, we are in your debt."

I smiled and kissed his cheek. "Then repay your debt by taking me away from here."

Victor sighed. "We must find another refuge it seems. The lion's den is too full for us to hide safely."

We started down the stairs, and Ares picked me up in his arms, cradling me against his chest. I frowned. "Why are you carrying me?"

He laid his head against mine and said, "So that I know you are safe. I will not let you out of my sight again."

I smiled and kissed his lips softly. "As my alpha wills it."

He rolled his eyes. "Isn't it supposed to be as my *king* wills it?"

I shrugged. "Alpha, king, same thing."

We were almost to the door when Koda yelled, "Get down!"

Ares turned and squatted down so that his body was shielding me from whatever was attacking us. I could hear a woman shouting and knew it was Isabella. I tried to get free of Ares' arms, but he held me. "I will not lose you again."

I stared at him in shock and for the first time saw the sadness on his face. "Ares, you have to help them."

"Can you stay here, out of trouble?" he asked.

I nodded.

He kissed my lips as though it were the only thing he needed to survive, and then disappeared out of the house.

I sat on the stairway, stunned from the kiss. I could hear them fighting and her rage-filled screams, and then everything went silent. I ran down the stairs and stood in the open doorway.

Maurice stood covered in moonlight over his dead wife's body. His dagger like fingers glistened with blood. I swallowed as he looked up at me, eyes burning with power. He asked, "Have you been harmed?"

I shook my head.

He asked, "Do you feel we have broken our treaty?"

I looked at Ares and he nodded. I shook my head in response. Maurice smiled and it made me smile back at him.

"Then my job is done." He turned and floated across the lawn, towards a limo and climbed in.

Ares rushed to me and glared at me. "You promised to stay there."

"I promised to stay out of trouble, and when I came to the door there was no trouble," I said with a smile on my face.

He sighed, and Koda laughed. "She's quick."

Ares snarled. "Don't encourage her."

I pressed my naked body against his and felt his body respond against me. "I think encouragement is what we all need."

He stared down into my eyes and then took a step back from me so that our bodies no longer touched. "No, not tonight. Tonight, I want to just hold you, while we sleep. To be a united pack again."

My heart pinched in disappointment. "Alright." I walked towards the second limo that I figured was waiting for us, and climbed inside.

Victor climbed in after me and frowned. "You are bothered?"

I wiped at the tears building in my eyes and knew I was being stupid and irrational. "No."

Koda climbed in next and frowned at me. "What's wrong?"

I pressed myself against the seat and stared out the window of the car. Once the door was shut and everyone was inside, the car drove off. I could hear the others whispering quietly, but ignored them, trying to console myself for the stupid feeling I was having. Ares had rejected me, but not because he was mad or didn't want me, and yet it was still rejection. I brought my knees up, hugged them against my body, and buried my face between them. I felt a hand on me and knew it was Ares and did not look up. I stayed in my ball, as I tried to convince myself of how stupid I was being, and yet the sting of his rejection was too much after the drama I had been through. Ares tried to pick me up in his arms and it was too much.

I moved across the limo as fast as I could to sit beside Jean Pierre. Ares snarled at Jean Pierre and he shrugged. "I did nothing Ares."

Ares asked, "Then why did she run to you?'

I hid my face behind Jean Pierre's arm as I answered. "He is not wolf and I need a second to clear my head."

Ares' voice was short as he asked, "Why?"

I opened my mouth to tell him and then stopped. I asked instead, "Why didn't you tell me I am half Sidhe?"

Everyone instantly stopped moving, so much so that I couldn't hear a heartbeat.

Ares asked, "Who told you?"

I whispered, "Isabella. It is one of the reasons she wanted me. They were trying to force me to learn my powers."

Ares sighed. "I did not tell you because the fey are not our allies right now. If they learned of your existence, they might join in the hunt for you."

I chanced a look at Ares and asked, "Why does everyone want me dead?"

"Everyone wants you because you're valuable," Ares said with a sympathetic smile. He then held his hand out to me. I stared at it and then turned my face into Jean Pierre's back. Ares snarled. "Why are you refusing me?"

I asked still pressed against Jean Pierre, "Why did you reject me?"

Ares laughed softly.

I looked up to glare at him. "You think this is funny?"

The car stopped at the mansion. I hurried out before Ares could stop me and ran up to the doors. The guards stared at me in shock at first. I realized that I was still naked.

I straightened my shoulders and spoke in as firm a voice as I could, "Open the doors for your Princess."

The guards bowed their heads and hurried to open the doors. Ares was close behind me now. I ran inside as fast as I could into the bedroom, surprised that I remembered how to get there. I ran straight to the bathroom and locked the door behind me. I turned the shower on and climbed in, letting the hot water beat against me as I cried for a reason I knew I shouldn't be. Sometimes being a woman means that your emotions don't always make sense. I heard the door crack and knew Ares had broken it down. I didn't look at him but continued to cry and face the back corner of the shower stall.

I felt his anger as he came closer to me and cringed as he opened the shower. I whimpered as his anger hit me like a waft of hot steam. He inhaled, then exhaled, and the anger was gone. He turned me around to face him, and I dropped my gaze immediately. He tilted my chin up and kissed my lips, but I pulled away.

"Artemis," he whispered, almost chiding and I turned away from him to face the corner again. He wrapped his arms around me and whispered into my ear, "Silly woman. I did not reject you."

I whimpered. "You did. You said you just wanted to—"

He nodded against my hair. "That I wanted to hold you and be a united pack. Not that I didn't *want* you. Artemis." He turned me around and stared at my face. His small smile vanished and he put his hands on either side of my face. "Artemis, I could never reject you. You are all I want and more. I just did not want sex with you tonight, because the thought of losing you was too much..."

Koda answered from outside the shower. "You should see the dining room."

Matt sighed. "It will take many days for the holes to be repaired."

Ares growled. "Who invited you?"

Koda and Matt stepped into the shower and stood on either side of us. Koda smiled. "She is our pack mate, too."

Ares frowned. "You see? Even if we had wanted time alone, we would not get it."

I smiled a little and then shook my head. "But you did reject me."

All of the men sighed. Ares asked, "Are you ready for that step? Are you sure that you want to do that?"

I thought about it and asked, "Why wouldn't I be?"

Ares smiled. "You have only known me a few days."

I smelled Victor come near the room and spoke loud enough for him to hear, "A good friend of mine said that love is not something that we should waste. That if I love then I should love. I have realized that… I do." I looked into Ares' wide eyes and said the only thing I knew truly in my heart, at that moment, "I love you, Ares. All I could think about when I let those men take me was how angry you were going to be at me and how hurt you were going to be… because I left…" I began to cry again, and Ares hugged me.

He kissed my cheek and said, "I was not angry or hurt, just, well…okay I was angry, but not how you thought. I'm just happy that you are alive and safe." He pulled back from me so I could see his face, and I realized that everyone else was gone. He smiled at me. The look in his eyes said it before he did. "I love you, too, Artemis. More than you will ever know." He kissed my lips, and I kissed him back. I let my hands travel up his body and into his hair and he pressed me up against the glass of the shower stall.

Ares' hands ran along my sides, but traveled nowhere else, as though he were worried of what I would and wouldn't allow. I grabbed his hands and brought them forward to cup my chest. I whispered, "I want to finish our connection, to truly be your mate. I want to be Artemis *Lupine*. I want *you*, Ares."

He stared into my eyes, his face full of conflict. Then his need took over, and he kissed me back.

What started in the shower, ended on the floor. It was a wondrous thing to have someone make love to you. I knew without a doubt in my heart that Ares and I loved each other. In those moments, it didn't matter to me that I had been destined for him or that he was a killer at times. He was mine and I was his. That was all I needed to know. We lay, breathing heavily on the floor, as our bodies tried to calm down. I turned my head and stared at his handsome face. He smiled at me, making his eyes shine with the happiness he felt. It was the first full smile I had seen on him. I asked, "Will it be like that every time?"

He shook his head and I frowned. He laughed and pulled me against his body, proving that he could go again if I wanted to. He said, "It's better, the longer you are together."

I smiled at him, and then Koda cleared his throat. I looked over the top of Ares' body at him and frowned. "How long have you been there?"

Koda smiled. "Don't worry, we just came in."

Ares sighed. "Koda, what is it?"

Koda blushed a little and spoke in a voice barely above a whisper, "I do not mean to interrupt, but we too have craved the attention of our pack mate." I stared at Koda in shock. He shook his head and waved his hands back and forth. "Not like that! We just want to sleep with you." I gaped at him, and Koda groaned. "Artemis! To sleep with you, you know… *Sleep*!"

Matt tossed two robes at us. Ares quickly put his on and faced his two pack members. I slipped mine on and stood beside Ares. "Are you asking for me to come to bed so we can sleep in our pack?"

Koda and Matt nodded in unison.

I smiled. "Very well."

We walked quickly to the bed and I hopped up in the center. Ares climbed in on my left side and I laid my head down on his chest, while Koda climbed in behind me and molded himself to my back. Matt lay down at our feet and wrapped his arms around my legs. I smiled happily and closed my eyes. "I love you all."

Koda kissed my cheek softly. "I love you as well."

Matt kissed my foot. "Me as well."

CHAPTER ELEVEN

We left France early in the morning, but without Victor or Jean Pierre. They were forced to stay behind to discuss some impending threat, which I assumed was regarding the attacks on the other countries. The connection between Ares and me was stronger than ever. I needed to have constant physical contact. We grabbed the first flight, and I felt my worry ease as we left France.

"Where are we going, Ares?" I asked as I relaxed against the seat.

Ares smiled happily. "My home, in Germany."

My eyes widened for a minute and I then smiled. He did have German features, as did Koda and Matt.

My smile left as a thought came to mind. "Great. Big, German, werewolf women. You couldn't have come from a country with small women, could you?"

Ares kissed my cheek. "You'll be fine."

I smiled evilly. "Maybe I'll just toast them with a fireball."

Ares shook his head. "You aren't allowed to use your Sidhe

powers unless absolutely necessary. No one must know that you have them."

I groaned. "Great. I finally get powers and now I can't use them." After a little accident, this morning, where I'd torched a hand towel, we realized I was able to use my Sidhe powers.

The plane touched down, and we walked through the airport to the waiting vehicle. A man, standing at least seven feet tall, leaned against the hood of a strange European vehicle. He smiled at Ares and bowed at the waist. "Greetings, Ares."

Ares bowed. "Greetings, Brother."

The man turned to me and smiled as he spoke to Ares. "I see your taste in women has improved."

My lip twitched in a snarl, and Ares wrapped his arm around my shoulders. "This is my mate, Ulger, and your Princess."

Ulger dropped to one knee in front of me. "Forgive me, Princess. I had not heard that Prince Ares took a mate."

I looked at Ares for help, but he just smiled. "Uh, you're forgiven," I said awkwardly.

Ulger stood and kissed the back of my hand. "Thank you, Princess."

Ares cleared his throat, and Ulger turned to him. "Darius wanted me to tell you that Darren has escaped our trackers. We aren't sure where he has gone, but we've sent additional trackers to pick up his trail."

"My dad got away? He's still alive?" My voice grew higher in pitch.

Ares wrapped his arm around my shoulders and whispered, "I won't let him hurt you."

His words and touch calmed my nerves, and I relaxed against his side. "I know."

Ares opened the back door of the car and smiled brightly. "Are you ready to meet more of our kind?"

I huffed. "No, but what choice do I have?"

We drove in silence for a few hours, and my mind began wandering. *What were these women like? Were they all as beautiful as the ones I had seen?* Ares tried to pull me into his lap, and I resisted, pulling away from him. He frowned. "What's wrong?"

I saw the look of concern on his face and forced the words out before I lost my nerve. "If I let you, would you leave me, for these women?"

Ares smiled, his blue eyes sparkling. "Not a chance. Artemis. I love you. I thought you were over this?"

"I'm sorry. I'm just nervous." I leaned against him and closed my eyes.

He whispered, "You are the only woman for me. Whether you feel the same for me or not, I will always love you."

I looked up at him and saw the pain in his eyes. He thought I was trying to tell him that I didn't truly care for him. I whispered, "I do love you, Ares."

Ares whispered, "It's our destiny to be together. Are you rehashing old issues because you don't want to discuss the new ones with me?"

"I don't know what you're talking about," I said indignantly and looked out the window to my left.

Ares whispered, "I know it's hard to deal with the fact that you aren't a virgin anymore, but isn't it satisfying to know that you'll be with the one that you gave it to, the rest of your life? Not many humans can say that."

I turned to him and kissed his lips. "I love you Ares. I'm just insecure."

He nuzzled my neck. "You have no reason to be insecure. I only have eyes for you."

Koda groaned and turned around from the passenger seat. "That was so cliché, Ares. You're how old and you couldn't come up with something better than that? I mean, you did work with Shakespeare!"

Ares frowned. "I was trying to be cute. Thank you for ruining our moment."

Koda winked at me. "Just here to help."

We drove for hours through a thick forest on an unmarked dirt road, until finally coming to a small gate with two male guards. Ulger rolled down his window and spoke in German to the guards. The guards opened the gate, bowing to our vehicle as we drove past. The trees began thinning, and we came to a large wooden barn. Ulger stopped the car, and we all climbed out. I stretched my arms up over my head, squealing as I moved.

Ares wrapped his arms around my waist and kissed my cheek. "You keep doing things like that and we won't make it to the village."

I blushed and tried to step out of his arms. "Ares, don't tease me."

He licked my cheek, holding on tightly to me. "I believe I was just saying that to you."

Ulger parked the car inside the barn and then returned to us, cracking his neck from side to side. "Ready?"

Ares nodded, smiling wide.

I asked, "Ready for what?"

Koda pulled his shirt and pants off, and then dropped to his hands and knees, shifting forms flawlessly in seconds. His wolf form was more beautiful than I remembered. I fought the urge to run my hands through his fur and turned towards Ares, who was taking his shirt off.

I sighed. "Fine, but I'm not changing back until we're somewhere I can get dressed. I don't want to parade around naked."

I took my shirt off slowly, noticing Ares watching me and folded it nicely on the ground. I slowly pulled my pants off, wriggling my butt excessively. Ares took a step towards me, and Koda stepped between us, whining and barking. I stripped my underwear off quickly and changed shapes. It felt good to be a wolf again. My wolf felt ecstatic at being let out and we stretched from head to tail. Ares sniffed my shoulder and I wagged my tail. *Let's run!*

Koda's tongue lolled out the side of his mouth. *Loser has to run around the house naked?*

Matt snorted. *No one wants to see you run around naked, anymore than we already have to.*

Ares whined. *Loser has to give the winner a back rub!*

We all ran down the dirt road, kicking up dust behind us. My muscles stretched and my blood pumped harder as I ran. The boys were lengths ahead of me when a familiar scent tickled my nose. I jumped into the forest to my right and ran through the trees towards the smell. *Mom.*

I could hear Ares, Koda, and Matt barking for me, but they could wait. I had to find my mom. Ares spoke through my head. *Where are you going? What's wrong?*

I ran faster trying to follow the scent before it disappeared. *My mom's here. I can smell her.*

I jumped over a fallen log and the forest quieted. I strained my ears to listen to Ares' approaching barks, but not even the wind whispered through my ears. I changed back to human and crossed my arms over my chest. "Hello?"

A bright light darted through the trees, coming towards me. I lifted my arm to cover my eyes and the light dimmed. A man with pale skin and blue vines etched in his arms and across his chest walked towards me. He wore only a pair of pants and was sleeker muscled than Ares, built more like a runner or swimmer. I swallowed in fear. "Who are you?"

He spoke and the leaves rustled. "I am Achilles."

"What are you?" I asked in the silence.

"I'm Sidhe." The leaves rustled again as he spoke making me shiver involuntarily.

"What do you want? Why are you here?" I asked, growing more and more nervous and wishing Ares was here.

He smiled and held out his hand, his body glowing slightly as though a light was turned on inside of him. "I'm here for you. I'm your fiancée and I'm here to take you," he said in a soothing voice.

Ares touched my shoulder and the sounds of the forest crashed into my ears deafening me. I dropped to the ground covering my ears with my hands and moaning in pain. Ares voice boomed like thunder, "You're not taking her anywhere!"

KISS OF A STAR

ARTEMIS LUPINE SERIES, BOOK TWO

USA TODAY BESTSELLING AUTHOR

CATHERINE BANKS

KISS OF A STAR

BOOK TWO

ARTEMIS LUPINE

Kiss of a Star by Catherine Banks.

Cover design by Covers by Juan.

Logo by Avery Banks.

Published by Turbo Kitten Industries.

www.CatherineBanks.com

Turbo Kitten Industries

PO Box 5012, Galt, CA 95632

ACKNOWLEDGMENTS

Pauline, you have quickly become one of my favorite people. Thank you for all of your help.

CHAPTER ONE

Ares, Koda, Matt, and I left France early in the morning, but without Victor or Jean Pierre. They were forced to stay behind to discuss some impending threat, which I assumed was regarding the attacks on the other countries. The connection between Ares and me was stronger than ever. I needed to have constant physical contact. We grabbed the first flight, and I felt my worry ease as we left France.

"Where are we going, Ares?" I asked as I relaxed against the seat.

Ares smiled happily. "My home, in Germany."

My eyes widened for a minute and I then smiled. He did have German features, as did Koda and Matt.

My smile left as a thought came to mind. "Great. Big, German, werewolf women. You couldn't have come from a country with small women, could you?"

Ares kissed my cheek. "You'll be fine."

I smiled evilly. "Maybe I'll just toast them with a fireball."

Ares shook his head. "You aren't allowed to use your Sidhe

powers unless absolutely necessary. No one must know that you have them."

I groaned. "Great. I finally get powers and now I can't use them." After a little accident, this morning, where I'd torched a hand towel, we realized I was able to use my Sidhe powers.

The plane touched down, and we walked through the airport to the waiting vehicle. A man, standing at least seven feet tall, leaned against the hood of a strange European vehicle. He smiled at Ares and bowed at the waist. "Greetings, Ares."

Ares bowed. "Greetings, Brother."

The man turned to me and smiled as he spoke to Ares. "I see your taste in women has improved."

My lip twitched in a snarl, and Ares wrapped his arm around my shoulders. "This is my mate, Ulger, and your Princess."

Ulger dropped to one knee in front of me. "Forgive me, Princess. I had not heard that Prince Ares took a mate."

I looked at Ares for help, but he just smiled. "Uh, you're forgiven," I said awkwardly.

Ulger stood and kissed the back of my hand. "Thank you, Princess."

Ares cleared his throat, and Ulger turned to him. "Darius wanted me to tell you that Darren has escaped our trackers. We aren't sure where he has gone, but we've sent additional trackers to pick up his trail."

"My dad got away? He's still alive?" My voice grew higher in pitch.

Ares wrapped his arm around my shoulders and whispered, "I won't let him hurt you."

His words and touch calmed my nerves, and I relaxed against his side. "I know."

Ares opened the back door of the car and smiled brightly. "Are you ready to meet more of our kind?"

I huffed. "No, but what choice do I have?"

We drove in silence for a few hours, and my mind began

wandering. What were these women like? Were they all as beautiful as the ones I had seen? Ares tried to pull me into his lap, and I resisted, pulling away from him. He frowned. "What's wrong?"

I saw the look of concern on his face and forced the words out before I lost my nerve. "If I let you, would you leave me, for these women?"

Ares smiled, his blue eyes sparkling. "Not a chance. Artemis. I love you. I thought you were over this?"

"I'm sorry. I'm just nervous." I leaned against him and closed my eyes.

He whispered, "You are the only woman for me. Whether you feel the same for me or not, I will always love you."

I looked up at him and saw the pain in his eyes. He thought I was trying to tell him that I didn't truly care for him. I whispered, "I do love you, Ares."

Ares whispered, "It's our destiny to be together. Are you rehashing old issues because you don't want to discuss the new ones with me?"

"I don't know what you're talking about," I said indignantly and looked out the window to my left.

Ares whispered, "I know it's hard to deal with the fact that you aren't a virgin anymore, but isn't it satisfying to know that you'll be with the one that you gave it to, the rest of your life? Not many humans can say that."

I turned to him and kissed his lips. "I love you Ares. I'm just insecure."

He nuzzled my neck. "You have no reason to be insecure. I only have eyes for you."

Koda groaned and turned around from the passenger seat. "That was so cliché, Ares. You're how old and you couldn't come up with something better than that? I mean, you did work with Shakespeare!"

Ares frowned. "I was trying to be cute. Thank you for ruining our moment."

Koda winked at me. "Just here to help."

We drove for hours through a thick forest on an unmarked dirt road, until finally coming to a small gate with two male guards. Ulger rolled down his window and spoke in German to the guards. The guards opened the gate, bowing to our vehicle as we drove past. The trees began thinning, and we came to a large wooden barn. Ulger stopped the car, and we all climbed out. I stretched my arms up over my head, squealing as I moved.

Ares wrapped his arms around my waist and kissed my cheek. "You keep doing things like that and we won't make it to the village."

I blushed and tried to step out of his arms. "Ares, don't tease me."

He licked my cheek, holding on tightly to me. "I believe I was just saying that to you."

Ulger parked the car inside the barn and then returned to us, cracking his neck from side to side. "Ready?"

Ares nodded, smiling wide.

I asked, "Ready for what?"

Koda pulled his shirt and pants off, and then dropped to his hands and knees, shifting forms flawlessly in seconds. His wolf form was more beautiful than I remembered. I fought the urge to run my hands through his fur and turned towards Ares, who was taking his shirt off.

I sighed. "Fine, but I'm not changing back until we're somewhere I can get dressed. I don't want to parade around naked."

I took my shirt off slowly, noticing Ares watching me, and folded it nicely on the ground. I slowly pulled my pants off, wriggling my butt excessively.

Ares took a step towards me, and Koda stepped between us, whining and barking.

I stripped my underwear off quickly and changed shapes. It felt good to be a wolf again. My wolf felt ecstatic at being let out and we stretched from head to tail.

Ares sniffed my shoulder and I wagged my tail. *Let's run!*

Koda's tongue lolled out the side of his mouth. *Loser has to run around the house naked?*

Matt snorted. *No one wants to see you run around naked, anymore than we already have to.*

Ares whined. *Loser has to give the winner a back rub!*

We all ran down the dirt road, kicking up dust behind us. My muscles stretched and my blood pumped harder as I ran. The boys were lengths ahead of me when a familiar scent tickled my nose. I jumped into the forest to my right and ran through the trees towards the smell. Mom.

I could hear Ares, Koda, and Matt barking for me, but they could wait. I had to find my mom.

Ares spoke through my head. *Where are you going? What's wrong?*

I ran faster trying to follow the scent before it disappeared. *My mom's here. I can smell her.*

I jumped over a fallen log and the forest quieted. I strained my ears to listen to Ares' approaching barks, but not even the wind whispered through my ears. I changed back to human and crossed my arms over my chest. "Hello?"

A bright light darted through the trees, coming towards me. I lifted my arm to cover my eyes and the light dimmed.

A man with pale skin and blue vines etched in his arms and across his chest walked towards me. He wore only a pair of pants and was sleeker muscled than Ares, built more like a runner or swimmer.

I swallowed in fear. "Who are you?"

He spoke and the leaves rustled. "I am Achilles."

"What are you?" I asked in the silence.

"I'm Sidhe." The leaves rustled again as he spoke making me shiver involuntarily.

"What do you want? Why are you here?" I asked, growing more and more nervous and wishing Ares was here.

He smiled and held out his hand, his body glowing slightly as though a light was turned on inside of him. "I'm here for you. I'm your fiancée and I'm here to take you," he said in a soothing voice.

Ares touched my shoulder and the sounds of the forest crashed into my ears deafening me. I dropped to the ground covering my ears with my hands and moaning in pain. Ares voice boomed like thunder, "You're not taking her anywhere!"

CHAPTER TWO

My ears still rang as I knelt on the ground beside Ares. Koda and Matt finally found us and moved to stand behind Ares in protective stances.

"What are you doing here, Sidhe?" Ares asked between clenched teeth. I'd never seen him so mad before. His hands were balled into fists at his sides as he glared at Achilles.

Achilles glanced from Ares to me. "What is this?"

My ears finally stopped ringing, so I stood up, slightly behind Ares, and placed my hand on his shoulder. The skin to skin contact allowed some of his power to seep in and heal the damage to my ears. "It's alright, Ares. He hasn't hurt me," I said softly.

Ares' fists loosened and he grabbed one of my hands in his. I could feel his anger and worry as if they were my own. Koda whispered, "Ares."

Ares looked at my face and exhaled. The anger and worry disappeared, allowing me to breathe. *When had I stopped breathing?*

"I'm sorry," Ares said softly to me.

I kissed his cheek. "It's alright."

Achilles began glowing again and he clenched his teeth as he said, "Do not touch him."

I glared at Achilles. "I don't know who you are, but I'm not in the mood. State your business."

Achilles' eyes widened in shock for a moment, but he quickly recovered. "Artemis, I'd appreciate it if you would step away from Ares."

Ares growled. "Not going to happen. State your business."

Achilles stopped glowing and rubbed his temples, looking weary. "Of all of the werewolves in the world, why did it have to be you protecting her?"

I looked Achilles over while he was babbling and felt a smile tug up the corner of my lips. He was incredibly handsome, very close in competition for most handsome with Ares. Achilles' blue vines were beautiful and throbbed like veins. His face looked familiar, but I couldn't remember where…

Achilles spoke, interrupting my thoughts. "Artemis, I've come for you. You're mine."

I looked at him and then at Ares. "There's a lot of that going around lately. Why do you think I am yours?"

He smiled making my knees wobbly. "You're my fiancée. You were betrothed to me at birth."

I shook my head. "I can't be your fiancée. I already have a mate."

Achilles glared at Ares. "Mate? She's your mate?!"

Ares smirked. "She's my *passt genau*."

Achilles shook his head. "You're lying. You just don't want to give her to me."

Ares snarled and his anger returned. "She's my match, Achilles. She's my *mate*. She's *MINE*!"

Why was he so easily upset by this Sidhe?

Achilles narrowed his eyes. "I will not give her up simply because she's your match! I was promised the first of her mother's children. I've waited *seven hundred years* for her and I will *not* just let you have her."

Ares rubbed his face, and his anger dissipated just as quickly as it had come. "I don't want to start a war between us, but if neither of us is willing to give her up, what do you suggest we do?"

"I do not have any suggestions as of yet, but we may be able to come up with something," Achilles said softly.

Ares looked at me. "Do you have any ideas?"

I laughed loudly. "Me? I just met this guy, the first of my mother's kind, and he tells me I'm his fiancée, but how can that be since I'm already yours? He says he won't give me up, yet he doesn't have me. What do you want me to say? Kill him? No, we can't do that because for some reason that would start a war. Give me to him? Hell no! No offense, Achilles, but I love Ares and my pack. I'm not going anywhere. So, I have no ideas."

Matt spoke for the first time, making me jump. "Maybe you could cut her in half, like that story of the children fighting over the doll?"

Ares growled at Matt, who raised his hands in the air and took a step back with his head lowered submissively. "I was just kidding."

Ares closed his eyes and took a deep breath to calm himself. "Artemis, don't worry. Achilles is the Prince of the Sidhe, so a war won't start, unless we tried to kill him, which we won't. Let's get to the village and we'll discuss it more there."

Matt growled and asked, "How do we know he's telling the truth?"

Achilles looked insulted. "I'm not a *pixie,* and I wouldn't lie about this. Besides, I didn't know she was Ares' match or mate."

I held up my hands. "Stop. Can we please just get to the village? I'm hungry."

Achilles nodded. "Alright. How far is it? Should I fly?"

I gasped. "You can fly?!"

He frowned and looked at me as though I'd asked what a nose

was. "Of course I can fly. You should be able to as well. Though, I suppose it depends on how strong your wolf is."

He was looking over my body, which made me realize that I was naked. A blush rushed to my cheeks instantaneously. "Enough talk. Let's go," I said as I tried to hide my embarrassment.

Achilles laughed. "She blushes? How endearing."

Ares, Koda, and Matt started running towards the village, leaving me and Achilles to catch up with them. Achilles ran beside me, watching me closely. I tried to ignore his stare, but my body began itching. I turned to him and was about to ask what his problem was when a tree appeared in front of me. I tried to stop, but couldn't slow down. At the last second, I dodged to the right.

"The trees are very interested in you," Achilles said from beside me.

"What do you mean?"

"The trees are alive, Artemis. That one that you almost hit was determined to get closer to you. I have not seen one do that in quite a while."

I groaned. "Great, now trees are out to get me. Why does my life have to be so strange? A few days ago, I was just another teenage human going to school and worrying about boys. Now I'm a half-werewolf, half-fairy, Sidhe, thing that is the mate of the Prince of the Werewolves and engaged or whatever to the Prince of the Sidhe. And *now* trees have decided they find me interesting. I would ask if it could get weirder, but I'm betting so."

We reached a clearing, and Ares growled at us in his wolf form. I dropped to my hands and knees and changed forms, rushing over to him and rubbing my head against his chest.

Don't let him touch you. Ares whispered through my mind.

Matt and Koda, also in their wolf forms, came to stand beside us. Darius, King of the Werewolves and the most frightening man I've ever met, walked towards us from around the side of a nearby house. The presence of him rose my hackles and made me back up underneath Ares until my head was below his chest and his body completely hid mine from sight.

Ares cocked his head to the side and looked at me questioningly, but Darius spoke, making him look away from me. "What is *he* doing here?" The hate was evident in Darius' voice as well as his defensive posture.

Ares looked at Darius intently for a moment and then Darius snarled. "You should have told me that he was coming with you."

Ares' body was completely still as he looked at Darius. I realized after a moment that he was communicating with Darius telepathically.

"Fine. Come meet with me in an hour," Darius said angrily before walking away from us.

You can come out now. Ares said to me.

I crawled out from under him and sat on my haunches. *He scares me.*

Ares sat beside me. *You don't have to be scared of him. He wouldn't dare hurt you now that you're my mate.*

Now? I asked in shock.

Achilles spoke softly, "Could you please stop communicating in wolf form? It's rude."

Matt growled softly at Achilles, his lips pulled back in a threatening snarl. Ares grunted, and Matt stopped, but I could still see the hate in Matt's eyes as he stared at Achilles. Ares nodded once and started walking. I followed close to Ares' side as we made our way through the town of log cabins. Men and women looked at us from the porches and from windows. Koda stayed close by my other side, scanning the houses as we passed them. Matt walked behind us with Achilles behind him.

We continued down the dirt road and past shops selling clothes and food. A small group of children stood outside one shop with ice cream cones. I stopped and stared at the cluster of toddlers and elementary-aged kids. *Children?* I mean, I knew they had children.

I'd seen the ones at the first werewolf village I'd been to, but so many young ones, just walking around?

Did Ares want children? Would he want me to have a child? A werewolf child?

Artemis?

I looked at Ares and shook my head. *Nothing.*

He looked towards the kids and lifted his lips in a wolfish grin. *Yes, we do have children here, just like at the other village.*

I moved away from him. *Can we just get to wherever it is that we're going? I want to change.*

Ares shut his mouth and looked upset, his tail tight against his body. *Alright.*

He led the way in silence as we passed more houses and more people. I couldn't believe there were so many werewolves in one place. If the humans knew about this, it would be chaos. Of course, with the preternaturals taking over the world, the humans already had plenty of chaos to deal with. Ares finally stopped at a two-story log cabin with a wraparound porch on both floors. It was beautiful, warm and inviting.

Ares changed forms and signaled for me to do the same. Koda and Matt changed forms and walked into the house without looking back at me. Achilles stepped onto the porch and spoke to Ares over his shoulder, "I'll wait inside."

Ares watched him walk inside with a fierce look on his face. He turned to me and his face softened. "Come on, Artemis."

I closed my eyes and pictured my human body. My body rippled, and I stood up in my human form. It still amazed me how easy it was to switch between forms. It also made me wish that I'd known about it sooner.

"Welcome to Lyngvi," Ares said.

"Lyngvi?"

Ares nodded. "That's the name of this town."

He picked me up in his arms and started walking up the stairs. "Ares!" I gasped.

He smiled and stopped in front of the door. "I want to carry you over the threshold."

"We're not married." The words left my mouth before I thought of the repercussions.

Ares' smile vanished and he looked at my face with pain pinching the corner of his eyes. "Artemis, you're my mate. That means we're married. How many times do we have to go over this?"

I had to fix the pain I'd caused him. I took a minute to plan out what to say before starting. "I'm sorry. I didn't mean it like that. I just meant that taking me over the threshold is only done when humans get married."

"This is my house, well ours now. You accepted my last name, 'Lupine', like a human married couple would have. Why can't you accept this?"

"Alright. You win. Take me into *our* house," I said quietly.

He kissed my cheek and smiled victoriously. "I always win."

He stepped over the threshold and then ran up the stairs, to the right and into a bedroom. He set me down on my feet slowly just inside the door. A large bed with luscious purple silk sheets took up most of the bedroom. A door across the room led to the bathroom with his and her sinks. A second door to the left led into a walk-in closet. The room was so welcoming and warm, that I instantly felt safe. I walked to the bed and ran my hand along the sheets. "It's beautiful."

He was still standing in the doorway, but was smiling, the full smile he so rarely wore. "I had the sheets sent from Paris specifically for you."

He started to walk into the bedroom when someone called from downstairs, "Ares."

Ares sighed loudly. "He's going to be a pest."

I walked quickly to him, feeling his irritation. "Ares, I love you and..."

Ares shook his head and kissed my lips, stopping me from

continuing. "Don't worry, Artemis. It'll be fine." He rested his hand against my face and gave me his full smile again. "You're so beautiful."

A blush covered my cheeks, which made him laugh. He kissed my cheek and then yelled, "Koda!"

Koda bounded up the stairs, taking them two at a time. He stopped at the door. "You rang?"

Ares stepped away from me slowly and stared at Koda. "You've been reassigned."

Koda's eyes widened and his voice rose a few notches higher. "What? You're reassigning me! What did I do?"

Ares placed a hand on Koda's shoulder and smiled reassuringly. "Brother, calm down. I'm reassigning you to be Artemis' guard."

Koda exhaled and put a hand against his chest. "Oh, thank the Mother. I thought you were kicking me out of the pack!"

Ares shook his head. "I couldn't kick you out of the pack. Besides, I trust only a few with her. Guard her while I speak to Achilles."

Ares kissed my cheek one more time and then walked quickly down the stairs. I watched his naked backside as he took the stairs. Koda cleared this throat. "Earth to Artemis."

I blushed again. "Sorry, Koda."

He walked into the bedroom and hopped up onto the bed. "They're going to be talking for a while."

"Why does Ares hate Achilles so much?" I asked as I sat down next to Koda on the bed.

Koda leaned back against the pillows and headboard. "That is a long story that Ares is better to tell you. I'm not trying to hide anything from you, but there's a lot to the story that I don't know."

"Is he bad?"

Koda laughed. "Bad? Well, it depends…he's not evil, if that's what you mean."

"What do you think they're going to decide?" I asked as I leaned back against the pillows next to Koda. His closeness was comforting, his scent, a mix of wolf and forest, was relaxing.

"I don't know," Koda said honestly. Koda stood up off of the bed and walked through the door that led into the closet. "You seem to be adjusting quickly," Koda said from inside the closet.

I looked down at my naked body and shrugged. "It just seems natural. I mean, I'm not going to walk around town naked or anything, but you, Matt and Ares are going to be seeing me naked a lot and, well, I just feel different now. It's like the connection with Ares has made me more mature in some ways. I'm not saying I'm completely mature, but in some aspects, I think I am. I don't know, you probably think I'm being ridiculous."

Koda walked out of the closet and tossed me a fluffy white robe. "I don't think you're being ridiculous. I think you're right. It may be your connection, or it may just be Ares."

I raised an eyebrow at him as I slipped the soft robe on. "Ares?"

"An alpha male has an intense effect on those of his pack. The alpha who cares for you after your first change, shapes you. Ares is a supreme being. He's kind, loyal, sympathetic and good. Sure, he can be intense, angry and scary at times, but overall he's smart and level-headed and very mature."

Ares stepped into the bedroom, wearing a pair of pants. "You flatter me."

Koda rolled his eyes. "I wasn't saying it for your sake."

Ares leaned against the bed post with his arms crossed. "We're still at a stalemate. I'm not sure what we're going to decide."

I crawled across the bed to sit beside where he was standing. "It's alright."

He smiled and kissed my cheek. "I've got to go speak with the king. Promise to stay away from Achilles?"

I nodded. "I'll stay here in the room with Koda."

Ares looked at Koda. "Don't let him near her and don't let anything happen to her while I'm gone."

Koda bowed at the waist. "Of course."

Ares rolled his eyes at Koda then kissed my lips. “Before I go, I want to show you something.” He took my hand and I hopped down from the bed to follow.

He led me into the walk-in closet and I gaped at the size of it. I’d thought it would be a normal closet, but the room was as big as the living room at Darren’s house. He led me past rows of pants, shirts and suits for men and to a back section that was recently added on. I knew it had been added on because there was still sawdust on the floor from the cabinets being put in.

Ares opened the doors to the cabinets, revealing rows of dresses, shirts, pants, undergarments and shoes. “Whose are these?” I asked in shock as I touched a soft white dress that stood out among the others.

“It’s all yours,” he said softly.

I turned to face him. “Mine? What do you mean mine?”

“When I started dreaming about you, I called here and had this area built for you. Then, when we were in Paris, I called again with your size and had these clothes and other items placed here.” He looked at the dress I was still touching. “I bought that for you in Paris.”

I smiled. “You’re full of wonderful surprises, Ares. Thank you.”

He took my hand. “There’s more.” He led me out of the closet, past Koda and to the bathroom. The bathroom was painted and decorated in a warm blue tone. The his-and-her sinks each had a toothbrush and holder next to them. Ares opened the cabinet doors under the sinks and pointed in. I looked inside and gasped. It was stocked full of feminine products, hair care products, hair brushes, curling irons, and devices I couldn’t name or even imagine how to use. “I wanted you to have everything you needed. I want this to be your home as much as it is mine.”

I wrapped my arms around his neck and hugged him tightly. “Thank you. You have no idea how much this means to me.”

I kissed him and he rubbed his thumb down my cheek. “Why are you crying?”

I laughed and wiped at my eyes. "Sorry, it's not you. I just... with Darren I never felt loved. Sure, he provided all of the necessary items for me and he kept me safe, but it was never a loving home. It wasn't really even a home to me. But with you...I feel loved and this feels like home to me already."

Ares kissed both of my eyes softly, stopping the tears. "I'm sorry your childhood was hard. I promise that I'll do everything in my power to keep you safe and happy. I love you, Sunshine."

I smirked. "Sunshine?" He'd been trying to come up with a nickname for me, but I'd rejected "baby" and a few others I simply refused to let him call me.

Ares frowned. "You don't like it?"

"Why Sunshine?" I asked as I played with his hair.

"Because you gave me sunlight in my darkest day. I thought I was going crazy before I met you. Now, even with all that is happening, every time I look at you, I feel happy and warm. So, yes, 'Sunshine' is your name."

I kissed his lips quickly. "I like it."

Matt cleared his throat. "Darius isn't going to like you being late."

Ares sighed. "Duty calls."

I kissed his cheek before walking out of the bathroom and towards the closet. "I promise Koda and I will stay in the room, away from Achilles, until you get back."

Ares stopped at the bedroom door and turned back to me. "After I return, we'll be going to dinner. The whole town will be there. Will you wear the white dress?"

I saw the hopeful look on his face and curtsied, bowing my head. "Of course, my Prince."

All three men laughed. Ares rushed over and kissed my lips hard, making my heart race. "Don't forget your necklace."

I touched the diamond heart necklace which was on my upper chest. It had been a present from Ares, a sign so that everyone would know that I had his heart alone. "I've still got it on."

Ares smiled happily. "Good. I should be back in an hour or two."

I hurried into the closet and to my cabinets. I'd never had so many clothes before. I took down the white dress and stroked the soft fabric. It had spaghetti straps, a v-cut neckline and an hour glass shape like I had. I hung it on a hook on the wall and stared at the assortment of shoes. "Koda," I called softly.

He walked silently into the closet. If I hadn't been watching for him, I never would have known he was coming. "Yes?"

I pointed to the cabinet. "I need you to help me figure out what to wear with this dress."

He smiled. "No problem." He stopped in front of the cabinet and whistled. "Wow, he went all out for you. Not that I suspected he wouldn't, but this is amazing."

"I know. I'm in awe," I said dreamily.

He looked at the white dress and then at me. "Hm…alright, here's what we're going to do." He took out a pair of white two inch heels and set them on the ground, underneath the dress. "Those." He started riffling through the underwear and I stared in shock at the thongs and lingerie in the pile. I'd never worn lingerie before. He picked up a white silk thong and set it on a chair that I hadn't noticed was next to the dress. "This." He turned to me now and frowned. "You're too big busted to go braless."

I frowned. "Thanks."

He shrugged. "Just being honest." He turned back to the cabinet and pulled out a white strapless bra. "Perfect."

I stared at the completed outfit and smiled. "You're good."

He smiled wide. "I know. Now go take a shower before you put all of that white stuff on. You've got dirt all over your legs."

I rolled my eyes. "Yes, father."

He smacked my arm playfully. "You want to look great for Ares, right?"

"Right." I gingerly took off the diamond necklace and handed it to him. "Keep it safe while I'm in the shower."

He took the necklace slowly and held it in one palm. "I promise. Now hurry. I want to tell you some things before we go to dinner."

I jogged to the bathroom and took off the robe. I started to reach for the door to shut it, but knew if Koda was supposed to be protecting me that he'd want it open. Plus, I felt safer having it open. The tub to the left of me was giant, big enough to fit all four of us in comfortably. "Koda, is this a spa or tub?" I asked curiously.

He laughed. "It's a spa."

"Why is there a spa in the bathroom?"

"Don't ask me. Ares designed this house," Koda said loudly.

The shower had no door, consisting of one long tiled wall with a shower head, which came out of the middle with a large drain in the middle of the floor. If I had been morea modest I would be running to shut the bathroom door now. I turned the shower head on and quickly scrubbed my hair and body. The shampoo and soap didn't have a smell, which was surprisingly refreshing to my nose. I hadn't realized how much the scented soaps bothered me until then. After drying off, brushing my teeth and blow drying my hair I finally felt clean. Clean for the first time in weeks. I strolled across the bedroom. "It's great to be clean."

Koda grunted. "Sure, rub it in."

My foot hit the floor awkwardly as I tried to stop in mid-step before turning to him. "What?"

He sniffed his arm. "I stink, but until Ares comes back I can't shower."

"Sure, you can. I'll just do my hair and makeup in the bathroom so that you'll be protecting me while you get clean," I said with a smile.

His eyes widened. "You'd be willing to do that?"

"It's not that big of a deal. Let me put on my underwear and dress." A patch of sun was shining on the dress as I walked in. It looked too perfect for me to wear, but Ares wanted it on. The underwear felt somewhat uncomfortable as I put them on, but after a minute I barely noticed them. Of course, there wasn't much fabric to notice. The bra fit well, but without straps I felt awkward. Finally, I slipped the dress on over my head and shimmied it down my body. It was snug, but not uncomfortable. After smoothing the dress down again, I walked out of the closet and twirled in a slow circle. "What do you think?"

Koda was sitting perfectly still. I couldn't even see his chest rising or falling with breath. "Wow," he said softly. He walked slowly towards me, making me stop twirling and blush. He smiled, but his eyes looked sad. "You're beautiful, Artemis. Ares is a lucky man."

"Does Ares know that you have feelings for Artemis?" Achilles asked from the doorway, making me jump since I hadn't realized he was there.

Koda frowned. "Of course, I have feelings for her and Ares knows. She's part of my pack."

Achilles smiled and it took my breath away. He looked like a Greek god. Wait? Achilles was a hero in Greek myths, right? Was he… "Achilles?"

Achilles looked at me and his smile faltered. "Yes?"

"Are you *the* Achilles?" I asked nervously. Being around him was uncomfortable, but not in a fearful way. He made me want to relax and be near him, which wasn't normal. Even Ares didn't feel like this to me.

Achilles smiled. "That is a long discussion that you and I will be having at a later time."

Koda grumbled. "Speaking of that, I need you to go back downstairs."

Achilles frowned at him. "Ares gave you orders to keep me away from her?"

Koda nodded. "I'm sorry, but he is my alpha and his orders were clear." Achilles looked like he wanted to argue, but Koda whispered, "Please."

Achilles sighed and rubbed his temples. "You were always my favorite, Koda. What do you want me to do, Artemis?"

"I promised Ares I would stay away from you. Please leave," I said quietly.

Achilles bowed at the waist in a graceful motion that made me stare in awe at him. "As you wish," he said before turning on his heel and heading down the hallway. The tone in which he said the words made me think of Wesley from Princess Bride and made me shiver involuntarily.

Koda handed me the diamond heart necklace and whispered, "It's a good thing Achilles is a reasonable male."

I clipped the necklace in place and walked towards the bathroom. "Come on. I want to be ready by the time Ares gets here."

Koda followed me in and started undressing. I pulled out the hair straightener and the box of makeup I'd seen earlier. Koda started the shower behind me and began singing. If he hadn't been such a talented singer, I would have laughed at him, but his voice was amazing and after a moment I hummed along as he sang. My hair didn't take long to straighten, but I was having trouble deciding what makeup to use. If I used too much makeup, I would smell funny, but I needed something to spice myself up.

Koda reached around me, making me jump and squeal. He laughed. "Sorry. I figured you had heard the water turn off."

"I was focusing on the makeup and what I should use," I said as my heart calmed down.

He held up the black eyeliner that he'd grabbed. "This around the bottom of your eyes and…" He grabbed white eyeshadow and black mascara. "These. Go light, but with just these things you'll look great."

He moved away from me and started brushing his teeth in the sink next to me.

"You have a great voice," I said to him as I applied the eyeshadow.

Koda smiled with toothpaste filling his mouth. "Thank you."

I giggled at him and finished with the makeup. My purple eyes stood out drastically with the makeup on and with the white dress below, I looked amazing. Was I conceited? "Koda? Do you think it's conceited for me to think I look amazing now?"

Koda shook his head. "No, just truthful. Sidhe women are generally beautiful anyways."

I heard the front door open and ran towards the closet. "Shoes!"

Koda followed me in and quickly got dressed in a pair of black slacks and a deep blue button up shirt. "Don't wear the shoes," he said quickly and quietly. "I forgot that we were going to dinner with the town. We don't wear shoes to events that the King and Queen are attending."

"Why not?" I asked curiously.

"Werewolves need to be able to change at any time and shoes are often destroyed in a change because it takes too long to take them off."

Ares and Matt were walking up the stairs, so I tossed the shoes back in the cabinet and adjusted my dress.

Koda whispered, "You look great. Stop worrying."

Ares spoke from the bedroom doorway. "I'm going to change before we go, Achilles. We'll be down after I'm ready."

I hid in the cubby area where my cabinets were.

Ares walked into the closet and started rummaging around in the front area. "Why are you hiding, Artemis?"

"I'm waiting until you're ready before I let you see me," I said.

Ares began speaking to Koda, "Darius wants to speed the process up. He wants it to be finished in six months."

Koda groaned. "That's crazy. I mean it's not like it can't be done, but why? Why not just let the chaos linger for a while?"

"I need to do my hair," Ares said before walking away.

Matt peeked his head around the corner making me jump since he hadn't made a noise. "Wow, you look great."

I smiled. "Thanks."

Koda cleared his throat. "Matt, shouldn't you be getting changed?"

Matt sighed and turned around. "Alright." Matt was acting different. I couldn't put my finger on what exactly it was, but something wasn't right.

Ares spoke from nearby, "Artemis? Are you ready?"

I smoothed my dress down, checked the placement of my necklace and took a deep cleansing breath. "Yes." My heart was beating faster than it should have, but I tried to keep the smile on my face to show I wasn't that worried.

Ares stood outside of the closet in a pair of black slacks and a black button up shirt. His eyes sparkled like diamonds, catching my attention. "It looks better on you than I would have imagined," he said softly.

"You look amazing, Ares." I managed to say between the backflips the butterflies were doing in my stomach.

Ares slipped his hand in mine and kissed me on the lips. "You're breathtaking."

I inhaled his scent and the butterflies disappeared. "Thank you."

Koda stepped out of the closet with his arms spread. "What about me?" Ares shook his head and I rolled my eyes at him. Koda twirled in a circle. "So?"

"You look great, Koda," I said as I tried not to laugh.

Koda frowned. "Ares is amazing and I'm only *great*? Now you've hurt my feelings."

Matt stepped out of the closet in a pair of dark blue slacks and a white button up shirt. "We better hurry or they'll eat without us."

Ares squeezed my hand. "Let's go. I can't wait for you to meet my mother."

I groaned. "Great, the mother-in-law."

Ares kissed my cheek. "She'll love you."

Koda and Matt were discussing females as we walked down the stairs, so I chose to ignore them.

Achilles stood by the front door, leaning against it. He was wearing a black suit that hugged the curves of his body.

The sight of him made me gasp, which made Ares growl, which made me blush.

Achilles frowned at Ares, but simply asked, "Are you all ready to go?"

Matt growled. "He's coming?"

Ares growled at Matt and turned to face him. "Be kind to our guest, Matthew. You forget your place and the fact that Achilles is Prince of the Sidhe."

Matt stopped growling, but his face still showed his anger. "The Sidhe's ranks have nothing to do with me."

Achilles folded his arms across his chest. "You were always the most volatile of the three, especially towards my kind."

Matt smiled. "Thank you."

"Enough," Ares barked. "Let's go."

Achilles opened the door and walked out first. Ares followed with me by his side and Matt and Koda brought up the rear. Ares stayed silent as we walked through the town.

I looked around and noticed how deserted it was. "Where is everyone?"

"They're all gathered at the dining hall," Ares said without looking at me.

"Does everyone always go to the dining hall together?" I asked.

Achilles answered before Ares could. "No, they're all gathered to see the return of the prince and to see his mate. Ares had quite a reputation with the females so I'm sure they're all dying to see who he finally chose."

"Oh. So, I'm going to have to deal with irate women? Again?" I asked quietly.

Ares pulled my hand up and kissed the back of it. "Just remember that you're the one that has my heart."

I looked down at the diamond necklace and smiled. "Right."

Achilles stopped in front of a large concrete building, the only concrete building in the entire town.

I could see the outer wall of a castle a mile or so away. "They have a castle?"

Ares nodded. "The king and queen live in the castle."

"Wow," I said just before the doors were pushed open.

Achilles stepped to the side, allowing Ares and I to walk in first. The room was filled with wooden tables and reminded me of a medieval movie I'd watched where everyone had gathered in the hall to eat, just before being slaughtered by a grotesque creature.

All eyes turned to me and the tension in the room quadrupled.

Darius stood from his seat at the front of the room. "Greetings! Everyone, please welcome back your prince, Ares, and his mate, Artemis."

Most of the crowd clapped, but at least four women glared at me. This was going to be wonderful; I could tell.

Ares walked up the center aisle with me and bowed to Darius.

I curtsied as low as I could, keeping my head down.

Ares stood up and I matched his movements. "Greetings, King Darius. It's good to be home. My pack brothers, Matt and Koda, have come with me as well, but also my guest Prince Achilles of the Sidhe." Ares smiled as he spoke, but as he said Achilles' name, his lips thinned.

Darius lifted a brow. "Greetings, Prince Achilles and welcome." Why was he suddenly so nice? Was it just because he was in front of the rest of the pack?

Ares looked around. "Where is the queen? I was hoping she would be here."

Darius opened his mouth, but a woman spoke from the farthest corner of the building. "I'm here, good prince. I'm here."

The woman walked towards Darius. She was older, she looked to be about forty, which made me wonder how old she really was. Her gray hair was braided nicely against her back and her face looked familiar. Of course! She was Ares, Koda, and Matt's mother! The Queen kissed Darius' cheek before walking towards Ares and me. Her presence made me bow my head in submission. She was definitely an alpha female.

"Ares, my son," she said just before wrapping her arms around his shoulders. I released his hand and took a step away from him to give her room.

"Hello, Mother," Ares said lovingly. "I'd like you to meet my mate."

She gasped. "So, the rumors were true! You did take a mate." She stepped towards me and then started walking around me. She stopped in front of me again. "Look at me. I will not harm you, daughter-in-law."

I looked up slowly and smiled at her.

She stared at my face for a moment before gasping and turning on Ares. "Ares! Why? How?"

Ares frowned at her. "She's my *passt genau*."

The room filled with gasps and loud discussions. I hadn't realized until then that while Ares and his mother were talking, no one else in the entire building had been.

Darius raised his arms and the talking stopped. The queen looked at me again. "Who are your parents?"

"Darren is my father, but I do not know my mother's name," I said softly as I tried to hide my face from her. Did she think I was ugly? Or was I just not good enough for her son?

"What do you mean you don't know who your mother is?" she demanded.

"My mother left us when I was five. I never knew her name and my father refused to speak of her to me."

"Then how did he explain your purple eyes?" she demanded. She was angry with me about something, but I hadn't done anything, had I?

Ares took my hand and pulled me so that I was standing next to him again. "That, Mother, is something that I have already discussed with King Darius. If you would like to hear her tale, I'd prefer it be done in private." He was angry, too. What had I done to upset them?

The queen smoothed down her dress and turned her head. "Very well." She walked past me to Matt and Koda. "Matthew. Koda. My sons."

Ares released my hand to wrap his arm around my waist. "She was just caught off guard by your eyes, Artemis. It's alright," he whispered.

I nodded numbly as he led me towards a table at the front of the building. Two thirds of the women in the building glared at me as I walked with Ares. It was starting out to be a wonderful night. Darius clapped his hands. "Come now, let's eat."

CHAPTER THREE

Ares pulled me down next to him on a wooden bench and kissed my cheek. "It's alright, Sunshine."

A woman a few rows back snickered softly, but still loud enough for me to hear. "He used to call me 'Sunshine'."

I growled softly, and Ares whispered, "They're just trying to get a rise out of you. Ignore them."

Koda and Matt sat down at a table behind us, and women instantly surrounded them. The sight of the women flirting with them set me on edge.

Achilles sat down across from me and frowned. "Why are you jealous?"

His presence made me relax and look at him. "What?"

"You're jealous of Koda and Matt, why?" he asked.

Ares looked at me curiously as I answered. "It's not jealousy. I just…I don't want to add another person to our pack yet. I just got here and I'm finally settling in. I don't want a female coming in and trying to fight me all of the time."

Ares smiled. "You don't have to worry, Artemis. Koda and Matt aren't allowed mates."

I blinked twice. "Why not?"

"We travel around a lot and as my guards, they need to be focused on me. If they both had a mate then their attention would be focused on her, instead of me."

"That's not fair," I said to him.

Ares shrugged. "They agreed to it. It's not like I just told them that's how it was and they didn't have a choice."

Men in tuxedos started walking out of a back door, carrying large trays of meat. The men set the meat on each table and then quickly retreated back to the door they had come through.

I inhaled and turned to Ares. "Humans? You have humans working for you?"

Ares nodded as he bit into a piece of steak. "They work for us, get paid well and if they want to, we'll turn them."

Ares set a large steak on my plate. I looked at it for a moment and then started eating. It was a little overcooked for my taste, but it was still delicious. I took a drink from the cup in front of me and nearly gagged. "What is this?" I asked quietly.

"It's wine," Achilles answered. "Flown here from the vampires' winery in France."

I sniffed the drink. "I can't get drunk off of this, right?"

Ares shook his head. "Not unless you drink three or more bottles."

The girls around Matt and Koda were still giggling loudly and starting to get on my nerves. "Ares, I need to use the restroom," I whispered to him. I needed to get away from the women or I'd lose the little control I had over my wolf.

He turned around to face behind him. "Koda."

Koda looked up from his plate and then quickly hurried from his table to crouch behind us. "Yes?"

"Artemis needs to use the restroom. You're her guard now, remember?" Ares said softly.

Koda winked. "Right. Come on, Sweetheart." Koda stood and started walking towards the door the humans had used. I kissed

Ares cheek before following Koda towards the door. "What's wrong?" Koda asked once we were away from everyone else.

I shook my head. "Nothing."

He rolled his eyes. "I can sense your irritation and worry. If you're worried about the women, you really shouldn't—"

I interrupted him. "I don't want to talk about it right now, please."

He pushed open the door without another word. It led into a hallway, lit with torches. He pushed open the third door on our right and waved me in. "Ladies' room."

I walked inside, and he closed the door, with him on the outside. At least he thought I was capable of using the restroom alone. I pushed open the first stall door and smiled. Indoor plumbing! Thank goodness, the werewolves weren't completely medieval.

After using the restroom, I stared at my reflection in the bathroom mirror. I looked and felt tired. The stress of everything was beginning to weigh on me.

Another stall door opened and an attractive red-haired woman walked out of the stall. She stopped moving when she saw me and growled. "You!"

I looked around the bathroom before looking back at her. "Me?"

She snarled. "Why did he choose you? What makes you better than the rest of us?"

I frowned. "He didn't pick me. I'm his match. Plus, I never said I was better than you."

She jumped towards me with claws extended from where her fingernails used to be.

I jumped sideways and slammed my back against the wall. "I don't want to fight you!" I yelled as she came at me again.

She was swinging wildly and using only her claws. "I'll kill you and then he'll take me!" she yelled.

Koda threw open the door as the woman crouched to jump at

me. He grabbed her around the waist and tossed her into one of the stalls. She hit her head against the back wall hard, stunning her. He rushed over to me and started running his hands over my face and shoulders. "Did she hurt you?"

I shook my head and batted his hands away. "I'm fine. She didn't touch me."

Koda turned to the woman who was holding her head in her hands and leaning against the wall of the stall he had thrown her into. "Attacking the prince's mate without challenge is illegal. Go visit the king after tonight's festivities," he said through clenched teeth.

The woman began sobbing.

Koda led me out of the bathroom and down the hallway. "I'm sorry, Artemis. I should have stayed with you."

I shook my head. "Nothing happened. I can take care of myself."

"I'm your guard, Artemis. It's my job to protect you," he said angrily.

I placed my hand on his arm, making him stop just before the door that led out to the main room. "Don't stress yourself over me. I can take care of myself. Besides, everyone dies some time. I don't want you blaming yourself if something out of your control happens."

He wrapped his arms around my shoulders. "I won't let anything happen to you," he said seriously. Apparently, he wasn't willing to listen to reason.

He released me and pushed open the door. I stepped out into the main room and stared at the women surrounding Ares. One woman in a short skirt was sitting beside him, running her hand along his arm. My lip rose in a snarl, and I started to rush towards him.

Koda grabbed my arm, stopping me. "Artemis, calm down."

Ares looked away from the women and towards me. His smile disappeared when he saw my face.

I pulled against Koda's hold, but he held tight. "Let me go," I growled.

Koda shook his head. "Artemis, they aren't doing anything. They're just—"

"Flirting," I said angrily.

The women noticed Ares was looking away and followed his gaze. I snarled at them, and they all smiled. I pulled out of Koda's grip and walked towards the women, fuming. Ares stood and one of the women ran her hand down his chest. "Don't go. We were just starting to get back into the hang of things with you."

"Don't touch my mate!" I yelled at her.

"What are you going to do about it?" she asked with a smug smile on her face.

My hands started to heat up, and my body began glowing. "I swear if you touch him again, I'll rip your still beating heart from your chest."

The smile left her face, and her hand dropped away from Ares.

Ares rushed over to me and a wave of invisible fire knocked me backwards. "Calm down."

My body stopped glowing and my hands cooled.

Ares reached out towards, me and I took a step back, away from him. He frowned. "Artemis—"

One of the women spoke seductively. "Come on, Ares. Forget about that little girl and come play with us."

My anger was feeding the wolf in me, and I felt her eagerness to tear the girl apart with our claws. My body started to shudder and Ares grabbed my arm. "No."

I stopped shaking and glared at the women. "If any of you come near my mate again, I'll tear you apart."

Ares stroked my arm. "Artemis, nothing happened. We were all just talking."

I turned my gaze on him and saw him flinch. "Talking? I think the correct term is flirting."

Two women stood up from the table and started to walk

towards us. One, a tall brunette who looked like a bull dog smiled evilly. "Why not let her fight to keep you? She doesn't deserve you, Ares. You deserve someone more beautiful, someone stronger."

I scoffed. "Look here, bull dog, I may be small, but I *know* I'm more beautiful than you *and* more powerful."

"Prove it," she said.

Ares released his hold on me and took two steps towards the girl. "Enough."

A woman two rows down leapt out of her seat, changing forms and shredding the skin tight dress she'd had on. She leapt at me, but I dodged, sliding to the right, and kicked her in the stomach. She yelped and landed on top of the table where the women were still sitting.

Achilles was a few seats down and stared at the wolf on the table next to him. "Always drama with the werewolves," he said quietly.

Two more females changed and started towards me from behind. Koda grabbed one of the females, but the other one jumped around him and charged at me. I ripped Ares' necklace from my throat, putting it on the table next to me and changed forms in a matter of milliseconds. Luckily the dress was short enough that it didn't tear and only slid up underneath my front legs. The girl growled at me, and my ears pinned to my head. I leapt forward, dodging her outstretched paws and bit into her throat. Why was her guard down? Was she so consumed by jealousy that she wasn't thinking right? I tossed her to the side, missing Ares by inches.

Three more females from the table changed forms and Ares yelled, "Enough!"

The females stopped moving and stared at him.

I growled, and Ares turned to me, his eyes were golden wolf's eyes and his wolf looked at me from within him. "Be quiet." I stopped growling, but started walking down the aisle towards the exit. "Change back," Ares commanded.

My body twitched once and then changed back to human. Two tears leaked out of my eyes before I stood. Being forced to change was not a pleasant experience. I continued walking down the aisle, away from the women and Ares. A woman stepped out in front of me and Ares yelled, "Stop!"

The woman's body instantly stilled. I couldn't move my legs for a moment, but I pushed through the command he had given and took one slow step at a time. A black-haired woman jumped at me, but I punched her in the chest, knocking the wind out of her and making her stumble backwards to fall on her butt. Ares growled and all of the woman cowered. They seemed to finally decide to obey him. The steps were becoming easier, the further away I got from Ares.

"Artemis," Ares said softly. The softness of his voice and the request in them made me stop moving. "Don't leave," he whispered.

My entire body hurt, begging me to turn around and run to him, but I wouldn't do it. "I'm going home," I said softly. "When you're finished, please come home, too."

"Artemis—" he began, but then Koda shushed him.

I hurried out of the building and away from the stares of the hundreds of werewolves who had witnessed everything. The cool night air felt like I had jumped into a lake of ice. I gasped and turned towards home. A human servant ran out of a shed to the right, carrying a box of wine. Alcohol. Ares said I could get drunk if I drank enough. I ran towards the shed and took three bottles of wine out. I hadn't been drunk before, but the euphoric look my friends used to get was enticing. If I drank enough, maybe I could attain that. The cork was a pain, but I finally managed to get it. I guzzled the wine and the liquor warmed my stomach.

Carrying the two unopened bottles in my left arm, I took long drinks out of the open bottle with my right hand.

"Artemis," Koda called when he stepped out of the building. I ignored him, heading towards home. "Artemis, wait," he said softly.

I turned to him and took a long drink from the wine bottle. "What?" I asked between drinks.

"What are you doing?" He tried to grab the bottle from my hand, which was now empty. I let him take it and jogged down the road as I opened one of the other bottles and started drinking from it. "Artemis, give me the wine."

"No," I said as I jogged backwards, away from him.

Ares stepped out of the building and stared at me. "What are you doing?"

I took a long drink out of the bottle, keeping my eye on Koda. "Drinking," I said through a hiccup. The bottle was empty, but I pretended to drink out of it again.

"Give me the bottle," Ares said calmly.

A smile crossed my lips as I tossed him the empty bottle and then ran down an alleyway as I tried to open the new bottle. "Artemis!" Koda and Ares called after me.

The bottle finally opened, and I guzzled the entire thing down just before Ares stepped in front of me. I tried to slide to a stop, but my reflexes weren't up to par. My foot slipped out from under me, and I fell on my butt, flinging the empty bottle of wine. Ares' hand shot out to the left as he caught the bottle. "Why are you doing this?" he asked. "I didn't do anything with them." He started to reach towards me and I scrambled backwards.

"They're right," I said as I backed down the alleyway.

Ares sighed. "Stop this. You're being childish."

The words stung worse than I had expected them to. I knew I was being childish, but for him to say it to me was worse than a slap in the face. Tears streamed down my face. "That's all I'll ever be to you, isn't it? A child. A stupid little girl who you got matched with."

Koda popped up behind me.

I squatted down and whispered, "I'll leave." Ares opened his mouth, and I jumped upwards as high as I could. Grabbing ahold of the roof, I swung upwards and started running on the rooftops back towards the shed.

"Artemis, *stop*!" Ares commanded.

My legs stopped moving just as I reached the edge of the house I was running on. I fell off of the house and hit the ground on my side. My arm crunched, and I screamed in pain. The pain released my body from Ares' power so I could move again. When I stood, my right arm hung limply beside me. Ares was coming around the corner, but I didn't want to see him yet. I ran the last few yards to the shed and grabbed another bottle of wine. There wasn't a way for me to pull the cork out with my hands now, but I improvised and grabbed the cork with my teeth to jerk it out. The cork tumbled out of my mouth, and I replaced it with the bottle, guzzling the liquor.

Ares took the bottle from my hand and chucked it at the ground, shattering it. "Stop this!" He grabbed my injured arm making me scream in pain.

Koda appeared behind him and growled.

Ares growled back. "I didn't know her arm was broken."

Koda stopped growling and stepped away from him.

Ares looked at my arm for a moment then sighed. "We need to set it."

The world started to spin from the mixture of pain and alcohol. My knees gave, and Ares caught me before I hit the ground. "Let me go. You don't want me. You should be with one of them…a woman."

"Shut up." He picked me up in his arms and the world spun more. "I love you, and you are a woman, a beautiful, pigheaded, wild, and crazy woman."

"Spinning," I said softly.

Ares started sprinting, and it took all of my willpower not to throw up on him. He set me on the floor of the bathroom in our house and pulled my hair back. Matt and Koda came into the bathroom and each placed a hand on me while I puked up everything in my stomach. The physical contact of my pack comforted me and soon the nausea and pain in my head disappeared. "So, alcohol can get me drunk."

Ares laughed softly. "Yes."

I stood, but my arm began throbbing. I whimpered in pain and Ares stood up quickly. "We need to set your arm. It's going to hurt…"

Koda stood on my other side and took my hand in his. "It'll be over in a second."

Matt grabbed a roll of gauze from underneath the sink and stood in front of me. "Ready."

Ares lifted my arm up and pushed on a bone in my upper arm. I screamed and all three men growled. Matt wrapped my arm to my body with the gauze in seconds and then they all wrapped their arms around me, giving me a group hug. The pain lasted another thirty seconds and then disappeared. Ares licked my cheek in apology for hurting me, and I nuzzled his neck.

My arm began throbbing again and then felt normal. Matt unwrapped the gauze and smiled. "Healed," he said.

I stepped away from them and quickly brushed my teeth. "I'm sorry," I said softly as I turned around. Ares and I were the only ones left in the bathroom. I hadn't heard the others leave.

"Artemis, I love you and only you. I'm sorry for flirting with them. I shouldn't have done that."

I folded my arms across my chest as the first tear fell down my face. "No, you shouldn't have."

Ares opened his hand, which held my diamond heart necklace with its broken chain. "Do you not want this anymore?" he asked softly, without looking at me.

I rushed forward and quickly took the necklace and chain. "I didn't want one of the women to break it or make me lose it. I'm sorry, Ares."

He wiped the tear tracks off of my face. "You're so beautiful. Every eye was on you tonight. Did you know that?"

I laughed bitterly. "Lots of women were glaring daggers at me, if that's what you mean."

Ares kissed my lips, pulling up my desire for him. "Lots of the males were looking at you. So many of them longing just to do this." He kissed me again and ran a hand up my arm. "If I were weaker, I would have a lot of challenges for you."

"Lots of women want to challenge me for you. They all want you. They all have pasts with you. How can I compete against those beautiful women?" I said softly.

"They have *pasts* with me, but only you have my present and my future." He ran a hand along my side. "This dress looks fantastic on you." I unbuttoned his shirt and ran my hand along his chest. He whispered, "I can't wait to see how great the dress looks on the floor, too."

He picked me up by my butt and set me down on the counter. My heart rate tripled, and I kissed him fiercely. He started to push up my dress when someone cleared their throat. Ares growled loudly. "Leave."

He started kissing me again and the person said, "Stop!"

I recognized the voice as Achilles'. Ares pulled away from me and the sight of his golden wolf eyes in his human face startled me. He glared at Achilles who was standing in the bedroom doorway. "What do you want?"

"I want you to stop touching her," Achilles hissed. His body glowed softly, and his hands balled into fists at his side.

Ares growled. "She's my mate. That means I mate with her. Leave us."

Achilles took a step into the bedroom. "No. While we're deciding what to do, you agreed not to do anything."

"I didn't mean that I wouldn't mate with her!" Ares snapped.

"It's not fair for you to share her flesh when I can't," Achilles said through clenched teeth.

"She doesn't want to sleep with you. She *wants* to sleep with me!" Ares bellowed.

Achilles eyes filled with pain, and he turned them towards me. "Artemis…"

I turned away from him. "Ares, maybe he's—"

Ares glared at me. "You agree with him?"

I hopped down from the counter and touched his arm. I opened my mouth to say something, but the anger he was holding in flooded over me like a wave of fire, scolding my skin. I screamed and the world went black.

CHAPTER FOUR

I woke up surrounded by heat and the smell of forest and wolf fur. "Mm, warm," I said softly.

"Artemis!" Koda yelled next to me.

"Shush. Not so loud." I groaned.

"Artemis, open your eyes," Matt said.

I opened my eyes and looked at their concerned faces staring down at me. "What happened?"

Ares spoke from somewhere in the room, "I hurt you." His voice was laced with pain.

I slowly sat up and looked at him sitting on the floor across the room. Achilles stood beside Ares, glaring down at him.

Frowning, I said, "I don't understand. I remember you were mad at Achilles and I said that maybe he was right and then your anger washed over me and…that's all."

Achilles spoke through clenched teeth. "He couldn't control his emotions. Your words upset him, and he caused you to faint."

I slid off of the bed and walked towards Ares. He stood up and turned his face away from me. "I'm sorry," he said softly.

I reached out towards him, but ended up touching the wall. I turned around and found him standing in the bathroom doorway. "Ares, stop moving away from me. I'm not mad at you. Come here."

Ares shook his head. "No, I should have more control than this…"

I sprinted across the room and knocked him to the ground, sitting on his stomach. "There, much better." Ares turned his head away from me. I grabbed his face and turned it towards mine. "Ares! Stop doing this. I'm fine. Sure, you made me faint, but I'm fine. I forgive you."

Ares smiled and hugged me against his chest. "I am sorry. I love you," he said as he kissed my cheek.

I stood up, taking Ares' hand as he rose next to me.

Achilles gaped at me. "That's it? Just like that, you forgive him?"

I shrugged. "He didn't mean to hurt me. Plus, I can't stay mad at him for too long."

Ares kissed the back of my hand. "It's one of her many great traits. She forgives easily and in turn allows us to forgive ourselves easily."

I looked at Achilles and then at Ares. They looked similar. "So, do you want to tell me why you two hate each other?"

Achilles rolled his eyes. "I don't hate him. He hates me."

Ares growled. "I hate all of you, but you the most."

"Why?" I asked.

Achilles smiled. "Yes, why don't you tell her?"

Ares shook his head. "I don't want to discuss it right now. It's painful enough that you're here and trying to steal my mate from me."

"I'm not stealing her! She was mine before she was yours." Achilles ground out.

I stepped between them and held up my hands. "Stop bickering!" They both stared at me in shock as I groaned. "You're both acting like two spoiled kids fighting over a toy. I'm not a *toy*! I have feelings and opinions, and my opinion is that I don't know how I feel about Achilles. What I do know is that if we are honestly discussing the issues he has with us, then we need to be fair. Achilles, you have to understand that because of our bond I need the physical contact with Ares. Now, can you two not try to fight each other and just…" I stopped talking as a wave of fear rolled over me. I turned away from the men and ran towards the window that looked out over the forest behind the village. Dark shapes darted between the trees one hundred or so yards out. "Ares!" I said urgently.

Ares rushed to my side and looked out the window. He growled loudly. "Koda, warn the town. Achilles protect the house. Matt, protect the village," Ares ordered. The men didn't hesitate. Each one ran to do his job.

I looked at Ares. "What are we going to do?"

He picked me up in his arms. "We're going to hide and keep you safe."

I shook my head. "No! Ares, the town needs you to help protect them. You're the prince for a reason."

Ares turned his head so I couldn't look at his face. "I can't."

"What? Why not?" I asked, confused.

"I can't…I can't lose you again," he said softly.

I turned his face to look at mine. "Ares, you have to protect the children. I can fight."

Ares shook his head. "No. You can't fight. I won't let you be taken from me again." He kissed my cheek and laid his head against mine.

"Ares," I whispered. "You have a duty to protect your village. Let Koda protect me, or Matt, or even Achilles."

Ares growled. "Not Achilles."

Matt ran up the stairs. "There's a group of twenty dhampirs and ten vampires surrounding the village. I smelled ogres, too, but haven't seen them. What do you want us to do? Do we try to talk to them?"

Ares looked at me and sighed. "Matt, guard Artemis. I'll go." I kissed Ares' cheek and smiled. Ares looked at Matt. "Don't let anything happen to her."

Matt nodded and held out his arms. "I swear."

Ares set me in Matt's arms and walked towards the bedroom door.

"I love you, Ares," I said softly.

Ares turned around and smiled. "I love you, too." He disappeared from my sight and I heard the front door open and close.

Matt set me on my feet. "We're going to stay in here. Achilles will keep them from coming in downstairs and if you're here by the bathroom I can keep them away from you if they get to the second story."

"So, you want me to hide in the bathroom?" I asked, narrowing my eyes at him.

Matt clenched his teeth. "My job is to keep you safe and keeping you in this room, where they have the least access to you, is the best way to do that."

"I can fight, Matt," I hissed.

Matt smiled. "I know, Love, but I need you safe more than I need to help your ego today. Just stay there and hide if I tell you to."

I groaned, but walked to the bathroom doorway and sat down. "I hope none of the children get hurt. Why would dhampirs and vampires be attacking us if we're allies?"

"I'm not sure." He turned away from me to look out the window nearest him. His answer seemed off, like he was hiding something.

Snarling, growling, and screaming, slowly filled the air. Matt paced from one window to the other as the sounds of fighting grew closer and closer to us. A window shattered downstairs.

I started to get up, but Achilles called up to us, "It's fine. He's dead."

Matt continued his pacing. He suddenly stopped and cussed. "Shit. Achilles, they're swarming us."

Matt ran to me and picked me up in his arms.

"What are you doing?" I squealed.

"I was wrong. We can't hide you. We need to run," Matt said as he ran from the bedroom down the stairs. He was talking so quickly that his British accent was making it difficult for me to understand him. "Achilles, they're coming for her."

Achilles blinked at me for a moment before answering, "Let me take her. I can fly her up away from them."

Matt shook his head. "No, Ares doesn't want you touching her. Just follow us. I need to get her away from here."

Achilles opened his mouth to argue, but the front door splintered as someone ran through it. A short black man stood in the doorway glaring at us. "Give me the girl, and we'll leave you alone," he said slowly.

Matt growled. "Not a chance, dhampir."

Achilles' body began to glow and then he shot blue fireballs from his hands at the dhampir. The dhampir ran to the right to avoid the fire, and Matt dashed through the door and out of the house. Ten men rushed towards us from the tree line. I spotted Ares across the town, fighting with a vampire. It surprised me that Ares was still in human form, but the vampire didn't look like he was giving Ares too much trouble. Ares turned his head, noticing me and started running towards us.

Matt ran towards the heart of the town. Ares caught up to us and yelled, "What are you doing? Why did you bring her out here?"

Matt didn't look at Ares as he ran towards the castle in the center of the town. "They're coming for her, Ares. They were swarming the house. I couldn't keep her there. She'll be safer away from the edges of the forest where they're coming from."

Ares ran beside us as Matt rushed into the castle and into a room that had no windows and only one door. Matt set me down in the back corner. "Stay here," he said sternly.

Ares smiled at me and then they both ran out of the room, leaving me alone. I knew it was stupid, but I was worried about

Ares. Just the thought of him being hurt or killed brought tears to my eyes. The sounds of fighting were still loud, but I couldn't figure out who was winning.

Why was my life so crazy now? It felt like years had passed since I was with my little human pack of Bret and Billy and their friends. I gasped as I realized why Darren had allowed me and Bret to be alone all that time and sleep in the same bed together. He knew that I wouldn't have wanted to mate with Bret, that he was just a pack mate to me. It made sense that I had craved physical contact even if it was from humans since I was, by nature, a pack animal. It would have been a lot easier on me if I'd known all of that back then though.

"What do we have here?" asked a female voice. I turned and looked at the doorway where an ugly woman with black hair and alabaster skin stood, smiling at me. "Now, why would they hide a girl in this room? You must be special for them to want to protect you."

"Leave if you value your life." I growled and stood with my back to the wall.

She laughed. "You don't scare me, girl. I bet you're the one all this commotion is over, aren't you?" She walked slowly towards me, her fingers elongating into six-inch daggers.

Fear consumed me. "I don't know what you're talking about." The words came out weak instead of strong as I'd hoped.

"I can't believe your mate would leave you unguarded like this. He must be overly cocky to think you'd be safe." She stopped twenty feet away from me and closed her eyes. Her face shifted and the ugly woman turned into a hideous monster with fangs and a distorted face. "I'm hungry, let's finish this."

She jumped at me, and I shot a purple fireball at her. I only had a moment to enjoy the color of the fireball, which matched my eyes, before she jumped to the side, my fireball only grazing her. She dropped to the ground and smacked the spot where the fire had caught on her clothes. She extinguished the flame, screamed in rage and charged at me. I lobed ball after ball of fire at her as she ran towards me, but she dodged them all. The daggers of her right hand jammed into my side making me scream.

"You were never meant to live. It's sad your mate chose you because now he'll have to deal with your death!" She jammed her other set of dagger-fingers into my stomach and smiled as I screamed again.

My skin began glowing brighter and brighter, until the vampire hissed and pulled her daggers from me. The anger I'd been holding in since I'd met Ares boiled to the top and spilled over. My skin glowed white and all logical thoughts left my mind. *Kill. Kill the vampire.* Lunging at the vampire, I grabbed onto her shirt and rode her body down to the ground. My right hand became covered in fire.

The vampire screamed, "Please. Mercy."

"You weren't going to give me mercy, so you shall receive none." The words came from my mouth and it was as though my wolf and I became one in that instant. No longer was it my wolf and me, but it was me and the animal instincts, urges, and thoughts, together. In one swift motion I plunged my fire covered hand into her chest and ripped her heart out. She screamed long and loud as I held her heart in my hand. The sounds were annoying.

I repositioned myself so that I was sitting above her head to get into a better spot. The heart had begun to blister from the fire in my hand, and long black smears surrounded it. With one quick squeeze of my hand, the heart turned to ash and sifted to the floor beside the vampire's head. Her scream turned into a high-pitched shriek. Ares appeared in the doorway and gaped at me as I picked her head up off the floor, gave one violent twist, and tore her head from her body.

The screaming stopped, and my anger dissipated. I dropped the head onto the ground, turned and vomited.

"It's alright, Artemis. Everything's alright now," Ares said softly as he stroked my hair.

I looked at my hands, expecting them to be covered in blood, but surprisingly they were clean. My wounds however were still open and blood poured from them, staining my white dress. "Ares, my wounds," I whispered as I started to faint.

Ares picked me up and ran. I faded in and out of consciousness, closer to out, than in. Ares kept talking to me, "Artemis, Sunshine, stay awake."

"I am awake. I'm awake and in pain. Where did you go?" I asked.

"I was protecting the front entrance to the castle. Matt was supposed to be protecting the back," he said through gritted teeth.

"Is he hurt?"

Ares shook his head. "He's not dead at least. I would have felt it if he had died."

Our house came into view as did Koda and Achilles. Ares set me on the porch and a beautiful blonde haired, blue eyed woman stepped out of the house wearing an apron. Who was she? Where had she come from? "What's happened?" she asked.

Ares ripped my dress off and everyone gasped. The woman knelt down beside me and started wiping the blood off of my stomach and side. "You're going to be alright. She didn't hit any vital organs and they're already beginning to heal."

Ares held my hand as she started chanting in a different language. "You did well against the vampire. I'm proud of you," he said softly.

His compliment made me smile. "Thanks."

The woman stopped and sat back on her heels, a bead of sweat rolling down her face. "She's fine, Ares. Your anger is becoming too much, please calm down," she whispered.

Ares took a deep breath and kissed my forehead. "I'm sorry, Gwen."

Gwen smiled. "I've never seen you so worried over a female before, or so gentle. She must be your mate."

Ares nodded and picked me up in his arms. "She is. Thank you again for your services, Gwen."

Gwen bowed her head. "Anytime, Prince."

Ares carried me into the house, up the stairs and to the bathroom. He set me down on the toilet seat and then turned on the shower. I watched him as he silently moved about the bathroom. He was bothered about something. My wounds were almost fully healed now, so I stood up and approached Ares, who stood beside the now warm water of the shower.

He turned to look at me, tears in his eyes.

"Ares, what is it?" I asked as I wiped the tears from his face and kissed each cheek.

He wrapped his arms around me and exhaled loudly. "I almost lost you again."

"Ares, I wasn't that close to dying. You heard Gwen—she missed the vital organs. Look, the wounds are already sealed." I grabbed his hand and placed it on my stomach where one of the wounds had been.

He ran his fingertip over the small pink scar that was quickly disappearing. "I'm sorry I failed you," he said softly.

"You didn't fail me. You were protecting one entrance while Matt was supposed to be protecting the other. How could you have known something would happen to Matt?" I pulled his shirt off over his head and kissed his chest. "Help me wash," I said as seductively as I could.

A smile lifted the right corner of his mouth and he unbuttoned his pants. "Alright."

I turned away from him and stepped underneath the water. The warm water felt good on my skin and helped erase the shock that was trying to set in. Ares began scrubbing my body with a soap bar, paying special attention to the blood on my stomach and side. He kissed my neck and turned me around underneath the water to rinse off.

For once, I wasn't overcome by my hormones and my desire to sleep with him, but instead the touch and caring fulfilled my needs. It was amazing to be loved like this. I hoped it never ended. He turned me around to face him and kissed my lips softly. "I love you, Artemis."

I kissed his lips and then rested my head against his chest. "I love you, too." Ares wrapped his arms around me and sighed.

"Excuse me." a female said softly.

My hackles, figuratively, rose, and I turned to the doorway, snarling. The young girl flinched and took a step back. "Sorry," I said softly.

Ares grabbed two towels and wrapped his around his waist. I wrapped mine around my body. "What is it, Lauren?" Ares asked in a soft voice.

"Darius wishes to speak to you, immediately," she said in a soft voice. Her strawberry blonde hair was naturally curly and hid her face from my view.

"I'll put pants on and be there in a moment. Wait downstairs for me," Ares said. Lauren curtsied and then rushed out of the room. Ares whispered, "She seems innocent, but she's been Darius' assistant for twenty years. I wouldn't be surprised if she was as cunning as he is."

I adjusted my towel. "I'm glad you're the one that has to deal with all of the political crap. I couldn't even stand listening to people in town debating about the presidential elections. Boring."

Matt walked in and smiled at us. "Who's boring?"

Ares blurred as he moved from the shower to the door in an instant to grab Matt around the throat. "Where did you go? You were supposed to be protecting the back entrance!" Ares yelled.

Matt's lip twitched for a moment as though he were thinking about snarling and then he whined. "Sorry. I saw two vampires attacking a child and so I went to help, but then got ambushed." He looked towards me and asked, "Did something happen?"

Ares released Matt's throat. "Artemis was attacked."

Matt looked at me with an almost sad look on his face. "Are you alright?" Was he sad I was attacked or that I survived?

I nodded. "I'm fine."

Matt smiled. "Good."

Ares looked at Matt a moment longer before yelling, "Koda!" Koda ran into the bathroom and looked at our faces. Ares looked at me. "Koda, guard Artemis."

Koda nodded, and Matt walked out of the room with Ares. "What happened?" Koda asked.

"Nothing," I said as I walked to the closet to change.

Koda leaned against the doorframe while I changed clothes. "Achilles said you used your Sidhe powers to fight the vampire."

I looked up at him in shock. "How did he know that?"

Koda smiled. "We can feel magic from those of our kind when they're being used in significant enough quantities. He said it's been a long time since he felt such a large pull."

"Well, she was trying to kill me," I said defensively as I buttoned my pants.

"Ares is having Victor come here to speak with Darius about this attack. They swear that it wasn't a sanctioned attack, and that they had no idea it was going to happen."

I looked at Koda's tight face. "You don't believe them?"

Koda smiled. "I believe Victor, but I'm not sure about Maurice."

Matt's attitude and response still bothered me, so I decided to tell Koda. After I'd finished Koda sighed. "I've been noticing it, too," he said quietly. "Something's bothering him, but I'm not sure what it is."

"Do you think he lied about why he stopped guarding the back entrance?" That part was bothering me the most. I couldn't explain why, but I knew he was lying about why he left.

Koda sighed and ran a hand through his Mohawk which I

noticed wasn't gelled up for once. "I don't know. I'll have to speak to Ares about it." He looked at my face for a moment before sighing. "Come on, you should lie down. You've had a lot happen to you."

I laughed and climbed onto the bed. "I never thought my life would be so crazy."

Koda laid down beside me and rubbed my back. "Don't worry, things will calm down, and we'll be able to show you the good side of life as a werewolf."

"I can't wait for that day," I mumbled as I relaxed and took comfort in Koda's touch. "Thank you," I whispered as I started to lose consciousness.

"For what?" he asked.

"For being you."

"Artemis?"

"Night, Koda."

CHAPTER FIVE

The sun rose earlier than I wanted, but waking up to Ares' arms wrapped around me definitely made it better.

"Morning, Sunshine," Ares whispered against my neck.

I shivered and asked, "Can't we sleep in?"

Ares chuckled and nipped my ear. "We need to go on a hunt. Come on. Everyone is waiting for you."

I groaned and rolled over until my face was pressed against Ares'. "I think we should stay in bed all day." I opened my eyes and stared at the handsome man looking at me. "You're too handsome for me," I sighed longingly.

Ares kissed my lips and rolled us over until he was lying on top of me. "Achilles left a couple minutes ago. He won't be able to tell that we've mated if we do it before the hunt."

He started kissing his way down my neck and it took all of my willpower to form conscious thoughts. "Ares, I thought you said Koda and Matt were waiting?"

"They can wait a little longer." He growled as he tried to work my shirt up.

"Ares, I know you don't like Achilles, but it really isn't fair.

What if the situation was flipped and he'd claimed me first? What would you want him to do?"

Ares groaned and pressed his forehead against mine. "Fine, but we need to figure out a solution soon. It's torment to be near you and not be able to mate with you."

I kissed his cheek softly. "I know. It's hard for me, too, but we'll figure something out."

I climbed out from under Ares and hopped down from the bed. It took my body a moment to change, but it was painless when I finally took my wolf form.

Matt and Koda yelled through my head. *Hurry up!*

I jogged down the stairs and opened my mouth in a wolf-grin at the two giant wolves sitting on the porch. *Morning.*

Ares walked out in front of me. *Come on, let's hunt. I need to kill something.*

I giggled, but the strange wheezing sound that came out of my wolf throat bothered me too much to continue. Ares glared at me with a tight mouth. *That'll teach you to laugh at me.*

Ares jogged away from the house and the rest of us followed behind him as he led us into the forest. We jogged for twenty minutes before smelling another animal. I twitched my nose in frustration. *What is it?* I couldn't figure out what animal I was smelling.

Deer. Ares said. He tilted his head to the right then turned to face in that direction. *There.*

We all turned slowly and stared at the herd of deer two hundred yards away. A ten point buck stood a little to the side of the herd. My mouth instantly started watering. Ares snorted softly, and Matt and Koda took off at a run. I started to follow, but Ares blocked my path. *Watch. You need to learn how to take down a buck first.*

Matt snapped at the buck's heels and Koda grabbed onto the distracted buck's throat. In only a few seconds they'd killed the buck. Ares trotted over and started eating. I sat down beside Matt and Koda who were sitting a few feet away.

Ares finished and looked at us. *Artemis eats next.* Matt growled and Ares growled back, his lips pulling up in a menacing snarl. *I'm alpha. I decide when my mate eats. She eats after me. You and Koda decide who eats after that.*

Matt stopped growling and then snorted in irritation. I trotted forward and took a bite out of the deer. *It's delicious!* It took only a minute for me to fill up on the deer. I licked my muzzle clean and trotted over to Ares who was licking one of his paws clean. *That was great.*

Ares licked my cheek. *Glad you like it.*

Matt whined. *There's another herd up ahead.*

Ares nodded once. *Let's go. This time, I take down the buck.*

Koda, Matt and Ares took off running before I could react. I watched as Ares ran, his muscles stretching and his fur pressed against his body. The buck lifted his head from the grass he was eating and then Ares was on him. I walked slowly towards the rest of my pack and laid down in a sunny spot a few yards away from the dead buck. *That was great.* I said quietly as Ares ate.

Koda snorted. *You're easily impressed.*

Ares finished eating and nodded at me.

I'm full. Thanks. I lifted my lips in a grin and rolled on to my back so the sun could warm my stomach. *We should have done this sooner.*

Ares laid down, placing his head on top of my stomach. *I'll make sure we take more time to hunt together.*

Matt walked towards us, and I felt uneasy, not wanting to be on my back anymore. I rolled over and sat up next to Ares. Matt looked at me quizzically, but didn't say anything as he sat down and waited for Koda to finish.

I was still bothered by Matt's lie and in wolf form I especially felt awkward around him. Ares draped his head across my neck and sighed in contentment. *How are you feeling today?*

Fine, thank you. I said quietly as I enjoyed his warmth and the smell of his fur. I noticed another slightly different, but familiar smell underneath Ares' fur, against his skin, but I couldn't place it.

Koda trotted over, licking his lips clean. *Okay, I'm done.*

Ares pulled away, and we all ran back towards the house. I changed forms at the door and ran inside and up the stairs. I stepped into the bedroom and stopped in my tracks. A slim, beautiful black-haired woman was lying, naked on the bed.

She sat up when I walked in and glared at me. "Where is Ares?"

I growled loudly and squatted down, preparing to attack. "Why are you on my bed, naked?"

She stood and glared at me. "I do not need to speak to you, *girl.* I came to see the prince. Now, step aside."

Ares walked up behind me and stared in shock at the woman. "Natasha? What are you doing here?"

She smiled seductively and posed against the bed post. "I was waiting for you."

I growled again, and Ares sighed. "Oh. I see. Natasha, you need to leave."

Natasha's beautiful smile wilted as she looked from me to Ares. "You would reject me for this…this *child?*"

Koda walked up the stairs and pulled me backwards, away from Natasha. Apparently, he guessed I was about to pounce on her.

Ares took a step towards Natasha and speaking in a soothing tone said, "You need to leave, Natasha. This is not your home, nor is this your pack. Leave."

She stuck out her bottom lip in a pout and took a step closer to Ares, running a fingertip over his chest. "Ares, you know you would rather have me."

Anger boiled up in me, tinting my sight red. I wanted to change forms, but I held the change and instead charged at Natasha, knocking her to the ground and punching her in the face before Ares pulled me away. "Let me go!" I yelled as I struggled to attack her again.

Koda knelt down beside Natasha's still body and then turned to smile at me. "You knocked her out cold. I'm impressed."

Ares wrapped his arms around me and exhaled. His magic wrapped around me like the warm hug he was holding me in and calmed me. "Artemis, relax. You know I would never, could never, cheat on you. Especially not with a trashy woman like Natasha."

I turned around slowly and asked, "Is she one of your former flings?"

"Yes, but I never felt anything for her."

Natasha moaned and sat up. "You bitch. You'll pay for that."

Koda picked Natasha up and started carrying her downstairs. "Time to go."

Natasha struggled against him, but decided instead to turn towards me. "You don't deserve Ares! You don't deserve to be in this pack. I challenge you. Accept, you *coward*."

Ares opened his mouth to speak, but I spoke up before he could. "A challenge for what?"

Her eyes brightened happily. Ares shook his head, Koda's mouth gaped, and Achilles walked inside the front door, staring at our group.

Natasha pulled out of Koda's arms and glared at me. "A fight to the death. Winner gets Ares and his pack."

"Artemis, stop this, you can't—" Ares began.

"I accept," I said over Ares' words.

Ares stared at me in complete and utter shock, as did Achilles and Koda.

Natasha nodded. "In three days at noon, meet me at the fountain." She winked at Ares and then jogged out of the house.

Ares' anger had been building since I had accepted and as soon as she was gone, he turned on me and yelled, "What are you thinking? Do you realize what you just did?"

He'd never been mad at me before, and it took all of my courage not to cower. "I'm protecting my place. None of the women here believe I should have you as a mate. I've been attacked and insulted, and I'm tired of it. I'm going to prove, once and for all, that I'm your mate and I'll die to keep that title."

Ares roared, "Did you think what would happen if you lose?" He stormed down the stairs without looking at me again.

Achilles was glowing and glaring at Ares. "You let her accept?"

Ares moved faster than my eye could track and suddenly had Achilles pinned to the wall of the entryway. "I did not let her! She did it herself!"

Achilles shoved Ares back, flinging him into the other wall. "You should have stopped her!"

Ares screamed and charged at Achilles, who charged at him, glowing brighter and brighter. The sound of their hits was like a jack hammer on concrete and soon I was covering my ears. Koda and Matt rushed into the fight and tried, unsuccessfully, to stop them. The metallic taste of blood hit my tongue from the air, and my senses finally returned. I rushed down the stairs and threw my self between the two men. Ares' fist stopped an inch away from my face and both men took a few steps away from me.

"Stop it. Both of you! I chose this and none of you could have stopped me. Stop fighting." The words came out loud and strong, like a drill sergeant ordering their cadets. I looked from one angry set of eyes to another and noticed that both had a split lip, but no other damage seemed present. "Please, don't fight."

Ares growled and stormed out of the house, walking towards the forest. Matt jogged after him silently. Achilles walked away from me and towards the room where he was staying. My legs started to give and only my arm reaching out and hitting the wall saved me. Koda rushed forward and picked me up. "Artemis?"

"I messed up, didn't I?" I asked in a small voice.

Koda nuzzled my cheek. "They're just worried." Koda shut the front door and walked up the stairs, keeping a tight grip on me.

"Are you mad at me, too?"

He kept looking straight ahead, avoiding looking at my face. "I don't think you should have accepted her challenge and I'm worried about the consequences. I am not mad at you though. Just worried."

"Is she that strong?" I asked nervously.

"She's one of the strongest females." He set me down and pushed me towards the bathroom. "Go take a shower. I'll keep guard."

I groaned as I started walking towards the shower. "It's ridiculous that I have a guard. I'm capable of protecting myself. I'm not a helpless female in need of a big man to protect me all of the time." Sure, sometimes it was nice to have backup, like when vampires and dhampirs attacked, but I could hold my own.

"Complaining won't change anything. No matter what you say, Ares is going to keep a guard on you."

The shower head groaned for a minute before turning on. My body suddenly felt very cold and the steam rising from the shower head was more than inviting. "Do you think Ares is going to come back?" I asked as I stepped into the shower and relaxed under the hot water.

"He'll come back. He's just blowing off some steam." Koda assured me.

I quickly showered and then dried my hair. Outside, a large crash sounded, making me jump. Koda rushed over and picked me up in his arms.

"Put me down, Koda. Why do you guys always pick me up and carry me? I'm not an invalid."

Koda set me on my feet and frowned down at me. "We pick you up because, as you're aware, touch helps soothe us when we're feeling upset. Plus, it's more effective to pick you up and hold you while we run somewhere to protect you."

"I'm sorry. I didn't mean to snap at you," I said softly.

Koda kissed my cheek. "It's alright. I forgive you. It was probably just Ares knocking over a tree anyways. Come on, we better get dressed so we can start training."

"Training? For what?"

He turned to me and all of the humor that usually lit Koda's eyes was gone, leaving them a dull blue. "You have to train for your fight. I won't lose my pack mate just because we were mad at you and didn't train you properly."

I followed Koda to the room and quickly dressed in jeans and a t-shirt. He dressed in only a pair of sweats and shook his head at me when I reached for shoes. "I need to teach you some tricks about changing to your wolf form. Put some sweats on instead."

"Ares didn't buy me any sweats," I whispered, feeling Ares' absence like a weight on my shoulders.

Koda handed me a pair of his sweats. "Cinch the string as tight as it will go on your waist and then roll the waistband so the legs are shorter for you."

I did as he suggested and then followed him back down the stairs. As we opened the front door to leave, Achilles walked out of his room. "Where are you going?"

"I'm taking her to the woods to do some training." Koda answered.

Achilles was frowning hard, but only a faint line creased his perfect brow. "I'll accompany you."

Koda looked like he wanted to object, but shrugged instead and pushed me towards the door. "Come on. We've only got three days to train you."

The three of us walked in silence through the woods. I felt nervous, but I knew Koda wouldn't hurt me. Although, I wasn't sure of Achilles' intentions, but I doubted he would hurt me either. Koda led us to a small circular clearing filled with grass and wild flowers. It was beautiful and yet I could smell dried blood on the ground. "This is our training field," Koda explained to me. He walked to the center of the clearing and motioned at me to come towards him. "I want you to attack me, but do not use your Sidhe powers, or change to your complete wolf form."

I nodded and walked to stand a few feet away from him. I took two deep cleansing breaths before moving forward as fast as I could and punching at Koda. He spun around me and, in an instant, had an arm wrapped around my throat, choking me. "You're too slow. You need to move faster. You also need to pay more attention to your opponent. As soon as you see me moving to go behind you, you should turn. Again."

For the next few hours, Koda drilled me again and again. He then started teaching me how to properly hit and kick and then how to use my elbows. My body was sore, and I was dripping with sweat when he said, "Now I'm going to teach you to half-shift."

Achilles stood from the spot in the grass where he had been sitting. "She's not ready for that."

Koda ignored Achilles and in a blink of an eye his body changed from Koda the man to Koda the man-wolf. His body was bulkier, but he could still walk on two legs, his hands were now paws and his entire body was covered in short fur. His face was more wolfish with a slight snout instead of just a nose and fangs in his mouth. It took him two tries before he could speak and when he did it sounded more like a growl than a human voice. "This is the best form to take when fighting because you have the benefits of the wolf strength while still being able to move on two legs. It's difficult to maintain though and so most of us prefer to simply take wolf form." He changed back to his human shape and leaned forward a little. "I need to practice more often. I'm getting rusty." He shook his entire body, like a dog flinging off water and waved his hand at me. "Your turn."

"How do I take that shape instead of my wolf shape?" I asked. Usually I just closed my eyes and let the wolf side of me take over to become wolf, or pictured my human self to become human.

"You just focus on keeping half your body human."

My body began to tingle all over in anticipation of changing. *Okay, only change part way.* I felt my bones shifting and then opened my eyes, but I was on all fours and, after wagging my tail realized, a complete wolf.

Koda shrugged. "We'll keep working on it. It's hard to do."

I changed back and sighed. "I'm sorry."

Koda smiled. "Don't be. Only a few are able to master this technique. Come on, let's get you some food."

Achilles followed behind us as we walked back to the house. Why had he come? He hadn't talked except when he thought I wasn't ready to learn the half-shift. Was he just worried about me? Was he spying on me? I shook my head and ignored all of the questions. I wouldn't know unless I asked, but I didn't want to. He still unnerved me in that weird, good way and I wasn't sure how to feel about that.

Ares stood on the front porch with Matt when we came up. He looked at my sweat covered body and ripped sweats and then at Koda's ripped sweats. "What were you doing?"

Koda smiled sweetly at Ares. "Nothing."

Ares frowned at Koda, but didn't press him further. I walked past him, knowing he was still mad and continued to the kitchen where Koda had already taken out three steaks. I sat down on one of the stools at the island and laid my face on the cold tile. "I'm sore."

Koda laughed. "Good."

I whispered, "Am I supposed to keep what we do a secret from Ares?"

Koda shook his head. "No, I just like irking him."

Ares walked in and looked from me to Koda. "What are you two whispering about?"

Koda turned on the stove top and put oil in a pan. "How I should prepare the meat."

Ares rolled his eyes. "You're the worst liar I know."

The closeness of Ares, but lack of touch made my skin itch. It'd been hours since we'd had physical contact, and I needed it bad. My arm started to reach out towards him, but I quickly pulled it back and closed my eyes. I didn't want to push him if he was mad at me.

He sat down beside me and when I opened my eyes, I found his head lying on the island next to me. "Are you feeling alright?" he asked.

"Tired," I whispered as a lump formed in my throat. The sight of his handsome face still sent butterflies whirling in my stomach.

He frowned for a second and then exhaled loudly before putting one of his arms around my shoulders. "Aw. Much better. Wasn't your skin tingling?"

"As if one thousand ants were crawling on it," I said honestly.

He moved his face closer to mine. "Then why didn't you touch me?"

I closed my eyes before answering. "You're mad at me. I didn't want to make you angrier by trying to touch you. I was letting you decide when we touched again."

He kissed my nose, shocking me and making me open my eyes. "Artemis, if you need to touch me, then touch me. If you need me to hug you, then tell me. No matter how mad at you I may be, I don't want you to suffer."

My shoulders relaxed and after scooting my stool closer to his, I rubbed my cheek against his. "Thank you."

Koda cleared his throat. I pulled away from Ares and took the plate Koda was holding out to me. Koda sat on the stool across the island from me and ate his food in silence, keeping his gaze down. Ares handed me a knife and fork and I quickly cut up the meat. Ares put his arm around my waist and I ate with my two favorite men. I tried to offer Ares a piece of the steak, but he just shook his head.

When the steak was gone, I leaned against Ares and sighed in contentment. "I love you both."

Ares kissed the top of my head and Koda smiled at me.

"Where's Matt?" I asked curiously.

Ares exhaled. "With a female, I believe. He asked for leave and since I don't need to go anywhere and I don't *actually* need a guard, I let him go."

Koda shook his head. "Something's not right with him. He's been different since we came back from the vampires' place."

Ares nodded. "I know. I've been trying to figure out what's different, but I don't know."

"Ares?"

"Hm."

"How'd you get the name 'God of War'?" I asked. I'd been wondering about it since the men who had kidnapped me for the vampire queen had discussed it.

I smelled Achilles as he walked to stand by the kitchen entrance. Ares shrugged and then said, "I was a good warrior and, because of my genetics, to the humans I appeared as a god."

Achilles scoffed from the doorway. "You withhold much from her. Why?"

Ares growled. "Go away, *Sidhe*." He said "Sidhe" with such malice that it made me pull away from him.

Achilles was rubbing his temples. "This hatred you have towards me is wrongfully placed. It was not my fault."

Ares stood and growled louder. "It *was* your fault! You could have prevented it! Instead you sat by and let it happen!" Ares had gone from irritated to ready to kill in two seconds.

"What happened?" I asked softly.

Ares shook his head and turned away. "I won't discuss it." He held out his hand towards me. I looked at him for a moment before realizing that he was playing a power game with Achilles. He wanted me to put my hand in his so Achilles got the hint that I was Ares' and Achilles couldn't do anything about it.

"Ares, why do you hide so much from me? I'm your mate." I whispered the words so that he wouldn't take them as a challenge.

His eyes glistened as though covered with a film of unshed tears. "This is not a topic I wish to discuss. Maybe at some point I will talk with you about it, but not now and not while *he* is here."

"You're just as stubborn as Father," Achilles said angrily.

Ares spun around and glared at Achilles, baring his teeth. "I have *no* father!" Spinning on his heel, Ares marched out of the kitchen and stomped up the stairs. I looked at Achilles apologetically and rushed up the stairs to the room where I found Ares staring out the window at the woods. "I'm sorry, Artemis. That was childish of me," he said quietly.

I wrapped my arms around him from behind and lay my head against his back. "Achilles does an excellent job of upsetting you."

Ares laughed softly and turned around to hug me. "That he does. So, what were you and Koda really doing?"

"Koda's training me," I answered honestly.

Ares grip tightened and his words came out clipped. "So. You're still going forward with the challenge?"

I nodded.

"You could die, you know this?"

I nodded again.

He pushed me back gently and looked at my face. "Why then? Why are you doing this?"

"I have to prove myself, Ares. Since I've met you, you all have been fighting for me and protecting me. It's time that I protect myself and prove to the rest of the pack that I'm not helpless."

Ares relaxed his grip and sighed loudly. "You could have just battled someone. You didn't have to do a fight to the death that would result in forcing a new mate on me if you lose."

"She challenged me, Ares. I couldn't refuse. Would you have refused if it were a man challenging you for me?"

Ares laughed softly. "No, I suppose I wouldn't have, but then again, I'm a veteran at fighting. You aren't."

I rubbed my sore shoulders. "I know."

Ares poked my shoulder, making me wince. "Come on, let's get you into the nice spa."

"Mm, the spa sounds wonderful," I said wistfully. Ares laughed and steered me towards the bathroom. He started the water while I stripped out of my dirty clothes. It hurt to raise my arms above my head, but I got my shirt off with only a little groaning. Ares tested the water in the giant spa and then stripped out of his own clothes. He climbed into the spa and held out his hand to help me in. I let him help me as I climbed into the hot water and then slid down against the wall of the spa, sighing happily.

Ares moved to sit down beside me and held one of my hands in his. "I love you, Artemis."

I snuggled against him as the hot water relaxed my sore muscles. "I love you, too. Have you thought of any ways to get Achilles to give up?"

Ares shook his head. "No. You?"

"No."

We sat in comfortable silence as we enjoyed the closeness of each other and the pleasantness of our contact. My eyes started to droop closed when Ares leapt out of the spa and growled loudly. I spun around and stared in shock at a woman with a dagger pinned against the wall by Ares. She struggled against his hold, her eyes fixed on me. "Female! Female, look at me!" Ares yelled at her, but she didn't take her eyes off of me or stop trying to get away from him. He closed his eyes for a second before shaking his head. "She's turning."

"Turning into what?" I asked.

"Turning rogue. Her wolf is taking control of her even in her human body. Artemis, run downstairs and stay there. Tell Koda to come here."

I obeyed Ares' instructions and ran down the stairs. Koda rushed up the stairs. "I just noticed the front door was open. We didn't even hear it."

I pointed up. "Ares has a woman who tried to stab me. He says she's turning rogue."

Koda cursed and ran up the stairs. Achilles walked towards me with a white robe in his hands.

I quickly put it on. "They have to kill her, don't they?" I asked Achilles.

Achilles nodded. "Yes. If you are of a foul mind and you let the wolf take over, you will kill whatever is in your path. Your own children included."

I looked at him curiously. "You talk as if you are one."

He shrugged. "I lived among the wolves for a number of years. I've seen a rogue attack twice. It is not something you easily forget."

The woman screamed and then the house was eerily silent. I shuddered at the knowledge that Ares or Koda had killed her. Even if it was necessary, it unnerved me. "Artemis, go in the kitchen and make us some dinner, please," Ares said from the bedroom.

I knew he was just trying to save me from looking at the dead woman's body, and I was thankful for the diversion. I quickly went into the kitchen and started pulling out steaks and vegetables to make for dinner. I even managed to find potatoes so I could make mashed potatoes. I kept my concentration on the meal and only when it was completed did I let myself step back and admire my work. The steaks smelled delicious, the mashed potatoes were perfectly smooth and buttery, and the vegetables were the perfect consistency, not too hard and not too soft. I grabbed plates from the cupboards and hurried to the dining room to set everything up. Ares and the others talked in the living room as I finished bringing all of the food into the dining room. I ran up the stairs and changed into sweats and a t-shirt and then called from the dining room, "Dinner's ready."

The men walked into the room, their somber faces changing instantly to smiles as they surveyed the food I'd made. Ares walked over to me, put his arm around my waist and kissed me on the lips. "It looks delicious."

I noted the hint of surprise in his voice and asked, "Did you think I didn't know how to cook?"

Ares laughed. "I was worried."

We all sat down, Ares and I at the ends of the table with Koda, Matt and Achilles filling in between. Ares raised a hand as I started to reach for the food. I set my hand down and stared at him as he closed his eyes, bowed his head and whispered, "Thank you, Mother of All, for keeping us alive and allowing such a great meal to be prepared for us. We, as always, are in your debt. We ask only that you keep our fur clean, our teeth and claws sharp and a meal in our bellies."

I looked around the table and found everyone, including Achilles, with their heads bowed and eyes closed.

The others mumbled something and then Ares opened his eyes. "Now you may eat."

It took a moment for the shock to wear off before I started putting food on my plate. They prayed? Who was the Mother of All? Was he referring to Asena, the mother of the werewolves?

The meal was eaten in relative silence, but even with Achilles and Matt there, it was comfortable silence. As soon as I filled my stomach, I started rushing around and picking up empty plates. Ares stood up and blocked my path to the kitchen. He gently took the pile of plates out of my hands and then nodded at the other men. As one, Koda, Matt and Achilles stood and started clearing the table. Ares bumped me to the side with his hip and I stared in awe as four men, no four *warriors* did the dishes. *Where's a camera when you need one?*

As soon as the men finished the dishes, they all walked out of the house. I followed them quickly as they made their way into the woods. *Where the hell were they going?* They all stopped in the training field and turned to face me. *Uh oh.* Ares looked grim as he stood in the center of the field. "Since you insist on fighting, I thought it would be good for us to train you, all of us."

Achilles took his spot on the grass and leaned against a tree. I looked back at Ares, Koda, and Matt and felt a lump form in my throat. "I have to fight all of you?"

Matt laughed and then spoke in his British accent that I used to love, "We all specialize in different areas of fighting."

I nodded, remembering one of my kidnappers in France talking about Koda being really good at karate. "Okay."

Ares exhaled and smiled. "Okay, come attack me."

"Can I use my Sidhe powers?" I asked.

Ares shook his head. "Nope, just your wolf ones."

I didn't want to fight Ares, the idea itself was ridiculous, but the wolf side of me was excited to play fight. I let my instincts propel my movements, but kept control of my body, not letting myself change. I punched at Ares, but he dodged. I kicked, but he pushed my upper body, making me stumble. The more I tried to hit him and the more he remained untouched, the angrier I grew. Soon I stopped *trying* to hit him and let my subconscious and the wolf take over. My fist grazed Ares' cheek and a jubilant smile broke out on my face. Ares smiled back at me and began attacking, putting me on defense. His movements were too fast for me to track and soon I was surviving his blows by instinct. Matt jumped from behind me and started trying to fight me as well, causing me to move twice as fast. Then Koda jumped into the fray, kicking and punching. With the three of them attacking, I was getting hit and kicked and left with no time to think. My fists hurt from hitting them, so I changed them to paws and began clawing at the men, opening a large gash on Matt's arm. I started to get the upper hand until all three men changed their hands to paws as well.

My arms and chest stung with the numerous cuts from their claws, and I lost my endurance. Slipping in the grass, I fell to one knee and then the flame of magic inside of me flared up and covered me in a bright purple light. The men couldn't get past the barrier of purple light surrounding me and were forced to stop their attack. Ares growled at me. "I said no Sidhe powers."

Achilles spoke before I could. "She did not intentionally use them. Her body recognized it was near losing and formed the ward for her." He walked towards me and reached a hand towards my ward. Ares growled, but Achilles placed his hand on the ward anyways. His eyes widened. "This is quite impressive. Most are not able to create as seamless a ward as this." He ran his hand along the ward making the purple light pulse everywhere he touched and making my body shiver as though he were touching my skin.

I pulled at the invisible force covering me and willed it back into my body. Slowly the light ebbed and then disappeared. I collapsed onto the ground gasping for air. Achilles squatted down next to me, smiling. "You have to learn to pace yourself when it comes to magic." Achilles stood and turned to Ares. "I need to work with her on her magic. Whatever qualms you have with me and whatever disputes we have between us regarding her do not matter in this instance. If she is not taught, she may cause a catastrophic event."

Ares nodded. "I understand, but you are not allowed to touch her."

Achilles smiled smugly. "It amuses me that you think one touch from me, and she would run into my arms instead of yours."

I growled loudly at Achilles, causing Ares and him to start in surprise. "I will *never* run into your arms. I am not yours. I am tired of you tormenting Ares. Why won't you just leave us and let us be happy!" By the end I was screaming even though I had not intended to.

Achilles looked hurt as he said, "Because you will see soon enough that I offer something for you as well." He strode out of the field and into the darkening forest.

Ares helped me stand and smiled down at me. "Well, that was interesting. You fought fairly well, but your reactions are slow. We'll have to work on that."

"Can we take a shower? My body is itching with all of the cuts and the grass covering me," I said as I leaned against him. He started to pick me up, but I pushed him. "I'll run."

He didn't seem as bothered by my statement as I'd expected, but simply held my hand as we started running towards the house.

Koda and Matt were arguing about something when we finally arrived at the house. People started coming out of the surrounding houses to see what all the commotion was about.

Matt growled loudly and yelled, "I challenge Koda for place in the pack and rights as second!"

I frowned. "Rights?"

Koda snarled. "I accept!"

Ares and Achilles were on the porch of the house talking quietly, leaving me alone beside Koda and Matt. "Hey, guys, let's just calm down and—"

Matt and Koda started fighting each other, their snarls and punches almost deafening me. I started to move forward, to stop them, but Darius grabbed my arm tightly. "You cannot stop a challenge once it has been accepted."

I stared at the King of Werewolves and felt his power. He pressed it on to me, and I realized I was staring into his eyes. I looked down and nodded in understanding and acknowledgement of my submission to him. He let go of my arm, and I moved away from him as quickly as I could without running.

Achilles moved down the steps and lifted the sleeve of my shirt to expose red marks where Darius had grabbed me. Achilles skin glowed softly as he turned to Darius. "I believe the king may have forgotten how to handle the Sidhe."

Darius frowned in confusion. "Speak freely, Achilles."

Achilles pulled me forward and lifted the sleeve of my shirt. "You've marked her skin."

Darius' eyes widened. "I did not mean to mark her. I was simply stopping her from interfering."

Ares walked down the steps and stood beside us. "Be careful, King. An offense such as this would have started wars not long ago."

Darius glared at Ares. "Perhaps you should teach your *halfbreed* bitch our rules, and I would not have to touch her."

Ares growled at him, and I felt his anger and Achilles' anger rising at the same time. It was like they were feeding off of each other's emotions. Ares whispered, "You should watch your tongue, Darius. You aren't as loved as you once were."

Darius snarled. "Watch your words. There are many who do not love you as much either, Prince."

Matt screamed in pain, and I remembered why we were there. I scolded myself for being distracted and yelled, "Stop fighting! Please!" I pushed around Ares to see Matt bleeding from his arm and Koda smiling happily. "Koda, please!" I begged.

Neither seemed to hear me though, as Koda grabbed Matt around the throat and choked him. "Submit to me," Koda growled.

Matt growled and struggled against Koda, refusing to submit.

"Ares, why are they fighting?" I asked.

Achilles whispered, "If the alpha dies, the second in the pack becomes alpha and takes the previous alpha's mate."

Me. They were fighting for the right to take me if Ares ever died.

"You stupid, idiotic men. Stop fighting!" I yelled at them.

Koda punched Matt in the throat and Matt whispered, "Submit."

The crowd clapped and cheered, and Koda smiled happily. I shook my head and walked inside the house, ignoring both men. "Idiots."

CHAPTER SIX

For the next two days, Ares, Koda, and Matt trained with me. Soon I was able to keep pace with Matt and almost with Koda, but Ares beat me every time. I had no doubt that Natasha wasn't as skilled as Ares, so I wasn't worried.

I continued trying to half-shift, but every time I tried, I only changed into my wolf, so we gave up.

As the sun rose on the day of my challenge, I felt my nervousness. I rolled over and snuggled against Ares, who wrapped his arms around me and held me tight. "You don't have to do this. You could rescind your acceptance to fight," he whispered into my ear.

I gaped at his serious expression. He'd stay with me even if I backed out of the fight? He knew I couldn't do that and keep face with the rest of the pack. He'd lose respect as well for having a coward for a mate. "Ares, you know I can't back out."

Koda whined. "Artemis, if you want, we'll leave with you. We'll run and make up some story that will convince the others we *had* to go."

I rolled onto my back so I could meet eyes with each of them. "Stop this. I'm not going to lose. Everything will be fine."

Ares and Koda nuzzled my neck and inhaled my scent at the same time.

My heart felt as though it were tearing apart. Tears trailed down my cheeks as I imagined life without my pack. Ares kissed my cheeks and whispered in my ear, "Artemis, please reconsider. I can't bear to lose you."

"I have to, Ares." No matter how much I didn't want to lose Ares, I had to finish the fight. With my mind made up, I focused on the amount of training I'd had with them and felt sure I would win.

Ares climbed out of bed and stretched. "I'm going to make breakfast." As he walked away, I noticed the tension in his shoulders and back. Matt followed Ares out of the bedroom. It didn't escape my notice that Matt had said nothing while Koda and Ares had tried to convince me to stay safe.

Koda sat up and looked at me. "Artemis, if you think you're going to lose, you can ask for mercy, and she has to refrain from killing you."

"And then be forced to have no Ares and no pack? No, I couldn't do that. I'd rather die," I answered with conviction.

Koda hugged me against him. "I can't watch you die. If you ask for mercy, I'll leave Ares' pack and join you. I know I'm not Ares, but wouldn't it be better than being dead?"

"You'd leave Ares' pack to be my mate? To be the mate of a worthless mixed blood?"

Koda pulled away from me and smiled. "You aren't worthless, and I don't care what bloodlines you have. I love you, Artemis. You're my pack mate and nothing will change that."

I kissed his cheek and climbed out of bed, surprised by his offer. "I'll consider it if the need arises." Though, we both knew I wouldn't. I couldn't continue living if I wasn't Ares' mate. It would be like cutting out an organ.

We'd all chosen to sleep in shorts and shirts so I didn't need to change before I went downstairs in front of Achilles. Ares and

Achilles both whispered in angry tones with one another when I walked into the kitchen, but I couldn't hear what they were saying.

Achilles looked at me with glistening eyes. "Good morning, Artemis."

I bowed my head towards him. "Good morning, Achilles."

Ares set a plate of bacon, eggs, and toast in front of me with a smile. I kissed his cheek and started eating. The men milled around the house in silence while I ate, a sense of doom clouding the air.

The time arrived, and we set out for the fight. The walk to the town center was filled with worry and sadness. In my mind, I was determined to win because I had finally found my pack, my family. But in my body, worry and fear resided, causing my hands to shake ever so slightly.

Ares squeezed my hand reassuringly and in an instant my worry was swept away and replaced with the knowledge that he loved me and no matter what, we'd always love each other.

Ares led us to a large grassy field where a large square had been marked out with white paint. It looked as if the entire town had turned out to watch my challenge, hundreds of people surrounding the square. Even the king and queen were sitting in chairs on the sidelines.

Koda stopped us at the sidelines and gave me a hard hug, whispering into my ear, "Remember what I told you."

Matt hugged me, too, and then both walked a ways back in the crowd. Achilles looked at me with sparkling eyes and softly glowing skin. The blue vines on his arms glittered like sapphires. "Win this battle Artemis," he said softly.

I nodded at him, and he quickly moved through the crowd. Ares rubbed his cheek against mine and inhaled my scent. Without thinking about it, I'd inhaled his scent as well and felt his unease within him. "I love you, Artemis. You'll win. I know you will."

Ares took my hand again and walked with me out to the center of the square where my opponent was waiting, bouncing on the balls of her feet and swinging her arms around. She smiled at Ares and then glared at me.

Ares raised his hand and the crowd silenced. "Today we witness a challenge between Artemis and Natasha, to the death. Winner earns the right to be mated to Ares, Prince of the Werewolves." The crowd gasped and began murmuring loudly. The queen stood up out of her chair, but the king put a hand on her arm and she sat back down. Ares raised his hand again, silencing the crowd. "No full changing will be allowed. Begin."

My skin itched, and my heartbeat tripled in pace as I watched Ares walk to the sidelines, never looking back at me. Natasha cracked her knuckles, bringing my attention to her. "Let's get this over with. I want to have your crap moved out of the room by sunset."

Her calm demeanor and cockiness made me seethe. "The only thing you'll be doing at sunset is paying the ferryman."

Her eyes widened for a moment before she recovered and charged at me. All thoughts shut off, and I went into battle mode. My wolf side took over, allowing me to use instinct to avoid most of her attacks. Unfortunately, she was faster than I'd thought, and I was soon bleeding from my lip and a cut above my eye.

I changed tactics and instead of being defensive, I became offensive, jabbing, upper cutting and attacking as fast as I could. I knew the crowd was cheering and booing, but all I could hear was Natasha, my breathing, and the dull thud of our fists hitting each other. My thoughts flickered to Ares and Koda as I turned to dodge her fist and noticed them in the back of the crowd, encircled by men restraining them. If I lost to Natasha, I couldn't stand to see her with Ares. I couldn't bear to see Ares with *any* other woman.

Natasha growled in frustration and changed her hands into paws. She swung her right hand at my face and I barely managed to dodge backwards, her claws slicing off a piece of hair that had come out of my ponytail. She screamed with rage and charged forward, slicing first into my forearms and then into my stomach. The wounds stung worse than I could have imagined. Natasha punched me in the face, making me stumble backwards. She took advantage of my imbalance and jumped on me, pinning my arms with her knees and began pounding my face repeatedly. She snapped my right wrist making me scream and fight to stay in my human form.

I was wrong, I couldn't beat her. I should have listened to Ares, but I hadn't and now I'd lose everything. I'd lose Ares and Koda. I'd lose my pack, my family. I'd lose my life.

She growled loudly. "You're nothing, but a worthless halfbreed! Your father should have killed you when you were born as he'd promised to do. You don't deserve Ares, and I'll make sure to erase every memory of you he might possess. One night with me, and he won't even remember your name." She punctuated every sentence with a blow to my head, but her words hurt me more than any physical attack could.

Anger boiled inside of me and before thoughts could form in my mind, I had exploded out from under her and grabbed Natasha, holding her up in the air by her throat. "Ares is mine," I said with conviction.

Natasha kicked and scratched at me. "Put. Me. Down."

I squeezed her throat harder. "Ares is my mate!"

I didn't want to kill her. I didn't want to kill anybody. I knew I had to end the fight, but I wanted to make her submit. As I debated what to do, she jammed her claws into my shoulder, making me drop her to the ground. I backed away from her, but she ran forward, slamming into me, sending us head over heels together.

She ended up on top of me and pinned me to the ground. "You're not meant to be the Beta's mate. You're too weak to be his."

She picked me up and threw me across the square. I landed on my face and felt a rib crack. She was on me again before I could roll over. She grabbed me by the hair and stood me up before kicking me in the side. The force of her kick knocked the wind out of me and broke another rib. She squatted down next to me as I gasped for air and writhed in the grass. "It's time to end this. It's time to finish you and take you out of Ares' life once and for all."

She turned my head, and I found Ares at the edge of the square being held back by four men. His eyes glowed golden as he looked at me. Koda and Achilles were near Ares, but both of them were also being held back by people. I reached out to them and brushed their wolves' energies with mine. My energy was depleted and it was only a matter of minutes before I died, whether by Natasha or the internal bleeding I could sense.

"I love you," I whispered. Tears leaked out of my eyes as I looked at the man I loved and my pack mate.

Ares growled angrily and struggled against the men holding him. "Artemis. No!" More men surrounded Ares and Koda.

Natasha turned my face back and smiled. "What a sweet goodbye." Her claws pierced my stomach as she drove them deep into my body.

I screamed and thrashed against her, pulling her hand out of me and smashing her nose with my fist. She stumbled backwards, eyes wide, and I pounced on her. I couldn't lose Ares. I couldn't die. Dammit, I couldn't lose.

In a matter of seconds, I had my arm around her throat and my legs around her waist with my left hand pushing her neck deeper into my arm. "Ask for mercy," I whispered.

She nodded once, and I released her, collapsing on the ground myself. I rolled onto my back and exhaled.

I'd won, but I could feel my life ending. *At least I'd won.* Natasha roared and jumped at me. I lifted my hand up, summoning what little energy I had left, and my Sidhe powers. A small fireball sped from my hand to her and disappeared through her chest. She staggered for a minute, looking down at the hole in her chest, before collapsing to the ground. Her lifeless body lay next to me, and I knew it was right that I'd won.

I took one more breath, whispered, "I love you, Ares," and then darkness consumed me.

~

The afterlife wasn't what I'd expected. First, I hadn't expected to be woken in the afterlife by a slap in the face. And second, I didn't expect to find Ares and Achilles sitting next to me.

"Artemis! Artemis, wake up!" Ares yelled at me.

"You're not dead. How can you be here?" I asked.

"Artemis, you're not dead," Achilles said through clenched teeth.

"My energy. It was drained," I said completely confused.

Ares put my hand against his face. "Yes, but Achilles and I have been loaning you ours."

The woozy feeling in my head disappeared, and I could feel my body. Everything hurt. Gwen, the healer, knelt beside me. "Artemis, where does it hurt?"

"Everywhere," I groaned.

She ran her hands along my body and then cursed softly. "Ares, how much of your energy are you willing to give up?"

Ares continued to stare at my face as he spoke. "I'll give everything."

She stared at him for a moment before shaking her head. "I won't kill you to save her, but that won't be necessary anyways because I'm sure the Sidhe Prince will loan me some of his energy as well, since he's already doing it."

Achilles nodded. "You can use as much as you need."

She looked quizzically at Achilles as he stared at me. It unnerved me to see the same look on Achilles' face that Ares' had on his. She studied the two men a minute longer and then shrugged. "Alright. Let's get started."

In ten minutes, she'd healed all of my wounds, including the internal bleeding and broken ribs. Her body slumped forward and her face looked gray as she finished. "She won't have enough energy to do more than rest in bed for the next few days. Keep her lying down as much as you can."

Ares picked me up and cradled me against his chest. "Thank you."

Ares turned around and I saw Koda unconscious on the ground. "Ares, what happened to Koda?" I asked with wide eyes.

Ares sighed. "You stopped breathing for a minute and he went ballistic, flinging the men around him away and trying to rush to you. I'd already gotten to you though, and he was so upset that he had started to change. Darius knocked him out. He'll be fine."

Matt walked over and smiled at me. "Hey, Love. Glad to see you're doing better." He picked Koda up and started walking back towards the house.

Ares followed him, nuzzling my cheek with his nose every few steps. Even though my body was healed, Gwen had been right, I felt exhausted.

I closed my eyes as I relaxed in Ares' hold. I felt safe and protected with his arms around me. Just as I started to doze off, I realized that I'd won. I'd beat Natasha and kept Ares as my mate. I'd actually won. Ares hummed softly and despite my attempts not to, I fell into a deep sleep.

THREE DAYS of bed rest was causing me to go insane. Ares wouldn't even let me walk down the stairs. If I started towards the stairs, he would pick me up and carry me down them, despite my protests.

My strength was finally back to normal as I sat in front of Ares and Koda, trying to convince them to go on a hunt. "Ares, come on. I need to get out of the house and I really want to do something as a pack."

Ares folded his arms across his chest and answered without hesitation. "No."

Koda frowned at me. "You *died* three days ago."

"I didn't die three days ago. I *almost* died."

Koda folded his arms across his chest. "*You* died. Achilles' and Ares' energies and magic were the only ones present in your body."

I sprang to my feet and stormed toward the front door. Achilles suddenly blocked my path. "Artemis, be reasonable." Ever since he'd donated his energy to save me, I'd felt a strange connection to him.

"You be reasonable. I *need* to go outside!" I yelled up at Achilles, not caring that he was a prince or that I shouldn't be yelling.

Koda walked out the front door, his shoulders stiff with anger.

Ares pulled me backwards and wrapped his arms around me. "We need to leave."

I pulled back from him to see his face. He looked tired and sad. "What? Why would we leave? Where would we go?" I asked.

Achilles cleared his throat. "Perhaps we could take her to my father's kingdom."

Ares growled softly. "No."

Achilles folded his arms over his chest. "She needs training anyways."

Koda ran inside panting. "Ares, we need to leave."

Ares looked at me with an I-told-you-so face and then turned to Koda. "Why?"

Koda exhaled. "Dhampirs, vampires, and ogres have surrounded the castle and are demanding Artemis."

Ares growled loudly and lifted his lip in a snarl. Achilles turned to Ares. "Let me fly her out of here while you deal with the intruders. You know I can keep her safe."

Ares shook his head still snarling. "No."

Achilles and Ares began arguing loudly with each other. Slowly, I backed away from them. Ares stopped talking and turned towards me. "Where are you going?"

"The bathroom."

His eyes narrowed, but Achilles said, "She would be perfectly safe in the Sidhe realm," and Ares attention was once again off of me.

I hurried to the bathroom and stared at my reflection. Every time I looked at myself, I could barely recognize the person staring back at me. I no longer looked like a teenage girl, but now looked like a woman. It hadn't been that long, but my features were noticeably different. Could it be from gaining my Sidhe powers? Or was it from the connection with Ares and all of the drama I'd been dealing with? Whatever it was, I was no longer a child. I'd killed people, and I was stronger than a human. I was strong enough to fight my own battles. "That's it," I whispered. My skin began glowing softly, and I knew what I had to do.

Quickly and quietly I moved from the bathroom, down the hallway and through the kitchen to the back door. Ares, Achilles and Koda were all arguing and yelling, so none of them heard me leave. I shut the door as quietly as I could and headed through town. Everyone stared at me as I walked by, but no one tried to stop me. Energy flowed through me and for the first time I felt the energy of the plants around me. Every living thing was filled with energy. Could I use that energy somehow?

A group of twenty people stood on the edge of the village at the beginning of the forest, while another group of twenty werewolves stood at the edge of the village facing them. Half of the werewolves present were in wolf form, so I knew I had to hurry because they would communicate to Ares telepathically that I was here without him.

I stepped just past the line of werewolves to stand alone between the two groups. The werewolves began murmuring, and the dhampirs and vampires in front of me simply smiled. My skin was still glowing softly, and it gave me hope that this would work. I squared my shoulders and spoke as loudly and as strongly as I could, "You are trespassing. Please leave the premises."

The dhampirs and vampires looked at each other for a moment before one of them walked forward. He was a short man, thin and unimposing, yet I could feel the evil radiating off of him in waves. How can you tell the difference between a vampire and a dhampir? Two ways. One, dhampirs are more muscular, not bulky like the werewolves, but not thin-built like the vampires either, an in-between of the two. And two, vampires ooze evil mojo whereas dhampirs only emit a creepy level of evil. He stopped several yards away from me and bowed elegantly. "Greetings, Artemis. I am Roger. It is a pleasure to meet you." He spoke with a slight English accent that would have made me smile if I hadn't been able to feel how evil he was.

"Who sent you here?" I asked.

He smiled. "If you would please come with us, we will take you to the one requesting your presence."

He was trying to be sweet, but nothing as evil as he was could be truly sweet. My skin began glowing brighter and my powers formed a shield around me as my fear of him grew. Any vampire who was so calm when faced with a group of werewolves had to be powerful. "I am not going anywhere with you. Leave this place or die."

The werewolves behind me began murmuring excitedly.

Roger's smile widened. "You think you can take us all on?"

I clenched and unclenched my hands and visualized fire covering them. Instantly, my visualization came true. Purple flames flickered around my hands as I smiled at Roger. "I can try."

One of the dhampirs yelled and began running towards me. I held up my hand, palm facing the dhampir and a fireball flew from my hand and through the dhampir's chest. The body fell to the ground and the rest of the vampires and dhampirs began rushing towards me. I backed up as I continued to send fireball after fireball into the group.

The werewolves behind me finally regained their composure and rushed forward to join the fight. I dropped my shield to conserve energy while I continued firing at my enemies. Roger dodged three of my fireballs and punched me in the face, making the flames around my hands disappear, and I stumbled backwards. His fists flew too fast for me to track and soon I was bleeding, in pain, and on my back on the ground. He jumped at me, and I flipped him over my body using my legs. I was up and fighting with another vampire before his body had even hit the dirt. More dhampirs and vampires poured into the area, easily outnumbering us.

I had been wrong. I couldn't take on this many. I could barely handle twenty. "ARES!" I yelled as loudly as I could. The connection between us would have notified him immediately when I was in pain so I knew he had to feel the fear I felt. "ARES!" I yelled one more time before Roger tackled me from behind while I was exchanging blows with a dhampir.

I grunted from the impact and tried to roll over, but Roger's fingers turned to claws, and he stabbed me in the side, holding me in place. "The boss didn't say you couldn't be hurt, just that you couldn't be dead. I have a lot of leeway between living and dead."

His arrogant attitude angered me more than the fact that he wanted to torture me. I grabbed his hand at the wrist and pulled his claws from my side. My skin began glowing and I smiled up at him. "It's going to make your boss really unhappy when he learns that you failed."

Roger tried to pry his wrist free from my hand, but I held tight and then faster than I'd ever been able to summon it before, flame covered my hand and instantly ate through his wrist, bone and all. I tossed his severed hand aside and plunged my hand into his chest like I'd done with the female vampire who'd tried to kill me. He began screaming and I quickly pulled his heart from his chest and turned it to ash. I pushed him off of me and stood up, the flames leaving my hand. Everyone was staring at me and the screaming vampire with a hole in his chest.

I felt Ares nearby, but didn't look at him as I walked around to Roger's head and picked him up by the back of his neck with his screaming head facing towards the other vampires and dhampirs.

"I asked you to leave. I even said 'please', but you still stayed to try to capture me. I am not as easy a prey as you were told." I had to shout to be heard over Rogers' screams. "You will find that my compassion only goes so far." The flames covered my hands again, and I placed them around Roger's neck. His screams intensified as the flames began covering his body. Apparently, vampires do burn easily by fire. Score one for Hollywood on that truth.

I dropped Roger's body to the ground as he burned and screamed, though his screams only lasted twenty more seconds because Achilles stepped forward and decapitated him with a sword.

The other vampires and dhampirs stood still in shock for a moment, staring at Roger's body before their eyes raised and they looked at me. As one, they screamed their rage and rushed towards me. Achilles sword flashed several times, decapitating those nearest me. Ares came to stand next to me in half-shift. I extinguished the flames covering my hands and set my hand against Ares' forearm, letting our bond heal the wounds on my body. He looked down at me, and his lips pulled up in what I guessed to be a smile. The smile only lasted a minute though because I'd angered the vampires and dhampirs more than I'd scared them, and they were coming towards me fast. Ares moved with deadly precision, killing one after another after another. I watched him in awe.

Achilles sword slashed down just to the right of me and I blinked at the severed arm that fell beside my body. Achilles decapitated the owner of the arm and then held his hand out to me. "Come, we must get you far away from here."

I looked towards Ares who was fighting with two vampires at once. "I can't."

Achilles groaned in frustration and picked me up in his arms. "He will get over me touching you as long as you're safe."

I looked around us and realized that we were vastly outnumbered as more dhampirs and vampires and even a group of ogres joined the fight from the depths of the forest. Achilles' body glowed and the blue vines on his upper chest and arms throbbed in time with his heart and then wings spread from his back. His wings matched the color of the vines on his skin. They were one of the most beautiful things I'd ever seen.

"Where did your sword go?" I asked curiously.

Achilles smiled down at me, making my breath catch in my throat. "Perhaps now is not the time to discuss that?"

I looked at the fighting going on and blushed in embarrassment. "Right." It wasn't my fault that I was easily distracted.

Achilles wings moved and we were suddenly above the fight. "Ares!" Achilles called. Ares looked up and growled loudly. "I'm taking her to safety. Meet us in your meadow."

Ares roared in anger and began attacking more fiercely, killing four vampires and two dhampirs in a matter of seconds.

Achilles moved his wings, and we were up above the trees and the people below looked like small ants. I wrapped my arms around Achilles' neck and trembled.

"What's wrong?" Achilles asked softly.

I closed my eyes and put my face against his neck. "I hate heights."

Achilles laughed, shaking his chest and me against it. "A fairy afraid of heights? Now that is original."

I pulled back to glare at him, but instead, found myself staring at the trees zooming past us like green blurs. We were flying incredibly fast and yet I felt no wind pressing against me. I looked up and noticed the slight blue tinge of a shield around us. "Why do you have a shield around us?"

"I thought it might frighten you more if you felt the wind while we flew."

"Oh." He was right. I probably would have been more scared. I took a deep breath and inhaled his scent. Instantly I relaxed and felt safe.

My grip loosened from his neck and Achilles smiled at me. "See, it's not so bad."

I refused to look down again. "It's not the fact that we're high up, it's the fear of falling down."

His smile disappeared as he grew serious. "Do you think I would drop you?"

I pulled my gaze from his lips up to his eyes. "I don't know. I hardly know you."

"Whose fault is that?" he asked sadly.

I looked over his face as I tried to gauge what mood he was in. He was mad, sad and yet seemed happy all at the same time. "Why didn't you come to me before?" I asked.

Achilles frowned a moment before sighing. "Your father forbade me from visiting you. I didn't understand why before, but now that I know he hadn't told you what you really are, it makes perfect sense. If you had seen me, then you would know that you aren't human and he wanted you to think you were human for as long as he could."

My heart was beating faster than normal as we flew farther and farther away from Ares. My skin started itching and my breath came in short pants. Achilles' wings stilled and we began falling down towards the ground. I grabbed on to his neck and closed my eyes as we fell. I knew that he wouldn't hurt himself and that I shouldn't be worried, but I couldn't control my emotions very well with Ares so far away.

Achilles was suddenly walking, and I realized we'd landed. I opened my eyes and looked at the beautiful meadow we were in. Wild flowers filled most of the meadow and added amazingly bright purples, pinks, reds and blues to the area.

Achilles walked towards an area with tree trunks set around a circle of rocks where a camp fire could be started. Achilles laid me down in the grass and wild flowers and looked up at the moon. My breathing had leveled out, but my heart was still beating fast and my skin still tingled. Could that mean Ares was closer? I sat up and looked at Achilles who was sitting on a log and starting a fire using his Sidhe powers. "Did you call this Ares' meadow?"

Achilles moved the pieces of wood in the fire around before turning to me. "Yes. We're actually halfway between the were-wolves and the Sidhe and this is Ares' land. This spot was his favorite to go to for meditations as I recall."

I approached Achilles with a purple wild flower in my hand. "You know Ares very well, don't you?"

Achilles poked at the fire with a stick. "Yes."

I sat on the log beside him. "What is he hiding from me? He hasn't told me anything about his past. I can only get bits and pieces from him."

Achilles tossed the stick into the fire and shook his head. "I cannot tell you. If he's withholding the information from you, then he must have a reason. I have no idea what the reason could be, but nevertheless he must have one."

I looked at the vines on his arms and watched as they throbbed. I lifted my finger and ran the tip of it down one of his vines. The vine sparkled brighter and then every vine on his body glowed brightly, and his skin exploded in white light. Achilles gasped and then groaned.

I yanked my hand back and moved away from him. I hadn't meant to hurt him. I'd just been mesmerized by the vines.

Achilles looked up at me, his eyes completely white, like two glowing pearls. "Don't be afraid," he said softly. I relaxed and he smiled. "Do you know what you just did?" Before I could answer, he shook his head and laughed. "Of course, you don't. You don't know anything of our kind." He shook his head sadly for a moment and then looked up at me again, a look of pure joy on his face. "You just released my powers with a single touch. It's rare because the one that can do that, is your destined mate."

I shook my head and backed up until the backs of my legs hit another log. "No. I can't be your destined mate if I'm Ares'."

Achilles gestured at his glowing body. "The results do not lie. You are my destined mate." He sighed, sounding exhausted, and his body stopped glowing. His eyes returned to normal and he shook his head sadly. "It's going to take years to come to an agreement with Ares."

I realized that my skin wasn't tingly anymore and my heartbeat was almost normal. "He's close by," I said.

Achilles frowned. "Hm."

I sat down beside him and sighed. "Can you wait to tell Ares about what happened? I'd rather deal with him being mad at me for trying to fight the vampires first instead of him being mad at me for touching you as well."

Achilles huffed a laugh. "I think you're right."

We sat in comfortable silence for an hour before I felt Ares approaching. I walked out of the ring of logs and towards the direction he was coming from. My heart beat faster each time I turned in the right direction, like a homing beacon.

Ares, Koda, and Matt finally came into view, and I exhaled happily. Ares sped up, running ahead of the others and picked me up in his arms, swinging me around a couple times before setting me back down on my feet. "Artemis, you're alright."

I kissed his face and lips several times before I looked into his eyes. "Of course I'm alright."

Ares kissed me roughly on the lips and hugged me tightly again. "Don't you ever try to fight without me again."

I nuzzled my nose into his neck and whined happily. "I'm sorry."

Koda and Matt finally arrived, and Ares released me so that I could hug each of them and rub noses to inhale each other's scents.

Ares picked up my hand and walked the rest of the way to the camp fire. "Thank you for protecting her," he said softly.

Achilles bowed his head. "Anytime, Brother."

Brother?

Ares growled. "We are not brothers."

Achilles sighed and poked at the fire with a new stick. Matt and Koda worked together and hung skinned rabbits and a skinned fox over the fire to cook. Looking at the cooking animals made me realize how thirsty I was. I stripped from my clothes, setting them on the log beside Ares and changed to my wolf form. I stretched and shook after the shift and then trotted over to the small stream I'd heard on the other side of the meadow. The men watched me until I started drinking from the stream and then turned back around and began talking.

After I had my fill of water, I jogged over to the logs, changed forms again and pulled my clothes on. It felt good and right to change forms now. I wish I'd known about it sooner so that I could have enjoyed it more.

I sat down beside Ares and rested my head against his shoulder. He was involved in a serious debate with Achilles, but he pulled me in against him so that his arms were around my shoulders while his thumb lightly stroked my skin. I tried to pay attention to what they were discussing, but I felt a presence out in the dark of the night. It was as if I was being poked in the stomach. I stood, and Ares grabbed my hand. I turned to look at him and saw his mouth moving, but I couldn't hear anything. I put my hands to my ears and then shook my head. Ares' and Achilles' mouths moved quickly and Koda and Matt ran off into the night. The poking in my stomach grew stronger until it felt as though something had pierced my skin. I screamed in pain and fell to the ground as I felt my energy being drained.

I couldn't see my attacker. I didn't even know *what* my attacker was. How could I fight it?

Ares had his hands resting against my face as he talked to me, but I couldn't hear his words. Tears streamed down my face as the unseen attacker continued to drain me. What could be so powerful that it could kill you without ever even touching you?

Achilles pushed Ares aside and grabbed me in his arms. His wings sprung from his back and then we were up in the air. I hung limp in his arms as he flew. Achilles' mouth was moving fast and then he pressed his forehead to mine. Images and thoughts filled my mind and I realized after a few moments that they were

Achilles' memories. I gasped and then the images and thoughts stopped, denying me the chance to make sense of what I'd seen.

Are you alright?

I gasped again as the question was spoken in Achilles' voice, but through my mind. "How can I hear you in my head?"

Achilles shook his head and I saw his chest heave as he sighed. *It would be best if you didn't speak out loud.*

"Is this like the werewolves' communication while in wolf form?" I asked out loud.

Yes. Now please stop talking out loud.

Sorry. Why can I hear you in my head anyways?

We'll discuss that later. For now, we must discuss what happened. You were attacked by the Queen of the Light Court, Hera—

Wait...isn't the queen your mom?

Yes, but...

Why did your mom attack me?

She was simply testing your powers first, which is why I didn't interfere, but when she realized that you are more powerful than her, she grew angry and tried to kill...

I'm more powerful than her? How is that possible? Does that mean that I—

Stop interrupting me! Listen to me, Artemis. We don't have much time. She's following us. I'm going to take you to my father's kingdom because he will protect you. My mother and he have been fighting for decades, and she's not allowed to enter his kingdom. It's the safest place for you. Ares will meet us soon.

Why is she following us?

She wants you dead. She's very jealous and has always tried to kill those more powerful than her. Vanity is one of her negative qualities that have caused many wars over the centuries.

Achilles landed on top of a hill covered in bright green grass beside the ocean and set me down on my feet.

Where are we?

Ireland.

How did we get here so fast?

Achilles rolled his eyes at me. *We're not as slow as birds or airplanes. We're preternaturals, which means we have extraordinary powers. Powers great enough to fly across the world in an hour.* He walked down the hill a little way and stopped in front of a square patch of dead grass. He placed his hand against the patch of grass and then his skin began to glow. The dead grass dropped down and the hole widened until it was at least ten feet by ten feet and a set of stairs was visible leading into the ground. Achilles picked up my hand and started walking down the stairs. I followed him down and swallowed nervously as the top shrank and the grass returned to cover the hole behind us. We continued down the steps in complete darkness.

CHAPTER SEVEN

We descended the stairs in complete darkness and I felt my nerves increasing.

Achilles?

Yes?

I know it's childish, but could you maybe... Before I could finish my thought, Achilles' skin began glowing and Lit the area around us. We were surrounded by stone instead of dirt and we walked down a narrow stairway that seemed to never end. I gripped Achilles' hand tighter as I began to feel claustrophobic. The wolf didn't like feeling trapped and deep underneath a hill in a stone stairway, close enough to a cage for us as a real one.

Achilles spun around suddenly and put his hands on each side of my face and stared into my eyes. *Easy. We're going to be fine. The door is just ahead and through that we enter into my father's realm. It's completely open. You're not trapped. This is not a cage—simply a passageway. You can't change.*

His touch and words relaxed me until I could breathe normally again. He turned back around and walked faster.

Why had his touch relaxed me? Only Ares should have been able to do that? Did it have something to do with his new ability to communicate telepathically with me? Did he do something? Or was he right about the destined mate thing?

I was trying to figure out an answer when he pushed open a door and sunlight temporarily blinded me. Achilles continued to pull me forward as my eyes adjusted. I tugged on his hand to stop him and rubbed my eyes with my palms. I slowly opened my eyes, and then my mouth dropped open.

In books, the fairy realm was simply an underground castle or a large underground room. They were completely wrong. It wasn't an underground anything. Birds flew in the blue skies above us and the oceans splashed against the cliffs nearby. I turned around and instead of seeing the door we'd come through I saw even more beautiful grassy land.

How?

The Sidhe do not live in the underground as humans like to believe. We live in a different dimension, which you can get to by using a portal, such as the one we used to get here.

A different dimension? That's crazy.

Crazy, but true. Come, we must hurry.

Achilles picked my hand up again and led me towards a giant stone castle. We had to walk through a village, and I stared in awe at the people dressed in fine clothes. *Why are they dressed as though they live in the medieval era?*

Achilles continued walking as he talked to me. *The medieval era is my father's favorite, so those that live in the Dark Court wear that period of clothing and even speak as they would during that time period. My father is somewhat egotistical, as you can imagine.*

The people all wore medieval clothing yet their skin was of every color of the rainbow with various designs on their skins. Some had their wings out, but most had their wings hidden. Men, women and children stared at us as we walked. Achilles seemed to ignore the looks while I couldn't help but look back. Were they staring at Achilles or me?

We made it to the castle and Achilles smiled. "Morning, guards."

The two guards, dressed in full armor, pushed open the doors and bowed their heads. "Greetings, Prince Achilles."

We started to walk past them when I caught their scent. I stopped walking and stared at them in shock. "Werewolves?"

I realized my hearing returned, and would have been excited if the two guards hadn't started sniffing at me. One of them reached out towards me, and I growled at him, snapping my teeth. He pulled his hand back and gaped at me. "Who are you?"

I opened my mouth to answer when a tall man with a long white beard stepped through the doors to stand beside Achilles. "She is Artemis, daughter of Darren of the Werewolves and Athena of the Sidhe, and fiancée of Prince Achilles of the Sidhe."

The man looked like Achilles, except he was slightly older and had a long white beard. I knew who he was instantly. I curtsied and bowed my head. "Greetings Zeus, King of the Dark Court of the Sidhe."

Zeus laughed happily. "I see you've started training her."

Achilles sighed. "We must speak father. It's important."

Zeus picked my hand up, and I straightened to look at him. He kissed the back of my hand and smiled seductively at me. "It's nice to finally meet you."

A blush instantly covered my cheeks, but I found my voice and said, "It's an honor to finally meet you."

Zeus took my hand and placed it on the inside of his elbow as he led us into the castle. The hallways were wide enough to ride three horses abreast and torches sat in decorative iron holders every five feet or so. Achilles walked on the other side of me as we made our way past large rooms filled with Sidhe of every color. I tried to stop to look, but Zeus continued to pull me along. He stopped in front of a set of large, ornately carved wooden doors and snapped his fingers. The two guards in front of the doors pushed them open and then stepped out of the way as Zeus led me inside.

The king's bedroom is expected to be elegant, but the King of the Sidhe's bedroom was magnificent. He kept to his medieval time period though, not having a single modern item inside. Zeus released my hand, and I walked quickly to the balcony, pushing aside the red drapes to look out over the ocean below.

The wind whipped against my face, sending a light spray of water to chill me. I'd never seen anything so beautiful. I looked up and felt the sun's rays heat my face. Everything felt so real, yet how could this exist without the humans knowing about it?

Achilles walked to stand on the balcony beside me and leaned his elbows on the stone railing. "This is my favorite spot in all of the Dark Court."

"I can see why," I said softly as I looked out over the ocean. A whale breached the waves a mile or so away from us and sprayed water up into the air.

Achilles picked my hand up and turned me to face him. "Your eyes are glowing with energy. You're even more beautiful when standing beside the ocean."

The wind whipped my hair from side to side as Achilles and I stared at each other. The desire to kiss him was almost as bad as it had been with Ares, but thinking of Ares helped cool my hormones and allow me to turn away from him. "Thank you."

A table had been set up in Zeus' bedroom while I'd been on the balcony. I hurried inside and sat down in a chair and began piling meat and cheese on to my plate.

"So, what brings you here?" Zeus asked Achilles.

Achilles sat down beside me and nibbled on some fruits and cheeses as he spoke. "Let's see, where to begin? Well, first let me tell you that Mother attacked Artemis and wishes to kill her..."

Zeus stood up and stared at Achilles. "Is that why you..."

Achilles held up his hand. "Yes, I only did it out of necessity."

"Did what out of necessity, my dear son?" asked a woman.

Achilles was instantly out of his chair and standing beside me, his skin glowing.

The woman was beyond beautiful. Her skin was like buttery cream with a beautiful filigree design which glowed as she looked at me and Achilles. "You had better explain why you are assuming an attack stance against me."

Achilles spoke softly. "She's my fiancée, Mother. I will not let you hurt her."

Hera looked at me with clear disdain. I met her eyes as I continued to eat. If she wanted to kill me, she probably could, so I would at least die with a full stomach.

I won't let her kill you.

My eyes flickered over to Achilles as he spoke to me, but I quickly looked back at Hera. *Can't she technically order you to kill me if she wanted to?*

Yes, but she won't do that because...

"Are you communicating telepathically?" she hissed.

Achilles glared at her. "You tried to kill her! What else could I do?"

"*You. Bound. Her?*" She asked in angry pants. Her skin began glowing again, and her eyes turned to white pearls as Achilles' had done when I'd released his powers.

Bound me? What did that mean?

"There was no other way. I had to save her," Achilles said through clenched teeth.

Hera stopped glowing and turned away. "You were always an impulsive man."

I turned to Zeus, since he wasn't involved in their conversation either. I might as well get as much information from them as possible while I was here. Who knew when the next time I'd be allowed to go to the Sidhe court would be? "Do all Sidhe have Greek names?" I asked.

Zeus smiled. "Technically we had the names first, but the

humans used to believe that we were gods and so their stories were based on us."

I looked from Zeus to Hera and then back to Zeus. "Is she really your sister?"

Hera gasped, and Zeus laughed. "No. Most of the family trees that the humans created are wrong. Hera is not my sister, only my wife."

"So, can you really use lightning bolts?" I asked curiously.

Zeus put his arm out, palm up. His skin started glowing and then a sizzling lightning bolt appeared in his hand. "Some of what the humans recorded about us is true," he said.

"Wow." I chewed on a grape when it occurred to me that "Ares" was a Greek name, too. "Wait. Are the Sidhe who the humans based their stories off of the only ones with Greek mythological names?"

Achilles opened his mouth to say something, but Zeus said, "Yes."

I stood up from my chair and walked quickly towards the balcony. *That was it. That was what Ares had been keeping from me. He is part Sidhe, too.*

Achilles stood next to me and put a hand on my back. "I cannot tell you his story. It's very personal, and I feel it is best for him to tell you himself."

"Who are you talking about?" Hera asked, narrowing her eyes at us. "I hate it when I'm out of the loop."

Achilles turned around. "Why is she here? In your realm?" he asked Zeus.

I turned around and found Hera sitting on Zeus' lap. Zeus sighed, "Well, son, you see…"

Achilles groaned. "You're dating again! You remember what happened last time?"

Hera shrugged. "It was a small battle."

Achilles scoffed. "A small battle? You call *World War Two* a small battle?"

Zeus turned to me and asked, "Do you have wings?"

I shrugged. "I'm not sure. I didn't know you had wings until Achilles showed me, and I haven't tried to get them out."

Zeus stood up out of his chair, helped Hera sit down in it, then walked to me and took my hand. "Focus on your surroundings. Do you feel the energy from all of the living things around you?"

I nodded.

"Good, now focus on those energies and ask them to loan you some of their strength."

If my life hadn't been as crazy as it was, I would have thought he was joking with me or that he was insane. Instead I closed my eyes and asked the plants to borrow some of their energy. I opened my eyes when I felt the excess energy flowing through me and lighting my body up like a fluorescent light bulb.

Zeus smiled. "Good. Now close your eyes and picture your back. In the center of your back between your shoulder blades I want you to picture two vertical slits, one foot long each."

I pictured exactly what he said and then felt my skin rip apart and my wings flare out behind me. The pain forced me to my knees, and my body sizzled as though I'd been electrocuted. Zeus helped me stand up and walked around me to look at my wings and body. "Interesting," he said as he came back to face me.

"How do I move them?" I asked after the pain had subsided.

Achilles smiled from beside me. "You just think what you want and they do it. Once you get used to it they move like your arms or legs, almost without thought."

I moved my right wing forward and stared at the purple wings with purple vines. "Purple vines?"

Zeus whispered, "They match your eyes, your new skin marks and the streaks in your hair."

"Streaks? Skin marks?" I started trying to pull my hair forward, but Achilles grabbed my wrists and then Hera snapped her fingers and a full length mirror stood before me. My black hair was now randomly streaked with purple. It was very punk and yet I loved it.

My skin was a lighter color and I had thin purple lines, like flower vines covering my arms and face and as much of my body as I could see. I loved it. I looked tough and beautiful at the same time. I looked hot! But...what would Ares think? Would he still think I was beautiful?

Of course, he will.

I looked at Achilles and smiled. "Thanks."

He smiled back. *Anytime.*

Zeus cleared his throat. "Okay, now to put them away you simply imagine your back, flat and devoid of any slits or wings."

I closed my eyes and the wings disappeared. My shirt flapped forward and I clutched it to the front of me. "Great, another way to ruin clothes."

Achilles laughed. "It's alright. I'm sure we have some clothes that'll fit."

Zeus disappeared through a side door and then came back out with a large t-shirt. "It's a little big for you, but it'll work for now."

I pulled the shirt on and smiled gratefully. "Thank you."

Achilles asked, "Would you like to explore?"

I nodded vigorously. "Yes, please."

Achilles took my hand and led me out to the balcony. His wings popped out of his back, and then we were up in the air. He made his way beside the water and then to the village we'd originally walked through. He set me down on my feet and then took my hand in his and led me through the town.

I stopped at a booth where a red and blue colored Sidhe woman was selling strange looking items. Achilles started steering me away then whispered, "They're magical items that you have no need for."

I rolled my eyes. "Why do men hate shopping so much?"

He continued leading me through the town and then out into the green fields surrounding the castle area.

I relaxed and asked the question I'd been dying to know the answer to, "So, were you really the hero of the Trojan war?"

Achilles rolled his eyes. “Yes, I was the one who thought of the Horse, but I’ve won many other wars besides that. Unfortunately, Ares was with me and as the ‘God of War’ they gave him more credit than they gave me.”

“So, you two used to be close then?”

Achilles sighed longingly. “It was a long time ago though.”

“So, why the ‘Achilles Heel’?” I asked, having been curious about that as well.

Achilles laughed. “If I had a dollar for every time someone has asked me that, I would be able to buy the world.”

I stayed quiet and waited for him to explain.

“Well, as you can imagine, a hit to my heel won’t kill me, but during the Trojan War I was in a terrific fight. I’d been shot by arrows and one of the Trojans was exchanging blows with me. I was growing weaker as the metal in the arrows stayed buried in my skin and then just as I was attempting to use a large portion of my magic some bastard shot me in the heel with an arrow. I screamed in pain and then my Mother appeared and, using her ability to teleport, took me to safety. Unfortunately, all the humans saw was me get shot in the heel by an arrow and then disappear in a flash of light. Can you believe that they all thought I exploded? Simply ridiculous!”

I laughed and then quickly tried to stifle it. “Sorry, I didn’t mean to laugh…”

He put his hands on his hips and said, “Really? You didn’t mean to…” and then he tackled me to the ground, tickling me in every ticklish spot I had.

I was laughing and struggling against him, but he seemed to be an expert at tickle torturing. I finally had to concede and yelled, “I surrender!”

He collapsed onto the ground beside me and laughed. “I haven’t had that much fun in a while.”

I sighed and sat up. “Me neither.”

He sat up beside me and pushed my hair behind my ear. "You have fun with Ares."

I nodded. "Yes, sometimes, but the fun times are always clouded over by the awful times."

Achilles smiled. "You'll have good times with him again. He's a lot of fun to be around when he's not trying to win wars or conquer the human world."

We sat in comfortable silence for a few minutes and then Achilles asked, "Has Ares told you where each of the main races come from?"

I shook my head.

Achilles twirled a blade of grass between his fingers as he spoke. "We are children of this world, though from different parts. For instance, the werewolves are Children of the Moon, which is why your power to change comes from the moon. Humans are Children of the Sun, though their species has a strange desire to forget their histories instead of remembering, and I'm sure none of them understand that. We, Sidhe, are Children of the Stars."

He paused, and I asked, "What about vampires?"

He tore the blade of grass in his hand into two and whispered, "Vampires are Children of the Darkness, which is why the sun harms them and they are so powerful at night."

"So, I'm half star and half moon?"

Achilles nodded. "Yes."

"Which is why I'm so powerful?"

"Which is why you have the potential to become extremely powerful. You are powerful, Artemis, but you are not able to harness your power like Hera or Maurice, who are thousands of years older than you. Though, with practice and time you will become more powerful than they."

"Which is why they want me dead?"

Achilles didn't respond, but I knew the answer. Now, it made more sense. With the combined power of two dominant races I had the ability to surpass any being who was a purebred of any one race.

We walked back to the castle and then out to the balcony. I asked, "Can I see my mother?"

Achilles smiled. "Of course, but she lives in the Light Court, so we'll have to wait..."

Hera stood and smoothed her dress. "Nonsense. We can be there in an instant."

Achilles rubbed his temples with his fingers. "Mother, please."

Hera smiled. "You have no need to worry now, dear. Achilles has seen fit to save you from any desire I might have had about killing you."

Zeus waved at me. "Goodbye, dear. It was nice to meet you."

Achilles walked to Zeus and quickly spoke in his ear before hurrying over and grabbing my hand. Hera grabbed each of our free hands and whispered, "This might make you a little queasy," and then we were in a black spinning vortex. At least, that's what it felt like to me. When everything stopped spinning, I dropped to the ground and tried my best not to throw up.

Achilles whispered, "You'll be alright in a moment."

"Guards! Take Achilles and Artemis to their chambers. Someone else go find Athena and ask her to report to the Prince's chambers."

I looked up and stared at the men standing in the hallway. Each of them was a different color and each had various patterns and designs on their bodies. Achilles helped me stand and then an attractive, white-skinned man with exquisite black scrolling designs stepped forward. "Greetings, Artemis. I'm Erebus."

Erebus, God of Darkness and Shadow. I was actually meeting *the* Erebus. How cool was that?

"It's an honor to meet you, Erebus," I said sincerely and as normally as I could when I secretly wanted to jump up and down as giddy as I was at meeting "gods".

Achilles took my hand in his. "Take us to our chambers."

Erebus frowned at Achilles, but he shook his head and turned around. "This way, please."

Why were you so mean to him?

Don't let Erebus deceive you. He's extremely powerful and very conceited.

It seems as though vanity runs through most Sidhe's veins.

Achilles laughed and squeezed my hand. "You're right about that."

We walked through several stone hallways much like the ones in Zeus' castle before finally coming to a bedroom. Erebus stood on the outside of the bedroom and smiled. "Here it is."

I smiled back at him and walked inside. The room was decorated in various shades of blue and was as large as Darren's house had been. Achilles shut the door and then walked quickly to the dresser. He opened the drawers and pointed inside. "These are all yours."

I stepped forward and looked down into the drawers and at the various folded dresses and corsets. I pulled out a dress that matched my eyes and held it up in front of me in the mirror. "It's perfect."

Achilles whispered, "You're perfect."

I turned and looked up at him, furrowing my brow. He ran his thumb down my cheek and bent down, his lips a breadth away from mine when someone knocked on the bedroom door. He stepped back, and I walked quickly to the bathroom to put on the corset and dress. Luckily the corset was the kind you tightened and then simply zipped up. I smoothed the dress into place and adjusted the bodice a few times before I was happy with the placement. I smiled at my reflection in the mirror and touched a couple of the purple highlights. The dress definitely looked great with the highlights and my new skin designs. I stepped out of the bathroom and stared at the doorway where my older, blonder, more blue twin stood. At least we could have passed for twins in the human world, if she hadn't been blue, but with her in the same room as me I could feel the power she possessed and the difference in age. She stared to walk towards me, and I felt incredibly nervous.

"Hello, daughter," she said softly.

I swallowed and tried to fight the tears in my eyes. "Hello, mother."

Are you going to hug her?

I don't know. Should I hug her? Do you even think she wants to hug me?

Before I could decide, she rushed forward and hugged me against her, crying. "Oh, I've been such a fool."

We held on to each other for a few more minutes, each of us crying softly. When we pulled back she looked from me to Achilles and then back again. "Why are you able to communicate mind-to-mind?"

Achilles actually began looking nervous, he stepped back a few feet and said, "Well, you see Hera was upset and was trying to kill Artemis so I bound her…"

Athena was known by the humans as being the Goddess of Wisdom, the one who was the best strategic planner. As her skin began glowing, and she turned on Achilles, I could see why a Goddess of Wisdom would frighten you and you might consider worshipping her. "You bound her! How could you do such a thing?"

"Hera was going to kill me," I said in defense of Achilles.

Athena stopped glowing and looked at me. "Do you understand what it means to be bound?"

I shook my head and Achilles said, "I haven't had time to explain it to her."

Hera took the opportunity to walk into the bedroom. "Aw, I see you've been reunited with your daughter."

Athena nodded. "Yes, but Achilles was just about to explain to Artemis what it means to be…"

I held up my hand and looked at Achilles. "How long until Ares is here?"

Athena and Hera both gasped. Athena asked, "What do you know of Ares? Has he hurt you?"

Hera's skin began glowing. "He better not show his mongrel face in my court."

I looked at Achilles frantically. "You said he was going to meet us here. You said—"

Athena interrupted me to yell at Achilles. "You let Ares near her?"

Achilles held up his hand. "You'd better sit down." Athena and Hera sat in a pair of chairs I hadn't seen before. Achilles sat down on the edge of the bed and sighed. "Where to begin?"

Athena spoke through clenched teeth, "How about start at the part where Ares was near my daughter."

"Artemis met Ares before I had a chance to find her."

Hera looked at me. "Well, explain."

I folded my arms over my chest, feeling angry at their reaction of Ares and defensive of him. "I am not just Artemis of the Werewolves or Artemis, Darren's daughter. I am Artemis Lupine, mate of Prince Ares of the Werewolves. I am Ares' *passt genau*."

Athena wailed and began crying. "No. No! It can't be true."

Hera stood and started towards me. Achilles stepped in her path and said, "You cannot kill her without killing me, too. We're bound, remember?"

I looked up at Achilles' back in shock. "What? What do you mean by that?"

Hera stomped back to her chair and tried to console Athena.

Achilles turned around and sighed. "I planned on telling you, but we haven't had time. When you're bound to someone if that person dies, then you die, too."

"So, if I die, you will die as well? Or if you die, then I die?"

He nodded.

"You're a fool! You should have let me die. I'm not worth your life!" I yelled. I wasn't ready to be responsible for someone else's life.

Athena sighed. "We should have killed her when we were supposed to. No, I should have never fallen for Darren."

I spun around and glared at her. "Ares is a good man. You have no reason to hate him like this. He has been great to me. Better than any of you have been!"

Athena stood up and glared back at me. "I will not allow my daughter to be mated with *him*."

My skin began glowing as I grew madder. "It's not your decision."

"The hell it isn't!"

"You lost the power to make decisions when you left me," I yelled at the top of my lungs.

She blinked at me a few times before stepping back and sighing. "I see the wolf is very present in you."

I gaped at her. "Just because I'm angry doesn't mean it's because of my wolf. You were just talking about how you should have killed me. What the hell is wrong with you people?"

Hera stood up and looked at me. "I will not allow you and Ares to bring another mixed blood into this world. Having two of you is bad enough. You will not be allowed to procreate."

My anger rose again and with it, my Sidhe powers. My wings popped out of my back, and my skin glowed brighter than usual. I started to levitate off of the ground and said, "I'd like to see you try and stop us."

Hera's body began glowing, and she began levitating as well. "One son is not worth a pair of mixed bloods breeding!"

I hadn't even felt him approaching, but then he was just there. A warm presence in the cold room. "Enough!" Ares yelled.

Hera spun around and glared at him. "You! Get the hell out of my Court!"

She started towards him, and I shot her in the back with a fireball. "Don't you dare touch my mate."

Achilles moved next to me and took my hand in his. "Artemis, please calm down. You do not need to fight."

Ares rushed forward and had Achilles in the air by his throat before I'd even blinked. "You had better do some quick explaining Achilles," Ares said through gritted teeth.

Achilles nodded, and Ares dropped him to the ground. Achilles rubbed his throat and whispered, "It was an emergency. Hera was the one attacking her in your meadow and she was sucking the life out of her. I only did it to save her."

Hera said, "I would have killed her if he hadn't done it. In fact, I'm still thinking about it."

Ares growled. "Unless you want a war with the werewolves, I suggest you wipe that idea from your mind."

"Ares," I whispered.

Ares turned to me and for the first time really looked at me. He walked forward and grabbed a strand of my purple hair, looked at my wings behind me and then ran a fingertip along one of my new vines. "I wouldn't have thought it was possible, but you're even more beautiful now."

I released my Sidhe powers and put my wings away and hugged him. He hugged me tightly and kissed my lips. "I'm sorry, Ares," I said softly.

He stroked my hair and shushed me. "None of this is your fault, and we'll deal with the predicament Achilles has put us into later."

Athena hissed, "Step away from my daughter."

Ares and I turned to face her, and I said, "You don't get to pick and choose when I'm your daughter. Either you want me dead or you don't. You can't keep changing sides."

Hera sighed. "We should have killed Ares when we had that slut abort their baby."

Ares growled and his eyes turned golden. I turned to Hera. "You killed one of his children?"

Ares turned away from everyone as he tried to calm himself. Hera sat down in the chair again. "He seduced and mated with one of the Sidhe women. Halfbreeds are not allowed, you and Ares are...*exceptions*, but we have strict rules for a reason. We made her abort the abomination before it had a chance to develop into," she gestured at Ares, "this."

Koda, who I hadn't noticed until then, rushed forward and began trying to console Ares. Ares shrugged him off and turned around. The pain he felt leaked through our bond and it became too much for me. I could feel how much pain he was in, and it summoned my rage.

I ran forward and attacked Hera. She was quick though and dodged my first punch and managed to get up out of the chair and to a more open area. I attacked her with all of the training I'd received for my fight with Natasha. I opened three cuts on Hera before she managed to land a hit on me. She stumbled backwards, and before I could move to attack her again, Ares was in front of me and holding me. Achilles rushed forward and stood in front of Hera.

"Artemis. Sunshine. Look at me," Ares yelled.

I pushed against him, trying to get to Hera. I wanted more of her blood. More blood from the one hurting my mate.

"Artemis, this is no longer a battle. You can't save the baby, its dead. The mother has moved on and is happily mated to a new man. I've moved on and am happily mated to you. Please. Stop."

I stopped moving and looked up at him with tears in my eyes. "They killed your baby. They separated you from your mate."

He nodded. "Yes."

Tears leaked down my face. "They want to do it again."

"I know."

I growled, the sound rumbling my chest. "I won't let them."

Ares kissed my cheek. "I know."

His tenderness stole my rage, and I sagged against him, letting him hold me up against his body. He kissed my forehead and rubbed my back slowly as tears leaked down my face from the emotions we were sharing.

Ares and I regained our composure and turned back to Hera and Athena. I whispered, "You do not get to decide who we mate with. You do not get to decide if we breed or not. If you try to separate us, we'll consider it an act of war against the werewolves. If we have children and you try to hurt them, we will consider it an assassination attempt and thus an act of war. Do I make myself clear?"

Hera glared at me a moment before saying, "You've learned a lot in a short time. I understand your views. I've heard your statements."

Athena stood up and smoothed her dress down. "We'll leave you alone now." She turned and left with Hera without a second glance back at me.

Ares rubbed my back and asked, "Want to stir up some gossip?"

I looked up at his smiling face. The change of subject so quick it made my head spin. "What?"

He tugged on my hand. "Come on. It's been a century since I've been here. Let's go walk around so you can see everything and people can have something new to gossip about."

I shook my head. "You always surprise me."

Ares laughed. "Oh, this is only the beginning, Sunshine."

Ares took my hand and lead me back through the castle hallways and then out a pair of large wooden doors. I'd expected a similar scene as the Dark Court, but the Light Court was different. Waterfalls, at least a hundred feet tall made a wall to the left. The waterfalls fell into a beautiful river that flowed through the center of the realm. Vines with beautiful flowers covered every building. The buildings seemed to be carved trees or trees grown into the shape of buildings.

Ares whispered, "A few of the Sidhe are gifted with nature abilities. They were able to charm the growing trees into the shapes of their buildings. The buildings, now being centuries old, are as sturdy as any rock fortress."

I sat down on a wooden bench and looked at Ares. "Who is your father?"

Ares turned and looked at me in shock. "What?"

I turned away from him and looked at the waterfall, suddenly nervous. "I know what you are."

"Oh." Ares sat down beside me and sighed loudly. "Who told you?"

"I figured it out by your name."

"I had planned on telling you later."

"Who is your father?" I asked again.

"Zeus."

I blinked at him and then laughed. "Of course! That's why you and Achilles look so much alike! Wow, I can't believe I didn't put two and two together sooner."

Ares picked my hand up gently and rubbed his thumb across my knuckles. "Are you mad at me?"

I closed my eyes as I enjoyed his simple touch. "Yes."

He bent and kissed my neck, nibbling lightly. "How about now?"

I growled softly. "Yes."

Ares laughed and stood up and started walking again. I caught up to him and linked hands. "Do you have any abilities?" I asked him as we continued through the town.

Ares sighed and looked up at the waterfall. "It was scandalous enough that Zeus bred with a werewolf female, but when his son showed no signs of power besides that of his wolf side, the Sidhe couldn't take it. I spent fifty years in the Dark and Light Courts only to be cast out after finding a mate who loved me even though I had no powers. I can't blame her for following the Queen's order. She would be terribly lonely in the human world and she would be especially sad to know that you were my true mate."

"How can I be your true mate if you already had a mate?"

"We broke our mate bond a long time ago. Many years before your parents even met, so technically I had no mate."

"Was she beautiful?" I asked as I looked around at the gorgeous Sidhe women walking around.

Ares stopped me and turned me to face him. "There are many

beautiful women in the world, Artemis, but none as beautiful and as wonderful as you."

"I have something I want to do, but I think you're not going to like it." I'd been thinking about it privately the past couple of days.

"What is that?" he asked as he pushed my hair behind my ear.

"Maurice wants to wipe out the humans. He wants them extinct. I can't let that happen. There has to be some way for us to save them, or as many of them as we can."

"He's not killing all of them. The humans are given a choice, be turned into a vampire or werewolf, be slaves, or be killed. The humans decide."

I frowned at him. "You do realize that most humans will simply choose death?"

Ares shrugged. "It's their choice."

"I can help them. If they see me and see that there are other races who aren't bloodthirsty vampires, more will choose to live."

Ares stared at me for a few moments before sighing. "Why do I get the feeling that you'll do this with or without me?"

I kissed his lips softly and whispered, "Because we're getting to know each other better. I have to try to save as many as I can. Humans should be allowed to be free, not just slaves."

Ares shrugged. "Alright. We'll go to the places left in Europe and try to save as many as we can."

I hugged him tightly and kissed his cheek. "I love you."

He laughed and hugged me back. "I love you, too. Now come on let's get back before Achilles has a brain hemorrhage from being separated from you."

I stopped him before he could take a step and whispered, "There's something I need to tell you."

Ares nodded. "Go on."

I let go of his hand and turned away from him, looking at the magnificent waterfalls. "I released Achilles' powers with just a touch. He said it means I'm his destined mate."

Ares was eerily silent. I turned around and found him glaring down at the ground. His hands were clenched into fists and I could hear his teeth grinding against each other. "When did this happen?"

"At your meadow, before you found us. I know you told me not to touch him, but I was just so mesmerized by his vines that I ran my fingertip along one and..."

"Have you kissed him? Or mated with him?" he asked as he continued to stare at the ground.

I rushed forward and picked Ares' fists up in my hands and looked up into his face where I saw not anger, but fear. "No. Of course not, Ares. You're my mate and I'd never cheat on you."

Ares teeth clenched again and he said, "He's also your mate. You're going to have the same impulses for him as you did for me. Will you fight it like you did me?"

I collapsed against Ares and sobbed once. "I don't know. I don't know what to do." I looked up at him and saw compassion now in his eyes. "What do you want me to do?"

Ares smiled and then shook his head laughing. "No, I'm not going to be evil. If you need to touch him, then go ahead, but until Achilles and I talk, I'd appreciate it if you didn't do anything with him beyond that."

I wrapped my arms around him and hugged him tight. "Okay. Ares, for what it's worth, I am sorry."

Ares wrapped his arms around me in a tight hug. "It's worth a lot to me. Thank you."

We walked back in silence, enjoying the peace for once and being able to be in each other's presence. We walked into Achilles' room to find Hera, Achilles, and Koda inside arguing vehemently.

"What's this about?" Ares asked.

Achilles glared at Ares. "You agreed to help her? How could you agree to a suicide mission? The humans are as likely to kill her as they are to listen to her!"

"I'll be beside her to protect her. No human will harm her with me there," Ares said through gritted teeth.

Achilles threw his hands up into the air.

"Achilles, you have to understand why I want to…"

The wall beside Ares and I exploded. Ares spun around and dropped to the ground, his body covering mine from the debris. Ares jumped back up and I gaped at the wolves growling at us. Ares growled. "Stupid vampires."

Hera yelled, "Guards!" but there was no need because a battle was already under way in the hallways. Ares ran forward and grabbed one of the wolves by its neck, quickly snapping the spine and killing it. The body reverted to the vampires' true form, with their scary face and six inch dagger fingers.

Ares turned to Hera. "These are not werewolves. They're vampires taking wolf form."

Hera nodded. "I witnessed your truth."

Ares smiled. "I'll assist in your defense."

Hera sighed dramatically. "Very well."

Ares kissed my cheek and pushed me into Koda's arms. "Take care of her."

Achilles and Ares ran side by side out the hole in the wall and began fighting with vampires and vampires in wolf form.

CHAPTER EIGHT

Watching Achilles and Ares fight side by side was an incredible turn on. I fought to control my hormones, but it was difficult, especially since both were my destined mate.

Koda tossed me on to the bed and shook his body. "I really wish you wouldn't think about things like that when I'm touching you. I'd rather not get in trouble with Ares. Again."

I blushed and adjusted myself on the bed. "I'm sorry."

The fight was over relatively quickly, with the vampires stopping the wolf charade and fleeing. Ares came back into the room, and I ran forward to hug him. He kissed my cheek and set me back down on the ground. "You shouldn't worry so much, Artemis."

I sighed. "I know, but I can't help it."

Achilles stopped near me, and I reached out to lay my hand on his arm. Ares' jaw clenched, but he stayed still. Achilles smiled at me in thanks then moved across the room to give Ares and I space.

Hera asked, "Why would the vampires attack here?"

"To start a war between the Sidhe and werewolves of course." Ares frowned.

Achilles folded his arms across his chest. "Surely they knew that there are connections within our races. They have to know that I would contact you to discuss this."

Ares rolled his eyes. "Because we are *so* fond of each other."

Achilles smiled. "Well, neither of us would have lied about something as serious as this. I could always tell when you were lying."

"Ares!" yelled a familiar voice.

Ares pushed me to the side of him and we both stared in shock at a group of Sidhe guards holding Matt between them.

Ares started to growl and then caught himself. "Release my brother."

Erebus, one of the guards holding Matt, shook his head. "I'm sorry, Ares, but we can't do that. We found him holding the portal open. He's the one who let the vampires in and out."

Ares blinked a few times and then looked at Matt. "Is this true?"

Matt growled. "All they wanted was her! All you had to do was just give her to them!"

Ares took a step forward and asked, "Why would you betray me? What have I done worthy of your treachery?"

"Did you really think I would stand by and watch you in mated bliss while I was forced to be your guard?" Matt asked. "She's nothing more than a mistake. She should have been put down. *You* should have put her down when you found her. You know what she will be capable of! Her being your match has blinded you. Love has blinded you!"

Ares took another step forward, his fury building. "Each time those vampires and dhampirs found us. You told them where we were, didn't you?"

Matt bowed his head in defeat. "Yes." I could see he was holding something back. Even during his hate filled tirade he hadn't seemed sincerely angry. What could he be holding back from us? Why would he want me killed?

Tears sprang to my eyes and I walked closer to Matt. "Why

would you do this? I've never been anything other than loving to you. I trusted you with my life. I loved you as a brother."

Matt looked at me, and I could see the regret in his eyes. "I had to. They have something of mine that I cannot live without. Surely you would do the same if Ares' life were in danger."

He *had* been holding out. I shook my head. "I would not substitute the life of a friend for the life of Ares and Ares would not want me to. Would you have done the same if it were Koda you had to hand over?"

Matt's eyes flared gold and he snarled. "No."

"Then why me, Matt? Why were you willing to let me die for whoever they have?" I asked as sorrow filled my body. I had never felt so hurt, so betrayed by someone before.

"There was no other way. I had to give you to them. He promised he wouldn't hurt you. He just needed you in his possession." Tears spilled down his cheeks as he looked at me. "You must know that there is no way to defeat him. He will get you one way or another. The only hope is to join him."

Ares took a step towards him and asked, "Who are you working for?"

Matt tried to pull out of the guards holds, but they held him in place. "The one who will rule the world whether he uses Artemis or kills her," Matt answered when he realized he wasn't getting away.

Why was he switching between moods so quickly? "Ares, I think he's tied to someone."

Koda walked up to Matt and inhaled his brother's head. He snarled and then turned, sadness and anger twisting his face. "He's been bitten."

Ares rushed forward and grabbed Matt by the throat, choking him. "Who do you work for? Tell me his name!"

Matt whispered, "Maurice."

Ares released Matt and walked towards me. "You were right. He wants to rule the world and knows of the prophecy."

"What prophecy?" I asked.

Ares shook his head and started back towards Matt. "Another time. First, I have to deal with this…"

The guards shoved Matt down on to his knees and held him as he struggled against them. Ares started to reach out towards him, but Achilles walked forward and held out his sword to Ares. "Here, this is more efficient and not nearly as messy as ripping off his head."

Matt began to whine. "Please Ares. Don't kill me. I love you. I wouldn't have done this if there had been another way. Surely you see that there was no other way!"

Ares snarled. "There is *always* another way. You could have come to me. We could have figured this out together. Instead you betrayed us all."

"No, Ares. Please." Matt begged.

I knew what Matt had done was awful, but part of me wanted to forgive him. There had to be some other punishment.

I started to move forward, but Koda grabbed me and held me back. "Matt, I loved you. I would have died for you," I whispered as tears fell down my cheeks.

Matt met my eyes and whispered, "Now is your first lesson. Trust few and guard your heart. I'm sorry Artemis. I truly am."

Ares took Achilles' offered sword and stood next to Matt. "I loved you as my pack mate. I loved you as my brother. You betrayed your alpha. You betrayed your pack sister. You betrayed all werewolves by assisting the vampire who wants to rule the world. Your punishment is death." Ares raised the sword over Matt's neck, pain and anger twisting his handsome features.

Koda hugged me tightly against him. Our bodies shook against each other as we prepared for our friend, our loved one to die.

Ares whispered, "I am sorry, Matthew. I should have seen the signs. I failed as your alpha and as your brother. I am sorry it had to end like this. May you run forever in the forests of the afterlife."

Ares started to lower the sword, and I turned my head into

Koda's chest, clenching my eyes closed and knowing that would not block the pain I felt.

The instant Matt's life ended, I felt it like a blow to the chest. Koda and I collapsed to the floor, still clinging to each other. I wailed my sorrow and Koda shifted to his wolf form and howled his.

I buried my face in his fur as I cried and felt the dagger of loss and also the heat of anger at his betrayal of us. It hurt so much and I could do nothing to ease the pain.

Ares dropped to his knees beside us. I looked up and saw unshed tears in his eyes and knew he was hurt from Matt's death as well, but it was a necessary evil he had to have endured many times. Matt being his brother though must have hurt the most.

I wrapped one arm around him and the other I draped over Koda's back. Koda howled again and Ares' human throat enlarged to form a wolf's in order to howl. My throat changed suddenly and then I was howling, too. My pack howled our sorrow at the loss of their brother, our hearts bleeding from his death.

I WOKE THE NEXT MORNING, my throat, eyes, and head sore from the howling, sobbing, and sniveling. I'd never experienced someone's death as I had with Matt's. There was a small space within me that felt as if it would never heal. I couldn't even begin to imagine how Ares and Koda were feeling, especially since both were acting as though nothing had happened. Achilles and Ares were talking quietly together while Koda sat next to me in the bed, reading a magazine. I sat up and stretched and Koda whispered, "Morning. Would you like some water?"

I nodded, and he handed me a glass of water from the side table. Ares stopped talking with Achilles to come over and give me a quick kiss on the lips. "If you want, go take a shower and freshen up. We're discussing our next move."

After grabbing another dress and corset from the dresser, I walked to the bathroom and stared at my haggard reflection. Dark bags hung under my eyes, which were bloodshot and nasty looking. I quickly stripped out of my clothes and started the shower.

The warm water felt amazing against my skin and helped clear my head. I wasn't sure what Achilles and Ares were discussing, but there was only one clear course of action in my mind. We had to get in touch with Victor and then face Maurice together. I knew it would involve a battle, and we would probably die, but it was the only way to stop all of this. I couldn't live the rest of my life with him sending hordes of minions after me. He wanted me, dead or alive, but I only wanted him dead. So, either he was dead, or I was.

I finished my shower and bathroom necessities and after dressing, walked out to the sitting area where Achilles and Ares were. "Can you get a hold of Victor?"

Ares frowned at me. "We already have, he is going to meet us here in five days."

I smiled. "Good."

Achilles frowned at me, Ares' and his looks remarkably similar, making me a fool for not noticing the relation sooner. "What are you planning?" Ares asked me.

I sat down beside Ares and sipped on the water Koda had given me. "Nothing. So, between now and when Victor comes, are we going to work on my plan?"

Ares and Achilles looked at me and then at each other.

With only four days to save as many humans as possible, I felt rushed. How was I going to keep the humans safe? How many could I truly save?

It was far away from our current location, but I knew the first place I had to go. "I want to leave in twenty minutes. Please don't argue with me. Please just get ready and come with me," I said to the three men in the room. Ares and Achilles watched me with worried expressions, but said nothing. Finally, both men stood up and began preparing to leave.

I sat on the bed and felt my nerves growing. There were so many things happening that it felt as though my nerves had been flayed open. My hands shook softly as I thought about talking to a group of humans and trying to convince them to listen to me.

"It'll be alright, Darlin'," Koda said as he rubbed his hands up and down my arms. "I think what you're doing is great."

"Is anyone else trying to save humans?" I asked as I leaned back against him, letting his touch and smell calm me.

Koda continued to rub my arms as he talked. "Everyone is allowed humans as slaves. The humans report to the camps and say, 'I'm Koda's slave' and they're kept alive and fed until we claim them. Those of us with a lot more power and thus a lot more slaves decide on a brand and for those humans we want as slaves, we brand them. So, we say the humans are our slaves, but when everything is said and done we let them go free. There aren't many of us who will let them go free."

That was how I would keep them free. I'd convince the humans to use Ares' brand and say they were his slaves. It wasn't the best plan, but it was a start.

"We're ready," Ares said from beside me.

I turned and found him dressed in sweatpants and a t-shirt. It was strange to see sweatpants strained to the point of breaking around his leg muscles. Every boy at my high school had been practically swimming in their sweatpants.

"What?" Ares asked as he looked at his clothes.

I shook my head. "Nothing, just comparing you to boys at my school and finding I'm extremely lucky."

Ares held his hand out, and I took it, standing up from the bed and walking into the circle of his arms. "I love you, Artemis."

"I love you too, Ares." His body was radiating more heat than normal and it felt good to be held by him. I pulled out of his arms reluctantly and turned to smile at Achilles. "I guess it's harder for Sidhe men to wear shirts."

Achilles smiled. "I could wear a shirt, but I prefer not to destroy clothes when releasing my wings."

Slowly, I walked to him and wrapped my arms around him. His body was stiff at first, but after a moment he relaxed and hugged me back. "I'm not used to this connection yet, but I've learned from being with Ares that it's better to give in and touch you then deal with the itching skin and irritation."

Achilles kissed the top of my head and whispered, "Thank you."

I pulled out of his arms and turned to face all three men. "I know you probably don't agree with what I'm doing, or at least are worried about my safety, but I have to do this or I'll regret it for the rest of my life."

Ares smiled. "We understand, Artemis."

Achilles cleared his throat and said, "Hephaestus, I require your assistance."

Two seconds later someone knocked on the door and then a man with forearms the size of my waist walked into the room. "You summoned me, Prince?"

Achilles stepped forward. "Artemis and Ares need a brand for selecting their human slaves. I'd appreciate your assistance in this matter."

Hephaestus looked at Ares and smiled. "Hello, Ares."

Ares smiled. "Hello, Hephaestus. You're looking well."

Hephaestus walked closer to me and then dropped to one knee and bowed. "It's an honor to meet you, Princess Artemis."

"Please, just call me Artemis."

He stood up and looked from me to Ares. "You want something simple or something dramatic?" he asked Ares.

Ares smiled. "Simple, if possible, yet still able to be easily recognizable from any others."

Hephaestus nodded. "Be back in fifteen minutes."

He walked out of our room through the giant hole in our wall and disappeared down the hallway.

Ares tugged me towards the table and pointed at the fruits and cheeses. "You need to eat anyways, so you might as well do it while he is making our brand."

I gave in and sat down, piling my plate high with food and then consuming the entire thing before Hephaestus came back.

Hephaestus held a cloth-wrapped bundle in his hands and smiled at us. "You didn't give me much time to work on it, but I hope you like it." He placed the bundle on the table before me and slowly unrolled the cloth. I pushed aside my empty plate and watched eagerly for the reveal.

I don't know what I was expecting, but the short, one-foot brand with a crescent moon and starburst was not it. It was beautiful. I said as much, which earned me a big smile from Hephaestus.

I stroked the moon and starburst brand and Ares said, "The moon and star are very fitting for us. I couldn't have picked a better design. We need you to make twenty replicas as soon as possible please."

Hephaestus laughed. "I should have known. Give me ten minutes to make them."

After Hephaestus left again, I turned to Achilles. "Can he really make twenty of these in ten minutes?"

Achilles nodded. "His greatest feat was making Ares five hundred swords in one hour."

That made my mouth drop. Five hundred swords in one hour? How is that humanly…. well there is the answer. Humans could never do such a thing, which is why they used to worship the Sidhe.

Ares sat down in a large chair and waved me over. I came over and sat down on his lap, sighing happily as he wrapped his arms around me. These little moments of relaxation with him were my favorite. Ares put his lips against my ear and began whispering too low for anyone else to hear. "You look so beautiful and smell so good. No woman on this earth can compare to you." Ares kissed my cheek and then nuzzled behind my ear, making me shiver. "I love you and hate the moments when we're separated. If it were up to me, I'd take you to the most remote place on earth so that we could be completely alone all the time."

I giggled and shook my head. "As long as it's not anywhere too hot or too cold."

Ares laughed. "But if it's cold it gives me an excuse to cuddle with you more."

I turned and nuzzled his ear with my nose, inhaling his scent. "I do like the sound of that."

Hephaestus came back with a wooden box in his arms and smiled at us. "Here you go. Twenty brands."

Ares stood, putting me back on the seat before taking the box and bowing to him. "Thank you."

Hephaestus bowed and smiled at Ares. "Anything for an old friend. Of course, you'll let me know if any battles are coming up with need of my skills?"

Ares laughed. "You'll be the first one I contact."

Hephaestus said goodbye and left.

Ares picked up the brands and asked, "So, where to first?"

"Where I was raised," I answered quickly.

Ares picked my hand up and kissed the back of it. "Alright, let's go."

We started to walk towards the door when it was flung open and Hera stepped through. "Good, I caught you before you left."

Ares and I looked at each other and then at her. "How'd you know we were leaving?" I asked suspiciously.

Hera waved her hand dismissively. "I'm Queen for a reason, dear. Now, I may not agree fully with what you're doing, but I'll agree to help."

Achilles walked forward and asked, "Help how?"

She smiled sweetly at him. "You shouldn't be so suspicious of your own mother. Of course, I did train you to be weary of everyone so I suppose that's my fault." She stood still a moment, thinking and then waved her hand dismissively. "Anyways, I'll travel with you so that we can teleport and get to every place faster."

She had to have another motive, but being able to teleport would make things much easier. "Alright," I said.

She clapped her hands together. "Wonderful. Alright, everyone join hands."

After forming a circle, Hera put her hands on Achilles and me who were on either side of her and she whispered, "Don't throw up on me." The world turned black and then we started spinning out of control. I gripped Ares' hand hard as I fought the nausea. The world came back into focus, and we stood outside the bar in the town I'd been raised in.

I pulled my hands free of everyone and looked around at the town. All of the houses were dark and the only light came from the bar. Where was everyone? It was night time, but it wasn't late enough that everyone should be in bed.

I heard shouting and arguments from inside the bar and turned to Ares and the rest of our group. "Ares, you come with me, but everyone else, please go wait in the trees. I'll bring them out here."

Ares handed the box of brands to Koda, picked up my hand and together we walked to the bar door. I stopped in front of it and took a deep breath. It was now or never. I pushed open the door and found the entire town inside, crammed together as they argued. All eyes turned to me and everyone stopped talking.

Billy's mouth dropped open as he looked at the vines on my skin and the purple in my hair and my purple eyes.

I straightened my back and looked at each pair of eyes. "You all know about the killings going on around the world. I've come to save as many of you as I can."

Skankzilla, my old arch nemesis, put her hands on her hips and glared at me. "And how are *you* going to save us?"

I smiled at her and said, "Everyone outside. I'll prove to you that I'm capable of much more than you think I am." I turned and Ares and I walked out of the bar, letting them all follow us. I knew they would follow because, well, what else would they do? I stopped when I reached a big enough open area that they could all gather and see me without being too close. I trusted most of them, but that didn't mean that they wouldn't freak out and try to hurt me.

Ares released my hand and took a couple steps away from me to give him more room to maneuver if he needed to stop any of them from coming after me. I could feel Koda and Achilles behind us in the trees, waiting. Everyone finally gathered near me in the clearing, murmuring nervously to each other. I took a deep breath and said, "You're going to be given a couple options by those coming, but I'm here to give you another option. Freedom."

People looked at each other in shock and then Billy asked, "What do you mean?"

I looked at Ares and he nodded. I turned back to the group and said, "We've been kept in the dark for centuries about the existence of preternaturals. Now, the preternaturals are taking the world back, taking control. Millions of humans have already been killed as you've seen from the news reports. The mist is vampires and the wolves are werewolves."

The group began murmuring loudly and then Glen, the oldest man in our town, stepped forward. "How do we know you're telling the truth? And if you are, what do you want from us?"

"I'll prove to you that preternaturals exist and all I want is for you to trust me and do what I say." I turned to the trees and said, "Come out. I don't really think we need all of us, but it'll be better to show them that it's not just me who's different."

Koda, Achilles and Hera came forward, standing just behind me. I closed my eyes and focused on the flame within me that was my source of power. I opened my eyes and knew my body was glowing.

I dimmed the light so that they could see me as I pulled my wings from my back. The crowd gasped in shock and everyone took a step back. "Don't be afraid. I won't harm you."

"What are you?" Skankzilla asked.

"I'm half werewolf and half Sidhe, or fairy as you call us."

"Werewolf?" Billy asked. "You don't look like a wolf."

His tone was mocking, as if he expected me to be lying about it. He could see me glowing with wings out of my back, but he still doubted I could be a werewolf. Had I been that dense?

Yes. Yes I had.

Ares said, "Artemis is telling the truth. She and I are the only mixed bloods. The only half werewolf, half Sidhe." He pulled his shirt off and I glared at Skankzilla who all but trampled those in front of her to get a better look. Ares kept his sweatpants on and took a half-shift. Koda came to stand beside Ares and changed into his wolf form.

A woman in the back screamed and I released my powers, letting my wings retract and said, "Don't be frightened. Ares and Koda won't harm anyone. They're simply showing you the forms we can take. As you can see, werewolves do exist."

Ares reverted back to his human form and shook his body like a dog flinging water off.

"In a short amount of time, a group of preternaturals, the vampires and wolves, will come to this town. They will give you the options of death, becoming one of them or becoming slaves," I continued.

I took one of the brands from the box Koda was holding and set it on the ground in front of me. "If you don't want to be turned, if you want to stay free, use this brand and they'll know you are Prince Ares of the Werewolves' slaves."

"How does us being your slave make us free?" Glen asked.

"Because I won't keep you as slaves. When things have cooled off we will let you go and you'll all be free," Ares said as he took my hand.

I looked at Billy and said, "Please. You have to listen to me. I lived with you all thinking I was human like you. What I've seen since then has changed me, but I'm still your friend. Please, do what I'm asking."

Hera put her hands on us and Koda and Achilles put their hands on her. "Heed Artemis' advice, humans."

I'd wanted to say more, but Hera had probably been right to make us leave. Though I would have liked to talk to some of the people in town whom I knew would listen to reason.

The nausea vanished and I opened my eyes to find us in a large plaza filled with people. I stood up on top of a table and yelled to get everyone's attention. "Listen to me! Everyone!"

We traveled from place to place, only sparing an hour or so to nap once in a while. Once we went to the last places left in America, we returned to Europe.

I stood in the Coliseum and raised my hands and wings up. "They're coming and there is only one way to stay free." Achilles translated for me as I spoke. "Choose to be our slaves and we will grant you freedom once everything is settled. If you agree, just use this brand on your arm and you will be spared."

Each time I finished my speech Hera teleported us out. It was great for time, but it also made our point to the humans that we really were telling the truth. We weren't human and we had powers they thought were reserved for fairytales and movies.

I looked up at our new location and blinked in shock. Russia. Since fully gaining my Sidhe powers, the cold didn't bother me as much anymore so I ignored the cold and looked at the beautiful snow. I walked around and looked at the buildings in awe. It was night time and there weren't many humans out so I couldn't make my speech now. "Maybe we should wait until tomorrow?" I suggested.

Ares rubbed his thumb across my knuckles. "Tomorrow is our last day."

I leaned against him, exhausted from the traveling and lack of sleep. "I know."

Ares led us through the streets and to an older building. After talking with the security guard for a moment, he let us in. Ares took us the top floor where a large penthouse took up the entire floor. I looked at Ares and he smiled. "I have a few buildings around the world. This is one of mine."

"You own this?"

He nodded.

I walked around and looked at the elaborate decorations and the set up. It was gorgeous and everything looked expensive. Even the light fixtures seemed to be made out of gold and jewels. I walked to the master bedroom and stared at the bed that seemed to be three king sized mattresses put together. The bed took up the entire room and I jumped up on to it as soon as I entered. The comforter was filled with down feathers and the mattress was like lying on clouds.

Ares hopped up on the bed beside me and kissed my cheek. "We should get some food before we go to sleep."

I nodded and sighed happily. "I think this is the most comfortable bed I've ever laid on."

Koda laughed. "It better be! Ares spent a lot to have this bed made."

Hera cleared her throat to get our attention. "There's a café just down the street that stays open late."

Ares helped me climb out of the bed and we all walked back out of the building and to the café. We all sat in a booth and I looked around at the faces of those with me and couldn't help laughing.

"What's so funny?" Koda asked.

"Here we are in the human world, sitting in a café with the Queen of the Light Court of the Sidhe, the Prince of the Werewolves, the Prince of the Sidhe and, well, me and you. It's just funny to me that after so many years of being human now I'm sitting here with all of you and it feels like its no big deal."

Ares slipped his arm around my waist. "You're adjusting, which is good. If you weren't adjusting that would be bad. Though, I do see your point and it is somewhat funny."

My mood sobered and I asked, "Do you think anyone will listen to me?"

Achilles whispered, "It's their decision now, Artemis. Even if they don't believe you now, when the others come to capture them, they'll know you were telling the truth. You're doing the right thing in giving them a choice. Not many of the preternaturals would give the humans a choice."

We ate in silence and then returned to Ares' building to sleep. I only had one more day to travel, which meant only a few more places we could visit. Even though I knew Achilles was right, I felt as though I wasn't doing enough. As if there was something more that I could do. Something I could do to save *all* of humankind.

ARES WOKE me up by gently rubbing my back. "Mmm," I said half-consciously. He started to pull the blankets down, but I held on tight. "Cold," I protested.

Ares nipped my earlobe, successfully waking me up. "Come on. I have a surprise for you."

I wanted to groan and protest, but I was too curious to do either. After stretching and forcing myself up and out of the bed, I pulled on clothes and shuffled to the bathroom like a zombie, arms raised in front of me to avoid running into anything and feet shuffling across the carpet. I think I even moaned a little, which earned soft laughter from Ares' direction. I ignored him and hurriedly brushed my teeth and used the restroom before returning to him.

Ares hugged me against him and kissed my cheek. "I didn't know that you were also part zombie."

I snarled at him. "I am NOT a morning person." I looked towards the window and my mouth agape. "The sun isn't even out yet! It is way too early to be up."

Ares' fingers intertwined with mine, and he kissed my lips gently. "Come on. You'll forget all about the time when you see what I have planned."

I doubted him, but obligingly followed. Besides, any time I got to spend alone with Ares was worth the loss of sleep. We walked silently out of the bedroom, past Koda, Achilles and Hera, who were all sleeping peacefully, and out into the hallway. Ares pushed open a door that had a sign with some type of warning, but I couldn't read Russian to decipher it's meaning.

"Ares, where are we going?"

He smiled his full, true smile I cherished so much and said, "It's a surprise."

I hated surprises, but for him and for that smile, I'd endure. We walked up a set of stairs and then Ares pushed open a door and we stepped out onto the roof of the building. The view was spectacular, even at night. I walked around the roof, but avoided getting too close to the edge. Even though I had wings now, I couldn't stand the thought of leaning out over the edge of the building.

Ares cleared his throat and I turned to find a blanket set on the snow covered roof with a picnic basket and wine. Ares had also set up two candles beside the blanket. I walked over to him and snapped my fingers, a small flame flickering to life above my finger, and lit the candles. I sat on the blanket beside Ares as he pulled out bread and cheese from the basket. He ripped a piece of the bread off and handed it to me. "It's come to my attention that we rarely have any alone time together. I intend to change that."

I took a bite of the warm bread and listened to him. He was right. We hardly ever got to enjoy time alone together. If he could arrange more dates like this, I was going to be a very happy woman.

"I'm sorry the beginning of your life with the preternaturals has been so difficult. I hope you know that I will do everything within my power to make up for this once the world has settled down."

I swallowed the bread and moved closer to him on the blanket, looking up into his blue eyes. "And how do you intend to make up for this?"

He smiled and my heart skipped a beat. "That is a need to know basis and you don't need to know. Yet."

I laughed and kissed his lips softly. "Tease."

The sun began to rise, and my breath caught in my throat as the lights changed colors in the sky and the buildings around us lit up. It was gorgeous.

Ares wrapped his arms around me and whispered, "I love you and every time I see the sun, I'll think of you, my Sunshine."

I relaxed against him and watched the sun rise, it was the best morning I'd had in a while. Ares and I ate the bread and cheese and then watched as the city's inhabitants began to rise.

"Ares?"

"Hm?"

"I have so many unanswered questions and it seems like I never have time to ask them. I don't want to ruin our date, but..."

Ares nodded. "You're right. Ask away."

I tried to think what to ask him first and my brain decided to draw blanks. I sat in the early morning light thinking for two full minutes until the first question popped into my head. "What's the prophecy you've talked about?"

Ares shifted until he was leaning back on his elbows and squinting at the sun. "Two hundred years ago an oracle made a prophecy which rocked the entire preternatural world. The oracle said, 'a mixed blood woman of great power will fight the evil which holds the world in darkness and right the balance of good and evil'. Many were confused since the current times weren't in darkness and so, we took it as an omen for the future. Most people forgot about the prophecy and decided the oracle was losing her touch and simply looking for attention. Now, it seems you may be the woman she was talking about."

"But the world isn't really unbalanced right now. I mean, I know the humans aren't ruling anymore, but that doesn't mean that the balance of good and evil is, well, unbalanced."

"Perhaps not right now, but if Maurice succeeds, he may tilt the balance."

Of course. "So, he wants me because he believes that after his plan is underway, I will be the only one capable of ending his tyranny?"

Ares wrapped his arms around me, growling softly. "I won't let him have you."

It was a very possessive gesture, but I scooted closer to him and allowed myself to relax in his hold. Strangely I enjoyed the possessiveness he showed. "I know. I trust you."

Ares rubbed his face against my hair and growled again. "Mine."

I leaned against him with all my weight, surprising him and forcing him onto his back. I straddled his body and pinned his arms down with my hands. "Mine." I nuzzled his neck and flicked my tongue along his pulse.

He smiled happily and pulled me down to squish me against his chest in a tight hug. "Yes. Forever."

I struggled out of his hold and then nipped his ear playfully before jumping away from him and squatting down. Ares sat up and smiled. I had to stop myself from shaking my butt since I didn't have a tail to wag and instead put my hands down in the snow of the rooftop and whined. Ares dashed towards me, and I tossed the snow I had in his face. He sputtered and wiped the snow off, but I was on the other side of the roof already, gathering up a snowball. He turned to me and I threw the ball, hitting him in the center of the chest. He looked down at the watery ball and watched as it slid down his stomach and to the ground.

He squatted down and began packing snow into a ball. "You asked for it now. You do realize this means war?"

I giggled and packed my own ball. "Bring it on, Your Highness."

His ball hit me in the stomach just as I threw mine and hit his shoulder. We both grabbed more ammunition and continued firing at each other. I packed my ball and aimed carefully, throwing it and watching with pure delight as it hit him on the head. The ball slid down his hair and plopped onto his shoulder.

I couldn't help it, I doubled over with laughter.

"You think that's funny?" Ares asked. I looked up at him, but couldn't stop laughing so I just nodded. His body blurred and I watched as he covered the distance of the roof to me in under one second. His body pressed up against mine as he smashed snow on the top of my head and squished it into my hair.

I gasped and pushed away from him, shaking my hair and trying to get the cold snow out. He laughed and returned to his side of the roof. I noticed he was inching towards the door and quickly threw the ball at him. At that moment, the door flung open, Achilles stepped out, and the snow ball hit him right in the face.

My hands covered my mouth as I fought not to laugh. The fight didn't last long as both Ares and I broke down and laughed hysterically. Achilles wiped the snow from his face and looked from me to Ares. "Now I understand what all the raucous was." He bent down and started making a large snow ball.

I shook my head and held up my hand. "No, Achilles, don't you even…" He tossed the large ball with deadly accuracy. It hit me in the chest and knocked me off my feet. I groaned as I sat up and glared at the laughing princes who seemed for the first time to have forgotten their differences as they shared a laugh at my expense. I made two balls and threw them at the two men, making them stop laughing and wipe at their faces.

Achilles looked at Ares. "Alliance?"

Ares smiled at Achilles. "Alliance."

Well, that couldn't be good. "Hey, no teaming up its not..." I screeched as I was forced to duck from the first few balls they tossed at me. I glared at the two men, but when I saw their smiling faces and saw them working together for the first time in who knew how many years, I couldn't get mad. So, I dodged as many of their balls as I could while throwing my own at them. We were all laughing and smiling until Hera walked out onto the roof with Koda and ruined our escapade by glaring at us. "It's time to eat and then you will speak to the last group of humans before we return."

"What a buzzkill she turned out to be," I muttered under my breath. Unfortunately, I'd forgotten that she had enhanced hearing just like everyone else with me. Koda snickered then tried to play it off as a cough, while Achilles and Ares worked to keep straight faces.

Hera rolled her eyes and huffed, "*Children*."

CHAPTER NINE

I was exhausted from all of our traveling. None of the humans had tried to attack me, though some had been frightened. I couldn't know how many I'd saved, if any, until after it was all done, but I felt good for trying. We returned to the Light Court and Achilles' chambers.

I lay in the bed between Achilles and Ares who had agreed to share the bed with me so that both could touch me while they slept. I stared up at the ceiling and wondered how we were going to work out something between the three of us. I knew I couldn't be with both Ares and Achilles, but my heart and the magic binding us didn't. Achilles suggested a fifty-fifty trade where I spent half the week with Ares and half the week with Achilles, but Ares refused to let me out of his sight, especially with our new knowledge that Maurice was after me.

Ares, Achilles, and Koda sat around a table inside Achilles' chambers discussing what to do next. I'd been sitting idly by, letting them debate with each other, but I couldn't hold back anymore.

"There's only one clear choice, but we need Victor in order to do it."

"What choice would that be?" Victor asked from the doorway.

I stood up and smiled at the handsome vampire. "Victor. It's nice to see you."

Victor was wearing all black and looking as sleek as ever. His all black eyes no longer bothered me, but made me realize exactly how powerful he was. He looked me up and down and smiled. "You're even more beautiful than you were when I first met you. Gaining your Sidhe powers has done wonders for you."

He walked forward and hugged me, ignoring Ares' growl. I stood on tiptoe and kissed his cheek. "You're such a sweet talker. I just hope you're willing to help us."

Victor and I stared at each other for ten full minutes of silence as I played out my plan in my head to him. Victor's vampiric ability, unlike any other of his kind, was to be able to hear people's thoughts. Victor listened intently and then arched one of his elegant black eyebrows. "Have you discussed this with Ares?"

I rolled my eyes. "Of course not. I wanted to discuss it with you first."

Victor laughed. "You're getting to know him better. That's good." He looked at Achilles and his eyebrow rose again. "You bound her?"

I groaned. "How can everybody tell that?"

Victor waved his hand in the air between Achilles and me. "Anyone with slight magical abilities can see the silver rope dangling between you two."

"I can't," I said with a pout.

Victor patted my hand. "You will. You're still very young. You have to remember, the rest of us have had hundreds of years to practice."

Ares cleared his throat. "Can we get back to the matter at hand?"

Victor laughed. "Yes, of course." He looked at me and sighed. "I fear Artemis is right. The only way to end the attacks on her and the craziness that is my father, is to fight him."

Ares jumped up and shook his head. "No! Absolutely not! I will not risk Artemis in a fight against Maurice and his flock."

"Excuse me," said an incredibly deep French accented voice.

Ares looked towards the doorway and then grabbed me in his arms while growling loudly and baring his teeth at the newcomer.

The man was obviously a vampire, sleek built yet omitting loads of evil. He should have had a sign above his head that read, "badass".

He smiled and spoke softly, "I did not mean to upset you, *Groll*."

Ares snarled. "State your intentions."

The man bowed. "I have come at Prince Victor's request."

Ares looked at Victor, his eyes narrowed. "You brought, *Fear*? You brought your father's number one assassin into the presence of my mate?"

Victor held up his hand, and Ares stopped his rant, setting me down on my feet. Victor pointed at the man Ares referred to as Fear. "One, he is not my father's assassin anymore. I blood bound him to me. Two, I brought him to assist me. Three, we will need his expertise if we are to fight my father's newest vampires. Four, I like him. He plays chess better than you and never turns me down when I ask for a match."

I raised my hand and everyone looked at me. I held up one finger. "One, why did you call him '*Groll*'?" I held up a second finger. "Two, why did you call him 'Fear'?"

Koda spoke from just behind me, having apparently moved forward when Ares growled, "He is referred to as 'Fear' because that's the last thing you feel before he kills you. You don't have a chance to look behind you or even to think someone might be behind you. All you know is that you feel fearful and then boom, you're dead."

Fear spoke then to me, "*Groll* literally means anger. Ares was the embodiment of *Groll* for centuries."

Ares had relaxed by then and linked his fingers with mine. "You will find that I no longer hold that title."

Fear laughed. "Oh, I think you do. Perhaps you are no longer *Groll* all the time as you once were, but he lives within you. Given the right circumstances, I believe *Groll* may resurrect himself. I believe when you fight to protect your mate you are not as calm as one should be."

Ares growled. "Careful, Fear."

The vampire bowed gracefully. "I meant no disrespect or threat."

"What's your real name?" I asked Fear.

He smiled and it made my heart beat faster in alarm. "You need not be frightened of me. I will not harm you. My name is Dmitri." He was suddenly in front of me and kissing the back of my hand. He inhaled loudly and smiled. "You smell good."

Ares growled. "Step back from my mate."

Dmitri winked at me and then was back by the door.

How did he move so fast? I couldn't even see a blurred trail of him. No wonder he was an assassin.

Victor, who had been standing idly by, now began speaking, "We need to go to my father and speak to him and if he won't listen to reason, attack him. He won't expect us to come there."

"He won't expect us to come there because it's a suicide mission!" Ares yelled as he started pacing around the room with his arms at his sides and his hands clenching and relaxing with each step.

Victor scoffed. "You have two of the most powerful vampires, the second in line of the Sidhe and Artemis at your side and you believe we cannot defeat an army of vampires and the King? You have no faith in us."

Ares rolled his eyes. "We have five, I will not count Artemis because I don't want her to fight. So, five of us against two hundred or more vampires, some of them three hundred years old, and you think we can win?"

Victor smiled with a gleam in his solid black eyes. "Yes."

Ares sighed. "I hate when you have that look. It means you have a plan that will involve me almost dying."

Victor groaned. "That was only once."

Ares said, "No, it was twice! The first time was when we battled the dragons. The second time was when we battled Genghis Khan."

Victor rubbed his temples. "The dragon incident was my fault, but you're the one who felt insulted by Genghis Khan. I didn't want to start a war with him."

Ares folded his arms over his chest. "You called his mother a whore."

Victor spread his arms out in emphasis. "She was! She took money from men in exchange for—"

"Dragons are real?" I asked loudly to sidetrack them.

Ares smiled. "They were real."

My mouth gaped. "You killed all the dragons?"

Victor said, "It wasn't our fault really. The dragons wouldn't stop attacking us and before we knew it, we'd kill all of them."

"What about their eggs?" I asked.

Ares and Victor looked at each other a moment before looking back at me. "What do you mean?" Ares asked.

I laughed. "You're kidding, right?" Both men just stared at me. "Dragons are born from eggs, like birds, right?" Both men nodded. "So, if you killed all of the living dragons that still leaves behind whatever eggs they had laid."

Victor laughed. "Well that explains the dragon sightings a few years ago."

Ares shook his head. "Why didn't we think about the eggs?"

Victor shrugged. "Perhaps because we were both trying not to bleed to death from the various wounds we had. It was a long, delirious trip back down that mountain."

Achilles raised his hand and everyone turned to him. "I could bring a few additional Sidhe with us."

Ares growled. "No."

"You would rather risk Artemis' life than have a few extra Sidhe around you?" Achilles asked angrily.

Ares' jaw clenched tightly for a few moments before he spoke. "I would rather not have to owe you any favors."

Achilles muttered under his breath and then said, "What if we agree that it's mutually beneficial for us to assist you and agree that you owe us nothing?"

Ares growled, and I ran my hand down his forearm. "It would help if we had some extra magic. Especially since fire is a big weakness for vampires."

Ares sighed and wrapped his arms around me. "I hate it when you're right."

I laughed. "No, you just hate it when you're wrong."

IT TOOK them two days to agree upon the Sidhe we would be bringing and then an additional day to agree on the plan. Each day of sitting made my irritation grow and with it, the need to kill something. It horrified me how easy it was for me to kill now. It was as if once you killed someone, the next ones were nothing since you'd already broken the barrier. I wanted to believe that things could be accomplished by simple discussions, but after living in this world for only a few weeks I realized that killing was the only way to solve anything with them.

My attraction to Achilles continued to grow and soon I found I needed his touch almost as much as I needed Ares'. Ares explained that my attraction and the need for touch were side effects from being bound to Achilles.

Every day we were in the Light Court, I practiced my magic. With Erebus' help I was able to summon fire as easily as twitching my finger. He also helped me learn how to fly and how to use my wings properly. Koda and Dmitri helped me with my fighting skills at other times. By the fourth day when we were preparing to depart, I felt as though I could take on the entire vampire army on my own.

Ares prepared a bag for me with some of the dresses and things from the dresser in Achilles' room. I sat on the bed behind him as he packed. "So, we're going to walk in the front door of the vampire estate and just ask to speak to Maurice?"

Ares stuffed a few pairs of socks into the duffel bag. "Yep."

"Are you scared?" I asked him.

He stopped packing and turned around to face me. "I'm only worried about you. Victor is right that Maurice will not stop hunting you. I won't let him have you."

I smiled. "I know that you'll protect me as best as you can. I'm not asking that. I'm asking what you feel as you prepare for a battle?"

Ares shrugged. "I've gone into thousands of battles. Two-thirds of those battles, I wasn't expected to win and I did. I guess it's like stage fright. After the first few times you get over the fear and just accept that you have to do it."

Ares and I were alone in the bedroom since everyone else was off preparing for the battle. I hopped down off the bed and ran my fingertip down his chest. "This could be our last night together," I whispered.

Ares tilted my chin up and looked in my eyes. "This will not be our last night together. I will not lose you." He kissed me with the same passion with which he spoke to me. It made my toes curl and my head spin. He picked me up and laid me down gently on the bed, as he began untying the dress and corset. He was being gentle when I knew he was holding himself back, the need to mate was driving us both crazy. With both hands I grabbed the collar of his shirt and ripped it in half, exposing his upper body. He had a truly splendid body. I ran my hands along his muscles and then kissed his upper chest. Ares moaned and then ripped my dress and corset in half, exposing me. It took me less than ten seconds to tear at his pants, but it was worth it. The first time I'd ever seen him naked I hadn't truly appreciated his glory. Now, I sat back and took in every inch of him, starting from the top of his head and ending at his knees.

"I love you, Ares," I whispered before I kissed his lips.

He pulled back from our kiss and smiled, giving me one of the most beautiful true smiles, and whispered, "I love you, too."

Ares and I walked hand-in-hand through the castle courtyard out to where everyone was gathered to step through the portal back into the human world. Various Sidhe watched us walk by, some with glares, while others had more curious expressions. Erebus, Eros, and Heracles, or as the Western States called him, Hercules, were the three Sidhe chosen to go with us.

Achilles kept his back to us as we walked up and instead of speaking to us, he simply opened the portal and stepped through, holding the door open for Erebus who was behind him. I could tell he was upset, but I couldn't figure out why.

Athena ran forward and hugged me tightly. "Stay safe, Daughter."

I kissed her cheek. "I am well protected, so do not worry."

She looked at Ares and sighed. "As much as I dislike this, I must admit that you are a different man with her. If she weren't so happy, I would press the issue." She stopped talking and looked at the ground before looking back up, a fierce expression on her face. "Keep her safe or you'll have to answer to me." She kissed my cheek and then walked away.

Everyone filed through the portal single file. Once inside, the portal closed and darkness surrounded us. Koda, Ares, and I growled softly and whined as we walked through the confined space. It still amazed me how a portal between dimensions felt like a stone staircase.

Achilles opened the other end of the portal and stepped out

into sun. Everyone hurried out. I basked in the light for a moment and then approached Achilles. "Hey."

Achilles turned away from me and pointed behind us, where a forest started. "This is the way to go."

He started to walk away, and I grabbed his arm. "Achilles."

He sighed. "Yes, Artemis."

I moved to stand in front of him. "Why are you refusing to look at me? You're acting like I did something wrong?"

Ares grabbed my other hand and started to pull me away. "It's alright. He just needs a few moments alone," he said softly.

I growled. "Dammit. Stop acting like a sulking teenage boy! Talk to me."

Ares released my hand, and Achilles looked down at me. "I'm trying not to be mad at you because I understand that you don't know how this bond works, but my emotions are on edge on the moment."

"Explain," I said softly.

He sighed and rubbed his temples. "Through the bond, it lets me feel what you are feeling. I can't read your thoughts, though we can communicate telepathically when you don't have a wall up. For some reason, you're blocking me out so you don't feel anything I feel, which is why you don't understand…" He stopped talking and looked up at the sun.

"Don't understand what?" I asked.

"I can feel your emotions, such as love, lust and…euphoria," he said through gritted teeth.

I blushed and stepped back from him with my eyes on the ground. "Oh." He'd felt my emotions while Ares and I mated. I hadn't even considered that. I hadn't even thought about Achilles at the time. "I'm sorry."

Victor cleared his throat. "We should keep moving."

Everyone started walking away, but I stayed still, wanting a moment alone with Achilles. Ares seemed to understand and followed Koda who was walking behind Victor.

I looked up at Achilles. "I'm sorry. I didn't know. You should have told me this before. I hate that you guys keep so much from me and then just let me stumble upon it like this. I really am sorry. I didn't mean to hurt you."

He smiled at me. "Thank you. All I wanted was a sincere apology." He pushed back a strand of my hair and whispered, "I love you, Artemis, which makes it incredibly difficult to stay mad at you."

I blinked at him. "You love me? Or do you mean you love me because of the bond thing?"

He shook his head and whispered, "I've loved you since you were born. Every summer I would sneak near your house to watch you grow up. Since the time you were sixteen, I could see how beautiful you were going to be. Now that I can see you since you've gained your Sidhe powers and can witness how great a woman you are, I love you even more."

I swallowed nervously. "Achilles—"

He put his fingertip to my mouth. "I know that you do not love me yet. I just hope that soon you will see that I love you as much as Ares does. Perhaps we can figure out a way for you to be happy with both of us. Whatever happens, it will not change the fact that for me, you're the only woman I want to be with. *Verus amor vincit omnia*. True love conquers all."

Before I could respond, he kissed me on the lips. The kiss started off gentle and then became more passionate. He caressed my back softly, and I lost myself in his touch. The barrier he'd been talking about in my head broke and images of him watching me as I grew up and then his current feelings bombarded me. He truly did love me and I knew he would do anything to keep me near him.

We broke apart and I gasped for air as I returned to my own thoughts. Achilles took my hand gently. "We should catch up with the others."

I realized his body and eyes were glowing and giggled. "Oops. Looks like I activated your powers again."

He sighed. "Yes, so it seems."

We started walking and Victor called from within the trees. "Could you turn off the light? You look like a damn Glowworm doll."

I giggled and then focused on my Sidhe powers and the connection I could now feel between Achilles and me. I poked him in the arm and said, "Off." His body returned to normal. I poke him again and said, "On," and he began glowing again.

Achilles smacked my hand as I reached towards him again. "That's enough. No more Glowworm jokes."

We caught up to the others, who had waited for us in a clearing, and I hurried to walk between Ares and Achilles.

Ares asked, "Aren't Glowworm's supposed to sing when you turn them on?"

I giggled. "No, they just play music."

Achilles snapped his fingers. "Darn. I forgot my flute."

Erebus said, "I just happen to have…"

Achilles sighed. "*Enough* with the Glowworm references."

We continued walking for three hours and then we came to the ocean. I frowned as I looked up and down the beach for a boat. "Um, how are we going to cross this?"

Dmitri's and Victor's bodies convulsed and shrunk as they changed shapes to two black bats. Vampires could turn into shadow, mist, wolves, *and* bats. I really needed a notebook to keep track of it all.

Erebus, Eros, Achilles, and Heracles let their wings out and I smiled. "Oh, I see." I was very glad that I'd put on a top with a low back as I let my wings out. I was glad I had practiced.

Ares and Koda stood in front of Erebus and Achilles, who picked them up, and then everyone was airborne. I flew after them and then followed the two black bats as they led the way to France. I trailed my hand in the ocean for a little bit and then flew up as high as I could, reaching for the moon before coming back down and joining the others. "I love flying," I said wistfully.

Erebus smiled and spoke in his incredibly deep voice, "The nighttime is the best for flying."

It only took us one hour to fly from Ireland to France, but I was tired by the time we arrived. We made camp in a wooded area which was a short trip from the vampires' nest.

I found an area with few rocks and laid down in the dirt. Ares appeared next to me, but in wolf form. He was as handsome in his wolf form as he was as a man. I ran my hands through his thick black fur and kissed the tip of his large nose. As far as I had seen, Ares was the only black werewolf. It made me wonder why. I'd also never seen another white werewolf like me. Was it because of our mixed genetics? Ares laid down in the dirt, and I scooted closer to him, letting his large wolf body circle around mine.

Koda approached us, also in wolf form and lay down facing Ares. He extended his paws so that they overlapped Ares'. Taking the hint, I laid my head on top of their front paws and let them arrange themselves comfortably.

The sun rose earlier than I would have liked the next morning. I started to stretch when I remembered the vampires. I bolted upright, knocking Ares' and Koda's heads to the sides as I searched for them.

Victor smiled at me, and I remembered he was a born vampire and the sun didn't harm him. "Your concern brings a smile to my face, *mon papillon*. Dmitri is safely buried so you need not worry for him," he said softly.

I exhaled and calmed my raging heart. "Sorry." I laid back down against Ares and he sighed, rearranging himself around me. I slept for a couple more hours and then my stomach grumbled incessantly.

Ares headed into the trees and came out a few moments later dressed in blue jeans and a t-shirt.

Koda was whining and kicking his hind leg as Ares walked back, but after a quick throat clearing from Ares, Koda was awake and groaning unhappily as he trotted towards the trees.

Ares wrapped his arms around me and asked, "So, what's for breakfast?"

Victor straightened his shirt and said, "I thought it would be nice if we took Artemis out."

I looked over at the black, white, and red Sidhe men, all with various vine and etched designs in their skin, sitting a few yards away. "Don't you think the designs on our skin might draw attention to us?"

The Sidhe men laughed and all stood up. Their bodies began to glow softly and then each of them had normal looking skin. They looked as though they belonged in Greece.

Achilles smiled. "We learned how to use glamour when we were going to be around the humans."

"Glamour?" I asked.

Erebus said, "It's a specific type of magic which alters our physical appearance."

"Oh. Well how do I do it?" I asked.

Achilles picked my hands up and whispered, "Close your eyes. Picture what you looked like before you came into your Sidhe powers, and pull at your powers."

I did as he said and when I opened my eyes, I couldn't believe that it had actually worked.

Victor stood and dusted his jeans. "Are we all ready?"

Koda came out of the woods in jeans and a t-shirt and nodded. "Yeah, let's go."

Victor led the way to a small café where we could sit outside in the warm sunlight. Ares ordered my food for me since I couldn't read the menu which was in French. It was nice having someone who could speak multiple languages so I didn't look like a dumb American traveler.

Our food came out quickly, and I ate every last bite. I hadn't realized how hungry I was, and I was thankful that Ares had ordered extra sides of eggs and bacon for me.

The men started talking in French, and I felt extremely left out.

Achilles smiled at me from across the table and then began talking to me telepathically. *They're discussing the best place to have the Sidhe wait. I will be going with you into the main door, but the other three will wait outside for our signal.*

What signal?

Oh you'll know it when you see it.

As the morning turned into afternoon, the men continued to plan and Achilles continued to translate for me. The plan was rather simple, but they were being very meticulous about the small details. We ordered lunch at the same café and sipped on wine until dinner time. I was feeling pretty lightheaded when dinner came, but my quick metabolism flushed out the alcohol the third time I used the restroom. Each time I went to the restroom, one of the men would accompany me, though each time it was a different man. After we finished our dinner, we walked back to the park and sat down in our camp spot.

As soon as the sun went down an arm shot out of the dirt in front of me, making me gasp and jump backwards.

Victor patted my arm and pulled me back down on the ground beside him. "It's just Dmitri, rising for the night."

Dmitri dug himself out of the ground and then shook like a dog to get the excess dirt off of him. Victor stood, and together they left to hunt for their meals.

I picked up a leaf and set it in the palm of my hand and then brought fire to my hand, burning the green leaf. I formed a ball of fire in one palm and then started tossing the ball back and forth in my hands.

Erebus watched me with a small smile of satisfaction on his face.

"Catch," I yelled as I tossed the purple ball at him. Erebus caught the ball of fire and it changed to a black ball of fire. He started playing with it before he tossed it to Achilles who changed it to a blue flame, played with it for a while and then tossed it back to me. As soon as I touched it, the flames turned purple.

"Why does the color change?" I asked.

Erebus said, "The flame changes to match our colors. So anytime you use fire or touch it, it will become purple while Achilles will always turn it blue. We aren't quite sure why it happens, but it does."

We occupied ourselves with that for the next thirty minutes while we waited for Victor and Dmitri. They returned and stood twenty yards away from us as they watched our game.

"Could you please put that out?" Dmitri asked.

Achilles tossed the ball up in the air. It went up and up and then disappeared completely.

Dmitri smiled. "Thank you."

Victor looked at Ares and smiled. "It's time."

Ares exhaled. "Alright. Let's go."

We ran for an hour through the city streets, just fast enough the humans wouldn't see us as we ran. As we approached the mansion, I could feel the evil that resided there—the hundreds of vampires and the king of evil himself, Maurice.

My heartbeat picked up and my palms began to sweat. What if we couldn't defeat him? What if Ares died? The thought of Ares dying ripped at my heart and brought tears to my eyes.

I couldn't let him die. I had to keep him safe.

Victor guided us through a back entrance and then we were at the front doors. The guards opened the doors and bowed as we walked by. Victor led the way through the giant mansion and into a large ballroom. Crystal chandeliers hung from the ceilings and made me feel as though we'd been taken back to another time period.

"Greetings," Maurice said. His voice sent shivers down my spine and would have made me tuck my tail between my legs if I were in wolf form.

Ares picked my hand up gently, and his reassurance gave me strength.

Victor walked forward and bowed. "Greetings, Father."

Maurice's gaze never left mine as we walked towards his throne. The throne seemed to be carved out of a single, giant piece of gold and glittered with gems. "I'm so happy that you came."

"Father, we have heard a rumor that the vampires and dhampirs that have been hounding Artemis may have been sent by you. Is this true?" Victor spoke in such a calm voice that I almost believed he was simply asking about a rumor.

Maurice began speaking, but I realized he was speaking to me. "I can give you anything in the world that you want. I could let you rule an entire nation if you wanted. Whatever you want, tell me and it'll be yours if you join me."

"I can't join you. I can't allow you to kill off the entire human race." I frowned.

Maurice stood up. "Join me, or those you love die!"

I looked at Ares and then at Achilles who were both smiling at me. It was then that I realized no matter how much I wanted to keep Ares and Achilles safe, they would have to fight beside me to accomplish our safety. I squeezed Ares' hand and looked back up at Maurice. "*Verus amor vincit omnia*. True love conquers all. No, I will not join you. I will not leave the ones I love. I will stand beside them and fight you, and die if I have to."

Maurice's face changed, and I saw his true face, his vampire face, and immediately my skin went cold. The King of Vampires in battle mode was something no human should witness. He was truly frightening.

The doors to the ballroom started to shake and Victor yelled, "Get ready!"

Achilles' body burst into bright color and he raised his hand straight up over his head, shooting a blue fireball through the ceiling.

That must be the signal.

Achilles smiled at me and then Erebus, Eros, and Heracles flew in through the ceiling. As soon as they landed, the fight began.

Hundreds of vampires poured in through the ballroom doors

and headed towards us. Ares body rippled as he took a half-shift and started attacking the vampires with Koda beside him in wolf form.

Achilles shot fireball after fireball at the vampires, catching some on fire and tearing holes through others.

Victor and Dmitri pulled out swords as they fought against their own kind.

Erebus, Eros, and Heracles fought in a small circle with their backs together.

I stood in the center of them all and smiled. It was my turn to fight. It was my turn to prove my worth.

Closing my eyes, I concentrated on the powers that resided within me, and focused on the plants outside of the building and all of the living things nearby to draw on their power. I summoned a portion of my energy, turned my hands into paws with extended claws and opened my eyes. My body was glowing brighter than anyone else's, making the vampires shield their eyes. I screamed my battle cry and leaped into the battle. Bodies fell before my wrath as my primal fighting instincts took over.

I thought we were winning, but as soon as we killed a portion of the vampires in the room, more would come in to replace them. I started moving further away from my group when I saw him…my dad.

Darren stood beside Maurice and was looking out over the battle. His eyes stopped on me and he growled, his lip pulling up in a snarl. He moved away from Maurice and towards me.

I tried to head back towards Achilles and Ares, but the vampires had clustered together to keep us separated. I couldn't fight Darren. I couldn't win against him.

"Ares!" I yelled frantically as Darren came closer to me.

Ares stopped his fighting and turned towards me, his eyes widening when he saw Darren. Ares started to make his way, but he was too far and there were too many vampires blocking him. I turned around in search of Achilles, but I couldn't see him over the vampires standing in front of me. I clawed and slashed and burned the vampires, but no matter how many I killed I couldn't get closer to Ares or farther from Darren.

Suddenly Darren's hand grabbed me by the hair and jerked me backwards. I yelled in surprise and he put his hand around my throat. "I should have done this eighteen years ago."

I struggled against him. "Please, Dad. Please."

Darren smiled. "Did you actually think I loved you? Did you think I could love a halfbreed? You were nothing more than a mistake. I wanted to mate with your mother, but I didn't want you. I never wanted you."

His words hurt worse than anything I could have imagined. "Then why did you raise me? Why keep me alive?" I asked as tears leaked down my face.

"I was training you for Maurice, but then you had to go and betray me by leaving with Ares."

"I didn't betray you. He's my destined mate. Please dad. Don't do this."

Darren laughed. "You're pathetic." His hand tightened around my throat and my air cut off. I gasped for air and clawed at Darren, but no matter how many gashes I opened, his grip didn't loosen. Spots crowded my vision as I began to go unconscious. Ares yelled, and then I was on the floor, gasping for air. I turned around and watched as Darren and Ares fought. I'd never thought of Darren as terrifying, but as I watched him fight Ares, he was one of the most terrifying beings on the planet.

Darren changed into his wolf form and jumped a few yards away for a chance to recover. Ares changed forms as well and charged after Darren. I wanted to keep watching, to help if I could, but the vampires surrounding me had started moving closer. Achilles yelled in pain at the same instant that Ares did.

Maurice yelled, "Join me, Artemis, and this can all end!"

White hot anger flowed through my veins. Death. I wanted all of these vampires dead. Permanently dead. I wanted my loved ones free. I wanted to be free. I closed my eyes and prayed to whoever or whatever might be listening to help me. I had to save them. Warm wind surrounded me in a mini tornado and then power filled me. I'd never felt so much power before and it made me dizzy. I stood up and whispered, "Kill the vampires." I felt as though my skin was going to burst and then all of the power left me in a giant explosion. I screamed as the rush of power left me and fell to the ground on my hands and knees.

The room was eerily silent as I opened my eyes and stood up. I soon realized why. Every vampire, except Maurice, Dmitri and Victor were gone. Ash sifted through the air, but no bodies remained.

Maurice yelled, "Now!"

I looked for Ares, but couldn't see him. I tried to stand, but strong hands grabbed me.

Ares and Achilles screamed, "No!" in unison and then I was traveling through a black spinning vortex I recognized too well. The spinning stopped and my nausea quickly vanished. I gaped at the house Darren had raised me in.

I spun around and glared at Hera. "What are you doing?"

Her body glowed and she never looked so much like a goddess as she did then. She placed her hands on each side of my head and whispered, "What is necessary for my son's survival." She started speaking in another language and then pain filled every cell of my body.

I started to scream, but horror froze my limbs as I realized what she was doing. She was stealing my memories. The fight with Maurice. The last night that Ares and I made love. Achilles telling me he loved me. The training with the Sidhe. Matt's death. Victor. Matt. Koda. Achilles. Ares. I screamed and fought against her, but she was too strong, and I was too weak.

Every memory that I cherished was pulled from me and increased the hole I felt widening inside of my heart. People's faces whom I loved began to disappear. I couldn't remember my mother.

I couldn't remember what Koda or Achilles looked like. I couldn't remember Ares scent or his face.

"Ares!" I screamed as the memories of him disappeared in a flash of painful magic.

Hera screamed and then released me as I fainted.

CHAPTER TEN

The woman standing before me was stunning. She was glowing as though an internal light was on. Part of me wanted to call it her powers, but I didn't understand what it meant.

She smiled down at me and held out her hand to help me stand up. "Are you alright, child?"

I rubbed my sore head and stood up on shaky legs. "I…I think so." I looked around at the place I was in and asked, "Where am I?"

She whispered, "You're safe and so is everyone else. That's all that matters for now."

"What do you mean? Who are you?"

She shook her head. "I'm sorry, but I cannot tell you that."

In a flash of light, she disappeared and I was alone. Had she been a goddess? Or perhaps a witch?

I rubbed my hands down my arms, realized I was naked, but decided it wasn't important at the moment, and turned to look at everything around me. I was in front of a house, but it didn't seem particularly special to me. A town was near, I could smell gasoline from vehicles, but I couldn't smell people. That seemed odd, but I didn't let it bother me at the moment.

I smelled trees nearby and that drew my attention. I stepped into the shelter of the trees and heard a wolf howl in the distance.

A wolf. Yes, I was part wolf. A...a werewolf. I could switch forms if I wanted to.

I closed my eyes and willed the wolf side of me to take over. My body changed and I ran deeper into the forest, calling out to any of my brothers or sisters that might be nearby. I felt lonely. So incredibly lonely that it hurt. Not just emotionally, but physically as well.

A pack of small wolves came from the shadows of the forest and surrounded me. These were obviously not werewolves like me, for one they were much smaller and didn't exude the same presence werewolves should, but I needed a pack to run with. I couldn't stand this loneliness anymore. I wouldn't survive this loneliness.

I dropped my head submissively and whined, asking to join their pack. The alpha, a grey wolf with a large scar down his throat, walked forward and growled at me. I dropped to the ground, and he moved forward to sniff my stomach. The rest of the pack came forward and I was recognized as a friend. The pack ran and I ran with it, now a member of it.

That was strange, too. Why would the pack accept me so quickly? So many strange things without answers. So many questions. So many unknowns.

There was something important I was supposed to be doing, but I couldn't remember what. I felt something missing inside me. Two big things. Yes, there were two things missing inside of me, as though pieces of my heart were gone, but I couldn't remember what to do to make me whole again. I didn't even remember what had happened to cause the emptiness.

I shook my head, cleared the human thoughts, and let the animal within me take over. I barked and ran after the others, happy in the moment of the chase as we raced after a herd of deer.

HEALED BY THE FIRE

ARTEMIS LUPINE SERIES, BOOK THREE

USA TODAY BESTSELLING AUTHOR

CATHERINE BANKS

HEALED BY THE FIRE

BOOK THREE

ARTEMIS LUPINE

Healed by the Fire by Catherine Banks.

Cover design by Covers by Juan.

Logo by Avery Banks.

Published by Turbo Kitten Industries.

www.CatherineBanks.com

Turbo Kitten Industries

PO Box 5012, Galt, CA 95632

ACKNOWLEDGMENTS

Mom and Dad, thank you for your endless support. You mean the world to me and your support means even more!

Lea, thank you for your PA-ing help and beta assistance on this series. You are a wonderful person and a great friend.

CHAPTER 1
CHANDRA

The sun was just cresting the mountains as I walked down the concrete sidewalk towards Preternatural Potions, the best magic shop within one hundred miles of the coven where I lived. I admired the buildings around me that still looked freshly painted even after thirty years, and I wondered which spell was used to protect the paint from dirt and sun bleaching.

I didn't remember what the human world looked like before the uprising, but from the pictures I'd seen I agreed with Selene that the preternaturally run world was definitely better looking. The leaders, however, were not better for the world. Now we not only had monarchs heading each of the races, but we also had a dictator who was worse than any human politician could have been.

A tall, light-skinned, red-haired dhampir stepped out of the store in front of me. I forced myself to lower my eyes respectfully and move out of his way instead of reacting as I desired. If only I remembered who I was, what my name was at the very least, it would help me understand more about my reactions.

"Good morning, miss," the dhampir said kindly.

"Morning, sir," I replied as I continued past him.

I snuck a glance back, but thankfully he was still rooted in the spot, following me only with his eyes. Only a few more blocks and then I'd be safely at my destination.

The sun rose and the true beauty of the town was revealed. Every vampire noble was given executive rights to decide what their territories would look like, except for specific restrictions that the Vampire King, the dictator of the world, gave. The buildings were constructed from wood and painted in what looked like a light blue color at night, but when the morning light hit the buildings it revealed its gorgeous bicolor. The paint was actually a dual tone of blue and purple, which changed continuously depending upon the way you looked at it.

"Owner?" asked a short, burly goblin at the crosswalk in front of me.

The goblins had been in the deserts of the Middle East and Northern Africa during the human reign. I wasn't sure if their resilience had come from living in the deserts for thousands of years or if their resilience had allowed them to adapt to living in the deserts, but the fact remained that they were a preserving and strong race which could adapt to any climate quickly. Once the preternaturals had taken over, the goblins spread out from the deserts to the more temperate climates around the world, mainly living in the Northern Hemisphere.

"Selene, leader of the Western Coven of Witches," I answered automatically.

The goblin, an enforcer for the vampires, nodded and waved me across the street.

How nice of you to let me pass. I continued on my way. Little did the goblin know that I could toast him out of his boots faster than he could yell for his mother. I was glad that he hadn't asked to see my brand since the one I had tattooed on the back of my neck wasn't the witch's. I actually didn't know whose it was.

I finally arrived at the store and pushed the door open. The scent of jasmine flooded my nose and the sounds of a rainforest inundated my ears. For a moment, I was teleported to a tropical forest where animals much different than the ones I was familiar with ruled and where humanity hadn't been able to overwhelm. The door closed behind, me and the spell broke slightly, allowing me to regain my senses while still being able to relax. It was one of the best spells I had ever encountered, and it did its job of allowing shoppers to browse stress-free.

The large store seemed small due to the wall to wall, floor to ceiling shelves. Various sized glass vials, bags, boxes and cages which held everything from toad tongues to herbs to test rats lined the shelves. Each had elegantly written labels hanging from them with product descriptions and prices. In the center of the store was a large circular wooden table which had sale items as well as the most commonly purchased potions, charms, crystals and other magical artifacts. I knew this was only a sampling of what Preternatural Potions offered and you only had to ask the clerk to run to the back for other items.

I looked towards the front counter, which was nothing more than a white elm trunk shaved into a rectangular shape. Not surprisingly, there was no one behind the counter. The clerk, Dionysus, had a drinking problem and was either drunk, crabby because he needed a drink, or passed out in the back of the store. I was actually pleased that he wasn't there to pester me. He was constantly toying with me and hiding ingredients that I required on a weekly basis so that I had to ask him, and ask him politely, for them.

One of the witches in my coven told me that he had interfered with something the Queen of the Sidhe had been planning for months because he had been intoxicated, so they sent him to operate the store. He hated every moment of it, especially since the vampires refused to let him decorate the interior in a more pleasing, non-sterile manner.

I walked to the first shelf and grabbed three vials of ingredients

I needed. I should have grabbed a basket from the stack sitting beside the door, but I moved on to the next shelf instead, grabbing another vial and cradling them all in my arms.

"Hello," said a voice like bottled sunshine.

I jumped in surprise and caught three of the four vials I'd had in my arms. I could have grabbed the fourth, but I was supposed to be playing human so I couldn't use my preternatural speed. I waited for the sound of shattering glass, but was greeted with only soft laughter.

I turned around and made my way past leg muscles straining against jeans, to an incredibly muscled stomach and torso to a smile that stole my breath and to eyes that made my knees wobble. To say that the man standing in front of me was handsome was like calling the ocean a puddle. His blue eyes sparkled like a clear summer's day. I dropped to my knees and bowed until my forehead touched the ground.

"I'm s-s-sorry, s-sir," I stuttered fearfully. "I didn't m-m-mean to l-look upon your f-face." I hated it when I stuttered, but it was a side effect from having been in wolf form for over ten years straight. Selene, the leader of the witch coven I lived with, had found me and helped recuperate me back into a human, or at least as much of one as I could be considering I was half Sidhe and half werewolf.

He sighed. "Broken. How can you be so broken?" My wolf snarled softly and as I feared he'd heard. "Did you just snarl?"

I swallowed. "N-n-no Sir." Words were still hard to say at times for me, especially when I was nervous.

He scoffed. "Stand up, Chandra. I'm not going to punish you. As if that would work anyways. Are you here to shop or browse?"

I stood up slowly and whispered, "Shop."

"How could this have happened? Doesn't even recognize me!" I kept still since he was obviously talking to himself and I had no clue what he was talking about.

My body trembled softly as I stood near him. He was the most dominant male wolf I'd ever met, and he was calling to every fiber of my wolf side. The urge to rub my face against his was almost overpowering for a moment as I fought with my animal urges. I knew he wouldn't be able to sense my wolf since Selene had given me a necklace with a charm which concealed my true genetics, one so powerful, no one except the most dominant of each race could break it, but I was worried. If he guessed for one second that I was a halfbreed, he would take me captive. I'd heard awful stories of halfbreeds seized from their home, their work, or even from the arms of their lover to be taken away and never seen or heard from again.

"Is this all or are there more items you need to shop for?" he asked, taking a step closer to me.

I stepped back from him and bumped into the shelves. "I have m-more."

"Very well. Finish shopping."

I waited until I heard and felt him walk away before looking up at the shelves again. I'd never *felt* somebody like I felt him. It was as if we were connected somehow. I shook my head and dismissed the ridiculous notion. I looked back up at the top shelf where Dionysus had placed my ingredient. I couldn't jump up and get it. I looked toward the register where the alpha watched me.

Why was one of the most powerful alphas working in a magic shop? Why did I feel so strongly towards him when I'd never met him before? How did he know my name?

"S-sir?"

He lifted a brow. "Yes?"

I pointed up. "I n-n-need that item. The usual clerk likes to t-toy with me by placing them out of reach. Could you perhaps... retrieve it for me?" The longer I talked with him, the less I stuttered and the surer of myself I felt.

He walked around the counter and towards me. I felt my heartbeat pick up as I watched his graceful movements, his feet light on the floor, barely making a sound as he stalked towards me. I forced myself to remain still as he walked up to me and stopped inches away. "Which item?" he asked softly. I inhaled the smell of him and closed my eyes as a memory of lying against him and inhaling his scent played across my closed eyelids. *A memory or a fantasy?* I wasn't sure.

I shook my body and cleared my throat before saying, "The bottle on the top shelf." I took two steps back to give him room and watched as he jumped up and grabbed the bottle easily.

He held the bottle out to me. "Anything else?"

You. No, you in wolf form, running with me in my wolf form. I bit my lip as I stopped the whine trying to escape. I'd been a lone wolf since Selene found me and being this close to a male wolf hurt. I wanted a pack mate. I wanted a wolf to run with me.

I bit my lip harder, drawing blood into my mouth, which helped clear my head. "I just have a few more things to pick up." I turned away from him and quickly grabbed the six other items I needed and set them on the counter in front of him.

He put the items in bags and set the bags on the counter. Since every preternatural group had slaves that contributed to the world, we no longer used currency. Basically, since everyone contributed, no one owed each other money. It was the vampire's ideal society, utopian socialism where they weren't the ones who had to contribute, only their slaves did.

I reached out for the bags, but instead of pushing them towards me, he carried them to the door and pushed the door open for me. Warm air blew into the store and his scent into my face. I inhaled and rememorized his scent. *Rememorized? When had I memorized it before?*

"Are you feeling alright?" he asked softly.

"Y-y-yes. Thank you." I took the bags from him, being extra careful not to touch him.

"Broken. I don't understand how she can be so *broken?*" he said angrily as he gripped his black hair.

I should have been afraid, but instead I turned around and demanded, "Why do you keep calling me *broken*?"

His face went completely blank, becoming the type of mask people wear when hiding their true emotions. "I did not mean to offend you."

I scoffed and rolled my eyes at him. "Right, because calling me *broken* shouldn't offend me. I know you're a bigwig in the werewolf community, but just because you're powerful doesn't mean you can go around calling people *broken*, especially when you have no idea what kind of crap they've been through!" I was yelling by the end of my tirade and my face was red with anger.

He smiled and bowed at the waist. "My apologies."

I thought I'd seen it all, but I never would have imagined that the Prince of the Werewolves would be bowing and apologizing to me. He straightened, and in doing so, spied the charm sitting at the base of my throat. Before I could react, he grabbed it and growled. I gasped as his eyes changed to golden wolf's eyes and a blanket of some invisible force surrounded my body. I'd felt power being used on me before, but it had never been so much and as strong as his. I couldn't move. I couldn't breathe. I was dying and he wasn't even touching me.

Spots began to cover my vision as he fought to break the spell Selene had placed on the charm, and his power continued to suffocate me. A spark of lightning burst from the charm to his hand, making him yell out in pain and drop the charm. His power disappeared, and I was able to breathe once again. I fell to the ground on my hands and knees, gasping and coughing for breath.

"Selene," he growled softly.

I looked up at him and could suddenly see the ghost outline of his wolf's face around his human face. Only werewolves could see the image, when a fellow wolf was close to changing. Against all warnings in my brain, I stood up, reached out, and touched the muzzle of the ghost wolf. "Black. You're a black wolf."

He spoke so softly I barely heard him, even with my enhanced werewolf hearing, "Yes."

I ran my hand along the ears of the ghost wolf and swore I saw him shiver. "I...I've had dreams about a black wolf, but I was told there was only one pure black wolf in existence."

His wolf side was close to taking over, and his words were short and clipped as though he was having trouble forming them, "Only one black wolf. Only me."

"Are there any white wolves?" I asked. I knew I shouldn't be asking him, but I had to know.

"Only one," he said. I looked up into his eyes and saw the smile I thought I'd heard in his voice. "Only you."

Before I could jump back, he grabbed my wrist. I gasped as he covered me in his power again. It felt like I was drowning in a sea of fire, making it impossible for me to breathe. The spell Selene had placed around me broke, the talisman around my neck shattered, and the world went black.

CHAPTER 2
CHANDRA

I woke up slowly and realized I was in my wolf form. I opened my eyes and found myself looking into another pair of amber wolf eyes. I scurried back away from him, and he whined softly. *It's alright. I won't harm you.*

My wolf whimpered and took control from me, running forward and rubbing our head against his chest. He licked my face gently and whined happily.

I regained control and pulled away. It had been years since I'd had problems with control of my wolf side. I wrestled with my wolf for one full minute until I finally regained control and changed to human form. I gasped from the quick changes and curled into a ball as the sharp tingling pains wore off.

His fur rippled like water and then he crouched before me as a man. "Are you alright?"

I backed away from him, covering my body as well as I could. "What did you do?" The desire to touch him was burning my fingertips. My lips burned with a memory of kissing his. "How do I know you?"

He held his hand out to me, and I backed away until my back

hit the wall. He dropped his hand and I could see the pain in his eyes.

"There is much to tell you. You and I are mates..."

I stared at him in utter disbelief, but my wolf side acknowledged him as our mate. How could he be my mate if I had never met him before? I shook my head. "No. You can't be my mate." I picked up my shredded pants and shirt and ran around him. He called after me, but I ignored his calls. I stumbled into my clothes as I ran out the door and then yelled as loud as I could, "Draco-blu!"

I heard the flapping of large wings and then the generated wind pressed down on me, flattening me to the ground. The alpha crouched down, walking slowly towards me, but I knew he wouldn't make it to me before Draco-Blu did.

Draco-Blu descended and I admired his beauty as he landed over me. He was the largest dragon I'd ever seen; the top of my head barely touched his underbelly. His build reminded me of a horse, four large, muscular legs which carried a sleek, but powerful body. Draco was the title given to the king of the dragons. Blu is the only blue dragon to be given the title in the history of the dragons. I asked him if there was a difference in power by their colors, but he simply answered that blue dragons were very rare. He was one of my friends and I had the special privilege of simply calling him Blu. His blue scales shimmered in the sun and the white talons resting on either side of me reflected my face.

"Oh, shit," said the alpha werewolf who had stopped advancing and now stood in front of Blu.

Blu roared, but the alpha held his ground. "Ares of the Werewolves! I challenge you..."

"Sorry, Draco, but I cannot accept. Chandra, we will see each other again. Soon," the alpha said before turning and disappearing around the corner of a nearby building.

Blu snorted a puff of smoke. "Well, that was interesting. Are you alright, Hatchling?"

I shuddered as I stood up. I grabbed onto his head and he lifted it up, setting me down just in front of his shoulders, at the base of his neck. "I don't know, Blu. I don't know what happened. I think I might know him from before. He…he knew I was part wolf. He said we were mates."

"You need to speak to Selene, and we need to visit the Council," he said. I swallowed nervously at the thought of visiting the dragon council. They were powerful and would know how to help me, but they scared me more than a horde of vampires overcome by bloodlust. I gripped Draco's scales, which were textured enough for me to hang onto yet not overly rough and painful after long rides.

He flapped his wings and zoomed up into the sky. I wished I could spread my wings and fly beside him instead of on his back, but if I did that and a vampire or a vampire ally saw me, they would try to capture me or just kill me. Mixed bloods were not welcome in the New Preternatural World.

"It's a good thing that I escorted you today and stayed just on the outskirts of the town while you shopped," said Blu as he glided across the winds.

I sighed sadly. "Yes, I suppose it is, although I do not like having to be protected to go out." I lifted my arms out to my sides, enjoying the feel of the wind on my body.

The concrete jungle that had once been the human world was gone, destroyed by the preternaturals to allow a more organic landscape to emerge.

We flew over various small towns and villages, children waving to Blu excitedly while the adults cowered in the doorways. Blu's massive shadow covered two buildings at once, scaring a coop full of chickens and a stable of horses at the same time.

"Are there any other errands you need to run or are we heading straight back to the coven?" he asked as he tilted sideways, making a large circle over a crystal blue lake below.

I looked longingly at the lake, wishing to go for a swim. I knew

I should head straight back to the coven to report to Selene, but I was shaky and needed to do something relaxing. "I guess we could stop for a short swim," I said finally.

Blu roared happily and dove straight down towards the lake, folding his wings in tight against his body. As he plummeted, I wrapped my arms around his neck so I wouldn't separate from him. The impact from slamming into the water almost dislodged me from Blu's back, but I managed to hang on. I fought the urge to gasp at the shock of the cold water surrounding me and released my hold, kicking my legs quickly to the surface. Blu spun around under the water, heading back towards me and shoved his nose under my feet, pushing me up and through the surface of the water. I flew up into the air thirty feet and then dove back down, barely making a splash as I reentered the water.

Blu swam in lazy circles, slicing through it with his tail. I splashed Blu's nose with a small wave of water, inviting play. Blu skimmed his tail across the water, sending a wave to cover me, which sent me back down below the surface.

Blu laughed hysterically, shooting fire from his nose in his delight. He was one of my best friends because he could go from being the fierce leader of the dragons to the silliest being on the planet and playing childish games with me.

We played until the sun stood in the center of the sky and both Blu and my stomachs growled loudly.

As we flew in the air towards the coven, I closed my eyes and enjoyed the warmth of the sun drying me. "Thank you," I whispered. He seemed to always know what I needed.

He hummed happily. "You are welcome, Hatchling. Now, let's get you home."

We flew the last ten miles in silence, enjoying the other's quiet, but pleasurable company and the moment of contentment. The coven came into view, and I admired my home.

The coven was a large fortress with thirty foot walls surrounding the one thousand acres property. The walls were really only there to keep out the local wildlife and for the perimeter spell, which alerted Selene to intruders. The main building was fifty feet high and had several hundred rooms, not including the kitchen and common areas. There were three smaller buildings, the larger of which was used for teaching the younger witches. The building to the left of that was the lab which was used for experimenting with new spells. The third building was a mystery to me. Selene had told me only that it was used for the witches' committee hearings. There was also a small stable area where we bred cows for Blu and the other dragons who visited to eat.

Two gardens took up three acres total on either side of the main building and a forest of twenty acres stood in the back corner of their property. The witches hardly ever used the forest, but I used it frequently.

Blu dropped down into the courtyard of the coven and roared a welcoming to the witches. Several witches were outside and they bowed respectfully to him. A teenage witch walked to the stable area to catch one of the cows for him. I slipped down his side and leg and smiled at the witches who were outside. I turned to Blu and bowed. "Thank you, Blu."

He flicked his forked tongue out across my cheek. "You are welcome, Hatchling. I will return with a summons once I've spoken to the Council. I will have Fira visit you in my absence."

Blu gulped down the cow the teenager brought out and then burped a stream of flame into the air happily.

He dropped his head down and I hugged his nose, laying a kiss on the tip of it. "Be safe and may the wind speed your flight."

He lifted one of his large front claws and brushed a scale off to land on the ground. "Take this. You may need the magic stored within it."

I picked up the scale and felt the power radiating from it. "This is a very precious gift. I will cherish it."

He rubbed his nose gently against my body once and then took to the sky. He roared a goodbye and then disappeared from my sight. I clutched the scale to my chest and raced to my room as the pain I'd been hiding intensified.

My heart hurt and the physical pain of the absence of the alpha was like a hot iron stabbing me in the stomach. I dashed inside the main building and up the three flights of stairs to my room in the west wing. Thankfully, I made it to my room unnoticed and unquestioned. I softly shut my bedroom door and sighed in relief.

"Who broke my spell?" Selene asked from behind me.

I growled and spun around, ready to attack. It took a moment for me to realize it was Selene and calm myself. "Sorry. Sorry," I apologized as I lowered my eyes and stepped back from her.

Selene was average height and build for a woman, but the incredible amount of power she possessed made her seem bigger and more intimidating. She had black hair that looked like it was streaked with blue in the sun and the deepest brown eyes I had ever seen.

She stood up from my bed where she had been sitting and placed her hand on my face. I closed my eyes as she closed hers and then she chanted magic words, which weaved a spell to replay the day's events in our heads for her to see.

Selene removed her hand and gasped as the last image of Blu diving into the lake finished. "No. No it cannot be true," she said in disbelief as she stepped back from me.

I fell onto my bed, tired from the changes and the magic which had been used against me. "What is it? Who is he to me? Is he really my mate?"

She shook her head, refusing to answer and then hurried from my room, closing the door behind her. The pain was intensifying so I closed my eyes and let myself sleep in an effort to try to heal myself.

~

"CHANDRA. Chandra, wake up! You're going to miss story time!" a young female yelled at me from beside the bed.

I opened one eye and looked at the seven-year-old girl standing with her hands on her hips beside me. She was small for her age, but what she lacked in height she made up for in attitude.

Once I had been rehabilitated, Selene decided that helping children find their powers would help calm the anger and despair that she insisted surrounded me. So, I taught the younger witches and the young girl in front of me, Juliana, was one of my favorite students.

I showered and dressed quickly so as not to keep the impatient child waiting too long. When done, Juliana grabbed my hand and dragged me down the stairs to one of the common rooms already filled with witches. This room was carpeted with soft blue shag ideal for lounging on. Many of the older witches smiled and bowed respectfully to me. I returned the salute and then sat down among the young children who crowded closer as I situated myself on the floor.

It'd been a long time since I'd come out of my room without my talisman on and many of the children ran their fingertips along the designs on my arms. I relaxed as their touch soothed the pack animal within me, but another part of me felt like a wire pulled taut. Somehow, I knew that this feeling wouldn't subside until I was near the werewolf prince again.

Selene stepped out in front of the room and the crowd instantly hushed their chatter. She sat in her chair with her head in her hands. "We will not be having story time tonight," she said softly. The children groaned and the adults looked at each other nervously. Selene began talking again and everyone silenced to hear her. "I am calling an emergency council of *all* fully realized witches to begin immediately. Jessica will be in charge of the teens and the children. Jessica, please take them to their rooms now. Everyone else please pick up a chair and form a semi-circle facing me."

I reassured the children and then grabbed a chair from the stack in the back. I started to set my chair beside one of the other witches, but Selene looked up at me and ordered, "Sit in the center, Chandra."

I swallowed the fear I felt and set my chair in the center. I waited until all of the other witches were seated before taking mine. I could feel the nervous energy around me and heard it in the shifting of chairs and the quickened breath of the witches.

"I have seen something which I need verified. I have seen something which may tell Chandra her true identity. The problem we are facing is Chandra herself."

I stared at Selene in shock. "Me? I'm a problem?"

Selene smiled. "Your powers are the problem. I think, as a group, we may be able to help you suppress your powers long enough to find your true self, but I am not certain."

"What about the dragons?" asked Angelina, one of the witches of whom I was most fond.

Every eye turned to me and I forced myself not to fidget. "Draco-Blu left earlier to speak to the dragon council and see if they would allow me an audience."

Selene tapped her chin with one long finger. "I'd like to hear all of your thoughts. My fear is that if we try and fail, we may permanently injure Chandra or ourselves. However, the dragons are a much older and much more powerful race and may be able to do it."

"Do you have her real name?" asked Silvia.

Selene avoided looking at me and simply nodded. "I have her first name."

I stared at her in utter disbelief. "You know my first name? My true first name?!" I asked, glaring at her.

She looked at me and licked her lips nervously. "Yes. I have not revealed it to you for fear of harming you. If you learned your true first name, but could not uncover the rest of your name on your own, it could destroy you."

"That's ridiculous!" I yelled, my hands forming fists.

"She's right," said the softest spoken witch in the coven, Mauve. "If you hear your first name and accept it as true, but cannot uncover the rest of it, the memories of your past could overwhelm you and cause you to go into a coma."

Every witch looked down at their hands in silence. I'd heard about the story of Mauve's sister, but hadn't believed it was true. Until now.

I looked at Selene. "What about the prince? Can't he help me?"

Selene sighed. "I do not know whether the prince is who he says he is or not and even if he is, I have no way of knowing if he is strong enough to assist you."

"So, either I have the prince and the coven help or the dragons?"

Selene shook her head. "The dragons will need the prince to help them as well. So, either the coven or the dragons will help you and the prince."

"Which prince?" asked Silvia.

"The werewolf one," I said quietly. "I forget his name."

Silvia opened her mouth and Selene placed a silencing spell on her before Silvia had uttered the first syllable. "No one is to reveal his name!" The room quaked with Selene's command and all of the gathered witches bowed in submission.

I stood up against her power and glared at her. "This is ridiculous! I want to know who I am and who he is! I've been alone for too long! I can't stand it anymore, Selene!"

"You won't have to," said a quiet male voice.

I'd never seen so many witches use the same spell so quickly. Before I'd even turned toward the voice, the speaker was off the ground and imprisoned in an invisible grip in the air. He was handsome, looked to be in his early twenties with black skin and white patterns down his arms. I could guess what he was instantly, but held my tongue until I knew for sure.

Selene walked towards the intruder slowly, her skin sparkling with magic. "Who are you and how did you get into my coven unnoticed?"

The intruder smiled. "I am a friend of those who have been looking for the woman you are protecting. I have come to offer her solace from the pain of loneliness that she has been enduring, until such a time as she can be reunited with her rightful pack."

Selene nodded and all of the witches released their spells and allowed the man to drop to the ground. He landed on his feet as though they'd dropped him one foot instead of twelve. "Come, we shall speak in my office," Selene said softly.

The man bowed his head respectfully and then walked slowly towards me. I inhaled, and my body quivered in excitement. He stopped in front of me, towering over me at more than six feet tall, and inhaled loudly. "What do they call you?" he asked.

I smiled up at him and inhaled again. "Chandra."

He looked into my eyes and asked, "Are you alright, Chandra?"

I kept eye contact, refusing to accept him as dominant over me. "I am better with your presence. What is your name?"

He dropped eye contact and recognized me as dominant. "My name is Theseus. I will return as soon as I am done speaking to your coven leader. Can you wait that long for a run?"

The scent of his wolf was stronger the longer he stood by me. I opened my mouth a little wider to catch more of his scent. "Yes, I will prepare myself mentally while you are speaking to Selene."

He smiled happily and followed Selene to her room. I dropped to my knees on the ground, smiling happily. A halfbreed wolf! I'd never thought I'd find another halfbreed wolf.

It was strange that I wasn't interested in him. Why wasn't I? He was attractive, yet I wasn't intrigued by him in any other way than for a pack mate and for our similar lineage.

Silvia dropped down next to me and looked in my eyes. "Are you alright, dear? Did he hurt you?"

I laughed and shook my head. "No." I looked up at all of the concerned faces of the witches around me. "You don't know?"

They all frowned in confusion. Silvia asked, "Don't know what?"

I smiled. Of course, they didn't know they couldn't smell him like I could. "He's a halfbreed wolf like me. He's the same mixture as me."

They all looked at me in shock as what I said absorbed and then they all started asking me questions at once. I raised my hand and silenced them. "I don't want to talk about it. I know what he is because I can smell it and feel it. If you want to know more, ask Selene." I stood up and hurried to my room before they could ask me any other questions.

I was finally going to run with another wolf! I brushed my hair until not a single knot could be found and then sat on the floor to meditate and calm my nerves. He wouldn't appreciate it if I bit his head off when I changed.

Just as I calmed myself enough to relax, someone knocked on my door. "Come in," I said softly.

Selene stepped into the room and closed the door behind her. "What he says is true," she stated simply, "He was sent here to be a companion for you until such a time as we can figure out who you really are. He is waiting out in the garden for you."

Standing up slowly, I watched Selene. She was hiding something. "What else did he say?"

She sighed. "He told me what he knew of your past and if what he says is true, you're in more danger than I originally thought. I hope Draco-Blu comes for you soon."

I followed her out of the room and out of the main building. "You are afraid. For me or the coven?" I asked.

She smiled at me. "Your ability to read me is a testament to the amount of time we have spent together. I am afraid for both. If you are who he says, the vampires will stop at nothing to get you before your true mate does. The vampires are powerful and I'd prefer they not view me as a threat."

"I will stay within our boundaries until Blu returns," I promised as Theseus came into sight.

Selene smiled. "Go on. Enjoy your run and your new friend."

I hugged her once and then changed forms before running to him. He was twice my size and a dark red color. *Are you ready for our run?* He asked through my mind.

I bobbed my muzzle up and down. *Yes, but we must stay within the boundaries of the coven.*

He sneezed. *As if you needed to tell me the dangers out there.*

Before I could ask what he meant, he took off at a full run. I yipped excitedly and chased after him. I pounced on top of him, knocking him to the ground. He rolled and jumped at me, but I dashed out of his reach and then dashed back to nip at his tail. He growled and snapped at me, but I was already ten feet away with my front half down on the ground and my bottom half up in the air. I wagged my tail happily. *You're pretty slow for a halfbreed.*

He lifted his lips in a wolf smile. *I haven't shown you my true speed yet. I've just been letting you enjoy yourself.*

Likewise.

His back paws dug into the ground as he prepared to charge me, and I sprang forward, darting right past him and nipping his flank before circling him and returning to my original spot. In truth, I had no idea how fast other werewolves or halfbreed wolves were since I'd never been around them, but I knew I was fast.

In a blink of an eye he dashed forward and nipped my flank. I spun around, but he was behind me again and nipped my tail. It was time not to hold back anymore. I followed his movements and then leapt up and over him when he tried to nip me again. He slid as he tried to stop and then I smacked into his side, slamming him to the ground and stood over him. *You're fast, but not fast enough.* I darted away and yipped happily. *Catch me if you can!*

For two hours, we ran and played in wolf form, stopping only to drink from a shallow stream which wound its way through the center of the coven's property. I watched the fish swimming through it, going with the flow of the current and wished for a free life to swim where I wanted.

After I had quelled the burning in my throat from our vigorous play I took off running again, but the beat of wings and the pressure of wind alerted me to the presence of a dragon.

"Run, Chandra!" yelled Fira, Blu's son.

I spun around just as Fira gripped Theseus in one of his front red claws. I changed forms in less than a second and shot Fira in the nose with my fire, stopping him just as he was preparing to toast Theseus. Fira dropped Theseus, and I ran forward to catch him, but he changed forms and released his wings just in time to soften his landing.

Fira roared at me. "Why did you do that?!"

"He is a friend, Fira, not an attacker. Besides, my fire does not hurt dragons so stop acting like I've harmed you."

Fira dropped to the ground and shook out his body. "No, your Sidhe fire does not harm us, but it is never pleasant to have unfamiliar fire touch your body."

"I had to stop you from killing him. Thank you for your protection and concern, but Theseus here is a friend."

Fira looked at Theseus a moment and then snorted. "A wolf-Sidhe halfbreed like you, Chandra. How interesting."

Theseus looked from me to the dragon and then back at me. "You know dragons?"

Fira dropped his head and allowed me to pet him. "Yes. I am friends with the dragons. Well, at least Draco-Blu and Fira here are my friends," I answered.

Theseus started towards me, but Fira growled.

"I do not trust him, Chandra," Theseus said.

I stopped petting Fira and looked at Theseus. "I do not care if you trust him or not. Fira is my friend and has been protecting me for the past several years. You will have to learn to accept the dragons or you will have to leave."

Theseus gaped at me. "You would send me away? You would live in solitude again?"

I shuddered and whispered, "I would not like it, but I love the dragons and I will not dishonor their protection of me just for companionship. Besides, you are only coming to me now while they have been protecting me for a decade. Who would you trust more?"

Fira yawned. "I need to return to the nest. Will you be alright for tonight?"

I nodded and placed a kiss on the tip of his nose. "Thank you, my friend."

Fira growled once more at Theseus and then took to the sky. I watched him, longing to fly with him and then turned to Theseus who was watching me with an intense curiosity. "I am sorry if I offended you," I said softly.

Theseus smiled and then wrapped his arms around me in a hug. "You are loyal, which is a wonderful quality, especially in these dark times."

I relaxed into his hold and inhaled his scent loudly.

"Well, isn't this cute? Two halfbreeds comforting each other," snarled a menacing voice.

I spun around and growled at the vampire standing before me. "How did you get in here?" I cast a Monitum spell, which created a butterfly that flew to Selene to notify her that I was in trouble and quickly moved back from the vampire, pushing Theseus backwards with me.

"I have my ways, female. So, you found her at last, did you Theseus?"

Theseus growled. "You know that I have to kill you now, right? I can't let you report back to Maurice."

The name Maurice sounded familiar and a headache began in the front of my skull. I rubbed at it and took a step back, hiding slightly behind Theseus instead of standing protectively in front of him as I had been.

I felt Selene's presence growing closer and hoped she would be there in time.

"Has she found herself yet?" the vampire asked.

"It seems we are all full of discoveries tonight. One of which is that I have a break in my barrier," said Selene as she finally arrived. The vampire hissed at Selene, but she only laughed and said, "Oh, you poor stupid vampire. Did you really think you could come into my coven and threaten one of my sisters? I think your kind has grown cocky." She raised her hands and then sunlight covered the vampire. He screamed once and then disintegrated into ash.

Theseus gasped and stared at the pile of ash. "I've never seen that spell before."

Selene smiled and put her arm around my shoulders. "Chandra discovered it." She looked at my pinched face and her smile disappeared. "What is it? What's wrong?"

"My head hurts," I said softly.

Selene looked at Theseus. "You swore you wouldn't reveal anyone's name!"

He swallowed. "I did not mean to. It was a name I thought she would have heard already."

Selene looked at him. "Who?"

"The vampire king," he said softly.

"Maurice," I whispered and then screamed in pain as my head throbbed and an image of a large winery in some foreign place and a handsome man whose smile was pure evil clouded my vision. "Why does it hurt when I say his name?"

Selene placed her hands on my head and started chanting. Theseus picked my hand up in his and then placed his wrist under my nose to distract my senses. Ten minutes later the pain was finally gone. Selene glared at Theseus. "You will remember next time. We cannot afford to lose her nor have her powers released."

Theseus bowed. "I apologize. I will remember."

Selene walked briskly away without looking back. I started to stand, but Theseus picked me up instead. I looked at his face and frowned. "You look familiar, like I've met you before."

He shook his head. "That's not possible."

"Maybe I know a relative of yours then?"

Theseus shrugged. "Perhaps."

I waited for him to tell me more, but he just walked in silence as he carried me back towards the main building. "Who are your parents?" I finally asked.

He sighed. "Chandra, I cannot say any names. You only heard one name of a person you aren't even tied to and it caused you pain. What do you think hearing a name of a person you are tied to will do?"

"You know my true name, don't you?"

Theseus sighed. "I hope Draco-Blu comes back soon. You ask too many questions which could kill you or everyone else."

I rolled my eyes. "And you are a dramatist."

CHAPTER 3
CHANDRA

Trying to work with the children was impossible with Theseus around. For one, they couldn't take their eyes off of him. The girls were mesmerized by his beauty while the boys were mesmerized by his masculinity. Second, my classroom had been transformed from a children's introduction to magic class to a coven's introduction to halfbreeds class.

Did it bother me that they wanted to learn more now that Theseus was here? Yes. Why wasn't I interesting enough for them to analyze? Or was it because I didn't know my past or how I'd learned my powers, while Theseus did?

Theseus stood at the front of the room shirtless with his back to us, his body shining as he called his power and released his wings. Those who were gathered watched intently as he pulled his wings out and put them back again and again.

"Does it hurt?" one of the girls asked.

He shook his head. "No, it feels good actually. Like when you have a spot in your back that needs to pop and then you turn just the right way and it pops."

"Unless someone forces your wings out. That hurts," I said quietly as I remembered the painful event.

He turned and looked at me in shock. "Who did that to you?"

"A full blooded Sidhe who likes to annoy me," I answered vaguely. I was not about to tell him it was Dionysus. As much as he annoyed me, he had kept my true lineage a secret.

"Can you show us the process of shifting to warrior form?" James, the smallest but most intelligent boy in my class, asked.

What would the werewolf prince's half shift look like?

Theseus closed his eyes, and his glow faded. I pushed myself off of the wall I had been leaning on and walked out of the classroom. Obviously, my services were not needed here.

I walked north and entered the arched hedge which led into the rose garden and the mini labyrinth Selene had created. The witches had a spell on the garden which kept the flowers constantly blooming. Once I entered it, no other scent except roses filled my nose. Bees hummed as they pollinated the roses and went about their business. The bees never bothered us, even when we entered the labyrinth, so we never bothered them.

I made my way through the small labyrinth, running my hands along the thick bushes. The first time I'd entered the maze I'd gotten lost and it had taken me an hour to find my way back out. I knew I could have just flown out, but I was determined to find my own way. Now, the path was as familiar to me as walking up to my room in the house.

I finally made it to the center of the labyrinth, which was a rectangular clearing about twenty square feet wide. I sat and ran my hand through the cool green grass. A small rabbit hopped out from underneath the nearest shrub and stopped in front of me, twitching his nose and moving his ears to pick up any sounds. Reaching out slowly, I began to stroke the rabbit's ears as I drifted off into my trance.

My thoughts always strayed to the prince and the strange connection I could feel in me. It was like a cord, one which if I focused on hard enough could be followed to him. But that was impossible, or it should have been. I also felt a second connection to someone or something, but I couldn't figure out what it was or what it meant.

If he was my mate, then why had I been alone as a wolf for so long? Why had he not found me until now? If he was really my mate then he should have been able to find me twenty years ago, or more. And why couldn't I remember anything?!

I had no idea how long I'd been a wolf because my mind had deteriorated into simple animal urges and instincts at some point and I would still be there if it hadn't been for Selene finding me and rehabilitating me. I knew that I'd gone through several generations of one wolf pack before leaving them for a new one and going through several additional generations with that pack, but I couldn't count the number of years. I was almost afraid to. I did and didn't want to know how old I was. I looked about twenty, but preternaturals age much slower than humans and in varying scales depending upon the race.

Maybe the prince didn't want me? No, I couldn't believe that. It hurt just thinking that.

I still vividly remembered the goddess, or Sidhe woman as I understood now, who was my earliest memory. I had tried to find her again and the place we had been at, but was unsuccessful.

My irritation was growing and the rabbit's fur twitched beneath my tense hands. My stomach growled and for a fleeting moment I thought about eating the rabbit.

"Chandra?" Theseus called.

"In here," I answered softly as I shooed the rabbit away, closed my eyes and started humming softly to meditate.

I felt his wolf as he sat down in front of me. It was strange to be able to *feel* someone like I did now. Had the interaction with the werewolf prince unlocked some of my powers?

I opened my eyes and asked, "How did you find me?"

He tapped his nose. "Scent trail. Are you feeling well?" he asked softly.

"Headache," I whispered. "I hope Blu returns with news from the Council soon."

"Do you know when your dragon friend will return?"

"No. It depends on how quickly the Council makes a decision."

"Would you like to go for a run?" he asked cheerfully.

I shook my head. "No, I think I'd just like to sit here for a moment." I started humming again and slowly slipped back into my meditative trance.

At least I was in my trance until a cold hand touched my face. "The dark approaches. Fire will consume and restore, happiness and pain must be experienced collectively. Death for three will be the end."

I opened my eyes and looked up at Margenta. Her eyes were opened wide, but only the whites were showing. A prophecy. Margenta was using her power of prophecy on me. "Who are the three?" I asked softly so as not to awaken her from her trance.

"Starlight, twice stars and moons. Those are the three."

"When?"

No response.

"Can the path be altered?"

"Fate can always be changed. Decisions must be made. But the death is unchangeable. Death requires the lives and Death will not be denied."

"Can another life be traded?"

"Death will not be denied the three. A decision will be made, but not by thee."

Margenta's eyes closed and then she gasped in a huge lungful of breath and dropped to her knees beside me. "What happened?" she asked.

"Prophecy," I whispered.

Her eyes widened and she looked at me in horror. "No, oh no. Chandra I am sorry."

I smiled and patted her hand reassuringly. "Your Sight is a gift and I thank you for using it on me. You should take a lavender bath to calm yourself."

She nodded and walked on wobbly legs out of the rose garden.

"I need to relay this to the ones who sent me," Theseus said.

I nodded and stood, brushing my backside off. "I need to seek Selene's advice as well."

"Are you alright?" he asked, concern evident in his voice and eyes.

I smiled. "Yes, I have heard many doom prophecies since coming here. I expected one day to hear my own."

He didn't seem convinced, but he left. I sagged to the ground and held my head in my hands. Why me? Why now? What the hell did it mean?

"Are you alright, Sister?"

I looked up and took Selene's extended hand. "No."

"Margenta came to me very distressed. Would you care to enlighten me as to what has happened?"

I exhaled and asked, "Could we go to your office first?"

Selene smiled and put her arm around my shoulders. "Certainly. And when we get there, I will brew you some relaxing tea."

"A shot of whiskey might be better."

Selene laughed, and my despair lightened slightly. She could always lift my mood. Of course, since she said I was surrounded by despair and darkness, that wasn't a difficult task. We walked into the main building and to her office in the east wing on the first floor. I sat down and watched Selene boil water and add leaves. She waved her hand and a pen and a piece of paper appeared in front of me. "Write down the prophecy and any answers she gave you to questions you asked."

I did as she asked and then flipped the paper around so that she could read it when she sat down. She set a cup of steaming tea on the desk in front of me and then sat down in her chair. I sipped my tea and looked around the room. The walls were painted black and aside from the desk and three chairs, only a small overhead light adorned the room. It was the perfect room for a witch to perform spells and meditate in privacy.

Selene's cup shattered as it fell to the floor, making me jump up out of my chair.

"Selene?"

She bent down and started picking up the broken pieces. "I'm alright, Chandra. I'm sorry I startled you." Our eyes met and she swallowed nervously. "Her prophecies have never been wrong."

I plopped down in the chair and sighed. "I know." I could smell Selene's fear and it made me worry. I'd never known the witch to be afraid. "Selene, why are you so frightened?" I asked.

"I need to do some research. You should return to your room and rest. I'm sure this has taken a lot out of you." She stood and walked to the door, opening it for me.

I had never been dismissed by Selene like this before. "Very well," I whispered as I walked past her.

I went to my room and sat on my bed. My room was small, just big enough for my dresser and bed, but it had its own bathroom and since only I lived in it, it was fine for me. It was like a little den where I was safe and could curl up in the dark, away from all of the scary things which hunted when the light disappeared.

Divinations were always tricky to decipher because sometimes they meant exactly what they said while other times they were metaphors. Plus, you couldn't figure out what it meant until it was happening and by then it was too late.

I could feel Theseus' approach before he walked in. He stopped in the doorway and looked at me with a carefully neutral expression on his face. "What did Selene say?"

I was still unaffected by his handsome appearance, which was strange. It seemed unnatural for a woman not to be affected by him. I could see that many of the witches were, so why wasn't I?

"Nothing. What did the werewolf prince say?" Just the thought of him sent my heart twisting. How could a man I didn't know affect me like this?

"He said quite a few swear words and then broke a few things. Then his second-in-command took the phone and told me that they would contact us if they deciphered anything." He sat on the bed beside me and wrapped his arms around my shoulders. "Are you alright?"

I scoffed. "I'm great. I'm being lied to by someone I thought was my friend. I discover a man who may or may not be my mate and who may or may not have abandoned me. And now one of my sisters foretells a prophecy that, I think, talks about my death." I flopped backwards onto the bed and growled. "Life is great."

"Let's go outside and play," Theseus suggested.

I shook my head. "No, I think I just want to sleep."

"We could fight if you wanted. I might even let you win once."

I smiled despite my mood and sat up. "You're on."

We walked out of the house with my sisters staring after me with solemn expressions. I gritted my teeth and followed Theseus out to the garden. Theseus stopped and turned to face me, his face serious as he stretched his legs and arms. "Are you ready?"

I smiled and charged forward, trying my hardest to hit him. He dodged left and right, keeping me at bay. I managed to clip his chin and then he was attacking me. I dodged his attacks, but my concentration wavered as I watched him attack. His style was familiar. I had an extreme case of déjà vu as I tried to remember who fought like him. My head throbbed from the effort, making me stumble and drop to my knees. I clutched my head as the pain increased.

Theseus dropped down beside me and rested his hand on my shoulder, trying to comfort me, and as he did so, we heard a noise above.

Blu roared overhead and wind pressed me down to the ground as he landed over me. I heard Theseus growl, but I was in too much pain to tell him to shut up. Blu placed his snout against my head and hummed, vibrating my entire body. After a moment, the pain in my head eased and then disappeared.

Blu growled again at Theseus and then nuzzled me gently. "Are you alright, Hatchling?"

I stood slowly. "Yes." I remained silent until I was sure that I could stand on my own. "Did the Council give you a decision?"

He muttered as his stomach growled. "First, do you have you any meat?"

Two witches who had been watching our garden play brought out a cow and Blu gulped it down. I waited until he was done licking his lips before asking again, "What did the Council decree?"

Blu looked at Theseus who was standing a few yards away. "How long will it take for your leader to make the journey to the Lair?"

Theseus answered quickly, "Two days."

Blu huffed. "Then you best notify him now that he needs to start his journey.

Theseus bowed and hurried into the house. "Blu! What is going on?" I asked in exasperation.

Blu flicked his tongue out in annoyance. "Your agitation is understandable, Hatchling, but you best remember your place when meeting the Council."

I bit my tongue and bowed my head, "I apologize, Draco-Blu. I have been in pain lately."

Blu pressed his nose against my head and exhaled. The sweet smell of his breath surrounded me as he used his magic to quickly view my memories of the time since he left. He snorted and pulled his nose back. "I see. Well, you and I will begin our journey to the Council and assuming all of the conditions are met, they will assist you in regaining your memory."

They'd agreed! I was finally going to find out who I was! "Wait, what conditions?"

Blu shook his head. "They are not conditions for you so you

need not worry until we arrive. Pack your things and let us head out."

I wanted to argue, but there are two types of beings you never argue with, vampires and dragons. So, I hurried up to my room and packed what little clothes and things I had. Theseus came into my room and watched me silently. I finished packing and turned to see him looking sad and fearful. "What is it, Theseus?"

He swallowed and smiled. "Just worried that once you regain your prior memories that you won't remember your time with me and we won't be friends."

I wrapped my arms around him and kissed his cheek. "You will always be my friend. You are the only one like me."

Theseus rubbed the back of his neck. "Actually, there are quite a few others like us."

I gaped at him. "What? When were you going to tell me?"

He shrugged. "I was told not to tell you too much. You'll meet the others once your memory is back though."

"How many others?"

Theseus whispered, "Hundreds."

Hundreds of wolf halfbreeds! How come I had never seen them? How come I didn't know they even existed?

"Let's go, hatchling!" Blu called from outside.

I pointed at Theseus. "You and I are going to talk about this later."

He smiled. "Of course."

I headed down the stairs into the main living room and found all of the witches gathered. The children were teary eyed, and the adults seemed more worried than sad. "This isn't goodbye. I'm still a part of this coven and will return. I promise," I said to the gathered women.

The children I'd grown to love took their turns giving me hugs and kissing me goodbye. Each of the witches bade me farewell and wished me luck. Selene stood at the exit and handed me a talisman. "This will hide your scent and Theseus' long enough for you to make it to the Lair. Be strong, Chandra, and return to me whole."

I hugged her and kissed her cheek. "I love you, Selene. Thank you for helping me regain my humanity."

Blu set me on his back and I slipped the talisman on. The designs on my skin faded and my hair turned blonde. She had to have put an extreme amount of power into the talisman for it to change my appearance so drastically. I looked at Theseus who was climbing onto Blu's back behind me and blinked. The markings on his skin were gone as well.

Blu roared farewell to the coven and took us up into the sky. The press of wind on my body felt wonderful. I leaned into it and lifted my arms beside me. I looked back at Theseus to find him sitting with his eyes closed and a smile on his lips as he enjoyed the wind on him as well.

"How long will it take us to get to the Lair?" I asked Blu.

"Two days. I will travel as far as I can the first night. I fear staying on the ground too long with two halfbreeds, even with Selene's talisman on you."

Theseus sighed longingly. "Someday the vampires won't have the power to make us hide in fear."

Blu laughed. "Yes, little halfbreed hatchlings, someday soon you will restore the balance."

We flew in silence until the sun rose and brightened the sky. Blu landed near a river, and we all slurped at the water. My nose twitched as I caught the scent of a deer, but before I could turn to chase after it, Theseus was already bounding into the forest.

I growled, yanked my clothes and talisman off and then charged after him. He stood in wolf form over a large buck, his muzzle stained red from taking it down.

I changed forms and walked forward, growling softly. *Step aside.*

Theseus dropped his head and backed away slowly. *Of course. I simply wanted to take it down for you.*

I turned so that I could watch Theseus then tore into the deer and ate until I was full. Once my stomach was full and my anger sated, I walked a few feet away and lay down to lick my muzzle and paws clean. Something seemed familiar about this situation, but during the years I'd spent as a wolf I'd gone on many hunts with the small wolf packs, so I pushed the thought away and changed forms. "I'm going to the river to bathe."

I jogged back towards Blu and then past him to the river. I shivered at the cold water and Blu plugged one nostril, snorting a jet of fire into the river around me, warming it instantly. I sighed happily and then started tossing him the fish which he'd killed in the process. I washed my body and then caught a few more fish for Blu before walking to the shore. I closed my eyes and called to the flame of power which resided deep within me. The flame brightened and then purple fire covered my body. I held the flame around me long enough to dry my body and then dressed and put the talisman back on.

"Your control over your fire has improved," Blu said as he used one of his large talons to pick at bones in his teeth.

I finger-combed my hair and smiled. "I had been working on it daily. The last thing I need is to offend the Council by accidentally shooting a flame at them."

Blu laughed. "Yes, that would be considered a grave insult."

I smiled. "Fira didn't like it much when I shot his nose with my fire yesterday."

Blu laughed, shaking the ground and me. "It was a good tactic, but it's never pleasant to have foreign fire on you."

"Have you learned to use your fire to deflect another's?" asked Theseus as he walked to the river and cleaned the blood from his body.

I watched him as he cleaned and grew angry at my incapacity to be interested in him. "Yes, I have. Have you?"

Theseus stood up and red flames surrounded him in a mini tornado. "As you can see."

I envisioned fire covering my hands and purple flames covered them instantly. I formed two giant streams of fire from my hands to his body and watched as the blue and purple flames swirled together and then my purple disappeared from his body. Theseus inhaled as he prepared to attack me back, but Blu snorted two twin jets of blue flames between us. "That is enough, hatchlings. We must rest."

"I was just playing," I grumbled.

Blu sighed at me and lay down. I climbed between his leg and body, underneath his wing and curled up into a ball. Theseus cleared his throat, and I smiled at him. "Come on. Blu won't mind if you lie with me here. He's large enough."

Theseus smiled and climbed beside me, curling around me.

"Good night, hatchlings. May your dreams be pleasant," Blu whispered as we drifted off to sleep against him.

The rain poured like a giant waterfall down my face as I scanned the forest. I wiped at the rain, but nothing helped. I put my hands over my eyes and screamed in frustration. I tensed as a wolf howled nearby, answering my scream. I walked backwards into the cave, pressing my back against the wall. My heart hammered against my chest, threatening to break through. I wiped the water from my eyes and stared at the black opening of the cave. Lightning flashed, allowing me to see outside, and my entire body stilled. A large black wolf stood in the doorway sniffing the ground. The wolf turned its head towards me and sniffed three times quickly. I tried to slow my breathing, but the adrenaline was pumping too quickly to allow it. The wolf walked into the cave and whimpered. I shook my head and closed my eyes. The sound of bones snapping and popping echoed in the cave. I hugged myself tighter, fear consuming my rational thought. A familiar male voice whispered, "It's alright. I won't hurt you. I'm your mate."

I woke up gasping for air, and my head throbbed in pain. Theseus whined beside me, and I realized he was now in wolf form.

"Are you alright, Hatchling?" Blu asked. "I feel that you are in pain."

I groaned. "My head...hurts."

Blu placed his nose against my head and exhaled. In a matter of seconds, the pain was gone, and I relaxed against Blu and Theseus.

"Thank you," I said as I fell back asleep.

Morning came faster than I wanted. I felt drained, emotionally and physically. The pain in my head was still present as was the pain in my entire body due to the connection with the werewolf prince. I felt it stronger than ever and knew I needed to see him soon, or I felt as though I would break.

Blu and Theseus ate quickly and after I forced down a few bites of food, we set off into the air again. Blu sang softly in the language of the dragons as we flew and after a few minutes I started to fall asleep again. Theseus wrapped his arms around me to keep me from falling off and I let Blu's magical song put me to sleep, healing the parts of me that it could.

I WOKE when Blu started rumbling beneath me. I recognized his angry growl and was instantly alert. Theseus stood on the ground beside Blu in wolf form, his fur puffed out as he snarled at something in the distance. I started to climb off of Blu's back, but he snapped, "Stay there."

I frowned. "What is it?"

"I landed to get water for you both and a group of strange vampires surrounded us," Blu said.

"Why don't we just fly away then?" I asked softly.

"Because we have archers with us," said a melodious voice which sounded vaguely familiar. A man with white skin and golden designs stepped out from the tree line. I didn't need to be near him to recognize that he was Sidhe.

"What do you want?" I asked. "And why are you working with vampires?"

The man smiled and there was something nagging at the back of my mind about him. He looked familiar somehow. "I was sent to intercept you."

Theseus changed forms and let his wings out. "You will not take her, traitor."

Blu roared and shifted his back foot. The signal. Blu had taught me this signal the first day we met. I screamed in rage and used all of the power I could without draining myself to send a ring of sunshine outwards away from my body. Vampires screamed and disintegrated in fifty puffs of ash. The Sidhe roared and jumped up to come at me, but Blu and Theseus shot him with their fire, forcing him to protect himself and drop to the ground.

Theseus jumped onto Blu's back as Blu continued to spray the man with fire and then we took off into the air and zoomed away. I looked back, but the man did not follow us, though we all knew this wasn't the last that we'd seen of him.

"How did they know where we were? How could they have known we would be heading this way?" I asked with a frown.

Theseus sighed. "That would probably be my fault."

Blu's head whipped around, murderous intent in his eyes. "You have two seconds to explain before I chomp off your head."

Theseus looked at me with pleading eyes. "I made a call to the werewolf prince, but spoke quickly before asking if he was alone. He has an ally who is a vampire, but sometimes his ally has minions around him who are not loyal. I should have asked first if it was safe to speak, but we were in a rush and...I am sorry."

Blu spoke rapidly in the language of the dragons, which meant he was saying harsh things he didn't want me to hear.

"You should be more careful next time," I said softly, "Apparently, I'm wanted by the vampires."

Finally, we reached the end of the landmass and flew out over the water. The ocean spread out before us in a seemingly endless expanse. The winds blew the scent of salt up to us, making my nose tingle and me sneeze. The sea was powerful and silent. It was eerie and yet reassuring. The only difference from the preternatural takeover and from when the humans ruled, is that now the ocean was *much* cleaner.

We flew in silence for the next two hours, passing over the sea and mountains until we finally came to the Lair. The mountain before us was the largest in the world, its peak over twenty-nine thousand feet high. It was also hollow. The dragons used their magic to hollow out the mountain yet maintain its stability.

The entrance was over fifteen thousand feet from the base and only accessible by air. It was also always covered in snow which made it a massive sight of splendor. Blu told me that there used to be other mountains around it, but the dragons thought they made a route for unwanted visitors so the dragons destroyed all of the mountains within a one-hundred-mile radius, leaving the behemoth dragon's nest by itself.

Blu approached the mountain slowly, making a wide arc so the guards had time to come to him and check him out.

Two dragons roared and then swooped down from above where they'd been making lazy patrolling circles. The first dragon was green and large, but still smaller than Blu.

"Welcome Draco-Blu. We are honored to escort you in," said the green dragon.

The second dragon, a gold colored dragon, glided besides Blu's left side. "Hail, leader. I am honored to be in your presence yet again." He was closer to Blu's size and as I recalled, one of Blu's friends.

Blu hummed respectfully, confirming my belief. "I am happy to see you again my friend."

The golden dragon tilted his head and flicked his tongue out, trying to catch my scent. "You must be the girl Draco-Blu is so fond of."

I bowed my head out of respect and then smiled at him. "I am Chandra, friend of the dragons."

The green dragon asked, "How are you faring at the moment?"

I bowed to the other dragon and said, "I am doing alright. My pulse is faster than normal and there is a pain in my head and heart, but nothing too serious."

The dragons glided as they approached the entrance and then formed a single file line with the golden dragon first, then Blu and then the green dragon. They landed inside the opening, which was only wide enough for one dragon with his wings fully extended to land at a time. Blu followed his friend through a pitch-black tunnel which made Theseus and me growl nervously. I hated confined spaces, especially ones under the ground. My head throbbed as I recalled walking down a narrow staircase underground with a man in a situation very similar to this.

I screamed in pain as I tried to recall his name or what he looked like.

Blu stepped out of the darkness and into the open mountain where the dragons lived. We stood on a ledge which dropped off to the bottom of the mountain. Rock outcroppings jutted out every twenty feet or so which served as nests for the dragons along the walls of the mountain. The nests were scattered along the full height and circumference of the mountain's walls.

Theseus grabbed me and jumped off of Blu's back, being careful to keep me from the edge and set me down in front of Blu. Blu and the golden dragon pressed their noses to my head and started humming.

The man in the staircase was connected to me. I recalled being able to speak telepathically with him, which was abnormal. I had been afraid, and he started glowing. He glowed because he was a Sidhe! He was tall and he had markings on his upper body...

"Hatchling!" Blu yelled. "Release the memory! Release it before it tears you apart!"

Release it? Why would I release it when I was so close? I could almost see his face. I could… Pain ripped through my body and stole the breath from my lungs, not even allowing me to scream.

Theseus bit my arm, and my eyes flew open, releasing the memory from my grasp. Blu and his friend hummed loudly, their magic wrapping around me in a soft whirlwind. The pain eased and then disappeared, allowing me to breathe.

"Speak to me, Chandra," Theseus whispered, "Please, say something."

I lay in stunned silence a moment and then whispered, "Ow."

The three dragons and Theseus exhaled in relief simultaneously, ruffling my hair with their combined releases of air. Blu rested his muzzle on my chest and whispered, "You need to be careful, Hatchling. That was too close."

I patted his muzzle reassuringly and then stood up slowly. "I'm sorry."

Theseus cleared his throat and the dragons turned to look at him. "Would it be alright if I flew down with you instead of riding?"

My eyes widened, and I looked at Blu hopefully. "Please, Draco-Blu. It has been so long since I've soared," I pleaded.

Blu locked eyes with his friend a moment as they communicated telepathically and then nodded. "You may follow us down to the floor level." Blu looked at me with concern and asked, "Are you sure you're alright to fly?"

I smiled and nodded vigorously. "Yes!"

Blu and the other two dragons sprang up and away from the ledge, extended their wings and soared over the giant expanse of the open mountain. Theseus pulled his shirt off over his head and then walked behind me, tearing open slits in my shirt so I could let my wings out while still keeping my shirt intact and covering my upper body.

I walked a few steps away from him and closed my eyes, calming my mind and body. Power flowed within the mountain and it generously lent me energy. I pictured my back and imagined my wings sliding from the two slits and expanding outwards. My back pulsed and then my wings were free. I opened my eyes and marveled at the colors of my body.

Theseus grunted and I watched as his body glowed and then his wings released. He smiled at me and then launched himself from the ledge.

I squatted down and then jumped up as high as I could, letting out a victorious cry of glee as I soared. I zipped past the others and made a circle around the entire mountain. If my calculation was correct, the area of the base of the mountain was at least twenty-five hundred square feet. Theseus flew after me and then folded his wings in and plummeted down towards the bottom. I followed close behind him but pulled up early to circle one more time before landing on my feet on the stone floor.

Blu landed beside me and roared happily. If I smiled any wider, my face would surely split. Mid-smile, I glanced at the floor of the mountain more carefully. Blu had described the mountain for me before, but it was incredible to witness firsthand. The ground was solid marble and several large tents were set up along the outer edge of the floor level.

"Who lives in the tents?" I asked curiously.

"Friends of the dragons when they visit," the golden dragon answered.

I turned to face him and said, "I must apologize for my rudeness. I have forgotten to ask what I may call you."

The golden dragon's lips pulled back slightly as he gave me a dragon smile. "Friends call me Fafnir."

I frowned as I recalled the name from a story I'd heard. "Doesn't that mean greed?"

Fafnir and Blu laughed loudly. Fafnir nodded. "Gold is not only my coloring, but my favorite treasure."

I smiled. "Aw, so your treasure holds more than just jewels and virgins waiting to be devoured?"

Blu snorted. "He wishes he had virgins again."

Fafnir sighed. "I do miss those days. Humans were so much tastier before they developed so many chemicals."

I turned to the green dragon and bowed. "I have not forgotten you. What may I call you?"

"I am Ryuu."

I smiled. "It is a pleasure to meet you Ryuu and Fafnir. I am honored."

Ryuu and Fafnir dipped their heads. "We are honored to meet you as well, Hatchling," they said in unison.

I'd heard Blu and Fira speak in unison before, but it was strange to hear other dragons do it as well. Blu said it was because of their telepathy. Sometimes they finished sentences for each other as well.

"Chandra," said five voices at once.

I turned and watched as the five oldest dragons, so worn with age that they rarely flew and if they did fly, only made it as far as the first nests two hundred feet overhead, walked towards me. They were all bi-colored, the only multicolored dragons I'd ever seen before. Were they more powerful because they were bi-colored or had they become bi-colored after becoming the Council? I wasn't sure since Blu never talked about it.

The dragons stopped a hundred feet away and held my gaze. I walked away from Blu and Theseus and dropped to the ground on my knees and bowed until my forehead touched the marble. I trembled inside, but I held my body tight as I bowed. I would not show fear to the Council. "It is an honor to have an audience with you, Council of Dragons."

"We are pleased to finally meet the hatchling of Draco-Blu," they answered in unison again. "Please stand, friend of the dragons, and be easy in our presence. You have nothing to fear from us."

I stood up and bowed my head politely. "Thank you."

"Please let us look upon your face."

I took off the talisman to reveal my true face. The dragons

stared at me and hummed in harmony as they each used their magic in sync to examine me.

I felt like a tuning fork that had been flicked. Their powers vibrated against me, infiltrating my mind and body. I tried to relax despite my fear so as not to disrupt their spell.

Images of events I did not remember started to play across my closed eyelids and made me cry out in pain. I fell to the ground on my side as the pain blacked out my vision. The images stopped and the dragons' magic dissipated.

"You are not ready to face this on your own. We must wait for him to come," the Council said.

Theseus picked me up from the ground where I was laying and carried me as he followed Blu towards one of the tents.

"Draco-Blu, I..." I began.

"Quiet. You must sleep and wait, Hatchling," Blu said with concern and worry evident in his voice.

I closed my eyes and a smile spread across my face as I whispered, "I can feel him coming."

Blu snorted in my face and the world went dark.

CHAPTER 4
CHANDRA

"I want to see her!" yelled a familiar deep, commanding male voice.

"She is resting," said Blu, growling.

"I'm awake," I whispered because I knew both would hear me.

Blu stuck his head into the opening of the small tent Where I lay. "How do you feel?" he asked.

"Like I got stepped on by a dragon."

Blu laughed. "You would not be alive if that were true, Hatchling."

"Please, I would just like to see her," said the werewolf prince.

Blu sighed. "Are you well enough to have visitors?"

I smiled at Blu and stood up slowly. "I am. Thank you for your concern."

Blu rumbled affectionately at me, much like a feline would purr.

I changed quickly and then took a deep breath for courage just as he stepped into the tent. He was even more handsome than I remembered.

He had started to move towards me but stopped and clenched his hands into fists. “How are you feeling?”

“I’ve been better,” I admitted.

“Did they hurt you?” he asked through gritted teeth.

I frowned at him. “Did who hurt me?”

His eyes flicked to the side. “The Dragon Council.”

I frowned at him. “They were trying to help me. I am sure they did not mean to harm me.”

Theseus walked into the tent with a tray of food but stopped when he saw the prince. “I…I’m sorry. I didn’t know you were here.” Theseus dropped his head in submission and started to leave.

“Wait,” I said. “Is that food for me?”

Theseus looked at the tray and then smiled nervously. “Yes, sorry. I’ll just leave it.”

I felt the prince watching us as I walked to Theseus and took the tray from his hands. I kissed Theseus’ cheek and smiled at him. “Thank you.”

The prince growled softly behind me, but made no movement besides that.

I ignored him and walked outside to eat beside Blu who still stood guard outside of my tent. Blu moved his tail so I could sit on it while leaning against him to eat as I’d done many times before. I sat down and patted his side before eating the meats and fruits on the tray.

“When will I speak to the Council?” the prince asked. His shoulders were tense, and his eyes glowed with magic.

Why was he so angry? Even if he was my mate, I hadn’t done anything that was considered inappropriate.

“As soon as she is ready,” Blu answered.

The prince started to move towards me, but Blu growled and wrapped his tail protectively around me, lifting me up to my feet.

The prince squatted down in an attack stance and changed his hands to paws.

I smacked Blu's tail. "You're being rude and possessive, both of you, and I don't like it."

Blu exhaled smoke. "I apologize. I did not mean to offend you."

The prince changed his hands back and his eyes returned to normal. "I'm sorry. I am not usually like this."

"The Council will see you both now," said the combined voices of the Council who were walking towards the center of the mountain.

I walked next to Blu, but felt the prince behind me like a weight on my back. We stopped in front of the Council and I dropped to the ground in a bow. "Thank you for seeing us, Council," I said as humbly as I could. I stood back up and rested a hand on Blu's shoulder for support.

"We have spoken to the Prince of Werewolves and know he has spoken the truth."

Then he was my mate! How? Why were we separated?

The Council continued, "But we cannot perform the recognition spell until the other man you are tied to has arrived."

"He should be here any minute," said the Prince.

I looked at the Council. "Wait. What do you mean the other man I am tied to? I thought you said that the Prince was telling the truth about me being his mate!"

"You are my mate, but you are also bound to another. It was an emergency action done to save your life," answered the Prince.

"But I do not regret it," said a voice like wind chimes.

I knew that voice, and I definitely knew the language with which that voice would normally speak. Sidhe. The man behind me was a Sidhe and judging by the presence I felt, a very powerful one.

What had I done in my life to warrant the attention of the Prince of Werewolves and the... I turned around and one look at his face released a torrent of memories. I screamed in pain as I saw the Sidhe holding me while I was in pain, saw him walk with me down a dark staircase and reassuring me with his presence. Heard his voice in my head whispering that he loved me…

I screamed again and my eyes flew open. Blu was lying across me, humming and singing in the magic of dragons. The pain in my head was subsiding, but my heart felt like it was going to explode. I turned my head and found the Sidhe and werewolf princes being held back by dragons. Yes, that was who he was, a prince. Wow. Two princes?!

The princes looked at me with fear and anger. Were they mad at me or with the dragons holding them back?

"Blu, I think you can let me up now," I whispered. The Dragon Council growled and I realized that I'd slipped and addressed him informally. "I'm sorry, I meant to say Draco-Blu. Please forgive my offense."

Blu let me up, but pressed his nose to my head. "I accept your apology. You're in much pain still though. Perhaps you should lie still while I heal you?"

"You cannot heal this pain, Draco-Blu." I looked at the princes. "They are the cause of the pain and I believe only they know how I can fix it."

Blu lunged across the opening and pinned each of the princes to the ground under his talons. "What have you done to her?"

I rushed to him and put my face in front of his. "No! You misunderstand! Don't harm them!"

"Let them up, Draco-Blu," said the Council.

Blu hissed at the princes and let them up, but not before pulling me back against his chest with his head away from the princes.

The princes both began to glow incandescently. "Step away from her," they said eerily in unison.

"We will begin our discussion now," said the Council distracting everyone.

I stepped away from Blu and walked to stand in the center of the circle of dragons. "I am ready and will humbly accept whatever decision you give."

"You are a valued friend of the dragons and we treasure your acceptance of us," they said to me.

The two princes came to stand on either side of me and I had to fight the urge to reach out and touch them. The Council looked at the Sidhe prince. "You are unknown to us, which is neither good nor bad as we are neither good nor bad, thus we are willing to assist you if you meet our small request."

"Anything for her," he said without hesitation.

The Council then turned to the werewolf prince and their mood darkened. "You are very well known by us. You almost destroyed the race of dragons, you and the vampire prince. You are no friend of ours."

"I will do anything you ask to make amends for the devastation I caused and for my ignorant and childish actions," he said quietly.

"You are no friend of ours and there is nothing you can do to make amends for what you have done, but we love the hatchling you are mated to and thus we will agree to ease the suffering in her if you agree to a test to prove your loyalty."

"Anything," he answered without pause.

The Council was silent a moment and then they said, "In addition to one task we will divulge later, you must retrieve the lost dragon egg."

I gasped and Blu snorted in surprise.

The werewolf prince asked, "Would this be the green egg which the vampires found eighty years ago?"

The Council looked at him suspiciously. "Yes, that is the egg we speak of. We have heard rumor that the King of Vampires has it in his possession and plans to hatch it and control the dragon within. We must not let this happen."

"So, if I get the egg and hand it to you, you will help Ar... Chandra regain her memories?" he asked.

The Council shook with anger. Why was he asking them to repeat themselves?

"Yes, if you hand the egg to us, intact and safe, and pass one more test, we will assist the hatchling in regaining her memories and thus returning her to you as she was before she was stolen from you."

The werewolf prince nodded. "Alright, deal. I will need Ach... the Sidhe prince to fly down to the bottom of the mountain to assist me, is this alright?" The Council nodded and the werewolf prince smiled. "Great. We will be back as soon as we can with your egg."

The Council was eerily silent as they talked amongst themselves, probably pondering what he had up his sleeve.

I turned to the princes. "You do realize that the King of the Vampires could capture you and kill you, right?"

The princes both smiled at me, their smiles bizarrely similar. If I didn't know better, I'd say that they were brothers. I wanted to get closer to the werewolf prince to smell him, but decided better of it and planted my feet on the ground.

The werewolf prince asked, "Are you worried about my safety?"

I stepped back and then glared at him. "I was just saying that it seems like a lot of trouble to go to for a girl who doesn't remember you." Both princes winced as though I'd struck them. I hadn't meant to be so harsh, but he was rude and I didn't like it.

The werewolf prince came to stand a few inches from me and whispered, "I would face the entire Flight of Dragons to have you back in my arms and have you remember the times we've spent together. I would cut off my arm and give it to the dragons as payment if they would accept it. You are the only important thing in my life and I will face a hundred Vampire Kings before I let something as simple as death make me hesitate in getting you back."

The conviction and feeling in his voice were overpowering and I would have fallen if not for Blu's tail catching me. "She needs to rest."

The werewolf prince smiled at me and said, "I'll be back. You don't need to worry about me."

I groaned as a memory of a weaker, non-magical me stood on the porch of someone's house watching the werewolf prince leave somewhere and say those exact words to me. Blu whisked me away from the princes and into my tent before I could say anything else. He laid his head on me and sang until I fell asleep.

CHAPTER 5
ACHILLES

I couldn't believe that we had finally found her. She looked even more beautiful than I remembered and yet I could see that she was not herself. The need to touch her was incredible, but I resisted so as not to cause her pain. She was so strong and yet so fragile since she had not found herself yet. I gripped Ares under the arms and jumped out of the Lair, letting the wind catch us.

"Could you please *not* jump." Ares hissed as his heartbeat quickened.

"I had forgotten that you are afraid of heights," I said.

He growled. "I'm not afraid of heights, I'm afraid of you dropping me."

We landed on the ground and I patted his shoulder. "I wouldn't drop you, Brother."

Ares grunted, cleared his throat and then howled as loudly as he could. I wished I could see the process of his vocal chords and throat changing shape when he went from a human's throat to a wolf's throat. Although I doubted slicing a man's throat in half to watch would then allow the process to complete.

A bat screeched nearby and I smiled. Victor loved being a bat when he could. I think he just liked being smaller and able to fly.

A small black bat came to hover in front of us and then changed into a six-foot-tall, black eyed man. If you were human you might think he was simply imposing, but it was just his raw, incredible power. Victor was one of the few vampires I genuinely trusted and did not fear. He shook out his body and then looked at me with a smile, showing just the tips of his fangs. "I do enjoy being smaller and being able to fly."

I pointed at him. "Stay out of my head."

Ares sighed. "If only that were possible."

We'd known each other so long that most times we knew what the other was thinking without the use of telepathic abilities, so Victor's abilities were not as intrusive as they once were.

Being one thousand years old made years seem like a human's minutes, but the last one hundred years had felt like a lifetime. I had finally revealed myself to Artemis in Lyngvi, trying to claim her, only to come up against Ares and the bond they had already developed. Then, after many fights and binding her to save her from Hera, I had told her that I loved her and showed her my memories only to have her taken from me by my mother. I understand why Hera had done it, but it didn't make the pain at being separated from Artemis any easier. Especially when we hadn't been able to find her where Hera claimed to have left her.

And now Ares had been the first to find her, the first to make contact with her. I hated that he had been able to find her first, but I could not direct that hate at him. I'd watched him suffer each night with only Koda there to console him as he lost the ability to hold shape and turned into a wolf. Not being able to maintain shape was something very uncommon for the Prince of the Werewolves. Every night he dreamed of her being taken and then turned into a wolf, howling his grief until he passed out from weariness.

A wolf's grieving howl was the most eerie and heart wrenching sound I'd ever heard. It made it that much worse to feel the same pain and sorrow echoed in my own heart. My soul howled right along with his as we ached to see and touch her.

The day Ares had come back from the town to confirm it was her, he had seemed defeated instead of happy. Now, seeing her and knowing she did not recognize us and did not feel for us as she had when we'd last seen her, hurt incredibly. She had been the love of my life since I had first seen her, and she had no clue who I was.

What had she been doing since we last saw her? Had she found a mate? Had she slept with someone else? What if she had a family? Could we really give her back her memories if she was already happy?

Theseus had said she was living in a witch's coven and that she didn't smell of a man, but it had been a hundred years; she could have mated with a human and had a family between now and then.

The thought of another man touching her made my fists clench and my skin start to glow.

"Achilles," Ares said softly, "It'll be alright."

I turned away from the concern on his face and ground my teeth together. "You have already established a bond with her. Of course, you think it'll be alright. I am, yet again, left to wait."

"Would you like me to answer the questions you were asking yourself a moment ago?" Victor asked me quietly. "I have seen some of her memories and know some of the answers."

It was tempting, extremely tempting, but I shook my head. "No, thank you. I shall wait to hear them from her lips."

Even if I hadn't been bound to her and she hadn't been my match, I wouldn't have been able to leave her or forget her. She was perfect. She was the only woman I wanted. The only one I thought about. She was everything to me.

Ares rested his hand on my shoulder and then turned to Victor. "We need the dragon egg your father has."

"That is the price the Council asked of you?" Victor gaped at us.

Ares smiled. "Yes, well I don't think they knew that you could just pop in and get it and come back."

Victor smiled. "Yes, translocation is a handy ability."

It would have been a much handier ability if he had had it when we were captured one hundred years ago. Of course, we had all learned some new ability which would help us should we be captured again. None of us enjoyed being imprisoned.

Victor closed his eyes, chanted a few words and then disappeared. Ares turned and met my eyes. "She'll remember you too, Achilles. She won't get only the memories of me back."

I sat down on the snow-covered ground and exhaled. "I know, Ares. It's just…"

"Painful," Ares offered.

I laughed bitterly. "Yes, painful. I see the way she looks at you now, even without memories, and it's like being back in Lyngvi again."

Ares sat down beside me and sighed. "I hadn't intentionally set out to find her first, to keep you second. I was just overcome with emotions when seeing her and her not knowing me. She looked so different, but then she yelled at me and I knew that she was still in there. I had to try."

Victor appeared in front of us holding a large green egg. "Got it."

I pointed at the small man latched onto his arm. "Someone grabbed on for the ride."

Victor hissed and handed Ares the egg. "I hate stalkers." He pried the other vampire's teeth from his arm and then snapped his neck.

Ares cradled the egg like a baby. "Let's go, Victor you come with us."

Victor sighed. "I knew you'd get me in trouble at some point. You better hope they don't try to kill me."

Ares smiled. "That would be a shame."

Victor smiled wide enough to flash all of his fangs and then changed into his bat form, squealing as he flew up towards the Lair's entrance.

I extended my wings and smiled. "Life has been entertaining with you two around the last hundred years. Losing Victor's comedic relief might dampen the mood."

Ares laughed. "Let's hope the dragons don't eat the winged rat before we get there."

I jumped up into the sky, flapping my wings to propel me higher. "We'd better hurry then."

CHAPTER 6
CHANDRA

I was really tired of sleeping so much. I woke up with Blu's heavy head still on my chest. "Blu, I need to use the restroom," I said as I pushed at his head.

Blu rumbled something incoherent and pulled his head out of my tent.

After freshening up, I walked outside to find the Council gathered around my two princes. I ran toward them and widened my eyes at the vampire standing in between them. He was tall with black hair and solid black eyes. I'd heard about him before, the vampire prince.

"Please accept my humblest apologies. I was a much more immature man then and very impulsive. I return what is rightfully yours in accordance with the agreement between you and the princes here. I hope you can heal her quickly for all of our sakes."

"I know you, too? What kind of woman was I? Do I even want to know about my former life?" I blinked and shook my head.

The vampire prince turned towards me and I saw several emotions flit across his face before happiness settled in. "You are even more beautiful than I recall," he whispered as he walked towards me, "and definitely more powerful."

I stepped back from him and then ground my teeth together. "I don't know why you are trying to frighten me, but if those two men are really tied to me in one way or another, then they will not allow you to harm me. Plus, I may seem fragile and *damaged,* but I still possess many powers."

The vampire laughed and the tension eased. "Even without her memories she is still just as assertive and wonderful."

"We are pleased with the return of our egg. We will now give you, Prince of the Werewolves, your final task," said the Council.

"I am ready," said the werewolf prince.

The Council stood in silence a moment and then said, "You must obtain approval from Rhea to continue being mated to this woman."

I gasped in horror.

"Very well. I accept the task," said the werewolf prince without hesitation.

"No!" I yelled. The Council looked at me in shock. I ran to the prince and looked into his eyes. "You can't do this. It's suicide! Please, please don't do this."

"Seeing your worry for me and feeling it from you is greater than anything I've felt in the past hundred years," he said quietly. He picked up a strand of my hair and inhaled deeply. "I will return to you. Nothing will keep me away from you now that I have finally found you."

"Don't go. We can start a life together now. I don't need my memories," I pleaded with him. "I'm not worth anyone's life."

He hugged me against his chest and kissed me fiercely on the lips. My head throbbed, but I ignored it as I enjoyed the easing of the pain in my heart and felt his love. He pulled back from me and I swore his eyes were misty with tears. "I will come back to you as soon as I can. I'm very powerful so you needn't worry."

I sniffed and wiped at the tears falling down my face. "Your power means nothing against the Mother. I should go. I should be the one who has to risk my life. I should…"

He kissed me again and then rubbed his face against mine, marking me with his delicious scent. "You should stay here and rest. The Sidhe prince will remain so you will not be apart from both of us." He turned to the Council. "May I ask two things?" The Council noddeds. "May I take a helper with me?"

"You may."

He nodded and I caught the vampire prince walking towards us. "My second request is to leave my younger brother here. I do not think it would be good for Ar…Chandra to see him, but I don't want to take him with me."

The Council said, "He may stay while you are on your journey and we will keep him separate from the hatchling." They turned to the Sidhe prince. "In fact, you will all be kept away from her so that she doesn't have any unfortunate episodes while the werewolf prince is away."

The Sidhe prince bowed, but his jaw bulged as he ground his teeth together. "Of course."

The vampire prince sighed. "We'd better not die. I want to live to two thousand years. If I stay your friend I may not live that long though."

The werewolf prince smiled. "Oh come on. You know you're excited to finally get a chance to meet Rhea. Besides, we haven't had a good challenge in a while."

"You're lucky I'm so fond of the two of you," the vampire prince said as he started walking away.

"Don't let him fool you. He's been worried about you as well. He was in an uncontrollable rage when we couldn't find you," the Sidhe prince said with a fond smile on his face.

"How long was I missing?" I asked curiously.

"One hundred and five years," he said without hesitation.

I hadn't known my eyes could open so wide or my mouth. "One hundred years!"

The werewolf prince nodded.

"No wonder it was so hard to control my wolf when Selene found me. I was in wolf form for…" I tried to calculate how long I'd been a wolf, but it was all a blur now. "If what you say is true, that means I was a wolf for around forty-five years!"

The werewolf prince stepped in front of me. "I'm leaving now. I expect you to stay out of trouble." He laughed and shook his head. "Saying that to you is like telling a vampire to stay away from the darkness." He sighed and pressed his forehead against mine. "Stay safe until I return. Please. I could not bear to lose you again."

I inhaled his scent and my hands found their way to his hard, broad chest. "I will be anxiously awaiting your return." I leaned into him and inhaled his scent again, trying to hold it in as long as I could. I wanted some way to keep his scent with me, but before I could ask, he was taking his shirt off and handing it to me. I held it away from my body and smiled at him. "Thank you."

He kissed me quickly on the lips then ran after the vampire prince. "If I don't leave now, I fear I never will."

The vampire prince put his arm around the shorter man's shoulders. "Don't worry, she'll look exactly the same when you get back. That's one of the many perks of mating with preternatural women."

The werewolf prince laughed and shook his head. "Always looking on the bright side, aren't you?"

The vampire laughed and looked up at the dragons in their nests around the Lair. "When you're a child of the darkness, that's the only place you can look."

I took a sniff from the shirt and exhaled softly. "Come back soon."

CHAPTER 7
KODA

Not only had I been forced to hide in this tent while Ares met with the Council and Artemis, but now I was being forced to wait while he went on a treacherous journey. I had been beside my brother since I was weaned and I did not like being away from him now. I trusted Victor to guard Ares, but was only seventy percent sure that he would give his life for Ares'. I would never even hesitate. Ares was my alpha, my brother, and my only true pack mate since Matt's death.

I had felt sorrow at Matt's betrayal and death, but nothing compared to the pain at Artemis' kidnapping. She was so pure and so sweet, the most perfect female in any race for a million years.

And yet she was not mine to have, except as a pack member. The one kiss we had shared resonated in my skull and burned my heart with longing. I knew she was Ares' and even Achilles' before she would ever be mine, but it didn't stop me from wanting and wishing.

Once she had fully accepted Ares as her *passt genau* I had given up on thoughts of courting her and simply enjoyed her company as part of the pack. Then when she had accepted the challenge from Natasha, there had been a glimmer of hope for me. If she had lost and asked for mercy, I would have left Ares' side to be with her, but her love for Ares was too strong. She had basically died to protect her claim to him.

I wanted to touch her, inhale her scent, bury my nose in her hair and listen to her heart beat. I wanted much and was allowed nothing. It took all of my control not to leave the tent and walk the one hundred yards to hers. She was so close and still so far away.

I'd tried being with other women, even fathering a few children, but it didn't diminish my feelings for Artemis.

I'd just received information from a credible source about the true reason of Matt's treason, but had not been able to discuss it with Ares yet. I stared at the letter in my hands and wished Matt had thought higher of us and had confided his problem in us. Ares and I could have helped him easily and he never would have needed to betray us. Clearly, he did not think much of our skills, which is why he had given in and played the rat.

"What is that?" Achilles asked softly from the stool he was sitting on across the tent from me.

I tossed the note to him and whispered, "Information in regards to Matt's treachery."

Achilles read the note and then looked at me with his neutral face. "Did you tell Ares?"

I shook my head. "There was not an appropriate time to discuss it."

"I am sorry that you have not been allowed to see her," he said quietly as he watched me. "It was not Ares' or my decision, but the Dragon Council's."

It bothered me that he could read me so well, but then again, he *had* been the first to notice that I was in love with Artemis.

"I know that," I said as I exhaled and ran a hand through my hair. "I just wish the Council wasn't making him go through all this bullshit."

"And that you could have gone with him instead of being left behind," finished Achilles.

I laughed bitterly. "You know me well."

Achilles dipped his head slightly in acknowledgment. "Yes, but I also know that I feel the same way."

This was why I liked Achilles so much. He was the heir to the Sidhe throne and yet he did not hold himself above anyone. Since I could remember, he had been kind to me and had treated me with respect even despite Ares' prior hatred of him. It made matters much easier on me now that Ares had forgiven Achilles and they had dissolved their issues. Although I do not think that would have happened if it had not been for Artemis' kidnapping and our imprisonment together.

We'd had many prison brawls, together and against other prisoners, which had brought us closer. Human women could not understand how fighting brought men together, but after a fight, whether it be against each other or against a common foe, our friendship developed and strengthened.

Victor and Ares' relationship had strengthened, while Achilles and Ares' had developed anew.

"I do not doubt Ares' abilities, but I do not like not being there to protect his back," I admitted.

"Do you doubt Victor?" Achilles asked.

I smiled. "You know as well as I do that Victor will protect Ares as best as he can, but he looks out for himself first, something which I do not."

Achilles' lips drew thin. "I agree."

I looked towards the east, where I could sense Artemis. "It's so frustrating to know she is so near and yet still out of reach."

Achilles sighed loudly. "You're preaching to the choir, brother."

Only he would obtain more kisses from her and, given long enough, possibly even be allowed to mate with her. I would never. I would only be allowed the bond of pack mates and the bond of friendship. Something which I was grateful for, but I craved so much more.

The woman of my dreams was within reach and yet so far gone that I knew she could not be mine, even if she did regain her memories. I would forever be left wanting.

CHAPTER 8
ARES

Leaving her side again after such a short and bittersweet reunion was extremely difficult. If it were for any other reason, I would have stayed, grabbed her in my arms and never let go. She looked exactly the same, but without her memories she wasn't the same woman. I could tell that she had the strongest connection to me still, but even after making amends with Achilles and letting myself love my half-brother again, I didn't want to leave her with him.

"The sooner we get this over with, the sooner you can be back in her arms," Victor said from my side.

I turned and smiled at him. "I know. I just—"

"Don't like leaving her with your half-brother, especially since you can tell she has some of her memories? Achilles is the most moral Sidhe I know and he won't make any advances on her while you are out risking your life. Besides, what you're doing isn't just for her to regain her memories. She is the key to everything."

"I don't think Achilles will try anything either, but…what if she starts remembering and I'm not there? What if she only remembers him and not me?"

Victor rolled his eyes. "You two dreamed again, right?"

"Don't patronize me, Victor. I know that we are still connected, but I have no way of knowing what Hera did to Artemis. If the dragons aren't as powerful as we think, she could end up dying." I wouldn't let that happen. I refused to let her die now that I'd found her.

"Let's just focus on getting to Rhea's Temple," he said softly.

We increased our speed and made it to the City of Rhea, which was the gatekeeper to the Temple, faster than I'd thought we would. Even during the human reign this had been left untouched. Of course, since it was in the Himalayas and freezing cold, I wasn't surprised that even after the uprising, Maurice had left it alone as well. Rhea was the strongest being on the planet and I for one would not want to be on her bad side.

"It's more deserted than I thought it would be," Victor said with a frown.

I looked over and saw his fangs fully extended, which was something he only did when scaring someone or when he couldn't retract them due to his overwhelming thirst.

"I told you to eat on the way here. You'll just have to settle for a rabbit to quench the fire for now."

Victor grumbled, and we started through the empty town. The buildings looked freshly made, but they had to have been at least a thousand years old judging by the architecture. The wolf side of me felt uneasy about walking into someone else's den, but this was for Artemis so I would just have to deal with the feeling.

Victor disappeared a moment and then reappeared with two rabbits. He drained the blood from them and then tossed them to me. "You need to eat too, in case Mother asks a price from you."

I ate the meat from the skinny rabbits and snapped off one of the rabbit's feet. I held it out to Victor. "Want a good luck charm?"

He swatted the foot away when I waved it at him and he shook his head in disgust. "I never understood why the humans used to believe that. And it was rather disgusting that they kept the piece of animal on their key chains of all places." I smiled and then Victor sighed. "I do miss the human world though. I miss the restaurants, the movies and most of all the women who threw themselves at me because they wanted to please me and were attracted to me and thought it was exotic to be with a vampire."

"You mean women don't throw themselves at your feet now?"

Victor groaned. "Yes, they do, but only because I'm the big bad vampire prince. I'm not my father, Ares, you know that. I don't like to be feared." I arched my eyebrow and Victor smiled. "Okay, I like to be feared a little, but not all the time and definitely not from the women I want to bed."

A loud growling brought my attention to the skies above us. The moon was gone and I couldn't see, but I definitely felt like I was being watched. "What is it, Victor? I'm blind here." I caught the dim shape of something flying through the air above us, but I couldn't make out the form.

"It looks like a griffin," he said with a bit of awe.

I started running and yelled, "Race you to the door!"

Victor caught up to me easily as the griffins began diving at me and pulling at my hair. Their claws raked my chest and back, drawing blood.

"I get the wolf. You can have the leech," said a deep and growly voice.

"No, he's a halfbreed and we agreed that I'd get the next half-breed that came through," argued a second voice.

I was beginning to worry when a commanding voice so beautiful and melodic that it made me stop running and stand still, yelled, "None shall touch him! He has a golden aura!"

Ahead of us was the temple steps and standing in the doorway was a woman more beautiful than any other I had seen. She had hair the color of wheat and eyes of emeralds. She was so powerful that I dropped to my knees instantly and bowed my head. "Mother," I whimpered.

She floated down the steps of the temple and knelt in front of me. She touched my face and frowned in concern. "You are in pain. What do you need from me, halfbreed son?"

She was right, I was in pain. Pain at having been separated from the woman I loved. Pain at not knowing for sure if she was alive or dead. Pain at not knowing if she'd been with another man in the past one hundred years. Pain at my love not knowing me.

"I need your consent to continue being with my mate. It is the price the dragons asked in order to assist me in recovering the memories which were stolen from her." I could barely whisper with her so close to me. She was the true Mother of us all, the Mother of even Asena.

"You love her more than anyone else. You have not touched another woman even though you have been separated for over one hundred years. I have not met a man so devoted as you and with a perfect golden aura in many years."

"Golden aura?" I asked.

She smiled. "When a man is pure of heart, void of evil and knows the love of a perfect match, his aura will glow golden. I will give you my consent..."

I looked up at her and smiled.

"...but you must defeat my champion," she finished.

"Your champion?" Victor asked.

Rhea turned to Victor and laid her hand against his cheek. "Oh, son of the Darkness. You are powerful, but not powerful enough. I think I shall grant you a gift as well if this task is completed. Yes, yes, I will give you more power if you and the halfbreed can defeat my champion."

"Who is your champion?" I finally managed to ask.

She wagged her finger at me. "You must agree or decline first."

"I agree. I will do anything to have my mate back," I answered without any more hesitation. I really hoped her champion wasn't that great of a fighter.

She threw her head back and laughed maniacally.

I looked at Victor, but he only shrugged. Women were weird, apparently from the beginning of time.

Rhea looked back at me. "I do not expect you to be able to kill my champion since I would not have picked a weak being for such an honor, but I do expect you or your vampire friend to be able to draw blood. If one drop of blood is drawn from him, then you will have what you ask for and your vampire friend will have more power than any other in the world. You agree?"

Victor and I nodded. I stood and brushed myself off. This was my chance. The one thing I had to do to get Artemis back. I would not fail.

The temple doors flew open, and I watched in awe as a tall man with thick cords of muscle and a perfect physique walked down the steps. His eyes were the purest blue I'd seen, even purer than my own. He stopped beside Rhea and asked, "You summoned me?"

Rhea hugged the man and whispered, "They need only draw a drop of blood from you. Fight well, Hyperion. Do not disappoint me."

Hyperion? Oh gods.

He stood, and I knew it had to be true. The father of the moon, stars and the sun. The father of all preternaturals.

"Oh, crap," Victor said softly.

I ripped my pants off, took a half-shift and then launched myself at Hyperion just as Victor charged at him, too. Hyperion smiled, rolled his shoulders in a circle and said, "It's been so long since I've had a challenge."

CHAPTER 9
CHANDRA

I jumped in the air as I dodged Blu's tail and then shot him in the back with fire. I blocked an attack from Theseus behind me, smiling at my quick reflexes. I grabbed onto Theseus' arm, tossed him over my shoulder and dropped onto his fallen body, delivering blow after blow to his face and body.

"Enough!" Blu roared behind me. I stood up off of Theseus and prepared to attack Blu, but he pinned me to the ground with his foot and growled at me. "I understand that you are worried about the princes, but you are taking it out on Theseus' body."

I hated being pinned. As a wolf I hated being trapped. my body began to glow in the reflection of Blu's eye. He grabbed me and then tossed me into the air. I pulled my wings from my back and flapped them furiously to keep from flying any farther away. I started to fly back towards Blu, but something slammed into my side and sent me careening sideways with my wings pinned against my body. I struggled against what held me until I looked up and realized it was Theseus.

He let us fall to the ground and then pinned me on my back to the ground. "I command you to stop."

I growled at him and bared my teeth. "Get off of me. You do not command me."

"Are you going to behave?" he asked in a reasonable and irritating tone.

I struggled against his hold, but then he used his power to make a shield and slammed it against me. I gasped and then anger overrode my other senses. I used my wings to push us up off of the ground and changed my hand into a paw to stab him in the stomach, but suddenly I was paralyzed.

"You are going to hurt someone you do not wish to harm if you don't control yourself, Hatchling," said the Council.

"I can't just sit here while he's out on such a dangerous mission! I can hardly sleep and I need to do something!" I yelled. I had never before yelled at a dragon, much less the Council and I expected a punishment, but at that moment I didn't care. The shirt the werewolf prince had given me had lost his scent quickly and I knew it was my own fault for smelling it and touching it so much.

"Very well, we will teach you a technique which will consume you, body and mind, until you have learned it. We warn you, it will not be easy to master and may destroy you if you are not powerful enough."

"Please. I need to do something," I said in a much quieter voice. I knew it was an honor for the dragons to teach anyone and that I should feel humbled, but the churning in my stomach at the thought of losing the prince was too much.

"Go wash, eat and then return to us with an open mind and quiet heart," said the Council.

I bowed to them and hurried to do as they asked. I washed my hair and body, ate some meat and bread and then sat in the center of my tent with my legs crossed as I meditated. Normally a request that I have a quiet heart was easy, but since meeting the man who claimed to be my mate and who I had an undeniable bond with, I couldn't. I closed my eyes and relaxed my body in sections. Once my body was relaxed, I focused on the inner turmoil consuming me and slowly released it.

The truth about who I was would be revealed once the prince comes back. The prince will return safely because he swore he would and because he is one of the most powerful beings on the earth.

Continuing in this fashion I released all of my worries and quieted my heart. Feeling better than I had in weeks, I walked out of my tent and to the waiting Council.

I bowed down before them and whispered, "I apologize for my discourteous behavior earlier. Please forgive my insolent actions and words."

"You are forgiven, Hatchling. Are you ready to learn what we are offering to teach you?"

I stood and bowed my head. "Yes. I am."

Blu stood off to the right, watching and waiting. I knew he wasn't just curious about what they were going to teach me, but he was also there to protect me if something happened.

The Council began humming and singing and then disappeared. I stared at the empty spot where five large dragons had just occupied. The humming returned behind me. I whipped around and found the Council now behind me. *Translocation.*

I moaned in pain as a memory of a beautiful woman transporting me from a fight to a strange town flashed across my eyes. I opened my eyes and found that I'd dropped to my knees and Blu was humming with his nose against my head as he tried to heal the pain.

"What did you see?" asked the Council.

"A woman, I believe Sidhe, though at the time I didn't know that. She teleported me from a fight with vampires to a town in the woods. There are periods of pain in between and I don't seem to have memories for those brief lapses, but..." I screamed again as I understood that she was the woman who had stolen my memories.

"Good, Hatchling. Now we know who the woman is that stole

your memories. She is a very powerful Sidhe and it will not be easy to break the barrier she placed."

"Barrier? You mean I still have my memories? She didn't steal them away?"

The Council looked at me in confusion. "Why do you believe they were stolen?"

I groaned. The pain in my head returned as I recalled specifics of the memory. "I remember that the images slipped out of my head, like mud slipping through my fingers. It was as though she plucked them from my head."

The Council went completely silent as they communicated to each other. It was rare that the Council was silent for such a long period of time and it made me very nervous. Finally, they said, "We will not discuss this further until the wolf prince has returned. Now, let us teach you how to teleport yourself and others."

I stood up and patted Blu's nose reassuringly. "Okay."

CHAPTER 10
ARES

My body hadn't ached so badly and in so many places at once in hundreds of years. Covered in sweat and panting like a child, I felt pathetic and weak. I looked over and found Victor in the same state, except his fangs were bared to their longest, reaching down past his lower lip. It was a situation neither of us had been in for a very long time. How could one individual be so powerful?

"We need to change our tactics," said Victor from beside me.

Hyperion was sweating slightly, but our two minute breaks completely revived him whereas we were still winded and still in pain.

"Obviously, but what do you suggest?" I asked with a growl. We'd been fighting for an hour and forty minutes and even with our combined attacks, Victor and I couldn't even scratch him.

"I don't know yet. I was hoping you might have an idea. You are the God of War."

I glared at him. "I'm the God of War against humans and other races, not the Father of Preternaturals!"

Hyperion charged at us, and I ducked just in time. I turned and slashed at his exposed back, but his fist smashed into my face as he spun around in a whirlwind. I crashed to the stone floor and snarled. This was not working.

Victor punched at Hyperion from the front, so I ran and jumped, trying to hop onto his back, but his foot rose without his head even turning and he kicked me backwards while he punched Victor in the chest.

"Do you have eyes in the back of your head?" I asked as frustration gripped me.

Hyperion laughed. "You know as well as I that your other senses can help you know when someone is approaching from the back. Your breathing is as loud as a baby rhinoceros."

I growled at him and attacked from the front, punching and slashing at his arms. No matter how fast I moved, my claws never reached his skin.

Rhea watched with glowing eyes from a throne the griffins had brought out of the temple for her to sit.

Victor rolled his neck and shoulders and said, "We need to use a cheap tactic."

I turned and stared at him. "You're serious?"

He smiled. "Do you really care if we win legitimately or not?"

Hyperion growled. "Are you two weaklings going to stand there and whine all day or are we going to fight? If you want to surrender, I'm fine with that, too."

"I will never surrender!" I yelled. I had to win. *I have to do this for Artemis.* I counted down from five and then charged Hyperion. His dagger pierced the side of my stomach just as Victor stabbed at Hyperion's other side. Without even turning, Hyperion swatted Victor, catching him in the side and sending him flying. Victor landed on his feet and skidded at least fifteen feet back. I pulled away from Hyperion and growled as I put a hand over my wound.

Victor hissed furiously and I saw his power release around him in a thick black cloud. "Ready?" he yelled at me as he disappeared.

I called upon the power of the moon, which hangs above us in her ever-present beauty, and charged forward. I exchanged blows with Hyperion and as my strength was waning shouted, "Now!"

Victor's body materialized from my shadow and he slid underneath my legs, between Hyperion's, and grabbed Hyperion around the arms.

I squatted down and slashed his leg, opening a small cut.

Hyperion yelled, broke free from Victor's grasp and picked me up by the throat. "No! I refuse to be defeated by a halfbreed!"

"You have been defeated, Hyperion. Release your grandson," said Rhea softly.

Hyperion looked as though he wanted to object, but after one look at Rhea's serious face, he dropped me to the ground and stepped back. "I admit defeat."

If only they would assist us in righting the balance of the world and killing Maurice, we could win the battle quickly and easily. I understood their desire to remain neutral, but it would make things so much easier.

Victor limped over to me and said, "That was easier than I thought it would be."

I forced back the smile which tried to surface and turned towards Rhea as I still clutched my bleeding side. "We have completed your task. Will you give me your blessing as you agreed?"

Rhea placed her hand on my forehead and said, "I, Mother Rhea, give you, Ares Lupine of the Werewolves and Sidhe, my blessing to continue as a mated pair with Artemis Lupine. May the dragons restore her memories and bring back the woman you love."

It felt like a weight had been lifted from my shoulders, yet I sagged to the ground and felt tears on my face. I'd done it. I'd completed the task and now Artemis was finally going to get her memories back!

"You, Victor of the Vampires, have shown great loyalty to your friend despite the differences in your races. Therefore, I pronounce you as Ruler of the Children of the Night and give you the power to hold that title. May your reign be brighter than your father's." Rhea's hands began to glow and she placed them on either side of Victor's head. He moaned in pleasure and then his body glowed with an eerie black light. It was like seeing a Sidhe glowing white, but his light was like the night instead of the stars.

Victor turned to me with flames flickering in the back of his black eyes. I smiled at him and asked, "Are you glad you came with me now?"

Victor laughed and reined in the power he'd been given. "That is a definite rush. I'm looking forward to using it against my father."

Rhea kissed each of us on the forehead and whispered to me, "Run home. She is close to breaking."

I blinked at her for a moment until the words made sense. Then I turned and ran without another thought. *Artemis.*

Victor caught up to me and asked, "What is it?"

"Artemis," I whispered, knowing he wouldn't need any more of an explanation.

CHAPTER 11

CHANDRA

I'd been training for an hour straight and had only managed to teleport two feet. The Council assured me that with more practice I'd be able to move farther. I closed my eyes and pictured the place I wanted to move to, the top of Blu's head ten feet away from me. Power built inside me, followed by pain, then nausea and then I was falling. My eyes snapped open and I straightened as I stood on top of Blu's head. "Yes!" I yelled victoriously. Blu huffed in mock irritation as I stood upon his head, but I could tell he was pleased.

I dropped to the ground, but just as I was landing pain erupted in my head. It felt like a crack had opened in something that encased my power and allowed it to leak out. The pain was more intense than anything I'd felt before and I couldn't even scream. I landed on my side, smacking my head against the ground, but didn't feel the additional pain.

Blu pressed his nose to my head and tried to help me, but the pain was beyond even his repair.

"Step back, Draco-Blu. She cannot be helped except by the two tied to her," said the Council.

On cue, the Sidhe prince dropped to the ground beside me with a grimace of pain on his face. "It's going to be alright. He's on his way and will be here soon."

Another man dropped to my side and placed his hands on me. I inhaled his scent and screamed in pain as a memory of him holding me while we both wept played across my open eyelids. Black dots began to cover my vision and I screamed again as my head throbbed in pain.

"Help us, please," the Sidhe prince begged the Council.

"Please, darlin', just relax. He's almost here. Just hold on for a few more minutes," said the man with a slightly southern accent.

My body began to twitch as the wolf side of me tried to find a way to save us. I growled and held my body together. "I…will…not…change."

Wind stirred above me and then the wolf prince dropped to the ground beside me. He tilted my face so I could look into his eyes. "Stay with me. I'm here now. Hold on." He turned away from me and said, "I have gained permission from Rhea. Please, help us now."

The Council said, "In order to restore her memories and give her full access to her power, you must divulge her full true name to her as well as both of the names of the princes she is tied to. Once you do that, her power will release, her memories will return and we will help you control her mind and body so that she does not become too overwhelmed."

"I understand," whispered the wolf prince.

"Me too," whispered the Sidhe prince.

"Begin," said the Council.

"You are Artemis Lupine, daughter of Darren of the Werewolves and Athena of the Sidhe, *passt genau* of Ares and bound to Achilles. You are princess of both the Sidhe and werewolf realms," said the princes together.

My head throbbed excruciatingly and black spots danced across my vision.

"I am Ares Lupine, prince of the werewolves and descendant of Beatrice of the Werewolves and Zeus of the Sidhe and your *passt genau*," said the wolf prince. My vision blackened completely and my body arched up off the ground as my power released.

"I am Achilles, prince of the Sidhe and rightful heir to the throne, descendant of Hera and Zeus of the Sidhe and your bound match," said the Sidhe prince.

Everything disappeared in a world of white and black. I knew I was screaming, but I couldn't hear anything besides the frantic pounding of my heart. Visions of Ares meeting me, fighting for me, making love to me replayed. Visions of Achilles fighting beside me, flying with me, teaching me to open my wings and telling me he loved me replayed. I saw my father. My mother. Koda. Matt. Maurice and his vampires fighting us. Hera taking me and stealing my memories.

The Council, Blu and every dragon in the Lair began singing as they tried to help me. There was so much magic in one place that it made me afraid of the possible repercussions.

I had no voice left for screaming and the power within me felt like it was going to rip me apart. Suddenly every memory I'd ever had fell into place.

"Ares. Achilles. Koda." I whispered their names.

The dragons sang louder than I'd ever heard before. Ares, Achilles, Koda and Theseus all touched me as they used their powers to help.

"I am Artemis Lupine!" I screamed. The pressure and power within me exploded outwards and left me feeling weightless. Every being screamed around me as my power was unleashed upon them.

CHAPTER 12
ARTEMIS

The magic and dust settled and I could breathe again. It seemed like a millennium since I had last opened my eyes, but when I did the joy was better than anything I'd ever felt before. Kneeling one foot away from me was the man who had loved me since discovering me in a small human town. The man who had been so patient with me while I learned about who I really was. The man who would protect me at any cost. His black hair was shaggier than the last time I'd seen him, but his blue eyes sparkled brighter than ever as he looked at me. I could see the hope and worry in his eyes.

How could he have survived the past one hundred years without me by his side? I doubted that I could have held myself together if I hadn't been able to locate him in one hundred years.

I felt my connection to Achilles, but nothing compared with the fierce pull, staggering desire, and love I felt for Ares. We both stood up off of the ground, and I walked slowly towards him. He stood perfectly still as he watched me approach him, but I could see the slight tremor in his arms.

He was such a magnificent man, and he was all mine, had

always been mine, and would always be mine. I wanted to jump into his arms and roll on him to cover myself in his scent, but this was not the place for that.

I stopped in front of him as my body quivered and said, "*Verus amor vincit omnia.* True love conquers all, even one hundred years of separation and a woman's plot to erase you from my memories."

He shuddered, and I wrapped my arms around his neck, kissing him fiercely. His arms were instantly around me in an almost painful embrace, but I didn't care. I was in his arms and we were together again. The kiss was intense yet tender. I felt like I could conquer worlds when he kissed me like that.

He pulled back first and stared into my eyes with tears in his. "Artemis, I've missed you," he whispered.

I buried my nose into his neck and inhaled his delicious scent. "Ares," I sighed. It felt so good to say his name.

Someone cleared their throat and I pulled back to find Achilles and Koda looking at me expectantly. It was almost painful as I tried to decide who to hug first, but Achilles won. I hugged him tightly to me and kissed his lips as his thoughts flooded my mind. *I've missed you so much. It's been so hard not knowing where you were. Or what condition you were in.*

I pulled back from him and smiled. "Thank you. I am truly sorry that I can't say the same. If I had had my memories, I would."

Koda pulled me from Achilles and wrapped me in one of his famous bear hugs. "I've been worried sick about you."

I laughed and relaxed in his hold. "I'm sorry."

Theseus stood back from our group and I remembered his worried words to me before we'd arrived. I walked to him and hugged him. "Thank you for keeping me safe and sane between the times I was able to see Ares. I have not forgotten you, my friend."

Theseus exhaled in relief and hugged me tightly. "Thank you."

Koda groaned behind me. "Great, now my son is taking her attention away from me. I'll never win."

I pulled back from Theseus and looked from Koda to him and

back. "He's your father?" Theseus nodded. I laughed. "No wonder you looked familiar to me!"

I pulled away from Theseus and walked into Ares' arms. Ares turned my face up to his and whispered, "I love you, Artemis."

My lips pulled up into a smile, and I wrapped my arms around him. "I love you too, Ares."

He sighed loudly. "It has been too long since I last heard those words." His lips were pressed to mine before I could say anything else.

I pulled back from him and stood between him and Achilles so that each could hold my hand. Their powers began to flow between me and I could feel the wound Ares neglected to inform us about. I placed my hand on his side, and he grunted in pleasure and pain as the wound knitted itself together.

I looked up at the Council standing near us and said, "Thank you, dragons. I am in your debt." I pulled away from Ares and Achilles and walked to the center to turn and look at each dragon. "I will always remember the great honor that you have given me."

The Council bowed their heads to me. "We will always remember you, Hatchling. It has been an honor to keep you safe over the years."

I turned to Blu and bowed until my forehead touched the ground. "Draco-Blu, you have been my greatest friend and guardian. I am forever in your debt."

Blu dropped his head into a bow. "There is no debt to be paid, Artemis. Just remember who your allies are and never forget the kindness of a dragon."

I held up the dragon scale which was secured on a string around my neck. "I will always remember you, my friend."

Blu wrapped his head around me and hummed against my body. "I will miss you."

Tears sprang to my eyes and I latched on to his neck. "I will miss you as well. Tell Fira goodbye for me."

Blu hummed louder and then pulled away. Ares and Achilles

each grabbed one of my hands and I exhaled in relief as their touch eased the ache in my body.

I turned from them to find Victor, who was standing off to the side smiling at us. I walked to him and hugged him tightly. "Thank you for everything you have done, Victor."

Victor hugged me back and kissed my cheek lightly. "I am glad to see you whole and safe *Mon papillon*."

I pulled back and wiped at the tears under his eyes. "I thought vampires weren't supposed to cry?"

He smiled and whispered, "It had been so long that I dreaded we would not find you. I am just...often in my experience these types of things end badly and I feared the worst might be true when we finally did find you."

I laughed. "Victor, you know me. I never get into trouble."

That received a round of laughter from all of the men gathered. I looked at Victor curiously a moment and then asked, "When did you gain so much power?"

Victor's tears forgotten, he smiled arrogantly, "Rhea gifted me for assisting Ares."

I looked at the lighter tint to his aura and asked, "Did she make you more human? Your aura is less black."

Victor shrugged. "I feel more like a vampire than I ever have before. I don't question what was done, just enjoy the powers that I've been granted."

Ares pulled me into his arms again and nuzzled my hair with his nose as he inhaled long draughts of my scent.

"Where are we going now?" I asked.

"We are going to prepare for the war," answered Victor.

I groaned. "You know, I'd hoped you would have taken care of that, not let the world fall into darkness as it has." I pulled out of Ares' arms and asked, "And what is going on with all of the half-breed kidnappings? I was scared out of my mind these past sixty or so years that I've been with Selene."

Ares sighed. "We have much to catch you up on. I'd prefer if we could make it at least to our base camp before we discussed it though."

Base camp? Since when had they started talking like military men?

Victor changed into a bat and screeched at us as he took off into the sky towards the Lair's exit. I turned and bowed to the Council one more time and then let my wings out from my back. Achilles and Theseus let out their wings and then Achilles picked up Ares and Theseus picked up Koda.

I giggled as I joined them in the air and said, "Koda that is so cute that your son can carry you!"

Koda stuck his tongue out at me. "I may be happy that you're back, but I will still kick your butt."

I rolled my eyes. "You couldn't take me even before I gained more power."

Every eye, including Victor's bat ones, turned to me. Achilles asked, "Gained more power? What do you mean?"

I waved at them dismissively. "I'll show you when we get to your 'base camp'."

The men grumbled their agreements, and we flew out of the Lair and out into the night. I reveled in my ability to fly again and somersaulted and spun in the air in a crazy dance of freedom.

"Been a while since you've last flown, Artemis?" asked Achilles.

I giggled happily. "Much too long. I was pretending to be human so I couldn't risk outing myself just to enjoy some flight time. I'd forgotten how wonderful the wind feels under my wings." I flipped onto my back and dove down and then back up again.

Theseus and Koda were discussing something with serious looks on their faces so I flew over to be nosy. "What's up?"

Koda asked, "Did you recognize the Sidhe who brought the vampires to attack you?"

I frowned. "He seemed familiar, like we were connected somehow, but I don't think I've ever seen his face before." I scoured my regained memories and shook my head. "No, I've never met him before. Why? Do you know him?"

Koda exhaled. "I might. We'll discuss it further at camp."

I flew over to Achilles and Ares and stayed by their sides the rest of the way.

"Where are we?" I asked as we dropped onto a beach where a large stone house sat alone.

"Ireland," answered Ares.

I grabbed Ares' hand and then Achilles'. Ares called, "Come out."

Over a hundred men and women walked out of the house to stand before us on the beach. All eyes trained on me and my instant reaction was to cower, but then I remembered who I was and straightened my spine, meeting all of their eyes. I expected some people to avert their gazes or meet mine defiantly. I did not expect them to all drop to one knee and bow their heads.

CHAPTER 13
ARTEMIS

I looked at Ares and Achilles. "What's going on?"

Ares and Achilles stepped away from me and walked towards the group. Achilles said, "We all knew this day was going to come. You've all been training hard and so, tonight we celebrate."

Ares took over. "We will celebrate the return of my mate. We will celebrate the return of the prophesied one. We will celebrate our impending victory."

The group cheered, but continued to keep their heads bowed in submission. *What the hell is going on?*

Ares turned to me. "We found a way to create an army to combat the vampires. An army which is stronger, more powerful and has fewer weaknesses."

Achilles said, "We have been training them hard in preparation for your return. I hope they are to your liking."

"What the hell are you talking about?" I asked. "What are they? Who are they? What do you mean you created them?" I looked from Ares to Achilles and then at the group.

Theseus stood up from amongst the group and said, "We are

mixed breeds, like you, though not nearly as powerful as you, Princess."

"Mixed breeds?" I walked to the group and inhaled their scents. "Oh, wow. Whoa." They were all half wolf and half Sidhe. "How did you create them?"

Ares smirked. "You see, Artemis. When a man and woman lie together..."

I stared at him in horror. "They're your..." I couldn't finish the sentence. I knew that I was gone a long time, but this was too much for me. I turned away from Ares and started walking down the beach, but Victor stepped into my path and shook his head with a smile on his lips. "You misunderstand, *mon papillon*. These are not Ares and Achilles' children."

I blinked at him. "But he just said..."

Victor silenced me with a glare. "Would I lie to you?"

A smile teased the corner of my lips. "You want me to answer that honestly?"

Victor laughed. "I am being truthful, Artemis. Neither of your mates has broken his vow to you."

I frowned at him as I looked back at Ares and Achilles talking quietly to each other. "I've never mated with Achilles, Victor. You know that."

He shrugged. "You are still bound to him as you are to Ares. It is not so different."

I rolled my eyes. "Not the point. So, if he didn't create them, then who did?"

Victor said, "Koda, among others from the pack who are on Ares' side."

"I'm sure that was a difficult task for them," I muttered. I felt like an idiot for storming away from Ares and Achilles.

Ares walked up to me and asked, "What's wrong?"

I buried my face in his neck and whispered, "I thought they were your children."

Ares pushed me back and held me at arm's length. "Artemis, you should know me better than that."

I blushed and said, "I was gone over a hundred years. I didn't know…"

Ares asked, "What about you? I won't be angry since you didn't have your memories, but…"

"No!" I yelled a little too loudly. I lowered my voice, "No, I didn't. I lived in the witches' coven surrounded only by women. Oh and Draco-Blu, but no, I didn't."

Ares hugged me again and kissed my cheek. "I still can't believe you're here after so long."

I laid my head on his shoulder and sighed. "It does feel like it has been an awfully long time since we've been together."

"Yes, well, could we finish with the introductions?" Achilles asked with a hint of anger in his voice.

"I'm still curious to see what Artemis meant about gaining power," Victor said behind us.

Ares walked with me back to the bowing group. "You just need to accept them as your followers and we can move on."

"Um, okay. I accept you as my followers," I said nervously.

The group stood up and then returned to the house. How could all of them fit in there?

"Alright, show us this new power," said Victor.

I looked around. "Are there any vampires who could be hurt by the sun here?" Victor shook his head. I lifted my hands up in front of my chest, palms facing each other. Warmth filled my body as I called upon my magic, which was much easier now that I was whole, and a ball of sun formed between my hands. I looked up and found Victor, Ares, Koda and Achilles staring at me in complete shock. "Sunlight," I said.

All of the men walked up to me and examined the orb of sunlight I held.

"Incredible," whispered Ares.

"I didn't know any of us could do this anymore," said Achilles.

"How big can you make it?" asked Victor.

Theseus said, "She sent it out in an expanding ring to turn a group of vampires who had surrounded us into ash."

Victor's eyes widened. "Show me."

I shrugged and released the orb and then formed a ring of sunlight around my body. I gathered my magic and then sent the ring out, expanding it as it moved farther away from my body. Instead of letting it go as I'd done previously though, I held it when it was about a mile in circumference.

"Remarkable," said Victor. "No wonder my father renewed his quest for her. Who did you do this in front of?"

I looked at Koda. "The guy you were asking me about. I did it in front of him."

Koda's eyes widened. "Oh no." He turned to Ares. "I think she met Apollo."

Everyone went still at the mention of his name. "Who's Apollo?" I asked softly.

Ares shook his head. "We don't have time to talk about him. We need to get everyone together and move. If it was Apollo, he'll be searching for her."

"Ares! Why are you still keeping me in the dark?"

Ares sighed. "He's the leader of a faction of vampires, which are stronger than the normal ones. Apollo is taking beings like trolls and Sidhe and turning them into vampires. He alone controls the group."

Vampire-Sidhe? Unbelievable.

Ares picked up my hand and smiled. "Come on, let's hunt first."

Koda shifted forms, shredding his clothes and then pranced along the beach as he waited for us. Theseus, Achilles and Victor walked to the house while I stripped. Ares watched me and I felt the blush on my cheeks before I realized I was embarrassed. I shifted forms and stretched. *Ah. It feels good to be a wolf again.*

Ares licked my muzzle, now in his wolf form. *Ready?*

Koda yipped and ran up the beach towards the distant trees. I chased after Koda and Ares ran at my side. I caught up to Koda and nipped his flank playfully. *Too slow.* I sped past him with Ares right on my heels.

Koda dove under my legs, making me tumble head over tail and then Ares was on top of me. We nipped and played for what felt like hours before collapsing into a pile together. Ares and Koda shifted positions until I was lying between, their heads and tails forming a circle around me. Finally, I was back with my pack. After so many years as a lone wolf I couldn't imagine a better place to be.

After our pack nap, we returned to the house which I thought would be filled to capacity, but it was strangely open. "Where is everyone?" I asked.

Achilles pointed down. "Underground. We built a lower level down there to accommodate the large number of our pack."

Victor asked, "Where did you learn that new sunlight power, Artemis? Did the witches teach you that?"

I shook my head. "A vampire attacked me one night while I was walking back to the coven. I just kept thinking how the fight would be a lot easier if I could use sunlight instead of fire and then, boom, sunlight burst out of my hand and poof went the vampire. It took a while, but Selene managed to create a spell which lets her do a similar thing."

Victor tapped his chin thoughtfully. "It might be beneficial to us if we contacted the witches and asked for their alliance in the upcoming battle."

Ares nodded. "I was thinking the same thing. I wanted to stop and talk to Selene anyways and thank her for protecting Artemis all these years."

I looked at the amount of space between Ares, Achilles and I. Why were they now staying apart from me?

Achilles looked at me, and I remembered he could hear my thoughts. He smiled and walked to me, taking my hand. "It was nothing intentional, we just didn't want to overwhelm you or cause problems."

I felt a piece of me calm and looked at Ares. "Are you still bothered by this? When I left, you two weren't really on the best of terms."

Ares smiled. "We have worked out our issues."

Somehow, I didn't think they had resolved the one major issue we had between the three of us while I was gone.

I walked to the living room which was sparsely furnished and sat in a rocking chair facing the rest of the couches. "Now, how about you all fill me in on the last one hundred and five years?"

The men all took seats facing me and looked at each other for several minutes before Koda began. "When Hera stole you, things went a little crazy. Ares and Darren were fighting, but when you got teleported to such a far distance, Ares strength sapped and Darren got in a few good shots. More vampires poured in and with both Ares and Achilles distracted, we knew we wouldn't win. So, we ran."

My mouth gaped open. "You ran away?"

Koda frowned. "Yep. We turned tail and ran. We escaped to Lyngvi, but when we got there Darius had us thrown in jail for some fake charges. He knew he couldn't have us murdered, but not even mom could get us out. So, we were all stuck in jail for fifty years."

"That's a pretty harsh punishment for fake charges."

Koda shrugged. "Fifty years isn't as long as it is to humans."

"How'd you get out of jail?" I asked.

Achilles said, "Hera."

I turned to him. "Hera got you out?"

He nodded. "She popped into our cells and took us to her Court."

"Why would she help you when she was the one who repressed my memories?" I asked with a bit of an angry tone.

"Because I never intended to keep you separated for so long," said a familiar female voice.

I spun around and before I'd even thought it, my wings were out, my skin glowed, and my hands became covered in flames. Every eye was focused on me as I floated above the ground and glared at the woman who had caused me so much pain and separated me from my pack and myself for so long. "What are you doing here?" I asked in a voice that boomed with power.

Victor circled me slowly while Ares and Achilles moved closer. "She really has grown in power. I thought she only meant that she had learned a new spell, but this...this is incredible."

Hera kept her gaze level with mine, but for the first time, I saw fear in her eyes. "Artemis, please let me explain."

Anger boiled inside me and in a millisecond, I moved across the room and had Hera up against the wall by her throat. "Give me one good reason why I shouldn't rip your head off right here and now."

"I only did it to save Achilles. Please, you must understand what lengths a mother would go to save her child."

"I know nothing of a mother's love!" I shouted at her. "Or have you forgotten that I was supposed to be killed when I was born?"

Ares and Achilles each touched one of my arms.

"Calm down, please," whispered Achilles.

Ares whispered, "We believe Hera and have forgiven her. Please, let her go."

My primitive side screamed for vengeance, but I subdued it and released her and my powers. "Fine, but if you so much as give me a cross look, I'll kill you."

Hera started to open her mouth and then thought better of it. "You're more a queen now than you were before."

I turned away from her and stomped to the other side of the room. "Why were you helping Maurice?"

"At the time, I thought he was the most powerful and couldn't afford to lose my people in a fight against him. Had I known that you were indeed the prophesied one, I would have never agreed to assist him. But I didn't follow his instructions exactly. You see, he wanted me to kill you, but due to Achilles binding you two together, that would mean killing my own son. I wiped your memory and sent you away from him so you would be out of Maurice's view and thus, safe. I did the only thing that could keep you both alive."

"Alive, but terrified," I whispered to the fireplace mantle in front of me.

"I am sorry, Artemis. If I could find a way to make up for what I'd done, I would," she whispered.

I turned back to Ares. "So, while you were locked up, Maurice took over the human world?"

He nodded. "He completed the take over and instead of being equal with the other races, the vampires ruled and he took over as king."

"And then the reign of terror began." I looked at Koda. "Why were halfbreeds being kidnapped?"

"The vampires kidnapped some in an attempt to find you and to build their army, but we also went to the already living half-breeds we could find and asked them to join our pack. Each that we asked came willingly."

I paced along the living room floor. "What's our plan? How does this Apollo guy figure into it?" Hera's body stilled and it looked like she wasn't even breathing. I walked towards her. "Who's Apollo?"

She swallowed and then her queen face was back on. "No one of consequence."

Before I could say anything, she disappeared. I growled and punched the wall, which buckled under my fist. "Why does everyone always hide things from me?!"

A man that looked to be in his late teens ran into the house. "Ares!"

Ares rushed to him. "What is it?"

The man caught his breath and then noticed me. "Oh. Wow."

I frowned at him and he started to move towards me, but Ares growled at him. "Speak!"

The man shook his head as though clearing it. "There's a group of vampire hybrids coming this way. That guy is leading them."

I rummaged through my bag until I found an open backed shirt which Selene made specifically for me to wear while my wings were out. All of the men looked at me questioningly as I stripped out of my current shirt, which was ripped since releasing my wings, and put on the new one. I shimmied out of my pants and put on a pair of short shorts and then put my fists touching in front of me. "By the power of the stars, grant me a weapon to fight this foe." I pulled my hands apart and a sword of light appeared between them.

"Who taught you that?" asked Achilles as his eyes went wide.

I shrugged. "I dreamed the words and when I tried them the next morning, it worked." I traced the outline of one of the vines on my face and whispered, "May the stars and moon aid me in my battle for peace." My power as well as the power of the moon and stars made my body glow bright and my vines surged. I smiled at Ares. "See you outside." I ran from the house and onto the beach where I could just make out the group coming my way.

Ares appeared at my side. "Artemis, please. Just wait in the house."

I laughed. "That didn't work before and it's definitely not going to work now."

Ares sighed. "Fine, but please, stay beside me."

I kissed his lips and whispered, "Yes, Alpha."

Ares kissed me a little bit longer, nipping my bottom lip at the end which made me growl in frustration. "Just think of that as incentive to stay alive for the private celebration afterwards."

The rest of our group and pack joined us, standing behind Ares and me. The man Koda referred to as Apollo stopped across the beach from us with his vampire hybrids fanned out behind him. "Surrender the girl and we will leave the rest of you alone."

Ares growled, but I laid a hand on his arm. "No, it's alright. Let him have me."

Ares gaped at me for a moment before he smiled, understanding that I had a plan. I walked slowly across the beach towards the stunned Apollo. He watched me in silence and then asked, "Who are you?"

I stopped walking and stared at his face. He looked like a male version of me. "I'm…Artemis," I whispered.

Apollo blinked a couple of times and then shook his head. "I've been sent here to collect you."

I scoffed. "I'm not a urine sample to be collected."

The vampire hybrids behind Apollo shifted nervously as I walked closer to their leader.

I started to reach out towards him, but a sword appeared in Apollo's hand, and I barely raised mine in time to block his strike. "Do not touch me," he growled.

"You're a halfbreed, like me," I whispered as our swords ground against each other's.

"I am nothing like you," Apollo growled as he pivoted and sliced at me.

The moment broken, the hybrids rushed towards the halfbreeds and the battle truly began. Apollo matched me strike for strike. I couldn't break through his guard, but he couldn't break through mine.

Ares appeared at my side and slashed at Apollo with his claws, but Apollo jumped backwards, and his wings popped out of his back.

Achilles ran forward and jumped into the air, his wings extending and his sword appearing in his hand.

Apollo blocked Achilles' attack, but fell to his feet on the ground.

Three hybrids rushed over to protect Apollo from us. I

decapitated one and rushed around the others who were distracted by Ares and Achilles. Apollo was ready for me though, and blocked my attack easily. I shot fire at him, but he deflected it away.

"Who are you?" I screamed at him. "Why do you look like me?"

Apollo growled, but then Darren was suddenly running down the beach towards us. I gasped, and fear made me freeze. Apollo swung his sword at me, but stopped with the edge pressed to my throat.

I whimpered, "Darren."

Apollo growled and pressed the blade harder against my throat, but still didn't draw blood. "Why don't I want to kill you? Is this some type of spell?"

Darren slowed and walked towards us. "Kill her, Apollo. Kill her now."

"You're my father! Why do you despise me so much?" I asked as tears leaked down my face. Due to my memory problem, I hadn't had time to deal with the words he had spoken to me during the battle.

"What do you mean *your* father?" Apollo asked in shock, his sword pulling slightly away from my throat.

Darren growled at Apollo who shuddered. "Kill her, Son."

"Son?" I gasped. I looked at Apollo and understood. "You're my brother."

Apollo shook his head. "No. That can't be. You told me I was your only child."

Darren groaned. "I thought maybe one of my twins could be a worthy child, but apparently, you are both worthless." Darren reached for the sword in Apollo's hand, but it disappeared into Apollo's skin. Only another Sidhe could use the swords we possessed.

"Explain this!" Apollo yelled.

Darren struck Apollo so fast that I only heard the sound and then Apollo was on the ground. I started to move towards him, but

Darren grabbed me by the throat and picked me up. "If you want something done right, you have to do it yourself."

I struggled against him and then relaxed. He was my dad and it hurt that he hated me, but I was a warrior. I was a powerful being and I would not be strangled by this man. I pulled my sword up and stuck it through Darren's stomach. He looked down and laughed. "You think that little thing will kill me?" His grip tightened and black spots began covering my vision. I couldn't move. I couldn't call my power. How could this man have so much power over me?

"Ares," I gasped with what air I had left.

I heard a responding snarl and then Darren was fighting with one hand while he choked me with the other. The power he possessed was like nothing I had ever encountered before. His aura was bright red and the sheer amount of strength frightened me. Darren tossed Ares backwards and then slammed me onto the ground. He touched the sword, making it disappear from his stomach and then changed his hand to a paw. He raised his three inch claws over my throat. "Time to finish your pathetic life," he said with a snarl.

I closed my eyes and waited for death. I didn't want to die, but Darren was *too* strong. He had to be close in age to Ares. His blood called to mine and I could not kill him. I opened my eyes a moment later to see his claws stopped an inch from my throat. I held my breath to keep them from getting closer to my skin and looked from Darren's shocked face to the blade protruding from his chest, where his heart was. Darren's body fell lifelessly to the ground.

I expected to find Achilles standing behind Darren, but it was Apollo. "None shall harm my sister," he growled.

"You saved me." I said through my hoarse throat. "Why?"

Apollo rubbed his temples and looked from me to Darren's body and back. "I…I don't know. I couldn't stand by and let him kill you. I just…my body moved on its own."

Ares growled from behind him and then Apollo took to the skies. "Fall back!" he yelled to what was left of the hybrids.

Ares started to go after him, but I grabbed his hand. "No! Let him go."

The hybrids and Apollo fled down the beach, disappearing around the turn.

Achilles squatted down next to Darren and checked his pulse. "He's dead."

I frowned down at the body. "Apollo killed him."

Achilles' eyebrows raised. "He killed his father?"

I stood and shoved my finger in his chest, pushing him backwards. "You knew? You knew he was my brother!"

Achilles stumbled back a couple steps and then caught my hands in his. "Yes, but he's our enemy," Achilles said softly.

I pointed to Darren's dead body. "Apollo saved me from Darren. Now, you tell me everything about him."

Theseus trotted up to me in his wolf form and whined. I turned away from Achilles and scratched under his chin. "What is it?"

He rubbed his head against my hand and then trotted away. I sighed and followed him to find a young halfbreed bleeding from gashes with Koda by his side putting pressure on the wounds.

I pushed him away. "Stay still." I put pressure on the wound and he winced. "It'll be over soon."

The boy nodded and then slowed his breathing as I closed my eyes. "By the blood in my veins, the power of the night, I call to the plants and ask for your help." Little bits of glowing energy danced across the wind towards me and with some focus, I pushed them into the wound. Instantly the bleeding stopped, the internal issues sealed and healed and the skin was blemish free.

"How many other spells did you learn?" demanded Victor in a near shout.

I patted the smiling boy on the head and stood up to face Victor. "Enough for me to be sure that if we can get your father and his whole army on the battlefield, I can obliterate every single vampire there."

Victor's eyes widened before he turned silently away to walk back to the house.

Theseus rubbed his head against my shoulder and I turned to smile at him. "Yes, I'm alright. No one hurt me."

Ares growled and Theseus whined in apology before backing away. I put my hands on my hips and glared at Ares. "He wasn't being possessive or overstepping bounds. He was acting as any other wolf in a pack would."

Ares' shirt was gone and as he walked towards me, the hormones I'd worked so hard to keep in control the past one hundred years surged forward. He inhaled, and I knew he could smell my desire.

Achilles turned away from us and walked into the house.

My emotions warred with me as my desire to mate with Ares and my desire to heal the feelings I'd hurt with Achilles gnawed at me.

Ares stopped an inch away from me and nipped my chin. "He understands."

My body wasn't responding to any of the commands I gave it, my arms felt like jelly, so I just nodded and allowed him to pick me up and dash off to the woods. Ares didn't stop running until we came to a densely wooded area where a bed of leaves awaited us.

I looked at it suspiciously. "Had this planned, did you?"

Ares smiled smugly. "It was only a matter of time before the need overcame your virtues. Besides, I am your mate."

He laid me down on the bed of leaves and kissed me fiercely. Everything felt so different than the first time we'd kissed and yet the same. I ran my hands along his sculpted chest and abs and to his muscular back, now slick with sweat from the fight. He nipped my shoulder, making me moan, which made him growl.

I didn't want to rush our mating, but I couldn't wait to become one with him again. I pushed him down onto his back and he laughed softly. Though I saw his eyes glint with gold, he let me force him to submit. I stood back and admired him in all his glory. "It's definitely been too long since I've seen you. I'd forgotten how magnificent you are."

Ares pulled me down and flipped us over, cushioning my head with his arms. "You almost died again today," he whispered softly as he kissed his way from my lips to my chin to my throat.

"No, I wasn't bleeding to death like all the times before."

Ares growled and nipped my chest. "If Apollo hadn't stopped him, Darren would have skewered you."

I arched up as he kissed his way down the center of my chest. "I'm sorry," I whispered.

"Say that again," he said with a hint of a growl in his voice.

I met his eyes and felt tears sliding down my face at the same time I saw tears falling down his to land on my chest. "I'm sorry, Ares."

He kissed me again and then made love to me until the sun rose above the trees.

CHAPTER 14
VICTOR

Artemis was much different than the first time I'd met her. She was still naïve in many respects, but I could see that whatever she'd been doing the past one hundred years had definitely changed her.

The most shocking change was her incredible power. I wouldn't admit it to Ares, but if she and I battled it would be a very intense and catastrophic battle. I would win, but I would be terribly injured and drained afterwards.

I couldn't outwardly choose sides, but I hoped Artemis continued to only mate with Ares. They belonged together and no matter what Achilles said, the two of them were not soul mates like Ares and Artemis were.

"Victor?" Koda asked softly, "Are you feeling alright?"

I shook my head and stood up from the couch where I sat. "I need to feed. I'll return shortly."

Koda watched me, not convinced that I was telling the truth and thinking those thoughts loud enough that I would hear even if my focus was elsewhere. I wasn't telling the truth, but I wasn't going to tell him that. We had known each other so long that he could tell when I was lying. I was not looking forward to the days when Artemis could read me as well.

I closed my eyes and focused on my favorite place to feed. The Red Bordello, a house of humans offering themselves for vampires to feed upon. Using my power, I shifted my body from one place to the other.

A woman screamed, and I opened my eyes, smiling. "Hello, *ma chéri*."

"Sir, you startled me," the doe-eyed petite woman said as she released her hold on her bed sheet. She had golden wheat colored hair and eyes the color of dark emeralds. Her negligee was white and she looked so fragile in the large, four poster bed.

The room was bare except for the large bed with extremely fluffy sheets and pillows. This room was where she slept so it was not as ornately decorated as the bedrooms where they entertained vampires when feeding them. I was the only one that I knew of who visited any of the feeders in their personal rooms.

I stood beside the bed, looking down on her. She had aged since the last time I was here and looked to have a bruise under her right eye. I picked her hand up and kissed it softly. "I apologize for startling you."

She smiled sweetly at me and then scooted over, patting the bed. "Sit with me a moment."

I obliged her and then turned her face to mine. "Who has harmed your lovely face?"

Most women would have turned away or been ashamed, but not her. She simply smiled and said, "It comes with the territory of being a blood whore."

I cringed, hating that term for the humans who offered their blood for vampires. "You are too sweet to be using such vile terms."

"You are too kind for being the Prince of Vampires."

I smoothed her hair back from her neck and she shuddered in anticipation. "I wish I could stay longer, but I have much on my agenda," I whispered in her ear as I kissed it softly and then made small tender kisses along her jaw line and to her neck.

Her jugular vein pulsed faster as I kissed beside it and my fangs lengthened in response. If I was not helping Ares, I would take this girl and keep her to myself, but I could not do that now. I would not promise her or even suggest the notion until I could do it. I was not one to go back on my word and I did not want to offer until I was sure I could keep it.

She ran her hand down my arm and then arched up into me as I kissed her stomach. I pulled the bed sheets down and then found my favorite vein on the inside of her leg.

My fangs extended fully and I bit down, sucking as her blood flowed from the bite. She hissed a moment and then relaxed on her back, enjoying the emotions I was giving her. Every vampire over the age of thirty could manipulate a human's emotions to make their bite enjoyable. Some used it negatively while others just didn't use the ability. I preferred to use it, enjoying the smiles on the women's faces as I fed.

I finished my feeding and pressed against the bite to ensure it stopped bleeding. "Lie with me until I fall asleep," she ordered quietly, still high on the feeding.

I should have said no, but I wasn't going to be needed until tomorrow, if at all by Ares. She was soft and warm as I laid down beside her, and she sighed softly. I stroked her hair and whispered to her in French, knowing she couldn't understand, but enjoyed it nonetheless.

She snuggled against me and giggled quietly. "I always dreamed of sleeping with a prince."

"Then go to sleep little Princess. And dream of happier days."

I watched her sleep with a smile on her face and then teleported back to the house.

"How is she?" Koda asked from the reclining chair.

I tried to hide my smile, but he saw it and smiled back. "Someday, my friend, we will both find females."

Koda shook his head. "We both know that we've already found them. Sadly, we are both unable to have them."

I patted his shoulder and whispered, "There are many more to choose from."

He scrunched his face and whispered, "How can I look past perfection to see them?"

Achilles and I were the only ones who knew of Koda's feelings towards Artemis. And I was probably the only one who knew the true depth of his feelings for her. "You must. Or you shall only wallow in what could have been. There could be a perfect one *for you* if you would just open your eyes."

He shook his head and stood. "I think I'll go for another run."

"Do not lose yourself in the wolf's mind for too long."

He bared his teeth at me. "I know."

I watched him go, trying my hardest to block out his pain and the thoughts in his head. If he got any worse I was going to have to talk to Ares about him.

He was dangerously close to losing himself to the wolf and it would break Ares to have to kill another of his brothers. I could do it to spare him the pain, but I had to hope he would keep the human side alive.

I couldn't judge him for his fascination on one being when I was fascinated on one, and she was human. I shook my head in disgust at myself and walked down to the basement area. The pack looked at me and then went back to their various activities. I walked to my room and lay down to sleep. Or at least to dream of what could have been.

CHAPTER 15
ARTEMIS

We woke to the sounds of whispering. Ares growled next to me and wrapped his arms around me protectively. "She's sleeping," he whispered.

"We discussed this, Ares. I know I agreed not to mate with Artemis, but you're not allowing me time alone with her," said Achilles.

Ares growled again as Achilles moved closer. "Back away."

"Ares," Koda said in an exasperated tone. "Stop acting so damn possessive. It's Achilles we're talking about, not some random wolf."

Ares nuzzled my hair and exhaled. He stayed in that position for two more minutes before finally releasing me and standing up. "I'm sorry."

I rolled onto my back and stretched. "What's going on?" I asked as I feigned naivety, looking from Ares to Koda and then to Achilles.

"It's time for breakfast," said Ares softly, pulling me to my feet and kissing my cheek.

I kissed his lips and then moved to hug Koda, but my stomach felt weird. I stopped moving and frowned as I tried to determine the problem. I stood perfectly still for thirty seconds as nothing seemed to answer what the weird sensation was. And then my stomach grumbled. I laughed at my ridiculousness and said, "I guess it *is* breakfast time." I hugged Koda before stepping into Achilles' arms. "Good morning."

Achilles smiled down at me. "Hello."

Ares and Koda took the lead and Achilles placed my hand in his as we headed back towards the house. Ares got dressed and tossed me clothes so I could dress as well before we all went down the stairs to the sub level of the house. The sub level wasn't what I had expected. I thought it would be wood and dirt and small and dark, but it was none of those things. Large wooden support beams held the sides and upper level from crashing down, but marbled tile and candelabras decorated the area. It was also much bigger than I thought it would be with two hallways leading to at least ten doors and three large main rooms, including a full kitchen.

The pack was sitting around the outer edge of the living room floor with empty plates in their hands, looking hungry. Victor stood in the center of the room tapping his foot impatiently, but once he caught sight of Ares and me, he just smiled.

Ares cleared his throat and the room quieted. "You all fought well yesterday and we're very proud. Now, let's eat!"

Five boys from the pack brought in platters of slightly cooked meat and set them down in a large circle in the center of the room. Ares picked up two empty plates and handed me one. I followed him as he took some meat from each of the platters and filled mine as well. Once our plates were full, Achilles and Koda took their turns, and then the rest of the room. Ares found an open spot against the wall and we all sat down with Ares beside Victor, me beside Ares, Achilles beside me and then Koda beside Achilles. I ate in silence as I listened to the pack around me discuss the small victory the battle was yesterday and what it could mean for the battle at large.

I finished my meat and leaned against Achilles who was sipping a glass of wine. He tilted it towards me. "Want some?"

I clapped a hand over my mouth to keep from throwing up. "No. I don't drink wine."

Ares and Koda roared with laughter. "Now, she doesn't drink wine," Koda said around his laugh.

Victor arched an eyebrow in question, and Ares said, "One night at Lyngvi she drank enough wine to get drunk and ended up throwing it all up in the toilet a few minutes later. I hadn't seen a young wolf drink so much in a long time."

I blushed and looked down at my hands. "I was upset because all those women were flirting with you and trying to kill me."

Achilles snorted. "Werewolves always have so much drama when they're together." The pack stilled and looked at him in question. He rolled his eyes. "Full blooded werewolves, not halfbreeds." The pack started talking and eating again. Achilles exhaled. "Your kind is so sensitive."

I rolled my eyes. "Right, because Sidhe are known for their loving, calm demeanors. Oh wait, that's right, I was supposed to be killed by them!"

Achilles sighed, but didn't pick up the argument. I relaxed against him to let him have his time with me near, but reached out my other hand to Ares so I could touch him as well.

Achilles smiled at me and kissed my cheek softly. I laid my head down on his shoulder and exhaled. This was heaven. I never wanted it to end.

Once everyone had finished eating, Ares called the pack outside for training, despite my wish to cuddle. The sand was somewhat restrictive for movement, but after running in it for a few miles I started to get the hang of it. I really enjoyed the wind blowing my hair back and the taste of the sea water as it splashed beside me.

Koda waved me over from farther up the beach and I ran to him, skidding to a stop and spraying sand at him. Koda stood across from me with a wicked smile on his face. "I have a feeling you're a bit out of practice, darlin'."

I rolled my shoulders and stretched my legs. "Perhaps, but even out of practice, I'm more powerful than you."

Groups began sparring around us, practicing everything from hand-to-hand combat to dealing with four or more opponents at once.

Koda rolled his eyes. "Powers don't matter in close combat situations. I'll drop you to the ground and stake you before you can even make a fireball."

I laughed and rolled my shoulders. "Bring it."

Koda charged forward and was in a half-shift before I noticed his hand was now a paw. I blocked the hit, but he scratched my arm. I gasped as it burned and dropped down to kick at his legs. He jumped up and swung at me again. I rolled out of his reach and shot a fireball at him. He growled and patted out the flames on his shirt. I stood and prepared for his next attack, a smile lifting my lips. Koda's eyes flickered above my head and I dropped to the ground just as an arm whistled over me. I flipped over to find Ares standing over me, smiling wide.

I kicked him in the stomach and then rolled between his legs to face them. Ares nodded at Koda and then they both charged me. I jumped up and released my wings, but Ares grabbed my foot and yanked me back down to the earth. I folded in my wings and then punched him in the face as they retracted completely. Koda swung at me, and I formed my sword. Ares knocked the sword from my hand and then Koda punched me in the face. I stumbled backwards and growled at them.

I felt my skin grow hot as I began to glow and my powers released. "Enough play," I whispered. I charged forward and swept Koda's legs out from under him and then punched him in the chest as he fell to the ground. Ares swung at me, but I caught his fist in my hand and punched at him. I, however, had forgotten that no matter how much more powerful I had become, Ares was *much* more powerful than me. He grabbed my hand, flipped me on my back and pinned me to the ground. I screamed in rage at being pinned and let my wings extend from my back to toss us up and him off of me. Unfortunately, Ares was prepared for this maneuver and held on to me.

He grabbed a handful of my hair, tilted my head back and placed his teeth, which were now four elongated wolf's fangs into my throat. "Submit," he said around my throat. I whined and relaxed in his grip. Ares removed his fangs and kissed my throat. "Thank you."

I stepped out of Ares' arms and rubbed my throat while glaring at him. Koda stood up from the ground. "Dammit."

A smile twigged my lip. "At least I beat you."

Koda sighed. "Yeah, whatever."

Theseus laughed. "Dad got beat by a girl."

Koda growled, but the rest of the pack laughed with Theseus, making Koda turn bright red.

WE CONTINUED the same daily routine of eating, training, and sleeping for four weeks until Ares and Achilles decided to relocate. I was surprised they'd waited so long to move since Apollo knew where we were, but they didn't seem worried.

We stood outside on the beach preparing to leave so I decided then was a good time to show them the trick the dragons had taught me. "Well, are we all ready to go?"

Everyone nodded and I said, "Will everyone please crowd around us and be sure to touch each other?"

Ares looked at me quizzically, but everyone obeyed my order, even Victor and Achilles. I closed my eyes, summoned my power and said, "Try not to puke."

The dizzying vortex sucked us in and then spit us out just in front of the entrance to the Light Court. All of the members of the pack groaned as they resisted the urge to throw up. Victor, Ares and Achilles stared at me with wide eyes. Achilles asked, "Who taught you that?"

I smiled. "The dragons taught me it so I wouldn't kill Draco-Blu or Theseus in my worry over Ares before I had regained my memories. They told me it would take practice to be able to do this, but once I felt the amount of power I'd had returned to me, I knew I could do it now."

Victor whistled. "You are quite an interesting woman. Ares is going to have to keep a tight watch on you."

I rolled my eyes. "Like that's not already happening."

All of the men laughed, and Achilles opened the staircase, which I knew was actually a portal to the dimension that contained the Sidhe courts. "Single file," he said as he started down the stairs. I summoned my powers so I would glow and be able to see as I walked down the stairs and smiled when I noticed the rest of the pack doing the same.

It didn't take long for us to make it through the door and into the open grassy field where I'd talked with Achilles the last time I'd come here. Hera was waiting for us, but as soon as Achilles walked to her, she took his arm and led him away. Erebos and Heracles stood guard and smiled at me as I stepped out. I bowed to them and they bowed back.

"Greetings, Artemis," said Erebos in his deep booming voice.

"It pleases us to see you well," said Heracles.

I smiled back. "Thank you. I am glad to see that neither of you was hurt after I was abducted."

Erebos and Heracles kept their smiles in place but did not respond. Hera and Achilles came back a moment later and Hera addressed Ares and me, "I have rooms for your pack, if you'd like my guards to show them there?"

Ares bowed his head respectfully. "I would greatly appreciate that, Queen of the Light Court."

Hera snapped her fingers and Erebos and Heracles waved the

pack forward. Ares pulled me against him and held me still. "Wait, I want to show you something," he whispered.

I relaxed against his warm body and waited as the rest of the pack, including Koda and Theseus were led to the castle. Achilles glanced at us, but then turned and followed his mother.

I'm still supposed to get alone time with you too, Artemis. Don't forget. Achilles said through my mind.

I smiled. *I have not forgotten and will be sure to pencil you in.*

Ares kissed the top of my head and then began leading me through the town. Sidhe peeked out their windows at us, but if we looked, they quickly turned away. I didn't understand their aversion to us. It wasn't like we were lepers or anything crazy. We were just two mixed bloods. Sadly, I knew that being a mixed blood was exactly why they hid. Once this was over, I intended to fix the Sidhe's belief system.

Ares wove his way expertly through the town's streets and seemed to know where he was going. I, on the other hand, was completely lost. I remembered coming here with him before, but we hadn't explored this area then.

Did it pain him to be back here? I tried to sense his feelings, but he had blocked me from them.

We made what felt like a circle around a large building and stopped. Amazingly there was a river there surrounding a small island covered in green grass, weeping willows whose branches dropped into the river and cherry trees whose pink blossoms drifted to the ground lazily. It was the most beautiful thing I'd ever seen, something straight out of a poem and yet here it was in front of me. We definitely had not visited this spot last time.

"It's beautiful," I whispered as we started across the wooden bridge to the island.

Ares stayed silent, but I could see the small smile tugging up the corners of his lips. We stepped onto the island and an immense amount of power in the plants and ground of the island pressed against me. A small sound escaped my lips as the power filled me and opened me up, my skin glowing softly and my vines sparkling.

We walked around the small island until we were underneath the cherry tree which had the most blossoms and the most power. Ares reached up and plucked one of the small pink blossoms and held it out to me. "This is an area of power. The Sidhe call the island the '*cor*' which means heart. This tree is the real center of all the power and is called '*mater*' which means mother."

I took the blossom from him and gasped as the power drained from the blossom and into me. I staggered backwards and ended up leaning against the tree. Power poured into me like a wave of fire, scalding me from the inside. I screamed, but couldn't move away from the tree to stop the overload of power. Ares grabbed my hand, but instead of pulling me away from the tree and releasing me from the power, the power spread to him and pulled him against me and the tree.

We screamed in our shared pain and pleasure as the power scalded us and yet filled us with euphoria. I felt as though my eyes were going to pop out of their sockets from the pressure of so much power in me. The power flared and then disappeared as Ares and I fell away from the tree.

I landed on top of Ares and we both gasped for breath and moaned in pain. I started to push off of him when I realized that I wasn't the only one glowing. "Ares," I whispered.

He looked up at me and frowned. "What? What is it?"

I pointed at his body. "You…you're glowing."

I moved off of him and he quickly walked to the river, staring in shock at his reflection. I stayed sitting on the ground as my body absorbed the power the tree had given me. How was it possible that I could hold so much power in me? When I borrowed power from plants I always had to use it or it tried to destroy me, but *mater* had given me power to store. Was *mater* a cognizant being? Could she really understand and did she know battle was looming?

A noise made me look at the bridge where I could see a crowd had gathered. No doubt they'd felt the power the tree was giving us and come to see who the lucky Sidhe was. Judging by their faces, they weren't pleased.

Ares laughed suddenly, making me jump. He ran to me and picked me up, swinging me around as he hugged me.

"Ares? Why are you laughing?" I asked nervously.

He set me down and I stared at the new marks on his body. I ripped his shirt off and gasped. Ares' arms and chest were now decorated with tattoo-like, black images of running wolves. I touched one of the little black wolves and jumped as it moved, biting the wolf in front of it, and causing all of the wolves on Ares to begin to run. The wolves ran together and even yipped.

I looked up and Ares' eyes were white pearls. I'd only seen this once before when I had released Achilles' power. "How is this possible?" I asked softly.

Ares smiled. "Do you mean the fact that you are my destined mate and can activate my powers?"

I shook my head at him. "No, we both already know I'm your mate. I mean, how is it possible that you have Sidhe powers?"

"Perhaps I had them all along, but since my wolf nature was so strong it lay dormant until you activated them."

"I didn't activate them, *mater* did."

Ares cupped my face in his hands. "You are always underestimating yourself. I touched this tree thousands of times when I was young in hopes that it would do this exact thing. The only reason this happened was because you were the one I touched."

"Out of the way! Make room," Hera yelled. Ares and I turned to find Hera pushing through the crowd which had gathered. She stopped at the edge of the bridge, just a foot away from the island and gasped. "No. It cannot be."

Ares walked towards her with his arms spread. "You see it. There are others here who witnessed it. My powers have surfaced. It seems you were wrong about me."

Hera pointed at me. "You! You did this!"

I shrugged. "That's what Ares said, but I didn't do it on purpose. I would do it again though."

Hera was glaring at me and looked ready to attack, but she held her ground and kept from releasing her powers. Was she holding back because of our truce or was she frightened of how much *more* powerful I'd become?

Ares exhaled and his eyes returned to normal and his body stopped glowing. "It seems I may be able to join the Sidhe's ranks after all."

Hera glared at him. "If that is the case, then I demand that you bow to me, your queen."

Achilles was standing beside Hera and up until that point, his face had remained perfectly blank. As soon as she said it, he rolled his eyes and shook his head in disbelief.

Ares bowed his head at the neck. "I acknowledge that you are queen of this domain, but I will join my father in his Court."

Hera glared harder at Ares, her skin starting to glow softly as she grew angrier. "Very well. Come now, let's return to the Prince's quarters and discuss this upcoming battle." Hera spun on her heel and marched back through the crowd of people.

Achilles walked down the bridge to stand in front of Ares. "You look better now," Achilles teased.

Ares laughed. "Don't worry, brother, I will not try to steal your throne. I have no intention of taking your title."

Achilles frowned. "You are a Prince of the Sidhe as much as I am and you will be given that title as soon as father sees you. I was simply meaning that I much prefer your decorated Sidhe body to the boring werewolf one."

Ares was frowning, too. "You will of course be next in line for the throne though."

Achilles smiled. "Of course."

Ares held out his hand with a smile. Achilles stared at Ares' hand a moment before clasping it and then pulling Ares into a hug.

Tears pricked my eyes as I watched the two men I loved hug and completely forgive each other for the first time in over four hundred years.

I realized one thing though as I stared at them. "Ares?" Ares and Achilles broke from their hug and turned to me. I waved them over, not wanting everyone to hear what I was about to say. They walked to me and the urge to touch them overtook what I needed to say. I reached out and clasped each of their nearest hands. I exhaled happily and then whispered, "Ares, I don't think you have wings."

Achilles' eyes spread wide. "She's right. Whenever she released my powers before, my wings automatically popped out." He pointed to my wings, which were out. "Even hers are out."

Ares shrugged. "It's alright. I don't like flying much anyways. I prefer the ground under my paws."

Achilles walked across the bridge and stopped when he noticed all of the angry looking Sidhe gathered. "From this day forward all shall recognize Ares, Prince of the Werewolves as Ares, Prince of the Werewolves *and* Sidhe. If any disagrees, let them challenge me."

The Sidhe gasped and then began whispering loudly to each other. Ares picked up his ripped shirt and smiled at me. "I wish this had been done in other circumstances."

I blushed and took the shirt. "I'm sorry."

He laughed and wrapped his arm around my waist. "Don't be. I liked it. Besides, I've ruined more clothes in fits of anger than you've probably ever owned in your life."

I giggled as I imagined Ares ripping his shirt off like when a comic book character gets angry and turns into a large green monster.

"What are you laughing about?" he asked.

The giggle turned into a laugh and I spoke in the deepest voice I could muster, "You won't like me when I'm angry."

Ares smiled and then lunged for me. "You think that's funny?"

"Uh oh, you better watch out! I think he's turning green!" I yelled as I jumped away from him and ran across the bridge.

Achilles laughed. "The Hulk is a rather fitting character comparison for you, Ares."

Ares snorted, a sound much better suited to his canine form. "I don't turn green."

"No, but you do get furry and rip your shirts off," I answered as another fit of laughter took me and I had to stop to hold my stomach.

"I think I'm more like Wolverine," Ares said seriously.

"Well you are grumpy like him and way too full of yourself," Achilles said in the same serious tone as Ares.

Ares flexed his abdominals and then lifted his arms, flexing his biceps and chest. "Have you seen me? How can I not be full of myself?"

My laughter disappeared as I looked at him. He was definitely way too perfect.

"Now you look like Koda," Achilles said with a chuckle.

Ares swung at Achilles, but he jumped back and Ares growled.

"Run, he's turning green!" Achilles said and grabbed my hand, running down the bridge with me in tow. A new fit of laughter forced me to stop running as I was bent over holding my stomach with tears falling down my face.

"Ha. Ha. Very funny," Ares said as he caught up to us.

Hera appeared in front of me. "Why are you delaying? Come, let's get on with our planning. We don't have much time."

I stopped laughing and took a couple of deep breaths to calm down before I let the anger control my tongue. "I apologize for enjoying the renewed time with my mate. I forgot that the world revolves around you, Your Highness."

Achilles groaned softly and Ares sighed. Hera's face turned red, but for once she held her tongue. She held out her hands and Ares and Achilles each took one and then took my hands. Hera started to draw power in, but I beat her to it and teleported us into her court room where she conducted her important business. We landed in front of a large conference table and eyes popped open from all of the Sidhe and halfbreeds gathered.

Hera's face was the most priceless of all. "You can teleport?"

I smiled. "A gift from the dragons to me for my friendship."

Several of the Sidhe gasped. Hera's face paled and she asked, "You're friends with dragons?"

I pulled out Blu's scale and showed it to the room. "I am."

"Perhaps now is not the time for this discussion? Let's work on our plan for the battle," said Achilles in a strong and demanding voice.

Victor sat in one of the many chairs and nodded. "Yes, we need to discuss strategy."

I dropped into one of the chairs. "Do we really need a strategy? We just need to have Maurice and as many of his vampires in the area so I can toast them. Wham, Bam, Thank you Ma'am and we've won."

"You think you're so powerful?" asked a female Sidhe with green filigree designs around her eyes. She obviously didn't like me and her glare was most impressive despite her small frame and delicate, doll-like face.

I covered my hand in sunlight and smiled as I said, "I know I am."

Victor nodded. "Yes, she is, but the problem is getting my father to the battleground. He prefers to let others fight his battles."

I shrugged, releasing the sunlight. "Then we storm his home and I toast him."

Koda sighed. "Darlin' it won't be easy like last time. Last time he was trying to capture you to make you his. Now, he just wants you dead."

"So how do we get him on the battlefield then?" I frowned.

"We have to offer him something he can't refuse," said Ares quietly.

Victor gasped. "No. There are too many variables and too many things that could go wrong."

"You think I don't know that?!" yelled Ares. "Unless you can come up with a better plan, that's the only way."

"We need to fight a battle which we lose first and then do that," said Victor.

"No! We cannot lose a battle on purpose. That would mean letting our people die!" I yelled.

"Artemis," Achilles started.

I stood up from my chair and slapped my hands down on the table. "No! I will not sacrifice anyone. We can fight one battle and then discuss whatever it is that Ares wants to do. We do not have to lose that first battle though. I can refrain from using my sunlight magic and that way Maurice won't know I can do it."

The room was silent for several minutes until Hera said, "I agree with Artemis. We can fight this first battle no matter the outcome. I would like to know what it is that Ares is suggesting."

Ares looked at the table a moment and then said, "The only way I can foresee Maurice coming out to the battlefield is if we agree to surrender and to give Artemis to him as a good faith gift."

"You want to give him Artemis?" Hera asked softly.

Ares smiled. "Well we wouldn't *really* be giving her to him, but we could make it look authentic. I could be bound and guarded by several of your Sidhe warriors while Artemis is bound with her hands in front of her. Then when Maurice takes the bait and comes near her, she can fry him and those nearest him."

"I like it," I said with a smile on my face.

Koda laughed. "You would like that idea."

"What's that supposed to mean?" I asked with a glare in his direction.

He held his hands up in surrender. "Nothing. Never mind."

Ares pulled me down into my seat and kissed the back of my hand. "Calm down. You're getting excited over nothing."

I took a deep cleansing breath. "Sorry."

"When will your pack be ready for the first battle?" Hera asked.

I looked at Ares' smiling as he said, "We're ready now, but you should begin the preparations of your Sidhe. We need to get word out that we're looking for a fight."

Victor smiled. "I'll spread word of that. I still have some allies who are undercover with my father's side."

Hera nodded. "Good. I'm sure the vampires will act quickly once they know we have Artemis with us again. I'll have Hephaistos start on the weapons."

CHAPTER 16
ARTEMIS

The full moon hung above us. Her presence made me itch to run as a wolf with my pack and hunt beneath her soothing and powerful light. I decided then that I would get the pack together and go for a run that night. I didn't feel right not having run with the halfbreed pack yet. A soft breeze blew around me, swirling cherry blossoms in a soft, soothing whirlwind. Energy from the blossoms seeped into me and filled me with a low level of power. My skin tingled and glowed softly as I absorbed the power and stuffed it down into the imaginary box that I pictured hiding within my soul. Over the last week, I'd been storing power there slowly, every time I visited the island.

"Artemis?" Achilles called from somewhere within the houses.

"Yes?" I answered, not bothering to move from my spot or raise my voice.

He walked around the house nearest the bridge that crossed to the island. He slowly made his way across the bridge and stopped in front of me. "Ares shouldn't have showed you this island. You're spending more time here than with us lately."

I held open my arms and he sat down, leaning against me and

letting me hold him. It wasn't a common gesture from me to him and he didn't delay in accepting it. "I'm sorry. I know I need to spend more time with you, but I've just needed some time to meditate and think."

He turned and pulled me into his arms, reversing our position and leaning me against his chest. "It's alright, Sweetheart. I've just been worried about you because you've been blocking me from your thoughts so deliberately." He slowly stroked my hair, calming me even more than my meditation had. Gently he titled my chin up and kissed me.

My control slipped the more time I spent touching him. Each additional time I touched him, the more I wanted to give in to him. His hands slid up and down my arms as he kissed me and I could feel the strength in them. My head swam, rendering logical thoughts impossible and allowing my hormones to rage. I turned completely around, wrapping my legs around his sides and sitting on his lap. I fisted my hands in his hair, loving the silky smoothness against my skin and kissed him deeply. He moaned and the sound made me smile and growl happily. He picked me up and then laid me down on the ground. The feel of him lying on top of me was incredible. I had wanted it for so long, but had been denying us both.

Was he as talented as Ares? The thought stopped me cold and dispersed my hormones. I couldn't cheat on Ares. If I mated with Achilles it would crush Ares. I put my hand on his chest and whispered, "Wait."

Achilles sighed, stood up and turned away from me. "I wondered how long until you pushed me away."

The raw pain in his voice hurt me. "Achilles, I'm sorry. I just..."

"Stop, just stop. Please, just leave."

His voice was so full of anger and pain that I actually flinched and took an involuntary step back. I headed towards the bridge, but stopped at the beginning of it. "I'm sorry I can't love you like you deserve, but know that I do love you. If I could release you from our binding so you could find a woman who loved you, I would."

He didn't move or acknowledge me, so I left him alone. The calm I'd gained was replaced by a depression and despair that soured my mood. If my life had been a cartoon, a storm cloud would be hovering over my head raining on me. I ignored the Sidhe watching me walk through the town towards the training grounds. Let them look. Let them talk. I didn't care.

Koda and Ares smiled at me from where they were fighting as I walked onto the grassy training ground. For the first time I ignored them, not returning their smiles and walked to a deserted corner of the field as far away from everyone else as I could. I needed to release this anger and despair. I needed release from the pain.

I inhaled, pulling my fire from my core and covered my hands in it. Ares walked closer to me, but I ignored him and his presence. I tilted my head up to look at the sky and raised my hands up over my head.

I had been making headway with Achilles. I'd been able to make him smile daily, even without mating with him. And with one word, one touch, I'd erased all of that.

I always screwed things up. I hurt Ares. I hurt Achilles. I even hurt Koda. All I wanted was to please them and I failed miserably at it. The anger and gnawing ache I felt grew unbearable. Tears streamed down my face and pain gripped my body. I closed my eyes and pictured each of their faces and the times that I'd hurt them. I took another deep breath and then screamed as I shot fire up into the air. The force of the power I was using, the pain I was feeling and the sadness sent me to my knees. I sobbed uncontrollably as I released it all and screamed and cried.

I reined in the power and dropped my hands to the ground, continuing to sob. Warm arms wrapped around me and pulled me against an even warmer body. "It's alright, Darlin'. It's going to be alright," whispered Koda.

I buried my face into his chest and snuggled into him as I continued to cry. "I'm always failing. I fail at being a woman. I fail at being a mate. I fail at being a pack mate. I fail at all of the relationships around me. How can anyone think that I won't fail at this prophecy that supposedly surrounds me?"

Ares squatted down in front of me. "What happened, Artemis? What made you feel this way?"

I turned away from him and whispered, "I've hurt you all. I've hurt all three of you. All I want to do is love you and make you happy and I can't even do that."

"You do make us happy. The sight of your face makes us happier than we have been in a hundred years," whispered Koda.

I shook my head. "I'm continually causing you pain by a wrong word or a wrong decision. I can't seem to do anything right."

"Life is all about learning from your mistakes. You think I'm perfect? You sure as hell know Ares isn't perfect," Koda said as he rubbed my back slowly.

"Hey," Ares protested. He reached forward and touched my arm. "We all make mistakes. The defining factor is how you handle the mistakes and what you do to try not to make them again."

"How can I not make a mistake when the choice will hurt one person no matter what?" I whispered.

"This is about Achilles, isn't it?" Ares asked. I didn't respond which was answer enough for him. "I know it's hard and I wish there was a way I could fix it for you, but I can't. I'd be lying if I told you it wouldn't bother me if you mated with him and I won't lie to you."

"What's going on?" Achilles asked with pain still evident in his voice. *Why hadn't I felt him approach or even heard him approach? It was odd that I hadn't been able to at least feel him when he was so close.*

I stood up and brushed myself off. "Nothing." I walked away from them all and towards Erebos who was sparing with Theseus. "Greetings, Erebos," I said as I smiled at him.

He smiled at me. “Greetings, Artemis. How may I help you this day?”

“Could you teach me some advanced magic techniques?” I asked.

Erebos blinked twice and then said, “I’m not sure that I can teach you anything. You know quite a bit more than me, actually.”

“I know witch magic and the magic I picked up, but I don’t know much Sidhe magic,” I answered.

He rubbed his chin a moment and then said, “Well, I could teach you a few of my special talents and some of the nature magic. It might be better if we had a few Sidhe who each possessed different abilities.”

“Whatever you think is best.”

He smiled. “I’ll round up some Sidhe and meet you back here after lunch. Is that okay?”

“Thank you.” I said with a smile.

Theseus touched my arm gently as I went to turn around. “Are you alright?” he asked softly.

I patted his hand reassuringly. “I’ll be fine. Eventually.”

He wanted to say something else, I could tell, but I walked away before he could. I could feel Ares, Achilles and Koda watching me, but I ignored them. I needed to be away from them for a while. I walked to a halfbreed and a full werewolf sparring with each other. “Mind if I join?” I asked them.

They turned and bowed to me. “Princess,” they said at the same time.

I waved my hand dismissively at them. “Call me Artemis. We’re pack members so there’s no reason we can’t be on a first name basis.”

The male werewolf on the left was quite possibly the tallest man I’d ever met. His body was corded with muscle and if I hadn’t heard him speak just now, I would have thought he could only scream at people. He did have bright green eyes that showed intelligence though and he looked older than the most of the others. “I’m Thor.”

I swallowed my laugh and asked, “And how old are you, Thor?”

He frowned a moment in concentration and then turned to Ares who was standing across the field watching us. “How long ago did we meet?”

Ares looked down at the ground as he thought. “We met around eight hundred Anno Domini I believe.”

Thor nodded, turning back to me. “So then I am around seventeen hundred years old.” He frowned a moment and then nodded again. “Yes, that sounds about right.”

I turned and looked at Ares, wanting to ask how old he was since he was older than Thor, but then remembered I was trying to ignore them. I turned back to Thor. “Well, then I shouldn’t be a problem against you.” I looked up his massive frame. “Not that I thought I could beat you physically anyways.”

The halfbreed was a woman who looked no older than twenty, but the looks she gave me made me think she was much wiser than me. “What’s your name?” I asked.

She smiled. “I’m Daisy Mae,” she said with a thick Southern accent. “It’s a pleasure meeting you.”

I shook her extended hand and smiled sweetly at her. “I love your accent. It’s a pleasure meeting you, too.”

“Why aren’t you just the sweetest thing ever? How old are you?” she asked.

“I’m over one hundred years old,” I replied. “And how old are you?”

“Only twenty-nine,” she said with the sweetest smile on her face. “I’m one of Koda’s daughters.”

I stepped forward and hugged her. “Well, then this is a more appropriate way to greet you.”

She laughed and squeezed me tight before letting me step back. “I’ve heard so much about you. I am so happy I finally got to meet and talk with you.”

I didn't want to be rude, but I wasn't exactly in the mood to socialize. "It's a pleasure to meet you, Daisy Mae." I turned to Thor. "So, how about that fight?"

Thor sized me up, looking from the top of my head to my toes. "You sure?"

I smiled, but it came out more as a baring of teeth. "Yes."

He smiled at me, apparently pleased at my reaction. "What are the ground rules?"

"No half-shifts, I don't need you bigger than you already are. Magic is permitted, but no lethal kinds. This is just a match for fun and to hone my skills."

Thor smiled wide, his teeth lengthening as he did. "Sounds fun. How about we start in full shift?"

I stripped my shirt off over my head and tossed it to Daisy Mae. "Sounds good." I pulled my bra, pants and panties off and gave them to Daisy Mae, too, and then dropped to my hands and knees as I shifted. The shift was smooth and pain free, but moving into my wolf form brought forth the feelings I'd suppressed. I clenched my teeth together as I fought the rage that tried to surface.

Thor yipped at me, and I turned to face him. He was almost as big as Ares, but still slightly shorter. A fight between the two of them could be catastrophic. I wagged my tail to show him I was fine and then crouched down and began circling him.

He circled with me with slow, graceful movements. I had no idea how an animal as big as he could be graceful, while I was such a klutz. He sprang at me, and I rolled to the right, spinning around and snapping at his flank, but he dodged before I could get him.

He was good. Fast and agile. I was incredibly outmatched. If this had been a real battle a smart wolf would roll on her back and beg for mercy. This wasn't a real battle though and I wasn't particularly smart. I charged forward, straight for his face and then slid underneath him, snapping my jaws around his forepaw. He yipped in pain and then spun around to attack me. I backed out from under his body, releasing his leg and danced around him.

You're good, but you're too slow. He said to me.

I lifted my lips in a snarl and smile. *Then why haven't you caught me yet?*

He lunged forward, his teeth flashing just to the right of my neck as I darted under his front legs and out the side. I knew he wasn't trying his hardest and it was only a matter of time before he caught me, but I would make him work to catch me.

He darted forward, and I barely had time to run away. I ran around him and bit his tail. He growled and before I could get away, jumped on top of me, pinning me to the ground.

This is cheating! I yelled indignantly. *A real wolf would never fight like this!*

Ah, but we are not real wolves, are we? I struggled underneath him, trying to get away, but he held me down. *Do you give up?*

NEVER! I yelled just before I whined.

"Step off of my mate, Thor," Ares said in a menacing tone from nearby. I couldn't see him since Thor was pinning my head to the ground with his neck.

I growled at Ares to butt out, but Thor stood up off of me. *You don't have to listen to him.*

Thor shook his head. *He is beta. I have to listen to him.*

I exhaled. *Sorry.*

Thor nudged my shoulder with his nose. *Did I hurt you?*

No. Just irritated that he stepped in when you weren't hurting me.

It's his place to protect you. He heard you whine and therefore thought I might be hurting you. He knows I would never purposefully harm you, but accidents do happen. What would you like to do now?

I shifted forms and took my clothes from Daisy Mae. "I think I'll go take a bath. Thank you for sparring with me. I look forward to sparring with you further in human form soon."

Thor bowed his wolf head and trotted over to his clothes.

"Are you hurt?" Ares asked from behind me.

I finished zipping my pants up and walked away, ignoring him. I shouldn't be mad at Ares, but I just wanted some time without them hovering over me. I couldn't even play fight with a member of the pack without him intervening.

My body was surprisingly sore so instead of walking, I teleported from the training grounds into Achilles' room. The room was thankfully empty and the wall where the vampires had attacked years before was blessedly fixed. I stripped my clothes off and started the water for the bathtub.

I was standing outside of the tub watching it fill up when I felt him behind me. "You know I can sense you so why bother sneaking up?"

"I'm concerned for you and I wasn't sneaking, I was just being quiet," Ares answered.

I stayed in my position, not facing him even though I needed his touch. I needed a bath and time to process my feelings as well though.

"Achilles told me what happened," he said softly.

There had been no inflection in his voice. So, either he was hiding what he was feeling, or he wanted me to ask. *Do I give in and ask, or do I stand here silently?*

I blew out air through my nose and gave in. It wasn't Ares' fault I was in a predicament. "And?"

"I understand why you're so upset now. It must have taken a lot to refuse him once you got that far. What made you do it?"

"You," I whispered as tears leaked out of my eyes silently. "I couldn't bear the thought of hurting you. Yet all I did was hurt Achilles."

Ares stepped in front of me, blocking my view of the tub with his chest. "I can't make this decision for you, Artemis. I don't know what the right answer is or what I should tell you to do. I love you and I'm a very jealous man. I don't want to share you, but at the same time I don't like seeing you or Achilles in pain."

I looked up into his face and saw the anger and pain twisting his handsome features. "You're my mate, my *passt genau*. How can I cheat on the only man that's ever given me a home?"

"He is your mate and *passt genau* as well."

I shook my head. "He's not my *passt genau*. You know it and I know it and Achilles knows it. I may be his destined mate because I released his powers, but that is different from the connection we have. I feel Achilles in my heart and my head, but I feel you in my bones and my soul. You may both share my heart, but only you have my soul."

Before I could wrap my arms around Ares, he squashed me in a hug, bruising my lips with his intense kiss. In two seconds my despair evaporated and the love Ares felt for me seeped in to lift my mood. He pulled back and wiped my eyes. "I love you, Artemis Lupine. I just wish I could fix this. I wish there were a way to make us all happy."

"If you let her mate with me that would help," Achilles said from the bathroom doorway.

"How long have you been there?" I asked in shock. *And why hadn't I felt him arrive for the second time in less than an hour?*

"Perhaps because you were too busy with Ares' tongue in your mouth," Achilles replied tautly.

I jerked at his hostility. "Achilles."

He rubbed his face and then slammed his fist into the wall. "I'm sorry, Artemis. This pain is eating me up. I can't sleep. I can't eat. All I can think about is you and the bond we have yet to complete."

"It is not fair for you to lay this burden upon her. She just returned to us!" Ares said as he pushed me slightly behind him. He was acting protective of me from Achilles, which was a very bad sign.

"She just returned to us and already you have mated with her! I know I agreed not to mate with her, but I had no idea how hard it would be," Achilles said as he stared at Ares.

Sensing I was not needed for this argument, I climbed into the now full tub and turned the water off. The warm water felt amazing against my skin and I relaxed into it. I had no idea what to say to Achilles or how to fix this issue, so I closed my eyes and relaxed, trying to ease the pain I was feeling.

"You are just being selfish and keeping her to yourself!" Achilles yelled.

"Listen to yourself! She's only back for a month and you're already pushing her and pressuring her!" Ares responded.

"You would be doing the same thing in my position!"

"I would be arguing with *you,* but not pressuring her and causing her pain! A male does not cause his female pain!" Ares bellowed, the walls shaking with the power which was leaking out as his control waned.

Achilles jerked as if the words had pained him. I clenched my eyes tighter, wishing to disappear. "Artemis? Is he right? Have I caused you pain?"

I didn't want to answer. I couldn't lie to him because he'd be able to tell. I couldn't tell him the truth without him getting upset. "Why can't we go back to how it was two days ago? Everyone was happy. Everyone was sharing well. Can't we just erase today and pretend it didn't happen?" Without a word Achilles spun around and left. This time I could feel him and his anger as he turned. "Achilles! Wait!" I called, standing up in the tub.

"Let him be, Artemis. He needs time to think," Ares said as he turned to face me. I could tell it hurt him to argue with Achilles so, but we both knew it was necessary.

"*I* needed time to think and no one left *me* alone," I complained as I settled back into the tub.

Ares smiled and grabbed the sponge and liquid soap. "I'm sorry, Sunshine, but I can't stand leaving you alone when you're in pain." He pulled a stool out from under the bathroom sink and sat down on it behind me.

"What are you doing?" I asked as he dipped the sponge in the water and squirted soap on it.

He pushed my head forward gently and then made slow, soft circles on my back. "I am washing your back."

I wanted to object and yet, I didn't. I loved it when he washed me. "I wish you hadn't intervened when I was fighting Thor," I whispered as he washed down my right arm.

"You whined and instinct overruled logic. I couldn't stand there and watch another male pin you under him while you whined."

He moved to my other arm, and I asked something I'd wanted to know since my memory had returned. "Did you ever discover the true reason for Matt's betrayal? Who it was they had?"

"Yes," Ares answered curtly and then stayed silent as he rinsed my back and arms off.

"And?" I prodded.

"And it doesn't matter anymore," he said.

"Ares."

He sighed and set the sponge down. I turned around and crossed my arms on the top of the tub and looked up into his eyes as he told me what had happened.

"The dhampirs took a female wolf he was fond of and held her prisoner. They beat her bloody and then sent him pictures. It would have been a simple matter for me to have Victor help us extricate her, but Matt tried to solve it on his own when we were in France and they caught him. I asked Victor about the girl when I found out, but that wasn't until we were at the Dragon's Lair, and he informed me that she had been killed a week after we left France. No matter what Matt would have done for them, the girl was dead."

No wonder he had been acting so differently. I would have sacrificed almost anyone to get Ares back. "Poor Matt," I whispered.

Ares growled. "The end result was his fault. Had he come to me early on I could have saved her and his life. I do not regret punishing him for his betrayal. No one who betrays the werewolves deserves to live among us."

He was sincere and yet I heard the bitterness in his voice. He wasn't only angry at Matt and the people who caused it, but he was mad at himself as well. "Ares, it's not your fault."

Ares sighed and leaned his forehead against mine. "I wish I believed that."

"If you think about it, it was my fault. If you hadn't been distracted by me and my immaturity, then you would have noticed..."

Ares grabbed my chin and stared into my eyes. "Stop. Matt's death was not your fault."

"He was jealous of us, Ares. He wanted to be loved like you love me. He was jealous of how much time you spent with me instead of him. I could see it, but I didn't say anything to you."

"What he did was his own decision. He betrayed you and tried to hand you to Maurice. No one should do that to a pack mate, especially not a pup like you had been. Do not blame yourself for another's reckless actions," he whispered as he stared deeply into my eyes.

I smiled at him and whispered, "You should take your own advice, Alpha."

Ares smiled and kissed my lips softly. "You've become very wise since I first met you."

"Being one hundred will do that to you," I whispered as I looked down at the water.

Suddenly water splashed over the side of the tub as Ares climbed in with me, wrapping his arms around me and holding me against him. "I tried to find you. I searched all over the world and threatened hundreds of people, but no one had seen you. Achilles couldn't find you with your bond either. It was as though you were invisible. I can't imagine how hard it must have been for you all these years. If I could take them all back I would."

I nuzzled his neck and kissed it softly. "I know."

CHAPTER 17

ARTEMIS

Over the days that followed, I continued sparring with Thor, and Erebos brought Sidhe out to teach me Sidhe magic I did not yet know. I was learning quite a lot in a short amount of time and I could tell they were impressed by me. Slowly my reputation built within the Sidhe community and changed from fear and hatred to awe and respect.

After a long training session, I sat on the ground and ran my fingers through the grass to calm myself. My training group dispersed and Achilles and Ares walked to my side. "We should visit Father," Achilles said with a smile on his face.

Ares nodded. "Alright."

I smiled and grabbed each of their hands. "Ready?" They nodded and I teleported us to the front steps of the castle. The two werewolf guards jumped in surprise and then bowed when they recognized Ares and Achilles.

Achilles led the way through the castle to his father's chambers where he knocked loudly on the door.

The door opened a moment later and Zeus stood before us with his long, white beard and handsome face. His power was extremely impressive, pressing down upon me in a way I hadn't noticed the last time I'd been here, which was strange.

Achilles stood in front of Ares who stood in front of me. I wanted to move forward, but Ares gripped my hand to still me.

"Achilles! Ares! My sons! To what do I owe the honor of your visit?"

Ares stepped around Achilles, spreading his arms and said, "Looks like I'm Sidhe after all."

Zeus' eyes widened in astonishment and then he regained composure long enough to pull Ares into a hug. "I knew you had powers."

He released Ares, and I stepped around Achilles. "Hi, Zeus."

Zeus' eyes met mine and he stepped around Ares quickly. He looked at Achilles and Ares and then back at me. "Artemis? You… you found her?"

Ares smiled. "Yes, Dad, it's her."

I smiled. "Yeah, they found me and made me whole again." I spread my arms out and released my Sidhe power, letting my wings out. I flapped my wings and wiggled my fingers. "All one piece again."

He grabbed my arms and pulled me into a hug, which nearly crushed my ribs. "I thought I'd never see you again."

I pulled my wings back in and relaxed into his hug. Why did he make me feel so at peace? Was it because he was Ares' and Achilles' dad? Or because he was the king of half of my bloodline?

He pulled back and looked at my face. "Your power has greatly increased. It's amazing." I felt a push against my body, like a person leaning on me and then it was gone. "By the goddess, how did you obtain so much power?"

I stepped back from him to stand between Ares and Achilles. "I gained some while I was without my memories and more from the dragons and then I gained most of what I have from *mater* when I channeled the rest of it to Ares."

Zeus stared at me for several moments and then clapped his

hands together. "This is wonderful! We need a feast!" He snapped his fingers and two beautiful Sidhe women stepped out of his chambers to stand beside him. He turned to them and said, "Prepare a feast in honor of the return of Artemis and to honor Ares now taking his rightful place as Prince."

The women bowed and scurried away to do his bidding.

"Come, you must tell me everything that has happened!" said Zeus as he put his arms around Ares' and Achilles' shoulders and pulled them away from me and into his chambers.

I followed behind them, a smile nearly splitting my face. Zeus sat down in his large, overstuffed chair and waved his sons and me over to a large couch. I sat down between Ares and Achilles and leaned against Achilles' side while Ares held my hand.

Zeus smiled at me and then said, "Artemis can you tell me where you've been the past one hundred years?"

I nodded. "For the first forty or so I was in wolf form running with wolf packs."

"Wolf packs? You mean you were with werewolves and they didn't contact Ares?" Zeus asked in shock.

I shook my head. "No, I mean wolf packs, like the actual animal."

His eyebrows raised. "Oh."

"I don't know this part of the story myself, but Selene said that they'd been hearing about an unusually large wolf in a local pack which wasn't afraid of people. Then they got reports of a naked girl seen begging for food and they were worried the vampires would get me. So, Selene decided that as a friend of the werewolves, it was her job to investigate. What she found was me separating from the wolf pack and trying to become human again. You see, I hadn't changed out of my wolf form in forty years so I couldn't even remember how to speak, and I barely remembered how to change forms. She thought I'd been abused by vampires or was on the run.

"As you can imagine, I wasn't in the best shape when she

found me. My body was filthy, my hair was matted and I had lice and fleas. She recognized that I had inherited witch's powers by the woman who had cursed my father so she took me in as a witch so that she could bypass contacting the werewolves or the vampires. She crafted a pendant which could hide my smell and my skin designs and made me for all intents and purposes human."

Ares exhaled. "Well, that explains a lot."

Achilles nodded. "Yes, it does."

I continued. "I lived with her coven for sixty years and was assigned as the youth counselor to help the young members of our coven come into their powers. I only left the coven's walls to go to the magic shop when Selene needed special items. That's when Ares first spoke to me."

Ares smiled. "Yes, and then you had your dragon attack me."

I frowned. "He didn't attack you and besides, he knew who you were and I didn't. He knew who you were because you killed off most of the dragons before."

"Most of the dragons? You have a dragon?" Zeus asked as he gaped.

Achilles nodded. "We went to the Lair for their assistance in removing the block on Artemis' memories. There were at least two hundred dragons in the Lair alone."

"Draco-Blu has thirty dragons in his flight," I said softly as my heart ached at the separation of Blu.

"We could visit him if you wanted to," Ares said quietly. "Of course it would have to be after the battle."

I smiled. "Thank you, but I know we have more pressing matters."

Achilles smoothed my hair back and kissed my forehead. "We could ask them to assist us in the battle. They'd be wonderful allies and the vampires would never expect it."

"Except that Apollo knows that Draco-Blu is a friend of mine," I said softly. "He also knows I can use the sunlight magic."

"Apollo? Sunlight magic?" Zeus asked his eyes expanded to their limit.

Achilles laughed. "There's still a lot you don't know."

"Apparently," Zeus said. "What is this talk of Apollo?"

"My twin's alive. He saved me from our father as he was trying to kill me," I said softly. "I don't think Apollo's all bad. I think..." I stopped talking because I knew what Ares would say. "And while at the coven I learned to use sunlight like I do fire."

"Can you show me?" Zeus asked curiously.

I put my hands out, palms facing each other and focused on the center of them. Picturing the bright orange sun and remembering the feel of sunlight on my skin, I called the power and a small orb appeared between my hands.

Zeus walked forward and ran his hand around the orb. "Incredible. It's been centuries since I've heard of someone being able to do this."

Achilles put his hand under the orb and asked, "Can you drop it into my hand? I want to see if I can control it."

I released the ball and the orb dropped onto Achilles' hand and then dissipated.

"So much for that idea," Achilles said in a light voice, but I could see the anger in his eyes. He didn't like not being able to do magic that I could.

I leaned against Ares and felt my eyelids droop. "Why am I tired?"

Ares stroked my hair and whispered, "You've been through a lot the past few days. You should rest. I'll tell the rest of the story to Zeus." I nodded and laid my head on Ares' lap and my legs across Achilles' legs. Ares started talking and the world faded into dreams of running through the woods with Ares and Koda.

CHAPTER 18

ARTEMIS

Ares woke me up a few hours later to attend the feast that Zeus had prepared, a feast coordinated to formally proclaim Ares as Prince of the Sidhe, second in line to the throne of the Dark Court.

I stood on the dais between Ares and Achilles and fought the yawn trying to come out. A short, rotund, brown colored Sidhe woman had come and forced a Renaissance era dress on me. I liked the dress, but would have preferred jeans. Ares and Achilles had changed into soft breeches that tied in the front and button up shirts. I asked the woman why she didn't give them puffy pirate shirts and she had scowled at me and stomped off. Some people have no sense of humor.

Zeus was wearing skin tight breeches like Ares' and Achilles' and a white shirt which showed off part of his upper chest. On him, the outfit looked stunning and very fitting. Who knew the God of Lightning would look best in Renaissance clothes?

"Thank you all for gathering on such short notice today. This is a joyous day in many regards," began Zeus. He gripped Ares' shoulder and smiled brightly. "My son, Ares, has released his Sidhe powers. He is now a member of the Sidhe realm and a prince of the Dark Court!"

The crowd clapped and a couple of the younger Sidhe cheered.

Zeus turned to me and extended his hand. I walked to him, being careful not to trip and embarrass myself. Zeus gripped my hand and said, "The second and most exciting revelation is the return of Artemis Lupine of the Sidhe and Werewolves." The crowd gasped and began murmuring. Zeus raised his hand and they stopped talking. "After being lost to us and as well as to herself, Artemis has returned and rightfully claims her title as mate of Prince Ares and Prince Achilles." The crowd clapped, but I got a few dirty looks from a couple of the Sidhe women. I rolled my eyes. I was not dealing with that again. Fighting jealous women was not fun and I'd already had more than enough of that at Lyngvi, the Werewolf home.

Zeus snapped his fingers and a beautiful bracelet appeared in his hand. It was made of thin strips of white wood braided together and it appeared to be holding a powerful spell. Zeus slipped it on to my wrist announcing, "So that you will never be lost to us again."

Achilles laughed and then pretended to cough. *He just put a tracking device on you.*

I smiled at Zeus and kissed his cheek. "Thank you."

Zeus released me, and I stood back between Ares and Achilles. Ares whispered, "Why hadn't I thought of that?"

I reached over and pinched his leg, making him rub the spot and smile.

"Let's eat!" Zeus yelled.

The tables in front of the crowd suddenly filled with food. I knew many forms of magic and had seen many spells used, but I had never seen that before.

"How? What?" I asked in shock.

Zeus winked at me. "I've got a few tricks up my sleeve too, daughter."

Did he just call me daughter? When I got over the initial shock, I smiled. I liked the idea of being his daughter. Ares picked my hand up and led me to the head table where Zeus, Ares, Achilles and I would eat. We ate a delicious feast of every kind of animal and at least ten types of desserts. I felt like I was going to pop by the time I finished stuffing my stomach.

I exhaled, feeling content, and leaned back. "I haven't eaten like that in a long time."

Ares smiled. "The Sidhe definitely know how to throw a party."

Achilles tapped my shoulder, and I turned to find him standing and half bowing. "May I have this dance?"

"There's no music playing," I said with a frown.

Achilles clapped his hands and a troupe of musicians walked in the side doors with instruments. "You were saying?"

I shifted nervously in my seat. "I don't know how to dance."

Achilles grabbed my hand and pulled me up and out of my seat. "Then I shall teach you." Ares growled and Achilles stopped, turning to face him. "Ares, please."

Ares exhaled and looked up at the ceiling. "Two dances and then we trade off."

Achilles half bowed to him in thanks and then twirled me out onto the dance floor.

"I don't know how to dance, Achilles and I especially don't know how to do that fancy dancing that everyone here is doing," I said nervously as I looked at the other couples around us.

Achilles smiled down at me and placed one of my hands on his shoulder and held the other. "All you need is a man taught properly and dominant enough to lead. Just relax and let yourself feel the music."

He spun us around and surprisingly I didn't trip over my own feet. I smiled up at him and let him lead as we waltzed along with the other couples. The music was incredibly beautiful and with Achilles leading me, I was left to simply enjoy it all.

He smiled brightly at me and said, "See, you can dance."

I laughed. "At least that is what everyone else thinks right now."

He winked. "I won't tell if you don't."

He made me twirl, and I laughed as the colors of everything around us blurred. He stopped my twirling and pulled me against him, holding me tightly to his body with an arm around my lower back.

I stared into his eyes and saw such passion and love in them that it made my breath catch. We stood still in the center of the twirling and waltzing around us and yet none of the noise and movement mattered to me in that moment. He bent down and kissed my lips softly, sending a pleasant electric surge through my body. I kissed him back and then leaned away. "How do we dance to this song?" I asked, in an effort to change the subject from our kiss.

Achilles smiled and led me in a strange dance. We kicked our legs, spun away from each other, he dipped me and then we looped arms and all of the couples switched from partner to partner until we returned to our original dance partner. I laughed as we performed the moves and the music made me forget all of my troubles. The song ended, and I curtsied to Achilles as the other women did the same to their partners.

Achilles kissed the back of my hand and smiled at me from his bowing position. "Thank you for the dances." He took my hand and gave it to Ares who was next to us.

Ares smiled at me. "You looked gorgeous out there."

"That was all Achilles. I don't even know how to perform these dances," I said as a new song started and Ares placed our hands in the appropriate positions.

"Then I shall make you look even better," he said with a smile.

He walked us into a circle of other couples, and we all joined hands. This dance was much more synchronized than the others. "What is this dance?" I asked as I learned the repetitive moves. *Step side to side, release hands and dance in a small circle, kicking your feet out. Come back to the others, rejoining hands and walk two paces to the left, then shuffle kick your feet forward three times. Step left twice and then right once and then dance in a small circle kicking your feet out again.*

"It goes by many names, but I call it the *Branle de Bourgogne*," he answered.

Soon I got the hang of it. Every time I danced in my own little circle I couldn't help but laugh and smile. It was the first real bit of fun I'd had in a really long time. Ares was smiling too, his perfect, true smile and the sight of him dancing and spinning happily with me made me happier than a hundred dead rabbits could.

"I have to say I'm surprised you're such a good dancer," I admitted as we continued the dance.

Ares smiled. "It is but one of the many surprises about me that you will soon learn. You have to remember that I have been alive a *very* long time, Sunshine."

As we neared the band, he cleared his throat. The band leader nodded and the traditional song changed to one song I remembered from my high school days. Ares pressed me close against him and began to grind his body into mine. I had seen my fellow classmates dance like this, but I had never done it, or experienced it. Ares moved behind me and helped me move my hips along with the beat and his movements.

I could feel Achilles' anger skyrocket as I reached back and wrapped an arm around Ares' neck, pressing us even closer together. I didn't want him to be mad, but at the same time I knew Ares was doing this for me. I deserved something for me.

Ares and I danced until the song ended and then he bowed to me, holding my hand and kissing the back of it softly. "Thank you for the dances."

I curtsied and said, "It was an honor to dance with the great Prince of the Sidhe and Werewolves."

He stood up and hugged me tightly. "You're too perfect for me."

I laughed and shook my head. "I am definitely not perfect. You, sir, are too good for me."

He nipped my ear playfully. "I could be bad if you wanted me to."

Achilles cleared his throat and we both turned to smile at him. "Did you enjoy your dances?"

I grinned. "I did. You're both incredible dancers! I never thought about you both knowing how to ballroom dance before."

"Perhaps you would like to dance with the man who invented ballroom dancing then," said Zeus from behind me.

I turned around and curtsied. "It would be a great pleasure for me to dance with the King of the Sidhe."

He picked my hand up and kissed my fingertips softly. "The pleasure is all mine, my dear." He winked at me and then spun me away from his two sons and back onto the dance floor. The song was slow, luckily, and Zeus led us in a simple box step. "I see there is still tension amongst you three."

I sighed. "Yes, but I don't see how to fix it. Achilles is upset because he wants me to mate with him, but Ares doesn't want that. I don't want to upset Ares, yet I do feel the draw to Achilles. But every time I start kissing Achilles I feel like I'm betraying Ares." I groaned and leaned my forehead against his shoulder. "What do I do?"

Zeus patted me on the back and then hugged me. "You need to make the decision that is right to you. I love both of my sons and want to see them happy, but I'm not going to tell you to do something that you might regret or that will make you uncomfortable. Give it time, dear. You've only been back with us for a short while. There is no need to rush things."

"Thank you. May we take a break? I would love to keep dancing, but I'm tired."

Zeus bowed to me and led me back to Ares and Achilles. "I return your beloved to you and thank you for allowing this old man to dance with such a beautiful woman." He leaned close to me and whispered, "Good luck."

I frowned at him and watched as he walked away laughing.

"What was that about?" Achilles asked.

"Just some fatherly talk from Zeus, nothing that needs to be discussed. I think I need a glass of water."

Ares and Achilles looked at each other a moment, communicating in that strange silent guy way and then they both ushered me back to our table. I sat down and accepted the glass of water Achilles handed to me. I hadn't noticed until I'd said something, but I was incredibly thirsty and a little lightheaded.

"You should have told me you were lightheaded," said Ares softly.

I shook my head. "I wasn't until I told you I needed a glass of water."

A Sidhe woman with green colored skin knelt before me. "May I assess your health, Princess? I am a healer."

I looked at Ares who nodded. "Sure," I said, "But I don't think it's necessary. I just got a little dehydrated."

She smiled sweetly at me and placed one hand on my stomach and one hand on the center of my chest. She was silent for four of my heartbeats and then pulled her hands away. "You're in very good health. Drink plenty of water and stay away from alcohol since it dehydrates." She stood up and turned to Achilles, motioning for him to follow her. He obeyed and they talked a few yards away.

Ares stroked my cheek. "How are you feeling?"

"I feel fine, Ares. I didn't mean to startle you both."

Suddenly, a pain flashed through me. Achilles' anger was like a whip of fire against my skin. I gasped and turned to face him. He stood alone where he and the healer had been talking a moment ago. Why was he so angry all of a sudden? His back was to me, making it impossible to gauge his problem from his face.

"What's wrong?" Ares asked.

"Achilles is very angry," I whispered.

Achilles straightened and turned to us, a smile on his face.

"Sorry, Artemis. I saw someone I did not wish to. How are you feeling?"

He was pretending as though he wasn't mad, but I could feel the anger and pain simmering beneath his smile. His eyes were also pinched, a sign of pain. "I'm fine. How are you? Why are you in pain?"

He sighed, looked down at his feet and then laughed. "This bond is burdensome in a few areas. I'm fine, just dealing with feelings about something I cannot deal with. You needn't worry, you have done nothing and I am not mad at you." He reached down and patted my hand reassuringly.

Why were men so stubborn? Why did they have to be hard asses all the time?

~

WE RETURNED to Hera's court and the rest of our pack to find a hundred Sidhe dressed in battle armor and practicing with swords, bows, and axes. Our pack watched from the sidelines, but I could see them taking it all in as they tried to memorize the moves.

Koda waved at us from the front where he was practicing using a bow and arrow with Erebos. I jogged over to him and asked, "Can I try?"

Erebos handed me a wooden bow instead of the silver one he had been using. I nocked an arrow, aimed and released. The solid "thunk" of the arrow hitting the target brought a smile to my face even before I saw that I'd hit the very center of the bulls-eye.

Erebos whistled. "Wow. You are definitely a natural with a bow." He turned and yelled, "Hephaistos!"

The tall Sidhe with forearms as big as my legs jogged up to us. "Yes?"

Erebos pointed to me. "You remember Artemis, right?"

Hephaistos dropped to one knee and bowed his head. "Princess."

I still wasn't used to this type of treatment, especially not after pretending to be human for so long. "Stand, please."

He stood and looked at Erebos who said, "She's a natural, as you can see."

Hephaistos smiled. "Indeed, she is."

"I would be greatly appreciative and honored if you would make me a bow and set of arrows. Your brand was great," I said.

He bowed. "Thank you. I'll return as soon as it's finished."

I spun around and jogged to find Ares. "Ares!"

He turned from his discussion with a pack member and met eyes with me. "What's wrong?"

"What happened to the humans? All those people we gave the brand to? I completely forgot to ask with all of this mayhem going on."

He averted his eyes a moment and said, "That's something we should discuss later."

"Why? What happened?" I asked frantically. "Where are the townspeople and all of the other humans from everywhere that we went? What happened to them?" Everyone had stopped practicing and turned towards me, but I didn't care. I had to know what happened.

Ares took my hands in his. "I'm sorry, Artemis. We were locked up so we couldn't help them. It's all my fault and I know it doesn't make it any easier, but…"

"They're all dead, aren't they?" I asked in a small voice.

He wrapped his arms around me and held me tightly against him, offering me his warmth and touch as my mate and pack mate to soothe me. "Yes. I'm sorry. Even if they hadn't been turned, humans don't live over one hundred years often."

Every person I'd grown up with in the town. Every person who had believed in me and wanted to be saved from the preternaturals. They were all dead and it was my fault. I knew that I should be sad, that tears should be pouring from my eyes, but the only thing I felt was anger.

I pulled away from Ares and saw my glowing body reflected in his eyes. "The vampires killed them?"

Victor walked over to me from the castle. "Yes, my father had anyone bearing Ares' marked killed."

"When is the battle?" I asked through clenched teeth as I tried to reign in my anger and power.

"We leave in the morning," Victor said softly.

I inhaled deeply and shoved the anger and power down. I could open it up and use it tomorrow. I noticed that everyone was still staring at me, so I turned away and walked towards the other side of town. With the anger pushed away, my grieving surfaced. Tears streamed down my face and body. Wrenching sobs forced me to stop and sit down as I cried over the losses. People had died because they trusted me. They might have lived if I hadn't come to them. If the vampires had come and given them the choices, they might have chosen differently and been allowed to live, albeit as slaves. My head and body hurt from the fierce sobs breaking out of me. How could I save the world from the vampires when I had doomed hundreds or thousands or however many people to death already?

"Artemis, it's not your fault," said Achilles softly from beside me.

There was no way I could defeat the vampires. I was just a worthless girl on a power high. I should have given myself to Maurice before Hera had stolen me. Then everyone would be safe.

Achilles squatted down in front of me and grabbed my arms. His body was glowing and his eyes were solid white pearls as he looked into my eyes. "You listen to me! Giving yourself to Maurice would not have accomplished anything except your torture and possibly our deaths as we tried to rescue you. Do not ever think about giving yourself to that monster! I would sooner give up my life than see you in his hands."

"If you died I would die too," I whispered softly as I wiped at the tear tracks on my face.

Achilles stopped glowing and the warm gentleness returned to his eyes. "Yes, I know. I was just trying to make a point." He sat down beside me and I let him take me into his arms. "It was not your fault. It was Maurice's decree and his vampires who executed them. The only person you should be mad at is Maurice."

He was right, but it didn't help the pain I felt in my heart. Inside it felt as though I had stamped their execution orders with my brand.

He rubbed his hands up and down my arms and started to sing in a language I didn't understand. His voice was amazing and the language was incredibly beautiful. We sat together for at least an hour and he didn't stop singing until Ares approached us.

Ares sat down and picked my hand up in his. I expected him to be angry that I had run off and he had found me with Achilles, but he did the most unexpected thing. He started singing where Achilles had left off. Achilles joined Ares and the brothers sang to me while the grief and sorrow I felt eased and then settled into a low ache.

They stopped singing when they determined I was no longer in pain and cuddled around me from both sides as comfort. Ares kissed my cheek and stood up. "I'll be on the training field when you're ready to return."

"Ares," I whispered. He looked at me and the sadness in his eyes made me struggle for a moment. "Thank you," I finally managed to say.

He dipped his head and disappeared around the corner of a building.

Achilles stroked my hair and whispered, "I love you, Artemis. I'm sorry that things are so difficult for you. If there is anything I can do to make it easier, please tell me."

"You've done so much already, Achilles. More than I could have hoped for."

He adjusted our position so that I was leaning against his chest and hugged me tight. "Will you please stay beside me during the fight tomorrow? I know you don't like the idea of us guarding you, but if it were up to me I would leave you behind for the fight. After you were gone so long, we've had so little time to spend with you."

"My life always seems to be hectic. We rush from one fight to another or one place to another. I just want this war to be over and the world to return to what it was, or as close as it can be."

"Will you stay by me?" he asked again.

I nodded and turned to face him. "Yes, but you have to focus on yourself and not me. If I get into trouble I can always use the sunlight magic."

Achilles smiled. "I will try to remember that." His smile wilted a moment and then he kissed me on the lips. Unlike Ares' kisses which filled me with a raging fire, Achilles' kiss filled me with an electric buzz, as if I was holding a live wire.

His hands ran from my shoulders to my stomach to my back and then he pulled me closer to him. It felt wrong to be kissing someone other than Ares and yet it also felt so incredibly right to kiss Achilles.

He pulled away first, and I knew without looking that both of our wings were out and that my eyes were pearl white like his. He smiled one of the first true smiles I had ever seen on his face, and yet I could sense sadness in him as well. He kissed my lips quickly. "Come on, we should get back. I'm sure Hephaistos has your bow ready."

I let him help me stand. It took a moment of intense concentration for me to calm my powers and bring my wings in. I was suddenly glad that he'd pulled back since I hadn't.

We walked back to the field where everyone, halfbreed and Sidhe, were now practicing together. It warmed my heart more than a million kisses could. Koda put his arm around my shoulders and pulled me away from Achilles and towards Hephaistos and Erebos. "You have to see what Hephaistos worked up for you."

"Sweet," I said excitedly as we increased our speed to get to Hephaistos.

Hephaistos smiled at me and then blushed. "I got a bit carried away, but I think you'll like what I've made."

I smiled at him. "I'm sure I'll love it. Your work is always beautiful."

He picked up a covered bundle from the table behind him and slowly unwrapped it, revealing a beautiful bow. Never before had I seen one so exquisitely crafted. The frame was covered in intricate carvings of vines which matched the ones on my face and arms. The string and frame were both a glowing silver color and seemed to throb as though alive. "I made sure not to use any silver since I know you're allergic to it, but I couldn't make you a bow simply out of wood."

Achilles and Ares had joined us and at the sight of the bow in Hephaistos' hands they both gasped. Achilles asked, "How long has it been since you made a bow this way?"

Hephaistos smiled. "Too long, but I believe Princess Artemis is the best recipient for such an item."

I cleared my throat and they all turned to me. "May I see the bow to understand why you are all so excited?"

Hephaistos laughed and held out the bow. "My apologies."

The bow was much lighter than I expected and as soon as it touched my skin I understood the excitement. My back arched in a mixture of pain and pleasure as the bow determined if I were suitable to hold it or not. After a moment the power of the bow receded and it vibrated slightly in my hand. "How did you harness starlight to keep the form of the bow?" I asked in shock.

"We are Children of the Stars and a mother is always willing to help her children," Hephaistos answered softly. "I am glad that you are able to wield it. I had not thought about the possibility of you being unable to."

I laughed and pulled on the string which was also made from starlight to test its resistance. "Do you have an arrow I can try?"

Hephaistos unwrapped another bundle and I gasped. "Starlight arrows?"

He smiled. "Starlight shafts with steel tips which have been dipped in sunlight."

Several of the crowd which had gathered gasped and started talking loudly.

I picked up one of the arrows and nocked it. I looked across the field and saw a target about two miles away. I aimed and released. The arrow sped across the field faster than any normal silver or wood arrow could and flew through the target and into the tree behind it.

"I never knew you were an archer," Ares said teasingly.

I shrugged. "It appears so."

I ran to the tree and pulled the arrow from the trunk. The tip of the arrow was no longer dipped in sunlight. I jogged back to the group, slung my bow over my shoulder and formed a ball of sunlight in my palm. I dipped the tip of the arrowhead in the sunlight and turned it slowly so that the sunlight coated it. "How does it stick?" I asked Hephaistos as I coated the arrow head.

"The iron is enchanted and the starlight can understand your desire and assists as best as it can," he said in an awed whisper.

I put the arrow back into the sheath and looked up at all of the eyes focused on me. "What?" I asked as I blushed.

"I was not aware that you could control sunlight," said Erebos from beside me.

I smiled at him. "Yes, I can."

"Ares!" Koda called. "We have a problem."

I followed Ares over to where Koda was standing with an unfamiliar Sidhe on the other side of the grass. The Sidhe left and Koda kept looking at me in a weird way, almost as if he was uncomfortable with me being there. "What's wrong?" asked Ares.

Koda looked at me a moment then sighed. "You'll find out anyways so I might as well just tell him in front of you. Ares, they're fighting a werewolf in the Games."

Ares folded his arms across his chest and it took me a moment to stop staring at his biceps. "Why is that a problem?"

Ares asked. "They've used a wolf before to fight one of the humans."

"It's a problem because the wolf isn't fighting a human. The wolf is fighting an elf," Koda said slowly as though trying to clue Ares into the secret without letting me figure it out. I really wished I could read his mind. Where was Victor when you needed him?

Ares asked, "What did the wolf do? Which wolf is it?"

"The wolf killed a vampire to protect a human that did not have his brand." Koda stopped talking, looking at me for a long moment before saying, "It's Bret."

"My Bret?" I asked in shock. Ares growled and I rolled my eyes at him. "You know I didn't mean it like that."

Koda smiled at me. "Yes, your Bret."

Ares sighed. "Crap."

"What are the Games?" I asked.

"They're like the old Roman gladiator fights to the death, but usually the humans are pitted against ogres or some other preternatural. It's rare that a preternatural has to fight another preternatural, but in some instances, they do it. Usually the fight serves as a public execution."

"And Bret is going to have to fight in it?" Dread overwhelmed me.. I turned to Ares. "We have to save him. We can't just let him die, especially if he was protecting a human."

Ares closed his eyes and rubbed his temples with his fingers, as though trying to get rid of a headache. "I knew you were going to say that," he whispered.

"That's why I didn't want to tell you in front of her," said Koda.

"Where're the Games held? How long will it take to get there? When is he fighting?" I asked frantically.

Ares threaded his fingers through mine, giving me reassurance and calming me. "Koda and I will take care of it. You stay here with Achilles."

"No way!" I yelled, pulling my hand from his. "You're not leaving me behind."

"Artemis, the stands are going to be full of vampires and Maurice will be there, sitting in the pulpit, watching over everything. Do you really think it's a good idea for you to go?"

"You're not leaving me behind. I'll teleport myself to the Games if you try to leave me." I was not giving up on this. No matter what he said I was going.

"She'd probably teleport herself right into the center of the ring," said Koda more to himself than anyone else.

Ares growled. "I am not taking you there! What if Maurice catches you?"

"I'll teleport out," I answered quickly.

"She has a point," said Koda.

Achilles walked towards us, a deep frown on his face. "What's going on?" He must have sensed my anger and come looking for me.

"Artemis' former friend is being fought in the Games. She wants to go with us and threatened to teleport herself if we leave her behind," summarized Koda.

Achilles gaped. "You can't go to the Games. It's not really even safe for Ares to go to the Games. What if you get captured?"

"I'll teleport out," I said calmly.

"It's not that simple," Achilles said with a hiss, "They could kill you before you had a chance to teleport. And we all know that you wouldn't leave us behind just to save yourself. You are not going, Artemis."

My mouth dropped open. Achilles had never spoken to me that way before. I expected it from Ares, but not Achilles. "You don't make the decisions for me," I said quietly trying to summon my anger, but in my shock I was unable.

"I am your mate, whether we've *mated* or not and therefore I do have a say in what you do, especially if it puts your life, and consequently mine, at risk. Plus, you're the Princess of the Sidhe and it's every Sidhe's job to protect you. Do you really want to fight off the entire Sidhe race just to go rescue Bret?"

Never in my life would I have expected Achilles to speak to me like this. "You're trying to push me into a corner."

He smiled. "No, sweetheart, I shoved you into the corner and shackled you there. Ares, Koda and I will go to the Games and save your friend. You will stay here, watched by Sidhe guards whom I know you won't hurt and you will wait for us to return. Are we clear?"

I turned to Ares. "He can't really do this, can he?"

Ares smiled sympathetically. "He just did."

Erebos, Heracles and Theseus walked towards us from the training ring where they'd been sparing. Without a word, Erebos grabbed hold of my left arm and Theseus grabbed my right and together they held me in place.

"Let me go!" I yelled as I struggled against them.

Ares said, "Maybe we should get Hades?"

Achilles smiled. "That's a much better plan. Hades!"

"What are you going to do, have him kill me?" I asked angrily.

Ares, Achilles and Koda all rolled their eyes at me at the same time. Ares stepped forward and kissed my forehead softly. "We'll be back as soon as we can."

Koda kissed my cheek and then Achilles stepped in front of me. "I don't like doing this to you, Artemis, but your safety is my top concern. I can't lose you again." There was such pain in his voice that it made my heart ache and made me wish to touch him and console him. Unfortunately, I was being held against my will so I found the strength to refrain.

"Achilles, please let me come with you. I can help you. I don't want to be sitting here on my hands fretting and wondering if you're okay or not."

He smiled and kissed my lips softly, sending a pleasant shock through my body. "You won't have to."

Hades stepped forward and smiled at me. "Hello, Princess. This won't hurt, but you're going to feel a little woozy."

"Ares! Achilles!" I called to them as they walked away from me.

Neither man turned back around towards me. I felt my heart hammering against my chest as they walked away and my hands started shaking. I didn't want to be away from them. I didn't want separation. Hades pressed his hand to my forehead and chanted a few words in a strange language. I struggled against Theseus and Erebos, but my limbs were growing heavy and my eyelids were becoming increasingly hard to keep open. "This. Is. Cheating," I panted out just before Hades' spell slipped me into sleep.

CHAPTER 19
ACHILLES

The look on her face tore at my heart. I hated forcing her to stay behind, but I could not bear to see her get hurt. Her indignant feelings would mend when we returned, but her death would ruin us all. Especially since if she died, I would. If we died, I wouldn't even be able to grieve for her, which would eat at my soul for eternity.

"You did the right thing, Achilles. I'm actually very surprised and proud of you," said Ares as we headed towards the main building and my mother's quarters.

"I know I did the right thing. I just can't stand the look she gave me. She feels as though I've betrayed her."

Part of me was still angry at Ares for what I'd learned from the healer, but I didn't want to tell him yet. I'd tell him soon, but not yet. And for now, I dismissed the anger and focused on the task at hand.

"She's only worried for your safety. She'll be asleep so she won't even have time to fret," said Koda. "Besides, she knows you only did it to keep her safe. She'll forgive you."

I wasn't so sure. She may forgive me, but that didn't mean she'd trust me again or look at me the same. I already missed the smell of her skin, the touch of her hand.

"You think Hera will be in a good mood?" Ares asked as we entered the building and headed down the left corridor towards her room. The paintings on the wall became progressively darker with scenes shifting from peaceful meadows to a stormy sea to a bloody war. They were the visual progression of my mother's moods when she was displeased, or at least that's what I thought.

"I doubt it, but she owes us much for the past one hundred years," I answered quietly as I knocked on the door.

"Enter," exclaimed my mother in her most regal voice.

I pushed open her door and found my mother, the Queen of the Sidhe, in a fluffy pink bathrobe sitting in a chair with maids painting her fingernails and toenails. "Achilles!" she said happily. "To what do I owe this visit?"

"We need your help," I said blinking at her. "We need to rescue someone from the Games and bring them back."

She stood up and all of her maids backed away. "A Sidhe is in the Games?" she asked, her lips thin.

I shook my head. "No, it's a werewolf, one who used to be a friend of Artemis'."

"Where is our favorite halfbreed?" she asked as she examined her fingernails, no longer worried now that she knew it wasn't a Sidhe in the Games.

"Hades put her to sleep because she was refusing to stay behind and threatening to teleport if we left without her," Koda explained.

Hera smiled. "She's very feisty."

Ares scoffed. "That's an understatement."

"What is it that you need from me?" she asked as she sat back down in her chair and let the maids resume pampering her.

"We need you to teleport us to and from the Games," I said as I plucked a grape from a dish on the table beside me and popped it into my mouth. The grape was perfectly ripe and extremely juicy. Of course, the Queen of the Sidhe demanded the best.

Hera sighed. "I was afraid you were going to say that. Very well, let me get changed and I'll teleport you all."

Ares, Koda and I walked out of her room and leaned against the wall in the hallway. "What's your plan for when we arrive?" I asked Ares.

He shrugged. "Find where they have him, take him."

"That's not a very well thought out plan," I said incredulously.

He smiled. "I'll figure something out. I always do."

I lifted a brow. "Like the time we stole Dad's Pegasus to race him against the elves and started a war?"

Ares smiled. "You're the one who called the elf names and started it all. I only gave you a way to end it. It's not my fault that my spear accidentally fell while we were racing and tripped their steed."

I shook my head and laughed. "Right. And it wasn't your fault that the elves' shields all disintegrated during the war either."

"I can neither confirm nor deny if that acid was from my personal stores or not," Ares said in a monotonous tone.

I laughed and then sighed. "That battle lasted five years. Father was furious with us."

"But, who won? We did, because elves are awful at battle strategizing."

"And because you pull crazy schemes out of your butt and they actually work," Koda said as he leaned against the wall.

Ares smiled. "You're both just jealous because I'm the God of War."

"Conceited," I whispered.

"Vain," Koda whispered at the same time.

Hera stepped out of her room and frowned at me. "I hope you aren't talking about me."

I smiled. "Of course not! I would never speak of my lovely mother in such a manner."

She didn't seem convinced, but she left it alone. "Ready?"

We all reached a hand out and touched her shoulders. "Try not to land us in the center of the arena, please," Ares said.

She sighed. "So little faith. I will transport us in the back area where they keep those to be fought."

She closed her eyes and sent us whirling through the vortex of teleportation. I hated the feeling more than anything else, preferring even to have a sword cut me than to spin around and around.

"You can open your eyes now," she whispered.

I opened them and found us in an underground room with stone walls, dirt floors, and a metal gate. "You teleported us to a prisoner's cell? How did you know to come here? When were you in a prisoner's cell?" I asked.

"There are many things that you don't know about me and many more things that I will never tell you. Just be happy that I had knowledge of this place and could get us here. Otherwise, we would be trying to walk through the front door." She pushed open the cell door and marched down the aisles of cells as though she owned the place. Ares and Koda searched each prisoner's face as we wound our way through the holding area, but they did not find who they were looking for.

The crowd roared above us and dirt sifted from the ceiling down onto us. "Perhaps he is already fighting," I suggested.

Ares sighed. "I did not want to go out into the arena."

Hera grabbed a guard who had been watching the fight through an iron fence. "Who fights right now?" she asked him as she pressed him up against the fence.

"A werewolf and elf."

She smiled and grabbed his keys from his belt. "Thank you."

She opened the gate and turned to Ares. "We run out, grab him and teleport, got it?"

Ares smiled. "Sounds like a plan to me."

We stepped out into the arena, and I nearly choked. Bret wasn't just fighting one elf, he was fighting six. His sides were smeared with blood and his chest was heaving as he gasped for breath. The six elves stood around him in a loose circle holding spears.

The crowd was roaring, but then all eyes turned to us and they silenced. Maurice stood from his seat in the **pulpit**, smiling down at us. "I've been waiting for you." He turned to the crowd and said, "It seems we have additional fighters." He looked at our group a moment and then frowned. He was probably annoyed that Artemis wasn't with us. For once we did not let her endanger herself, and her hurt feelings no longer bothered me.

The crowd took a moment to understand the shift in the situation, but then they cheered in anticipation of bloodshed. I looked around the stands and was surprised to see beings from every race, *including Sidhe,* attending the Games.

Ares turned and smiled at me. "I'd always dreamed of fighting in the Arena, but father wouldn't allow me to in the Roman days. That's why I owned that group of gladiators and trained them instead of fighting. Oh, Spartacus, that was one hell of a gladiator. I do wish he had let me turn him." He stopped his reminiscing and looked at the elves. "You think the elves remember me?" He ripped his shirt off and took a half shift, growling at the crowd, sounding more like a lion than a wolf.

The elves turned and fixed their gazes on him. Yep, they remembered him. Ares charged forward, slicing one of the elves' heads almost completely off with his claws. Bret limped towards Ares, clutching his side and a wound which was dripping onto the sand.

The cool night air caressed my skin as I took a step forward. Small glass balls enchanted with a light spell sat in little holders around the arena and throughout the stands so the attendees could see everything even though it was night time. The smell and feel of the sand at my feet and the roar of the crowd brought back many memories of my younger days in Rome. Of course, back then I'd been revered as a god, sitting in the pulpit, watching, and determining the fates of the gladiators, not participating. Like Ares I had always wanted to participate, but father had forbidden us from fighting. I looked around at the eons old architecture and wished Artemis was here, knowing she would have enjoyed seeing the coliseum. Although it was not nearly as spectacular now as it was in its original days. I did have to admit that it was nice to be able to look in the stands without finding couples fornicating though. Romans were such vile creatures.

I turned back to the issue at hand and ran forward, releasing my powers, but not my wings and used a fireball to push back the elves. Koda ran at my side, now in wolf form and snapped his teeth at them.

Hera walked behind us at a leisurely pace as though we were simply walking through a park.

"What are you doing here?" asked Bret with more growl to his voice than human words.

"Saving you," Ares said. "Now shut up and go stand by the Sidhe Queen."

Bret looked like he wanted to object, but he limped his way to Hera and stood beside her. "I hope you know what you're doing," he whispered.

I came over to stand beside Ares and smiled at the elves. "It's been so long since I've seen elves bleed. I should like to draw this fight out a bit."

Ares laughed, sounding incredibly creepy in his half shift. "The crowd craves blood, let's give them a show!"

The elves charged forward, their eyes burning with blood lust. I dodged the spear one threw at me and kicked him in the chest, making him fly backwards to land on his back. An elf charged at Ares, but Ares snapped the spear in half and then impaled the elf with the end he'd broken off.

The crowd cheered madly, standing up and raising their fists in the air. Koda walked backwards and sat beside Bret, apparently deciding that we didn't need help in this fight.

The elf I'd kicked jumped up and flung dirt at my face. I

covered my face, but he punched me in the ribs, knocking my breath from me. "Dirty little elf!" I yelled as I backhanded him across the face and then kicked his legs out from under him. I dropped down onto his body and began punching his face as hard and as fast as I could. Blood sprayed and it took me a minute to realize that he was dead. I stood up and walked to stand beside Ares. I had a moment to feel excited that I was standing beside my brother again in battle, before refocusing on the situation.

Two of the elves charged at us, so we grabbed them both in headlocks and snapped their heads off simultaneously. That maneuver pleased the crowd who were all on their feet, screaming themselves hoarse.

Ares and I looked at the final elf who now seemed scared. "How should we kill this one?" Ares asked as he began pacing in a wide circle around the elf. "The crowd wants a messy death. They want someone ripped in two."

"Or perhaps sliced up into multiple pieces," I suggested, "we did end this fight too quickly."

Ares ripped the spear from the body of the elf he'd killed. "That is a good suggestion, but I think beheading him might be the most pleasing to the crowd. Plus, I grow bored with these Games."

Ares spun around and sliced the elf's head clean off. The elf's body fell to the ground twitching and Ares stabbed the spear into the bottom of the head, holding it up above him and then flung it into the crowd.

Maurice raised his hand and four men blew on their trumpets. A gate to the left of us opened and the crowd grew silent in anticipation.

"What do you suppose he's kept hidden from us?" I asked as I stood beside Ares, watching the gate.

"It would have to be something extremely powerful to take out both of us," Ares said with a somewhat demented smile on his half wolf-half man face. "I hope its ogres."

The trumpets blew again and a spear flew from the darkness of the gate. Ares and I dodged separate ways, avoiding the spear by mere inches. The spear imbedded into the stone wall behind us. I turned and inspected the spear, knowing Ares would warn me of any attacks. "It's embedded over two feet. Something strong is waiting for us."

Ares scoffed. "I could have embedded it five feet at least, with your body hanging from it."

Standing beside him once more, I stared into the open gate. "You think it's a machine? A preternatural should have come out by now instead of cowering in there like a scared whelp."

A roar quite similar to Ares' sounded and then a werewolf in half shift walked out of the shadows.

Ares growled. "Darius. I should have known since he was always awful at all of the sporting contests we held in Lyngvi every century."

"Why would your King fight in the Games against you?" I asked. Such a thing would never happen among the Sidhe.

"He thinks he can best me and wants it to be public. He will soon learn the error of his ways."

"Why would Darren and Darius betray their own race?" I still could not understand it.

Ares smiled. "Because they think Maurice is stronger than he really is. They don't realize how strong Victor is since he's been hiding it and only lets me see his true power. In order to keep from being overtaken, the two cowardly wolves bowed to the Vampire King to save their own hides. That's why Darren betrayed his own daughter and the wolves. They're scum and I plan to kill Darius now so the pack is clean of his cowardice."

Darius stopped once he'd reached the center of the ring and then tilted his head back and howled. Six wolves ran out of the gate to stand behind him, all snarling and frothing at the mouth.

"He brought some pups with him," Ares said with a smile on his face. "It has been a long time since I've fought my own kind."

"Ares," I whispered, moving closer to him, "Won't you be unable to move against him if he commands you since he's your alpha?"

Ares laughed. "That fool has never been my alpha. He knows that I am the true alpha of the werewolves and that's why he can't even fight me on his own. I should have killed that bitch years ago, but my mother had seemed happy with him." He frowned a moment and then said, "I hope she likes being a widow."

Maurice raised his arms and the chattering of the crowd stopped. "Today we have a rare feast for you. Today the Alpha of the Werewolves fights the Beta of the Werewolves in a fight to the death!"

"I've grown tired of your annoying presence," Darius said to Ares. "I only wish your halfbreed bitch was here so I could kill her too."

Ares growled loudly. "You've done nothing, but sully the name of Werewolves. I intend to fix that presently. Once I've killed you and ripped your heart from your body, I will take my true position as Alpha and see that we are restored to our original place of honor. No longer shall we be second to the vampires, but soon we will be their equals as we should be!"

Ares sprinted forward, slashing and punching at Darius so fast that it was hard for even *my* eyes to track. The other wolves started to move towards Ares, but I ran forward, cutting them off, forming a wall of fire between me and them. Koda ran from his spot beside my mother to jump on the back of the nearest wolf. He bit into the scruff of the wolf and shook his head fast. The wolf struggled against Koda, but with one more quick shake he snapped the wolf's neck and released his hold to let the dead body fall to the ground. The other wolves turned and growled at Koda. He shifted to his human form and said, "Submit or die!"

The wolves' knees trembled as they fought against his command. Being third in the werewolf hierarchy made Koda's commands very difficult to ignore. I released my wall of fire and turned to see how Ares was faring.

Ares' left arm bled from three cuts he must have received from Darius' claws. Darius was the worse for wear as he had cuts littering his body and a pool of blood forming at his feet in the sand. Both were fighting fiercely however, so Darius wasn't hurt enough to be slowed down.

I saw movement out of the corner of my eye and turned just as one of the wolves jumped at me. He knocked me to the ground, snapping his jaw at my throat. I shoved him off and stood up. "Thanks for the warning, Koda," I said as I looked for him.

"Sorry, I sort of have my hands full and didn't see that one slip away," he said where he was sitting on top of a pile of five men all whining and whimpering.

I turned and grabbed the wolf by its throat as it charged at me again and held it up. "Charging madly will not win the fight. You must learn to be stealthy and silent."

I tossed him towards Koda who grabbed him and forced him to change back to man. "Lie down and be still like the rest of your brothers," commanded Koda.

I laughed and shook my head as the five men lay down and remained still. Perhaps Ares was not the only one capable of being Alpha. With the wolves taken care of, that only left Ares and Darius left to battle it out. I returned to Hera and sat down on the ground beside her. "How has the fight gone?"

"Darius has opened a few cuts and landed a few hits, whereas Ares has opened at least a hundred cuts and has landed as many hits. Unfortunately, Darius does not seem to be slowing or weakening." She closed her eyes a moment and then opened them to stare intently at Darius. "I wonder if there is some type of spell keeping him from feeling pain or from weakening. He should be slowing by now."

"I don't see anything," I said as I watched Darius and Ares exchanging blows.

She frowned. "It could be a talisman or a stone enchanted with the spell."

I watched as Ares and Darius fought and sighed. "I can't tell from so far away. Ares! He's got a talisman or stone that's keeping him from weakening! You have to get it away from him before you can defeat him, short of ripping his head off!"

Ares growled and slashed at Darius' throat, but Darius stepped back in the nick of time, missing Ares' claws. "Can't even fight me fairly, can you Darius?" Ares yelled as he attacked him. Darius swung at Ares, and Ares dropped to the ground, picking up a spear shaft. He swung the shaft into Darius' upper right leg and then into his left. Darius growled and tried to grab the shaft, but Ares swung it up, connecting with Darius' jaw and making him fly up into the air. Darius landed on his back on the ground and started to get up, but Ares straddled his chest, pinning his arms with his legs and shoving the shaft against his throat. Ares ripped a necklace off of Darius' neck and tossed it towards me. "Is that it?" he asked as he punched Darius' face again and again. Blood sprayed from Darius' nose as Ares broke it, but Darius just continued to struggle against Ares.

Hera took the necklace and shook her head. "Nope."

Ares spun around Darius in a wrestling move I'd often seen humans in the mixed martial arts competitions use and grabbed Darius' leg in a leg lock. He reached up with one hand while Darius struggled to free his leg and stuck it inside Darius' pocket. Darius yelled and tried to grab Ares' hand, but Ares held him down with his leg across his chest and tossed the stone to us before he could reach him.

Hera caught the stone and gasped. "Yes, this is it. You can kill him now."

Ares stood up off Darius who was now lying on the ground gasping in pain and moaning. "You thought you could defeat me with a cheap stone? A stupid spell! I could have just ripped your head off when I had you pinned on the ground, but that's too swift a death for you."

Darius shifted to his human form and whispered, "You're not wolf enough to be Alpha. They will not bow to you."

Ares laughed. "You can't even hold your form and you say *I'm* not wolf enough? I'm more wolf than you could ever hope to be!"

Ares kicked him in the ribs. "That is for frightening my mate." He grabbed Darius' arm and bent it backwards, breaking the bone. "That is for ordering me around the world on stupid missions simply because you couldn't stand seeing all of the females crawling all over me." He grabbed a spear and snapped off the tip. He sat down and with skill that suggested he'd done this many times before, cut open Darius' chest and tore his heart from it. "And that's for giving Matt's female to the vampires to assist in his treachery and death!"

The crowd exploded in cheers and began chanting, "Ares!" over and over again.

Ares threw the heart up into the pulpit at Maurice's feet. "A gift from the new Alpha of the Werewolves to the King of the Vampires. Don't say I never gave you anything."

Maurice glared at us from his seat. "You've won this time."

Ares smiled and touched his pointer finger to his forehead in a mock salute. "We'll see you soon, Maurice."

We walked back to my mother, and she grabbed onto us, teleporting us back to the training ground. I looked down and sighed. "I'm covered in blood and dirt."

Ares shrugged, motioning to his own body. "I'm worse." He shifted back to full man and looked around expectantly. "Where would they have taken her?"

Bret dropped to his knees on the ground, winced, and grunted. "Thank you."

Ares pushed him on to his back and started examining his wounds. "You're welcome, but I didn't do it for you. I did it for Artemis. She would have been very upset if you were dead."

"Artemis? She's here?" Bret asked eyes widening, trying to stand up.

Ares pushed him back down. "Stay still. Yes, she's here, but she's sleeping. You need to lie still for about an hour for your wounds to heal properly."

"I need to get back. I need to find my people," Bret said as he tried to sit up again.

"Lie still!" Ares commanded. Bret stilled, unable to ignore Ares' command. "What people? Tell us how you got into the Games in the first place."

"I found the villagers from the town Artemis and I grew up in. They all had your brand, but they were living in the middle of nowhere on the run from vampires who had apparently tried to kill them. I've been protecting the descendants for the past hundred years."

Ares groaned. "Artemis is going to want to run out and find them when she hears of this."

"Do we have to tell her?" I asked.

Ares smiled. "As much as I would like to keep it from her, we should tell her. Besides, Bret won't lie to her about it. Bret, we will wait until after tomorrow's battle to tell her though. I do not want to have her focus waver during the battle. Do you understand?"

Bret nodded. "Yes, Alpha."

"I'm going to clean up. Ares, you should probably do the same so Artemis doesn't faint when she sees you." I started for the main building where my quarters were.

"You don't think she would view it as sexy?" he asked as he stood up and flexed his biceps.

Koda laughed. "Artemis would if she had been in the battle with you, but since she was left behind she would only be worried."

Ares fingered his left arm where Darius had scratched him. "I hate when it's healing and it starts to itch. If you scratch it too hard you reopen it and it has to re-heal which then makes it itch again."

Koda smacked his hand. "This is why you have to suffer through it until it doesn't itch anymore."

"You'd be scratching it too if you were covered in dirt and

blood and had cuts that were healing," Ares grumbled as he headed towards the main part of town where a public bathhouse was run by Poseidon, a blue Sidhe who loved water.

I looked down at Bret who was still lying on the ground. "You can't move, can you?"

He shook his head. "I can't sit up at least."

"I'm going to wash up and change quickly and then I'll be back. Just relax and let your wounds heal."

"As if I can do anything else," Bret grumbled.

I ignored him and continued to my room. I really wished to soak in a bath, but I felt bad leaving Bret alone. I would feel much better once the blood and dirt was washed off my skin.

CHAPTER 20
ARTEMIS

My eyes opened slowly as I regained consciousness. I was surprised that I did not dream while I had been asleep, but being put in a spelled slumber was not the same as *falling* asleep. The room was dark, no lights anywhere. I sat up and was met with three pairs of eyes watching me from chairs in front of the bed. My night vision kicked in and as I looked around, I recognized my surroundings as Achilles' chambers. "Have they returned?" I asked nervously.

Theseus smiled. "They returned a few moments ago and are waiting for you in the training grounds. We are to escort you there."

"I've no need of an escort." I closed my eyes and focused on the image of the place I wanted to go and summoned my power.

Nothing happened.

"You cannot teleport while restrained in magical chains," said Erebos in his deep voice.

I opened my eyes and sighed. "Fine, escort me."

"You know we do not like doing this. We were ordered to guard you," said Heracles as he came to unchain me.

I sighed. "I know. I do not blame you or hold anger towards you."

Surrounded by the men who had been holding me prisoner, I now walked in a circle of protection. I knew that Ares and Achilles had forced me to stay behind to try to protect me and not having to wring my hands in worry had been good for my nerves, but I felt betrayed.

We walked through the halls of the main building of the Sidhe court and out through a set of large doors to the open grassy area used for training. Our pack of halfbreed wolves was all around Ares with eyes intently fixed on him. Ares looked up and smiled at me. There was something different about him. He seemed bigger somehow. I shook my head at the ridiculous thought. He couldn't have gotten bigger. So what was it?

The closer I got to him, the more I felt like bowing to him. That was a feeling I had not had in quite a long time around him. The pack made a path for me, but as I walked by, those nearest reached out to touch me. I smiled at them and held my hands out to touch some as I walked. The touch of the pack was even more reassuring than ever before. Had I changed somehow? Had Hades done something that permanently affected me?

I finally made it to Ares and looked over his body for marks. I couldn't see any, but then again, he was wearing a t-shirt and jeans. He leaned down and kissed me deeply, winding a hand through my hair and around my hips, pulling me against him. I melted into him and felt the fire building within me that Ares always ignited. He pulled back from the kiss and smiled at me. "Did you have a nice nap?"

"Yes." I wanted to be mad, but I couldn't even feign it while I was still high on the kiss. . I looked into his eyes and asked, "Why are you more, more wolf than normal? No, it's not that you're more wolf it's just that your aura is stronger. What changed?"

Ares said, "I've always been like this, but now that I've claimed my proper title it's more evident to you."

"Your proper title? What do you mean?" I asked, my nerves growing.

"I killed Darius. I'm the new Alpha of the Werewolves," he said with a wide grin.

"Alpha," said the pack behind us.

"You killed Darius! When? Where? How?" I asked. I stopped my questions and asked the question I should have asked first, "Did you save Bret?"

Ares grabbed my shoulders and turned me around. "See for yourself."

Bret stood from where he had been kneeling among the pack and walked slowly towards me. He stopped in front of me and smiled nervously. "Hey, Chicky."

Varying emotions warred with my mind, but I ignored all of them and threw my arms around his shoulders. Bret stiffened a moment and then wrapped his arms around me in a tight hug. We inhaled each other's scents, and I whispered his name. I pulled out of the hug and smiled at him. "I'm glad you're okay."

He picked up my hand and traced one of my vines. "You look even more beautiful than the last time I saw you."

I cringed, waiting for my power to release from his touch and my life to be even more chaotic and stressful than it was, but nothing happened. I exhaled in relief and heard Ares do the same behind me. "Thank you," I said softly.

Koda cleared his throat from beside us. I jumped, having not heard him walk up. I turned to him and hugged him. "Are you unhurt as well?"

He nodded as he hugged me. "I am. I also brought you a present."

"A present?" I asked as I stepped back from him.

Koda stepped to the left and motioned at the line of men who had been standing behind him. "Darius brought them to fight Ares, but I made them submit to me instead. They're our newest pack members and as Alpha Female I thought it appropriate that you meet them."

"Alpha Female?" I asked in shock. I turned to Ares. "What about your mom? Isn't she Alpha?"

Ares shook his head. "When a new Alpha male takes the position he either takes the former Alpha's mate to be his, or his current mate takes the position. Obviously, I'm not going to take my mom as a mate, so you're now Alpha Female of the Werewolves."

I was Alpha Female!

"Whoa," I said as I comprehended all that had happened. I turned to the wolves in line in front of me and walked so that I could see them all. Most appeared young looking and middle level in dominance. "Whom do you serve?" I asked them.

"The Alphas," they said together.

"Whom do you protect?" I asked as I walked down the line.

"The Alphas."

"Who am I?" I stopped in front of them at the center of their line.

"Artemis, Alpha Female."

I walked up to each man and inhaled his scent at his neck and rubbed my cheek against theirs to scent mark each as mine. Luckily being short let me do it without having to bend down at an awkward angle, though two of the men were so tall that I had to stand on tiptoe to reach their cheeks. When I'd finished I turned to the rest of the pack and said, "Embrace your new brothers."

The pack surged around the men and greeted them. Ares walked to me and wrapped his arms around my waist. "You did that very well."

"Thanks. I learned it from the real wolves. Well obviously not the talking part, but the rest," I said as I leaned back against him. I looked around and frowned. "Where's Achilles?"

"I'm here. I was just freshening up from our excursion."

I watched him walk up and felt my heart flutter. How could he affect me so? My reaction to Ares was different, but Achilles still raised my pulse and made my legs wobble. It wasn't right to be in love with two men at the same time and yet I was. Sometimes I really hated magic.

I pulled away from Ares and turned to face him and Achilles. "I wanted to show you something. I watched the dragons doing this and I'm pretty sure I can duplicate it, but I'd appreciate it if you two would stand nearby in case it gets out of my control."

Ares frowned and Achilles sighed and shook his head. I took that as an "okay".

I stepped out onto the field and waited until everyone else was off of the field and Ares and Achilles were relatively close. I closed my eyes. Selene had taught me to meditate to better control my powers, and I really hoped it worked now. Inhaling slowly and grounding myself with the earth around me and beneath my feet, I channeled my power to my hands. I raised them slowly up, heels of my palms touching while the rest of the palm turned up to create a funnel for the power. I pictured the one time I'd seen Blu perform this technique and opened my eyes as fire burst out of my palms in a swirling purple tornado. I focused on the energy of the element and lowered the swirling fire until it formed a solid, protective circle around me. With a deep breath, I ground my feet into the ground and the fire spread out, increasing its circumference until it surrounded the entire field. Sweat began to drip down my face as the pull of controlling the wild element strained my magical ability.

"Release it, Artemis!" yelled Ares.

I shook my head and slowly and painfully pulled it all back into me. With each foot of returned element my magic returned and my body refilled with energy.

"By the Mother of All, I have never seen something so incredible," whispered someone.

"She has to be the most powerful being on the planet," whispered another.

"No wonder halfbreeds were forbidden. We couldn't defeat her unless we used a large group of our top soldiers," whispered one of the Sidhe soldiers.

I pulled in the last bit and felt completely revitalized. I turned and smiled at Ares and Achilles. "I did it!"

Hera was standing behind them, having snuck up while I was testing the magic. She snarled and started glowing. I only had a second's notice to prepare as she shot fire at me from her palms. I formed a shield of fire around me and absorbed her shot at me. Those gathered now stared in terror at me instead of awe. Hera's eyes turned solid white as she drew on all of her power and increased the amount of fire directed at me, but my shield simply absorbed it. Ares started to move towards her, but she released her powers and stopped the fire. Her body and eyes returned to normal, with fear in them. "Who taught you this magic?" she asked in a shocked whisper.

For a moment, I didn't want to tell her, but Ares bowed his head slightly to me, telling me it was okay. "The King of the Dragons taught me to create the fire shield and the other he had to use once to protect me," I answered. "A group of vampires found us in the woods together and ambushed us. One of them grabbed me by the throat before I could shift and in his anger, he used it."

Hera swallowed before asking, "Could you contact the dragons?"

I nodded. "Yes, if I needed to, but we won't need them tomorrow."

She shook her head. "I wasn't speaking about tomorrow."

I shrugged. "If we need them, I can contact Draco-Blu, but I don't know if they will help or not. They prefer to stay neutral."

Ares walked up to me and stared into my eyes. "How are you feeling?"

I smiled and kissed his lips. "I feel perfect. By drawing the element back into me, I replenish myself and thus have no loss and no negative side effects."

He smiled and put his arm around my shoulders. "That's quite a trick you've got there. Perhaps you should start teaching me to use some of my Sidhe powers."

I shook my head. "I think your father or brother should teach you that."

He laughed. "Right."

Hephaistos cleared his throat, drawing our attention to him. "I have something else for Princess Artemis as well."

Ares and I followed Hephaistos back to the table and I noticed that the Sidhe backed away from us and made a path quicker than usual. Was I that powerful? Or that frightening?

Hephaistos stood in front of the table and blocked our view. "I took measurements by eye only so I hope it fights properly, but if not I can always remake them." He took a step to the side and there lay the most beautiful armor I'd ever seen.

I walked forward and gingerly touched the armor. "It's beautiful," I whispered, "I've never seen such incredible armor. Thank you."

Hephaistos bowed. "You are more than welcome, Princess."

I shook my head. "No, you can call me Artemis. Anyone who would go to such great lengths to create something as beautiful as this for me has to be a friend."

Hephaistos smiled. "Thank you, Artemis."

Ares asked, "Do you want to try it on?"

Of course I did, but I also didn't want to diminish the beauty of the armor by placing it against me.

Achilles groaned. "Really, Artemis? Here, let us help you put it on."

Ares looked at Achilles questioningly, and Achilles whispered into his ear. Ares groaned. "She'll never understand."

Achilles shook his head. "No, I don't think she will."

Before I could ask what they were talking about, they started lifting pieces of the armor and placing it on me. In a matter of seconds, I was dressed and, surprisingly, I didn't feel weighed down. I stretched and moved around to test the restrictions out. Ares held up his fists in the universal sign of "let's fight" and I threw a few punches and kicked at him a few times, all free of limitations. "Wow my movements aren't restricted at all and it's not any heavier than a sweater."

Hephaistos smiled. "Sidhe enchanted."

"It's great, Hephaistos. I love it."

He bowed. "I'm pleased you like it."

Ares and Achilles stripped me out of the armor and set it back on the table on top of the cloths it had been wrapped in. I yawned and Koda put his arm around my shoulders. "Tired, Darlin'?"

I nodded. "Yeah. It's been a busy week."

He led me away from the table and the group which had gathered. "Well, let's get you some food and then get you to bed. Tomorrow is a big morning."

I leaned my head against his shoulder and inhaled his scent. "It's good to be back with you again."

Koda smiled down at me. "It's good to have you back again. I missed you more than you'll ever know."

CHAPTER 21
ARTEMIS

As the sun rose the next morning, the sounds of activity were already high as people prepared for battle. Ares, Koda, Achilles and I lay in the giant bed in Achilles' chambers staring up at the ceiling. I knew they were all worried for my safety and the possibility of losing me again. I was worried about the possibility of losing them and I admit, about the possibility of my prophesied death. Luckily, I had avoided the topic with Achilles and Ares, but it still bothered me. Even though I didn't know the date of my death, I knew others would die with me and that was what truly worried me. I had accepted my upcoming death, but I couldn't accept others dying with me.

Victor walked into the room and said, "It's time we all started to get ready."

Ares nodded, but instead of getting up, he rolled over and molded his body to my side. He whined softly and nuzzled my hair with his nose.

I rubbed his back with one arm while I held hands with Achilles with the other. Koda lay at the bottom of the bed and snuggled my feet against his chest.

Victor sighed and then inhaled before he yelled, "Ares and Achilles! Quit acting like a couple of sniveling cowards! You've fought thousands of battles and this one will be no different! Now get up and get ready!"

Ares growled and stood up out of bed. "Damn pushy vampires."

Achilles sighed and climbed out of bed too, muttering to himself. Koda kissed the top of my foot and followed the other two men into the bathroom to prepare. I fluffed up my pillow and smiled at Victor. "You're nervous, aren't you?"

He sat on the edge of the bed facing me. "I have a bad feeling about today, but I'm not sure why."

"Where are we fighting?"

"France. Hera and you will have to teleport us all."

I finger combed my hair. "Okay, but I've never teleported from this realm to the human realm. Maybe we should use the portal and then once we're in the regular realm again I can teleport everyone."

Victor smiled. "Okay."

My stomach churned, and I clamped a hand over my mouth.

"Are you alright?" Victor asked with concern in his voice.

I shook my head and ran into the bathroom, shoving past the three men who were showering and brushing their teeth and made it to the toilet just in time.

Ares dropped to his knees beside me and pulled my hair back as I threw up everything in my stomach. "Artemis, what did you eat?"

I shook my head but couldn't talk as my stomach constricted and I dry heaved. *Achilles, I didn't eat anything. I was just talking to Victor and had to run in here.*

Achilles relayed my thought to Ares, Koda and Victor, who had followed me into the bathroom. Achilles was acting off, distancing himself from me. Was he just worried about today? He hadn't spoken to me or Ares much last night, but he didn't seem mad either. He was blocking me so hard that the corners of his eyes were pinched from the strain.

"She's probably just worried about the battle," said Victor quietly.

I wanted to argue with him, but I *was* nervous. Finally, my stomach settled, and I could lean back. "He's probably right."

Ares helped me stand up and handed me a toothbrush. "If you notice anything abnormal, tell me right away. I don't want you going out on the battlefield if you're sick."

"I'm a freaking halfbreed. I thought we weren't supposed to get sick," I complained around my toothbrush.

"We're not, but you're also unique," Ares said as he ran his hand through his hair.

His bicep flexed and then relaxed as his arm moved. How was I so lucky that I snagged a guy with such a great body? He ran his other hand through his hair and I watched his bicep again.

All eyes turned to me and I realized that I'd moaned. "Sorry," I whispered as I resumed brushing my teeth, a blush on my cheeks.

Achilles climbed into the shower and turned the water on. His back was tense, but he relaxed after the water flowed over him a few minutes. Obviously, I wasn't the only one nervous.

Ares kissed my cheek and walked out of the bathroom. Koda laughed and I spit the water I had in my mouth at him.

He jumped out of the way and stuck his tongue out at me. "Missed."

Achilles pushed up the shower head and then used his powers to increase the flow of water to reach Koda, soaking the shirt he'd just put on. "I didn't."

Koda groaned. "You're not supposed to gang up on me. What happened to 'bros before hoes'?"

I finished putting my hair up into a ponytail, pointed at him and glared. "You better not have just called me what I think you did."

Koda raised his arms in surrender. "I was joking."

"And besides, which one are you?" I asked teasingly.

Koda's jaw dropped. "That's just mean."

I walked out of the bathroom and started putting on the armor that Hephaistos had designed for me. I slid the sheath of arrows onto my back and then draped the bow across my body diagonally until I needed it. Seeing all of the people I loved preparing for battle, preparing for their possible deaths, made me start to tear up. I walked back into the bathroom and wiped at my eyes before anyone could see me.

Ares rubbed my back reassuringly. "It's alright to be nervous."

I whispered, "Ares, if I lose you…"

He moved in one blink and had me wrapped in a hug against his body. "Don't think like that. I promise that we will not be separated. Not even death could keep us apart. *Verus amor vincit omnia.* Remember?"

I pressed my nose against his throat and inhaled his scent, drawing him in and holding the smell in for as long as I could. "I know. I love you, Ares."

"I love you too, Artemis Lupine."

I giggled and rested my head on his chest for a moment before pulling away from him. "I'm ready."

He slipped his fingers through mine and we walked back into the bedroom and ate. Once I started eating, the food stayed down and then we made our way out to the field where the portal to the human world existed. Hera, Zeus, our pack of halfbreeds and at least one hundred Sidhe stood waiting for us.

Everyone looked nervous and twitchy. One of the halfbreeds turned to talk to his neighbor, and I saw the brand on his arm, a crescent moon with a star. Ares and my brand. The anger I had shoved down the night before resurfaced and with it rose my powers. My body glowed bright, my wings popped out of my back and my vines sparkled.

I looked at the gathered warriors and said, "We are going to fight the vampires. I know some of you are fighting at the request of your king or alpha, but I want you to know *why* we are fighting. The vampires have turned the world which was filled with light and happiness into a world of darkness! A world where humans can't live freely. A world where Sidhe can't go out alone!" I paused to allow my words to sink in and then continued, my voice gaining momentum, "A world of hate and fear and misery. A world where the only important thing is feeding the vampires! They've killed millions of innocent people. They have killed my friends. They tried to kill me, which, in turn, would have killed Prince Achilles. They do not deserve to live. They are evil! They are darkness given form and it is our duty to kill them and right the balance!"

Everyone cheered and those with weapons raised them in the air. "When you go out on that battlefield, I don't want you to fight for your king or your alpha. I want you to fight for the rights of every race! I want you to fight for the return of humanity! I want you to fight for the return of the light!"

The warriors all cheered and then started filing through the portal to the human world. Ares smiled at me. "Nice speech."

I smiled at him and said, "Let's go kill some vampires."

Ares sighed dramatically, his hand against his forehead like a woman swooning over a man. "Isn't she dreamy?"

Zeus laughed. "Yes, son, she is definitely a perfect match for you."

I turned and headed into the portal, folding my wings close around my body as I walked up the staircase portal. We stepped out into the human world and I noticed that we had split into two groups, but they were mixed groups of halfbreeds and Sidhe as opposed to a halfbreed group and a Sidhe group. Finally, we were making headway. Hera stood in the center of the first group so I walked to the next group and waited until the last person had walked out of the portal and the ground had closed up behind him.

"Ready?" I asked those gathered around me. Everyone placed a hand on each other so that we were all connected by touch. Hera nodded at me to express her readiness. "Try not to throw up on each other," I whispered just before I closed my eyes, and we spun through a spinning vortex. I opened my eyes and smiled at the sight of the Eiffel Tower lit up by lights in the distance. Several people groaned as they tried to settle their stomachs from the trip.

It was eerily quiet now that the humans didn't inhabit France and as we followed Victor through the empty streets towards the battleground, I shivered. Straightening my back, I focused on my anger and ignored the chill of fear creeping up my spine.

Achilles slipped his fingers through mine and moaned when just the touch brought his powers. His wings popped out of his back, almost hitting Ares.

"Watch it," Ares growled.

Achilles whispered, "I didn't mean to do that."

I rubbed his hand with my thumb and said, "Sorry."

He shook his head and kissed my cheek. "You have nothing to be sorry for. That has never happened before so I wasn't prepared."

Victor gave us a scalding look so we stopped talking.

We walked for what felt like hours before finally coming to a field of burned wood and ash that used to be a lush forest. Several of the halfbreeds, including Ares and I, growled at the ruined forest. Thousands of trees had been destroyed in the obviously man-made fire. Whatever their reason had been for destroying the forest, it just added to the anger and the need to tear something apart in all of us, the Sidhe who value nature included.

The presence of evil pressed down upon me as we walked farther into the opening and then we saw the vampire army. A familiar figure stood at the front with hybrid vampires beside him. I swallowed nervously as I thought about the possibility of having to fight my brother. I pulled my bow over my head and nocked an arrow.

Apollo stepped forward and spoke in a commanding voice, "You are acting in treason against the King of the World, Maurice. Drop your weapons or we shall be forced to attack you."

Zeus turned to Ares, Achilles, and I and waved us forward. "You're the leaders."

Ares and Achilles shrugged and Ares asked, "You want to respond?"

I smiled. "Sure." I walked out past our group and let my wings fully extend and my body glow brighter. "There is no king of the world, only an old vampire overstepping his place and committing extreme crimes, including murder, treason and torture. We are all equals. Unless you drop your weapons and allow us to pass so that we can kill Maurice for his crimes, we will be forced to fight you."

Apollo's shocked face was priceless. He took a moment to compose himself and then he said, "You will not see reason. I have no other choice but to punish you."

The vampires and dhampirs all hissed at us and licked their lips in excitement. I aimed my bow and released the arrow. Apollo jumped to the left, narrowly escaping the arrow, and it passed through the four vampires behind him, making them burst into ash at the touch of the sunlight on the tip of the arrow.

"Then let us fight!" I yelled.

Our army surged forward and the vampires and dhampirs ran to meet us. The screams of rage and pain covered everything else. Achilles, Ares, Koda, and Theseus took protective positions around me, preventing any from coming too close to me. I shot three more arrows, which killed an additional twelve vampires and two dhampirs. Vampires and dhampirs died all around me, while very few of our group fell, a good sign so far.

Ares and Koda fought side by side in half-shifts, cutting down our enemies with a speed that I only hoped to attain with practice. Achilles' sword flashed, quick as lightning, as he attacked, his focus never wavering from the battle.

Despite all of the vampires and dhampirs the men around me killed, the enemy continued to crowd closer, pushing the men even closer to me and preventing me from fighting. The battle finally grew too close so I hung my bow over my shoulder, placed my fists together and then separated them, forming my sword of light.

I held the sword in readiness, but Ares and the others were still keeping the vampires and dhampirs a safe distance away from me. In this moment, I watched the skill of Achilles' blade and the swiftness of Ares' movements with awe. The vampires pressed closer and forced the men to move even closer to me. "Stop protecting me and let me fight!" I yelled over the sounds of the battle.

Ares growled, but after killing two more vampires he stepped forward to break the circle around me. A vampire charged in and I brought my sword up, slicing him cleanly in half. My blood pumped harder and my body quivered in excitement as I started fighting. The men moved out a little farther, opening their circle and killing faster as they plowed deeper into the advancing enemy. My wings retracted due to the now limited space, but my body continued to glow as I fought with everything that I had. Bodies piled up around us and I realized that the vampires weren't just fighting, but fighting their way towards me. That realization didn't frighten me like it would have years before. Instead, it made me smile and renewed the vigor with which I fought.

We had to move deeper into the swarming masses due to the immense amount of dead bodies around us, which were making it impossible to walk. Achilles stayed beside me while Ares, Koda and Theseus were separated from us by the crowding enemy. I reined in my power to keep my reserves up and laughed joyously as I killed again and again. When I thought I was human, I never would have enjoyed killing. Now I knew what I was made for. I was made to end the evil in the world and right the balance. Dhampirs backed away from me when they got too close and I followed after them, cutting off whatever was closest to me and finishing off the being as it screamed.

I turned to find Achilles and Apollo battling each other, but surprisingly Apollo was holding his own against Achilles.

I turned around in time to decapitate a dhapmir running at me.

I battled with vampires while trying to watch the fight between Achilles and Apollo at the same time. A vampire grabbed my sword hand and twisted, trying to break my wrist, which only pissed me off. Sunlight began seeping out of my pores and the vampire burst into flames and then turned to ash, drifting along the wind.

Achilles gasped in pain. I spun around and stared in shock as a blade was shoved through his chest and its bloody end dripped out the back. I moved towards him, but it was too late. I was always too late. Too slow.

"No!" I screamed as Achilles' light faded and then my own body dropped to the ground. Darkness surrounded me and cold spread through my limbs. The last thing I heard was Ares scream my name as I died beside Achilles.

CHAPTER 22
ARES

My soul split in two, sapping half of my strength and making me stumble forward. Koda's heartrending howl confirmed what I knew had happened before I turned. I spun around and screamed Artemis' name, but it was too late.

Terror and dismay washed over me as my beautiful mate dropped to the ground beside Achilles and both of their lights faded.

I ripped through everyone and everything blocking my path to her. Vampires and dhampirs fled in terror and Sidhe and half-breeds dove out of my way as I ran to her.

Koda made it to her body first and kept the vampires at bay, snarling and slashing at them in his half-shift. I dropped to the ground and picked her limp body up into my arms. Her head lolled to the left and her arms hung limply by her sides instead of wrapping around me as they should have. I howled in pain and cradled her against my chest as tears streamed down my face. My body reverted back to man and my throat changed with it.

"NO!" I screamed as the loss of her presence began to resonate within my body. "Please Artemis, wake up," I whispered as I stroked her hair.

Not a single sound came from her. Her beautiful voice was gone. She was gone. I screamed and heard the keening sound I was making, which I knew sounded pathetic, but I didn't care. My mate was gone. I had nothing now.

The sounds of fighting ceased and Hera and Zeus dropped to their knees on the ground beside Achilles' body. Hera placed her hand against Achilles' face and screamed her despair.

Zeus looked from Artemis to Achilles with tears in his eyes, but made no sounds of loss. He stood up and said, "This battle is over for today."

Artemis' body was beginning to lose its warmth. I rubbed her arms to try to warm her and cradled her head against my shoulder, but she remained cold. Koda shifted to his wolf form and howled in grief. She was the love of my life, magical influence or not, I loved her more than anything else in the world. She was the greatest gift I'd ever been given and now she was gone.

I couldn't lose her! She had just come back into my life. I'd waited one hundred years to find her again and we'd only just been reunited. This couldn't be happening. I wouldn't let this happen!

"Hades!" I yelled as loud as I could. "Hades!"

A Sidhe as dark as night itself walked through the crowd and dropped to his knees in front of me. "I am here, Ares," he said in a voice as deep as the night was dark.

"Send me," I whispered.

The crowd which had been murmuring quietly a moment before, instantly went silent.

"Ares, I don't think..." Hades began softly.

I growled at him and stared into his eyes. "Send me!" I yelled.

"We can't do it here. We need to wait until we're somewhere safe so that we can protect your body as well as Artemis' and Achilles'," said Zeus from beside me.

Koda wrapped his furred body around me in an attempt to comfort me and I pushed him away. Comfort meant there was something to be sad about. I couldn't be sad about this because that meant that she was dead and I couldn't get her back. I would get her back. "I won't let her die. I promised her that I wouldn't let anything separate us, not even death. I have to go!"

"I understand. Hades will send you once her body is protected," Zeus said. I nodded in understanding and then he started to reach down towards Artemis.

I growled at him and spun up and around to protect her body from his touch. "Mine!" I yelled angrily. I held her body against mine, wishing my warmth would bring her back. Wishing this was just a dream.

Zeus raised his hands in the air. "I'm sorry," he said sadly, "Come, let's leave this place."

Hera picked Achilles up in her arms and let her wings out. She flew up above everyone's heads and wailed as she cradled her dead heir against her bosom, just as she'd done over one thousand years ago, when he had been born.

Zeus waited until Victor was beside me and then took to the skies after his wife.

"Let's go, Ares," Victor said quietly. "We need to hurry before the vampires change their minds and come back."

"Let them come. I will tear their hearts from their chests and feed it to them," I said as I started walking.

The sound of someone softly sobbing a few feet away made me turn. Apollo sat on the ground staring at nothing. "I didn't know. I didn't know," he repeated over and over again.

"Didn't know what?" Victor asked angrily.

"I didn't know she was bound to him. If I had known…I wouldn't have told them to…I never wanted her to die. I just wanted to scare her and make her stay off the battlefield. I didn't know who he was to her," Apollo whispered as tears flowed down his face.

Koda snarled and lunged at Apollo who made no move to protect himself. I stepped into Koda's path and said, "Bring him with us. Alive."

Victor grabbed the halfbreed by the back of the neck and forced him to walk in front of us. The crowds parted as we walked and I growled at anyone who came too close. She wasn't going to be dead for long. I had to save her. I had to save her or give my life trying.

We'd known about this prophecy and yet it had been forgotten in the hectic life that we led. I might have been able to save her had I remembered it and consulted the other Sidhe. I might have kept her from dying if I'd only forced her to stay at Hera's Court. How could I have forgotten the prophecy?

Anger stirred within me, and I wanted to break something or someone. She had been taken from me again! I was supposed to be one of the most powerful beings on Earth. Only two generations from the original beings and yet I could not protect her. When the wolves had kidnapped her for the Vampire Queen, I'd wanted to tear down every building in search of her. Then Hera had stolen her and blocked her memories. Of all the times I'd wanted to kill that woman then had been the only time I might have actually done it. And now Artemis was actually dead. Her cold, lifeless body lay in my arms as evidence.

Every part of me ached, and I shook in misery as her loss and distance became more evident. If I couldn't get her back, I would never see her smile again. I would never hear her laugh. Never see her blush. I'd never run with her in the forest.

She was my world. Nothing else mattered, but having her beside me. Not the fate of the world, not even the fate of my pack. How could I possibly continue to live without her hand in mine?

Dmitri led the way, claiming to know a place that was safe for us as well as him and not visited by other vampires. We walked for two hours before finally stopping at a lone building in the middle of a flower field. It was an old cathedral that had somehow survived the uprising of the preternatural world. Surprisingly even the stained-glass windows were still intact. I looked up to see the gargoyles staring out across the field as though to ignore our presence. The saints carved around the entrance glared accusingly, but I ignored their prejudice. Zeus pushed open the doors, which groaned at him for disturbing their peace.

"Koda check inside," I said as I adjusted my hold on Artemis' body.

Koda walked into the cathedral and came out a moment later, sneezing. *Only rats and dust in there.*

We walked into the cathedral, and I stopped a moment to admire the building. The stained-glass windows cast multicolored shadows upon the wooden pews. A wide red carpet led to the front of the cathedral where a skeleton sat in a chair. Judging by his robes he must have been the priest.

Victor leaned over a basin of water which stood at the entrance and whispered, "I've always wondered if this worked on us or not. Father told us that it didn't, but none have been willing to test the theory in front of me before." He put his hand into the water and splashed some onto his face. He frowned a moment and then smiled. "Guess not."

Dmitri led us through a side door which opened to a hallway where saints carved into the stone watched our passing with great sadness. I wanted to yell at them and tell them her death was not permanent, but remembered they were only stone carvings and did not understand our situation.

We rounded a corner and started down a narrow set of stairs which led underground to the catacombs I'd heard about long ago, but never visited.

Zeus' body glowed as we descended into the darkness, giving us enough light to see. Koda snapped up a rat which squeaked its disapproval of our presence.

I looked at Koda and asked, "What are you doing?"

I'm hungry. He said just as his stomach growled.

"That's disgusting, Koda. You don't know where that things been," Victor said as he kicked another rat out of his way.

The ground was dirt, but it was packed down so tightly that it resembled stone. Despite the exquisite cathedral above us, there was no architecture in the catacombs to speak of save the wooden skeletal structure that kept the earth from caving in on itself.

We weaved our way through the catacombs, following behind Dmitri, who stopped at a tomb with an x marked over it.

Dmitri broke the door open and walked inside. "X marks the spot," Apollo said softly.

Despite the circumstances a soft chuckle slipped past my lips, as well as Victor's. Victor nudged Apollo forward into the tomb and we filed inside.

Dmitri sat beside a stone sarcophagus with an image of a young woman carved into its lid. He rested his hand on top of one of her carved ones and whispered softly in French.

"Who's that?" I asked Victor softly.

"His wife. He was turned while he was still with her and he could not control the bloodlust when he went back to visit her."

"Is that why this cathedral hasn't been destroyed?" I asked.

Victor nodded. "My father agreed to leave this building intact at Dmitri's request."

A second sarcophagus sat beside Dmitri's wife, but its lid was blank. "Who is that?" I asked as I motioned towards it.

"No one lies there. That was supposed to be Dmitri's burial place when he died."

I walked to it and laid Artemis' body along its cold stone lid. Dmitri was still whispering quietly beside his wife's sarcophagus and I felt immense pity for him and a determination not to be in the same situation. I arranged Artemis' body comfortably and placed her hands on her stomach. She looked like an angel.

Hera was elsewhere in the catacombs, wailing through the wall of the tomb, her power beating against the stone walls. I knew I should be mourning the loss of my brother, but I couldn't think of his death while I held Artemis' lifeless hand in mine.

I walked with Victor and helped him secure the front door so that any passersby wouldn't walk in.

"Ares, think about it before you do anything rash," Victor pleaded with me as he followed me back into the room.

"I've thought about it enough. I'm going to get her and bring her back," I answered.

"Let us discuss it first. Seek council from Koda and your father. Please," Victor said with such concern in his voice that it made me stop to look at the vampire.

We'd known each other one thousand years and he'd never spoken to me with such evident worry. "Very well," I answered quietly. I turned to Koda who had been listening passively. "Koda?"

Koda turned his head, breaking the silent stare he'd had on Artemis' body. *Huh?*

"Do I go after Artemis or stay here and let her rot?" I asked.

Victor groaned and threw his hands up into the air. "You're impossible! Koda, does he go, possibly to his death, to *try* and possibly fail to get Artemis? Or does he stay here safe, happy and alive?"

Koda looked at Artemis' still body and then met my eyes. *Bring her back.*

Koda was the most emotional of my brothers' and the lack of emotion in his eyes frightened me. It could only mean one thing; he was bottling it up. That could result in a catastrophic event if he didn't release soon, especially since he was staying in wolf form. I debated whether to force him out of wolf form, but Zeus walked into the room, interrupting my thoughts.

"Finally, someone who thinks logically. Please, talk some sense into your son," Victor begged.

Zeus ignored all of us and walked to Artemis' side. He dropped to his knees and cradled her small hand between his two giant ones. "I am so sorry, child. We should have been there to save you.

I should have been fighting beside my son. I have failed you." Silent tears slid down his face as he kissed the back of her hand. "I will never forgive myself for this."

Victor sighed softly. "So much for logical."

"Father," I whispered.

Zeus placed Artemis' hand on her stomach and walked to us. "Yes?"

"Do you think I should venture to Death's realm to try to barter for Artemis' soul? Or let her death be?"

Zeus shook his head. "I will have no part in this. I've lost one son and one daughter. I will not help you decide and possibly cause your death as well."

"Tell him not to go," Victor pleaded. "Tell him to stay."

Zeus shook his head again. "No, it is his decision. If he goes than he does so with my blessing. If he stays than he does so with my blessing. I am neutral and will remain neutral."

"Thank you, Father."

Zeus gripped my shoulder in a sign of affection and left the room.

"I'm going, Victor. I must. And I need to go now, before her body fully dies and Death permanently holds her."

Victor hissed and turned towards the door. "Well I'm not going to sit by and watch you die."

"Thank you, Victor."

He met my eyes and shook his head. "I hope you get her back. I do not wish to bury your body."

"I love you, too, man," I said in a silly tone, reminiscent of the human's stereotypical hippie voice to try to lighten his mood.

Victor shook his head and left the room.

Hades had followed us in and now stood silently beside me. I could sense he did not want to do what I was asking, but I also knew that he would do it if I asked.

"Send me. I have to get her back," I whispered without taking my eyes from Artemis' face.

"You know you might not be able to get her back. If Death decides to keep you there, too, I cannot return you to your body either. You may both die this night," said Hades in warning.

"I have no reason to return to my body if I can't bring her back," I answered. I kissed her lips and whispered, "I'm coming, Sunshine. I'm coming to bring you back from the darkness."

I lay down on the ground beside her and closed my eyes. "You're in charge," I told Koda who only huffed in response. I should have tried to console him since he was my only living pack mate at the moment, but I didn't want my focus to waver from Artemis.

Hades put his hands on my head and chest and spoke quickly in Latin. Pain surged through my body, but it was nothing compared to the pain I felt losing her. This pain I could handle. This was only physical pain. Darkness rolled over me, through me and then surrounded me.

Nothing moved. Nothing breathed. Nothing was anywhere. Anger overcame me and I growled and closed my eyes, focusing on my senses and searching for any movement. Any sound. Any smell.

"Death!" I yelled into the void.

I still couldn't sense anything and my wolf side did not like that fact. It was too close to being in a cage or being trapped for me. I inhaled and yelled, "Death! Show yourself!"

The darkness stirred and a hooded figure stepped out in front of me. Its cloak looked like it was formed from the darkness that surrounded us and made me wonder if it could consume a person if placed over them. The scythe it carried was at least seven feet long, a full foot taller than Death and had a wicked sharp edge that gleamed even in the darkness.

It raised its hand and instead of the black void where I had been, I now stood in a royal chamber and Death sat upon the throne. The carpet and upholstery were black instead of red like most kings would have. I supposed that black was a fitting color for Death's throne room, though I personally would have gone for a less cliché color myself, probably blue. Or purple, like Artemis' eyes.

Death stroked the scythe, which was now sitting beside it like a king would stroke his scepter. "Ares Lupine," it said in a voice like rocks grinding against each other, "I have longed to see your face in my realm."

"I regret to inform you that I am not yet dead."

Death laughed and said, "I am aware of that, Ares. I am also aware of the fact that you are here for two of the souls I received during your battle." It was odd not to see a face while talking to someone, but then again, Death wasn't really a person.

"I will take Achilles' soul back with me if you permit, but if you only allow me one soul than I will take my mate back. It is not her time. She still has a prophecy to fulfill." I walked closer to Death, wondering what game I was going to have to play to get Artemis back or what price might be asked of me.

Death stood and motioned for me to follow. It walked down a hallway lined with what looked like black velvet and with sconces made of bones. Pictures of beings in various states of torture hung every ten feet along the wall on the right side while paintings of battlefields pooling with blood lined the left side. I knew this was all just a conjured image, but it was going a long way to keep up the charade for me. Was there some point it was trying to make?

The sounds of moaning and wails began to echo down the hallway. The hair on the nape of my neck stood up and the wolf within me grew uneasy. Was this a trap? Or perhaps it was going to test me somehow?

The hallway ended at a large metal door, and Death pushed it open. The wailing grew incredibly loud as I stepped through the door to stand on a stone balcony overlooking a black river. Glittering silver specters swirled around inside the river and I realized that's where the moaning was coming from. "The river Styx?"

Death nodded. "Some of the beliefs of each religion are true. It is unfortunate the humans could not come together to understand the complete truths of each."

A young girl, no older than seven years old, walked across the bank on the opposite side of the river towards the water. Her eyes were lost and full of fear as she stepped into the water, but as soon as it closed over her head her fear evaporated and a smile spread over her face.

I stared at the writhing black water a moment longer before asking. "Why did you bring me here?"

"There are some who would die to see this," Death quipped.

Death was trying to joke with me. At another time I might have laughed, but there was no humor in my heart at the moment. "Are you going to make me swim through it to find my mate's soul?" I asked.

Death laughed. "You would not survive the waters. The others would eat you alive if the water did not take you first. No, Ares Lupine, I have brought you here to see the truth of fate. There is no heaven or hell. Your soul simply glides around the waters until I release it to disappear and let you rest."

That was partially reassuring since I'd always assumed I was going to Hell for all of the beings I'd killed, but also slightly disheartening to know we simply vanished.

Death walked back to the first room and sat on the throne. "Why have you come to me?"

"You know the answer to that question," I growled.

"Yes," Death said with amusement in its voice, "But apparently, *you* do not."

It waved a hand and Artemis appeared in human form beside Death. A light pulsed where her heart was, her soul, but a second light pulsed in her stomach as well.

"I'm surprised that you would so easily give up the soul of your unborn child," Death said mockingly.

I gaped at the small pulsing light in my mate's stomach as Death's words sunk in. Artemis was pregnant. That's why she had thrown up. I'd thought it had been nerves, but obviously, it was more than that.

"What price would you pay for your mate and your child's souls?" asked Death as it ran a hand along Artemis' side.

I did *not* like it caressing my mate in such a manner. I tried to rein in my anger so as not to upset it. I couldn't afford to piss it off and lose my mate and my child. How could I have been such a fool? How could I have let this go unnoticed? "I have given you thousands of souls and I will give you thousands more for their lives. Give my mate and my child back to me!" I commanded, losing control at the sight of it continuing to touch Artemis.

"Only gods may command me, Ares of the Werewolves," Death answered slowly. The taste of its fear tickled my tongue and excited the wolf within me. How long had it been since Death had been afraid? I wasn't naive enough to assume I was the first to frighten it, but I was angry enough to want to be the last to. It grabbed its scythe, standing up and blocking my view of Artemis.

My body began glowing as my anger grew and my Sidhe powers released. I moved faster than a human eye could track, stopping inches from Death. I had no fear of this thing and I had no fear of death. It had angered me, and I was tired of its games. I yelled, "I am the God of War! Give them to me!"

BATTLES OF THE NIGHT

ARTEMIS LUPINE SERIES,
BOOK FOUR

USA TODAY BESTSELLING AUTHOR

CATHERINE BANKS

BATTLES OF THE NIGHT

BOOK FOUR

ARTEMIS LUPINE

Battles of the Night by Catherine Banks.

Cover design by Covers by Juan.

Logo by Avery Banks.

Published by Turbo Kitten Industries.

www.CatherineBanks.com

Turbo Kitten Industries

PO Box 5012, Galt, CA 95632

ACKNOWLEDGMENTS

RJ, thank you for all of your help, insight, assistance, guidance, and most of all, thank you for being my friend.

CR, thank you for your PA-ing help and all of the other things you help me with. You are amazing and I'm so lucky to have found someone like you to help me.

CHAPTER 1
VICTOR

I was over one thousand years old and felt as helpless as a newborn human.

There were few people whom I truly cared for. Ares was one I unashamedly loved. I stared at his lifeless body and hissed at my uselessness. Here I was, the most powerful vampire in the world, and I could do nothing, but wring my hands and pace.

I turned from Ares only to have my eyes come to rest on Artemis' body, which lay next to Ares' on top of the sarcophagus that should have been for Dmitri, had my father not made him an immortal vampire.

Artemis was small, beautiful, and enormously powerful. When I had first seen Ares and Artemis together, I was not sure what to make of the awkward, shy girl, but she soon proved that she was just as loyal and good hearted as the prophesied savior of the world should be. She was certainly capable of killing, but she had a good soul and most importantly she made Ares happy.

Ares and I had been through many battles and he had saved my life numerous times. He had also put my life in danger just as many times, but no matter what we encountered, he never backed down and he constantly proved his loyalty to me. I wanted to prove my loyalty to him, to repay him, but I could do nothing.

"Any change?" asked a deep, growling voice from far away.

I walked out of the room and down the dark catacombs until I reached the stairs which led up into the cathedral where we were currently taking our refuge. A dark blue dragon's head snaked through the doorway of the cathedral and wound his way as close to the catacomb stairway as he could.

Draco Blu, leader of the dragons, had come an hour after Artemis' death demanding to know what had happened and seeking blood.

It was a good thing that Apollo, Artemis' twin brother and cause of her death, was locked deep within the catacombs or the dragon might have torn him apart and I did not think I would have been able to stop him. Draco Blu and Artemis had developed a friendship, which had shocked the entire world since the dragons had previously only kept to themselves. Knowing Artemis though, I felt that many would change their views after meeting her.

I met the dragon's eyes and shook my head.

He growled in frustration and asked, "How much longer can Hades hold him?"

Hades yelled, "Not much longer. I'm not strong enough to hold him more than another hour at most." Hades was a full-blooded Sidhe who had the unique power of being able to send people into Death's realm and bring them back…usually. He was currently the only thing keeping Ares alive, and the only link that would bring Ares back to the living realm.

Of course, that also depended on Death as well. If Death decided that he wanted to keep Ares' soul with him, then there was nothing any of us could do.

Draco Blu pulled his head out of the cathedral and then returned only a few seconds later with one of his scales between his teeth.

I stared at it a moment before taking it from him and returning to the room where Hades was bent over Ares. I set the scale in Hades' hand and he gasped as the power flowed out of the scale and into him.

Hades blinked at it several times and then spoke to Draco Blu as I walked back to the stairway, "Why would you do this? Giving me some of your energy is an extreme gift, but you do not know me."

He simply said, "She is my friend."

I stared after the leader of the dragons.

In one thousand years, the dragons had not been friends with anyone. Now, the leader was giving his energy, his essence, to strangers to try to save a girl he viewed as his friend.

Times were definitely changing.

The dragon withdrew from the building and I returned to the room, leaned against the wall, and watched Ares again.

Koda walked into the room, still in his wolf form. Most werewolves were clean in their wolf forms because they switched forms a lot, but his fur was matted and looked oily and dingy. His eyes were glued to Artemis' body as he walked, as if she were the only thing in the room. The usually joyful and teasing man who always had a mohawk and crazy hair color had transformed with Artemis' death. As soon as Artemis had died, Koda shifted forms and refused to change back. I was slightly worried that he might go rogue, but more importantly, this was not like him.

He walked past me without even an acknowledgment and sat on the floor beside Artemis. He put his nose against her hand, inhaling her scent, and shuddered. He rubbed his face against her palm and then walked to Ares', repeating the movements. There were other wolves around, so he was not a lone wolf, but he had lost his brother Matt when Ares had had to execute him for being a traitor. To lose Artemis and Ares was too much for Koda to handle as a man, so he chose to stay a wolf. He jumped onto the stone, curled up at Artemis' feet, closed his eyes with a sigh, and fell asleep.

I left the room to find food before I lost control. Sidhe and wolves moved out of my way as I walked down the underground passageways. I realized after a moment that there was no food here, and I needed to teleport somewhere to find some. I closed my eyes and began to gather my magic to teleport to my favorite girl when a hand came to rest on my arm. "Victor," Dmitri whispered. "Take me with you please."

I opened my eyes and saw his pinched eyes and slightly elongated fangs and realized that I was failing as his leader. "I apologize. I should have remembered that you would need food as well."

I closed my eyes again and teleported us both to Las Vegas, not wanting to tell even Dmitri about my favored female. Vegas was one of the only areas that my father had not changed. For some reason he liked the bright lights and busyness. It was now home to hundreds of shapeshifters and vampires.

Dmitri smiled as we started walking and asked, "Are we going to get in a fight while we are here?"

I shrugged. "It depends on my father's minions. Most should know to steer clear of me and let me do as I want, but perhaps some will try to gain favoritism by attempting to capture me."

"Attempt would be the main word in that sentence," Dmitri said with a smile.

We walked down the sidewalks, passing by potion shops, clothing stores, strip clubs, and restaurants. The patrons of the town veered out of my path, which made me smile.

Or perhaps it was Dmitri they were avoiding. He was known as Fear and had been my father's right-hand assassin until I had freed him from my father's grasp.

With him beside me, I doubted we would have any trouble in this town, but one could always hope.

I stopped in front of a ten-story building with no markings on the front except for the address. "Here we are," I said with a smile as I pushed open the door.

A tall woman with exotic eyes sat behind a counter with a

bored expression on her face. As soon as I entered, she stood up and smiled pleasantly at me. "Prince Victor. It has been too long since I have seen your handsome face."

"Alexandria, I have missed our meetings," I said with a bit of purr and sexual innuendo added along with some power in my voice.

Her body tightened in response to my power and she stepped around the counter to place her hands on my chest. She was slender and had thick blonde hair down to her butt. "What can I get for you?" she asked with heat in her eyes.

Dmitri rolled his eyes.

I smiled. "I need two donors for each of us. We are very thirsty."

She nodded and walked to an intercom, speaking in Russian and bending over just enough to make her skirt inch up her long legs. She motioned for us to follow her with a flick of her finger and tongue.

Dmitri shook his head at me, and I followed him without reading his thoughts, knowing well enough what he would be thinking.

Alexandria stopped at the first door and pushed it open. "Dmitri, you will feed here."

Dmitri stepped into the room and two beautiful Asian women stepped out from behind a curtain. "Hello, Dmitri," the identical twins said.

"Come, Victor," Alexandria prompted.

I waved to Dmitri and followed Alexandria to the room directly next to his. Alexandria pushed open the door and waved me in. "I hope you enjoy your meal."

"I appreciate your hospitality," I said and then picked her hand up and kissed the back of it.

She flushed and quickly turned away, retreating out the door she came through.

I opened the gate which I kept closed over my mind and focused on the two women sitting on the couch in front of me. I was strong, but even the strongest could fall prey to a trap and be killed. Women were often used as traps for men because we so often forget that women could be just as deadly. If men would only think about the lion and the fierceness of the lioness, the hunter of the pride, they might not forget to keep a knife nearby after lowering their defenses for a woman.

I never forgot.

The female vampire was just as capable at killing me as a male vampire. That was part of the enticement for me when mating with vampire women. They could turn from giving you sweet kisses to tearing open your throat with their fangs in a millisecond.

He's scary. I hope he isn't a messy eater.

Oh, he looks powerful. Look at those black eyes. I hope he chooses to feed from me first.

The humans who became cattle for vampires, were not usually the brightest, but I was surprised at the fierce look in the second's eyes and her desire to be fed from first.

I sat down on the couch between them and turned to the second girl. "I think I will start with you." I let my fangs extend fully, and she turned her neck to the side, presenting me with a perfect angle to puncture her neck. It was nice to have such pretty food sometimes.

CHAPTER 2
KODA

Miss Alpha.

Miss Alpha female.

Want pack back.

Lonely. So lonely without.

Need to eat. Need to rip into something's stomach. Mm, fresh liver. Blood smells good in forest. Blood. Want blood.

No. Alpha and Alpha female not happy if I kill.

Want her back. Want her warmth back.

Whine.

Pain. Hurts. Need her back.

CHAPTER 3
ZEUS

This battle had not gone anything like I had thought it would. My youngest son, one of the strongest of the Sidhe, lay on top of someone else's grave, cold to the touch. My other son lay on another grave in Death's realm trying to retrieve his mate's soul. Poor Artemis, who had been through more than one being should be forced to go through was dead just like Achilles, her death caused by their bond which he had created to save her.

Hera, my wife, still sat beside Achilles, holding his hand as if she expected him to awaken and sit up from a dream. How I wished this was all a dream! In one day, I could lose both of my sons and my daughter-in-law. It was too much for a parent to bear.

I should have been strong enough to take out Maurice myself, but the sad fact was that I had lost most of my magic when I had battled Goliath, the former Werewolf King and Beatrice's father, and he had torn one of the wings from my back. My wing had regenerated, but my magic was a quarter of what it had been.

None of this was right. Achilles was supposed to live thousands of years after I died. He was supposed to rule over the Sidhe with Artemis at his side.

Achilles had always been a loving and caring child. I had been proud to see him carry that on into his adulthood. He had been shaping up to become an amazing king.

Despite all of the issues surrounding Ares, Achilles had always loved and looked up to him.

Hera and I had caused the rift between the brothers. I had caused my sons so much pain during their lives.

I had failed as a father, I already knew that.

My two sons had finally started to mend the rift between them and now this had happened.

Now, I had failed as a king.

Tears slipped silently down my face and I covered my eyes with my hands.

It should have been my son mourning me. Not me mourning my son. I shouldn't have had to listen to my wife mourn our boy.

CHAPTER 4
VICTOR

I sat dozing in one of the chairs in the room where Ares' and Artemis' bodies lay. I had fed and returned quickly, not wanting to miss Ares' return. Two more hours had passed, and I was quickly losing my ability to stay awake.

Hades gasped. "Victor! He's coming back."

I was alert and instantly on my feet. Koda climbed down from where he had been lying at Artemis' feet and stood beside me, facing Ares' body. We stood side by side, both rigid in anticipation and worry. Hades closed his eyes in concentration and grunted just as Ares took a gasping breath and sat up.

His eyes met mine, and he whispered, "Find me a steak."

Koda whined and wagged his tail, and Ares frowned down at him. "You thought I wouldn't come back?"

Koda flattened his ears to his head and crawled on his belly towards Ares.

Ares set his hand on Koda's head and smiled. "I would not leave you alone, Brother." Ares turned and looked at Artemis' still body a moment before looking at me with a small smile. "She's pregnant."

I stared at him a moment before comprehending what he had

said. Had he forgotten what had happened? Had he dreamed instead of going to Death's realm?

"Ares, she's not alive," I whispered to him.

He waved his hand dismissively at me. "She will be in a little bit. I just need to take her outside so she can be resurrected."

"Resurrected?" I asked.

He stood slowly, testing his body, and whispered, "Death agreed to let me have both of their souls back."

That was not uncommon. Many had traveled to Death and had a life returned, but all was done at an extreme cost. "What price was asked of you?"

Ares walked to Artemis and stroked her hair, looking at her with so much love that it felt like an invasion to even witness him next to her.

"Ares, what price was asked of you?" I asked again.

He picked her body up in his arms and cradled her against his chest. "Come, their souls need to return to her body."

I grabbed his arm and his lips pulled back over his teeth as he snarled at me.

"Ares, tell me," I insisted.

He smiled. "None, because I demanded their souls back as the God of War." His smile became darker and he said, "And I smelled Death's fear."

I stared at him in astonishment. "You think Death will leave it at that?"

Ares smiled brightly and said, "I will deal with that when the time comes. For now, let's go enjoy the moonlight and the last bit of quiet before Artemis wakes up."

The joy on his face, the absurdity of everything that was happening, it broke the shell of worry surrounding me.

With a chuckle, I followed him out of the room.

CHAPTER 5

ARES

I hated Artemis feeling, smelling, and looking so dead in my arms. I hurried from the room, out of the catacombs, through the cathedral, and out to the open grassy area outside.

My mind was still reeling from the conversation with Death, but that was something I didn't have to worry about for a long time. For now, I had only to focus on Artemis and our child inside of her.

I laid her down on the grass and Draco Blu approached.

His huge body towered over us both, his scales gleaming in the fading sunlight, and yet his eyes were soft as he looked down at my mate. "What happened?" he asked.

I smiled at him. "I came to an agreement with Death. Artemis will be alive again as soon as the moon's and the stars' lights shine upon her face."

Draco Blu lowered his head until it was level with mine, his eye staring straight into my own, and whispered, "I will help you with the price, if you need it. I know Death asks a lot of those souls it releases."

It was the greatest offering any could give, especially considering I had almost killed off his entire race.

I bowed my head and whispered, "I am honored at your offer."

He snorted softly, dual rings of smoke rising from his nostrils. "I offer only because she is my friend and valuable to all. You alone should not be forced to carry the burden just because she is your match."

I had known he was not offering for me, but I found it amusing that he felt the need to point it out.

I was barely able to keep the smirk off my face. "Luckily, no price was required," I whispered to him.

He snorted again, this time in disbelief, and I smiled, enjoying the shock on his face.

The sun began to set and a crowd started to gather. Koda, still in wolf form, kept everyone back to give us room.

I kissed Artemis gently on the lips and moved a little ways away from her.

Zeus made his way through the crowd and sat down next to me on the grass. His face was drawn, his eyes pinched, and for the first time in his life he had bags beneath his eyes. Achilles' death was taking a toll on my father. He most likely had found some way to blame himself, as he often took the blame for things not his doing. And, he was likely mourning Artemis as well. He had grown attached to her rather quickly.

"Will you help protect those gathered?" I asked him.

He nodded. "I will shield everyone else, but you must shield yourself from her when she wakes up."

The return of a soul to a being of power was often catastrophic for those nearby. Artemis' return was bound to be cataclysmic due to her amount of power. Hopefully, it wouldn't be nearly as bad as when she had broken the barrier and regained her memories since we only had four dragons with us this time.

I nodded at Zeus and prepared a shield around myself. Koda stepped out into the circle of people and Zeus raised a shield of power around all of us. I raised my shield and spread it to cover Zeus. Draco Blu and the other dragons that had come also put shields around us, singing to invoke their magic.

I only hoped it was enough.

The sun set and everyone became silent in anticipation. The moon rose and the stars glittered brightly, yet Artemis lay still.

I started to move, but Draco Blu whispered, "Look."

The moon's light flared, and a beam like a spotlight highlighted Artemis. The stars flared brighter and they formed a unified beam down on her. Her body twitched once and lay still again. Her chest rose and fell with breath, but I dared not move. The stars and moon shone brighter than our eyes could handle, forcing us to close them. Power greater than any I had ever encountered before pressed down upon us, and then Artemis began to scream.

I forced open my eyes, squinting against the light, but needing to see what was happening to my mate.

Artemis floated in the air, her wings extended, her skin the source of the shining. Her eyes were orbs of white and her stomach glowed blue. She stopped screaming and sighed as the power left her in a wave of fire that burned through our shields and knocked those nearby to the ground.

I crawled to her body, ignoring the pain and the still sizzling grass.

She lay on the ground, sleeping peacefully.

After pressing my ear to her stomach and hearing Artemis' heartbeat as well as our child's, I cried. The sorrow I felt at her death, the pain from carrying her lifeless body from the battlefield, the hurt knowing she loved Achilles, and the grief I felt at losing Achilles. I released all the pain and wept at the return of my soul mate, my *passt genau,* while those around me cheered.

CHAPTER 6
ARTEMIS

My body felt stiff and uncomfortable, but I knew I had to get up because something was happening. I could feel Ares touching me, but people around us were shouting and dragons were roaring so loudly that I could not hear him.

I opened my eyes and whispered, "What's going on?"

The ground around us was burned and some bits still smoking. It looked like all of our allies were gathered around us, most sitting on the ground with huge smiles on their faces. Some were even crying.

Ares lifted his face from my stomach but the wetness of his tears remained. "Are you hungry?" he asked softly.

Of all of the things I had expected him to say, that was not one of them.

I nodded and started to stand, but he picked me up in his arms and cradled me against his chest. I relaxed against his familiar touch and the wonderful warmth of him, letting his body heat warm my chilled body.

He walked past a crowd of smiling people who all looked at me with awe.

What had happened while I was asleep?

Ares set me down on a padded pew in a large, empty cathedral and a young girl brought a bowl of soup to me.

I sipped the soup, and then my hunger took over and I gulped it down in eager swallows.

Ares took the empty bowl and handed me a plate with two slabs of meat on it. He ate a third slab of meat. I ate my meat just as quickly as I had eaten the soup, and more food was brought to me. After thirty minutes of stuffing my face, I was finally full.

I leaned back against the pew and patted the spot beside me.

Ares sat down next to me and hugged me tightly, wrapping his entire body around mine.

I gently rubbed his back. "Ares, what has happened? Why were you crying when I woke up?"

He pulled away and ran the back of his hand gently down my face, caressing me and smiling tenderly. "What is the last thing you remember?"

I tried to think, but the last thing I remembered was the fight and…

I gasped. "Achilles! Oh no, Ares please tell me that he is alright." My heart constricted, and I knew the truth without Ares having to say it.

Ares took my hands in his and whispered, "During the battle, he was stabbed in the heart and instantly died. You both fell and because you were bound to him. You…" He choked on his words and couldn't finish the statement.

"I died," I whispered.

Ares swallowed, trying to keep his emotions at bay. "Yes."

I shivered and climbed into his lap, hiding my face against his chest. I couldn't believe that I had died. "How did I come back?"

"I demanded your life back from Death," Ares said in a serious tone.

I looked up at him. "You did what?"

He smiled. "With Hades' help, I entered Death's realm and

demanded your life back." He put a hand on my stomach and whispered, "As well as the life of our baby."

I stared at his hand sitting on my flat stomach and said, "You're joking."

He shook his head. "You're pregnant. That is why you were throwing up and why you were so moody."

I was pregnant. I stared in disbelief at my stomach a moment before closing my eyes and focusing on my body. There, in the center of my stomach, I felt the power of another being, small, but still very much there. I was pregnant.

"I'm going to be a mom," I whispered. I looked at Ares' happy face and smiled. "We're going to have a baby."

He kissed my lips and I melted against him, kissing him back as though it had been years since we had last kissed. His lips burned mine, and I shivered from the difference in our body heat. How long would it take my formerly dead body to heat back up?

After a few minutes, he pulled away with a somber expression on his face. "I am sorry that our news is tainted. I would have preferred we were able to fully enjoy this."

I stood up and stretched my stiff body. How long had I been dead? I was not sure what to expect, but I would have thought that my body would be stiffer than it was. "I agree, but we have had our moment of joy. Perhaps it is time to deal with our grief and begin grieving," I said.

Until I saw Achilles' body, I could not believe that it was true that he was dead. It had to be a cruel joke. He had been so alive. I remembered his fierce face during battle and the compassion he showed me when we were alone. I could not believe he was dead now. It did not seem possible.

Ares linked his fingers with mine and led me down a stairway into dark catacombs.

Koda bounded inside in his wolf form and knocked me to the ground, licking my face.

I laughed and pushed his face away, wiping the slobber off. I pet Koda's head and asked, "Why are you in wolf form?"

"Because he thought you and I were gone and not going to return," Ares answered for him with a bit of anger in his tone.

I tapped Koda's nose in a playful discipline. "You should know better than that."

Koda grunted and then looked up at Ares. Apparently, he had been in wolf form too long and could not change back on his own.

Ares grabbed Koda by his scruff and growled into his face as he used his power to force the change.

Koda whined and then moaned as he shifted into his human form.

Ares released Koda and grabbed my hand again. "Eat something and then wait for us to summon you."

"Yes, Alpha," Koda said softly as he panted, naked on the floor.

Ares led me down a hallway to another room which had five Sidhe males guarding it. The guards gaped at me for a moment before stepping aside and opening the doors. Apparently, they weren't used to seeing people back from the dead.

The room was cold and empty except for Hera, Zeus, and a table with Achilles' body lying on top of it.

I pulled out of Ares' hand and walked to Achilles, feeling like I was in a dream. He looked so much more handsome than I remembered him being and so at peace. I reached out slowly and rested my hand against his cheek. Instantly tears rolled down my face as the warmth that usually radiated from him was gone.

He felt cold, like stone.

I sobbed and cried as I held his lifeless hand in mine. He had died protecting me. It was cruel that I was alive again while he was not. He had watched me and loved me since I was a child. He had bound me to him to protect me and had endured so much for me. I had not been able to spend enough time with him. I loved him, but not as he had deserved to be loved and he had not been allowed to love me as he had wanted.

Ares wrapped his arms around me to comfort me, but that only increased my sorrow.

If Achilles had found me first, what would things have been like? Would I be carrying Achilles' child now instead of Ares'? Would I have been fighting this war or would we have been somewhere safe, away from the battle which took both of our lives?

The sounds of sorrow poured from my mouth, but all I could see or hear were memories of Achilles and the awful understanding that I would never experience them again. I would never see his smile. I would never see his vines glow or his power open when I touched him. I would never see his wings spread and watch him take flight. I would never again hear his voice in my head. I would never again hear him speak Latin to me.

He was gone before I had ever gotten to have him. It wasn't fair!

I felt my body begin to heat up, but I did not care about the repercussions. Ares said something to me, but I pushed him away from me. I climbed onto Achilles, straddling his body, and called my power. I called to all of the plants and trees. I called to the moon and the stars. I called to the goddess or god or whatever being created us. I called them all to me and pulled the power into my hands.

Ares was yelling at me, but I ignored him.

I raised my hands and prepared to pour the power into Achilles to try to resurrect him when Zeus touched my arms and whispered, "You must not mourn the times you did not have, but remember and cherish the times you did have."

"I can raise him. I can bring him back," I said in a voice that sounded strange even to me.

Zeus shook his head. "You could raise him from the dead, but he would not be the Achilles you loved or the son I loved. His soul has been gone for too long. Besides, you would not be bound to him anymore."

"I can bring him back," I insisted.

Zeus gently grabbed my arms and whispered, "He died to save you because he loved you. Do not let his sacrifice be for nothing. Release the power before it kills you and the child you carry. Let his soul rest."

I screamed in grief, pain, and loss and released the powers.

Zeus caught me before I fell and whispered, "Remember, Artemis. That is all he would want. He would only want you to remember him."

Ares reached for me, but I jerked away from him. I could not let him comfort me over Achilles' death. It was not fair to Achilles.

I used some of my power and teleported to Ares' house in Russia, knowing that no one would be there and that it was one place Ares would not look for me.

The living room looked just like I remembered it and thankfully there was no one inside. I collapsed onto the couch and let the tears flow again. Achilles was dead, and I had not been able to help him. If only I had been faster. If only I had not been a burden to him. I had been pushing him away and now he was gone forever. All I wanted was one touch. Just one whispered word. I wanted to hear his voice and feel his skin touch mine. I tried to stop crying, but could not.

Hours passed as my sorrow poured out of my body in cries, sobs, and screams of agony. I was tired of losing people whom I loved.

The day turned into night and the river of tears turned into a trickle. I knew I should eat, but the grief I felt over losing Achilles was too much to bear. I buried my face into the pillows and let more of my grief lose by way of tears and uncontrollable sobs.

DAY TWO

The pain became so unbearable that my wolf took over, and I shifted forms despite the small fear I had that I would not be able to change back again. My wolf felt as sad as I did and instead of cries and sobs, I released my pain in heartbroken howls.

Why hadn't I been able to protect him?

I missed him.

DAY THREE

Part of us missed our mate, but part of us was too sad about losing our other non-wolf, sort of mate. He had been nice and warm and smelled great. We missed his scent.

Pain made me whine and then the howls tore out of our throat again.

DAY FOUR

My stomach hurt, and I needed food to feed the baby I was growing. Despite the weakness that I felt, I shifted to my human form and opened the door, walking down the stairs until we reached the bottom floor, and opened that door.

Cold air pierced my skin and I welcomed its pain. This pain meant that I was alive. It was good to know that I was alive, even if Achilles was not. I shifted forms again and raced towards the nearest restaurant, searching for scraps in the dumpster, too tired to hunt anything formidable. Luckily, I was able to find meat scraps outside of a butcher's shop, and I ate what I could find, fighting off rats and stray animals.

The wind whistled down the alley and a bright blue light shone at the end.

Achilles!

I ran down the alley, yipping in excitement as I chased after him. I knew he couldn't be dead! I ran as fast as I could and pounced at the light, slamming into a building. I shook myself and looked up, stunned to see a blue lantern affixed to the building. No Achilles.

I whined as pain filled my chest and then growled at my stupidity. He was gone, and I had to deal with that fact. No matter how much I wanted him, he was never coming back again.

I ambled to the house, shivering in the cold as snow landed on my back and muzzle. I shifted forms to open and close the doors and then crawled into the bed which had a very warm blanket on it and fell asleep replaying the memories which Achilles had shared with me when he had bound us together.

DAY FIVE

The pain was gone and replaced by a vast numbness. I sat very still and became aware that I was not handling my grieving process very well. I growled in frustration and shook my head. I missed Achilles, but I could not be so immature and inconsiderate. Ares had saved me and I had abandoned him. I needed to finish my grieving and return to Ares.

The memory of Achilles' dead body flashed before me, and I curled up into a ball on the bed.

Tomorrow, I would return to Ares.

DAY SIX

At some point I had moved from the bed to the couch, only to be awoken by the scent of vampires drawing near me. I held my position and kept my eyes closed, waiting for them to get closer.

"We heard rumors of a wolf howling and assumed it might be someone from your pack," one of the vampires said sounding very arrogant for only seeing me and not having captured me yet. He still had to capture me before he could sound that smug.

I opened my eyes and was shocked to find myself surrounded by vampires.

Okay, maybe his smugness wasn't so hard to believe.

I growled and sprung from my sleeping position up into a crouch, ready to attack and shift if need be. "What do you want?" I asked as I assessed my options.

There were twelve vampires in the room in a circle around me and several more out in the hallway, though I had no idea how many since they were not in view so I could have been vastly outnumbered. I could use my fire, but then I would end up burning down Ares' house, which I was sure would not be okay with him. He would forgive me, but I did not want to burn down the pretty building. If I'd had any energy, I could have teleported.

"We want you to come with us peacefully to see the King," he said pleasantly.

I could use my sunlight magic, but I had to be sure to get every vampire here, otherwise if I missed one, he would go to Maurice and spill my secret.

Wait.

If I was taken to Maurice, then I could kill him there! Even if they bound me and blindfolded me, I could still use my sunlight magic. It could be a quick end to this entire battle! No one else would die needlessly.

"Will you promise not to hurt me?" I asked softly, trying to feign a little bit of fear. "I am pregnant."

The vampires all blinked at my news, but the leader nodded. "I swear we will not cause you or your unborn child harm if you come with us willingly."

I stood up and smoothed down my clothes. "Okay. Let's go."

My answer seemed to surprise them more than my announcement of being pregnant, but after a second of gawking, two of the vampires took me by my arms and led me out of the house. A third vampire came and tied my hands behind my back as we walked. I had wondered what measures they would take to secure me at least in some way. Not that I couldn't break out of the ropes easily, but I let them have their imaginary safety. Now that we were out, I could finally count the total number of vampires and was surprised and a little prideful that they had sent thirty vampires after me. Not that one hundred could have captured me if I had not wanted to be captured, but it still meant that they thought I was a threat.

The vampires whispered to each other for a couple of minutes and then the leader asked, "If we allow you to fly, will you try to escape?"

Were they really giving me this option? In normal circumstances, I would have agreed and then immediately escaped. "I will not try to escape. I want this war over before anyone else I love dies."

He sensed my truthfulness and must have seen the pain on my face at the mentioning of my loved ones dying. "Very well. We will tie your hands in front of you to allow you to fly beside us. If you try to escape, I will kill you."

I kept a grim look on my face and said, "I understand".

One of the other vampires untied my hands from behind my back and retied them in front. Once the vampire was sure the ropes were tight, he nodded at the leader.

"Let's go," he said. As one the vampires transformed into bats. It happened in the blink of an eye and was quite impressive. I took a deep breath and gathered my magic, urging it into my back and forcing my wings out. The cool night air swirled around me and I drank it in in big gulps. I had stayed cooped up in the house too long and denied myself the outdoors.

The vampires circled overhead as they waited for me to make a move. I could fly away and return to Ares. Or I could follow the vampires and confront Maurice. Part of me wanted to escape and return to safety, but a larger part of me knew I needed to face Maurice and end this war.

I flapped my wings and joined them in the sky. One of the bats squeaked and then they all took off. I flew along beside them, trying not to think about my impending fight and possible death. I had to live or Ares' journey into Death's realm would have been for nothing.

We flew for what felt like an hour before finally seeing the Eiffel Tower. Why had they left the Eiffel Tower intact? Memories of my first visit to the city made me cringe and miss Ares. I had put my mate through more than any living being should have had to endure. I had to end this war so that we could begin a normal life together. A life that did not involve me or anyone else dying until we were very very old. I laughed at the thought of how old

Ares already was. I wasn't exactly a spring chicken either. Where had the time gone? I was over one hundred years old and having my first child. That would have been something I would have laughed at before I had met Ares. Before I had met Ares, I had thought it was crazy for a woman over forty to have a child. Things had changed so much.

The vampires switched forms, landing lightly on their feet in front of a palace. "Where are we?" I asked.

"This used to be the king and queen's when they were ruling here," the leader said.

How fitting that the vampire who thought he was supreme ruler would live in a palace that used to be a monarch's. I followed them inside the building and was shocked to find it full of vampires. Several hissed at me or bared their fangs when they caught sight of me. I showed them my teeth and growled. I may have surrendered, but I was not afraid of them and would protect myself if they attacked me.

A man who was completely covered by a large black robe stopped our group. "What's your business?"

"We are bringing Artemis Lupine to King Maurice. She surrendered herself to us."

I took long draws of air in through my nose trying to catch the robed man's scent, but I could not find it. Who was he? Better yet, *what* was he?

"I will accompany you," the robed man said and walked to the back of the group of vampires escorting me.

"Who was that?" I asked, hoping to receive an answer, but sadly I only received silence from them.

We continued forward, walking to a large ballroom where Maurice sat on a throne watching vampires dancing and talking. The vampire women were all dressed in extravagant gowns and wore hundreds of diamonds while the vampire men were dressed in tuxedos. As we entered the room his eyes found mine and a smile spread across his lips. "Welcome, Artemis Lupine, Queen of the Werewolves and Princess of the Sidhe. It has been too long since we last met."

I played polite dignitary and curtsied to him. "Thank you for your warm greeting, King Maurice. Your new place is lovely."

"Thank you. I enjoy it here."

"May I have my hands untied? I am with child and surely no threat to someone as powerful as you."

"With child? Is it the Sidhe's or the werewolf's?" he asked as he motioned at the robed man to untie my hands.

"It is Ares' child," I said as I fought to keep the pain from my voice and hold in the whine that wanted to escape.

The robed man stopped in front of me and I tried to catch a glimpse of his face, but the robe hung too far over. I took in a deep breath and still could not smell him. He cut the ropes with a dagger, being sure not to let his skin touch mine and then stepped away from me.

I rubbed my wrists and smiled at Maurice. "Thank you."

"Come, sit beside me, Artemis, and rest your feet. I hear women's ankles swell during pregnancy."

I walked towards him and wondered what he was up to. How could he be so calm and so at ease with me approaching him? I sat down and looked at the large group of vampires inside the room and the robed man. What were my best options for killing them all?

"I bet you are wondering about my plan to defeat the little rebellion your group is involved with, aren't you?" Maurice asked.

I did not say anything because I figured he was not looking for me to speak, only for me to listen to his *wonderful* plan.

"At this moment my vampires are moving to strategic points around the world. They will sit in hiding, waiting until they are given the word from me to attack. Once your group comes and challenges me, the deployed vampires will attack, killing those that have been left behind. All of those submissive wolves, Sidhe, and elves won't stand a chance against my vampires."

He was right that he would kill hundreds if not thousands, but now that I knew his plan, there was no way he would get away with it. Or did he think it did not matter? Did he want to try to scare me into stopping the assault on him?

Did he not view me as a threat? Did he really think that I was captured and now his prisoner? My anger boiled over and I let my magic fill me. I pictured Achilles' dead body and let it fuel my anger until my body was shining too brightly for any to keep their eyes open. I formed sunlight around me in a circle and sent it outwards in an ever-expanding wave, killing the vampires in the room before they could even draw in a breath to scream.

I looked at the throne and felt terror run through my body in a wild chill. Maurice sat calmly on the throne, examining his fingernails as the sunlight drenched him. "Why isn't it affecting you?" I asked as I backed away from him, stirring up the ashes of the dead vampires on the ground.

"I am the original vampire, the first," he said as he stood up and let his fangs fully extend. "Did you really think that a little thing like sunlight would kill me?"

I gathered my magic and tried to teleport but doing so made me dizzy and nauseous. Was it from being pregnant? Or was it because I had not eaten in two days? I had to teleport. I had to escape! I tried again but could not move anywhere.

The robed man stepped forward and removed his hood. He was tall, ugly with a much too large nose for his face and had an evilly confident smile. "You cannot teleport so long as I, Merlin, the greatest sorcerer in the world, am alive."

I focused on my wolf, transformed into a half-shift and said, "Then I shall fix that issue."

I charged at him, but a sword appeared in his hand and he swung it at me, barely missing my stomach. I jumped backwards and formed a sword from my body. I would not let him win. I charged at him again, blocking his sword with mine and trying my hardest to disarm him. He parried each strike I made and did it with a smug smile. I formed claws from my left hand and sliced at his face, hoping to rip that smile off, but he dodged, and Maurice stepped between us.

I swung my sword at Maurice's chest, but he turned his torso into mist and my blade went through him. "You cannot win, Artemis. I do commend you for your effort, but you are no match for me."

I screamed at him and formed fire, the only other thing that scared a vampire as much as sunlight. He turned into mist and flew quickly across the ballroom, out of the fire's path. Before I could gather enough magic to engulf the entire room in fire, Merlin attacked me, using a magic staff in addition to his sword. Something about the staff made my hackles rise. I wasn't positive what was wrong with it, but I knew I needed to keep it from touching me. He struck at me with the staff and I recoiled from it and the smell of death which permeated from it.

I focused on my magic and the plants outside of the building we were in, drawing all of the magic to me while still battling Merlin. Maurice appeared behind me and I released my magic in the form of a fire circle. As I had expected, Maurice turned to mist and flew up into the ceiling. I formed a ball around myself with the fire and grunted as I thrust the fire out, adding additional fire to it as it moved and making it expand. Maurice cursed and I smiled, knowing I had trapped him. The fire expanded until it engulfed the entire room, setting Merlin on fire and catching part of Maurice on fire just before he slipped out one of the doors.

I wanted to chase after him, but I had pressed my luck too far as it was. I teleported back to Ares' Russian house and found Ares and Victor sitting in the living room on the couch. How the hell had they found me?

"You want to explain to me why you let vampires capture you and take you to see Maurice?" Ares asked calmly with his arms crossed over his chest.

"I had a plan. It was a great plan. It would have worked too if that stupid Merlin had not been there." I said as I took deep breaths to slow my racing heart.

"You thought you could kill Maurice with sunlight and end the war," Victor said. "And no, I did not read your mind. I just know you."

"That is very like her," Ares grumbled. "Risking herself to try to end this battle. Although I had hoped she would not do those types of things now that she is pregnant."

"They swore they would not harm me or the child while they took me to Maurice," I said irritated. "It would have worked if he had not been immune to sunlight. I almost got him with fire, but he misted out a door."

Ares shook his head sadly. "And here I thought you would be in need of consoling, not saving."

"I was grieving and then they showed up," I whispered, feeling insecure about not still grieving for Achilles.

"One has little time to grieve in times of war," Victor said, reading my thoughts.

"How did you find me?" I asked without moving closer to them. Part of me wanted to run to Ares, but part of me felt like it would be a betrayal to Achilles whom I *was* still grieving for.

"We thought of all of the places that we would normally think you would go to and then immediately crossed those off of our list. Then we made a list of all of the places that you knew of and picked the few that we thought you would go to and think we would not think of going," Ares said. "It's simple Artemis logic really."

"Simple," Victor said with a chuckle.

I glared at Victor and then turned away, looking out the window and trying to sort through my feelings. Once I was calm again, I turned around and they both gave me the look. "What?" I asked.

"You cannot go off by yourself and try to take out the King of the Vampires," Ares said sternly, as though he were lecturing a teenager. "You have duties, responsibilities and a child to think about now."

I resisted the urge to answer with "Yes, Father" and simply bit my tongue. Of course, Victor read my mind and laughed, turning away from us and heading into the kitchen.

"I was thinking about my responsibilities. I *almost* killed him," I answered as I plopped down on the couch. Now that I was not in a fight, a headache had decided to rear its awful head and begin torturing me.

"What's wrong?" Ares asked and then sat down beside me, moving my hands away from my face.

"I just have a headache," I whispered, wishing for once that his touch was not so soothing. Would the pain of Achilles' loss ever leave? Or would I always feel this regret and pain when Ares touched me? Why did I feel like I was cheating?

"It will get better," Ares whispered as he pulled his hands away.

I was not so sure about that. The only way I could see it getting better was to forget him and I would *never* do that.

"We have had many die around us, Artemis. Trust us. In time it will be bearable," Victor said as he poured himself a glass of whiskey from the cupboard in the kitchen.

"Are you here to bring me back?" I asked Ares. How could I face Hera and Zeus? Would they ever be able to forgive me for causing their son's death? Was Ares upset at me for causing his brother's death? They had only recently become close and now his brother was gone forever.

"We mainly came to ensure that you were not getting into any trouble," Ares said.

"Which of course you were," Victor said as he walked to the large reclining chair and sat in it with his glass of whiskey.

I ignored his comment and asked, "When do we have to go back?"

Ares shrugged. "Probably soon since Maurice will be angry that you killed a lot of his vampires, the warlock, and that you almost killed him."

"There are probably fifty or more vampires headed our way as we speak," Victor said with a strange light in his eyes.

"So, are we going to stay and kill them or are we leaving?" I asked. It was strange that Ares wasn't whisking me away to safety knowing that we would soon be attacked. It was especially strange since I was pregnant.

"We will be leaving in a moment," Victor said sadly, "Before the vampires arrive."

"You sound like you want to get in a fight," I said.

Victor smiled. "I do."

"We all do," Ares said with a growl.

My headache intensified, causing me to double over in pain and hang my head between my legs. "Can we go now?" I asked.

"Yes," Ares said, standing up and then picking me up from the couch.

"Can you teleport us?" I asked Victor. "I am in too much pain to do it."

"Of course," he said as he stood up and walked to us. He chugged the rest of his whiskey and then set a hand on each of our shoulders. "Just throw up on Ares if you need to."

The world twisted around us and then we were in the underground of the cathedral again, inside the room with Achilles' body. "Why are we here?" I asked, swallowing back the tears that tried to surface.

"Because I want to speak to you," Zeus said from behind us. Ares turned around so that we were facing Zeus who was sitting on a stone bench.

I felt more nervous facing him than I had anyone else. Hera popped into the room using her teleportation and sat down on the bench beside Zeus. "Did I miss anything?"

Zeus shook his head. "They just arrived."

"Good," she said.

"What's up?" I asked nervously.

"Victor, would you please leave us?" Zeus asked.

Victor bowed to Zeus and Hera and said, "Of course." He winked at me and then disappeared in a whirl of mist.

"How are you feeling?" Zeus asked me as he and Hera just looked at me.

What was going on? Why had they called me here? "I'm okay. I have a bit of a headache, but I'm sure that will be cured when I eat some food."

"When was the last time you ate?" Hera asked.

"Two days ago," I whispered, wishing Ares was not there to hear.

"Two days?" Ares hissed, setting me down on my feet. "Why haven't you eaten in two days?"

"Ares," Zeus reprimanded, "Calm down."

"You cannot starve yourself. You have a baby inside of you now and you must take care of it above yourself," Ares said with a rumble in his voice. "I will leave her here with you and get food for her."

"Ares, don't leave me," I begged him.

"Zeus will protect you if you get yourself into trouble, yet again, while I am gone," Ares said and then walked out of the room.

I stared at the door in shock. He rarely got angry with me. Was it because of the baby? Or was this also because of Achilles?

"Are you able to fully use your magic and fully change?" Hera asked.

I sighed. "Yes."

"Do you have any side effects that you have noticed?" She asked.

I frowned. "No."

"Good. You are one of the few that have returned from Death's realm so we wanted to make sure that you were doing alright," Zeus said.

I cringed, knowing that if it were up to them that they would have wanted Achilles back as well.

"We brought you here to check on you and to tell you that we do not blame you," Hera said.

I trembled to my core. "What?"

"We do not blame you for our son's death," Zeus said, glancing quickly at Achilles' body before looking back at me.

I didn't know what to say. The only thing I could think to do was apologize to them and they did not seem like they wanted my apology, so I just stood there.

I blamed myself. How could they not blame me?

Zeus came over to me and wrapped his arms around me in a hug. "You cannot blame yourself for his death," he whispered. "He would not want you to. He died doing something he loved, protecting you, and he should be remembered for his heroism."

"If I hadn't…" I started.

"Enough," Hera said. "You will not blame yourself." She walked to me and grabbed my chin in her hands. "Grieve for your lost one and then square your shoulders and rule as the Queen that you are. You have priorities and you must not act so disparagingly about the war."

"There's something I have to tell you," I said.

She released me and frowned. "What has happened?"

"Maurice is immune to sunlight."

Zeus and Hera's eyes widened and she asked, "How do you know this?"

"I attacked him," I said. "I used sunlight on him, and he sat in it, examining his fingernails."

"Hope is not lost for the war," Zeus said, "He is still vulnerable to fire."

"I fear I cannot defeat him," I whispered. "He is too strong."

"We will figure something out," Zeus assured me. "I have already called a meeting and hopefully there we will formulate a plan."

Ares returned empty handed. "Are you ready to leave?" he asked me.

"Leave, where?" I asked.

"To eat. Come, you need to eat and then rest," Ares said softly.

I let him lead me away from Zeus and Hera, wanting to get away from Achilles' body before I started crying again. I knew I should ask Ares if he was mad at me about Achilles, but I was too chicken to ask, fearing his answer. I was surprised and relieved that Hera and Zeus did not blame me and would take Hera's instructions to heart. She was right, I had to lead as the Queen of the Werewolves. There were many more lives at stake than my own.

CHAPTER 7

ARTEMIS

"Why are you sad?" Achilles asked me softly as he stroked my hair. We were in a beautiful meadow with a softly bubbling brook a few yards away. The sun was warm against my face and a soft wind caressed my skin. How could it feel so right when everything was wrong?

"You're dead," I whispered miserably as I lay in the comfort of his arms. "I will never see you again."

He smiled and whispered, "I will always be with you, Artemis. I live inside of you and Ares. I am a part of your past which has shaped your future. As long as you do not forget, I will always be with you."

"I will never forget you. I love you," I whispered as I looked up at him.

He pressed his lips against my forehead and whispered, "Then live, Artemis. Fulfill the prophecy, raise children with Ares, and live your life. I will always be in your heart and your memories. That is the best any man could ask for. Do not blame your brother for my death but embrace him and reconcile, as Ares and I did after so many years. Do not make the same mistakes as we did.

Remember, *verus amor vincit omnia*. True love conquers all. Fulfill the prophecy and right the balance of light and darkness."

"Achilles!" I yelled as the dream dissolved and I opened my eyes to find Koda and Ares looking at me. I wrapped my arms around Ares and cried, needing to be comforted by him despite feeling like it might be wrong.

Koda wrapped his body around me from behind and my two-man pack comforted me.

After several minutes, I calmed myself and wiped the remaining tears from my eyes. "I'm sorry," I whispered.

Koda rubbed my back slowly and Ares kissed my cheek.

"You have nothing to apologize for," Ares answered. My stomach growled and Ares said, "That's our cue to get you food. Come, on, let's eat."

I really wanted to just lie in bed and weep for the loss of Achilles. I wanted to let my body release the pain it was feeling in some way, but Achilles did not want me to lie around. He wanted me to live, so that was exactly what I was going to do. I would not hide in my room and weep. I would use the time I had to plan and seek revenge on Maurice for Achilles' life.

I looked around in shock as I realized that we weren't in the cathedral anymore, but in a room with a bed. "Where are we?"

"We are in Zeus' realm," Ares answered.

"How did we get here? When?" I asked, feeling like I had missed something.

"After you ate last night you fell asleep and Victor teleported us here," Koda said.

"I don't remember eating," I admitted.

Ares and Koda looked at each other but did not say anything.

A servant brought in plates piled high with food. I ate until I couldn't hold any more and then changed into clothes I found in the dresser.

"You should visit the dragons today. They have been waiting

patiently, but I am not sure how much longer their patience will last," Ares said softly.

"Blu's here?" I gasped, turning away from the mirror where I had been staring at my haggard self. I was in desperate need of a shower.

"He is not far, but not in this realm. He felt you die and flew to the cathedral. According to Victor, Blu is the reason I survived," Ares said.

Without another word I flung open the bedroom door and ran down the hallway towards the exit.

Ares raced after me and caught up to me just as I pushed open the outside doors.

"Wait for me," Koda called from behind us.

I grabbed each of their hands and then asked, "Where to?"

"We are simply walking out of the passage," Ares said.

I dropped their hands, raced up the stairs, and flung open the hatch.

Blu roared from the sky where he had been circling and dove to the ground, landing heavily and making me wobble. Ares steadied me with a hand on my shoulder and then released me.

Blu wrapped his neck around me, humming loudly. "Hatchling, I have been worried about you," he said in his deep and familiar voice.

I wrapped my arms around as much of his neck as I could. "Thank you for coming, Blu. I have missed you greatly."

He backed away from me and said, "I am sorry for the loss of your bound Sidhe. He would have been a great king."

I sniffed as tears threatened to leak out. "Thank you."

Ares picked my hand up, helping drive away the sadness by his comfort.

Zeus stepped out of the portal and smiled when he saw me. He walked to me and wrapped me in the biggest hug I had ever received, other than Blu's. "Artemis, I am so glad to see you."

"Sorry about the other day and going a little crazy with my powers," I whispered, warmth heating my cheeks.

He shook his head and pulled back, holding me by the arms. "Do not apologize for grieving over my son. I expected nothing less." Zeus looked at Ares and said, "The ceremony will begin in one hour. Will you assist me?"

Ares bowed at the waist. "It would be an honor."

"What are you talking about?" I asked softly.

"The funeral," Zeus answered.

I leaned my head against Zeus' chest. "When do we get to kill vampires again?"

Zeus squeezed my shoulders. "Killing your enemies is always more fun than burning your loved ones. We will resume the fun soon."

Blu asked, "Would the Sidhe mind if some non-Sidhe attended the ceremony?"

Zeus turned and smiled at Draco Blu. "The Sidhe would be honored if the dragons attended. I'm guessing you are more interested in the announcement at the end?"

Blu nodded once. "Yes, we know your protocol and are interested in the announcement after the funeral. Plus, we would like to pay our respects to Achilles."

Ares tugged on my hand. "Come on, we need to get changed."

Zeus kissed my cheek and released me. "I will see you both in an hour."

Ares led me back to the room where Victor was waiting for us. Victor stood when he saw me enter and enveloped me in a hug. "*Mon papillon*. It is good to see you breathing and not getting yourself into trouble."

I hugged the vampire back and then stepped out of his arms. "How long did you see me not breathing?"

"He stayed at yours and Ares' sides the entire time," Koda answered from the chair he had sat down in.

I looked at Victor. "You did?"

Victor shrugged. "It is not important."

He was hiding something, but I let it go since Koda needed comforting. I sat on his lap and let him cradle me for a moment, not long enough to be rude to Ares, but also not too short to worry Koda. Ares held out a black dress and advised the others of the funeral time.

After putting on the dress and tying my hair up, I sat on the edge of the bed pondering over everything. In order to fulfill the prophecy, I had to restore the balance of good and evil, of light and darkness. To do that I had to defeat Maurice. To do that I had to destroy most of his vampires. I knew what I had to do, but to effectively do it I needed my brother's help. "Ares?"

Ares turned around, finishing buttoning up his black dress shirt. "Yes?"

"Where's Apollo?"

Koda snarled and Ares asked, "Why do you want to know?"

I exhaled and said, "I had a dream and Achilles told me not to blame my brother and to embrace him."

Ares stopped his buttoning and said, "He's locked in a dungeon cell right now. Even if he had never meant to harm you, he killed Achilles. The Sidhe aren't going to just let that go."

"Are they going to execute him?" I asked nervously.

Ares looked at Victor who said, "They haven't told me anything, but I think they were waiting for your return before making the final decision. I'm sure they will make the decision tomorrow though."

I exhaled. "Okay."

Ares looked at Victor again and Victor shook his head. "I have no clue who they're going to choose."

"Choose for what?" I asked feeling left out yet again. It was a problem that happened far too often with this group and was something I intended to fix.

Ares smiled. "You'll just have to find out with the rest of us after the funeral."

I rolled my eyes and followed him out of the room. He led our small group out the back of the building and to a large wooden platform. Wood was piled high underneath it and an enormous crowd, consisting mostly of Sidhe, had gathered.

Victor and Koda joined the crowd and Ares pulled me off to the side. "I'm going to be part of the procession, so you should go stand beside Hera."

I kissed his cheek before making my way through the crowd to Hera.

Athena stood beside Hera and when she saw me, she lunged forward and wrapped her arms around me. "Artemis, I am so sorry for how I have treated you. Please, forgive me."

I patted my mother awkwardly on the back and then released the anger that had begun simmering at her presence and hugged her back. "You're forgiven."

Athena smiled at me and kissed my cheek. "Thank you."

I took my place next to Hera who acknowledged my presence by grabbing my hand in hers, her grip tightened until it was almost painful, but I said nothing. Athena stood on Hera's other side and Hera latched on to her just as quickly.

A horn trumpeted and all of the Sidhe released their wings from their backs. Athena nodded at me, and I released mine as well, letting my body glow with the rest of the Sidhe.

Zeus began singing and then Ares joined him. I had never heard Zeus sing and was surprised at how wonderful they sounded. They sang a sorrowful song in a language I could not understand and carried Achilles' body on a plank towards the wooden platform in front of where we were all standing. The sight of father and son singing brought back a memory of Ares and Achilles singing to me in Hera's court what was probably only a few weeks ago but felt like years.

The Sidhe in the crowd joined the song one by one until all of the full blooded Sidhe were singing their sorrow and mourning together. Even Hera sang, her voice carrying above the others in her extreme grief. I had never before heard something so eerily beautiful and at the same time heartbreaking. I didn't need to know the words to know that they were singing their mourning for Achilles.

The song stopped as Zeus and Ares laid Achilles' body on top of the platform. Zeus turned to Ares and Ares' body began to glow, and he created fire in his hand. He dropped the fire onto the wood and then walked to me, his body still glowing as mine was. He took my free hand as tears streamed down his face.

I cried in silence with the rest of the Sidhe as we watched until the fire died.

The crowd turned as Zeus flew up into the air near the building. "As is customary after the death and funeral of the heir, I will announce my new heir. Hera, please join me." Hera released Athena and my hands and flew up into the air beside her husband, taking his hand. Zeus smiled at her, but she simply nodded at him. "Achilles was the heir to both the dark and light courts. Therefore, a new heir for both of the courts needs to be chosen. In the past, each court has been allowed to choose a separate heir, but Hera and I have decided to choose a joint heir again."

The crowd was thrumming with anticipation at the announcement. I only felt exhausted and sad.

"I, Zeus, King of the Dark Court of the Sidhe, with the consent of Hera, Queen of the Light Court of the Sidhe, hereby declare that Artemis Lupine is the new heir to both the Light and Dark Courts of the Sidhe."

Of all of the surprised gasps, mine must have been the loudest. Ares squeezed my hand and whispered. "If you accept, you need to fly up to them."

I stared at him, unable to process this. "I…I..." How could they spring this on me? Why hadn't they talked to me about it before? Wasn't Ares technically the next heir?

He released my hand and smiled. "It's what Achilles would have wanted."

I exhaled and flapped my wings, pushing myself up into the air and flying to Zeus and Hera. I hovered in front of them and said the only thing that I could in the situation, "I accept this great honor."

Hera was handed a purple bag and from it she pulled a small tiara. "We are glad that you accept and will do our best to prepare you well before your ascension to the throne." She placed the tiara on my head and whispered a spell which released a block that had been on the tiara. Power flowed from the tiara into me and then memories of past bearers of the tiara began to stream into my head. I closed the barrier as I had learned to do before, and the memories stopped. My right ring finger began to tingle and then a small tattoo appeared around it.

I turned to face the crowd and Zeus said, "All hail Princess Artemis, Heir to the Sidhe Throne!"

The crowd dropped to their knees and bowed with their foreheads touching the ground, everyone except Victor, Ares and Draco Blu. Victor, Ares and Blu did bow their heads in respect though.

I swallowed nervously and prayed that I could live up to their expectations. As long as Ares was by my side, I knew we could get through this together.

CHAPTER 8
ARTEMIS

"No, I won't allow him to be executed!" I yelled at Zeus.

Zeus was trying to control his anger, but bits of his power flared. "He killed Achilles, the Prince of the Sidhe. There is no punishment, except death, harsh enough for such an act. If we let him off easy, then others will attempt the same thing."

I turned to Ares, who sat beside me. "There has to be something. Please. Help me."

Ares rubbed the stubble on his chin and said, "I might have an idea, but it's not something we have used in generations. It was considered too barbaric by the Sidhe. It may be fitting for the current situation though."

Zeus looked at Ares a moment and exhaled. "Have you even talked to him? Do we even know if he wants to switch sides? He *was* a servant of Maurice's."

"He didn't know!" I said through clenched teeth. "Darren gave him to Maurice's people to raise. He saved me and killed Darren and surrendered after I died. That has to count for something."

Ares rested his hand on my arm and tried to calm me with our bond, but I pushed his hand off and paced across the room.

"I will speak to him and determine if he is willing to pledge loyalty to Artemis. If he is, and he makes the vow, then will you agree to the punishment I speak of?" Ares asked.

"I don't even know the punishment," I said in irritation.

Ares whispered, "I was asking Zeus."

I blushed and looked down at my hands. "Oh."

Zeus frowned a moment and then exhaled. "The others will not like it, but I do believe it is a severe enough punishment. Speak with him and return. Artemis and I need to discuss other matters anyways."

Ares stood, kissed my cheek and left. I sat down in the chair next to Zeus and exhaled. "I don't like making decisions."

Zeus laughed. "It gets easier with age and practice."

"That is hard to believe," I muttered.

"Artemis, as heir you do not have to make decisions, but I think it would be good for you to at least weigh in on the topics and listen to Hera and I making decisions. You know that you won't need to take over our reign until we die, which won't be for a long time unless there are extenuating circumstances."

"Can we not talk about your deaths? There has been enough already."

He rested his hand on my shoulder and smiled. "Soon we will finish this war and you will raise your child in happy times."

I rested my hand on my stomach and asked, "What if I can't do it? What if I can't defeat Maurice?"

"There is not a doubt in my mind that you will. He has grown arrogant these past one hundred years. You will be able to defeat him. You just have to figure out how."

He made it sound like it was a simple task. How do you kill a vampire who is the one of the most powerful in the world? Fire, but that would mean getting close enough and cornering him to use it. Plus, I was sure that he had ways to protect himself from fire if he had survived this long.

"Artemis," Zeus said softly, "Why don't you go rest? We can discuss everything else later."

I was tired, but there was too much at stake. Too much that still needed to be done, like killing Maurice. I had thought many times about popping back into his chambers and toasting him and popping back out, without anyone knowing. But I couldn't risk my life like I had been willing to before. It was strange to know a being was growing and living inside me, but I had accepted it and vowed to be the best mother that I could be.

"Alright, I'll rest, but we still need to figure out our plan for attacking Maurice. The world has lived in darkness too long, and I don't want to raise my child in it," I said to Zeus as I stood. I stopped at the door and said, "I do have one more question though."

"What is it?" Zeus asked.

"Why did you make me heir when Ares was already the next in line? Why isn't he now the heir?" Zeus had held a feast in his honor, naming Ares an heir to the throne so it did not make sense to me.

"Normally Ares would have become the next heir for the Dark Throne, but that still left the Light Throne open. Ares, Hera and I discussed it and we all agreed that you were the best person to be our heir, besides, Ares is your mate so naturally he would be your king which would still allow him to be heir."

I frowned. "So, Hera did not want Ares to be heir to her throne is what you are saying."

Zeus exhaled. "My wife holds grudges and unfortunately Ares has received much of her wrath because of my indiscretion with his mother. She is making strides to stop being so one sided when it comes to Ares, but it will take her time. This is a great step for her."

Great was not really the word I was thinking, but I let it pass.

Koda followed me out of the room and towards Ares' old chambers, which Zeus had given us. "How are you feelin', Darlin'?"

He was always asking me that. Ever since I had returned from being dead, he had renewed his job as my guard and stuck to me like glue. "I'm fine, Koda. I am just tired and queasy."

"Do you want me to get a healer?" he asked.

I shook my head. "It's just morning sickness. Maybe I need to try to eat something?"

"I'll get her some food," Victor said from beside me.

I refrained from jumping or yelling in surprise, but knew I couldn't lie to him mentally since he could read minds. "Not funny," I grumbled.

Victor smiled. "I didn't mean to startle you. What would you like to eat?"

He had also been incredibly nice to me since I had returned, not that he wasn't always nice, but everyone treated me differently now that I was pregnant. Like I was a porcelain doll that needed to be pampered or I would start crying.

"Fruits and cheeses would be nice," I said with a smile. "Thank you."

He kissed my cheek and then disappeared in a flash, using his ability to teleport. If only I could use that ability to my advantage against Maurice.

Koda pushed open the door to the bedroom and I waited patiently as he searched inside to ensure that it was safe for me to enter. It frustrated me that he insisted on doing this since I was more powerful than him and extremely capable of protecting myself. I hadn't died because I was careless.

My throat constricted at the memory of Achilles' death and tears filled in my eyes.

Koda stepped out to tell me it was safe and saw my face. "Darlin', let's lie down while we wait for Victor to return."

I nodded and wiped at my eyes, but that seemed to only open the flood gates.

Koda took my hand, led me to the bed, and curled up around me as soon as I lay down. "I know it hurts. I'm sorry."

"I miss him so much," I whispered. And I felt awful for how our relationship had been. I had tortured him emotionally and physically with our bond that we never sealed.

"He wouldn't want you to blame yourself," Victor said as he set a tray of food down at the end of the bed and touched my arm. "He knows why you made the choices that you did, and he never blamed you."

If anyone else would have said it, I wouldn't have believed them, but Victor was one of the few who actually knew what people were thinking and feeling.

"Will it ever stop hurting?" I asked.

"No," Victor said seriously.

"Victor," Koda hissed his name.

Victor smiled. "No, it will never stop, but it will turn into a low ache that you can deal with. You must focus on the positive memories. Remember how much he loved you and how much you loved him. Remember the fun times you had together and soon it will be bearable."

"He's right," Koda said. "As much as I loved Matt, now his death is simply a dull ache within my chest. If you focus on the good times, you can get through it."

"Come and eat. The baby is sure to be hungry," Victor said as he softly tugged on my hand.

I sat up and did as he asked. "Thank you."

Victor sat in one of the chairs in the room and closed his eyes. "You are welcome."

"Victor?" I asked softly.

"Hm?"

"The prophecy says that I am the one to restore the balance of good and evil, but it doesn't specifically say who is supposed to kill Maurice. He's your father and… Are you planning on killing him or should I be?"

Victor kept his eyes closed, but his lips lifted up into a wide smile, showing the lower part of his fangs. "As the next in line for the throne it doesn't matter if I kill him or not, but I would prefer if I killed him. However, he has caused you an enormous amount of misery, so I would understand if you wanted to kill him."

"That didn't answer my question," I said, eating some of the food he had brought me.

He shrugged and folded his hands in his lap. "We shall see when the battle starts, *mon papillon*. Then we shall decide."

I couldn't argue with that, so I lay down instead of trying to find an answer now.

Koda wrapped himself around me again. "Sleep, Artemis. Sleep and I will protect you."

"Two weeks," I whispered. "I want to fight Maurice and his group in two weeks."

"We will discuss it later," Koda said sternly. "Rest or I'll call Hades in here."

"Alright," I said as I snuggled against him. "Koda, promise me something?"

"Anything," he whispered.

"Don't let Ares die."

"Darlin' I've been trying to keep him alive since I was ten," he said and chuckled.

"I'm not strong enough to raise this child without him. I can't lose anyone else. I can't lose Ares or you," I said and sniffled.

"Go to sleep, Artemis," he whispered. "Everyone will be safe while you sleep."

I closed my eyes and sighed. "Okay, but only for an hour or two."

"ARTEMIS," Ares whispered as he ran his hand along my stomach. "Wake up, Sunshine."

"So tired," I whispered as I opened my eyes.

Ares smiled down at me. "I know, but you need to eat. It sounds like the baby is roaring in your stomach."

I sat up and then fell back. My body was burning up, like I was covered in blankets. "It's so hot," I whispered.

Ares ran his hand over my forehead and then yelled, "Healer!"

The healer from the feast hurried into the room. She put her hand on my head and stomach and frowned. "She has a strange illness. We must get rid of this fever before it begins to affect the baby."

"Ares," I whispered as the healer began chanting. "Don't leave me."

He gripped one of my hands with his and stroked my hair. "Never."

After a few moments, the fever began to dissipate and the strange lightheadedness I had been feeling disappeared.

"How do you feel?" the healer asked me.

"Much better, thank you," I said as Ares helped me sit up and handed me a cup of water to drink.

"Ares, a word please," the healer said as she headed towards the door.

Ares kissed my hand and followed the healer outside the chambers.

Even though I had slept for at least three hours, I felt exhausted again. What was wrong with me? Preternaturals never got sick. Was there something wrong with the baby?

Ares stepped back into the room and smiled at me. "Don't worry. She said the baby is perfectly healthy and you are now as well."

He was telling the truth.

I exhaled. "Okay."

"But she did order you to stay in bed today."

"All day?" I asked, my mouth dropped open.

He nodded. "Yes. She doesn't want you overexerting yourself and possibly hurting the baby."

"What good is it to be a preternatural if I can't even get out of bed?" I grumbled with a frown.

He sat down next to me and began massaging my shoulders. "With your metabolism, whatever got into your system will be gone soon. Plus, it gives us an excuse to cuddle all day," he said as he continued his massage.

"Maybe it's not so bad after all," I murmured as I relaxed more and more from his expert hands.

Ares kissed the back of my shoulder and moved his hands down to my back. "Are you hungry?" he asked.

"Yes, but I don't want you to leave," I admitted to him.

"I won't. I'll just summon Koda."

"Where is he?" I asked, shocked he hadn't stayed glued to my side.

Ares' fingers kneaded the knots around my shoulder blades. "I sent him away when I came in. I wanted some alone time with you."

"Alone time? What's that?" I asked as I leaned back against him, smirking.

He wrapped his arms around my upper chest and sighed. "Yes, it is a very scarce commodity for us. Soon, we will end this war and then we will have all the alone time we want."

"You're dreaming," I told him. "With you as Alpha of the Werewolves, and me as Heir to the Sidhe thrones, we will *never* have alone time."

Ares laughed. "I suppose you're right. That just means that we have to treasure every alone moment we have."

"You summoned?" Koda asked as he walked in.

"Can you get me some food? I'm on bed rest so I can't get up," I answered.

"Bed rest?" he asked with worry evident in his voice.

"Easy, she just had a fever and the healer wanted to be sure she and the baby were fine, so she ordered bed rest," Ares said reassuringly as he ran his hands down my arms.

"What do you want to eat?" Koda asked.

I thought about some of my options and then nausea spiked, and I had to jump up and run to the bathroom to throw up.

"Crackers and water would be good," Ares told Koda as he came to me and pulled my hair back.

My stomach finally stopped convulsing, but I was still exhausted, so I just leaned against the toilet. "I'm so glad Zeus has indoor plumbing," I whispered.

Ares laughed softly and stroked my back. "Who do you think invented it?"

"How's Apollo?" I asked him as I leaned back against his chest.

"He's fine."

"Did he agree to whatever it was you and Zeus were talking about?" I asked.

Ares rested his chin on top of my head. "I gave him until tomorrow to decide."

"And what exactly is he deciding to?"

"It's difficult to explain, but basically he would be pledging himself to my service for the rest of his life."

"You're making him a slave?" I asked, horrified, and pulled away from him.

Ares sighed. "He would only be a slave by the spell, but I wouldn't actually force him to be a slave for us."

"That's awful," I whispered and pulled away from Ares to stand up, gripping the sink to keep from falling from my dizziness.

"It's the only way Zeus will allow him to continue to live. It's either that or he's killed for his crimes," Ares said matter-of-factly.

I brushed my teeth and then walked back to bed, lying on my side.

Why were things always so easy for Ares? Kill or be killed. Punish him by death or slavery. I couldn't think that way all the time. Especially not about people I loved.

"I want to attack Maurice in two weeks," I told him.

"So soon?" he asked as he settled behind me. "I had hoped you would allow more time for you to recuperate."

"I want this war over before the baby is born. I want the world to have some semblance of balance before we bring a newborn into it," I told him.

Ares rested his hand on my stomach and sighed happily. "I hope it's a boy."

I laughed. "All men want boys."

"That's because we want to raise a man to take our place."

"Well I don't care what gender it is. I just want it to be healthy and safe," I said and looked down at my stomach.

"I'll rip off anyone's arm who even tries to touch it," Ares said with a menacing growl.

"I'm sure no one would be that stupid."

Ares kissed my neck. "Many have tried to hurt you," he whispered.

I closed my eyes as I relaxed against him. "Yes, and we've killed them all."

"Not all, we still have Maurice."

"Yes, Maurice, but soon enough…I will kill him."

"I don't want you fighting. I can't lose you and our baby again," he whispered as he rubbed my stomach and kissed my neck. "I'll go crazy and Zeus will have to put me down," he said softly.

I set my hand on top of his on my stomach. "I must fight. I must right the balance. I must end Maurice's life."

"Can't we wait at least until after you have the baby?" he suggested. "Then if you are determined to fight, we could ensure our child was safe somewhere."

"Food's here," Koda said as he entered the room again with a tray of cheese and crackers. "I figured you would be ready to eat by now."

I sat up and took a piece of cheese, chewing on the soft and delicious goodness. "Thank you."

Koda sat down on the end of the bed and looked at Ares. "Mother is here," he said softly. "She asked to see you privately."

Ares sighed. "I was hoping not to have to deal with this until later. Did she seem mad?"

Koda shrugged. "Not particularly."

"I'm not leaving Artemis' side, so bring her here to our chambers. I'm sure we can manage to be civil," Ares said.

Koda nodded and then looked at me. "You alright now? You need anything else?"

"There aren't any *Sprites* lying around are there?" I asked hopefully, but already knew the answer.

"Sprites? You mean little pixie beings?"

I laughed. "No, lemon-lime soda. You know, from the human era."

Koda laughed. "Oh that. I'll see what I can dig up."

"You're the best," I said as I chewed on my cheese.

Koda winked. "I know."

Ares laughed at his brother's conceitedness and then stole a piece of my cheese. "Stolen food always tastes so much better," Ares said with a wicked smirk.

I growled. "My food."

Ares growled back, but there was no real anger in his growl. "Everything that is yours is mine."

"Haven't you ever heard the line, 'what's his is hers and what's hers is hers'?"

Ares lifted his lips in a playful snarl. "Not when I'm involved."

"So territorial," I said as I snatched the last little bit of cheese he had stolen and popped it into my mouth.

He wrapped his arms around me. "You're mine."

I laughed. "Yes, I'm yours. All yours," I said softly as my sadness over Achilles' death returned.

"I miss him, too," Ares whispered.

Someone knocked on the door, breaking the mood thankfully. I stood up and walked to the restroom, closing and locking the door.

"Enter," Ares said.

"So commanding," his mother, Beatrice, said as she entered. I stared at my reflection, unsure if I was ready to face her again.

"It's great to finally see you, Mother," Ares said to her.

I opened the door but stayed just out of sight to see how their meeting went.

He walked to her and hugged her.

She hugged him, but as soon as they separated, she slapped his cheek. "That is for killing my mate."

I growled softly, not liking seeing her slap him, but stayed still.

"He challenged me," Ares said. "I had no choice but to kill him. I am sorry for any grief I have caused you."

"You should have killed him one hundred and fifty years ago," she said angrily. "How could you leave me in his hands for so long?"

Ares gaped at her. "You never told me you were unhappy. You never acted unhappy."

"I couldn't act unhappy in front of him," she said. "I was a queen. I had to keep our people united."

"You could have told me," Ares snapped. "If I had known, I would have killed him. I thought you loved him."

"How could I love him? He killed my mate!" she screamed.

"Mother," Koda chastised. "You should have told us."

She inhaled, and her queenly face was back on. "I'm sorry. I let my emotions get the better of me."

Ares smiled at her. "It's understandable."

I stepped out of the bathroom and walked to Ares' side. "Hello."

Beatrice looked at me and then blinked twice. "Wait? Isn't she supposed to be dead?"

"She was dead," Koda said. "But Ares retrieved her soul from Death."

"My soul and our child's," I said as I rested a hand on my stomach.

Her eyes widened and she looked from my stomach to Ares. "A child?"

"Yes, you're going to be a grandmother," Ares told her as he put his arm around my hips.

"You are sure that it is yours?" she asked Ares with narrowed eyes at my stomach.

I growled. "How dare you insinuate I have cheated on Ares. I would never cheat on my mate. Even if I am a halfbreed, half of me is still a wolf."

She smiled at me. "I like her. She's feisty."

"Yes, very," Ares said as though exasperated.

I pinched his arm. "Don't be rude."

"May I?" she asked as she pointed at my stomach.

I looked at Ares, unsure what she wanted. "She wants to speak to the baby."

"Oh. Sure," I said and pulled my hands out of the way.

She crouched down and put her ear against my stomach. The smell of lilacs and wolf fur drifted up to me and I realized that it was Beatrice's scent. "My, what a loud heartbeat you have, little one. You must grow strong and big. You are going to be the Alpha someday." She was quiet a moment and then whispered, "You will be protected from harm. None shall hurt you. Do not worry. None shall hurt you or your mother ever again." She stood up and met Ares' eyes. "I'm joining you in the battle against Maurice."

"No," he said definitively.

Beatrice snarled at him, and her eyes turned amber. "Even if you are old and powerful, I birthed you. I created your power within me. You cannot stop me."

Ares' eyes had turned amber as well, but after a moment of staring at his mother, they finally returned to normal. "You're as stubborn as ever."

She patted his cheek softly. "Good boy. Alright, I'm off to find a room."

"I'll escort you," Koda said with a wide smile and held the door open for his mother.

"Such a good boy," she said as she kissed his cheek and placed her hand on his bent elbow. "Goodbye, Artemis. Keep Ares in check while I am gone."

The door closed and I turned to Ares with a wide smile. "I like her."

Ares laughed. "Of course, you do, now get back in bed."

"Yes, master," I said in a mocking tone as I sat on the edge to continue eating.

We remained sitting in silence for a few minutes, and then Ares said, "Artemis, I have wanted to ask you something since you came back but have not found the right opportunity."

"You know you can ask me anything," I told him and turned to face him.

"Do you remember being dead?" he asked. "Do you remember anything after you died, I mean?"

I shook my head. "No. I remember seeing Achilles fall and then my strength gave out and I dropped to the ground. Then I woke up when I came back to life."

"Good," Ares said with evident relief as his shoulders relaxed.

"Were you worried I had been frightened while in Death's realm?" I asked and placed a hand on his shoulder.

He picked my hand up and placed it against his cheek. "Yes."

I smiled. "I wasn't. Even when I died, I wasn't scared. It all happened too fast."

"I'm sorry."

I rubbed his cheek with my thumb. "Don't apologize. You saved me from Death. That is the bravest thing I have ever heard."

He stared into my eyes and said, "I love you."

I smiled wide. "I love you too, Ares and I always will. Even when you're being a stubborn, pain in my butt or trying to order me around. I will always love you."

CHAPTER 9

ARTEMIS

One week of nothing was driving me insane. The healer came to check on me every day and though my fever had stayed away I was still exhausted and dizzy quite often. She wasn't sure what to make of it and gathered a council of healers to discuss the matter.

Being trapped in my room was not fun and brought back so many memories of prior times in my life with Ares.

Finally, the healer said that as long as Ares kept his arm around me in case I fainted, I could go for a walk.

So, we strolled through the Dark Court along the beach and watched as dolphins played in the sea with water nymphs.

"When this is all over, where will we live?" I asked Ares as we walked, and I shuffled my feet in the warm sand.

He tilted his head back and let the sun highlight his handsome face a moment. "Well, that's something I have not thought about yet. I own multiple properties in several countries."

"I guess we will just have to travel to each one until I find the one I like," I said with a smile.

Ares looked down at me with a wide smile. "Sounds like a plan to me."

"Will my pregnancy be nine months?" I asked him, having forgotten to ask sooner.

"No, it will be three months."

"And I am already one month?" My eyes widened at the realization that delivery was going to be much sooner than I had anticipated.

"Actually, you are starting on your second month in three days."

I didn't really believe him since my stomach was still flat, but I did not say that.

"What if I can't defeat Maurice? What if I can't right the balance?"

"Then you will teleport us to Darren's old house, and from there we will travel around until we find a place to live, alone and safely," he said like it was an easy plan.

"Hm," I mumbled, not wanting to say anything because I would not teleport and leave everyone to die. I couldn't do that.

"We should head back. It's time for the meeting with Zeus," Ares said and pivoted us back towards the castle.

Birds high up in the sky circled lazily.

I was watching their circles when something extremely larger than them dove and scattered them. "Ares!" I gasped and pointed. "What is that?"

Ares looked up and watched the flying animal a moment before laughing. "That is an old friend. Would you like to meet him?"

"A friend?" I asked.

Ares put two fingers in his mouth and whistled.

The flying being swerved away from the birds it had been chasing and headed in our direction. The body moved away from the sun, and I could finally see the shape.

"A Pegasus?" I asked. I had assumed that there were other preternatural beings alive that I had not met yet, but I had never dreamed I would meet a Pegasus.

The Pegasus in question landed and bobbed its head at Ares. "Ares! It's been so long!"

I kept my mouth closed even though my jaw wanted to hit the ground. How could a Pegasus, with a horse head, speak English?

Ares scratched its ears affectionately. "I've missed you as well, Starling."

"Who is this?" Starling asked as he bobbed his head towards me and nickered. "She's pretty."

"Starling, I would like you to meet Artemis Lupine, my mate."

Starling snorted and opened his eyes wide. "This is the infamous Artemis Lupine? It's an honor to meet you." Starling lowered the front half of his body in a bow.

"Thank you, it's an honor to meet you, Starling," I managed to say like I wasn't still reeling in shock.

Starling stood up and then tilted his head sideways to look at Ares. "Need a ride?"

Ares smiled. "Actually, we would love a ride. Artemis is pregnant and a bit wobbly on her feet at the moment."

"Hop on!" Starling encouraged. "I'll take you to the castle."

Ares helped me on and then hopped onto Starling's back behind me, holding me against his chest. "Hold on to the mane," Ares whispered.

"Here we go," Starling said and then started running down the beach. Sand kicked up around us, wind pressed against my face and the water sprayed us softly.

After running a little ways Starling leapt and flapped his wings, carrying us into the air. "You seem a little out of shape, old friend," Ares teased.

"You seem to have gained some weight," Starling said back.

I laughed and Ares said, "I've only gained muscle."

"Or perhaps it's the fat in your head," Starling said and then whinnied loudly in Pegasus laughter.

"Ha. Ha," Ares said. "You are as funny now as you were four hundred years ago."

"How long does a Pegasus live?" I asked, my eyes widening.

"As long as we want," Starling answered. "Some of us prefer to live a normal horse's age while others, like me, enjoy living a long life."

Starling landed in front of the castle and Ares hopped off and then lifted me from Starling's back and set me down on the ground.

"Thank you," Ares said and bowed.

Starling nudged Ares' chest. "Anytime. You take care of your baby."

"I will."

We watched Starling fly away again before walking into the castle.

"That was fun," I said. "I've always wanted to meet a Pegasus."

"If you didn't have wings of your own, I would suggest getting one, but then you would not be able to use your own wings."

"Yeah, I would much rather use my own," I admitted.

We walked down the large hallways and into the gathering room where the meeting for the battle was being held. Hera, Zeus, Beatrice, and Koda were standing off to the side talking while the rest of the people sat in seats murmuring.

"Chandra," said a voice I had missed deeply.

I turned to my right and a smile split my face. "Selene!" I said with a smile, pulled away from Ares and hugged her. "I've missed you."

"I have missed you as well, sister. How fare you? I had heard that you were dead and couldn't believe the rumors," she said as she smiled at me. She wore a beautiful black and purple dress with moons embroidered on it.

"Well, I did die, but then came back and we found out that I'm pregnant." I grinned.

Selene's shock was quick and then she smiled again. "How wonderful that you are with child. We must catch up after the meeting."

"Of course," I said and stepped back into Ares' arm.

"Artemis," Zeus called. "Please come up here."

Ares and I walked to the front of the room where they were standing, and Koda pulled out a chair for me next to Beatrice.

Ares sat beside me, and Koda took his position behind my chair as my guard.

The room quieted and people took seats in the audience.

"As you all know, the upcoming battle with Maurice and his followers will not be an easy one. This battle will determine the fate of the world," Zeus began.

Victor popped into the room in the back with Dmitri beside him and Victor winked at me in hello.

Damn flirtatious vampire. I thought at him.

He smiled wide, flashing his fangs and walked forward.

"Victor, thank you for joining us," Zeus said as Victor took a seat beside Ares up front.

"My pleasure," Victor said. Dmitri stood behind Victor like a bodyguard but smiled pleasantly at me when he saw me looking at him.

"We're calling in all the help we can get," Zeus continued. "We are continuing to add to our allies and we're planning a battle like none before. I would like to welcome Selene and her fellow witches."

Selene bowed her head respectfully. "Thank you for contacting us. We look forward to the battle ahead."

"We welcome the Elves and Alianna, their leader."

A silver haired, pointed eared Elf stood up and bowed. "Thank you."

I hadn't even noticed the group until then, but now I could see at least two dozen elves in the audience.

I needed to pay better attention to my surroundings.

"We welcome the Dwarves and their leader, Klaus."

"Thank you," the leader, one of the midgets with thick beards, said in very rough English.

"We welcome the Trolls and their leader, Razi."

The troll leader stood up and up and up. He was well over ten feet tall. "Thank you," he said in an elegant British accent despite the tusks in his mouth.

How had I not seen any of these creatures in here before now? I was seriously lacking on my observation skills.

"And we welcome the Shapeshifters and Wereanimals of every group and their leaders."

Ten women and men stood up and bowed.

I had so many questions for Ares, but I could not ask any of them. I needed a notepad to write them all down.

"Let me introduce those here in the front. I am Zeus, King of the Dark Court of the Sidhe. This is Hera, Queen of the Light Court of the Sidhe. To her left is Beatrice, former Alpha female of the Werewolves. To her left is Artemis, Alpha female of the Werewolves and Heir to the Sidhe throne." Several of those gathered murmured loudly, but Zeus continued. "To her left is Ares, Alpha of the Werewolves and Artemis' mate. To his left is Victor, Prince of the Vampires."

Razi, leader of the Trolls, stood up. "I do not mean to sound stupid, but I had heard Artemis had died." His voice was rough and deep, and it hurt my ears a little.

"She did die," Ares answered.

"Yet she is sitting beside you?" the Troll asked, obviously perplexed.

"Ares reclaimed my soul from Death," I explained.

"Death gave your soul up?" Alianna asked, eyes wide.

"Yes, mine and my child's," I answered.

The audience began murmuring even louder.

"How do we know this isn't just a trick? That Artemis isn't still dead and that you are not just going to lead us straight to our deaths? How do we know you aren't lying, Zeus?" asked another of the Elves angrily.

Having someone accuse Zeus of lying really made me mad. My

power released and I began levitating in the air without even thinking about it. "Zeus is an honorable king, and you should not accuse such a man of lying without proof," I said as I floated closer to the Elves. "Do you believe this is a trick?" I asked as I folded my wings in so as not to hit anyone.

"Your power has grown," Selene gasped. "You have so much power."

"We believe," Alianna said as she smiled at me. "We apologize for any offense towards Zeus."

"Thank you," I said as I released my power and dropped to my feet on the floor. As soon as my feet hit the dizziness set in, and I started to fall forward, but Victor teleported to me and caught me.

"You must be careful," he whispered too low for anyone else to hear. "There is something not completely right with you."

"I'm just clumsy," I said loudly and growled a bit. "I was in wolf form for many years and dead not too long ago."

Victor teleported us back to the front and helped me sit down.

I sat and took a drink of water before smiling at Zeus. "Excuse my interruption, please continue."

Zeus nodded and turned back to everyone. "We have scheduled the battle for next month and Victor has been using his spies within his father's network to let him know. Now, how should we fight this battle?"

FIVE HOURS LATER, nothing had been decided, but almost everything had been argued. Ares and I had left as soon as the meeting was adjourned for the day and returned to our room.

Selene met us at our room with a somber expression on her face and asked, "What aren't you telling me?"

Ares and I exchanged a look of confusion and then Ares said, "We do not know what you mean."

Selene walked to me and took my hand, chanting a searching

spell over my body to look for illnesses, spells or anything abnormal. She dropped my hand and then looked at Ares a moment with a startled expression. She asked Ares, "Why aren't you seeking treatment?"

"Treatment for what?" Ares asked, growing angry.

"Have you not noticed Chandra's…I mean Artemis' dizzy episodes and fevers?" she asked.

"Yes, but the healer treated them and put me on bed rest saying it was nothing to worry about," I said, feeling fearful at what she was going to say.

Selene looked at me a moment and I could see sadness there. She sighed and said, "You are in good health. You and the baby are fine. Ares on the other hand needs to be treated for a small illness which is affecting you by his nearness and your bond. Ares, may I speak with you outside?"

"No secrets," I said with a scowl.

Selene smiled. "I must speak with him alone a moment to cast a spell. I do not want you near him while I do it."

Ares kissed my cheek and walked out the door with Selene beside him. I sat on the bed and growled. I hated secrets. Most of my time with Ares had been in the dark because they hadn't wanted to scare me and had kept so many things from me. I had to hope that Selene was being truthful and that she would tell me if anything serious was wrong. I could not lose Ares.

CHAPTER 10
ARES

"Is there somewhere we can go to speak in private away from Chandra?" Selene asked me with a sad expression once outside of the room.

"Yes, follow me," I said suspiciously. I did not like the look on her face. And I really did not like the lie she had told Artemis about the illness I supposedly had.

We walked in silence down the hallways passed many Sidhe and several of my pack. I was confident that Selene would not harm me as she and I had a civil past and she and Koda used to date when he was in his early hundreds. I did keep my guard up just in case she tried anything funny though. I never trusted anyone completely, except for Artemis.

I knocked on the door to Zeus' office and opened it. Seeing no one inside, I waved Selene in and then shut the door behind us.

"I don't understand how you could see an illness that the healer could not," I said honestly to her. "I do not mean to insinuate your skills are flawed or insult you, but the healer never even looked at me."

Selene smiled. "Which is exactly why she doesn't know what is wrong. She is so focused on Artemis and why Artemis is sick that she did not think about the fact that you and Artemis are tied to each other and that your illness is affecting her."

"Are you sure that I am ill?" I asked.

I felt great. I felt like I could take on an entire army.

Selene closed her eyes and began whispering a spell to look at my body and everything going on with it. I felt tingly and wanted to rub my arms to rid them of the goosebumps covering them, but being an alpha meant not showing weakness, so I held perfectly still and kept my breathing even to keep her from noticing my discomfort.

Her eyes opened and she said, "It is worse than I had originally thought. This is Noctum, the black illness. It starts off slowly with just fevers and dizziness, and then builds until the infected can't get out of bed and can't eat or sleep. Seizures will begin and then, ultimately, death."

"Why am I not showing any symptoms?" I asked.

"This illness is created so that it affects the person closest to you, magically and nearest you, physically. What I mean is that it is affecting Artemis through your bond, but if Artemis were not here it would most likely show on Koda. If Koda were not here it would go to the next person linked to you, perhaps your father or mother. The illness does this so that you do not treat the correct person and the person, and the one it is affecting, die before you realize that it was always the stronger one who was sick. Thankfully, some of us know about it and can see the signs and have spells to confirm it."

I stared at her in utter shock and disbelief. Not only was I dying, but because of my bond, Artemis was as well. "How did I receive this?"

"Only one gives this cursed illness, Death."

I grabbed the chair nearest us and threw it into the wall to my right. "No! That bastard did this because I forced him to give me their souls. No. This cannot be."

My child would be born soon, and I would continue to hurt Artemis until this illness killed me and her. There had to be some way to fix this. Even if I had to send Artemis away or if I had to isolate myself, I would do it.

"Is there a cure?" I asked after calming down a moment.

"Yes," she said, but not cheerfully which meant that it was complicated.

I sat down in a chair and met her eyes. "What is it?"

"It's not easy and not a cure most would go through with."

"Tell me!" I commanded and then sighed. "I apologize."

"It's quite alright. I understand that you are worried for Artemis and your child due to this illness affecting them. It is understandable." She paused a moment and then said, "To cure Noctum one must perform the appropriate spell, which uses dragon's blood and a soul."

"A soul?" I gasped and then sighed. "A sacrifice. I would need Dragon's blood and a sacrifice."

"Yes," Selene said as she nodded. "The spell makes the being, and whoever they are tied to, practically immortal. There are many who would abuse the spell, such as Maurice. The spell was hidden from the world because of this and only the leaders of the witches know of the spell. I am willing to use this spell on you because I have known you a couple hundred years and know you will not abuse your immortality, especially not with Artemis by your side. I am sorry to be the bearer of such bad news, but Ch-Artemis is one of my sisters and her safety is of great concern to me. I will leave you and visit with your mate another day." She walked out of the office and closed the door behind her softly.

I slumped in the chair and ran a hand over my face. What was I going to do? I needed to get a cure before the illness affected Artemis and the baby any more, but Artemis was not going to take this well. I could hide it from her while I searched out an appropriate person to sacrifice, but knowing her, she would think the worst and panic and overreact. If I tried to send her away, she would just teleport back to me. And if I left, she would try to track me.

I did not particularly like the idea of sacrificing someone to keep myself alive. If it had been Artemis in danger, I would do it in a second. I could not leave my child now that I was finally going to have one. I had waited too long for this moment.

"Ares?" Mother said as she opened the door and entered the room. "What is wrong?"

"What?" I asked as I looked up at her.

She smiled. "I am your mother. I can sense your unease a mile away. What is troubling you?"

My mother, Beatrice, was a smart and level-headed person. Well, as level-headed as any female wolf could be. She was probably the best person for me to discuss the matter with to get help in making my decisions.

"I am having a dilemma and I am not sure how to deal with it," I said.

She sat down in a chair beside me and then noticed the chair embedded in the wall across the room. She smirked and said, "I see. Maybe I can help you."

I took a deep breath and said, "You must promise not to speak of it to Artemis or Koda."

Her eyes widened. "You have never kept secrets from your brother before. Is this so terrible that you must now?"

I nodded and she smiled. "Very well. I promise."

I described to her in detail what had happened in Death's realm and every word Selene had said. Mother listened passively and stayed silent a long time after I was done, mulling everything over in her head as she weighed out the choices. She had been a good Queen and had had to make many hard decisions. "I am not sure what your dilemma is, to be honest. Are you just unsure as to who to pick for your sacrifice?"

That was the woman I knew. Sure of right and wrong and

capable of making choices that others might cringe at if it would ensure the safety of her pack.

"I am worried about how Artemis will react and yes, I am unsure of who to choose."

"Does your conscience really worry about picking someone to die for you? For your child? I would think you would go out and snatch up the nearest being from the cells and snap his neck right away if that would do it."

I smiled. "Normally, that would be my reaction, but it is not the child's life on the line. My life is the one on the line."

"Artemis is a strong woman and might make it through your death, but then again she might not. She did just lose the man she was bound to. I'm not sure if she could handle her *passt genau* dying as well."

I had already thought the same thing, but didn't want to admit the weakness in Artemis.

"Plus, Selene said that both of you would die and if she died before giving birth, that would mean the death of your child as well. I can have a list made of potential sacrifices if you would like? I will go and personally handpick the person to be sacrificed. I do not want to see another one of my son's bodies lying before me. You are supposed to far outlive me, not the other way around," she said seriously.

"A list would be helpful," I admitted. Though the slight nagging on my conscience would not go away. It was one thing to kill to protect someone or yourself but using someone for a spell was not something I was used to. I did see her point about saving Artemis and our child though.

"Are there restrictions on what type of being it is? Or their health?" Victor asked from beside me.

I had felt him appear a second earlier but had not acknowledged him. Mother growled at being scared by his sudden appearance, plus she had never liked him anyways.

"I don't know," I said with a shrug. "I did not ask Selene."

He paced across the room with a cloud of black hanging around him. It was rare to see the vampire in such a state of worry. "We need to ask her. If we could find someone who had a serious illness and wanted to die soon then your conscience would be eased with using them."

I smiled at Victor. My oldest friend knew me better than most.

The door flung open and Artemis rushed to me. "What happened? What did Selene say?"

I pulled her onto my lap and held her against my chest. She was warm again and shaking slightly. "You were supposed to stay in bed," I said with no real anger in my voice as I was happy to touch her and smell her.

"Don't change the subject," she murmured as she buried her nose into the side of my neck, inhaling my scent for reassurance and to help her calm down.

"The symptoms you are having are actually Ares'," Mother said. "He is dying and if you stay near him then you will die as well." So much for her not speaking of it to Artemis.

Artemis stilled, her heartbeat slowing with the lack of breath. "No," she whispered after a moment, "Selene has to be wrong."

"There is a cure," Victor said as Artemis' fear began to build.

"What is it? Why aren't we working on it now? Is that where Selene is? I can go help her and..." she stood up and then her legs gave out.

I caught her easily and pulled her back on my lap. "Easy, Sunshine."

"Victor and I will go speak to the witch. We will get this started now," Mother said as she motioned for Victor to follow her.

Artemis grabbed my face between her hands and forced me to meet her pale face. "I can't lose you. I can't. I am not strong enough to deal with your death."

I kissed her nose softly and smiled. "You won't lose me. However, you are losing the use of your legs because I am now forbidding you from walking anywhere for the next twenty-four hours." I picked her up and carried her down the hall to our room.

"What needs to be gathered for the spell?" she asked.

I clenched my teeth, not wanting to discuss it with her. I had forgotten for a moment that she had been Chandra for a long time and that she was well acquainted with the steps needed to perform spells.

"There are a couple items which Victor and my mother will work on gathering. You do not need to worry about it."

"Of course, I'm worried," she said with a sob. "Why is there always so much death around me?"

I kissed her head and set her down on the bed. "This is not your fault, Artemis. I have not led a very virtuous life."

"Tell me what needs to be collected for the spell," she said in her best alpha voice.

It was a good tone, one that would make lower dominance wolves bow in submission. I was impressed.

"Dragon's blood and a sacrifice," I said softly.

"A sacrifice. Why does it have to be a sacrifice? The dragon's blood I could get easily, but a sacrifice will be harder to find," she whispered. She tapped her chin a moment and then snapped her fingers. "I know! We will just go to the dungeons and take the worst criminal there and use them."

"I had already thought of that," I said with a smile. "I just don't particularly like the idea of someone being killed for me. If it were a battle and I had to kill or be killed then it would be an easy choice, but this is not a battle."

She turned my face to meet her gaze. "You listen to me. I will get you cured. I will not let you die. Maybe there is a way around the sacrifice. I will not let this illness hurt our child either."

I smiled and kissed her cheek. She was learning too much from me. She was right about one thing though. I could not let my illness harm our child. I had to stop being cowardly and be an alpha and a father. I had to choose a sacrifice.

"Ares?" Koda called through the door. "May I enter?"

"Yes."

Koda entered and immediately rushed over to Artemis. "What happened? I felt your fear and rushed here."

"Protect Artemis, I'm going to speak to Zeus," I said as I pulled out of her hold.

Artemis grabbed my arm. "Ares—"

I kissed her cheek. "You cannot stop me from protecting you and our child."

"Let me contact Draco Blu first. Maybe the Dragon Council knows of a different way. One that doesn't include a sacrifice," she pleaded.

"Sacrifice? What the hell is going on?" Koda asked.

"Artemis will explain while I am away. Keep her on the bed and do not let anyone inside and do not let her walk," I ordered him. I pulled away from Artemis and walked out the door to find my father.

CHAPTER 11
ARTEMIS

"Artemis, what is going on?" Koda asked. "Why does Ares need a sacrifice?"

I sat down on the bed and cried, unable to hold it in any longer. "Ares is dying," I croaked out between sobs.

"What?" Koda bellowed. "How?"

"Death's way of getting one over on Ares for getting my soul back. He cursed Ares with Noctum, the black illness."

"Is there a cure?" he asked.

I wiped my eyes, trying to calm myself down and recompose myself into the leader that I was. "Yes, but it requires a sacrifice."

"Done," he said seriously. "I will sacrifice myself."

I wanted to slap him. "No!" I screamed. "You are not dying! We need you."

"Darlin' you don't need me. As long as you have Ares, that's all that matters. Besides, if I can ensure he will live then I would gladly give my life."

"Koda stop it. You are not dying," I snarled.

"Alright, calm down," he said, but I knew he wasn't being completely honest with me.

I rolled onto my side and put my head in his lap. "I can't live without you."

"That's sweet, Darlin', but the only one you can't live without is Ares. I'm just your packmate."

"Stop it," I ordered him.

He stroked my hair and whispered, "I missed you so much those hundred years. And when you died, it tore a piece of my heart out. I thought I would never feel whole again and then you came back and I had never been so happy in my life. I realized then that even though I can never have you as my mate and you will never love me like you do Ares, I could at least be happy knowing you're alive."

I sat up and stared at Koda. "What are you saying? That you love me?" I asked him. He had never spoken to me in such a way before.

"Yes," he said seriously, "but I do not expect you to say anything or even acknowledge my feelings for you. It is enough for me that I am in your life."

"Does Ares know?" I asked, still reeling from this news. How could he say such things?

"I assume he does, but we have not discussed it. Do you understand now why I would sacrifice myself for Ares and you? To save either of you from death would be the greatest death for me," he whispered.

"I order you to stop," I said to him. "You are not going to die. No one is going to die!" Tears were streaming down my face and I couldn't see. Why was this happening? Why did everyone have to die around me?

"Alright, easy," he whispered as he pulled me closer to him. "Let's drop the subject."

"I can't let anyone else die. Never again," I whispered. A plan formulated in my head and I knew it would work. I only had to convince Ares and Zeus to allow it.

~

THE NEXT DAY the meeting was called again. I sat down and listened as they argued for an hour and held my tongue, but as nothing was accomplished still, I raised my hand, and everyone turned to stare at me. "I have information regarding Maurice's plan and another bit of information that I feel everyone here must know."

"What information? Where did you acquire this information?" Zeus asked. I knew he wasn't trying to be rude to me, he was just exasperated with the situation of everyone arguing in circles.

"When I was grieving over Achilles, I allowed myself to be captured by the vampires. They took me to Maurice, and I used my ability to create sunlight and surrounded him and all of the vampires in the room in sunlight. All of his vampires died instantly, but he didn't," I said.

"He is resistant to sunlight?" Victor gasped. "I never knew. He wasn't born and never went into the sun, so I assumed he could not."

I nodded. "He sat in the sunlight with no pain whatsoever. He is in fact able to walk in sunlight."

"We are doomed! How will we defeat him?" one of the trolls asked.

I waited until the room was quiet again and said, "He is still vulnerable to fire."

"So, why didn't you use fire?" Alianna asked.

I smiled. "I did, but he escaped, and I was too weak to pursue him. I returned back to Ares after that."

"What is the information you have about his plan?" Ares asked. I could see he was irritated that I had not mentioned it to him before, but I had been a little preoccupied with finding out about his death.

"I have a plan that I believe will ensure the demise of his reign.

It will take a lot of coordination and will require you all to trust me, but if we do this, I am sure we will win."

"Is it suicidal?" Ares asked.

I sighed in exasperation. "No."

"Has anyone contacted Draco Blu since the funeral?" I asked.

"No," Zeus said, "The dragons have always preferred to be neutral, so we did not contact them to discuss our battle."

"I'll contact him tomorrow," I said, "I am sure that they will come when I tell him of the news."

"What news?" Hera asked.

"I would prefer to reveal it to all of the races at once. I do not wish to cause undue alarm. I would ask that we reconvene tomorrow morning and I will reveal everything then and we can begin to arrange our attack."

Zeus tapped his chin. "Agreed. We will reconvene tomorrow at eight in the morning."

I stood and Ares linked hands with me, walked beside me as we headed out of the room and to our chambers. "You seem different," he said softly as we walked.

I smiled up at him. "I am just remembering that I am not a little girl anymore. I am over one hundred years old and I am the leader of the werewolves just the same as you are. I have to start acting like the alpha that I am."

He wrapped his arm around my waist and whispered into my ear, "I like it when you talk like an alpha."

I laughed and pulled away from him when we got to our chambers. "As soon as Victor pops in I will tell you what I learned since I know you will pester me until I tell you."

"I do not pester people," Ares said indignantly, "I order them, and they surrender and grovel at my feet."

I rolled my eyes at him. "I am not going to gravel at your feet."

Amber flickered over his eyes and he said, "That would be a very fun thing to see though. Perhaps I should give you an order as your alpha."

I smirked at him and backed up towards one of the chairs in the room. "You could try."

I started to sit, and Victor said, "While I do find our friendship has grown, I had not known it had moved to the point where you would sit in my lap."

I growled and spun around, sitting in the chair opposite him. "I hate when you do that."

He smiled. "Ah, but I do love the shock it gives people."

"Hopefully he gets over it within the next hundred years," Ares said.

"So," Victor said, drawing us back to the topic at hand, "What news do you have? You have guarded your mind so well with thoughts of unicorns and kittens that I have not been able to discern it."

"Unicorns and kittens?" Ares asked.

I shrugged. "I had to figure out a way to keep him from hearing my thoughts and I figured he would grow bored of me thinking about those animals."

"Well played," Victor said, "Although I did see that whatever it is will cause widespread panic across the world."

Ares sat down in the chair beside Victor and I took a deep breath and began. "Your father believed that I was permanently in his hold so he thought it was okay to divulge his strategy to me because there was no way I could get the information back to Ares and let him know. Maurice has stationed vampires all around the world in anticipation of our group attacking him. When we lead our attack, he will signal his vampires who will attack all of the defenseless beings who were left behind. They will march into Lyngvi for example and his vampires will kill every female, child, and submissive male that has been left there."

Ares growled and began pacing around the room. Victor linked his hands together and rested his chin on top of them with his elbows resting on the arms of his chair. "It's a brilliant plan."

"Even more brilliant now that we know," Ares said in a deep growl.

"How so?" I asked.

"Now that we know what he is planning, we will have to split up our attack force. Instead of all of our strongest attacking him, we will have to send some of each to protect our weakest. He has successfully separated us and diminished our force," Victor said. He looked at me a moment and then said, "But you have a plan for that." I smiled and started thinking about a kitten riding a unicorn. He scoffed. "Think about all the kittens and unicorns you want. I will wait until tomorrow to hear your plan." He stood up and bowed to me. "Goodbye, *Mon Papillion*."

He disappeared and Ares plopped down into the chair he had just vacated. "You have a plan?"

I nodded.

"Are you going to tell me it?" he asked.

I shook my head.

He sighed. "I am your mate and you will not tell me your plan?"

I smiled and said, "I have a plan and I will reveal it and these details to everyone." Something moved inside of my stomach and I looked down at it in shock. "What was that?"

Ares walked over to me and rested his hand on my stomach. "Did the baby kick?"

I shrugged. "I don't know. It felt like a weird bump." I looked at my stomach, which was noticeably larger now. When had my stomach expanded so much?

He titled his head to the side and placed his ear to my stomach. The strange feeling happened again, and Ares smiled. "The baby's kicking."

I smiled and rested my hand on top of Ares' head. "In order for my plan to work, we will have to wait until after I have our child."

Ares lifted his head up and rested his chin on my stomach so that he could look at me. "Why do I get the feeling that I am not going to like this plan?"

I leaned forward and kissed his forehead. "You are a very perceptive man."

He growled. "You are infuriating."

I closed my eyes and felt exhausted. Would we be able to cure Ares before I had our child? "Am I going to have stretch marks?" I asked him with my eyes still closed.

He laughed softly. "Yes, but they will heal almost instantly. After you have the baby your body will repair itself quickly."

"I'm scared," I whispered.

He moved and before I could inhale, we were lying on the bed and he was cuddling with me underneath the blankets. "I will do everything that I can to keep you safe."

I nuzzled his throat and intertwined our legs together. "I'm not scared because of that. I'm scared of childbirth."

"Speak to my mother. She can talk with you about it and ease your fears," he whispered.

I kissed his neck and then settled against him. "Sometimes I wish we could pause the world and simply live in moments like this."

"So do I," he whispered.

"Ares?" Koda called through the closed door. "Has Artemis eaten yet?"

"No," Ares said, "Please get her something and me as well."

We heard Koda's footsteps walk away and only after I was sure that he was gone did I relax against Ares again. I dozed in his arms until Koda returned and then tried to eat despite the nausea which had decided to return as soon as I sat up.

"Get Selene," Ares whispered to Koda when he thought that I was not paying attention.

"She is at the door," Victor said from the chair beside me.

I lifted my head to look at him and immediately regretted it. Victor grabbed me and a moment later set me on the floor of the bathroom with my head over the toilet and my hair pulled back in his hands.

"Thank you," I thought as I threw up everything that I had just eaten.

"You're welcome."

Ares came into the bathroom and took Victor's place holding my hair. "Selene is here, and she has good news."

I took a deep breath and forced my stomach to stop squeezing its contents out. I hoped this was not going to be a constant thing. After being sure that I was done throwing up I sighed, and Ares picked me up and carried me out to the bed.

Selene placed her hand on my forehead and chanted a fever reduction spell and then made me drink a disgusting tasting anti-nausea potion. "Better?" she asked. I nodded and she sat down beside me on the bed. "I spoke with Draco Blu yesterday. He and two thirds of his flight will be joining our battle against Maurice."

"That's great," I said with a smile. Having the dragons would be a huge advantage for us because of the fire they produced in an endless quantity.

"And," she continued, pulling a chain from underneath her shirt which lifted a vial that was attached to it, "he gave me this."

The vial had green liquid inside of it that glowed softly.

Ares walked towards us and Selene placed the vial and necklace in his hand. "Is this dragon's blood?" he asked.

She smiled and eyed the vial. "It is Draco Blu's blood to be precise?"

"The Draco of the dragons gave you his blood?" Victor asked, furrowing his brow.

I smiled and felt extremely grateful for the friendship that I had created with him. He had given me many gifts and had protected me many times when I was Chandra. I would need to find a way to repay the large debt I now owed him. It would not be easy, but it was necessary.

Selene said, "She was the favored hatchling of Draco Blu and his flight. It is a very rare honor."

"She is very good at getting people to like her," Victor said.

I wasn't sure what he meant by that, but I did not think he meant any disrespect, so I let the comment lie. "Have you chosen a sacrifice yet?" I asked Ares.

He shook his head and Victor said, "We have one chosen for him."

"Who?" Ares asked, obviously not happy with that news.

"A prisoner who was sentenced to be put to death, but whose sentence has yet to be carried out. He committed violent crimes that are unforgivable and as such there is no reason why he should not be used for a sacrifice."

"Will the death be painful?" Ares asked Selene.

Selene glanced at me and I knew as well as she did that sometimes sacrifices in spells were very painful. Often times the person would scream for the duration of the spell. "It will be painful but will not last more than two minutes."

Ares did not look reassured by that answer. "I will pick the sacrifice myself."

"You had better choose in the next day or two," Selene warned. "Artemis is getting worse and the baby is beginning to suffer."

My hand instinctively went to my stomach and I felt fearful for my unborn child. Ares set the vial of Blu's blood in my hand and walked towards the door. "Victor, would you please protect Artemis for a few hours?"

"Of course," Victor said and then stood up.

Ares shut the door behind him, and I gaped at it. "What just happened?"

Selene stood up and smiled at me. "I will come see you tomorrow. We should be able to perform the spell then."

She left and I looked at Victor who was frowning. "What just happened?" I asked again.

"Ares went to blow of some steam and then to find someone suitable for the sacrifice. Now that he knows the baby is in danger, he will not hesitate in picking someone. Don't worry. He will be back soon."

I laid down on the bed and asked, "Why is he being so stubborn about choosing a sacrifice?" I really did not understand it. I would have chosen someone as soon as I found out about it if I had been able to.

"He does not like the idea of picking someone to die in his place. It is different when that person is attacking you and it is either them or you then it is to choose someone to be used in a spell. Many consider using a sacrifice to be a dark art and stay away from it."

"Selene told him already that I would die as well as him and so would the baby. So why is he now going? Why has he been putting it off?" I frowned.

"I understand your frustration, but Ares is very old and is very set in his ways. He is not used to not being in control. He is used to taking care of everything himself, but now he cannot. He is upset because you constantly put yourself in danger and he is upset that you and your child are in danger and he is upset that he cannot rip off Death's head in order to fix it all."

"Artemis?" a soft male voice asked from outside my door. "Can I come in?"

"Who?" I started to ask.

Victor whispered, "Apollo. I do not think Ares would like it if…"

"Come in," I called, not letting Victor finish.

Victor sighed. "Ares is going to have a brain aneurism when he learns that I let him in here with you."

I smiled. "You'll protect me if I need it."

Victor rolled his eyes. "Don't patronize me, Artemis. I am over a thousand years old."

Apollo walked into the room and I was awestruck again by how similar we looked. His hair was incredibly blonde now though. It looked almost magical. "Hello, Apollo," I said as I sat up. He was wearing blue jeans and a white t-shirt. He was a halfbreed like me so didn't that mean that he could switch to a wolf form?

Victor set pillows behind me so that I was propped up and discreetly shook his head at me. "What business do you have with Queen Artemis?" he asked Apollo when he turned around to face him.

"I heard that you were not feeling well," he said as he walked closer to the bed.

"Just a slight side effect to being pregnant," I said with a smile.

He smiled back at me. "You lie very poorly."

Victor stepped between Apollo and the bed and said, "That is close enough."

"Is he your bodyguard?" Apollo asked me. "I thought they said you were the prince or something?"

"He is a friend and yes, he is the Prince of Vampires," I said before Victor decided to show him how strong he was.

"You have a lot of friends," Apollo said. He sat down in one of the chairs in front of the bed and said, "I came to apologize to you."

"Now is not the time for your apology," Victor hissed.

"Victor, it's alright." I hated that everyone was babying me.

"No, he is right," Apollo said. "When you are feeling better and your mate is back then I will come visit you again."

"Apollo," I called, stopping him. He turned around and faced me, waiting for me to talk. "Why did you surrender after the battle?"

"Another time," he said with a shake of his head. "We will talk about that at a later time."

"Thank you for coming to see me," I said with a smile.

He smiled back. "I am glad that you are alive. I felt…strange when you died, and I did not like it." He frowned at what he had said and left without another word.

"I do not trust him," Victor said.

"He saved me from my father and killed him for me. I trust him." Plus, Achilles had told me to make amends with him and I would.

"Artemis, it was not..." Victor started, but I glared at him and he stopped talking, raising his hands in surrender. "Alright."

Koda came into the room with his mother behind him. She smiled at me and hurried over to put her hand on my stomach and whisper to the baby. It was strange, but I was not about to disrespect her by telling her I thought she was weird. Victor smiled and then sat down in one of the chairs to relax.

She stood up and asked, "How are you feeling?"

"Same," I lied.

She tsked at me. "You cannot lie to me sweetheart. I am older than even Ares."

"I'm scared," I admitted. "I'm scared because the baby is beginning to suffer according to Selene. I'm scared because my stomach is expanding very very quickly, and I am scared because I have never had a baby and I'm afraid of what it is going to be like." Tears filled my eyes and I wiped them away, hating that my emotions were getting the better of me.

She sat down on the bed beside me and put her arm around my shoulders. "It is alright to be scared sometimes. I was scared when I had Ares. I was terrified that Hera would try to kill him. I was even scared when I had Matt and Koda because I was huge with twins."

"Will it hurt?" I asked her.

She gave me a kind smile. "Yes, but you will survive. Our deliveries are usually very quick and although they are painful, our bodies repair the damage right away. You will be exhausted for the first couple of hours afterwards, but then you will be good as new."

"Will the stretch marks heal?" I asked softly.

She laughed. "Yes, child. You will look like it never happened."

I exhaled in relief and rubbed my stomach. "We haven't even picked a name yet."

"I believe the healer will be coming today to tell you the gender. I would wait until Ares is here though," Koda said.

Of course, I would wait for Ares. Why did he think I would do something so rude?

"Where is my eldest?"

"Seeking out a sacrifice," Victor said from his chair.

"Good," she said as she stood up. "It is about time he took charge of this."

I laid down again and closed my eyes. "Why am I so tired?"

"You are growing a being inside of your body," she said. "It takes up a lot of your nutrients and energy. In fact, Koda, would you get us some food?"

"Yes, ma'am," he said with a bow of his head and left the room.

Beatrice looked at Victor. "May I have some privacy to speak with my daughter-in-law?"

Victor frowned. "Normally I would leave, but Ares asked me to protect her."

"I am not going to hurt her," she said, narrowing her eyes at him.

Victor shrugged. "I don't know that for sure. Besides, I would rather not leave her alone with anyone but Ares. She is very vulnerable right now and needs as much protection as possible."

"And you think that I would not be able to protect her? You forget that I am older than even you, Victor of the Vampires. I could be Alpha still, if I so desired."

"I do not doubt your strength. I am simply refusing to leave Artemis without me as an additional defense," he said adamantly. I had never seen him so serious about anything before.

She glared at him, but finally relinquished and turned to me. "The mind reading vampire already knows this so I might as well discuss it in front of him. Have you talked with Ares about Koda's feelings for you?"

"I only found out about his feelings yesterday," I said uncomfortably. Was it just obvious to everyone that he had feelings for me, or had he talked to his mother about it? Which was worse?

"And I did not think it was a good idea to bring it up to Ares due to his recent mood."

She sighed. "My sons have mostly gotten along, but I fear this might ruin the bond they had formed. Koda looks up to Ares and loves him like any younger brother should, but his feelings for you have only escalated since your disappearance and then death."

"He told me that it was enough just to be in my life," I said. "I'm hoping that he keeps that mentality."

"He might for a while," she said, "But his jealousy might also grow and…" She stopped talking and then the door opened as Koda entered with food.

He smiled at me and set a tray of food on the bed beside me with a glass of water. "Sorry it took so long. I got sidetracked on my way to the kitchen."

"Thank you," I said and then picked up some food and started eating.

"You have always been the politest of my sons," she said with a smile at Koda.

He took a seat in a chair next to Victor and then sat very still. It was weird looking, and I was about to ask what he was doing when Ares flung open the door and charged inside. "Why do I smell Apollo?"

He was seething with anger and I could almost see a red cloud encircling him. "Ares, what's wrong?" I asked as I stood and started towards him.

"Get in bed," he said. "Stop moving around," he growled. He had never growled at me or been seriously mad at me before. I continued walking towards him and he growled again. "I order you to get in bed," he snapped, his order as alpha pressed against me like a net pulling me backwards.

I growled back at him and held my ground, trying my hardest to slide my feet forward.

"Stop, Ares. You're going to hurt her," his mother said.

"I wouldn't be hurting her if she would obey," he said. "For once in your life, obey."

"Come here, Ares," I ordered him in my best alpha voice and using as much of my dominance as I could.

His body jerked towards me and his eyes widened. He apparently did not know that I could order him around just as he could me. He held his ground and gnashed his teeth together.

"Even if you prove your point," Victor said, "You will only feel bad about hurting her afterwards. We all agree that Artemis needs to start taking some orders."

"I just want to touch you," I said to Ares. He was being obstinate, but I was much better at it.

"Why was Apollo here?" he asked me again.

"He came to visit me," I said. "He wanted to check on me because he had heard that I was ill."

"Who let him in here?" Ares screamed.

He was getting too worked up and soon would let his bloodlust take over if he was not careful. I had never seen him in such a fit before. I had to do something, but what could I do to diffuse the situation?

"Victor," I said softly. "Teleport them out of here so I can speak to my mate alone."

"No one is going anywhere until I get answers," Ares said.

"I let him in," I said. "Victor was guarding me, so I was perfectly—"

"You let him in here with my sick mate?" Ares screamed at Victor as he walked towards him.

Victor stood and I could see the slight worry in his eyes and the tension in his body. "Artemis allowed him in and I stood between him and her and forced him to keep his distance from her. She was not in serious danger."

Victor was the only one who saw the punch coming because he turned to mist, and Ares' fist went through him.

"Ares," I yelled. "Stop it!"

Victor drifted away and reformed across the room. "I know you are upset, but you do not want to fight me."

Ares shifted into warrior form and charged Victor. Koda tried to grab him, but Ares flung him across the room. Koda spun at the last second, bouncing off the wall with his feet instead of slamming into it. He ran forward and kicked Ares in the back of the knees, making him stumble as he lunged at Victor who was teleporting around the room trying to stay out of his reach.

"Ares, calm down," Victor said in a soft voice. "I understand that you are stressed out, but you do not want to hurt me."

Ares roared at Victor--logical thought gone as he tried to attack him. Koda jumped onto Ares' back and tried to wrap his arm around Ares' throat, but Ares simply grabbed Koda by his arm and tossed him across the room, straight into Victor who thankfully misted before Koda hit him.

"Ares," Beatrice said. "Calm down, son." He turned and growled at her and she took a step back, fear emanating from her. I wondered why she was so afraid when she was older than him.

I approached Ares and set my hand on his forearm. He jerked away and spun towards me, ready to attack me until he saw my face. He lowered the hand he had raised at me and instead snarled at me. I took his clawed hand and gently set it against my face. His hand flexed and the claws bit into my skin just enough to draw blood.

Koda growled, and Ares started to turn towards him, but I grabbed Ares' other hand and set it on my stomach where the baby was kicking up a storm. He looked down at my stomach and his lips lowered, closing over his teeth and his body slowly started to return to his human form.

"Everyone out," I whispered.

Koda started to protest, but Victor grabbed him and teleported before he could move.

"I hope you know what you're doing," Beatrice whispered.

"Mate," I whispered, drawing Ares' attention back to me and away from his mother as she walked slowly out of the room.

He looked up at my face and growled. "Mate."

I took a step backwards, towards the bed, holding onto his wrists and keeping them on my face and stomach. "Artemis," I whispered, hoping that he could slowly regain his control.

"Artemis," he whispered back as he looked down at my stomach from another of the baby's kicks.

"Baby," I whispered. "Your baby."

"My baby?" he asked.

I nodded and sat down on the edge of the bed, keeping his hand on my face. "Your baby. Your mate. Artemis."

The gold melted out of his eyes and he plopped face first down onto the bed on his stomach. "Artemis. Sorry."

I kissed his cheek and wrapped myself up in his arms and whispered, "Sleep."

He nodded, and we fell asleep together.

CHAPTER 12
ARTEMIS

I woke up the next morning alone. *Completely* alone. I got out of bed, changed and peeked my head out the door. The hallway was empty too. "Hello?" I called, but only received my echo back. I walked down the hallway, running my hand along the wall in case I had a dizzy spell to keep from injuring myself and made my way out of the castle. I looked in each room that I went past, but all of them were empty, which was very strange considering that there were usually servants running around everywhere. Where was everyone?

I pinched myself and growled at the pain. I was definitely awake. My stomach grumbled, and I sighed. I was definitely hungry.

"Victor!" I called, hoping he would be listening or would be nearby. "Victor, where are you?" He did not appear in front or behind me, so I continued towards the front doors. I pushed them open, straining with the weight a moment. The doors opened and bright sunlight blinded me. I blinked my eyes until I could finally see and felt my heart drop at the sight before me.

Hundreds of beings were gathered in a circle in the field in front of the castle where Ares and Koda were standing in the center facing each other. I saw elves, wolves, Sidhe, halfbreeds and even a couple of dwarves and ogres standing in a circle around them, waiting. Koda was shirtless and judging by the amount of amber in his eyes, very angry. Victor was standing between Ares and Koda, talking quietly and quickly. No doubt he was trying to calm them down and talk sense into them.

"Victor," I whispered urgently.

He looked towards me and his eyes widened. He said something to Ares and then Victor teleported to me and picked me up. "Why are you out of bed and walking around?"

"I was alone," I said, "I'm never alone so I was worried. What is going on?"

He teleported so that he was standing between Koda and Ares again. "Koda, Artemis is here."

Ares reached to take me from Victor, but Koda growled at him and swatted his arms away from me. "You do not deserve to touch her."

"Set me down," I ordered Victor. He obeyed but gave me an irritated look so I apologized silently. "Koda, what is going on?"

He pointed at Ares and said, "He hurt you yesterday. He does not deserve to have you as his mate."

"Do not do anything that you will regret, brother," Ares warned him.

"Koda, he was experiencing bloodlust. It happens to even the best wolves. You cannot blame Ares for losing control once in over a couple hundred years. He has a lot on his plate right now and—"

"It is inexcusable that he hurt you," Koda roared, cutting me off mid-sentence.

"I am not hurt," I said, "It is not his fault—"

"He cut your face with his claws," Koda roared again. "I challenge—"

I punched him in the stomach as hard as I could, making him

gasp for breath and stop talking. "Shut up before you do something you will regret."

He got his breath back and whispered, "He is letting you die for him. He is going to kill you."

"I am not letting her die," Ares growled.

Koda stood up straight, pushed me to the side into Victor's arms, and then charged Ares. I tried to move towards them, but Victor held on to me and due to my weakened state, I was unable to break free.

Ares blocked Koda's punches and kicks but did not hit him back. "Stop this," Ares said. "Let's talk about this in private."

Koda growled and shifted into his warrior form. "I challenge you for the position of Alpha of the Werewolves."

"No!" I screamed. "Koda, don't do this. If you kill Ares, I will never forgive you. Do you hear me? If you take him away from me, I will kill you myself!"

"Listen to her, Koda. She isn't bluffing," Victor urged.

Ares stayed where he was, watching and waiting for Koda's decision. I could see the tension in his body as he waited and knew that if Koda attacked him that he would not hold back.

Koda turned to me with hurt in his eyes. Part of me felt bad for threatening him, but I knew he needed to hear how I felt. I loved him as a pack mate, but Ares was my mate and the man I loved unconditionally. I would never forgive anyone that took him from me. "Why do you want him when he treats you poorly?" he asked. "I would treat you like the queen that you are."

"I love him, Koda. He is my *passt genau*, my one true love and the father of my unborn child. He treats me well and you would see that if you were not blinded by your emotions. No one can replace him."

"Fine, a fight to yield for the position of alpha," he said.

"I will not be your mate," I told him sternly.

He growled. "I am not fighting to take you as my mate, Artemis. I am fighting to take his position as Alpha."

"Why?" I asked. "Why is it suddenly so important for you to be alpha?"

"Because I have lived in his shadow for too long. It is time that the world knows me for who I am, and the wolves have a leader that will lead them properly," Koda said.

"I accept your challenge to yield for Alpha of the Werewolves," Ares said.

"What are you doing?" Victor asked, releasing me and walking towards Ares.

I looked around at the crowd, hoping to find a Sidhe who was manipulating Koda like Achilles had done before.

"He wants to take over as alpha, so I am willing to let him try. If I do not accept his challenge it will make me look weak and now is not a time that I can appear weak," Ares said angrily. "He has wanted to do this since Artemis went missing and I will let him." Ares looked at Koda and said, "I will not hold back just because you are my brother. If we go forward with this challenge, I will fight you with all of my strength and power."

"I would have it no other way," Koda said.

"This is ridiculous," I said angrily.

"What's going on?" Theseus, Koda's son, asked as he walked up to us.

"Your father is challenging Ares to become Alpha of the Werewolves," I said, trying to portray how ludicrous it was and hope that he would talk some sense into his dad.

Theseus folded his arms across his chest and said, "I wondered how long it would take him to do this. I guess your health finally pushed Dad over the edge."

My jaw dropped to the ground. "Are you serious? Aren't you going to try to stop him?"

He put his arm around my shoulders and squeezed. "It'll be alright. Dad won't kill him."

I screamed in frustration and stepped away from the idiot brothers and said, "I refuse to watch this." I teleported to the dragon's hive, letting Victor know where I was heading. I knew Ares would be mad, but I was safer in the hive than anywhere else in the world. I popped into the hive, in the tent where I had slept while waiting for the dragons to help me unlock my memories and found it empty, thankfully. I stepped out of the tent to be met by the Dragon Council.

"Greetings, Artemis Lupine," they said in unison.

I bowed to them as well as I could with my enlarged stomach. "Greetings, Council."

"What do we owe the pleasure of your company to?" they asked.

"Werewolf quarrels that I have no desire to witness. I came to see Blu, I mean Draco Blu, if he is available and to seek your counsel regarding some issues."

"Draco Blu has been missing for several days," the Council said. "We sent Fira to contact you, but due to your lack of knowledge we must assume he is now missing as well."

"Missing? What do you mean missing?" I asked in shock.

"We do not have the ability to speak telepathically over long distances," they said.

I paced back and forth in front of them nervously. "What could have happened? Do you think it is possible that he was taken hostage or killed?"

"All things are possible," they said.

I refrained from rolling my eyes and asked, "Did the dragons acquire any enemies recently?"

"No."

Could Maurice have found out that the dragons were going to assist us, and would he have been able to capture Blu, or kill him? I shuddered at the thought but could not believe that the dragon would be easily taken down. Fira was a smaller dragon, but almost as strong as Blu and not easily killed either.

"We had planned to send scouts, but…"

"But you did not want them to disappear as well," I finished for them. "I will investigate myself," I said, "It is the least I can do after everything the dragons have done for me."

"You should not travel alone in your condition," they said.

"If I return, my mate will not allow me to go search for Draco Blu. I cannot return there to find someone to go with me," I said as I resumed pacing.

"Then I will go with you," Victor said from behind me. I spun around, angry that the vampire had gotten the drop on me again. He bowed to the Council. "Greetings, Dragon Council."

"Greetings Victor, Prince of the Vampires," they said.

"I will accompany you while you search for the dragons so that you are protected and so that I can teleport you to a healer if your condition should worsen," he said to me.

"Are Ares and Koda alright?" I asked.

He shrugged. "They were still fighting when I teleported to check on you, per Ares' request."

Of course, he had sent Victor to check on me. "Fine, but just remember that I can teleport just like you can so if you teleport me away and I am not ready to leave, I will just teleport right back."

He smiled. "I know, Artemis." He turned to the Council and asked, "Can you give me the specifics of your last communications with the two dragons who are missing?"

"Draco Blu left three days ago to head for the Sidhe's ground opening. He usually contacts us by magical reflection once he has arrived at his destination to check on the status of the hive while he is away. This is not the first time that he has not contacted us, but it is very rare."

I knew the spell to speak by reflection and it was very easy. In fact, Blu and I had used it to communicate when he was away from me while I was with the witches.

"Would he be able to contact you if he was captured?" Victor asked as he began pacing back and forth in front of the Council.

"He should be able to find some way and that is the other reason we are worried."

"Has Fira contacted you since he left?" I asked.

"No."

My fear for the dragons grew, and I put out a hand to lean against Victor as I took deep, calming breaths. Victor said, "We will travel the path to the Sidhe's opening and look for any sign of a struggle and search for the dragons. We will report to you periodically."

"Thank you," the Council said.

"How are you feeling?" Victor asked me as he watched the dragons walk away.

"I actually feel a lot better than I have in a while," I admitted to him. "Perhaps it is because of the physical amount of distance between me and Ares."

He nodded his head. "Selene did mention that it would affect those closest to him. It may be a good thing that you are away from him for a while."

"How long will the battle between Koda and Ares last?" I asked nervously. I did not doubt that Ares would win, but I was nervous that he would get seriously hurt.

"Two or three days," he said.

"Days?" I gasped.

He nodded. "Koda is alpha material. I noticed it the day we went to rescue your little friend, Bret. If Ares were not around, Koda would be the logical choice for alpha. He is dominant enough and he has a leader's mind."

"Part of me does hope that he takes over as alpha," I admitted.

"Why?" Victor asked.

"Because then it would mean that Ares and I could relax and raise our child together in peace somewhere," I said longingly.

"You would still be the next in line for the Sidhe throne," he said.

"Do you really think Hera or Zeus are likely to die anytime soon?" I asked sarcastically.

He shrugged. "Stranger things have happened."

I thought of Achilles and his early death and turned away from Victor. Victor patted my back and said, "We should head out. I have a feeling that we are going to be in for a very long night."

"What if your father has them?" I asked him. "What can we do?"

"Let's deal with that later if it comes up. You need to start thinking positively."

I pushed my wings out of my back and flapped them, sending me up into the air. "Fine. Let's start looking. I am getting more worried about them the longer that we stand here."

Victor transformed into a bat and flew after me as we headed out of the mountain and towards the Sidhe mounds which were entrances to the Sidhe realm. The cold air blasted against us as we exited the mountain, and I was forced to squint my eyes against the snow and wind.

We flew and scanned the terrain below us. Halfway there. I began to get lightheaded and was forced to land, but I was happy to have not found anything yet. I sat on a log and looked at the forest around us. It was so quiet and peaceful and relaxing that I did not want to get up.

"It seems the closer we get to Ares, the worse your symptoms become. Perhaps it would be best if you returned to the Dragon's lair and stayed with them?" Victor suggested as he watched me from the tree he was leaning against.

How could he look so normal in a forest where he should seem so out of place? "I cannot sit on my hands and worry. I have to do something." Plus, me having idle time was not the best idea. I would think of the worst outcomes and freak myself out more than was necessary for the baby.

I stood up and walked towards Victor. "I never thanked you," I said to him.

"Thanked me for what?" He asked.

"You have been a great friend, Victor. Thank you for protecting Ares and staying beside him when I was away. I can't imagine what it must have been like to deal with him those hundred years that you were all searching for me."

He smiled. "Ares is my best friend. You do not need to thank me for anything."

The baby started kicking and I grabbed Victor's hand and placed it on my stomach. "Feel it?" I asked him.

He stared at my stomach with such awe and softness that it almost made me forget that he was a vampire and capable of as much, if not more, damage as Ares. "Such strong kicks," he whispered. "Does it hurt?"

I huffed. "No."

He pulled his hand away and smiled. "I am glad that Ares has you. He is a very lucky man."

I laughed. "*Right*. He is so lucky to have a troublemaker like me. I think I have caused him more headaches than he was expecting."

Victor smiled. "You may be right about that, but I saw him when you were stolen and again when you died and know that he would rather have you giving him headaches than you no longer in his life."

We made camp since it was so late and slept until the sun rose before heading out again. The day lagged on and still we found no trace of Draco Blu or Fira. I was just starting to lose hope when I inhaled to say something and smelled smoke. "Do you smell that?"

He nodded,and we both flew up into the air. I followed the scent of the smoke and gasped when we came to the scene. The forest abruptly ended in a ten-mile wasteland of ashes. There was no doubt in my mind that this was a scene of a dragon's fight. I hovered above the destruction and searched for any clues that might answer what the outcome of the battle had been.

"There are a lot of dead vampire ashes here," Victor called to me from the ground.

"How can you tell?" I asked him. To me the ashes looked the same as the burnt trees and bushes.

"I can tell," he whispered as he examined another streak of ashes.

I flew to the edges of the burnt forest, searching for signs of escape. Halfway around the damaged area I finally found marks, but the sight of them made my fear and worry skyrocket. Victor teleported to me and sighed when he saw the very large drag marks. He followed the marks and then returned to me. "They dragged him about a mile and then picked him up. He must be at my father's castle."

"Will he kill him?" I asked. And who was it? Was it Blu or Fira?

"No, he will not kill him. He will keep him prisoner to bait you into trying to rescue him and he will try to find ways to use him to his benefit," Victor said seriously.

My stomach clenched so hard that it made me gasp in pain. Victor grabbed me and said, "There is nothing we can do right now. We need to return and advise everyone what has happened."

"No," I said through gritted teeth.

"Hello, Victor," a deep voice said from behind us.

Victor did not turn around, but his entire body tensed up. Judging by his reaction, he had not heard the being arrive behind us. "Hello, Bartholomew," he said bitterly.

"I had expected Artemis to come in search of her dragon friends, but I had not expected you to be with her," Bartholomew said as he circled around to stand in front of us.

He was tall, dark and handsome. He was also very powerful and judging by his calm demeanor, not scared of Victor, which was not a good sign for us. I looked at Victor. *Is he susceptible to sun?* Victor shook his head.

"I came to assist her in her investigation," Victor said.

"Ah. You have always had a soft spot for the werewolves," Bartholomew said with a shake of his head. "Your heart is your biggest downfall."

"Would I be able to use fire on him without you getting burned as well?"

Victor laughed once and shook his head. "You only think that because you have no heart."

"Better to have no heart and be able to think clearly then to have a heart that clouds your thoughts and judgments."

"Where is the dragon?" I asked Bartholomew. The conversation between Victor and him was not going anywhere that would help us.

"He is with the king," he said, "Don't worry, you will be united with him soon, after I take you there."

"I have visited the King recently and I have no desire to go back to him so soon," I said with a smile. I turned to Victor. "What are we going to do?"

"First, Victor will die and then you will accompany me willingly to go see the king," Bartholomew said.

I rolled my eyes.

Victor smiled. "He has always been overly cocky. I think we have a couple of options, but I would prefer not to discuss them in front of Bart," Victor said as he moved a step closer to me.

I knew he wanted to teleport, and I knew that we probably should, but at the same time I did not want to return to Ares and have him force me to stay in the Sidhe realm. I needed to find Blu and Fira and I needed to do it quickly, before any harm came to them. I made up my mind and before Victor could say anything, I unleashed fire, covering Bartholomew.

He screamed and tried to turn to mist, but it did not matter, I kept the fire on him until he was forced to fly away from us to save himself. Victor turned to me and laughed. "I cannot believe you made him retreat. That is the first time he has been forced to retreat in one hundred and eighty years."

I shrugged. "I needed him to leave and I did not want you to teleport us."

"Clearly," he said with a shake of his head.

"Alright, let's go. We need to find Blu and Fira," I said, taking a step towards the path of the drag marks.

Victor touched my arm, stopping me. "Let's not get ahead of ourselves. We should at least talk with Zeus..."

"No!" I yelled. "He will tell Ares and then I will be held captive. I have to do this without telling Ares. I thought we had already gone over this?"

"I know, Artemis, but if Bartholomew is involved then that means that all of the highest leveled vampires are involved. It is something too dangerous for just you and me to tackle," he said, grabbing my shoulders and forcing me to look at him so I could see how serious he was. "It is something that not even I should face alone. I will need the help of allies to face them."

"Then why don't you teleport and get Dmitri, Theseus, a couple other vampires still your allies and a couple other halfbreeds if you think we need that many."

"And what are you going to do while I do that?" he asked me suspiciously.

I sat down, crossing my legs and said, "I will be right here."

He stared at me a moment and then asked, "What is the real reason that you do not want to return to the Sidhe realm?"

"I have been over this with you. I do not want Ares to keep me there."

"And?" he prodded.

I growled. "You can already read my mind so why are you asking me to say it out loud?" Vampires were so frustrating.

"Because you must say things out loud so that you make them real and realize your fears. It is not healthy to bottle things up."

"Do you pull this with Ares?" I asked him.

He smiled. "Yes, and that is one of the only reasons that he is sane right now."

"Fine, I will answer you. I am afraid to return to the Sidhe realm and to Ares' side because the closer I am to Ares the sicker I get. If I stay away from him the baby will not be in as much trouble."

He smiled. "Was that so hard?"

"You're an ass."

He laughed. "Alright, Artemis. I can tell that you are determined to go after the dragons so I will teleport and bring back enforcements. I do not like the idea of leaving you here, but I agree that it is better for the baby if we keep you farther away from Ares then he would normally let you be. You better be here when I get back."

I smiled. "I cross my heart." He rolled his eyes and then disappeared. I exhaled and rested my hand on top of my stomach. "What are we going to do little one? Your father is going to be extremely displeased with me for running away from him despite the fact that it is best for you. You will learn that he is very stubborn." I laughed. "But he is the greatest man I know. He will love you and you will be the greatest gift he has ever received."

Thinking about Ares made me think about the current predicament he and Koda were in. What would happen if Koda became the alpha? What would that mean for Ares and me? Would we be able to raise our child in peace while Koda helped the pack? The thought alone made a smile spread across my lips. A life where we could enjoy each other and spend time alone sounded mythical. I had to hope though. I had to keep hoping that someday it could happen.

Victor, Theseus and Dmitri popped into existence in front of me. Victor smiled and I smiled back. "You didn't think I would be here, did you?"

He laughed. "I have to admit that I assumed you would be on your way after the dragons already."

I stood up and said, "I'm trying to act mature. I believe a being over one hundred years old should start acting their age."

"Father and Ares are…" Theseus began.

I held up my hand, stopping him. "I do not want to hear about it. I will find out the result of their stupid fight when I return."

"Ares did ask about you when he saw me teleport in," Victor said.

"What did you tell him?" I asked.

Victor smiled. "I grabbed these two and teleported out without answering him. I did hear him roar before we left though."

"Good. He can deal with not knowing for a while."

"Shall we go?" Dmitri asked. "The night will fade soon."

I nodded, and Victor grabbed my hand, helping me stand. "I'm not that pregnant yet," I said teasingly.

He smiled. "No, but it is gentlemanly to assist a lady."

"So, did you wear one of those white curly powdered wigs back in the human time in Europe? The ones like the judges wore?" I asked him.

He walked next to me and said, "I did wear a peruke and I looked fantastic in it."

"He looked like a ninny," Dmitri said.

Victor rolled his eyes. "You did not look any manlier in knee length breeches and stockings."

"Can we please not focus on the fashion of such a dreadful time period?" Dmitri asked. "Can't we focus instead on the nineteen seventies? Those were wonderful years."

"That was a terrible time!" Victor exclaimed. "You have terrible taste in dress."

"Says the man wearing a puffy pirate shirt in the twenty-two hundreds," Dmitri said as he pointed at the shirt Victor was currently wearing.

I tried not to laugh, but I could not help it after the indignant look Victor gave Dmitri.

"Artemis," Apollo said behind me.

We all spun around and Victor moved in front of me in a protective stance.

"What are you doing here?" Victor hissed.

"I came to aid Artemis," he said.

"How did you locate us?" I asked him. "And how long have you been able to teleport?"

He shrugged. "I don't know. I just closed my eyes and focused on the tingle that tells me where you are and when I opened my eyes, I was behind you."

"Wait, you can locate me?" I asked him.

He nodded his head. "Don't you feel it? Can't you feel the tingle in the center of your head?"

Now that he mentioned it I could. I had just assumed it was part of the sickness of Ares' or because of the baby. I never imagined it was because he was my twin. "I never really thought about it," I answered softly.

"Go back," Victor commanded. "Ares is already fighting one person because of you."

"That is hardly fair." I frowned at Victor. "Apollo has done nothing to me since he surrendered and has tried to prove his desire to turn around from his previous life."

"He killed Achilles," Victor reminded me.

I turned my head away, fighting the emotions inside of me and the tears trying to leak out. "He did not know what he was doing. He had been brainwashed."

"Achilles would not so easily forget your death," Victor hissed.

I slapped him across the face before I thought better of it. "How dare you!" I screamed. "I have not forgotten Achilles' death. I ache from his loss every day but dwelling on the dead does not bring them back. Achilles came to me and told me to make amends with my brother and that is what I am trying to do."

"She slapped you," Dmitri whispered. "She actually hit you."

"I know," Victor said.

I wasn't sorry that I hit him, and I was not going to apologize for it just to calm him either. He had deserved that slap and he knew it. Victor laughed and shook his head. "I'm sorry, Artemis. Still, I cannot allow him to accompany us."

I groaned. "Why are you all so stubborn?"

"It's alright," Apollo said, "Just promise me that you'll be careful?" he asked softly.

I smiled. "I'm always careful."

Every one of them laughed at that, which I found incredibly rude. Apollo closed his eyes and disappeared. "Let's continue," Dmitri said.

I opened my mouth to say something to Victor, but he rested his hand on my shoulder and shook his head. "Let's forget it," he whispered, "I deserved your slap for being cruel."

The sound of a dragon screaming filled the night air from far away and instantly brought tears to my eyes. Without waiting for the others or even thinking about the possibilities of this being a trap, I flew up into the air and flapped my wings for all they were worth.

"Artemis, wait," Victor called.

"No," I said as I flew faster. "I will not abandon them in their time of need. I will rescue them. No one makes the dragons bleed. No one!"

CHAPTER 13
VICTOR

I had hoped to shelter her from the fight that we would encounter when we found the dragons, but once she had heard the pain-filled scream of one, she would not be stopped. She flew ahead of us, her body glowing as she prepared to rescue one of the dragons whom she called friend.

It was still incredibly strange to me that the dragons and she were so fond of each other. Then again who was I to judge a strange friendship? Many had found Ares' and my friendship strange and unnatural and many still did. Perhaps I was too quick to judge others despite my attempts not to.

We raced through the wooded area, following the path they had created by dragging the dragon and the sound of the fight ahead of us. It was hard to keep up with Artemis, but I refused to leave her side since Ares was not here.

The sound of fighting grew louder and then we finally witnessed the chaos that was ensuing. Forty vampires were attacking Draco Blu and the dragon was holding his own, biting, clawing and decapitating vampires faster than the vampires could defend themselves. I took in the scene in less than a second, but it was already too slow because Artemis had joined in the fight. She grabbed a vampire, ripped him in half and then tossed the halves of his body into two other vampires, which allowed Draco Blu to grab them and bite their heads off. The two work easily together, never getting in the others way and seemed to anticipate the other's moves. It was incredible, and after two minutes, my presence was completely unnecessary.

Bartholomew ran from the shadows of the trees and leapt at Artemis, attempting to grab her. She saw him coming and teleported behind him. Bartholomew spun around and would have grabbed her if Draco Blu had not been there. Draco Blu grabbed Bartholomew with one of his giant Dragon's feet and slammed him into the ground, digging his claws into the dirt and pinning Bartholomew in place. Draco Blu growled at him and was about to engulf him in fire, but Artemis placed her hand on Draco Blu's shoulder and the dragon stilled.

"What is Maurice planning?" she asked Bartholomew, landing on the ground and folding in her wings so that she could stand and stare into his eyes.

"The King is planning on ridding this planet of the existence of werewolves and sidhe," he said.

"You don't have an army big enough for that," I said.

Bartholomew smiled and I did not like it at all. "Our plan is strong."

"You mean your plan to send vampires to kill the people who are not protected since all of the strongest warriors will be at the main battle?" Artemis asked.

Bartholomew's face scrunched in anger. "How did you know that?"

"Your king told me."

"No matter, we will still rule."

"Your plan will not work. We will kill any vampire who opposes us," she said looking as regal as ever.

She turned away from him and walked to the still body of a red dragon and knelt at its side. "Blu, you may dispose of the vampire however you wish."

"You need me," Bartholomew said.

"You killed my son. The only one who needs you is Death," Draco Blu said and then breathed fire onto Bartholomew until even his bones disintegrated.

Artemis wept as she lay across the dead dragon's neck. "I am sorry, Fira. I should have gotten to you sooner. I should have kept you all away from this."

Draco Blu lay down beside Artemis, wrapping his neck around her and his dead son and hummed a sorrowful tune. We watched them in silence, but after an hour Dmitri whispered, "The sun, Victor."

I rested my hand on his shoulder and teleported him and I to the darkened chambers he was sleeping in at Zeus' place and then teleported back to Artemis. When I returned she had stopped crying and was glowing as anger replaced her sadness. "Let's go get the egg back."

"We already got the dragon's egg back before you regained your memory," I reminded her.

"They took the Pegasus egg that I was bringing as a gift," Draco Blu said. "One of the vampires left the group as soon as they took it and returned to your King."

"If we go there now, we will be outnumbered and outmatched. We should wait for others to go with us," I pleaded.

Artemis looked at me and I had never seen her look so much like a Queen before. "Then we will return, and the war shall begin."

CHAPTER 14
SELENE

The battle between Ares and Koda was intense and very bloody. The ground around them was soaked in blood as they cut each other again and again, but their bodies healed the wounds and allowed them to continue on.

The audience had originally numbered in the thousands, but after two days of fighting it had dwindled to just their other pack members, Artemis' twin Apollo, and myself. I had seen Artemis teleport away the first day, which was probably for the best. The further away she was from Ares, the better she would feel and the more likely the baby and she would get healthy again. If it were up to me, I would send her and Ares to opposite sides of the world, but sadly it was not up to me.

The sounds of Koda and Ares' growls were the only noises in the Sidhe realm. It seemed that they were trying to be respectful, but part of me wondered how many of the Sidhe were hoping for Ares' loss, and even his death. They had agreed not to end this fight by death, but in the heat of the moment, things were known to happen, and more than one werewolf had died by the angry hands of another despite their prior agreement.

I doubted Koda would kill Ares, if he could, due to Artemis' declaration that if Koda killed Ares, she would kill Koda. I had seen the hurt in Koda's eyes, and like everyone, I knew that he loved her. How much pain was he enduring mentally as he fought his only remaining brother, knowing that if he killed him, the woman he loved would attempt to end his life?

I shook my head and sat down on the ground, smoothing out my dress as I did. Werewolf politics were always crazy, and it seemed even with Ares and Artemis in charge, that had not changed. I had already prepared my spell to use on Ares to cure him from Death's curse and I was certain I would not fail. I just prayed to the Goddess that we could perform the spell before Artemis and her child were affected too badly.

Koda and Ares backed away from each other and squatted down to rest for a moment. Koda's face was a mask of anger, while Ares' was stoic as usual when Artemis was not around.

Did he realize that his regal mask shattered the instant his mate was near him? I had known him hundreds of years, and it was good to see him so happy with a mate.

Two of Koda's sons walked out to Koda and Ares and gave them each one cup of water. Ares sipped it slowly, while Koda gulped it down. The brothers were not so different from each other really, but men refused to see the similarities in one another, especially when they loved the same woman.

Ares turned and looked at me, his eyes the molten gold of his wolf. "Artemis?" he asked in a clipped word. He was so tired and so frustrated that he could barely speak.

I shook my head. "Still gone."

He growled.

My hair rose at the predator's rumble. "She is safe. Victor, Dmitri, Theseus, and a couple others went after her to keep her safe."

He stood and growled again. Then he stretched out his body and regained control of his wolf. He stood straight and tall and even though his eyes were still his wolf's eyes, he was calm and collected once again. "Let's finish this so I can go find her."

"I would advise you to stay away from her," I said.

He turned and looked at me and I could see that his control was a hair's breadth away from slipping if he was pushed the wrong way. "Why?"

"The farther apart you are, the less sick she will be," I explained.

He growled. "I don't like being away from her or trusting others with her safety."

"You will like it less if your nearness causes her death," I admonished him with a scowl. I had grown attached to Artemis while she lived in the coven as Chandra. How I hadn't put two and two together was truly a mystery. Perhaps it had to do with Hera's spell? Or, I had just been blinded by the desire to protect Artemis like so many of these men were.

Ares growled and took a step towards me. I was only slightly afraid because I could incapacitate him long enough to get away and I knew he really did not want to hurt me. I did not have to do anything though, because Koda tackled Ares, taking advantage of his distracted opponent and not for the first time protecting me.

Seeing Koda's children had been hard, as I had fallen for the wolf at one time, but I'd let him go a century ago. Koda was a wonderful person, but we were not a good match.

The brothers attacked each other again and again and despite my gnawing hunger, I stayed where I was. Artemis would ask for details, and I would be sure to have answers for her when she finally returned.

"Would you like some bread and cheese?" Zeus asked as he sat down beside me on the grass.

I took a piece of cheese and swallowed it whole before answering him. "Thank you. I am famished."

"I see not much has changed in their fight," he said, letting my rudeness slide without remark.

"Pretty much. They are both slower and more tired, but aside from that there has not been any progress," I reported. "And both are still in control of their wolves." Which was a very good thing. We did not need a rampaging werewolf on our hands, especially not one as strong as these two.

"Any sign of Artemis?" he asked with pinched eyebrows and a tight jaw.

"No, but I am sure she is fine. Victor and Theseus would never let anything happen to her," I assured him.

Zeus laughed and said, "I never expected the friendship between Ares and Victor to last so long. Most of us figured they would end up killing each other within the week, but thousands of years later their friendship is as strong as ever."

"The hatred between the races seems to have died out, especially in the last hundred years. It gives me hope that perhaps after we defeat Maurice, we will be able to unite all of the races and live peacefully," I whispered.

"That is the dream," Zeus said wistfully. We ate the food and watched the brothers fight in silence after that.

As the sun set, I prepared to nap a moment, but then Artemis appeared in front of me and sat down without even looking in my direction.

"Zeus, can you ask a servant to get me food?" she asked in a deep voice.

"They are already on their way to the kitchen," he said, moving closer to her.

"Stay back," she warned him. "Ares is losing control and I'm not at my best either. It would be better if everyone stayed a bit away, so we do not feel threatened."

"What happened?" I asked her.

"Vampires killed Fira and stole a Pegasus egg. We're leaving to start the war in three days."

"Ares and Koda will need time to heal," Zeus reminded her.

"They will be left behind then," she said coldly. "We don't have time to wait for them."

"I take it you have a plan," Zeus asked.

Why was he so calm and relaxed about her appearance and actions?

I wanted to drag her to her room and put her on bedrest as it was, but since she had told us to stay back, I assumed that meant her wolf was a bit too close for comfort.

She nodded. "Split up in teams. Save my Pegasus egg. Burn down any who oppose us."

"What about your baby?" I asked her, my eyes wide and shock almost palpable.

"He will be born tomorrow," she answered. "You will deliver him, and he will stay here in the Sidhe realm while we fight."

"What do you mean 'he'?" I asked, eyes wide.

"A mother knows," she whispered as she watched her mate and her packmate fight.

What must she be feeling, watching them battle?

"How do you know he is ready to be born tomorrow?" Zeus asked her.

Her eyes stayed glued to the fight as she continued answering us. "Victor told me the baby is ready. He said he wants out now."

"What?" Zeus and I gasped at the same time. I knew he could read minds, but how could he read a baby's mind?

She waved her hand dismissively. "Don't ask. It's not important. Just be ready to perform the spell and deliver my baby tomorrow."

"Why the sudden change in attitude?" I whispered to Zeus.

He shrugged and then whispered back, "It could be the dragon's death. She becomes emotionally attached to her companions, and it makes sense that she would become focused after an event like this."

I wasn't so sure, but I dared not question her when she was so close to the edge. I rose and headed to my chambers to prepare for the spell and prayed to the goddess that everything would go according to plan.

For once.

CHAPTER 15
ARTEMIS

I switched forms while I slept and when I woke, I was still in my wolf form, lying on the grass outside.

Ares and Koda were still fighting which astonished me and angered me at the same time. I wanted to march out there and slap some sense into them, but I knew I could not interfere with the challenge and had to let them finish.

One of the Sidhe servants brought me out a plate of meat and set it down a few feet from me.

"Anything else, Princess?" she asked softly.

I shook my head and waited until she was gone before eating every last piece of meat and licking my paws and snout clean to get any traces left. The baby was making me very hungry and I was having cravings for sugar and meat, although those cravings were not altogether abnormal for me.

Ares and Koda separated to catch their breaths and Ares finally noticed me.

I locked eyes with him a moment and then turned my head away to show my disapproval.

"Artemis," he whispered, "are you alright?"

I turned around, flicking my tail at him and let him look at my butt as I laid down again with my head between my paws.

I can still communicate with you, even if you want to show me your cute butt.

I sighed, really hating werewolf telepathy. *Hurry up and finish your fight. Our child is going to be born today.*

"What?" he asked out loud instead of telepathically.

"What's wrong?" Koda asked.

"She said the baby is going to be born today," Ares answered.

"Then I will stop toying with you and end this." I heard Koda slam into Ares and I cringed, thankful that he could not see me wince at the impact.

I turned around and watched, shocked that their fighting intensified despite this challenge having lasted multiple days without any food.

Was I that strong? Could I handle a fight like that?

Of course, you could, Ares said. He ducked underneath Koda's punch and caught Koda with a sidekick as he darted away.

I growled. *Focus on your fight.*

Our pack had slowly moved closer and closer to me, subconsciously yearning for the nearness of their Alpha female while their Alpha male was engaged in a fight that they could not help him with.

I stretched out and pretended to doze in the warmth of the sun, and they all moved ten feet closer to me, the fear of Ares the only thing keeping them so far from me as it was.

Apollo was among them, but he was the farthest from me, which was smart.

"I submit!" Ares yelled.

I sat upright and growled. What had happened? Why did he submit?

Koda stood over Ares, his claws too close to Ares' throat. "You never could figure out how to counter that attack," Koda said. He plopped to the ground beside Ares and groaned.

"Sneaky," Ares said. He stood up and cleared his throat. "By submission I announce the new Alpha of the Werewolves, Koda."

The pack cheered, everyone except Ares, Koda, and me. Ares walked to me, his body stiff and weariness in his movements. "Let's go to our room," he said.

I stood up and touched my nose to his hand and then teleported us into our room. He collapsed on the bed and sighed. "Thank you. I do not think I could have made it to our room if I had had to walk all the way."

I shifted and then laughed at him. "Of course, you could have. You would not have let the others see such a weakness."

"Are you upset?" he asked me.

I weighed my answer. "I am not sure how to answer your question. Can you be more specific?"

"Are you upset that I submitted?" he asked.

I shook my head and sat on the bed beside him, resting my hand on my handsome mate's face. "No. In fact it feels good knowing that we do not have to rule the werewolves and that the pack is in such good hands."

"You know I submitted on purpose, right?"

I laughed. "Of course, I do. You would not be so easily defeated."

He smiled. "Let's not tell Koda, alright? It's best if he and the rest of the world believe that Koda is the rightful Alpha. I am weary of trying to wrangle you and a thousand werewolves at the same time."

I kissed his cheek and then wrinkled my nose in disgust. "You need a shower."

He rolled on his back, grabbed me, and pulled me down onto my side with my head on his chest. "All I need is you."

I put his hand on my stomach and whispered, "He wants out."

"He?" Ares asked.

I nodded and smiled. "Our son is ready to come out. I suppose that means we should give him a name."

"It's too early for him to come out," Ares said despite the happiness I saw at the news of having a son.

I shrugged. "Victor told me that the baby is ready to come out, and I feel that he is right."

"So, what shall we name him?" Ares asked.

"You can think of names *after* you shower," I said, sitting up and pushing his side.

"Fine," he said, dashing to the bathroom and returning a few minutes later smelling like roses. "Cratus."

"What?" I asked since I had not been paying attention.

He sat down on the bed beside me and spoke in a soft voice as he ran his fingers through my hair. "I would like to name him Cratus."

"Cratus," I repeated, letting the name roll off my tongue so I could try it out. I nodded. "I like it."

Ares smiled. "That was easier than I thought."

"I'm not *always* difficult," I said defensively.

"Only ninety percent of the time," he teased me and then kissed my temple.

Dizziness overwhelmed me, so I gracefully fell onto my side, thankful I was already sitting on the bed.

"Artemis?" Ares asked, concerned at the sudden movement.

"Dizzy," I whispered.

"I'll call Kod—" Ares stopped and laughed. "I guess I can't summon Koda anymore. I'll go get Selene."

I grabbed his hand before he could stand up. "No, don't leave. It'll pass in a moment." The baby started kicking and I groaned at the fierce kicks. "Never mind, get her."

He rested his hand on my stomach, lowered his face until his lips were pressed against my skin and growled, "Calm down, pup."

Surprisingly, the baby listened, and the kicking stopped. "You're amazing," I whispered in awe.

"Let's hope this still works when he is a teenager," Ares said with a laugh.

"What age do you consider a preternatural a teenager?" I asked him curiously. "Humans consider thirteen to nineteen a teenager, but that's not really a teenager for a preternatural."

Ares said, "Trust me. You will know when he is in the teenage years. When he starts rebelling it will be obvious."

"Let's hope he does not tear down an entire civilization during his teenage years like his father," Zeus said as he entered the room.

Ares sighed. "You're never going to let me live that down, are you?"

Zeus frowned at him. "You obliterated an entire civilization. That is not something to easily forget."

"Who are you talking about?" I asked curiously.

Zeus threw his hands up into the air and said, "That's the point! No one even remembers them."

"I was young and angry and stupid," Ares said. "And I will not let my son get so out of control."

"Good luck," Zeus said.

Selene entered the room and asked, "Are you ready, Ares? We should begin the spell to remove Death's sickness as soon as possible, especially if your child really is going to be born today."

"I need meat and about an hour of sleep and then I will be ready," Ares said.

One of Zeus' servants walked in with a tray piled high with steaks and set it on the table before quickly leaving.

It always interested me how Zeus' servants were so frightened of Ares. Had they seen him at his worst and that was why they were so frightened?

Ares sat at the table and ate his food in silence.

I closed my eyes and then smelled and heard Selene walk over to me. "Are you feeling alright?" she asked.

"I got dizzy for a minute, and then Cratus began kicking and hurting me, but Ares made him calm down."

"Cratus? Him?" Selene asked. "How do you know?"

"I sort of let it slip," Victor said, materializing beside Ares. He looked down at Ares and said, "So, you passed the reins on to your brother?"

"He beat me," Ares said with a shrug. Victor was silent a moment, so I knew Ares was telling him about keeping the fact that he had let him win a secret. Ares resumed eating his steaks and I closed my eyes to rest.

Selene whispered a spell so softly even I could not hear it and then the baby kicked. "Ow," I said. "Don't get him riled up again."

She smiled. "I will try to keep him calm while I check him out." She resumed running her hands along my stomach and then said, "Well, he or she, is in good health, but strangely has grown exponentially. You are right that you could go into labor any time now."

"Okay, everyone out so I can take a nap," Ares said. "If I don't get some sleep, no one is going to like being around me." I started to get up and he shook his head at me. "Not you. You are staying right here with me."

Zeus and Victor left, whispering conspiratorially to each other and Selene stopped at the door. "I'll be back in two hours to get you for the spell."

Ares nodded and laid down on the bed beside me. He scooted over and draped his arm across my waist, below my bulging belly. "I'm surprised that he grew so quickly without hurting you, but I'm glad too."

"Let's not look a gift horse in the mouth," I said. "Honestly, I don't even know when it happened. I know that while I was searching for Blu with Victor, I felt heavier, but I thought it had something to do with the sickness Death gave you."

"I can't wait to hold him," Ares whispered.

"Will he come out in human form?" I asked.

He nodded and kissed my cheek. "You know we don't change until after we hit puberty."

"Yes, but you and I aren't exactly normal werewolves. Stranger things have happened."

He kissed my cheek again and whispered, "Let's sleep. Soon we will not have time for naps like this."

~

THE NAP WAS INTERRUPTED before I wanted it to end and no amount of begging kept Ares in bed with me.

Ares left with Selene to perform the spell and I was ordered to stay in bed and as far from the place of the spell as possible. Victor was left to guard me, and I stayed lying on the bed despite knowing how rude it was of me. I wanted to pace or to run out to watch everything, but I could not. I hated being helpless.

Food was brought to me and I sat at the little table in the room and ate it while Victor watched me with a strange expression on his face.

"What?" I finally asked. "Why are you looking at me like that?"

"I'm listening to Cratus," he whispered. "I've never listened to a baby's thoughts before. It's intriguing."

"What's he thinking?" I asked.

"Well, children in general think less with words and more with feelings, especially Cratus since he has not been outside of your womb to see anything yet. He wants to stretch but it's too tight in your stomach."

"He'll be out soon enough," I mumbled.

"Are you going to talk to Koda?" Victor asked.

I grit my teeth and sat up slowly, my belly even larger now. "Eventually."

"He challenged Ares because he injured you. He felt he was defending your honor."

"He is an idiot. Hurting Ares only angers me."

"He wouldn't have hurt—"

"He was going to fight him to the death!" I screamed, interrupting him.

"He would have stopped before that," Victor said. His tone told me that he knew that for certain, which he probably did since he could read thoughts.

"Only after I told him that I would kill him if he killed Ares," I said adamantly. I had meant it, too. Even now, the thought made my blood boil.

"You shocked him when you said that," said Victor with a shake of his head. "You broke his heart."

"Hopefully, he will go find a mate now." It would be good for him to be on his own.

"You'll miss him," Victor said softly.

"Of course, I will, but it's time that Ares and I go off on our own."

"Your mother-in-law is coming," Victor whispered.

I heard her approaching footsteps and then she knocked twice on the door, not waiting for permission before she entered the room and closed the door behind her. She hurried to me and rested her hand on my round belly. "I hadn't believed the rumors, but they are true! How could you have progressed so much so quickly? How are you?"

I smiled at her and patted her hand. "We are fine. I thought you would be with Ares."

She smiled. "He and Selene can handle the spell. Are you ready for labor?"

I dipped my head and admitted, "I'm frightened of the labor."

She patted my hand reassuringly. "It will hurt, but you are strong, and you will do fine."

"Have you heard news about the baby's gender and name?" I asked her. I had wanted to tell her, Zeus, and Hera right away, but we had not had the time.

She narrowed her eyes, and her body stiffened. "You picked a name?"

"You will have a grandson and his name will be Cratus."

"Cratus," she whispered as if trying to recall a memory. She tapped her finger twice and then laughed. "Ares picked the name, didn't he?"

"How'd you know?" I asked, narrowing my eyes suspiciously.

"It was an alter ego of Ares' when he was younger. It's fitting that your halfbreed child inherits it," she answered.

"I had forgotten about that," Victor said.

Cratus kicked hard and then tried to stretch out. I moaned and lay down onto my back to give him more room.

Beatrice rested her hand on my stomach and then looked at Victor. "See how long until the spell is over."

I screamed as my stomach contracted again and again in quick succession.

Beatrice frowned and held my hand. "Your son is coming."

CHAPTER 16
VICTOR

I teleported to the Sidhe mound outside the portal where they were performing the spell. Surprisingly, the spell was done, and Ares and Selene were sitting side by side, panting on the ground.

"Did the spell work?" I asked.

They both nodded.

"Then come with me."

Ares and Selene stood stiffly, and Ares asked, "What's wrong?"

I smiled. "Your son is being born."

~

AFTER TELEPORTING Ares and Selene to Artemis, I teleported to Anabelle, my love. Artemis was adamant about attacking father as soon as she was able to, which meant that I had very little time to say goodbye, and I intended to use all the time I could. I pictured Anabelle's face as I teleported, but arrived as mist to surprise her.

As soon as I arrived, the scent of her blood engulfed me. I materialized and dropped to the ground, taking in the scene before me. Blood covered every wall, piece of furniture, and the floor. The blood was only a couple of days old.

Anabelle lay in pieces across the room, her head motionless on the pillow, a scream stuck on her face. Her beautiful hair was matted with her own blood and stuck to the pillow. I turned towards her mirror to find a message written in her blood. I recognized the writing instantly as my father's.

You can't hide from me, son.

I had kept Anabelle a secret from everyone. She was the first woman I had fallen in love with in my entire life. The first woman whose smile alone could brighten my day.

Now, she was gone. I would never see her smile. I would never hear her laugh. I would never hold her warm body in my arms again.

The emotions I had been holding in broke free.

I screamed in sorrow and anger.

The one woman I had dared to love had been taken from me by my own father. I would kill him for this. I would rip his wretched heart from his body and tear him into pieces like he had done Anabelle, and my heart. And then I would burn every last piece of him.

Two men spoke outside her house and before I had even consciously made the choice, I was outside feasting on their blood. I lifted my blood-soaked face to the sky and screamed.

Tonight, I would feast on every man I saw and tomorrow, I would kill my father.

CHAPTER 17
ARES

Artemis dozed on the bed, still recovering from the 20-hour labor, two days later.

Cratus was perfect. With my hair and Artemis' purple eyes, he was going to be a ladies' man.

"You're spoiling him," Artemis whispered.

"And I will continue to every day I am with him," I whispered back, rocking the tiny baby in my arms.

Mother walked in and set a tray with a salad, fruits, and meat on Artemis' lap. "Eat every piece," she ordered her.

"Yes, ma'am," Artemis said, and tucked in.

Cratus moved and then started fussing.

"He can't be hungry already," Artemis said with a groan. We had been awake most of the last two days with our incredibly hungry newborn.

"I'll feed him," I offered as I walked to Selene who had already prepared a bottle for him.

Due to Artemis' desire to leave for battle tomorrow, she had opted not to breastfeed. So, the Sidhe had prepared their substitute for breastmilk and were supplying it to us. They had also taught

Selene and Artemis how to create some replacement milk magically in case of emergency.

I walked around the room slowly as he ate his bottle and let him hold one of my fingers in his tiny hand. I burped him occasionally, and then when he was done and had fallen asleep, I set him in Artemis' arms so that she could bond with him more.

The instant his skin touched hers, he drew in a deep breath and sighed happily, cuddling up against her. Artemis cradled him to her chest and lay down, cuddling with Cratus as she dozed. She looked so peaceful as she held him, and I felt that peace in me as well.

This was what I wanted after the war was over. As soon as the victory was declared in this war, we would go to one of my properties and bond as a family.

Zeus walked in and hugged me with one arm. "He's going to be a handful."

I smiled and said, "I think I've become used to it with Artemis."

She did not respond which meant she was finally asleep.

"Have you heard from Victor?" Zeus asked quietly as we walked to the other side of the room to avoid waking either of them.

I shook my head. "No. The last time I saw him was when he teleported me here for Cratus' birth two days ago. I thought he was just giving us space."

"No one has seen him in those two days. Not even Dmitri," he said.

That was not like Victor. He had disappeared randomly before, but it was usually just to feed and then he would return in less than half a day's time. Most of those times he took Dmitri with him, though.

Someone knocked softly on the door, and then Theseus poked his head in. "You need to come outside," he whispered to me. I could smell his fear and judging by the whiteness of his skin, he was not accustomed to what he had witnessed.

Mother waved me out, sitting in a chair facing Artemis and

Cratus. I could not ask for a better bodyguard than her, so I followed Theseus and Zeus outside of the castle.

The sun was beginning to set, and there, in the center of the grass, sitting on his knees was Victor, covered in blood. I inhaled and was surprised to find that none of the blood on him was his own.

"Victor?" I asked. "Are you alright?"

He looked up at me and the pain in his eyes reminded me of when I had lost Artemis. "Are we ready for battle?" he asked with a lisp due to his fangs extending past his lower lip.

It had been centuries since I'd seen him fail to keep his fangs within his mouth.

"We're leaving tomorrow morning," I said, moving closer to him. I continued to keep my composure because in situations where someone went ballistic, one person needed to remain calm. I had seen him snap before and I had seen him slaughter an entire island of people in minutes. "Artemis needs one more night of rest."

He took a deep breath and stood up, the emotions locked away and his Court face on. "I'll go wash up."

He walked into the castle and I said, "Keep everyone away from his chambers for the next hour. He is composing himself, and if someone bothers him during that time, he could snap again."

Theseus trotted off into the castle obediently.

Zeus asked, "What do you think happened?"

"I have no idea," I whispered. Although I had a feeling that whatever had happened had just ensured our victory over Maurice.

CHAPTER 18

ARTEMIS

"Waah," Cratus cried, waking me up from my peaceful sleep.

I opened my eyes and kissed his little head where it lay on the bed beside me. "Shh, it's alright, Cratus. Mommy is here." I sat up and Beatrice handed me a bottle to feed him.

"Ares was hungry all the time, like him. I thought he was going to suck me dry," she said with a laugh. "Part of me wished I could have fed him while in my wolf form because that form had three sets of teats to feed him from instead of one pair."

I laughed and cradled Cratus in my arm as I fed him his bottle. "Are you going to watch him while Ares and I go to fight?" I asked her. "I won't feel safe leaving him with anyone, but you." I was extremely thankful for her help since Cratus was born. She had stayed in the room to lend me a hand anytime I asked and had even slept in the chair by my bedside.

"Of course, I will stay and protect him," she said. She looked around and then whispered, "I don't fully trust the Sidhe still. Part of me is worried that they might try to hurt Cratus while you and Ares are gone."

I didn't say it aloud, but I agreed with her, and sadly felt exactly the same. Even though Hera had seemed to have a change of heart about me after Achilles died, I did not trust the stableness of her emotions, and I did not trust her to be alone with Cratus. They'd already killed one of Ares' children. I wouldn't let them kill another.

"Five more minutes," Ares groaned from the bed beside me.

Beatrice and I rolled our eyes at the same time and she said, "You stop being Alpha for three days and suddenly think you get to sleep in? You're still Beta, you know?"

"I've always been Beta," he said through his pillow. "I'll always be Beta, too. That does not mean that I never get a day to sleep in."

"It is attack day," Victor said. "No one gets to sleep in."

Cratus jumped at the strange voice and spit out his bottle. His little eyes filled with tears as he started crying, and then suddenly stopped. He looked at Victor and then took his bottle back and relaxed against me.

"What was that?" I asked softly, shocked by the sudden rapid changes in his mood.

"Victor used his powers to calm him," Ares said from under his pillow. "I'd appreciate you not doing it again."

"I was simply calming him down since I startled him by my sudden appearance. I would never use my powers on him for anything else," Victor said.

There was something off about Victor. Something different in the way he was acting today. Had something happened?

Ares lifted his head out from under his pillow and lifted a brow at Victor.

Victor smiled and said, "I am fully in control of myself now."

"Are you going to tell me what happened?" Ares asked.

I was right!

Victor sat in the chair beside Beatrice and sighed, "Another time. Let's not get anyone else riled up before we get to the fight."

"The troops are ready," Zeus said as he entered the room.

"Just once, I'd like a room where people didn't pop in unannounced or whenever they wanted," I muttered.

Ares sat up and kissed my cheek. "Soon enough, we will be on our way to our own house where no one but our family of three will be."

"As if you could keep me away," Beatrice said and scoffed with arms folded across her chest, leveling Ares with a challenging glare.

"The dragons have arrived outside the mound," Koda announced as he entered the room. "Artemis, I need you to go greet them." He looked taller and bigger, but I knew he had not grown, and it was simply because he was the Alpha now. Despite still being angry at him, I had to admit he looked good, and being Alpha seemed to suit him.

I gritted my teeth and closed my lips tightly to keep from baring them at him. "I will get dressed and go see them," I said in a clipped tone.

Koda softened and became the friend and packmate I remembered. "Artemis, please don't be mad at me."

I did not answer him and instead, handed Cratus to Ares and walked to the bathroom to get ready.

After the war was over, Koda and I would talk, but until then I needed to stay away from him, or I would punch him in the face… a few times.

Victor chuckled, and I sighed, knowing I was being childish again.

I braided my hair and got dressed into the battle gear that Hephaestus had made me. I was thankful for being a preternatural and being completely healed and recovered from giving birth already.

Tears built up in my eyes, and I wiped them away quickly. It was harder than I thought to think about leaving Cratus, but I had to do it. I had to end this war and right the balance between all of the races. Beatrice would protect him and take great care of him, and hopefully it would not be too long before I returned and was able to hold him again.

Ares walked inside the bathroom and hugged me. "You don't have to go," he whispered. "You could stay with Cratus here, where it's safe."

I hugged him back and kissed his cheek. "You know I won't do that."

He sighed. "I know, but I had to try." We stayed in the bathroom holding each other for another minute, and then reluctantly separated.

I walked out to Beatrice who was still holding Cratus and took him for one last snuggle. I hugged him tightly and kissed his forehead. "Mommy loves you, Cratus. I'll be back soon."

Cratus looked at me in silence and I felt tears building again. I inhaled his scent, memorizing it and the feel of his baby soft skin, and then handed him back to Beatrice.

"I'll protect him with my life," she said, cradling him against her chest.

I nodded and left the room without another word, afraid that if I said anything else, I would not leave. I grabbed my bow and arrows as I walked out, slinging them over my back.

Koda followed me, but I ignored him and headed to the portal. We walked up the stairs, and I composed myself to face the dragons. My heart still hurt from the loss of Fira, but now was not the time for sadness. Now was the time for fierceness and battle.

I stepped from the portal and found fifty dragons waiting in the field. Stunned, I walked to Blu.

Blu wrapped his long neck around me in a hug, humming softly. "Hatchling, you look well. How is your child?"

"He is beautiful and perfect," I said with a wide smile. "He will stay with his grandmother while we destroy the vampire king."

"Thank you for coming," Koda said. "The werewolves and the alliance appreciate your assistance with this fight."

Blu looked at Koda a moment and then at me. "You are no longer Alpha?"

I shook my head. "Koda is now the Alpha of the Werewolves."

Blu dipped his head to Koda. "I did not know."

"I will go check on everyone else and let you know when we are ready to head out," Koda said. He looked at me a moment, words on his lips and a sad frown on his face, but then he strode back into the portal without a word.

"I did not know you and your packmember had had a falling out," Blu whispered.

"It's nothing worth discussing," I said and waved dismissively. "Did you leave enough dragons to guard the Hive?"

He nodded. "The Hive is well guarded."

"Good. When we arrive at the vampire's castle, I need your dragons to burn and destroy as much of the building as possible. You and I will go to Maurice's chamber and search for the Pegasus egg."

"It may have hatched already," Blu said with a growl. "The demon spawn may already have the baby in his hands."

"Then I shall cut his arms off and take the baby from him."

Blu roared in approval, and the other dragons roared with him.

Ares stepped through the portal but stopped at the sight of the roaring dragons. I held out my hand, and he walked slowly towards me, lifting a brow.

"Everyone is ready," he said once he took my hand.

I hugged him and kissed his lips softly. "Stay safe," I whispered.

He nuzzled behind my ear, and we inhaled each other's scents. "I love you."

I hugged him tighter. "I love you too, Ares."

He pulled back and looked at Blu. "I leave her in your capable claws. Please, keep her safe while we are apart."

Blu bowed his head. "I shall protect her like she is my own."

Ares kissed me again and then stepped into the portal.

It had been incredibly hard to convince him to fight separately, but I had finally won the argument when I had reminded him that he was needed to kill as many vampires as possible. Plus, I would be with Victor, Apollo, and Blu and with the three of them beside me I was sure to survive. I thought of Achilles and cringed. This fight would be different.

Apollo and Victor stepped out of the portal.

Apollo wore armor similar to mine. He smiled and said, "Hephaestus thought it would be fitting if the two of us had matching armor since we're twins."

"It looks good on you," I said with a smile.

"Ready?" Victor asked.

I took a long, deep breath before answering. "Yes."

Apollo took my hand and smiled reassuringly at me. "Let's kill some vampires, Sister."

I nodded, set a hand on Blu to teleport him, and closed my eyes as the other dragons who had the ability to teleport began humming. I opened my eyes after we arrived and found Hera standing at the front of the fight beside Zeus and Ares with the rest of our army behind them.

The dragons took to the skies and Apollo, Victor, and I joined them, circling around the top of our army.

The vampires were standing in formation across the field from our army, fear on their faces despite the fact that they still outnumbered us two to one.

"Tonight, we fight to end the false king's reign," Ares bellowed. "Tonight, we fight for our lost brothers and sisters. We fight to end the slaughter of the humans who cannot protect themselves. When this battle ends, the world will be rebalanced and all shall be equal. Humans, Sidhe, vampires, werewolves, elves, dwarves, ogres, and halfbreeds will all be equal! Kill all who oppose us. Kill them all!"

Our army cheered, screamed, roared, and howled. Then they all flew across the field into the waiting vampires, tearing into them before they were ready to start fighting.

"Now," I screamed.

Blu roared, and twenty of the dragons flew over the field. Starting at the vampires who were not yet engaged by our army, the dragons made a wall of flames that none could escape. They burned the vampires and any who stood with them as they flew towards the castle. In seconds, a third of the vampire army was destroyed. The rest of the dragons, Apollo and I headed to the castle.

The dragons began spitting out fireballs which grew hard as they flew and broke the castle everywhere it landed. Archers began to shoot at the dragons, so Apollo and I broke away, shooting them back with our sun-tipped arrows. Vampires exploded into ash as we shot them, and soon there were no more archers firing upon the dragons.

"There," I shouted as I pointed at the part of the castle where Maurice's chambers were and where Victor was standing on top of the building.

Blu spit a fireball straight at Victor who jumped out of the way. The fireball made the roof collapse, and we dropped into the giant room.

Maurice stood up from his throne and his eyes widened at the sight of Blu. "What are the dragons doing here?" he asked.

"Ensuring the world is returned to its rightful balance," Blu said. "And to watch you die."

Maurice held an egg in his hands.

I growled at him. "Give me back my egg."

He smiled. "This is my dragon egg."

"It's not a dragon," Victor said.

Maurice looked at Victor, noticing him for the first time. "My own son is here to fight against me."

"You killed her, and you thought I would forgive that and come to your side?" Victor asked with a snarl. "You're psychotic."

"You should have never taken that damn halfbreed's side!" Maurice yelled, pointing a finger at me.

"Your reign is over," Victor said. "It is time that I take the throne from you."

"You'll have to kill me first," Maurice hissed.

"I intend to," Victor said with a smile.

I darted forward at the same time as Apollo, as we tried to take the egg from Maurice.

Several vampires poured into the room from the side door and interrupted us. I turned my fingers into claws and began tearing into the vampires, ripping their heads off as I went.

"Back!" Blu shouted.

I grabbed Apollo and teleported back behind Blu as he doused the room in flames, killing all of the vampires who had come inside. Maurice and Victor fought to the right of the room, steering clear of the fire. Victor knocked the egg out of Maurice's hand, and I teleported to him, grabbed the egg, and teleported back to Apollo. "Protect Blu. I'm going to teleport this to the Sidhe realm and then I'll be right back."

Apollo nodded. I teleported to Ares' and my chambers, set the egg down in one of the chairs and smiled at Beatrice. "Guard this, too. It's a gift for Cratus from the dragons."

She nodded, cradling Cratus in her arms. I closed my eyes and teleported back to the battle.

Apollo fought a group of vampire-sidhe who were flying above Blu, trying to shoot him with arrows.

I used my sunlight magic, turning them all to ash.

"Thank you," Blu said and then blew out a jet of flames through the door as vampires began to surge inside.

"You alright?" I asked Apollo.

He nodded, gasping for air. "Just catching my breath."

Victor and Maurice were still battling it out, and it looked like an even match. I wanted to help him in some way but did not want to end up hurting Victor in the process.

What could I do? How could I help him?

"Artemis!" Apollo yelled.

I spun around and ducked just in time to avoid an arrow aimed at my chest. Apollo returned fire, hitting the vampire with his arrow and turning him to ash.

That had been too close for comfort.

"Apollo, fly up and check on the other dragons," I said.

He obeyed instantly, flying upwards out of the hole in the ceiling.

"Are you okay?" I asked Blu. He nodded, and I flew up and out to the battle where Ares was tearing vampires apart in his half-shift. I flew down to him and joined in the battle.

"You're unhurt," he yelled so I could hear him. "I'm surprised."

"It's still early," I teased him.

He growled in response, and we took a moment to smile at each other before resuming our vampire killing spree.

It seemed strange that these vampires were so easy to kill. Were they all new? Had Maurice turned others just to increase his numbers for battle?

That wouldn't surprise me. He didn't view others as equals, but as pawns for his use.

After a bit, when there were fewer vampires around Ares and me, I teleported to Lyngvi and was happy to see a pile of dead vampires with Koda standing next to them in his half-shift, and children walking around unhurt.

"Everything went well?" I asked him.

He turned and his eyes raked my body, looking for wounds. "Yes. No one was hurt." He walked towards me with shaking hands.

I had mine behind me so he would not see the fists I was making.

"Good," I said.

"How is the battle going?" he asked, stopping a little ways away.

"Still going. I have to get back." I started to teleport, and he grabbed my wrist.

"When are we going to talk?" he asked me, pleading with his eyes.

I turned my head to avoid his eyes and whispered, "I don't know."

"Artemis, I—"

I jerked my hand away and teleported back to Blu.

Was it sad that the battle against the vampires was easier for me than my warring emotions about Koda? Part of me wanted to rip him apart for threatening Ares and for fighting him, while the other part of me wanted to forgive him and go back to being friends, before he told me he loved me, before it had all gone sour.

Blu was still fighting vampires, but he was definitely winning. In fact, he looked bored. I stood next to him and watched Victor and Maurice fight. I could hardly keep track of them.

Victor hit Maurice somehow and it hurt him enough that he stopped and put a hand against his ribs.

"You'll never defeat me!" Maurice screamed at Victor.

Victor ducked under his father's attack and then shoved his hand into his chest, grabbed ahold of his heart, and ripped it out. "You lost the moment you touched Anabelle."

Anabelle? Who was Anabelle?

Maurice's eyes widened and then he fell to the ground.

Victor squatted down and tore apart his father into small pieces . Once finished, he backed away and looked up at Blu. "Would you please torch him to ashes so that I may scoop up the remains and scatter him around the world?"

For someone who had just torn a being apart into tiny pieces, he was rather calm.

Blu exhaled a jet of flame onto the dismembered body until it was all ash.

Victor scooped up the ashes, putting them inside a clear vial, which he then put inside a leather pouch that smelled of sage and rosemary mixed with something faintly smelling like blood. He tied the pouch shut and held it in front of his face. "It was a long reign, Father, but you should have known it would come to this."

Apollo dropped down and said, "The vampires stopped fighting everywhere, even in the locations across the world."

Victor smiled. "The war is over, and a new king has taken the throne." Victor looked at me and said, "You will never have to worry about the vampires again."

It seemed too easy. It seemed like it had ended too quickly to be real.

Victor placed his hand on my shoulder and whispered, "It is over. With your help, I learned to love, and having that love taken away from me prompted my decision to kill Maurice." He kissed my cheek and said, "You are right, there is no reason that every race cannot live together peacefully, and we should remember that we were once humans as well. Come, let's go speak to the world." He took my hand and I flew up into the air and out to the field where the two sets of troops stood facing each other uneasily.

I landed in the center, and Ares rushed out to me. "Are you hurt?" he asked, looking me over.

I took his hand and kissed his cheek. "I'm perfectly fine."

"Selene," Victor called.

She stepped from our battalion and approached Victor. "Yes?"

"Would you mind creating a global broadcast?" he asked.

She took a big breath and then spit into her hand.

Victor cocked an eyebrow and stared at her with an expression of confusion, which made me smile and laugh softly.

Selene drew a square on her hand in the spit and then held her hand up into the air. She chanted a spell I had never been able to master, and a large square appeared in front of Victor. "You may begin," she said.

Victor looked into the square and began his speech. "The world has been living in darkness, overshadowed by the preternaturals' desire to rule over the humans and subjugate them as they had done to us. The former King of the Vampires killed any who opposed him or any who he viewed as a possible threat. That king is dead. I, Victor, am the new King of the Vampires. As king, I vow to work with the Council of Beings to create a world where everyone can live peacefully together, including humans. From this moment on, there will be no more war."

Everyone cheered, throwing their hands up into the air or hugging each other.

Victor cleared his throat, and everyone calmed down again. "Any vampire who attacks another being, unprovoked, will answer to me, and I will not take it lightly. From now on, I own all vampires and you will all listen to me."

"Actually, we own everyone," said a female voice.

All eyes turned to face a woman of immense beauty and power with a man of equal attractiveness and power beside her. She looked out over the crowd until her eyes settled on me. "Hello, Artemis."

Ares appeared at my side and dropped to one knee, bowing to the two. "Greetings, Rhea and Hyperion."

Rhea smiled and the man Ares had called Hyperion folded his arms across his chest.

Rhea said, "Greetings, Son. Rise."

Ares stood and took a small step in front of me, which I hoped the visitors did not understand meant he was trying to protect me from them.

"I see that you were able to save your mate," she said and smiled sweetly.

Ares dipped his head. "Thanks to you, I was."

"She and you are a fitting couple," Hyperion said with an approving nod of his head and relaxed his arms.

"How is the child?" Rhea asked.

"He is doing well," Ares said.

"He," Hyperion said happily. "It is good that you have a male to continue on with your genes. You are a worthy offshoot of me."

"Have you chosen a name?" Rhea asked.

Why were they so interested in us? And what had they meant about owning everyone? What the hell was going on?

"Cratus Lupine," I answered her.

She smiled. "That is a fitting name for a halfbreed baby like him." She turned and looked at Hyperion, who I was beginning to believe was her mate. "Did you bring it with you like I asked?"

He pulled off a bag that had been hanging over his shoulder and opened it. "Of course, I did."

She reached inside and pulled out two beautiful silver rings that gleamed in the sun with strange symbols. "We have come baring gifts to those who are deserving," she said to the crowd. "Artemis Lupine, you and your mate, Ares, have shown true strength, devotion, and unwavering love despite times of trepidation. For your loyalty to the world, and each other, we present you with immunity to silver and absolute immortality." She placed one of the rings on my finger and the other on Ares' and then whispered, "May your love guide the hearts of others."

My finger burned a moment and then the silver stopped hurting. I looked at Ares.

He asked, "What do you mean absolute immortality?"

Hyperion pulled out a sword and cut off Ares' head. I stared down at the head of my mate and gasped. Seeing his head on the ground confused me enough that I couldn't move to react.

Rhea sighed, "You could have just told him. Why must you be so dramatic?"

"It is better that the world see the truth now so none try to test him," Hyperion said.

Rhea squatted down and picked up Ares' head, placed it on his shoulders, which I realized was even more strange because Ares' body had remained standing. Then, in total awe, we all watched as his neck reattached itself to his body and Ares shuddered and said, "That was unpleasant."

"You get used to it," Hyperion said with a smile as he patted Ares' back.

"You can shift back now," Rhea whispered to me.

I looked down and realized I had taken a half-shift. When had I shifted? I was still in too much shock and it took me a minute to focus enough to shift back to human form.

"Why are you giving so much to them?" Athena growled as she came up. "Why have you forsaken the rest of your children?"

Rhea looked at Athena with the sorrow of a mother whose child had gone astray. "You were given a chance to prove you were different, but you betrayed your daughter for your own selfish needs. Even if your daughter has forgiven you, it does not mean you deserved her forgiveness. Should I give you a gift for treachery?"

Athena stormed away with shame written plainly on her face. I felt bad for her, but in the same token, what had she expected Rhea to say?

Rhea turned to Ares and asked, "Are you sure that you do not want to be King of the Werewolves?"

Ares nodded. "The title rightfully belongs to Koda. I want to raise my pup with my mate without the stipulations of being Alpha."

"None are more dominant than you," Hyperion said and then added, "Except me."

Ares smiled. "Yes, but I am not fit to rule them as I would not put them before my mate or my pup."

Hyperion nodded in understanding.

Rhea said, "Then we have a proposal for you."

Ares tensed beside me, and I held my breath as we waited for her proposal. These beings were very old and anything they offered had to be weighed before an answer could be given.

"We would like you and Artemis to return to our home after your son and daughter are old enough to shift. At that time, we will teach you and your children all that we know, and you will become guardians of this world. Will you accept?"

"We don't have a daughter," I answered right away.

Rhea smirked and said, "Give it a year."

"What does being a guardian of this world entail?" Ares asked and moved closer to me.

"You are a smart boy," Rhea said with a laugh. "Very inquisitive."

"You would be charged with watching and preparing your children for restoring balance to the world should things get too out of hand," Hyperion said. "I believe you will have a very long time before the balance is shifted again."

"Why didn't you assist us if that is your charge?" I asked, frowning.

Rhea placed her hand on my cheek and whispered, "We have always been with you, child. We created you and protected you from your father and mother, and you flourished into a greater woman than I could have dreamed you would become. Through you, beings who thought they were soulless learned to love. How many can say that?"

I glanced at Victor and he smiled at me, though I could see pain within the pinched corners of his eyes.

"What say you?" Hyperion asked me with a stern expression.

I looked at Ares, and he whispered, "We knew we wouldn't be able to live alone forever anyway."

I laughed and then looked at Hyperion and gave him my most serious face. "We accept."

He smiled and clapped his hands together. The earth shook, causing everyone to wobble as we tried to maintain our balance, and then Hyperion grew taller and taller until he was too big to even fit on the planet. He continued to grow until he looked down at us from outer space and spoke with a voice that boomed. "By the powers as the Father of the Universe, I appoint Artemis Lupine, Ares Lupine, and their children as the Guardians of Peace."

"We accept," Ares and I said at the same time and then gaped at each other since we had not planned on saying anything.

The earth shook again and the tattoo that I had noticed on

Hyperion burned like fire as it was drawn on both Ares' forearm and mine. I growled at the pain but did not cry out.

Hyperion shrunk back down, landing lightly on his feet beside Rhea.

Rhea hugged me and kissed my cheek. "You have turned into a spectacular woman. I am so proud of you," she whispered into my ear.

Tears filled my eyes at the heartfelt approval, and I realized that Rhea was my true mother. Athena and Darren had simply been vessels, which had failed the test Rhea had given them.

"Thank you," I whispered and hugged her back.

She placed a necklace with a red heart around my neck and whispered, "Whenever you want to talk, press the necklace to your chest and Hyperion and I will be able to communicate with you."

I threw my arms around her neck as peace consumed me and I felt fulfilled for the first time.

She patted my back and laughed.

Beatrice cleared her throat and held out Cratus to me. "I figured you wouldn't want to wait another minute, since the battle was over."

I smiled my thanks to Beatrice, took Cratus, and nuzzled his neck, inhaling his scent and realizing that it was all over. Ares and I would be able to raise him in a peace-filled world, and we would be able to do it wherever we wanted without interruption.

Cratus nuzzled his face against mine and then Ares hugged me from the other side of Cratus and rested his face against Cratus' cheek. Cratus exhaled and relaxed between us.

"May I?" Hyperion asked, placing his bag on the ground and extending his hands out towards us.

Ares took Cratus from my arms and handed him to Hyperion without hesitation.

Rhea reached into the bag and grabbed a silver chain necklace and a golden rattle. "For Cratus."

"The necklace is the same as our rings?" I asked.

"Yes." She walked to Cratus and shook the rattle. "May I?"

Ares nodded, and she placed the necklace around Cratus' neck.

Cratus fussed a moment, but Hyperion bounced him in his arms softly and made soft shushing noises. The necklace shortened around his neck so that it was more of a choker than a long necklace like it had been.

Rhea put the rattle in Cratus' hand and showed him how to shake it.

He put the rattle in his mouth and relaxed.

"Why is he developing so quickly?" I asked Ares. "Humans don't develop this fast."

"We aren't human," Ares whispered to me. "He is developing as all preternaturals develop. By tonight he will be crawling and in a couple of days he will be walking."

Rhea turned to Victor and smiled. "You did well, Son of the Darkness. I will take the remains from you."

"Will you dispose of them?" he asked her as he held out the bag.

She nodded, took the bag, and threw it up into the air. It disappeared from our view and she said, "He will burn in the sun's flames."

Hyperion continued to play with the rattle and make cooing noises at Cratus, which dimmed his super tough persona and made me like him even more.

Rhea walked to Hera and Zeus, and considered them with a somber expression. "I cannot bring back your son permanently, but I can bring him back so that you may all say goodbye."

She waved her hands and Achilles appeared in front of Rhea. Hera gasped, but before she could reach him, I ran forward and threw my arms around Achilles' neck.

"I'm sorry," I cried as I hugged him.

He hugged me back and kissed the top of my head. "You have nothing to be sorry for. You and Ares belong together, and I was a fool to think that I could intervene."

"I—"

He put his finger against my mouth and stopped me from talking.

"Where is Apollo?" he asked, scanning the crowd over my head.

Apollo stepped forward, looking afraid and very young despite being over one hundred years old just like I was. "I'm here," Apollo said as he approached.

I stood beside my twin protectively, afraid that Achilles might try to harm him. Achilles looked down at him and said, "I forgive you for killing me, and as Prince of the Sidhe I give you a full pardon for my murder."

Everyone gasped, including me.

"Thank you," Apollo whispered, eyes wide, and then he dropped to his hands and knees with his forehead touching the ground. "Thank you."

"Protect Artemis and Cratus," Achilles whispered. "That is your duty now."

Apollo nodded and stood, putting an arm around my shoulders. "I will."

"Achilles," Hera whispered as tears flowed down her cheeks in a steady stream.

Achilles turned and smiled at his mother. "Mother, I am so proud of you," he said. She sobbed and he wrapped her up in a tight hug. "I love you."

"I love you, too," she choked out.

Zeus hugged Hera and Achilles at the same time, and then grabbed Ares and pulled him into the hug as well. Achilles and Ares smiled at each other.

Ares said, "I am sorry that I could not save you from Death's hold."

Achilles shook his head. "You were right to save Artemis and your child. I would have done the same thing had I been in your shoes. Can I speak with you privately a moment?" He asked Ares.

Ares nodded and Hera reluctantly released her hold on

Achilles. The brothers walked away together, far across the field away from everyone else to talk.

Apollo patted my shoulder reassuringly as he hugged me against his side. "It is good for them both to get some closure," he said.

I knew he was right, but I desperately wanted to know what they were saying. "How relieved are you that you've been officially pardoned?" I asked with a smile.

Apollo whispered, "More than you know. I only hope that in time, the Sidhe learn to forgive me as Achilles did."

I watched Ares and Achilles who were still talking to each other with their arms folded across their chests. Ares nodded briskly a few times as Achilles talked and frowned deeply a few times. They seemed to have finally finished when they hugged each other and headed back towards us.

Achilles stopped at his parents, and Hera hugged him again.

Ares walked to me and Apollo stepped aside so that Ares could put his arm around my shoulders.

"So, what did you two talk about?" I asked.

One side of Ares' mouth quirked up in a smirk. "None of your business."

I sighed, which made him laugh.

Achilles made his rounds, saying goodbye to everyone, but saved me for last. He held my hands in his and smiled at me. "You have grown into an incredible woman," he whispered. "I am glad that I got to see it happen."

My throat was too tight for me to speak and tears were threatening to break free at any moment, but I forced my lips to move. "I will never forget you. I will tell my children about you and your brave sacrifice. Everyone will know what a great warrior you were and how wonderful you were."

He bent down and whispered into my ear, "I will always love you and watch over you, and I will always be in your heart. Do not let your relationships with others fail as I had with Ares. *Verus amor vincit omnia.* I love you." His lips touched my cheek in a gentle kiss and then he was gone.

I wanted to scream at Rhea and make her bring him back, but I bit my tongue and walked to Zeus who pulled me into a tight hug, letting me bury my face into his chest as tears escaped, despite my greatest efforts to hold them in.

"Now is the time for rebuilding and peace," Rhea called out. "Any who oppose this peace shall answer to us. Let the Earth unite as one world instead of different nations. You may all be different beings with different backgrounds, but you are all children of the All-mother, Gaia."

People cheered all around me. I took a deep breath, shoved my feelings down, and turned away from Zeus, walked to Ares and took my place by his side. Cratus squirmed in his arms and I took him, cradling the baby against my chest and kissing his forehead.

Even though in the end I had hardly raised a finger in the final battle, it was finally over. Ares and I could finally build a house and raise our child and live as a normal family should. Despite the pain I had experienced over the years and the pain Ares had endured, it was all worth it to finally have our happily ever after.

Ares kissed Cratus' head and then kissed my lips softly. "So, where are we going to build our house?" he asked as people crowded around Rhea and Hyperion for a chance to meet them.

I smiled and grabbed his hand. "I believe your meadow is the perfect place, don't you?"

"I was hoping you would say that."

I lifted our clasped hands and kissed the back of his hand as I pictured the meadow where flowers were blooming, bees were buzzing, and animals ripe for hunting awaited us. "Let's go home."

EPILOGUE

Immediately following the battle, the Council of Beings was created and each group was given a headquarters where the leaders were to live. However, everyone else was instructed to live together and that we were not to section ourselves off anymore. Areas like Las Vegas, Rome, and Paris were rebuilt, and millions moved together, opening businesses and helping each other.

Victor made a lot of changes within the vampire community and despite his battles, he still had a long way to go. It was hard to change people who had been set in their ways for hundreds of years, but with Dmitri's help, he was making headway. I only hoped that they both might find love again so that the sad looks they had when looking at Ares and I together would leave.

I made up with Koda, deciding that I should take Achilles' words of wisdom and not lose a friendship like ours. Despite being very powerful and being known around the world for his skills, he was challenged to fight many battles. However, he won all of them easily and even found a mate who was just as quirky as he was. Anastasia was standing on the sidelines during one of his fights and the sight of her pierced nose, lips, and eyebrow, and half shaved head caught his attention. He flirted with her during his fight and in the end, convinced her to go out with him. The two had been inseparable ever since.

Ares took Apollo under his wing and was teaching him everything he knew. I worried at first that he might snap one day and hurt him, but it seemed that due to Achilles forgiving Apollo and whatever Achilles had said to Ares, that he forgave Apollo as well. We built a house for Apollo a few miles away from ours, and together they trained every single day. Cratus watched and listened, and I had no doubts that he was learning just as Apollo was.

Beatrice built her own house deep within the forest, about ten miles from ours, but visited Cratus every day and took him and Apollo on hunting trips with her. She was taking her role as Grandmother like a full-time job, which was nice because it gave Ares and me time alone.

Cratus loves Blu, and we visited the hive at least once a month. Cratus' powers and skills have developed much faster than I thought they would, and his magic was even more powerful than a child his age should have been. With the Council's help, we were helping him understand how to control his emotions and his powers, but even the Council was shocked with his quick growth. He is a sweet boy though, and I had no doubt that he would become one of the greatest leaders in the world when he was older and might even surpass Ares in power.

Our daughter, Solara, was born exactly a year from the day Rhea had told us. She takes after her father when it comes to anger, but her powers were primarily sun based. She loved creating little balls of sunlight at night to dance with fireflies.

I loved seeing my two children playing together and with our other children in the pack.

The number of halfbreeds increased quite a bit and I knew the population would continue to grow now that Maurice and his evilness was gone.

The world is far from perfect, but the fear is slowly evaporating, and people are smiling a little more every day. Every type of being can be seen working and living side by side and even though we know the peace won't last forever, we are enjoying it while we can. Together we were stronger than ever and together we could accomplish anything.

THANK YOU

Thank you for reading the Artemis Lupine Series. This was the first series I ever wrote and published and holds a special place in my heart. Knowing that you took the time to read the full series makes me happier than you will ever know.

If you enjoyed it, please consider leaving a review.

BONUS SCENES

BONUS - HALLOWEEN

"What are you doing?" I asked Koda who stood in front of the open window in warrior form.

"Trying to scare some little kids," he responded honestly. "You can't let humans see you like that," I said angrily.

"It's Halloween. They'll just think it's a really good costume," he said, "We've been doing this for a hundred years."

"Ares, are you going to let…" I stopped talking because Ares had walked into the room with jeans, a jersey, and a high school letterman jacket on, in his warrior pose. "Teen wolf, really?" I asked him with a sigh.

He smiled at me, or tried with his wolf head. "What are you going to be?" Matt asked me. "I'm not dressing up," I said.

"We're going to a party. You have to dress up," Ares told me. "We're going to a party? A human party?" I asked. All three

nodded their heads. What was wrong with these men? "Just take a warrior form," Ares suggested.

"I don't want people trying to touch my head," I said.

"They won't while I am standing next to you," he said with a jealous gleam in his eye.

“Maybe some pirate will sweep me off my feet and steal me away to his boat,” I teased, placing the back of my right hand against my forehead and fanning my face with the left hand.

“He won’t get very far without his head,” Ares growled.

“We’re in Wisconsin, there are no pirates here,” Koda pointed out.

“I might have to go find some,” I said with a wink at Ares.

He shifted back to his man form and wrapped his arms around me, “You’re mine and I’ll fight off any pirate who tries to steal my treasure.”

“Remember when we stole Blackbeard’s ship?” Matt asked with a wicked smile.

“Blackbeard was so furious, but we had already sailed out too far so they couldn’t catch us,” Koda added.

“That and they were too drunk,” Ares said.

“Only because someone gave them two barrels of whiskey,” Koda said, pointing at Ares.

“You stole Blackbeard’s ship? Blackbeard?” I asked in shock. “We were bored,” Ares said with a shrug, “And the whiskey

was awful. I was glad to get rid of it. Plus, we returned the ship to Blackbeard.”

Someone knocked on the door of the house we were staying in and Koda opened it. Three kids in varying ages stared at Koda a minute, processing his appearance and then they smiled and gave him high fives. He gave them candy from a bucket I hadn’t seen a minute ago. The kids waved at Koda, who waved back and then shut the door. “See, the kids like it,” Koda said.

“Pick a form,” Ares said, “And let’s go.” “Who’s going to give out candy?” I asked.

“We leave the bowl on the step with a note,” Matt said, “Most kids around here know us and they’ll only take a couple pieces of candy.”

“That’s because Matt stayed home one time, but set the bowl

outside with the note and hid in the bushes so when a kid tried to take too much he jumped out and scared them," Ares said.

"You three are terrible," I said with a shake of my head.

We walked out of the house and Matt said, "Everyone likes to be scared on Halloween."

"I don't," I said honestly, "I hate being scared."

A man dressed up like Dracula leapt out in front of me and hissed. I punched him in the face before I could scream. His fake teeth fell out and he clutched his face. "What the hell?" he said.

"Sorry," I said, wincing. Ares, Koda, and Matt laughed hysterically. "I'm so glad I could amuse you."

"We better remember to duck and weave when we try to scare her tonight," Koda said.

Ares had shifted into warrior form and growled at me. I glared at him and shook my head. I was walking down the street with three werewolves in warrior form. Everyone looked at us and yet no one freaked out. We walked into a large warehouse which had been converted to a club with tons of Halloween décor. Ares took my hand and spun me out onto the dance floor. The crowd parted for him and we found a spot on the crowded dance floor. People complimented Ares on his costume. Ares danced with me until I was too thirsty to ignore it anymore. At the bar, I ordered two waters and then whispered into Ares' ear, "It's too bad you're in that form because now I can't kiss you."

He grabbed my hand and towed me to the back of the room, outside and into a deserted alley. His body returned to normal and he kissed me. "Better?" he asked.

I smiled and said, "Everything is better if you're here."

He smiled, pleased with my comment and asked, "Want to howl at the moon?"

I placed my hand on my heart and pretended to hold back tears as I said, "I thought you would never ask."

We shifted into warrior form, tilted our heads up to the moon, and howled. Koda and Matt howled inside the warehouse, but we could still hear them where we were.

"Want to go back and dance?" I asked.

He nodded his head and we went back inside to dance the night away as werewolves, the humans none the wiser.

BONUS - KODA

The wind ruffled my fur and blew familiar scents across my nose. The high grass swayed with the wind and its scent held more happy memories for me than any other scent in the world, well except for one person's. The moon was high, its magic humming through me and making the switch from man to wolf much easier. I could change whenever I wanted to, but when the moon was full the call to become wolf was its strongest. I was more than a couple hundred years old now so I could control myself enough even while in wolf form that there really was no difference in me between forms. Although I do bite more often in this form. Ares was on one of his walkabouts although I followed him long enough to figure out where he was heading so I could rush to his aid if need be. Not that my older brother really ever needed help. He was the strongest man I knew and a very skilled fighter, which helped him obtain the nickname of God of War. The jerk had even been worshipped as a god for a long time. I knew my twin brother Matt was also following him so I didn't feel too bad about taking some time for myself.

I loved my brother and as his packmate I craved time with him, but I hoped he took a while longer on this walkabout. I was having a *very* good time. An owl flew over my head, heading for a mouse in the field of grass who had mistakenly thought it was a safe time to make a voyage across the green area. He was now the owl's dinner. I watched the owl dive into the grass and then fly away with his prize in his talons. Sometimes I wished that I could fly. I refocused on my hunt in front of me, crawling forward on my belly as slowly as possible to close the distance just a little bit more before I made my attack.

The woman in front of me had no idea I was here. She stood in the middle of the field picking flowers which only bloomed in the light of the full moon and putting them in the little wicker basket she was holding. She was gorgeous. She was powerful. I was going to pounce on her and pin her to the ground. Her black hair waved in the wind like a welcoming flag. I dug my claws into the ground and bunched my muscles to prepare for my leap. It was a long distance, but I could leap a lot farther than a normal wolf. She looked behind her at the sound of a rabbit being chased by something in the forest. This was my chance! I leapt up and at her, my legs spread wide to knock her to the ground. Two feet short of her she looked up at me with a smile on her face and I froze in midair.

"You're louder than you think, Koda," she said as she smiled at me. I growled at her and she laughed. "You do not frighten me."

I could if I wanted to, but I didn't want to frighten this gorgeous woman.

She walked up to me and kissed my muzzle. "Go hunt the little things in the forest and then come see me in the morning."

The spell released and I spun around to land on my feet. I watched her walk away swinging her basket and then ran into the forest to sidetrack myself for the rest of the night before going to see her. I had a lot of energy to spend. As a rule I only hunted predators. I was at the top of the food chain and although I enjoyed burgers and steaks as a human, I felt it was only fair to hunt other weaker predators. My hunger tonight would need to be filled for the fun I was planning to have with my friend in the morning when I went to visit her. It took down a male brown bear since they were heavily populated here and ate my fill. Scavengers began to fill up the area, keeping their distance, but waiting, but I made them wait longer as I cleaned my paws like a cat. I made my way to a creek nearby to clean myself off and then jogged back towards the witches' compound. The women on night watch waved to me as I jogged inside and I hurried to the top of the stairs where the coven leader slept. The door was left open a crack, which made me smile a wolfish smile. She was always so considerate.

I nudged it open and then closed it behind me. The room was dark, but I could see her chest rising and falling as she slept in her bed. I walked over to the bed and looked at her beautiful face as she slept. Selene. She was one of the most powerful witches I had met yet. She was also one of the most kind hearted women I knew. I had seen her help a child she didn't know and even take an arrow to the stomach for a werewolf she didn't know during a battle. I shifted forms and kissed the scar on her stomach before crawling in beside her and falling asleep with her in my arms. I knew she would never be my mate, but I enjoyed every moment I spent with her and I would cherish every moment I spent holding her.

"KODA," Selene whispered, "Wake up, darling."

I opened my eyes and smiled at her beautiful face hovering over mine. "Good morning."

She kissed my cheek and said, "Every morning with you beside me is great, not good."

I pulled her down, hugging her against me and said, "You are right. Great morning."

She laughed and kissed my cheek again. "Go brush your teeth, you beast."

I tickled her until she begged me to stop and then walked to the basin in her room. "Bear breath isn't sexy?" I asked as I scrubbed at my teeth and tongue.

"Not particularly," she admitted, "But there isn't much about you that isn't sexy so you need a flaw every now and then."

"Stop staring at my butt," I told her as I spit into the spittoon beside the table.

"It's so cute though," she purred from behind me.

I turned and leapt on to her, pinning her to the bed with my body weight. "Ha!" I said victoriously.

She laughed. "I let you pin me. I could have frozen you midair again."

"Stupid spell," I muttered.

She leaned up as if to kiss me and whispered a word in Latin that I did not know. I should have learned it by now since she used it on me often to send me flying across the room. "Rude," I grunted as I struggled against the spell holding me to the wall.

She stood up and let the sheet fall to the ground around her feet like a puddle of silk. "You my dear have gotten too comfortable. What if I decided to stab you while I held you in my spell like this?"

"A world where you would betray me is a world I would not want to live in," I said mournfully.

She released the spell, letting me stand on the ground on my own feet and kissed my lips. "You are very crafted with words."

"Would you have found me so interesting if I wasn't?" I teased. "Oh you are interesting in very many ways. You also know it." "To know one's strengths is to also know one's weaknesses," I whispered in her ear.

"What weaknesses do you have, Wolf of Lyngvi?"

I nipped her neck and said, "A wolf does not reveal his weaknesses, my little Goddess."

I felt him before I heard the howl. "Who is that?" Selene asked in shock.

"Ares," I whispered. I kissed her neck and quickly got dressed. "It was lovely seeing you again. I hope to see you soon."

She blew me a kiss and said, "The pleasure is always mine." I winked and said, "That was the plan."

She blushed and I darted out of her bedroom, running down the stairs and out the door without saying bye to anyone I past. I ran out of the compound and slid to a stop in front of Ares who was in his wolf form. "Hi," I panted.

He sat on his butt and looked at me. "*Selene?*" he guessed. I smirked. "A gentleman does not kiss and tell."

He rolled his eyes and turned around. "*I need some clothes.*" "Have a mishap?" I asked him.

"*No, some woman stole my clothes.*"

I laughed. He had had this happen several times. "She thought you would stay if she held them."

"*Yes.*"

"Did she faint when you turned wolf and walked away?" "*She was asleep,*" he mumbled.

My mouth dropped open as I looked at him. "Wow."

He growled. "*Not because of that. I just sort of helped her fall asleep.*"

I shook my head at him. "Some ending to your walkabout." I looked around and frowned. "Where's Matt?"

Ares stopped and narrowed his eyes as he looked at me. "*What do you mean?*"

"He was following you," I answered honestly.

We both looked at each other in silence a moment and then burst into laughter. No doubt some woman was holding him hostage for his clothing as well. He'd eventually get free and come find us.

"So, where are we going?" I asked as we continued walking. Obviously, we were going towards the closest town so I could get him some clothes, but he knew that wasn't what I meant.

"*Away from Lyngvi,*" he answered simply. "That's vague."

"I believe that I have a passt genau."

If my jaw could have, it would have hit the ground. "What?!"

Ares stopped and looked at me. *"I can't really explain it, but I started feeling this way a little while ago. I went to that house yesterday and had no interest in them. None, Koda. Zero. It was like you showed me a piece of cake and I just didn't want anything sweet."*

"So, what are you going to do?" I asked when I finally found my voice again.

"First I need some clothes and then I'm going to need to stay away from Lyngvi."

The most eligible werewolf bachelor, the prince of werewolves, was now off the market because of a girl he hadn't met yet. He was going to have a lot of angry women on his hands if he went back to Lyngvi so I didn't blame him for his decision. "We're going to Russia, aren't we?" I asked with a sigh.

Ares smiled a wolfish smile at me and said, *"It's not so bad there."*

"It's cold," I muttered, "And the women are always dressed in lots of layers."

"We could go to the Bahamas," he suggested. "Really?" I asked.

"No," he said with a snort.

"That was cruel," I growled at him. "Why can't we at least go to Florida or somewhere like that?"

"Maybe," he said in consideration.

"I could let you stay a wolf and not get you clothes," I suggested.

"I could bite your finger off," he growled.

"You'd have to catch me first," I teased him, "I doubt you would want the humans to see you chasing me through town. I bet they'd put together a hunting group."

"It could be fun," he said seriously, *"It's been a while since a human has tried to hunt me."*

"We are not antagonizing the humans. We don't need them killing all of the real ones again just because you're bored."

He whined. *"It wasn't my fault! Matt was the one who ran into the town."*

"You left the paw prints."

He winced. *"Right. So, how about those clothes?"* "Miami?" I asked.

He sighed. *"Fine."*

"We should get Matt first." *"He's behind you."*

Before I could turn around my twin brother tackled me and licked my face. *"Yo."*

"Yuck," I grumbled as I pushed him off me. "So, some girl stole your clothes too?"

"Yup." He answered with glee.

I rolled my eyes at my brothers and headed towards the town to purchase clothes for them. "Matt, we're going to Miami."

"Woohoo!" he yelled in our heads.

If Ares was right and he did have a *passt genau* then our lives were going to drastically change. What did she look like? What was she like? It honestly shocked me that he would have a *passt genau* with his lineage. There weren't any other half werewolf, half Sidhe in existence. Would she be powerful or would she be weak? Sometimes the matches ended up being complete opposites so I could see Ares' match being a completely submissive wolf. It might do him some good to have a submissive wolf as a mate. Perhaps she could calm him down a bit.

"Are you going to keep taking a stroll through the forest or are you going to get us some clothes?" Ares asked.

"Sorry," I mumbled and started jogging through the forest. The town was about five miles away. Ares and Matt would hang back in the forest while I went into town and got them some clothes. We would have to go to a werewolf town nearby to get some cash, but I didn't want to mention that to Ares. No matter where we went women would throw themselves at him for a chance to be his mate. I didn't envy him for having women throw themselves at him, I had that myself, but I did envy that he could take a mate. I knew when I took the job as his guard and as part of his pack that I could not have a mate, but sometimes I wished for a mate of my own. Then I saw something else shiny and it took my mind off of it.

"Be careful when you go into town. The Justinson brothers are still out for my head," Ares reminded me.

How could I forget? Those idiot brothers had almost exposed us to a group of humans a few months ago. If Victor hadn't been with us and been able to use his vampire powers on them then it would have ended much differently. Speaking of Victor…

"Where's Victor? Are you going to invite him to Miami?" I asked.

"That's not a bad idea," Ares mumbled.

It was always strange to hear someone mumble *inside* your head. The telepathy we shared was extremely convenient for the most part, but it had taken a long time to get used to. "I can call him when I get in town," I offered.

"Okay," Ares agreed.

The edge of the forest came into view so I slowed down to say goodbye to my brothers before heading into the town. "Any specifics that you would like?" I asked them.

"No, torn jeans," Ares said. *"Stupid fad these kids are having in the '90s."*

Torn jeans were definitely the fad right now. "Matt?" I asked. *"No fishnet,"* he growled.

Ares and I laughed and then I jogged away. The sun was just cresting the mountain when I made it down to the city and shops were just beginning to open. I slowed to a walk and acted like I was taking an early day stroll through the town. The shop I was heading for was owned by the witches and run by them as well. It was the farthest shop on Main Street which meant I had to take my stroll past a bakery that smelled like heavenly sugared bread, a coffee shop with fresh roasted coffee beans and the butcher's shop. My stomach was growling fiercely when I finally made it to the witches' spice and herb store and I was sure Janice, the witch behind the counter, heard it when I walked in.

"Koda," she said with a pleasant smile, "How can I assist you?" She was beautiful, but not as beautiful as Selene. Where Selene was dark and mysterious, Janice was light and sweet.

I leaned against the counter and smiled sweetly at her. "Ares and Matt had a little mishap and need some clothes."

Janice laughed and asked, "When don't you guys have mishaps with clothes? You should just call your werewolf towns, nudist colonies."

"We tried that once, but a lot of weirdos came and tried to join us," I admitted to her.

She laughed even harder and then turned around to walk in the back. "We've got some clothes back here you can go through. Your kind drifts through here a lot so we keep spares in case you need them." She showed me the boxes of clothes in various sizes and walked back to the register in case a customer came in.

"You're the best," I praised her.

She winked at me and said, "If you only knew." If I hadn't been so fond of Selene I might have taken her up on that offer.

The clothes were pretty normal, jeans and t-shirts, but I wanted to find something annoying or embarrassing for Ares to wear. I pulled out jeans in Matt and Ares' sizes and then searched through the box until I found a ridiculous Hawaiian shirt for Ares and a tie dye shirt for Matt.

She gave me a small backpack and said, "Selene asked me to give this to you when you came by."

"Thank you," I said as I walked out of the store. I opened the bag and a smile split my face. She had put cash, jerky and a note in the backpack. I opened the note and laughed since it only said, "xoxoxo Selene". I was going to have to thank her next time I saw her.

"*What took you so long*?" Ares asked when I came back. He and Matt were lying on the ground dozing.

"I had to find clothes in your sizes," I said, "There wasn't much to choose from."

I dropped the clothes in front of them and Ares growled. "*This is the best you could find?*"

I shrugged and said, "Beggars can't be choosers." They changed forms and then got dressed quickly. "You're still here?" a voice asked behind me.

I didn't need to turn around to find out who it was because I could smell his and his brother's stench from here. The Justinson brothers.

"We're on our way out of town," Ares said, "Not that it is your concern what I do."

"Of course you're running away," the youngest one scoffed. That was probably the dumbest thing he could have said to

Ares. My brother never ran away from anything, especially not a being so pathetic when compared to him. I knew better than to intervene and so did Matt. We both walked a little way off and turned around to watch the carnage.

"See, even your brothers are afraid of us," the oldest sneered. "No, we just don't feel like getting your blood on us," I

explained.

They looked at me dumbly and I almost felt bad for them. They were pretty high level within the werewolf society, but no one was higher than Ares, even the current Alpha who hated that fact.

"You have one chance," Ares said calmly, "Apologize for insulting me or I will have to punish you."

The brothers looked at each other and laughed. "Apologize to you?" the oldest asked with a scoff. "You're not as tough as you think you are."

Ares kept a tight lid over his power so that very little of his true dominance leaked out. When he let it go it was like a boiling pot of water was poured over you and if you did not fall to your knees instantly you would be boiled alive. These idiots were about to find out what it felt like to be boiled alive.

Ares took a deep breath and then the men in front of us fell to their hands and knees. Matt and I were unaffected because Ares was shielding us, but I winced anyways, remembering the feeling. "Do you submit to me?" Ares asked.

The men groaned and the eldest even tried to stand up, but it was impossible. No one could withstand him. "Submit!" Ares roared.

The men fell flat on their stomachs on the ground and both whispered, "We submit."

Ares inhaled and the world started moving again. It was funny how you didn't notice that everything had gone quiet until the animals started moving and making noise again.

We left the men lying on their stomachs and started our journey towards the airport. It was about fifty miles away, but it was good to walk and get some of our energy out before we got there, especially for Ares since he so rarely took that lid off.

"Well that was fun," Ares said with a smirk. "Did you tell Matt?" I asked him.

"Tell me what?" Matt asked nervously. He hated surprises. "Ares has a *passt genau*," I answered instead of letting Ares. "What!" Matt screamed.

"Easy," Ares said in a soothing tone.

"So, you have a match? Somewhere out there?" Matt asked, motioning out to indicate the world.

Ares nodded his head. "Yes." "How do you know?" Matt asked.

"I can't explain it very well," Ares admitted, "But I felt something in my heart that was exciting and loving and peaceful and when I went to the brothel down the way I suddenly...didn't want anything to do with them."

Matt stopped walking and I could feel his jealousy. He had volunteered to be part of our pack and to give up the chance of having a mate to properly guard Ares, but he still craved a mate as much as he denied it. "So why aren't you going out to find her?" Matt asked.

"I believe she may have just been born," Ares admitted sheepishly.

"Woah. Woah. Woah!" I said in shock. "What do you mean?"

"Why would I just now get the feeling if she had been alive all this time?" he asked angrily. "If she had been alive for years wouldn't I have felt her before now?"

"Maybe she just hit puberty or just changed for the first time," I suggested.

"Everyone I have talked to said that you feel your match as soon as you or they are conscious enough to understand it," Ares explained.

"So, you have to wait eighteen years?" I asked softly. Ares sighed. "Yeah."

"You can't even just go see her or check up on her occasionally?" Matt asked.

Ares shrugged. "There really isn't a standard protocol for this, but I don't want to freak out her family or her. Plus, I don't know if I could watch someone grow up knowing that eventually she was going to be my mate. I will just wait until she is eighteen, an adult, to go see her."

Ares had a *passt genau*. How much would our lives change once we met her? I could only hope for great things and pray that my pack stayed together for eternity. Only eighteen years to wait until we met the mystery girl. I hoped she was worth the wait.

ORIGINAL CONCEPT ART BY AVERY BANKS

ARTEMIS

ARTEMIS & ARES

ARTEMIS
LUPINE

ARTEMIS

DRACO BLU

VARIOUS ART

ARTEMIS
LUPINE

I really appreciate you reading my series! I hope you enjoyed it. Please consider leaving a review at your favorite site.

Here are some ways to connect with me:
www.catherinebanks.com

Join my newsletter:
catbanks.co/Newsletter

Follow me on Amazon:
www.amazon.com/author/catherinebanks

Follow me on BookBub:
www.bookbub.com/authors/catherine-banks

Purchase signed paperbacks and items handmade by Catherine:
Etsy.com/shop/TurboKittenInd

ABOUT THE AUTHOR

Catherine Banks is a USA Today bestselling fantasy author who writes in several fantasy subgenres and has multiple pseudonyms. She began writing fiction at only four years old and finished her first full-length novel at the age of fifteen. She is married to her soulmate and best friend, Avery, who she has two amazing children with. After her full-time job, she reads books, plays video games, and watches anime shows and movies with her family to relax. Although she has lived in Northern California her entire life, she dreams of traveling around the world. Catherine is also C.E.O. of Turbo Kitten Industries™, a company with many hats including being a book publisher and Etsy store full of nerdy fun.

facebook.com/catherinebanksauthor
twitter.com/catherineebanks
amazon.com/author/catherinebanks
bookbub.com/authors/catherine-banks

MORE FROM CATHERINE BANKS

YOUNG ADULT PARANORMAL & FANTASY ROMANCE SERIES

Artemis Lupine Series

Song of the Moon

Kiss of a Star

Healed by the Fire

Battles of the Night

Artemis Lupine, The Complete Series

Little Death Bringer Duology

Mercenary

Protector

Little Death Bringer, The Official Coloring Book

Pirate Princess Series

Pirate Princess

Princess Triumvirate

ADULT PARANORMAL & FANTASY ROMANCE SERIES

Zodiac Shifters Paranormal Romance Series

Centaur's Prize
Tiger Tears
Lion About

Ciara Steele Novella Series

True Faces
Barbaric Tendencies

ADULT REVERSE HAREM PARANORMAL & FANTASY ROMANCE SERIES

Her Royal Harem Series

Royally Entangled
Royally Exposed
Royally Elected
Royally Enraged
Her Royal Harem, The Complete Series
The Demon's Fair
Her Royal Harem, The Coloring Book

Wings of Vengeance Series

Of Dragons and Cruelty
Of Minotaurs and Sacrifice
Wings of Vengeance, The Complete Series

Anderelle: Minloa Trilogy

Queen of the Stars
Empress of the Galaxy
Goddess of the Universe
Anderelle: Minloa, The Complete Series

MORE FROM CATHERINE BANKS

Bonds of Madness Series

Sealing the Deal
Racing the Clock

Her Super Harem Series

Lucky Strike

Her Hellish Harem Duet

A Demon's Heart
A Demon's Soul*

*Coming Soon

MORE FROM CATHERINE BANKS

STANDALONE YOUNG ADULT PARANORMAL & FANTASY ROMANCE BOOKS

Monster Academy
Daughter of Lions
Lady Serra and the Draconian
Of Sky and Sea
The Last Werewolf
Sybil Deceived

STANDALONE YOUNG ADULT PARANORMAL & FANTASY REVERSE HAREM ROMANCE BOOKS

Moon Academy

STANDALONE ADULT PARANORMAL & FANTASY ROMANCE BOOKS

Demonic Contract
Anja's Secret
Dragon's Blood
Last Ama Princess

Transforming Rose
Alys of Asgard
Phoenix Possessed
Stone Heart

STANDALONE URBAN FANTASY BOOKS

The Pawn

CHILDREN'S BOOKS

Calvin's Alien Adventure

MORE FROM DAISY EMORY

The Boyfriend Deal

Their Purple Girl

ACCIDENTAL MOBSTER SERIES
Accidental Mobster
Unintentional Pirate
Suddenly Baroness*

*Coming Soon

www.ingramcontent.com/pod-product-compliance
Lightning Source LLC
Chambersburg PA
CBHW030344310726
48979CB00001B/186

9781946301550